MY ALPHA'S BETRAYAL

BURNING IN THE FLAMES OF HIS VENGEANCE

BOOK 1

MOONLIGHT MUSE

Edited by Morrigan Sinclair
Cover Design by Moorbooks Design
Typesetted by Eacodes

My Alpha's Betrayal

To all those who believed in me.

CONTENTS

There was no love nor emotions in the eyes of the man before me… only the flames of hatred burning brightly consumed them.

"Tell me… what are we?" I asked softly. The pain in my body was suffocating, and no matter how strong I tried to remain, I couldn't keep the pain from my voice.

"Nothing more than Heaven and Hell." His voice was equally cold, destroying the last of my resolve.

"Then kill me," I whispered hoarsely, trying to ignore the pain of betrayal that was tearing me up from within.

A ruthless smirk graced his handsome face. His fingers curled under my chin and made the sparks from his touch rush through me; pleasurable, yet equally painful. He was so close… yet so far away…

"That would be far too easy… but I assure you, when I'm done with you, you'll wish you were never born."

"You don't mean that…"

"Watch me." He turned away, pushing me to the ground roughly. "Burn her."

My heart sank, my head hanging as the pain of his rejection tore through me. Even when I was doused in gasoline, I didn't move, trying not to gag on the strong, pungent smell that cloaked me entirely, keeping my eyes clamped shut. Didn't he realise I was already burning in agony from the pain he had inflicted within me?

My eyes stung as I forced them open, watching him retreat, hoping… praying… that he'd turn back and change his mind. That perhaps deep inside of him, that man that I loved still existed.

He once said that I was his kryptonite… was it all lies?

He paused, and my heart leapt with a glimmer of hope, but then I saw it – the blazing match in his hand as his eyes met mine…

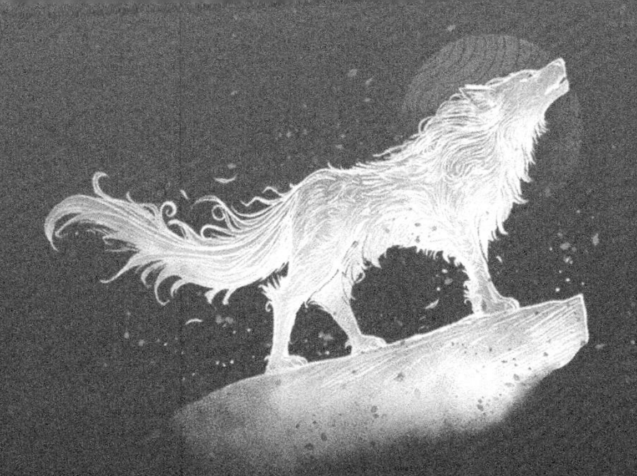

The White Dove

YILEYNA

THE SMELL OF BEER and mead laced the air, mixing pleasantly with the sound of men and women chatting and flirting in the White Dove. Despite it looking like the local pub, everyone knew that the White Dove was a brothel, one that was busy every day, no matter the season.

Night had fallen in the streets of Westerfell. The heat of the sun still lingered in the air despite its absence. The soft breeze dancing along my skin was warm as I wrapped my hand around the delicate wrist of my best friend, Charlene. Her green eyes widened, and the lights from the lanterns that hung from every wall cast shadows over her delicate features, highlighting the peppered freckles that adorned her cheeks and nose.

"Yileyna, really?" She whispered, her heart thumping as I looked down at her from the low wall I was crouching upon.

"There's no show to see from down there, my queen," I replied, my eyes sparkling with excitement.

No, we were not meant to be there, and I was sure if either of our parents found out, they would surely disapprove, but what's life without a little risk? Being the daughter of the Alpha and Beta couples, we were both of high class, and everyone knew who we were, so we'd better not get caught.

"Okay," she huffed, blushing as she allowed me to hoist her onto the wall

We both jumped down over to the other side silently. I was glad there were no guards around this side, but I knew that. I had timed it so well. The last time I came here, I had seen a lot, and I wouldn't lie, I was curious to see what was going on down there. Or better yet, ruin Charlene's innocence. I loved the girl, but she was far too prim and clueless.

We squeezed through the bushes, and I placed a hand on my blonde hair as it snagged on the branches behind us. Making it out the other side, I gathered up the skirt of Charlene's dress. Unlike me, who had dressed in pants and a backless top, she wore a pretty summer dress that was all caught up in the branches.

"Ouch," she winced.

"You are the future Alpha Queen. Are you really wincing from this pain?" I whispered as I helped her free.

"It still hurts. There were thorns." She pouted, making me feel sorry for her.

I was about to reply when the sounds of grunts and moans reached my ears, and I placed a finger to my lips. Her eyes were as wide as saucers, making my lips curl in a smirk.

This was exciting.

I pulled her along until I reached my spot, a hand-span wide gap behind the ivy curtain that covered the wooden planked fence that seemed to have been broken and no one had realised. Slowly, I reached forward and moved the ivy aside, motioning for Charlene to move too. It was just a few feet above one of the windows in the brothel. In this warm weather, the window was open, giving us the perfect view of what was happening inside.

Charlene gasped, and even my eyes flew open at the scene before us: two well-muscled men, whom I could tell were warriors from the thick muscles in their legs and arms, were standing facing one another, both pounding into the same woman. Her arms and legs were around one of the men, whilst the other man held her hips from behind as he thrust into her. The erotic sounds of their skin meeting and their lust-filled moans and grunts filled the air, making my cheeks heat up. The woman's pale, cream skin was coated in a sheen of sweat, her breasts slapping against the chest of the man she was facing, her lips meeting his hungrily.

"Goddess, Yileyna! No wonder you are so sinful! How often do you come to taint your eyes?" Charlene hissed.

I pouted as I dragged my eyes away from the male's shaft, wondering how the hell that could fit up her ass. She was rather small…

"No, this is the first time I've seen anything that's caught my attention." I suppressed a giggle when she gasped.

"You're into that...?" She asked, blushing as she dared not look again.

"Hmm, it looks fun." I shrugged.

What was I into? My heart skipped a beat when a certain face came to mind, and my cheeks burned as his gorgeous amber eyes filled my mind—the one man who could make my stomach knot and my core throb with desire. The first and only man I ever craved in an intimate way.

"Oh my goddess, you are!" Charlene exclaimed, completely misinterpreting my blush.

"Who's there?" Someone shouted, snapping me from my thoughts of having a certain sexy werewolf make love to me.

"Shit!" I hissed. Despite having used a small scent disguising enchantment we had purchased from a vendor a few days ago, it seemed they had realised we were here. "Run!"

In a flash, I was on my feet, grabbing Charlene by the wrist and rushing down the narrow path. It wasn't physically possible for any of the grown male wolves to fit down here, so I knew we were safe for now.

"Oh goddess, protect us! If Father finds out we were here," Charlene whispered, her heart thundering as I continued down the narrow path, trying not to hiss in pain as I squeezed through the gap between the fence and the large bushes behind us. My breasts snagged against the rough wood of the fence in front of me.

"I think I saw some runts down back! I'm sure it's those lads from earlier!" I heard a man growl. We continued on, praying that we weren't caught.

"Yileyna, you are not going to fit," Charlene whimpered in panic as the gap became narrower.

"We're almost there."

I paused, trying to hear if we were still being followed, but it seemed whomever it was had given up. I exhaled in relief, giving Charlene a reassuring smile before I glanced up at the dark, clear sky, noticing that despite the fact that there were no clouds, the stars were hidden. Strange.

"Just a little further, then we climb up. No one will see us by the marshes."

She nodded, and I glanced at the starless sky before taking a deep breath, feeling a little claustrophobic in the tight place. Charlene was a lot slimmer with smaller breasts, but I knew I was not going to be able to go any farther. We had to climb up.

"I'll go first."

I motioned upwards and reached up. I grabbed hold of the fence and squeezed myself out. I knew my back was going to be covered in scratches, and it was going to be messy to make sure none of the splinters or anything was left inside of me.

I took a deep breath of fresh air, happy to be out of there, when I froze. A distinct, rotten smell seeped into my nose, replacing the smell of the warm night and the bushes.

My heart thundered as I looked over the marshes, my stomach sinking when I saw the pack of wolves that were inching closer. There were far too many to count, their heads low, their dark fur matted and dirty. Their red eyes glowed with hunger as they stared ahead towards the outer wall of Westerfell.

Rogues…

We were under attack.

"Stay down," I whispered to Charlene as quietly as possible.

"What is it?"

"Nothing, don't move and stay out of sight," I replied calmly. "Promise me."

She hesitated before nodding in defeat.

There was no way they could get to her in that narrow alley, she would be safe as long as she stayed there, but the city wasn't. I needed to alert everyone.

Staying low, I stuck to the shadows and began edging towards the city wall. How did they even get out here in the marshes? This place was empty, with the forest to the left and the patrol, not to mention that it was a danger to even cross this place.

I kept my eyes on the growing glow of the city lights. All I needed was to get close enough to alert one guard who was able to sound the alarm and pass on the message.

I had just reached the wall to the outer city when a low menacing growl made me spin around just as one of the wolves leapt towards me. I jumped back, my heart hammering. My cover was blown.

I turned, grabbing the blazing torch from the bracket above me, and swung it at the wolf.

"ATTACK! WE ARE UNDER ATTACK!" I screamed at the top of my lungs, knowing that someone would hear me. My heart was a storm of emotions as I hit the wolf over the head with the torch. "All of Westerfell knows you're here," I hissed.

I am my parent's daughter, the future beta of this pack, and I will not...

My mind went blank when I suddenly saw the huge influx of dark wolves that were running towards me. How many were there?

Something flew past my head, and I gasped in horror as the entire section of the wall blew up. Rubble and debris went flying in all directions, and I was thrown off my feet due to the impact. Flames erupted and began spreading high and fast, faster than was naturally possible. What was this?

"Yileyna!"

My heart leapt at the voice that called me just as the same wolf lunged at me once again.

"Dad!" I shouted.

"Beta William! Don't go out there!"

"My daughter is out there!" I heard dad growl.

"Beta! It's dangerous!"

I saw Dad running towards me, shifting mid-jump and biting into the neck of the rogue, stopping it from attacking me.

"Get inside, Yileyna!" Mom shouted.

I turned, spotting her just before she shifted. My hair blew in my face as I gave her a nod, brushing it back and running towards the broken wall. As much as I wanted to help, I would only be a distraction. I needed to get inside and make sure the area was clear at the very least.

More men and women were coming to join Dad and Mom, some in human form, others in wolf form.

"Goddess, help us!" I whispered, observing the destroyed outer wall of the city, wondering what kind of enchantment had been able to break through our defences.

I climbed over the rubble, but if I had thought the inner walls were going to be better, I was wrong...

Fear and panic pierced my heart as I took in the scene before me. The anguished screams of my pack members filled my ears. The stench of coppery blood and burnt flesh filled my nose, making my stomach churn.

The rogues were mauling whomever they could reach, ripping them to pieces with their bloody mouths. The carcases of our people were scattered on the ground, and the pain in my chest was suffocating. It was as if I was drowning underwater, but there was no surface to break through to find any reprieve. There seemed to be no end to the horror that was ravaging my pack.

I saw Gamma Henry's seven-year-old son, Rhys, crying as a huge wolf covered with blood and dirt launched itself at him. His eyes were burning with hate.

"No!" I screamed in panic, running towards them. I swung the torch in my hand at him, only for him to swipe it from my hold. "Rhys! Run!"

He remained frozen in his spot. I looked around, but every side was in chaos, and it was then I realised they had ambushed us from all sides.

The wolf before me growled menacingly, his claws ripping through me as he brutally slammed me to the ground.

I jumped up, shouting at Rhys to move. The rogue growled, his blazing red eyes burning into me. I grabbed the torch from the ground and rammed it into his eyes, taking my chance and dragging Rhys away from the chaos.

"The Beta's down!" Someone shouted, making me freeze.

I spun around, my heart in my throat. The blood was pumping through my body loudly, and a cold chill enveloped me. Goddess, no....

I forced my body to move, trying to rush back outside. I had to get to Dad!

Someone blocked my path, and I slammed straight into a hard, muscular chest. I jerked away, trying to get past them, but a strong pair of hands grabbed my waist.

"Yileyna!"

"Let me go! Dad's out there! Mom too!"

"*Yileyna*!" His deep growl made me freeze. "Listen to me."

I stared up into the amber eyes of my crush. His hands cupped my face, a frown creasing his brow. This time, it wasn't his beauty or touch that hit me, but the words that left those plump lips.

"It's too late. They're dead."

And just like that, my world crashed down around me, tearing me apart with pain and guilt. Even I didn't realise the scream that ripped through the air belonged to me...

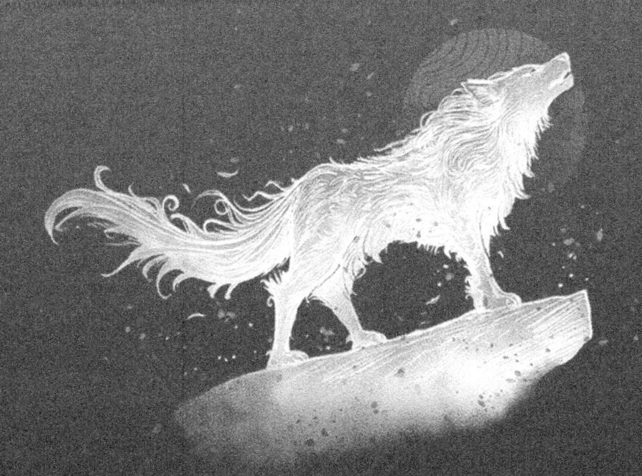

Down by the Coast

YILEYNA

TWO MONTHS HAD PASSED since the night of the massacre, but the horrors of that attack still haunted the dreams of many. We lost thirty-four people that night and another seven later on due to fatal injuries. What hurt the most was that I knew Dad left the safety of the walls for me, to protect me and to make sure I was safe, and with his death, I lost Mom too. True mates who have marked one another will die together.

A lot had changed since then. People looked at me with contempt and hatred. I knew they blamed me for the loss of their Beta couple, but I blamed myself too. It was my fault.

"The cheek that she's showing her face here…" one of the two women who walked past us muttered. I smiled sadly, not bothering to look back at them.

I don't think they realised that they may have lost their Beta couple, but I lost my parents. The familiar painful hold on my chest returned, and I swallowed hard, trying to focus on the destination we were heading towards.

Charlene turned, glaring at the back of the two women.

"Ignore them," she said, wrapping her arm around mine.

"I do, my beautiful queen." I smiled at her; among everyone, she was the one who didn't change towards me.

Sure, the Alpha and Luna were okay with me, but I didn't see them too often, and I did feel a hint of hostility from the Alpha... I still remembered when he asked what I was doing out there, how my carelessness had cost us all…

"Come on, we better hurry before Theon realises we are no longer in the baths," she giggled.

Theon. That was someone else who treated me indifferently, the same as ever. The most emotion I saw on him was when he told me their fate…

"You know, he's going to get angry. Again," I smirked, brushing away the thoughts that flooded my mind.

"Oh well, you are one of the strongest people I know. In the last two months, you have taken that to an entirely new level. He'll know I'm safe," she stated confidently. She was exaggerating. I was skilled, but I was by far one of the strongest.

Charlene… what would I do without her? But it didn't take long for someone to turn on me… would I lose her too?

Since my parent's death, I had focused on working harder and pushing myself to my limits. I was seventeen, but I still hadn't gotten my wolf. Werewolves usually shifted at any age from thirteen, and the latest recorded shift was at nineteen, but the average age was fourteen to sixteen for most wolves. Charlene had shifted at fifteen, and I was nearly eighteen with no sign of a shift happening.

I knew it was something that everyone talked about. I was the daughter of the Beta couple, I should have shifted by now.

In the kingdom of Astalion, there were ten packs, with the centre and the largest territory belonging to King Andres, father of Charlene and the Alpha of the Silver Storm Pack.

I knew the expectation of shifting and proving my worth to take the Beta position had only grown since my parents had passed away, but there was nothing that I could do to force it to happen. I just had to bide my time and wait for the shift.

We walked through the bustling streets and past the lines of trees heading towards the coast. The sun was already low in the sky, and we would only have an hour at most.

"Finally! Some space to breathe," Charlene whispered as we headed down the rocky path.

I didn't blame her. Things had been rather tense as of late, and I knew there was something troubling her. If she wanted to share, she knew I was there for her when she was ready to tell me.

We reached our destination, and she smiled, slipping off her shoes and beginning to take her dress off. It was safe down this side; well, as long as we were gone by nightfall. That was when the waters became a threat.

The coast this close to Westerfell was, for the most part, not too bad, but the sea was the kingdom of a dark species, and it was common knowledge not to linger anywhere close to the waters at night.

I unzipped my boots, unbuttoned my leather pants, and stripped them off, leaving the white shirt that I had tucked into my pants on. It only partially covered my derriere, which was clad in tiny underwear.

I was five-foot-seven, in comparison to Charlene's five-foot-ten. For werewolves, I was slightly on the shorter side, and unlike Charlene, who had a toned, slender body, I had slightly curvier hips and an ass that had a little more fat than the average she-wolf. With double D breasts that made me appear more like an Omega at times, I was a little more self-conscious about stripping bare even though we were alone.

Charlene was only in her lingerie and already splashing around in the water. I walked into the water, allowing the soothing tides to wash over me. I loved the sea, the feel of the waves rippling against me, the calmness of the fresh air and the smell of the clean salty water. It was more relaxing than anything else.

"Yileyna!"

My eyes flew open just as Charlene grabbed my ankle, dragging me into the water and making me gasp as I stumbled, tumbling backwards into the water. I gasped again as I broke the surface, brushing back my wet hair and giving her a mocking glare.

"Charl! Oh, you asked for it!"

We splashed each other, shrieking and giggling when we managed to shove the other under the water. I think for a while, I was able to forget all my troubles when the red glow of the sun bathed us in its warm colours. I looked at Charlene.

"I think we better head back now. I'm sure Theon found out we're missing," I suggested reluctantly, not wanting to leave the warmth of the water.

"Not that I'd mind him showing up. He's so stiff and indifferent, I wonder if seeing us almost naked would even bother him?" She mused, swimming away.

"I doubt it, nothing bothers him. Charlene!"

"Five minutes! One swim, and I'll be back!" She called out, swimming away.

I sighed, staring out at the glittering water and taking a deep breath. I ducked under the water, looking at the fish that were swimming around. I held my breath for several moments, enjoying the beauty beneath the surface, before my body begged for oxygen, and I broke the surface, taking in a deep gulp of air as I brushed my hair off my face.

"Get out."

My heart skipped a beat, and I turned, staring up at the man that stood at the edge of the water. His coppery brown hair was brushed back, his amber eyes burned with a fury that was barely contained, and his chiselled jaw set taut as he clenched his teeth. His bulging arms were crossed over his broad chest, and the tattoos that peeked out from the collar and sleeves of his clothes only added to how hot he looked right then. The sun made his hair look like it was on fire, emphasising every angle and curve of his face.

"Excuse me?" I raised an eyebrow, very aware that if I got out, my shirt would be sticking to me and reveal my lacy lilac lingerie.

"You left without telling me."

"Obviously, or you wouldn't have allowed us to leave. I'm surprised it took you this long to come here."

"Get out now."

"You're not my guard. Charlene's gone for a swim, go find her instead," I suggested, sinking lower into the water, leaving only my eyes above water.

"You know the waters are dangerous once night falls, Yileyna, we need to head back." His deep, sexy voice only made my core clench. "Do not make me get you out."

That wouldn't be a bad idea...

I sighed and swam to the edge in defeat. Getting out of the water, I glared at the taller man, wishing I was wearing my boots. At least I would have had a few extra inches on me. Standing at six-foot-five, he towered over me.

"I never knew you were so scared of Sirens," I smirked tauntingly.

"I'm not. I just don't think you'll be of much use with a few missing limbs," he remarked, his gaze dipping down to my soaking body.

I kept my eyes on his, trying to gauge his reaction. His eyes seemed to burn through the flimsy fabrics that covered me, and I felt very bare. My white shirt was now see-through, clinging to my curves, and the lace of my bra was clearly visible. My nipples were stiff from the water that had cooled considerably, either that or due to the man that stood before me.

Not one movement… not one hint of desire. His gaze ended at my thighs, and then I got the tiniest reaction. His tongue slid over his bottom lip, his eyes glimmering with a hue of gold before he turned his back on me smoothly.

"Get dressed and get Charlene. The Alpha wants to see the both of us."

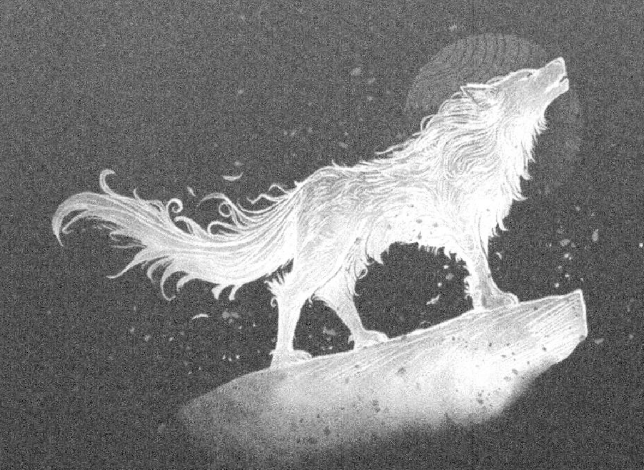

The Alpha King

YILEYNA

SURPRISINGLY, THEON SAID NOTHING to Charlene when she returned, not even casting her a glance as we made our way back towards the castle. We split up, with Theon escorting Charlene to her room whilst I headed to my quarters, the Beta quarters. A place that was so empty since Mom and Dad were gone.

I quickly showered before pulling on a fitted navy top, black pants, and boots, and I pulled my wet hair back into a ponytail. I exited my room and almost knocked into Theon, who was leaning against the wall.

"Goddess!" I gasped, jumping back, my heart thumping. "You scared me."

"For someone so audacious, I didn't know anything could scare you," he replied emotionlessly.

"What's life if you don't live it at full throttle?" I replied, making sure the door was locked before we both fell in step.

"Let me guess, not living, simply existing?" He raised his eyebrow.

"Are you mocking me?"

"I'm glad you figured it out," he whispered huskily, leaning down.

My heart skipped a beat as our eyes met, making me feel giddy. His sexy masculine scent invaded my senses, the thrum of his steady heartbeat making my own pound louder.

"Jerk," I managed to retort, pushing him away.

Theon had only been in this pack for two years. We didn't know where he had come from or who he was. The only thing he remembered when he regained consciousness was his name: Theon.

It had actually been Charlene and me who had found him a few weeks after her shift. We had been out, sneaking away as usual, when we saw a Naga, a half-human, half-serpent-like being. Unlike the ones who lived on land, the sea Naga were as dangerous as the Sirens, and this one had been no different.

Seeing the bloody body in the Naga's hold, Charlene had frozen in horror, and although my instincts told me to run, I couldn't leave someone to die, so I had swum out. With nothing but my sword, I had managed to injure the Naga just enough to free Theon from his hold. Despite him having elemental powers, I had managed to pull Theon to safety, and we had then called for help.

But Theon didn't know that. Charlene had asked if she could say she had saved him when she saw how handsome the young man was. As much as I would have loved to taunt him, this was even better. Now I often reminded him that he had been saved by a princess.

We weren't sure about Theon's age, but he looked to be in his early twenties.

It had taken time for everyone to trust him, but slowly he became one of us and was initiated into the pack. He never regained his memory, but he was hard-working, strong, and an excellent warrior, so he had risen through the ranks. He was now an Epsilon-rank warrior, which meant there were only four ranks above him and that included the Alpha rank.

Being the princess' bodyguard was an honourable job. It meant that the Alpha trusted him and knew he was capable of protecting her.

We walked down the hall. I turned towards the Alpha King's office only for Theon to take a left.

"The office is this way."

"I know, but did I say he was in his office?" He replied as if it was obvious.

"Right..."

Alpha Andres, no matter how many times you go before him, was still intimidating and powerful. He was the biggest man I had seen at around six-foot-seven or eight inches. He just looked far too large around everyone else. There was a handful of men around Theon's size, but they were rare too. The king was a beast and a king in all aspects.

Theon walked out of the double doors that led to the back grounds, and I grabbed the door before it swung shut in my face.

"Ever heard of manners? That's no way to treat a lady," I remarked.

"Never knew you were one," his emotionless reply came as he glanced at me over his shoulder. His gaze flicked to my body for a moment before a small smirk crossed his face. "Yeah, definitely not a woman."

I'll get you back for that…

I glared at his back, my gaze falling to his ass. I couldn't deny that he was sexy, yet he was equally irritating. Although both Charlene and I found him incredibly handsome, he didn't give us any attention. Although lately, I felt he teased me a little more… or maybe that was me being wishful.

I followed him out just as the king slammed two men to the ground, making the ground shake at the impact. His torso was shirtless, a man made from pure bulging muscles. His tanned skin was littered with scars and tattoos of runes. Symbols and images depicting war and victory mapped his entire torso, and his straggly chocolate-brown hair fell below his huge muscular shoulders. He was the opposite of his daughter, who had taken after her mother.

"Just on time. Who's next?" He asked with a grin as he turned to us, his gold tooth glinting under the lights of the courtyard.

"I wouldn't mind sparring with you, Alpha, but I fear I may not make it out alive," I replied with a small smile. It felt good to know he was still talking to me, even if it was just the adrenaline of beating us to a pulp that put him in a good mood.

"I hear you have been training a lot more… let's see."

That was a command. One I couldn't disobey.

"Don't die," Theon remarked mockingly, crossing his arms and placing one hand under his chin, as if he was about to enjoy the show.

I stepped out and looked up at my Alpha, amusement clear in his eyes. He knew I wouldn't even last a few minutes. The two men who had been thrown to the ground got up as the king jerked his head in dismissal.

"I'm not sure if you are reckless or brave," the king stated, grabbing a towel and wiping his face, which was coated with a layer of sweat.

"A little of both?" I suggested when he turned back to me.

A predatorial grin crossed his face, and he raised his fist, lunging at me without warning. My eyes flew open, and I ducked to the left just as his fist hit the ground, creating a crack. He turned and threw another punch, using all his brute strength. Of course, I wouldn't last when it came to a battle of strength.

Was it disrespectful to defend or attack the king?

I kept dodging when the king growled.

"Do not run! Attack! I'm sure Will showed you something!" The sudden anger and irritation in his voice at the loss of his closest confidant was raw and clear, sending a stab of pain through me.

Of course he had... I would never let my father's name be tarnished...

I knew that he blamed me too. I could see it in his eyes, even if he never voiced it... but didn't they realise it hurt me too?

A flash of anger overcame me, but I didn't let it show. The urge to release this pent-up irritation was rising within me. If the king had strength, then I had speed.

This time when he lunged at me, fist raised, I didn't duck, blocking it with my arms and gritting my teeth as I felt something break. I twisted, grabbing the king's thick forearms, and with all the force I could muster, I kicked him straight in the stomach. I do hope he realised I could have kneed him where the sun didn't shine, but I didn't think it would have been very respectful. He staggered slightly, and I glanced at Theon, a flash of surprise crossing his usually arrogant, emotionless face.

"Hmph... talent but no strength," the king grunted, turning away, a clear signal that we were done.

My arms screamed in agony, but they would heal. I looked down, noticing my right one was at a slight angle, but I was not going to snap it into place in front of the king. I didn't reply, bowing my head in submission. I knew what he meant... the fact that I hadn't shifted or come into full strength...

He picked up a bottle of water, downing it in a few gulps and leaning against one of the pillars as he looked at both Theon and me. I could feel Theon's gaze burning into me, but I refused to look at him.

"Do you know why we are constantly attacked?" He asked.

"Everyone wants a slice of the power that the Alpha king holds, and possibly the legend that the one who conquers Astalion ultimately has within their hold the power to rule the thirteen kingdoms and the seven seas," Theon replied.

That old folk's tale? I know people believed it, but I didn't think Theon was one for old wives' tales. The king nodded with a smirk.

"Well, that's a whole load of bullshit, but every myth and legend comes from somewhere." His smirk vanished, and he looked up at the sky. "I trust you both. Theon, we may have only had you here for two years, but you have proven yourself as a loyal warrior and an honoured member of this pack. I have placed my greatest treasure in your care, and I know you will protect her with everything. You will honour the oath you took when you joined us."

I glanced at Theon, who was simply watching the king indifferently. Both men were regal and powerful. I felt like an unnecessary extra here. Why did he want to speak to me?

"She saved my life. That isn't a debt that I'll ever forget," he replied. The king nodded.

"Yileyna, you are the… daughter of my closest friend and confidant, and you are also Charlene's best friend. I know you mean the world to her, and despite everything, you do protect her. There is something I need to share with you both…." His gaze scanned the area, making sure we were alone. Why did it feel like whatever he wanted to tell us was very important?

"The myth you speak of, Theon, the so-called treasure given to the middle kingdom; the heart of Kaeladia, of our world… it's not a tome or a magical crystal. It's something entirely different… and the reason no one has ever found it. It's said to be revealed every few centuries..."

I frowned as I began to piece the puzzle together. He mentioned Charlene... Was she somehow connected?

"You mean…" Theon murmured, but I could tell from his tone that understanding had dawned on him.

"Yes. My daughter is the heart, the treasure that every kingdom seeks."

Theon's eyes flashed a brilliant gold, but it was only for a split second as he frowned.

"That makes sense… a treasure to reveal itself every fifth century… because it's reborn," Theon mused, realisation flooding his face. The king nodded.

"Yes, in an Alpha female. However, the thing is, Charlene has not shown any signs of unlocking this power. Trouble is rising from all sides, we cannot delay."

Well, I knew how that felt, having something expected of you and yet… unable to do anything about it.

"What if she isn't the one to have this ability? You said yourself, once every few centuries, maybe it's not Charlene," I reasoned, trying not to clutch my broken arm.

"She is the heart of Kaeladia. Before her birth, a prophecy was revealed. My daughter is the one holding the heart of our world, the powers that everyone on the planet seeks, and I want you, Theon, to train her, to push her to her limits until she unlocks those powers by luck or by force." His cold grey eyes met Theon's amber ones. An agreement was made without even a word spoken.

The king dismissed us soon after, and as we walked down the hallway in silence, I didn't know what to make of it. Something big was worrying the king for him to actually think of pushing Charlene to her limits. I knew he chose Theon because everyone knew he followed rules without thinking of the consequences.

"Do you think you can do that to her?" I asked, knowing exactly what pushing her to her limits meant. I was doing the same to myself; sometimes, I wasn't even able to move after training and even fell unconscious at times.

"Why not?"

"She saved your life, and you want to break her?"

His smouldering eyes met mine, and he turned, making my heart thunder under the intensity.

"If it's for her benefit, then yes, I'll break her willingly." A small smirk crossed his lips as he tilted his head. "What's wrong, little storm, jealous?"

"Oh please, jealous of what? Being beaten to a pulp by you?" I growled, when suddenly he grabbed my arm and snapped it back into place, making me whimper at the jarring pain that shot through my arm and neck, and my eyes watered.

"No." He leaned closer, the heat of his body invading my personal space, his chest grazing mine. I felt his warm breath on my ear as he whispered the words that sent a rush of pleasure through me. "To be broken by me."

My Worth

YILEYNA

Last night's events were fresh on my mind, along with Alpha Andres's and Theon's parting words, I hadn't even been able to thank him for helping fix my arm, something that I could have done myself, but it's a lot easier when you're not the one snapping your bones back into place. I hadn't shifted yet, so I didn't heal as fast as those who had.

I had woken up with Theon's words playing on my mind and an ache between my legs that begged for only one man's touch. As much as I was sure I could find a man to satiate the hunger, I didn't want just anyone.

I had changed and come out to one of the smaller, less frequently used training fields. No one really came this far out often, and since the pack had, in a way, shunned me, I felt more comfortable training out here alone.

Rain had fallen heavily all through the night, and it was still ongoing. The ground beneath my feet was muddy, and my boots were completely covered in it, squelching with every move I made as I punched the tree repeatedly, venting my frustration.

I was wearing a tank top with a leather jacket and pants; my hair was open, and I was completely drenched despite the overhead branches that partially shielded me from the rain. I didn't mind it; I was simply relieved that there was not a soul in sight. I guessed the regulars were all training in the indoor courts and halls.

I punched the tree again, the Alpha's words ringing in my head.

"Talent but no strength."

The tone of his voice made it obvious I was just a failure...

I punched the tree harder, staring at the blood that streaked the trunk. Despite the bandages I had wrapped around my hands, I had still bruised them. The once-white wrap was covered with dirt, water, and blood.

Useless.

A failure...

I was a shame to the De'Lacor name. I was meant to be my father's legacy... someone who he'd be proud to call his daughter, the future Beta, but without my wolf, I didn't think that title was going to be mine.

It had been two months, and I knew the rest of the ranked wolves wanted the king to pick a new Beta... no doubt the Gamma and Delta wolves had their eyes on that position. A position that was rightfully the De'Lacor's.

I felt an all-too-familiar stinging in my eyes as I continued to hit the tree. My grunts, whimpers of pain, and effort faded into the sound of the downpour, weather that truly fitted my mood.

I kept going, no longer focusing on anything but the pain in my entire body. I knew I was going to end up in bed for an entire day after this. I stumbled, my feet skidding in the mud. I fell forward, bracing my hands on the tree as my knees hit the ground.

"Now I think that's the best position for you to be in," a haughty voice from behind came.

Irritation flashed through me as I got to my feet, turning to look at the two young men who stood there. Nikolai and Kyson, warriors that were of the same rank as Theon, but unlike him, both were trash in my eyes. It had been Nikolai who had spoken. With his dark hair and blue eyes, one might think he was handsome, but his personality was far from it.

"I don't think anyone was asking you what the best position for me to be in is," I replied, acting unbothered as I began to unwrap the bandage on my right hand. I was shaking from exhaustion, and the number of splinters embedded in my hands was far more than I realised.

"Curvaceous, beautiful, and wolfless. I think we have ourselves an Omega... and what are they good for, Kyson?" Nikolai asked, a smirk on his face. Anger flared inside of me at the insult. I was no Omega!

"Fucking," Kyson added arrogantly, his brown eyes glimmering with lust.

"Exactly," Nikolai replied, his voice laced with amusement.

"Say that again, and I'll show you what you will or won't be capable of when I'm done with you," I hissed, clenching my fists.

"Ah... I see you have quite the tongue on you. Maybe we could put it to better use."

Kyson stepped forward; his shoulder-length blond hair was pulled back in a pony, displaying the scar that ran across his jaw. If he carried on as he was, I wouldn't mind adding another one to his face.

I scoffed as I stared at them in disgust. There was no one around for miles, and in the exhausted state I was in, I didn't want to be alone with those two...

"How about we do just that? Just looking at her makes me want to bury myself into the little whore."

"Touch me, Nikolai, and I swear by the goddess I will have you castrated."

"I think you forget you have no rank anymore; don't you know what they are saying in court? Theon might be taking the Beta title... and once he does, you become an Omega by default. But play for the right team, and we might just make that experience very pleasurable for you...."

His words shook me, but I refused to admit that. Was it true? Theon may become Beta?

He advanced towards me, making my heart thunder. His eyes were predatory, like the animal he was. Unmarked women were just targets for men like them, and one without a wolf was the perfect plaything...

"I am Yileyna De'Lacor, and until the king himself strips me of my rank, I am still the Beta candidate," I warned, my voice sounding breathless and shaky even to me.

"And a beautiful name it is for the flower you are. The king can strip your title, but allow me to strip you of a little more," Nikolai remarked, his eyes darkening with hunger as his gaze fell to my front, and I realised my shirt was sticking to me, almost completely see-through, thanks to the rain. In a flash, he grabbed my arm, spun me around and tugged my jacket off roughly. I heard Kyson's sadistic chuckle and felt their eyes on me. Nikolai's hand reached around, grabbing my left breast.

"Don't touch me!" I hissed, ripping his hand from my body. I twisted back towards them and yanked free from his hold, only for him to grab my hand and squeeze it painfully. I winced as I felt something break, making me gasp in pain.

I needed to get away from there. Now.

He slammed me against the tree, the jagged edges of the splinters I had created in the trunk cutting into my back. I could feel them embedded into me, making my eyes water in pain.

I raised my hands, using both to try to push him back, but he was a wall of muscle and one that was not going to budge no matter how hard I tried. I was as weak as a pup, and he was a full-fledged werewolf.

My gaze flickered to Kyson, who stood there watching, a smirk on his face. As much as I wanted to plead for him to help me, I knew he was waiting his turn... the very thought made me sick...

"Let go of me, Nikolai," I growled coldly.

He sneered in response and instead stepped right up to me. Reaching down, he forced my legs apart. I shoved him hard, but he didn't budge.

"You will pay for this, Nikolai!" I hissed.

"Will I?"

Probably not... he was the respected son of one of the highest-ranked families. No, he wouldn't pay because I didn't have my father to protect me anymore. Right now, I was the one who was a no one... even if no one said it... I knew.

He pushed me back roughly, pinning my arms to my side as he forced himself between my legs, and I felt my stomach churn as I felt his hard shaft pressing against me. Immense rage flared inside of me, like a brewing storm, as I struggled in his hold. Did he really find pleasure in this?

If there was a time to shift, now would be it. I was using all my willpower and strength to fight him, but I had worn myself down. I felt helpless... useless. Even though I tried so hard and trained so hard, I was still weak.

"Calm down, beautiful. Let's put this body to good use," he rasped huskily, making me glare at him in disgust. Had he always been so... ugly and sick?

"Let me go!" I hissed, trying to kick him, but he had my legs clamped between his, restricting me completely.

He bent down, one hand squeezing my neck as he forcefully pinned my head back against the tree trunk. His eyes fell to my lips as he licked his hungrily, a move that could look appealing on one person's face but was sickening on Nikolai's.

Using all my might, I tried again and pushed him, making him momentarily loosen his grip. I needed to escape! Taking the chance, I darted to the side, ready to make a run for it, when a hand twisted in my hair and yanked me back.

"Now she wants to do this the fucking hard way," Nikolai spat.

Something hit the back of my head, and I heard Kyson murmur something as I fell to my knees. He tossed whatever he had hit me with to the ground.

"She's done." Nikolai's voice came before I was pushed backwards into the mud.

My vision was slightly hazy as my top was ripped off, leaving me exposed in my bra. Nikolai climbed on top of me, pinning my thighs under his knee as he began to unbuckle his pants.

"The Alpha will not forgive you!" I shouted. He scoffed,

"He won't care… you aren't even Beta's Williams's own blood… I think you were right, Kyson, she was probably born from an Omega whore."

His words hit me hard, my heart thumping in fear. What were they saying? What did he mean?

"I'll show you exactly what someone like you deserves…."

He reached down, ready to unbutton my pants, but I forced myself up. I'd ask questions later, I needed to get away from there! No matter how terrified and helpless I felt, I was not going to let this happen. My body screamed in response as I brought my knee up and kicked Nikolai in the leg, making him fall back onto the muddy ground.

I lurched to my feet and barrelled into Kyson. He staggered, and I turned away. I needed to run as far and fast as possible before they succeeded in raping me.

"Grab her!" Nikolai growled at Kyson.

I ran blindly, the mud slowing me down, my feet squelching as they sank into the ground. Both men were gaining on me, but luckily, being heavier, they were finding it harder to keep up, sinking deeper into the muddy ground.

"Don't do something you will regret, you bitch!" Nikolai growled just as I stumbled, falling face-first into the mud.

"I would say the same to you too, Levin."

My head snapped up as a pair of hands grabbed my elbows, lifting me from the ground. Wet strands of coppery brown hair fell over his forehead, rainwater trickling down his perfect features, and I found myself staring into a pair of seductive yet dangerous amber eyes.

"Theon…"

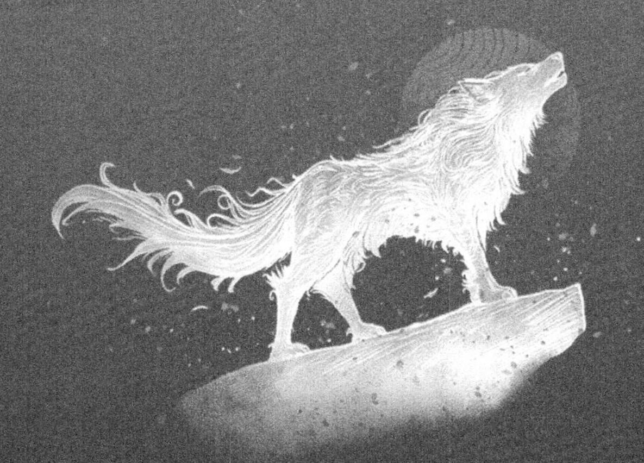

A Hot Brew

YILEYNA

THE RAIN CONTINUED TO beat down upon us, washing away most of the mud that had splashed on my face. He reached up, brushing my dirty hair back from my face. My eyes fluttered shut under his touch, a touch that I welcomed…

A wave of relief washed over me. Theon was many things; mocking, aloof, cold, and arrogant, but he was not a monster.

"It seems you can't stay out of trouble for even a moment," he murmured quietly before his eyes sharply snapped to the two men who stood a mere few feet away.

"You should leave, don't interfere where it's not your business," Nikolai's cocky voice came from behind.

The gold flash in Theon's eyes made my heart skip a beat. Even if the rest of his face remained emotionless, the anger I saw in those eyes… for me. My stomach fluttered before Theon moved me behind him.

"As warriors of the pack, it's a nice example to set."

"This has nothing to do with you. Leave. You saw nothing," Kyson added coldly. I stared at the back of Theon's head as I crossed my arms over my breasts, hugging myself.

"I saw enough to take this back to the Alpha." Theon stepped forward, and both men tensed.

I frowned as realisation hit me. They weren't scared of Theon but of the fact that he may be the future Beta… how rank made you everything or nothing…

The two exchanged looks, mind-linking before they glared at me coldly. The silent promise that this was not over was clear in their eyes. Both men walked past us, only for Theon to grab Nikolai by the collar and punch him across the jaw.

"What the actual fuck?" Nikolai hissed, clutching his face as he stumbled back.

"Touch her again, and I will kill you," Theon replied, his voice dangerous and cold.

Both men walked off, but Theon turned towards me. I suddenly felt very bare, despite having paraded in front of him only yesterday. Today was different. I suddenly felt dirty and used, the sheer weight of what could have happened crashing down on me. I turned my back on him, not wanting him to see the vulnerable state I was in, the fear that rattled me. My entire body was beyond the point of exhaustion.

I gasped when I felt his fingers brush my upper back. I bit my lip when he tugged a lint of wool from me.

The silence between us was loud, but I had nothing to say today. My heart thudded when I felt the warmth of his jacket being placed around my shoulders, his scent invading my senses. I closed my eyes. Despite the intensity of the comfort it brought me, the sheer reality that I was a no one… pretty much alone in this world, hit me hard.

My parents were dead… I couldn't uphold the De'Lacor name, and I had no one…

You have Charlene and Theon… I tried to tell myself, but did I?

"Let's get out of here." I nodded, clutching the jacket around me tightly as he turned away.

To my surprise, he took hold of my wrist, glancing at my bruised hands. A frown creased his brow as he led me away. I looked at his large hand wrapped around the sleeve of his leather jacket, my heart skipping a beat. He had saved me…

Theon may become Beta…

I glanced up at him sharply, wondering how true that was. Did he know?

I was so lost in thought that I didn't even realise we had come to a stop. He pushed open the door to the small cabin.

"Where are we?" I asked.

"My place." I raised an eyebrow.

"You live at the castle..."

"I have a room at the castle, but this is mine," he corrected, looking over at me. I realised that I had actually never been here... but how much did I really know about Theon? Not much. He didn't really share, nor did I bother to ask. "Are you planning on letting the rain continue to flood the place?"

I blinked and quickly stepped out of the doorway, about to shut it when he leaned over me, snapping it shut. My heart skipped a beat as he flipped the light on, and I took a good look around me. It was simple and clean, with a small kitchen area and a table with two chairs was standing to one side. On the other side, a two-seater sofa was opposite the fireplace, with a coffee table before it and two large bookshelves on either side of the fireplace. Two doors led off the room, most likely to the bedroom and bathroom.

Theon walked across the room and through one of the doors. I peered inside, seeing the edge of a bed from where I stood. I turned away, glancing up at the ceiling with the wooden beams and the iron filigree light shades. I had to admit the place looked very cosy.

His scent lingered in the air. I wondered how much time he spent there. I looked down at the mud we had stained the floor with and slowly stepped out of my boots, not wanting to spread the mud and water everywhere. I clutched Theon's jacket around me. Must I give it back?

"Go shower."

I looked up as Theon stepped out of his room, holding a shirt and some sweatpants. His clothes.

"Thanks," I replied, walking over to him. I took the clothes gingerly, careful not to dirty them.

"Wear the shirt back to front. I'll check your back over," he said just when I turned away, making me freeze. Check my back? He was going to check it?

"I don't need -"

"It's that, or we go to the royal healer, take your pick," he cut in coldly.

I frowned. What happened wasn't something I wanted others to know. It wasn't going to help my case in any way, and the rumours would spread fast.

I entered the bathroom, shutting the door behind me, and hung the clean clothes up on the peg behind the door before I took his jacket off. Mud covered the lining, and I felt guilty.

I'll rinse them off once I rinse the mud off myself, I decided.

I turned the showerhead on and placed my hand under it, waiting for the water to warm, and quickly stripped out of my clothes, carefully placing my panties aside. They weren't as wet as the rest of my clothes, and I needed to wear them. I stepped into the tub and under the water, welcoming the warmth of the hot water and letting it soothe my aching bones.

Once I had soaped myself clean and realised that I smelt a little like Theon, thanks to his body wash, I stepped out of the shower and grabbed one of his towels. I dried myself quickly and walked over to my muddy clothes, dumped them into the tub I had just gotten out of and quickly felt inside Theon's jacket pockets. Taking out a few explosive enchantments and two small daggers, I placed them aside and dumped his jacket into the bath too. Scanning the bathroom, I looked in the drawer under the washbasin but didn't find any washing powder.

I guessed he took his clothes to the castle to have washed. Omegas or the human staff would usually do all the chores like that, and someone of Theon's status would have one or two Omegas attending to him personally, that I was sure of.

Remembering what Nikolai said made a pang of jealousy flood inside of me. Theon was a young man, one who would obviously have needs… did he have Omegas for his sexual desires? Or maybe he visited The White Dove.

A deep frown settled on my face as my thoughts got darker and darker. After wringing out the clothes, I draped them over the edge of the tub and towelled myself dry before slipping my panties on. My body was screaming with exhaustion, and the urge to just curl up into a ball and go to sleep threatened to consume me.

I examined the pants before pulling them on, tying them tightly by the drawstring at my waist. Last of all, the shirt. I slipped it on backwards, flinching slightly as I reached behind and closed one button.

I looked at my bruised hands and sighed, picking out a few splinters before I clutched the towel and stepped out of the bathroom. I looked around, noticing the curtains were drawn. The lights were switched on, the floor was clean from all the mud and water, and both our shoes stood by the front door, clean. The hearth was lit with a blazing fire that warmed the entire room up.

I looked over at Theon, who was pouring what smelt like coffee into two mugs. I couldn't resist a small smile from crossing my lips. I didn't think I had ever seen Theon do anything so… ordinary? I wasn't sure if it was the right word, but he still looked far too handsome whilst doing something like that.

He glanced at me, raising an eyebrow, and I shook my head quickly, turning away and trying not to blush. I went over to the sofa and took a seat staring at the shelves. Most looked like history books, although there were some training ones and others on other subjects.

"Don't be nosy," he remarked, placing the two mugs on the table, and I took a moment to drink up his muscular biceps.

Oh, Goddess, this man is made to sin... may I be the subject of that sin?

I frowned at the thought, remembering the incident with Nikolai.

"Drink it whilst it's warm," he said, taking a seat on the sofa. I suddenly became very aware that it was the first time we were in a private place, alone.

I reached for the mug, my arms screaming with agony when he grabbed hold of my wrist and pulled me back.

"Are you simply stupid or incredibly reckless?"

He raised an eyebrow, giving me a cold gaze. My heart skipped a beat when he took my hand in his, using the other hand to feel my bones, cracking a few as he went. I bit my lip at one point, trying not to pay attention to the tingles that danced up my hand and arm at his touch. He dropped my hand, taking the other, and picked out a few pieces of wood that my body hadn't automatically rejected.

"Ouch," I winced when he pulled out a thin piece of splinter that was embedded in my finger. He glanced up at me before he let go of my hand.

"You didn't answer that question."

"I didn't realise it was a question," I replied.

Reaching over, I grabbed the mug. The shirt I was wearing slid off my shoulder, and I placed my free hand on my chest, moving back slowly. I inhaled the milky coffee, relishing the smell before I took a sip. Theon had made coffee. For me...

Oh, I couldn't wait to tell Charlene. *Wait, can I tell her this?* No, if she knew what happened, she wouldn't be happy...

I sipped the coffee, enjoying the silence as Theon picked up his own mug and downed it in a few gulps making my eyes widen.

"Wasn't that hot?" I asked in surprise. He raised an eyebrow.

"Not for me. I can handle the heat; we aren't all babies." His mocking arrogant tone made me narrow my eyes.

"I am not a baby..."

"No... maybe not. Want to share exactly how stuff went down that path?" He asked, the mood darkening instantly.

I shook my head. I didn't know what to say. How do you tell someone you didn't even do anything wrong or anything to instigate that? Nikolai's words were spinning in my head, only adding to the exhaustion I was feeling.

...Aren't even Beta Williams's own blood... Theon might be taking the Beta title...

"Turn around."

His command pulled me from my thoughts, and I glanced down at the white shirt that was covering me before staring into his eyes. A glint of something I couldn't make out flickered in them, but his gaze didn't falter, as if challenging me to refuse.

I clutched the shirt tightly and slowly turned my back towards him, holding my mug steadily with both hands now. I bit my lip, trying to ignore my hammering heart that I knew he could hear too. I stared down at my mug as I felt him tug on the shirt slightly as he undid the button. His eyes were burning into me, and my stomach fluttered as the shirt fell open, revealing my back to him. His heart was steady, and I wondered why he had such an effect on me.

I hissed when he pulled the first of the splinters from my back.

"You have a few, and you've begun healing, embedding them into your skin."

"Great."

"Hold still." I rolled my eyes. *I was still!*

My eyes flew open when his hand went to my waist, gripping it tightly, sending a strong jolt of pleasure through me. *Goddess, don't let him hear my heartbeat.* He pulled out another splinter, making me flinch as a sharp stab of pain shot up my back.

"That one was deep."

I nodded, unable to focus with his hand still gripping my waist. Goddess...

His touch was like a drug, intoxicating and dangerous, yet so, so... tempting. It made me feel all lightheaded.

I felt a trickle of fresh blood drip down my back and Theon's thumb brushing it off, igniting a trail of sparks in his wake.

"Perfect."

I turned just in time to see him lick the blood off his thumb, making my stomach flip and my core throb with a desire that he alone could ignite. His gaze flickered to mine, and those intense amber eyes fell to my lips, and then I heard it, the slight change to the beat of his heart…

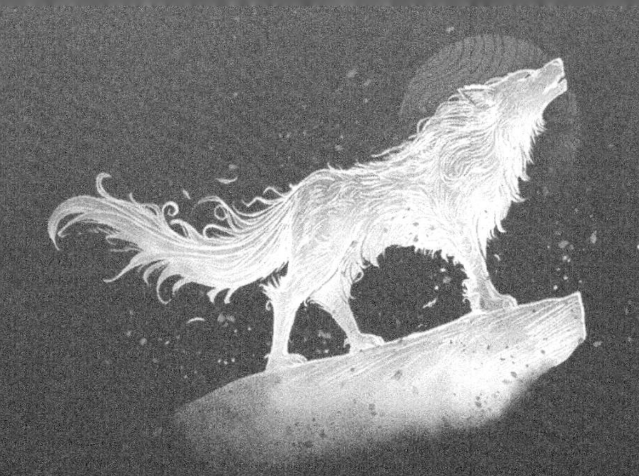

Two Questions

YILEYNA

I quickly turned away, my cheeks burning as I gulped the rest of the coffee down. I felt him move away, so I quickly placed my mug down and stood up, trying not to groan at the ache in my muscles. I slid my arms out of the shirt, holding it firmly as I twisted it around and slid my arms back in and buttoned it up.

I turned back towards him, his arms spread over the top of the couch as he glared into the fire, his brows creased in concentration.

"Thanks for saving me," I remarked gratefully, tugging at the sleeves of the shirt and staring down at the ground. *I surely must look a sight in these oversized pants and shirt. Now, what do I do?* I sat down on the small couch and pulled my knees up against my chest, feeling exhausted.

"You may not have been at their level, but you shouldn't push yourself to the extent where you cannot even defend yourself, especially somewhere secluded."

"Hmm. I didn't think that would happen. I just thought to train… I'm lacking in far more than shifting," I whispered, very aware of his hand near my head on the back of the couch.

"Are you? Or are you allowing others to dictate that?" He asked, tilting his head as he looked at me. His hair almost glowed a gorgeous copper in the light of the fire from the hearth.

"It's true, though, isn't it? I'm not strong enough. I'm nearly eighteen, but I haven't shifted…" I glanced into the flickering flames, frowning. "There's already talk that I may be stripped of my rank."

I looked up into his gorgeous eyes, waiting for a reaction, anything to tell me what his opinion on that was. He looked away and into the flames for a second before his gaze snapped back to mine.

"Who told you?" He asked, making my stomach sink.

So, he knew. He knew the Alpha wanted to make him Beta. I didn't know why that hurt as much as it did. What was I expecting? For him to care? For him to come and tell me?

"Does it matter?" I countered, looking down at my knees, unable to hide the bitterness from my voice.

"The Alpha only mentioned it a week or so ago. Nothing is finalised. There's still time."

Each word was like a punch in the gut. The tears that I had been suppressing seemed to be on the verge of breaking their dam. Still time…

"If he gives you the title, you will take it because he is your king," I said, forcing a smile. His face remained emotionless as he looked at me.

"No one refuses the Alpha."

Yeah…

I needed to get out of there… I shouldn't be there. We weren't friends… just two people who were always by the princess' side.

"I'm going to head out. Thank you," I whispered, sounding weaker than I was meant to.

"Yileyna…"

I stood up, staggering slightly. My legs felt like lead, and my entire body was aching from the workout.

"I'm going to head back." I walked to the door, my eyes on my shoes. Just like that, the De'Lacor name would vanish.

"You can't even walk straight." I could smell him behind me. Goddess, he moved so silently.

"I can manage," I replied coldly. "I need no one."

I had just about pulled one shoe on when he grabbed my elbow, yanking me back roughly. I gasped, almost stumbling, but before I could fall, he slammed me up against the wall.

"What are you doing?" I hissed venomously.

"Proving my point. You are not leaving this place until you are up to it."

"You can't keep me here!"

"Nikolai and Kyson are out there. Are you sure you want to go back in this weather all alone?"

"I never knew you cared," I shot back.

For a moment, he stared into my eyes before he let go of me, letting me fall to the ground.

"I don't. Get out," he replied coldly.

I'll do exactly that.

I pulled on my shoes with weak hands, realising that if I stepped out into the rain, my shirt would become entirely see-through again. I looked around before walking back over to the couch and picking up the blanket that was draped over the armchair.

"I'll return this."

"No one's allowing you to borrow it." And with that, he yanked it from my hold, his gaze dipping to my breasts which were moving far too much without my bra. "If you want to leave, it's going to be like that."

He turned away, throwing the blanket onto the sofa. I was leaving, one way or another. I yanked the door open without another word and hurried out into the rain, my arms crossed over my chest as I became instantly drenched. I didn't glance back, and when the door shut, it didn't bother me.

The future Beta… Beta Theon. Nice. I knew I was being bitter, but it hurt.

I dragged my feet towards the castle. I needed to speak to the Alpha… Nikolai said I wasn't my father's blood. What did he mean by that?

I was relieved that I didn't really meet anyone on the way home, and when I snuck into the castle, I was glad that there weren't many people around save the guards on duty. My body was ready to collapse by the time I reached my quarters. I cursed, realising my key was in the pocket of my pants. Pants I had left at Theon's, along with my bra… *Oh, Goddess, now what?*

I looked down the hall, tempted to go to Charlene, but it wasn't the time to disturb her. I was sure she was having dinner with her family. I'd ask the head Omega…

Or I'd just wait there… I felt far too tired to go in search of anyone, so I slid down the wall and curled up in a ball, wrapping my arms around my shivering cold body tightly.

I'll just rest a little…

I felt someone move me, but my eyes refused to open. In the hazy state of my mind, I had a feeling that the scent was somehow familiar as strong arms lifted me from the ground. The sound of a key scraping in a lock could be heard.

Open your eyes, Yileyna…

I couldn't. I felt like dead weight as my head lolled backwards. Whoever was holding me didn't really seem to care. The familiar scent of Mom's cocoa butter candles seeped into my nose. *Home?*

The man's footsteps creaked on the wooden floor. I managed to crack them open ever so slightly, but I felt like I was somewhere far away. I wasn't sure…. I was in my house, I could see that much from the angle my head was tilted. It was all I saw before my eyes fluttered close once again.

Get up…

But I was far too gone for that. I felt myself being placed on a bed, my bed. Felt fingers brushing my hair back ever so slowly. It almost reminded me of Mom's soothing touch… but it was different. I couldn't explain it… comforting, but…

And then I heard the door shut before darkness welcomed me back into its folds…

"Seriously, Yileyna, who trains out in the cold like that? We are werewolves, not immortals," Charlene scolded as she motioned with her eyes for me to eat the bowl of soup.

"You know I hate soup."

"You don't hate it, you dislike it, but it's good for you. Now, eat," she cajoled firmly.

I was sitting in bed the following afternoon, and I had slept most of the day until Charlene had shown up an hour ago, banging on my door, which was locked, and I had found the key on the floor.

Theon.

It had to be. He must have found the key in my pants. What was he doing looking in them in the first place?

Anyway, Charlene had shown up, demanding entrance and made me take a hot bath, which, I won't lie, made me feel much better. But the bowl of soup from the head chef wasn't appetising. The truth was, the only soup I ate was Moms…

I promised her I'd only eat her soup or none… and somehow, I just couldn't stomach the bowl before me.

"I'm not hungry, Charl… please," I pleaded. She looked down at me with concern in her green eyes.

"What is it, Leyna?" She whispered, sitting down on my bed and taking my hands in hers. I shook my head, refusing to let my emotions get the better of me.

"I only eat Mom's soup," I managed to reply, trying to remain strong.

"Oh, darling." She wrapped her arms around me tightly, and I rested my head on her slender shoulder, fighting back my tears. "I'll have something else brought right away."

"I'm not really hungry." I refused, moving back.

I was wearing a large, oversized shirt that used to belong to Dad. I loved stealing his clothes because they were so comfortable, and now that he was gone, it was all I really had of him. Memories… this entire place held memories…

Would I have to move out?

"Is the Alpha working today?" I asked casually.

"Dad is, as always," she responded.

Maybe once Charlene left, I'd go visit him. I needed to ask what Nikolai meant about me not being Dad's daughter…

A light knock on the door to my quarters reached my ears, and Charlene jumped up, her ginger hair bouncing around her.

"I'll grab it."

I nodded and dropped back onto my pillow once more, looking around my room. The walls were painted off-white, and the floor was solid wood. My furniture was all wood, including my bed. There were paintings on the wall, some with just quotes, others made by Dad or me, and a few that I had brought from our journeys out of Westerfell; one from when we went on a journey out of our Kingdom of Astalion. *Dad…*

Two pairs of footsteps approached. I quickly pulled my shirt down over my thighs just as Theon and Charlene appeared at the door. Charlene was holding a brown bag that clearly contained food.

"You brought food? I never knew the princess's guard was also a delivery boy," I remarked, trying to calm the nerves that erupted inside me as I sat up. The memory of what had happened at his place yesterday was fresh in my mind.

Our eyes met, and I swallowed, seeing his gaze flicker to my bare thighs before he looked back into my eyes, and I quirked a brow.

"Seems you're healed," he remarked, turning away and crossing his arms as he leaned against the door frame as Charlene brought the bag over.

I rolled my eyes, almost scoffing. My legs didn't have bruises... I wasn't ready to tell Charlene what happened, but I did want to ask Theon if he was the one who brought me inside.

"Alright, eat the sandwich up, and there's apple pie."

She unwrapped the items, and I took the sandwich, lost in my thoughts. I needed to talk to the king immediately.

Once Charlene had finished fussing over me, I tried not to meet Theon's burning gaze as he stood there before I was finally left alone. Luckily, the queen had called Charlene to meet someone or other, and both had left, but not before Theon's burning emotionless gaze met mine. Once again, I couldn't make out what was going on in that mind of his.

Quickly getting dressed, I left my quarters feeling tired and exhausted. The aftereffect of the rain and training still left its mark, and my muscles groaned with every step I took. I saw a pair of guards walk past, and I called out to them.

"Excuse me! Do you know where the Alpha is?" I asked. One of them raised an eyebrow whilst the other one's eyes softened slightly.

"Of course, dear, he's out in the courtyard. He was training, but he is done for now," he replied.

The perks of the mind link. That was another one I heard from the people. *If she had her wolf, she could have prewarned us about the attack.*

"Thank you," I replied politely before turning and hurrying down the hall. I hoped the Alpha would be willing to talk because I needed answers.

I reached the courtyard to see him sitting on the steps, peeling the skin of an apple. On the stone steps next to him was a bowl of fruit. I glanced around, but he appeared to be alone.

"May I speak to you, Alpha?" I asked.

Once upon a time, as a child, I used to address him as uncle, but as I got older, I started calling him Alpha, and that stuck, more so now that Dad was gone. That connection was also no more.

"Sure, what is it, Yileyna?" The Alpha turned. His hair framing his face only added to his dangerous look, and I lowered my head before stepping down onto the grass and turning to face him. The knife in his hand was large, and I watched as he made slices out of the apple. "Speak up." I blinked and nodded.

"I had two questions, Alpha Andres. Yesterday, an Epsilon-ranked warrior told me that I… that I'm not my father's blood," I began. The words hurt even as I spoke them. It still hurt so much. His face didn't change as he ate a slice of apple, munching on it before putting two more in his mouth.

"Rumours. People want to spread those rumours because you're not living up to your status," he replied.

A wave of relief flooded through me, despite the insult that was thrown in there. I was my father's daughter. Of course I was! But his following words felt like a few punches in the gut.

"But the truth is, all rumours start somewhere… I never saw your mother pregnant, so who knows exactly where you're from? Was your mother unable to carry? Did your father have you by a whore? It doesn't matter. He was always adamant you were his, as was your mother. Whether I believe it or not, they stuck by it… but the truth is, you hold no power to show that you are part of the De'Lacor family."

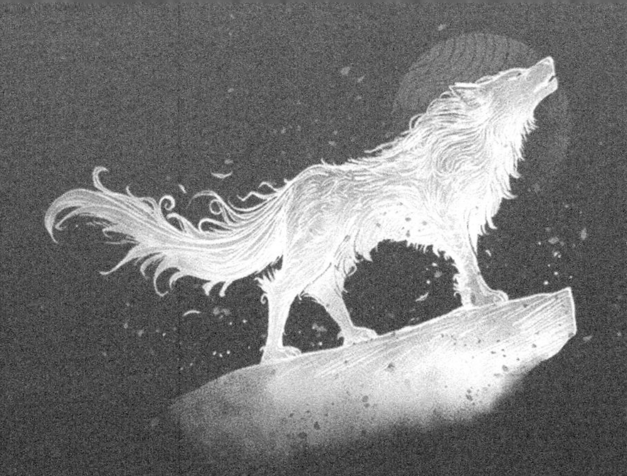

A Word of Warning

YILEYNA

His words stung. Was he saying that although Mom and Dad said I was theirs, there had been rumours… meaning there was something there…

I looked into the Alpha's hard, emotionless eyes, feeling very alone. Sure, he was our Alpha, his job was to take care of his pack, his city… and as king, his responsibilities were far more than that, but if even for a second I thought I'd get any compassion from him, I was wrong.

"I understand, Alpha, and that brings me to my second question; is it true that another will take my place as future Beta?" He leaned back on one hand, eating his sliced apple as he looked up at the sky.

"I need a Beta soon. I can't wait for a wolfless pup to shift to take that position. I'm afraid, yes, I will be choosing another."

His eyes fell on me once more, and I did my best to remain emotionless despite the pain in my chest. I bowed my head, trying to force a polite smile.

"I understand, Alpha. Will I be given at least some time to prove -"

"To prove what? You didn't shift when Will was killed in the proximity you were in. I don't think anything will trigger your shift." That stung. Guilt enveloped me, and I knew it was my fault they died…

"I understand. Will I need to move from the castle?" From my home?

My parents' home? It hurt so much more than I could express.

He sighed heavily, picking up a pear and slicing it.

"Come sit down."

I tried to remain passive as I sat down on the steps a few feet from him, sitting one step lower than he was. He didn't speak as he sliced the pear and peeled the skin of another apple.

"I know that place holds sentimental value for you, but they are the Beta quarters. When he takes the position, you are welcome to move to another room in the castle. You won't be asked to leave the castle." He pushed the fruit plate closer to me, but I had no appetite. I picked up a slice of apple out of respect and took a bite.

"Thank you for your explanation, Alpha." I bowed my head and stood up.

I needed to stop feeling sorry for myself. I needed to prove I was good enough, not for the Beta position but for my father. I couldn't let him down.

"It's nothing personal, Yileyna."

"Of course. Thank you once again."

I turned, leaving the warmth of the courtyard. The sudden coolness of the halls felt far more chilling than they were.

Nothing personal, just the pack laws and rules.

In this big world, I was just one more in the throngs of thousands…

The blanket of darkness had fallen over the city of Westerfell, and from where I sat on the roof of the Goddess' Citadel, the tallest building in the city, I stared down at the bustling streets lit with lanterns. Vendors were still running busy, and late-night stalls were as full as they were throughout the day.

The Moon Goddess Festival was coming up soon too. I guess everyone was busy shopping for it. I hadn't thought over what I'd wear. After all, usually, Mom had my clothes sorted.

Although the majority of the city was part of our pack, there were others who resided there; humans, mages, and fae. Being the middle city, the capital, we were the home to many, but along with that status and privilege, the risk was always heightened.

I ran my fingers through my hair as a sharp wind blew, and I turned my attention towards the outer wall. The wall that had been destroyed two months ago had been resurrected, and I knew it had been reinforced. There was still no news on what those rogues had wanted or how they retained that much sanity to think straight and plan something like that. Unless, of course, it was as rumoured - that there was a bigger force at play…

I sighed, turning away. The way the streets were thriving below, one wouldn't think we had lost so many…

Charlene told me earlier that her training began the next day and how I had to be there. It was good for her to train harder. Anything could happen…

The night of the attack, she had managed to sneak away from the place I had left her. I knew it was so I didn't get in trouble. If anyone knew that she had been there… that I had almost risked her life…

"I'm surprised you're not down by the White Dove." A deep, seductive voice that I recognised came from behind me.

My heart skipped a beat. I hadn't even heard him approach. My cheeks flushed at what he just said, and I raised an eyebrow.

"How do you know I go down to the White Dove?" I retorted, not even turning to look at him. What was he even doing there? After what happened at his place last night, I didn't think being alone with him was ideal.

"Isn't it where you go often? Clearly, getting a free show is the most excitement you will ever have in your life." I couldn't resist turning and giving him a scathing glare.

"Oh please, I could get a man if I wanted one," I declared.

Yesterday's events returned to the forefront of my mind, and I felt my stomach churn with distaste. He cocked his eyebrow.

"I highly doubt that." The mockery in his tone grated on my nerves, and I raised an eyebrow in return.

"And you knowing I go down to the White Dove must mean you're a regular there?" A strong flare of jealousy reared within me, but I fuelled my irritation into the glare I was directing at him.

He didn't reply, stepping forward and dropping to the ground. Even a simple move like that from him made my heart jolt. He leaned back against the bar behind him, looking at me. A single strand of his hair fell across his forehead, and a piece of straw was in his mouth.

Take me right now…

"I don't need to go to a whore house to get a woman," his reply came, bringing me out of my daze and making me pout at what I had been thinking.

I glanced over at him. True, he didn't need to go to an Omega… I was sure any woman would happily want him, but then I was sure he'd love the Omega females too… curvy, dainty, yet stronger than humans so that they don't break. Men and women alike loved Omegas…

I frowned as I glared ahead.

"And what did you come here for?"

"I come here often. It's a coincidence that you're here," his cold reply came.

Guilty… I found this place when Charlene and I were spying on Theon, although he slipped away. Later on, I had searched the area until I got to the top of this citadel.

"Or maybe not," he added, tilting his head as he looked at me. His sexy eyes made my heart skip a beat. Again. Goddess, I hated him.

"It has a nice view."

He didn't respond, and we fell silent. The passing breeze, the damp ground, and the glittering lights of my home city somehow felt… distant… like I was an outsider looking in.

"Did you go through my pants to find my house key?" I asked suddenly. He raised an eyebrow.

"The key was on the floor in the bathroom, so I thought I'd drop it off since you could barely walk. Pretty stupid for someone who was almost raped to fall asleep in an empty hallway."

Raped. I shuddered at the thought.

"The guards make their rounds…" He gave me a pointed look, and I trailed off. It was guards who had tried to rape me. "I didn't think."

"You're not a child anymore, and although you shouldn't trust anything I say or do, trust me when I say that many men have their eyes on you."

My heart thundered as our eyes met, grey against amber. They say that our eyes are the doorway to our souls, yet just like him, his eyes held mystery. One that even I could not break through…

"You're contradicting your own words," I remarked, standing up and trying not to wince at the pain in my body.

"I warned you. The rest is up to you." I tried not to focus on the way his voice sounded. Goddess, what was my problem?

"Because my father's gone, so now I'm open game? Wow, how nice. I think you forget that I'm not even worthy of being Beta. There's nothing beneficial for trying to claim me," I remarked, staring out at the city before I turned away to leave.

I gasped when he grabbed my arm, spinning me around roughly and slamming me against the rail he had been leaning against only moments earlier.

"This is not a joke. Grow up, Yileyna, and stop acting like a child," he growled, making my heart thud. His hand wrapped around my throat as he flicked the piece of straw that was in his mouth to the ground.

"Excuse me?"

"This has nothing to do with you being a De'Lacor. It's your physique that's the talk of the fucking town. Keep acting the way you are, and you will get into more trouble than you'll be able to handle."

My heart was thundering with nerves, yet at the same time... the tingles of pleasure that coursed through me at his proximity and the way his hand was wrapped around my throat sent a sharp jolt of desire to my core. His chest almost grazed mine, but it was the anger in those eyes that cleared my mind.

"I'm not acting like anything."

"Reckless and stupid."

A flash of hurt rippled through me, and I frowned. Was I stupid?

"You don't know anything about me, Theon, so just leave me be," I shot back coldly, trying to yank his hand from my throat, but he only tightened his hold.

"Then use that feisty attitude of yours to get free since you're strong enough to handle yourself," his husky reply came, the challenging glint in his eyes only making me glare at him.

I clenched my jaw, ready to bring my leg up and hit him where the sun didn't shine, but it was as if he knew what I was thinking. He forced my legs apart, placing his knee between my thighs, trapping my left leg between both of his. My chest heaved as I struggled to pull free, trying not to focus on how his body felt against mine.

"Theon, just because you saved me once does not mean you have the right to call me stupid or reckless," I hissed.

He needed to let me go before my arousal perfumed the air, and he found out how turned on I was getting.

"I'm stating facts. Next time, I might just stand by and watch. Seems like you don't really care what happens anyway."

"Why the hell are you getting so worked up?" I shouted in anger.

He let go of me roughly, and I fell to my knees. His jaw clenched as he looked down at me.

"Pathetic."

He walked away, leaving me alone on the roof. I stared at the ground in front of me.

Stupid, pathetic, reckless, useless. The list sure was growing.

I massaged my throat, knowing his hold would leave a bruise.

I had to remember I wasn't the daughter of a Beta anymore. I was just Yileyna, and I needed to grow up. Maybe he was right... maybe I was immature...

I stood up and climbed down, deciding I needed to return home. Maybe it was time I began to look for another place to stay. I wouldn't take pity and remain at the castle. I'd leave before I was told to.

Theon was right. I needed to grow up.

Pushing Our Limits

YILEYNA

The following morning dawned clear yet cold. The sun was shining, deceptive of the temperature outside. Great, the weather was getting worse as winter approached.

I had just bathed and was towelling my hair dry as I stood in front of the full-length mirror in my room. I paused, tilting my head as I observed my body. An hourglass body with larger breasts than average. With the light of the sun shining through the window, the water that clung to my body almost looked like little crystals clinging to me. Creamy smooth skin that Charlene always said looked breathtakingly flawless. Curvy hips that irked me as they reminded me of the Omegas, and thighs far thicker than the lean ones I was used to seeing on most werewolf women.

I sighed, turning away from my reflection and tossing my towel aside.

Today was the day Charlene was going to begin her training. Perhaps I could also pick up on some of the stuff that Theon would teach her.

I grabbed some black leather pants, squeezing into them and picking out one of Dad's oversized white shirts before tying it up with one of my leather corset belts. I rummaged through Mom's items, selecting a checked black and white hair scrunchy and smiling fondly.

Mom loved to do her hair. She often styled and braided mine as well. I was no good with that sort of thing myself. I tied my hair into a high pony, remembering when Mom did about thirty small braids in my hair. Oh, I had loved them, and when I opened them, my hair had been really pretty and crimped. She had told me that on my eighteenth, she'd do the same… I swallowed, exhaling deeply.

I shouldn't have been there… I cost them their lives…

I pulled on some boots, left my apartment, and headed towards Charlene's quarters. To my relief, she was just exiting her bedroom, whilst Theon stood leaning against the wall, arms crossed in a dark maroon T-shirt with a V-neck and some black pants and boots.

"Ready?" Charlene asked.

Her hair was pulled into a sleek bun on top of her head. She wore tan pants and a matching crop top. My girl is sexy. I was sure Theon was going to secretly enjoy teaching her. Yes, I liked the guy, but if there was one person I wouldn't be bitter over having him, it was Charlene. I'd die for her.

Although I didn't think Theon had anything but his damn looks going for him. Arrogant jerk.

"Shall we go, my angel?" Charlene asked me, a smile on her face as she linked arms with me.

"Right away, my queen."

"Where to?" Charlene asked Theon.

He didn't even look at her, stepping ahead of us and leading the way without even speaking a word. I rolled my eyes, exchanging looks with Charlene.

"At least we get a nice view," she mouthed, pointing at Theon's ass.

I smirked and nodded my agreement. Damn… that man had an ass you just wanted to touch. Urgh, we were as bad as all the men around.

Theon led us away from the castle, past the trees, and down towards the coast. It wasn't far from where we had gone the other day, but he didn't stop there. He kept on going, making us head down the rock path, the water not far from our feet.

"If we were to go down here, wouldn't travelling in wolf form be better?" Charlene asked as her foot skidded on the wet path. Theon paused and turned towards us.

"Not everyone is capable of shifting." His eyes met mine, and I raised an eyebrow.

"Good things take time," Charlene defended. "Besides, if we shifted, I'd carry her."

"No."

"Theon, can -"

"Have you ever carried someone on your back, Princess?" Theon's voice was cold as he continued walking.

"No, but -"

"Are you used to rocky, uneven terrain?"

"No, but I -"

"So, is the plan to drop her on her head and crack open her already empty skull?"

"Hey!" I frowned. Charlene furrowed her brow looking down, clearly disappointed.

"It was a suggestion."

"Unthought-out suggestions can kill. Use the brain you're given." His words were cold and harsh. I saw Charlene flinch at them.

"At least he knows you have a brain?" I comforted, giving her hand a squeeze. I held onto her tightly as her foot skidded once more.

Theon was right on one point; Charlene hadn't really had the experience in such places. Dad used to take me to all kinds of places to train. I remember fighting Dad on a plank in the middle of the ocean, and every time I fell in the water, I had to be careful something didn't attack me. But then again, I loved the water, even if it was dangerous.

We finally came to a stop, and Theon turned to face us, inspecting both of us. Charlene was a little breathless, and I was simply frowning.

"Begin sparring."

"What?" Wasn't that his job? To teach Charlene?

"Why else are you here? Now start."

I turned to Charlene. We had sparred many times, but something told me Theon didn't mean a friendly match...

Charlene fell into her stance, and I motioned for her to throw the first punch. She preferred defence, but Theon would be watching her. She lunged at me, and I blocked through my own jab.

"Fight like it's real," Theon's voice cut in.

"I'm not hurting her," I replied, sensing the irritation in his cold voice.

"The Alpha has given me a job... and unless you want me to take your place, you will do as I say."

"Listen to him, Leyna," Charlene replied. Her face was serious. I wondered if she knew about the prophecy. She must be feeling the same pressure that I was to live up to the expectations set out for us.

"Then attack me," I replied softly.

She frowned and nodded before she spun and lashed out at me. I raised my arm, blocking her before spinning around and hitting her chest. She stumbled and my eyes widened.

"Sorry!"

"Continue," Theon's voice cut in sharply.

Charlene threw a punch and I ducked, kicking her legs out from underneath her. She gasped when she hit the rough ground, and my heart leapt in worry. I held a hand out to help her up, when Theon knocked it aside.

"Useless. The both of you."

"We're trying," Charlene said struggling to her feet, massaging her head. My stomach sank when I saw the blood that mixed in with her ginger hair and stained her fingers. I couldn't. I just couldn't do this.

"So, the future Alpha of the pack is being defeated by a wolfless woman?" Theon questioned, a small sneer on his face as he looked at Charlene.

I hated his words, but the fact that he called me a woman… that sent my stomach into a fluttery mess, much to my irritation.

"She doesn't like to hurt me because I'm her friend," I added in her defence.

"The weak always die. Very well then, I'll spar with you." Theon stepped forward, and Charlene paled.

We both knew no matter how handsome and sexy we found him, he was ruthless, and he wouldn't hold back from doing actual damage. They began sparring, and it was obvious that Theon wasn't even giving it his all. With every fist that connected with Charlene's slender frame, my anger began to rise.

"This is far too brutal for her first day!" I growled.

"She's been training all her life," Theon remarked, his boot-clad foot connecting with her stomach, knocking her back a few feet before she tumbled to the ground. She rolled over several times before she came to a stop. "Get up."

"Theon…" I went to help Charlene up, but Theon grabbed my arm, stopping me. "One more step, little storm, and you're next." His cold eyes turned to me, and my irritation arose.

"This isn't teaching, it's beating."

"It's called survival, and it's high time you both learned that."

I stepped back when Charlene gave me a smile telling me she was okay. Was this what was wrong with me? That I wasn't doing enough? Was I really not pushing myself hard enough?

I watched them spar, and every time Charlene got up, he knocked her back down, criticising her footing, her strength, and her analysing skills. My nails dug into my palms as I clenched my fists. Every time Charlene hit the floor, it was painful to watch, and I wished it was me getting hurt.

"Enough!" I shouted when Charlene hit the floor once again, and Theon's fist stopped inches from her stomach. This time, Charlene didn't protest as she rolled onto all fours and struggled to sit up. Cuts and bruises covered her, and she was bleeding. "I don't think the Alpha will approve," I hissed, helping her up to a sitting position.

"He gave me permission to train her as I deem fit. And I'm getting irritated with you constantly challenging my orders." His eyes flashed with a hue of gold, and he yanked me away from Charlene, gripping both of my upper arms as he glared down at me. "You had the chance to spar with her. You failed."

"So, this is my fault?"

"Watch and learn," he said icily, looking down at Charlene before pulling me away from her. I wrenched free from his hold as he rolled his neck.

"Let's see how long you last in comparison to our future Alpha."

The insult in his tone grated on my nerves, and I fell into my stance. I didn't wait for his signal and spun forward, feinting a kick to his thigh but instead, I aimed a hit for his chest. He blocked both. Grabbing my wrist, he twisted and pulled me closer. My back grazed his chest, his seductive scent filling my senses.

"Far too slow."

He pushed me away, and I spun around, not wasting another moment, and aimed a few kicks. Each one was easily blocked by him, and then I realised he wasn't throwing any hits.

"Can't find an opening?" I taunted, raising an eyebrow.

"Sure I can. Just find it pretty amusing that you're trying so hard," his mocking reply came.

I narrowed my eyes. If he wanted to play like that…

I twisted around, about to kick him in the crotch, when he frowned, his hand shooting out and wrapping around my neck at the same time he knocked my foot aside.

"And if this were a real fight, I would have snapped your neck by now." He looked down at me, his gaze dipping to my heaving chest, and he smirked, "Out of breath already… weak." He wasn't even breathless. This wasn't fair… but fights usually aren't.

"Is grabbing someone by their throat your favourite move?" I snipped in.

"If it's yours... yes."

My eyes flew open, my core clenching at the words that could mean something entirely different…

"Well then, it's getting boring," I shot back, trying to swallow, only for him to tighten his hold. He leant down, his lips almost brushing my ear and his voice dropping a few octaves.

"Then maybe we should take it up a notch."

His minty breath fanned my ear as his thumb caressed the centre of my neck. My eyes fluttered shut, unable to stop the intense surge of emotions and desire that coursed through me. Goddess…

"No thanks." I managed to whisper, forcing myself back to reality.

"Then stop disobeying me."

"I don't answer to you," I reminded him, glaring into his eyes in defiance.

Not caring that his arm was now pressing against my breasts, the urge to hurt him and show him that he wasn't invincible consumed me. I was once told the ear is quite a sensitive part of our body…

"Either you like a punishment, or you really are stupid."

"Who knows…"

Taking the chance as his eyes locked with mine, I yanked his head forward, snaking my hand around his neck, and sank my blunt teeth into his earlobe, tugging hard. Oh, how I wished I had my canines!

A low growl reverberated from his chest, and I thought I felt something throb against my stomach, but it was fleeting. My heart hammered when he yanked away as if he had just been burned, and for the first time since I'd seen him, his eyes were filled with surprise. A trickle of blood dripped down his neck from his ear.

Our eyes were locked on one another, and I was unable to stop myself from licking the droplets of blood that coloured my lips. His eyes shimmered a dazzling gold as they dipped to my lips…

The River

YILEYNA

"She wins, right?" Charlene's tired yet happy voice asked, snapping us both out of our trance.

"We're taking a break," Theon's cold reply came, turning away swiftly as he walked down towards the water. My heart was thumping as the moment played out.

"O, M, Geeeeee!" Charlene hissed, grabbing my arm, her eyes wide as she stared at me. I blinked, trying to focus on what was happening.

"What?" I whispered.

"You two had a moment," she hissed, her eyes alight with excitement. My cheeks burned, and I rolled my eyes.

"We didn't. I bit his ear," I pouted.

"Umm, Leyna… do you think you could have gotten that close without him noticing? He was far too distracted by you, and that growl… it sounded more possessive and like one of approval than an angry one.

Okay, she had officially lost her mind. I rolled my eyes again, shaking my head.

"Stop rolling your eyes before they vanish into the back of your head!" She hissed. *Yeah, then I'll be wolfless and eyeless…* I shook my head, trying to focus.

"Okay, I think you really hit your head harder than I initially thought. Charl, you have no idea what you're going on about. Trust me, Theon dislikes me."

"Well, not once did he knock you on your ass. Instead, he kept pulling you into his arms or holding you when fighting you. I want that," she whined with a pout, making me giggle as she stomped her foot.

"Ah, my beautiful queen, how can I make it up to you? Shall we head back and make him panic?" I suggested, slyly wiggling my eyebrow at her. Her eyes widened before a sly smile crossed her face.

"Ooo, let's hide instead!" She decided, grabbing my hand as she pulled me away from the rocky edge.

I glanced over my shoulder to see Theon running his fingers through his hair, his back to us as he gazed out at the water, and then he disappeared from view as Charlene tugged me away.

"This is totally on him if we get lost." She groaned, "I feel awful all over."

"You know we still have more training, and I swear he's going to torture us for this when he finds us," I whispered, stumbling on some loose rocks and glancing down at the water that hit the rocks.

The water was a lot harsher here, crashing against the walls of the rocks as if venting its anger. I frowned, watching the dark colours. It was interesting how narrow River Rosewyvern was and so different from the waters of the Mighty Gulf just around the corner.

Enraged, dark… almost bitter.

"Yileyna?"

I blinked, dragging my eyes from the water to see Charlene point to what looked like a large rock.

"We can hide down there, and the water will disguise our scents."

"I don't know… that's too close to the waters…"

"It's not night yet, darling," Charlene rebutted, linking arms with me as she tugged me onwards.

I glanced back towards the angry water, trying to look into its depth, but the darkness was far too deep. The sun was shining. It was okay, right? The stories of avoiding the dark waters that Mom used to tell me hummed in my mind, and I shook my head.

Okay, I needed to stop being paranoid. Pushing my thoughts aside, I followed Charlene down the path, grabbing hold of her arm when she stumbled.

"I'm fine." She smiled up at me.

"I don't want anything to happen to you," I murmured, glancing at the water again.

"Relax, my beautiful angel," Charlene replied, almost as if she was trying to soothe me. We reached our destination and hopped onto the rock that jutted out of the water, then crouched behind it. "Now we wait for Theon to track us," she giggled. I smiled, amused, as I leaned back against the damp surface of the rock.

"You know he's going to be pissed," I murmured, reaching over and placing her head on my shoulder. She smiled and nodded.

"Of course. It's payback for beating me black and blue. Honestly, when I thought of Theon training me, I imagined something a little more like what went down between you two, all up in each other's personal space…"

I frowned, no longer able to focus on her voice. There was another sound… something alluring... coming from somewhere. A soft song, maybe? Music? My eyes were fixed on the water ahead.

It was still raging roughly, a few broken logs and branches were riding the waves, and the way the wood splintered against the rocky cliffs on the other side told me it was indeed rough.

Charlene was still talking as I felt a pull towards the waters. I leaned forward about to reach for it, wanting to feel it against my fingertips, when I was pulled back.

"Yileyna!" Charlene looked startled as she stared at me in concern. "What are you -"

A splash in the water made both of us turn, and to my utter horror, I saw deep red hair floating just beneath the surface before it emerged from the water. My heart thundered as I stared at the thing before me, something I had only heard of in stories. I knew they were there… I knew they were forever close… but never did I think I'd see one so clearly in broad daylight.

Her skin was smooth, and a soft violet sheen seemed to glow from it. The water clung to her like sparkling gems, and her eyes… they were a mix of purples and silvers, rimmed with long thick lashes. She was terrifyingly beautiful, and when she smiled, her teeth were sharp like razors, giving away that she was indeed a monster.

Her eyes were fixed on Charlene as she licked her plump lips. Her breasts were bare, with just a thin woven piece of seaweed squeezing them together covering her nipples. I didn't need to look down to prove that I was looking at none other than a Siren. Her tail, which shimmered in hues of deep purple that looked almost black, was behind her, and when she launched herself at us, a scream left my lips as I pushed Charlene behind me. Her long claws slashed into me, and I hissed in pain.

"Charl, run!" I shouted as the Siren grabbed my leg. A soft song began to leave her lips, and I saw Charlene's eyes become hooded. "No! No, Charlene!"

Reaching over, I managed to slap her across the face, knocking some sense into her. I needed to shut this Siren up before she did more damage.

"Theon's coming!" She whimpered.

Thank the goddess for mind links! Charlene lashed out, but the Siren was winning. Charlene grabbed my arms, trying to keep me from being dragged into the depths of the water.

"Just let go!"

"No!"

The Siren suddenly grabbed onto her, her long nails digging into her arm, dragging her into the water.

"Yileyna!"

My heart skipped a beat at the sound of Theon's voice. It was the last word I heard before I was pulled under, and the ethereal song filled my ears once again.

Was Charlene okay? I couldn't see her; my only consolation was that Theon was coming for her. I struggled against the iron grip of the Siren, but…

Was it worth it? The pain… the agony… the loss of my parents... this felt…

My eyes fluttered as I stared into the beautiful eyes of the Siren. Goddess… she was gorgeous… welcoming… but this wasn't right…

The enchanting song continued, but it wasn't having the effect she wanted on me, I could see that…. It came to an abrupt end, and I didn't feel as confused anymore.

"Come to me, my love," she whispered seductively, despite the confusion within her eyes.

The haze seemed to have lifted, and when her arms snaked around me, yanking me against her, alarm bells went off in my head. The moment her cold lips touched mine, I suddenly felt as if my body was weighing me down, but then, she was ripped away from me.

Blood tainted the water, and I saw her head torn from her body, my eyes blurry as I looked at the man before me. Her body fizzled away into foam, and then it was just… gone. The powerful waves hit me, and I felt myself being pulled deeper. A strong arm wrapped around my waist, and I looked into the handsome face of my saviour.

Theon...

He swam upwards, and soon we broke the surface.

"Fuck," he cursed, pulling me onto the rocky ground. His hand checked my pulse, the other brushing my hair back.

Charlene... where was Charlene?

"... bleeding..." I couldn't understand him until I felt my corset belt being torn off and my shirt being lifted up.

"Charl...ene," I croaked, coughing up water. My lungs heaved as they sucked in the air that I direly needed.

He tensed before he pulled back and jumped back into the water. I rolled over onto my side, hissing at the pain in my left hip. I pulled my top up, staring at the claw marks embedded deep into my skin. When did she manage to hurt me there?

A gasp made me look to the water to see Theon with Charlene in his arms. To my relief, she looked unharmed as he placed her on the rocks next to me, his eyes on me. My heart thundered, seeing the anger clear in his. Involuntarily, I found myself moving back, almost ready for his wrath to be unleashed.

"You almost died," he hissed, glaring at me. His anger was obviously directed at me, and it made sense.... I should have taken better care of Charlene...

"I... we didn't think something like this would happen," I whispered.

"It's not her -"

"I am not talking to you," Theon cut in dangerously, raising his finger at her in warning. His gaze was fixed on me. "Do you really want to die? Because if that's your wish, I wouldn't mind fulfilling it." His words cut me deeply, and I frowned.

"It was daytime. I didn't think that there would be a Siren out here."

"Also, she said not to! I was the one who was behind this!" Charlene intervened; her eyes filled with guilt as she stared at my hip.

"Well, congratulations, Princess, your spoiled behaviour and petty quims almost cost you your friend." He stood up, whipping his hair off his forehead as he glanced back at the water. "Let's head back. We will continue with training tomorrow."

I gripped the side of the rock, struggling to my feet as Charlene did the same. She was exhausted. I could see it on her face even when she grabbed my arm, wrapping it around her neck to support me.

Theon glanced back at us as we began walking, pain shooting up my hip and waist. *Fuck, I wish I had my wolf so I could heal faster.* He stopped, looking at me with anger simmering in his eyes. *Boy, if looks could kill...*

He turned, yanking me away from Charlene's hold, making me wince in pain at the rough tug. I gripped my hip as I bumped into his hard chest, almost tumbling back. His arm snaked around my waist, keeping me against him before he scooped me up bridal style, not even bothering to look at me as he adjusted me in his arms and continued walking.

My heart fluttered, very aware of his hand that was on the side of my breast, the other hooked under my knees. I snaked an arm around his neck gingerly, looking at Charlene over his shoulder. She was grinning widely and gave me the thumbs up. I wasn't sure if she sensed the anger that was radiating off him or the tension that was clear in his taut muscles.

Would I have to thank him for saving me again? I supposed I should be humble and thank him; the silence was becoming too much.

"Theon, I..."

His burning gaze fell on me, and my stomach twisted when I saw the gold hue that had overtaken his usual amber eyes, making all words die on my lips. He wasn't just angry... he was absolutely fuming.

My stomach sank as he turned his gaze back on the rock path. Something told me this was not over...

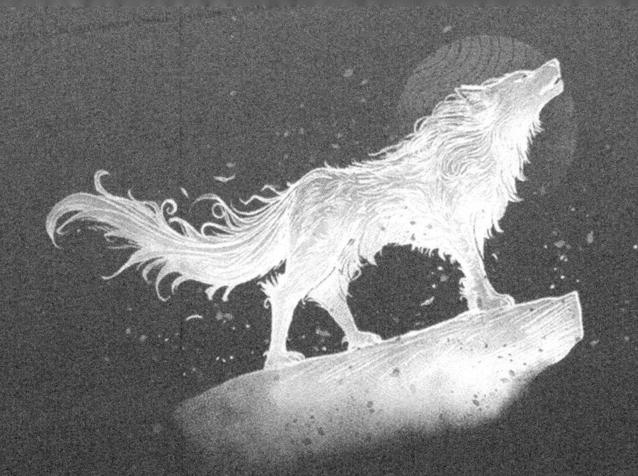

His Rage

YILEYNA

The moment we returned to the palace, Theon had told one of the other royal guards to escort Charlene to the healers for a check over.

"Don't I need to go…" A withering glare made me go quiet. I needed a healer too…

"She needs to be checked ov-"

"Take care of yourself first, Princess," Theon's icy reply came, cutting Charlene off.

I exchanged looks with Charlene, but neither of us spoke, knowing that if he told the king what happened… we were entirely screwed.

All the way back, Charlene kept on saying it was her fault and that she was ready to take responsibility, but Theon had ignored her. I knew she was trying to drill it into him that I had nothing to do with it, but I did… I should have been more responsible.

"I can walk," I declared as we headed towards my quarters.

He came to a sudden stop, not even looking at me and dropped me, making me gasp as I landed hard on my ass on the floor. Pain jolted up my side, making my eyes sting with tears. Goddess…

"Walk then."

He crossed his arms, his eyes simmering as he looked down at me

I frowned, forcing myself to my feet. The pain from the injury was excruciating.

"See?" I replied haughtily, clutching my injured side as I limped along, gripping onto the wall. I needed a healer, but I couldn't even mind link. Why didn't he let me go straight to the infirmary?

"Sure, the poison from a Siren's claw will kill you slowly," he remarked to my annoyance, following me down the hall.

This was so hard as it was. I paused, unable to go further, needing a break. I leaned against the wall, breathing heavily as I looked up at him.

"Yeah, I've heard. How about you be so nice as to call a healer for me?" I asked, trying not to scream as a flare of pain shot through me.

"You seem capable enough." I felt my irritation grow.

"What is your problem, Theon? What have I ever done that made you so angry towards me? Just get me a damn healer, please!" I turned away, not wanting him to see my tears. I gasped when his hand went to my shoulder, spinning me around rather harshly, but just then, we heard footsteps, and we both turned to see one of the healers walking toward us.

"Miss De'Lacor, Master Theon. I came as fast as I could," the elderly male with a long white beard remarked, his eyes instantly assessing me. So, Theon had called a healer. "Bring her to her quarters, Master Theon," he ordered politely, leading the way to my room.

I glared at Theon, warning him not to touch me. I turned to follow Healer Ulric when I was suddenly lifted by my thighs and tossed over his shoulder.

"Ouch!" I gasped, feeling the pressure on my stomach only tugging at the injury on my side.

"C-careful, Master Theon, she's injured, is she not?" Healer Ulric exclaimed. Healer Ulric was a healer mage and one of the heads at the royal infirmary.

"She isn't in that much pain, are you?" Theon asked, yanking me off his shoulder and into his arms. I gasped in pain, clinging onto his shoulder and glaring at him murderously.

"I didn't say that! I said I could manage; you are hurting me," I hissed, trying not to focus on his perfect jawline.

"Don't like a little pain?" He taunted quietly. My heart skipped a beat, and he quirked an eyebrow. "Key, little storm."

I blinked, realising we were outside my quarters. I quickly took it out and handed it to the healer. I glanced down at Theon's neck. My nails had drawn blood. Well, he was being a jerk to me, too.... Our eyes met, and aside from his anger, I couldn't make out the emotions in them.

"Lay her on the sofa."

"Or more like drop me," I remarked as he walked over to the sofa.

"Ahh, please don't, master..." Ulric said nervously.

Theon clenched his jaw as he let my legs down instead before he pushed me with a mocking flick back onto the couch.

"Good enough?" He remarked, glaring at Ulric. He didn't wait for an answer, walking out and shutting the door behind us with a snap.

"Sorry about that," I apologised. Healer Ulric was a respected elder, but it seemed Theon had no care for it. He smiled warmly at me and began to open his bag.

"Don't worry, I deal with brutish men all day long; he just has thick skin. He does care... he was very clear I must come immediately. Now, tell me, dear, where are you hurt?" I lifted my shirt, his words ringing in my head.

Theon was a mystery. I didn't get if he cared or not. Sometimes he did things that I was sure my delusional mind made me think he cared... but then I knew that was not true.

I zoned out as the healer got to work, a soft orange light around his hands as I pondered on everything. Was it possible to crush on someone who my mother would say was a total bad boy? One I should stay away from. However... no matter what a jerk he was, I couldn't get over the way my heart raced in his presence, the way those amber eyes lit my entire body ablaze with a dangerous desire. The fact that he was the only one who made me forget the emptiness that I felt inside...

"I'm surprised the poison didn't spread as deeply as I assumed it would. A Siren's touch is nothing more than death itself," he mused, sitting back and taking out a roll of gauze.

I frowned, remembering the Siren's Kiss of Death, and shuddered. There were rumours that when one is kissed by a Siren, their death is inevitable. It had been strange... they say when a Siren sings, one becomes completely enraptured and is lured to their death without even realising what fate they faced. Was that a blessing or a curse?

"Rest, Miss De'Lacor... the healing herbs will make you feel rather drowsy. I'll show myself out."

I didn't reply, letting sleep envelop me in its embrace...

"I don't know, Leyna, maybe you imagined the kiss?"

The following night, Charlene and I were in her quarters, discussing what had happened yesterday. Luckily, the king didn't question us, but it seemed Theon had had a word with him, and Charlene had told her father that she was fine.

"I couldn't imagine being kissed by that thing." I rolled my eyes, lifting my top as I looked at my healing wounds in her ornate, gold-framed, floor-length mirror. She gave me a sheepish look. Her gorgeous ginger hair seemed to glow in the warm lights of her bedroom.

"I know, but it's… you know they say it's bad luck," she mumbled, looking down at her organza gown and fiddling with the hem.

"Yeah, no one lives after the Kiss of Death, and if by some miracle you make it back alive, you will die soon? I've heard that old tale. I don't believe in it. We all know that they kill by ripping our hearts out, not by the kiss."

"But if you speak of it… people will associate you with bad luck. I would never think that, but just… be careful." I looked at her reflection in the mirror, our eyes meeting. I knew what she was saying… that it would just make me in whole look worse… I nodded.

"I get it… Theon probably saw it, but he won't tell anyone, I know that much, aside from the Alpha, if he hasn't already told him."

"I doubt it. Father didn't say." She shook her head confidently. "He just said Theon once again proved himself."

"Well, he did save us." I pouted. Saved me again…

"Did you hear what he said before we were dragged into the water?"

"Hmm?" I asked, turning away from the mirror and letting my top fall over my stomach.

"He called your name… he saved you first…." She wiggled her eyebrows pointedly, and I tilted my head, rolling my eyes.

"Oh, for Goddess's sake, Charl, stop it. He probably did that as the Siren had a hold on me. It was probably easier to save me first, or he just thought I was useless and probably would die before you." I dropped onto her luxurious four-poster bed and stared up at the canopy. The organza curtains blew gently, thanks to the wind that came in through the open balcony doors.

"I don't know… I just think maybe I need to stop gushing over him," Charlene murmured, watching me. I turned my head to look at her as she slowly lay back on the bed next to me, placing her hands under her cheek.

"I'm serious, Yileyna… I think maybe he's into you." I stared into her eyes and smiled sadly.

"I'm a nobody, Charlene… besides, this full moon he cannot avoid you," I stated. The last two full moons, Theon hadn't been around.

We can only find our mates once both have shifted and are in the vicinity under a full moon. Plus, this full moon was also the day of the Festival of the Moon Goddess. They say couples who find each other under the Moon Goddess Festival's full moon will hold great blessings throughout their life.

"Hmm, I highly doubt it," she said. Rolling onto her back, she stared at the ceiling. "I have training tomorrow. You don't need to come, I'll be okay. I need to do this… as future Alpha Queen… you know, Yileyna…" She sat up, staring at her lap. Her organza gown was open, and she was drawing invisible patterns on the silk of her pyjama buttons with a finger.

"Hmm?" I asked. She turned to me, and I was surprised to see the tears in them.

"When I become Alpha Queen, I'm going to make you my Beta. I don't care what happens now or who Dad chooses. You will be my Beta. It's your birthright… and not only that, but you are the one person I trust the most."

I was unable to hold back my tears as I sat up, about to get up from the bed to hide my tears, when she wrapped her arms around my shoulders.

"You are strong and perfect. Don't let anyone ever tell you otherwise."

I nodded, a few tears trickling down my cheeks. I couldn't tell her… but it wasn't that easy. As future queen, her job was to do what was best for her kingdom. One day she'd probably think the same as her father, and when she did, I wouldn't hold it against her…

The sound of crickets chirping and the distant hooting of owls filled the night sky. Silence had blanketed the castle, only then did I take my leave. The festival was the day after tomorrow and I still hadn't gone shopping for any clothes. I had even tried to fit into something of Mom's, but it was futile. We were far too different in body shapes.

I strolled through the silent halls of the castle. Charlene had been falling asleep when I left but I felt far too fresh to even consider sleeping. I decided to go for a stroll around the grounds. Perhaps that would tire me out.

I stepped out of the castle, the guards at the door giving me a nod which I returned with one of my own and began walking swiftly. A good jog may help. I picked up my pace, and soon I was jogging along. The wind rushed past my face, the adrenaline in my body fuelling me as I sped up until I was running as fast as I could, jumping and skipping over the steps or the low walls.

I couldn't stop the smile that crossed my lips. For a fleeting moment, I felt free, simply enjoying myself without thinking of anything else. I turned the corner and found myself in one of the far training grounds, freezing in my tracks when I saw none other than Theon.

My heart pounded, and it was not because I hadn't seen him since he left angrily yesterday… but because he was shirtless as he slicked back his damp locks, his arm flexing as he did so. His pants stuck to that sexy ass… tattoos of engravings ran down his spine, and there were some symbols on his lower back. He turned, his amber eyes flashing gold when they met mine. Anger…

I stepped back, raising my fist to my breasts. What did I do now?

"I didn't know you were here…" I said defensively.

I couldn't stop myself from letting my gaze trail down his tattooed torso and felt my pussy clench as I swallowed hard. Three chains hung around his neck, and his chest heaved as he breathed hard. A trickle of sweat ran down his torso and between his defined abs. The urge to lick it up was overpowering… his Adonis belt was perfection, dipping into those pants and -

I snapped my gaze back up to him, my cheeks burning. He saw me staring… Goddess…

He walked towards me slowly, and I stepped back, my gaze dipping to the bandages he was unwrapping from his hands slowly.

"So, once again, you're out alone when you know exactly how weak you are." His words hurt, and I knew his next words would be equally harsh. "Tell me, little storm… are you that desperate to be defiled?" A flash of anger rushed through me, and I glared at him.

"Don't assume. I was out for a run," I snapped icily.

He tilted his head, unwrapping the other hand as he leaned down close to my ears. His scent, mixed with sweat, made me giddy, my heart thudding at his closeness, and my core clenched in anticipation and confusion.

"Then tell me this…" his deep, husky voice whispered in my ear. "Why do you smell so fucking aroused?"

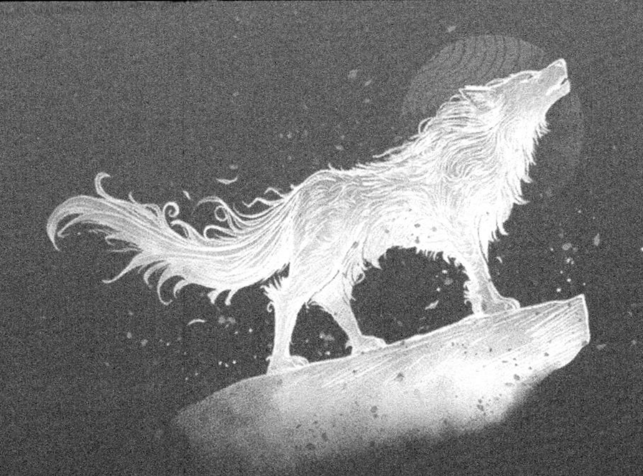

The Perfect Dress

YILEYNA

I GASPED, MY CHEEKS FLUSHING.

"I am not!" But before I could push him away, his thumb flicked one of my hardened nipples, sending a sharp sizzle of pleasure to my core.

"Your mouth can lie, but your body cannot," he smirked slightly, looking into my eyes. "Tell me, Yileyna... do you taunt me on purpose just so I pay attention to you?"

"Don't get so full of yourself. If I wanted you, I'd say so," I lied, turning my back on him. Was I that obvious?

My heart and stomach were a mess of nerves. I heard a small, breathy chuckle leave his lips before his arm snaked around me, placing his hand firmly on my lower stomach as he pulled me back against him, making a small, whimpering gasp escape me. I could feel his entire body against me. The bulge in his pants pressed against my lower back only added to the ache in my core.... The way his chest felt, rising and falling behind me...

"Then tread carefully... because in the end, don't forget that I am a beast worse than any other."

I closed my eyes, unable to reply. His hand ran up my stomach slowly, making me suck it in, my breasts rising and falling heavily. Suddenly he pulled up my top, exposing my injured hip. The cool air against the sore skin made me snap out of my daze just as he stepped away from me.

"You are lucky to have survived." His voice was emotionless once more as he dropped my top and turned away.

I felt as if anger was radiating off him. A tiny part of me wondered if there was any truth in Charlene's words. Could I deny that I'd love it if someone cared for me like that? I couldn't deny the attraction I felt towards him, but did he feel the same?

No one came to check up on me after the injury. None of the Gamma females or even the Luna... it seemed since Mom and Dad were gone, I was just no one, just another forgotten orphan.

"I... how were you not affected by the Siren's song?" I asked, trying to change the subject.

"Who isn't? I just knew how to keep my sanity." He tilted his head, and I tried not to pay attention to how sexy he looked. That sheen of sweat was driving me crazy.

"How?" I asked, my gaze dipping to his lips when he licked them.

"What? Planning to jump into the ocean again?" He gripped my chin, rubbing his thumb along my lips, sending my heart racing even faster. "She kissed you." I tensed, my heart thudding as I tugged away.

"D-did you tell the Alpha?"

"That you are more of an ill-omen now than you already were?" His words cut, and I forced a small smile onto my face.

"Yeah, I guess, so did you tell him?"

"No." I felt a wave of relief wash over me.

"Thanks."

"Don't mistake it for compassion. I just found it unnecessary. I don't believe in superstitions." I nodded. Of course. I would be a fool to think it was anything else.

"Goodnight, Theon."

I didn't wait for a reply, jogging back the way I came. *I think that was enough for tonight.* I felt his piercing gaze burn into me until I disappeared around the corner, letting out a deep breath I didn't know I had been holding.

Theon. The man was a mystery that, two years on, I had not even managed to make a dent in learning about. Who was Theon? What life did he have before he lost his memory?

Charlene and I had observed and noted his tattoos over time, but they were just strong proverbs or messages. Nothing to link him to where he may be from. They just gave the impression that he was someone with a strong will who was powerful and believed in striving for what he wanted. I could have told anyone that without reading his tattoos.

Theon… one day, one day, I'm going to learn more about you. I promise.

The following day, I did as Charlene had said and didn't attend training with her. Instead, I decided I'd do my own light training. Although I was almost healed, I was advised to take it easy. Then I needed to find something to wear, so I spent the entire afternoon in the bustling markets as everyone seemed to be doing last-minute shopping.

The cobbled streets were full of life; men, women, and children alike chatted, bartered, played, and simply enjoyed the occasion. I smiled, remembering coming down here with Mom and Dad two years ago. It was one of the rare times Dad would accompany us; as Beta, he didn't have as much time, but that year he did.

Smiling at the memory, I stopped at a stall selling pretty dresses, ones with the customary floral embroidery that the Kingdom of Astalion was known for. Despite the stunning designs, her stall was far emptier than most.

"Can I help you, my sweet?" The middle-aged woman asked from behind the counter.

I looked at her, smiling. She was part fae, part human, or mage, I wasn't sure… but it made sense as to why people weren't bothering to buy from her—a shame. Even though we were at peace, the discrimination remained… just how it would be like this for werewolves residing in a fae kingdom.

"I need a dress for tomorrow's festival, and your dresses are stunning…" But all looked a little too small on the bodices, well, those on display anyway. "Would you have anything that may fit me?" I gestured at my tan halter-neck top and flared black pants.

She smiled and tilted her head. Her dark hair had a few stray whites shining under the afternoon sun.

"Do I… well, I have this yellow fabric I bought down in the town of Khinesh." She pointed at a stunning yellow gown. "I have this embroidery all the way from Eastmoor…" she carried on, pointing at several dresses.

"I can adjust them to fit your bosom, I assure you. Now, tell me, my sweet, have any caught your attention?"

I chewed on my bottom lip. Mom always did this... I didn't even know how to shop!

"They are all so beautiful –"

"You should go over to the stalls over there, dear." I turned as someone tapped my shoulder. Her haughty nose turned up as she looked at the woman behind the stall.

"No, thanks, I like these dresses," I replied firmly to the elder she-wolf. Her eyebrow shot up before she stepped away.

"As you wish. A bad seed..." she muttered, walking off. I smiled apologetically at the woman.

"Ignore them," I said without thinking, instantly worrying if I offended her. Her eyes crinkled as she shook her head. The wrinkle lines around her eyes gave away that she was far older than she looked.

"I'm used to it. I have not sold one dress despite setting up shop every day for the last two weeks." She chortled, moving aside some of the boxes that contained folded dresses.

"Well, today you will because I need a dress." I touched the yellow, tilting my head. It was pretty... but I'd stand out. I turned my attention to the ivory and maroon; it was also nice...

"I think I have a dress that doesn't even need adjusting!" The woman exclaimed suddenly, her dark eyes sparkling as she turned away and bent down to get something from under her desk. "It's been collecting dust for the last few years... but it is a timeless piece, and I think it may be just what you are looking for..."

My curiosity was piqued. I think I did need someone to just choose for me. I was so indecisive. She took out a plain box that had probably once been white, yet it had taken on a yellowish hue over time. Unlike the rest of the pretty boxes that her stall held, which were tied with ribbons, this one was plain.

"The fabric isn't the latest. It's something I picked up on a visit home. Open it."

My heart skipped a beat as I looked at the box. From a Fae kingdom, maybe? I lifted the lid from the box, staring inside at the folded dress. A smile crossed my lips, and I didn't need to ask her to take it out.

This was it—the perfect dress. I knew it was going to fit me, just as she had said.

"Oh, thank you, madam..."

"Ailema." She smiled

"Thank you, Madam Ailema! I love it. May I know the price? It's perfect," I complimented, running my hand over the fabric before lifting the short dress from its box. She chuckled.

"You have already paid for it." I frowned.

"No, I haven't."

"You have, with kindness, child."

"No, kindness isn't something to use as payment, I have money."

"You don't argue with an old woman, my sweet! My word is final! However, I have some accessories and shoes to match, and you can pay for those! I need to make an earning too." I couldn't help but smile, nodding in defeat.

"Then you better show me your finest heels."

"Shopping for tomorrow, it isn't like girls to leave it until the last day."

I turned, recognising the voice of none other than Raiden Bolton, one of the future Gammas and also the older brother to Rhys, the boy I had protected that fateful night.

"As you may have heard, I'm not really the ordinary 'ideal girl' now, am I?" He smirked, his curly black locks tumbling in front of his eyes.

"Of course not ordinary. Yileyna De'Lacor is one of a kind and absolutely ideal." I rolled my eyes.

"It's far too early to flirt, Raiden. I'm sure Kahlia wouldn't be happy," I replied, picking up a pair of pretty heels.

"Kahlia?" He looked confused for a moment before smirking, "She was three women ago, my little flower. The only name I cannot forget is yours."

"Go away, Raiden." He chuckled and glanced at Ailema, who was watching him firmly.

"I'll see you tomorrow… by the way, that dress is gorgeous." I gave him a glare, but he simply winked one of those bright blue eyes of his before he walked off.

"Well, he is charming," Ailema replied with a knowing smile.

"He's a player."

Raiden was a year older than me, and he always flirted with me, but it was just that. Playful flirting. But somehow, I was beginning to look forward to tomorrow. Maybe what I needed were some fun and merriment. That is what tomorrow promised. Food, dancing, games, and happiness. And I planned to look as good as I wanted to feel.

"These ones," I said, picking up a pair of heels…

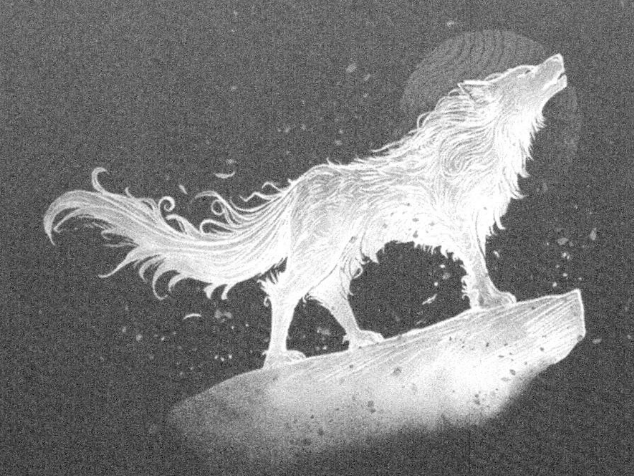

The Moon Goddess Festival

YILEYNA

THE NIGHT OF THE Moon Goddess' Festival arrived, and, like every year, the skies were clear, the full moon gracing us with its presence, and the sheer ambience of the night was warm and welcoming. The merry music drifted through the open windows, making you want to get up and join.

I was getting ready with Charlene. She had been adamant that I spend the afternoon getting ready with her, although this was usually a time one spent with their families, and every year before this one, she and her mother got ready together just as I did with mine.

"Those curlers look ready to be removed," Charlene said to the human woman who was helping us.

"Yes, Princess," Belinda replied, bowing her head before she came over to me and began to remove the curlers from my hair.

I stared in the mirror at my face. My make-up was done; having been told my skin was perfect without a base, she said she'd do subtle touch-ups… but I looked entirely different. I looked older, more mature. My cheeks were accentuated, a shimmer dusting my cheekbones, with a vibrant deep pink lipstick coating my lips. My eyelashes were layered with mascara, making my long lashes stand out even more with a touch of shimmer on my lids.

When she began to open my hair, letting my now curly hair frame my face, Mom came to mind and her promise to curl my hair on my birthday. I felt a little emotional, but before I could delve into those thoughts, the door to Charlene's room opened and her mother, Luna Soleil, stepped inside.

She was an inch taller than Charlene, with features that were very similar to her daughters. Her red hair was braided and twisted into an updo woven with sprigs of fresh flowers. She wore a gorgeous pale blue dress with coloured embroidery along the entire skirt that fell to the ground, spreading around her stunningly. I stood up and lowered my head to the Luna.

"I thought I'd come to check how you girls were getting on. My, you look breath-taking, Charlene," Luna Soleil complimented, looking over at Charlene, who was wearing an off-shoulder ivory dress with a green leafy pattern along the sleeves and bodice. It reached just below her knees, and she had accessorised it with deep green jewellery that only enhanced the green in her eyes.

"We are almost done. I'm ready," Charlene replied, smiling over at me.

"Perfect, we need to leave," Luna Soleil reminded her.

The royal family would walk down the main street before taking their place in one of the marquees. The Luna wasn't often seen out. Being the true mate of the Alpha, if she were killed, it would kill the Alpha too, and so she was always kept inside. Even for this festival, she would spend the majority of the time inside and under heavy security, away from the public. Even Charlene would not be able to enjoy the festival as I would.

"You look lovely as well, Yileyna," Luna Soleil remarked, looking me over. I didn't miss the way her eyebrow shot up as she looked at the dress that I was wearing. "Interesting choice. Now come along, Charlene." I smiled politely, although I didn't think it was exactly a compliment. Was it the fabric?

"Ah, I got to go! I will see you for the banquet," Charlene whispered, giving me a tight hug. She smiled, her red-coloured lips only complimenting her snowy skin. I nodded.

"See you later."

I watched her until she disappeared from the room before I looked back in the mirror. The lace dress I wore was fitted to the waist, with thin straps and a bow on each shoulder. The skirt was four layers of tulle with a matching belt tied around my waist. The fabric had tiny sparkling stones sewn to it, giving the dress a stunning sparkle every time I moved.

Belinda finished doing a braid along the crown of my head, adding a few sprigs of flowers and leaving the rest open. I reached up, tugging a few strands out and letting them frame my face.

"Thank you, Belinda."

I bent down and pulled my matching heels on, tying the ribbon that went around my ankle in a bow before I put in the drop earrings that I had selected from Mom's collection. I stood up and smiled at my reflection, trying to imagine what Mom and Dad would say to me.

Dad would compliment me and joke that he needed to hide me away from all the lads. Mom would get emotional and say I've grown so much.

The first round of fireworks that signalled the Alpha and his family had stepped out made me turn.

"Have fun tonight!" I called out to Belinda, knowing that once her chores were completed, she'd be able to enjoy the festival if she wanted.

Humans would join in too. Although they didn't worship the same deity as us, the festival was still a place of fun for all. The food alone was enough to get anyone to step out of the confines of their homes.

"Thank you, Miss!" She called as I left the room, clutching onto my little pouch that hung from my wrist.

I was going to make sure I won some toys so I could donate them to the kids at the city orphanage. I rushed from the castle, my excitement growing with every step…

"I win!" I jumped up, punching the air as the man behind the counter chuckled.

"Finally, but well done, now which one would you like?"

"Finally? I used seven gold coins there! It is not easy to hit three targets when they are moving," I pouted. "Oh, that white bunny!"

"Yes, yes, but can't have it too easy, now can I, lass?"

"I guess not." I smiled, taking the bunny teddy and walking along the bustling streets.

Couples, families, and groups made their way around the vendors or simply enjoyed the treats they held in their hands. Laughing and joking, some newly mated couples were obvious to point out, staring with starry eyes into their mates' eyes—that, or making out with one another, like they only existed in each other's worlds.

Mates, it wasn't very often that we actually found our fated mates. They say one in five people will find their true mates. It's rare, considering they could be anywhere in the world. Since I had stepped out, I had received a lot of attention, and a lot of it was from young men.

I stopped outside a food stall, the smell of the fried steak fries filling my nose, and I waited patiently for my turn to purchase them. I tried to ignore the two young girls in front of me who were staring at me very openly.

"Hey…" I waved, hoping they realised they were staring.

"You look like a princess," one of them exclaimed.

"Yes, you only need a tiara," the second added.

Both looked cute themselves. They were no older than ten and were dressed in stunning organza dresses with floral embroidery on them.

"Well, I believe that we don't need a crown to be a princess," I replied with a smile. "Just like the two princesses before me." They giggled, turning away when it was their turn to order, just as two adults came hurrying over.

"Thanks, aunty!" One of the girls said, smiling at the woman who had paid for them.

I turned my gaze to the sky above, glancing at the full glowing moon, enjoying the soft wind whispering past me. They say when we die, we go to the realm of the Moon Goddess... were Mom and Dad there now?

"Next!"

"One cone of fries, please," I spoke, stepping forward and taking out the money to pay for it.

"My! You look stunning!" The woman behind the counter complimented me as she tossed salt and pepper over the square of paper containing my fries before giving them a good shake and holding it out to me.

"Thank you!"

"Next!" She called, giving me a nod as I moved away, and a group of five stepped forward.

I picked up the little wooden fork and began eating, balancing my bunny under my arm. The sound of upbeat folk music reached my ears, and I followed it until I saw a large crowd of young adults clearly seeming to have some sort of dancing show going on. A large group had gathered around to watch the twelve young women in the middle dance to the current song, all dressed in vibrant colours. The crowd sang along, clapping and cheering them on. I munched on my chips, pushing my way through the crowd until I got to the front.

"Oi, stop pushing!" A woman growled.

"I'm short!" I protested apologetically. Well, short in werewolf standard anyway.

I moved my hips to the music, eating my chips and enjoying the show. I had just about finished my chips when one of the stunning women dancing grabbed my wrist.

"Join us!"

I blinked as the crowd cheered. I looked around, scanning the crowd, wondering if there were any of the high-ranking wolves there. Seeing none, I tossed my bunny to the ground behind us and started watching the other women's footwork. I placed my hands on my hips, copying them as we danced to the music. I swayed my body sensually as I twirled, hoping my dress didn't ride up.

"Go, Yileyna!"

My eyes widened as I spun around, scanning the crowd when a head full of black hair caught my attention. Raiden stood there, looking handsome in a navy shirt tucked into a pair of black pants and a belt around his waist. His arms folded as he watched me, giving me a wink. Confidently, he strode towards us and fell in step by my side as he began dancing alongside us. The crowd only seemed to get more excited.

"Seriously, Raiden?"

"Only way to get a dance with you," he replied, smirking as he took my hand and spun me out. His eyes dipped to my breasts as his hand went to my waist, his eyes flashing before locking with mine. "You've always been the most beautiful girl in Astalion… but tonight, I don't think there's even one woman on this planet who can match up to your beauty."

"How poetic." I smiled, raising my eyebrow. "But thank you. It's a pretty dress, isn't it?" He spun me around, his hands on my hips as he danced behind me.

"Not as pretty as the girl in it."

"Don't make me your next pursuit, Raiden, it won't work. I am not interested," I said lightly, pulling away and dancing by his side once more.

"You can never be just another one of my escapades, Yileyna. I genuinely…" he trailed off, spinning me back into his arms and pressing me against his firm chest. I could feel his entire body against mine and blushed in embarrassment as I tried to pull away. "Don't look now, but I think many are jealous of me right now." He chuckled.

I was confused, wondering what he had been about to say, when I felt a chill run down my spine as the song came to an end. Through the cheers and clapping, I looked in the direction Raiden was staring, my heart thundering when I saw Theon standing there, his arms crossed. His eyes shimmered a dazzling gold, the hostility in them clear as he glared at Raiden…

The Alpha's Announcement

YILEYNA

"Maybe I was wrong..." Raiden murmured, confusing me.

I pulled him to the side as the next song began, and more people began to join in with the dancing.

"Hi, Theon," I said as I collected my bunny from the ground, dusting it off. His eyes snapped to me, and I saw the tick in his jaw as he clenched his teeth.

"Yileyna."

My stomach fluttered, as it always did when he called my name. He looked handsome in full black, his sleeves were pushed up, and his pants hugged his thighs. A white belt with a silver chain on it was around his hips, only emphasising his incredible body.

"It's a pleasure to see you, Theon," Raiden offered, smiling respectfully. No one needed to announce it for me to know that everyone already saw him as their soon-to-be Beta.

"Wish I could say the same," Theon's cold reply came.

I looked between the two men. The humour that had danced in Raiden's eyes moments earlier was gone, replaced by curiosity and a hint of something else.

"Well, enjoy the evening. Yileyna, it was an honour to dance with you tonight." He gave me a charming smile and took my hand. He raised it to his lips, kissing it softly.

"Enjoy the rest of your evening…" I replied, trying not to let Theon's glare affect me.

Charlene's words came back to me. *If there was any truth in what she said, then...* My heart skipped a beat, and I was unable to stop myself from reaching up and pecking Raiden on the cheek.

"Thank you as well for being such a pleasure to dance with."

My heart was going crazy, and I dared not look at Theon. My eyes were fixed on Raiden's blue ones. A smile crossed his face, and he nodded.

"Anytime, beautiful."

He gave Theon a final nod before walking off, and I dared to gather my courage to look at the amber-eyed man next to me.

"Hey." Wait… didn't we already greet one another? I fiddled with the strands of hair that framed my face, almost dropping my rabbit. The silence was deafening.

"Didn't I warn you to stay away from men like him?" I looked at him, surprised.

"I don't need to stay away from anyone if I don't want to. Besides, he's nice," I stated, trying not to pay attention to the way I was feeling. Was it just me, or was he acting like a jealous, possessive male? Maybe I was delusional, and it was just my wishful thinking that was confusing me.

He grabbed me by the wrist, making me gasp at the power in his grip as he turned and dragged me along with him away from the glittering lanterns and music.

"Theon! You're hurting me!" He didn't reply, pulling me around a corner roughly and down a dimly lit alleyway. "Theon! Stop it! What is your problem?" I snapped.

He turned, his eyes shimmering with irritation as he grabbed my arms and slammed me against the stone wall behind me, making me gasp at the brutal force he had used. One of his hands was still wrapped around my wrist, pinning it to the wall next to my head. He didn't reply, simply glaring at me as if he wanted to burn holes through my head. His heart was beating a little faster than usual, and my gaze dipped to his lips.

"My problem is that your stupidity knows no bounds."

"Or is it that maybe you want me?" I whispered softly. "I'm not stupid, Theon... otherwise, care to explain why seeing me talking to Raiden really pissed you off? I'm not Charlene. You're not my bodyguard. What I do is none of your concern. You need not get pissed off." Call me crazy, but I couldn't just let him get away without explaining himself.

"Was that your aim? To piss me off?"

His husky voice was making me breathless. I tried to focus on anything but how close he was now standing. How could someone irritate you yet at the same time make you want them so badly?

"Not exactly…"

His scent invaded my senses, and my core clenched when he stepped even closer. My breasts that were already sticking out, thanks to him keeping my arms captive against the wall, pressed against his chest.

"Then… was the aim to make me jealous?"

My eyes flew open at his words, gasping when he released one of my wrists and instead wrapped it around my neck.

"Did it work?" I braved, my heart thumping. I watched him as his gaze dipped to my cleavage before slowly running back up to my lips. *Say something…*

I could smell my arousal… which meant he sure as hell could.

We were too close… I could feel his body barely centimetres away from mine. The bulge in his pants pressing against my lower stomach only made my core throb. The urge to reach down was overwhelming, but instead, I wrapped my hand around his wrist as he held my neck.

"I warned you that I'm a beast and I will destroy you. You're playing a game far bigger than you could ever imagine... keep tempting me, and I'll ravish you in a way... that you never could even imagine in your wildest dreams."

I slowly ran my hand down his forearm, trying to comprehend what was happening. He wanted me, even if it was just a desire he wanted to satiate… a pang of hurt clawed at my chest, and reality hit me hard.

No. No, he was right. He'd destroy me… but… I still needed something. No. I wanted him. I wanted to feel what he could offer, even if it was just once before he realised he had made a mistake.

"Then show me. Show me exactly what you can offer…" I whispered, running my hand down his waist, feeling his hard, muscular body through his shirt.

The slight racing of his heart made my own speed up. Our eyes locked as his hand tightened around my neck. We knew it was reckless. I could see the battle within his gorgeous amber eyes as he fought himself. Which side would win? Logic? Or Lust?

His thumb caressed my neck, making me sigh.

"I'm glad you aren't wearing a necklace because the only thing that looks good wrapped around your neck is my hand."

Goddess… His words sent another sizzle of pleasure through me. How could he make me so crazy with just his words? I ran my tongue along my upper lip sensually. A wanton moan escaped them when I felt him throb against my lower stomach and a low growl escaped his lips.

"Fuck, Theon…" I whimpered the moment he crushed his body against mine completely, closing the tiny gap that had separated us moments earlier.

He leant down, his lips near my ear. The warmth of his breath made me giddy with anticipation when he tensed, freezing. His heart thudded, and I knew reality must have settled in.

Don't pull away… I couldn't let him… I didn't want to be alone.

In a futile attempt, I ran my hand over his package. My pussy clenched at just the light feel I had managed of his large shaft. I heard him suck in a sharp breath as he moved his head back, looking down into my eyes.

"The king has summoned us. We need to get to the banquet now."

He let go of me, turning away, his voice once again cold and emotionless before he walked off, not even waiting for a reply. The absence of the warmth of his body made me feel strangely cold.

He had left me alone in this dark alley, feeling... empty.

I headed for the banquet field, wondering why the king had summoned us and feeling confused.

It was clear that there was something from Theon's side. I wanted him, he wanted me, but all we did was clash… I wasn't a fool. I knew Theon didn't seem like the type to want anything more. But… I couldn't deny how I felt in his presence.

I looked around the tables, unsure where to sit. Once upon a time, I sat at the Alpha table with my family. I saw Charlene watching me and gave her a small wave, and forced a smile.

"Sit down, dear," Raiden's mother, Andrea, said. She was probably one of the only ones who weren't entirely hostile to me for saving their son, I guess. Although even then, they kept it neutral.

I sat down at one of the long tables covered in white cloth with flowers and wine set in between the luxurious platters of food. I looked around slowly, scanning the area until I spotted the king talking to Raiden's father, Gamma Henry, as well as Gamma Grayson.

"Do you know what's happening?" I asked. Andrea smiled sympathetically.

"Oh, nothing at all." She was lying. I nodded, not saying anything else, as Rhys flashed me a smile.

"You look beautiful," he commented, blushing lightly.

"I said the very same thing," Raiden's drawling voice came as he pulled the seat next to me out and sat down.

After what happened with Theon, I didn't want Theon to see me sitting next to Raiden, but there was nothing I could do or come up with that would be a good enough excuse for me to leave the table. I forced a smile, and he frowned slightly, looking concerned.

"Are you okay?" He asked quietly as the king walked to the Alpha's table that stood on a dais, a table where his two Gammas and usually the Beta family would sit…

I nodded in response to Raiden, reaching over and helping myself to part of the lamb joint. A pleasant hum of chatter filled the room as everyone began to eat. I picked up my knife when Raiden's hand closed around my forearm.

"What is this?" His voice was sharp yet full of concern, and I looked down to see the clear handprint Theon had left on my wrist. My heart thundered, and I wondered if there was a mark left on my neck as well. I didn't dare look up at him, hoping my hair covered it if there was any. I pulled out of his hold, slipping my hand under the table. Andrea was watching us curiously.

"It's nothing… I just…"

"Can I have everyone's attention?" Alpha Andres's voice boomed around us, and I felt a wave of relief wash over me, turning to look at our Alpha. "Tonight, we pray to our goddess and celebrate everything she has blessed us with; power, prosperity, and peace."

Everyone had fallen silent, listening to the king. Peace? Did everyone forget that there must be more to the attack that happened two months ago? "However, two months ago, I lost a dear friend, William De'Lacor, a loyal companion, a brave warrior, a strong Beta, along with his mate, Hana, in that attack…"

And a loving father... did you forget that one, Alpha Andres?

It hurt the way he talked about my dad as if he was nothing to me. Why didn't he pre-warn me that he was going to mention Dad tonight? I saw Charlene try to stand up, but her mother pulled her down. She glanced at me, and I forced a smile.

"With a heavy heart, I have finalised on a new Beta. Someone strong, smart, and efficient," Alpha Andres continued.

A murmur rippled through the crowd of seated people, and I knew that through the open mind link, those who weren't close enough to hear would receive the news. I felt a few heads turn toward me, but I kept my gaze ahead.

"A new Beta."

"She doesn't even have a wolf?"

"Someone else?"

"I hear it's the young warrior, Theon…"

"I present to you your new Beta! Beta Theon, a man who has proven himself worthy countless times! Someone I can trust and someone I know can hold this kingdom together by my daughter's side!"

My heart squeezed as Theon, who stood to the side, remained passive. Despite the cheering, he didn't go onto the dais. Our eyes met, but from this distance, I couldn't make out what he was thinking. It hurt so much…

Everyone began cheering with approval, but it all became a haze, the remarks and clapping becoming a loud, painful echo in my mind. *Will you not acknowledge the daughter of the Beta you so loved? At least you could have let me know that today I was to be stripped of my future.* Yes, I knew it was coming, but still…

"…leyna? Yileyna?"

Someone was calling me, but I couldn't understand who it was. My eyes were fixed on the Alpha. *Maybe, just maybe, he'll still say something…*

"Come sit in your spot, Beta Theon. We will hold the ceremony this coming week…"

I stood up, unable to sit there any longer.

"Yileyna!" Raiden whispered, trying not to cause a scene as he took hold of my hand gently. I tugged free, doing my best to walk out of there with my head held high.

Give me strength, Goddess. Mom… Dad... you're still watching over me, right? My vision blurred with unshed tears as I kept going, ignoring everyone around me. The moment I was out of sight, I broke into a run, only for Raiden to call me again. The sound of his footsteps grew as he jogged to catch up to me.

"Yileyna, wait!"

"Leave me alone. What do you want?" I asked, quickly blinking away the tears as I stopped running, not wanting to cause a scene.

"The marks on your wrist…" He walked over to me swiftly, taking hold of my hand.

"It's nothing, Raiden, please, just go away."

He was concerned about the bruises? Didn't he realise it was the pain inside of me that was destroying me?

"I'm sorry… I…" he trailed off, his gaze falling to my neck and his concern vanished. His eyes narrowed as he stepped closer, cupping my cheeks tenderly. "Did Theon hurt you, Yileyna?"

"No, he didn't. Raiden, please -"

I saw someone approaching from the corner of my eyes and stopped mid-sentence, turning my gaze to see Theon. His face was emotionless, his eyes hard as he looked at us both. It hurt to see him after knowing he was the one to take my birthright, but at the same time, a part of me needed him, needed something from him. His touch or just something…

"Theon -"

He turned without another word, walking away, anger rolling off him in waves.

Please don't turn your back on me…

But he didn't look back, not even once.

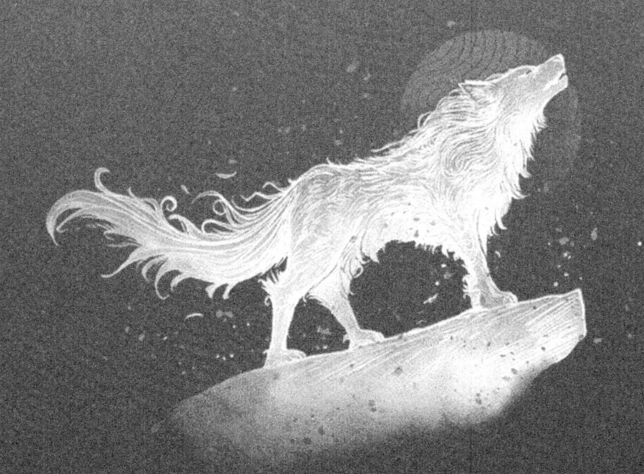

A Moment of Want

YILEYNA

I WANDERED THE STREETS THAT were a lot less busy than before, with most at the banquet, although many teens and children roamed the streets rather enjoying more street food than that at the banquet. I walked along with no destination in mind, refusing to allow the tears to fall.

After a good hour of walking around, I decided that I needed to start packing. The Alpha said the passage of the title would be in a week's time, meaning I needed to get out of there. *First thing tomorrow, I'll go looking for a place.*

Turning back, I decided to head home.

I gathered a few discarded boxes on my way to the castle that had probably contained items for the festival; they would come in handy to pack up my belongings. I guess once Theon becomes Beta, he won't be Charlene's guard, but I'm pretty sure he'll still be training her. As long as I don't need to see him.

I picked up two more boxes and knew I wouldn't be able to carry anymore, so I headed back towards the castle. The guards opened the door.

"Need help?" One of them asked.

"No, thank you," I replied, carefully squeezing past with my boxes.

The castle was silent save for the sound of music that still seeped through the open windows. I paused, rebalancing the boxes in my grip, realising I had left my bunny at the banquet…

A sudden wave of sadness washed over me. The poor bunny… I meant to win more for the orphanage, and now I didn't even have one… I reached my quarters feeling gloomy. My high spirits from earlier were dampened. I placed the boxes down, took my key from my pouch and unlocked it.

The smell of Mom's candles lingered in the air, and I inhaled deeply. Home.

I bent down to pick up the boxes.

"Already planning to pack up?"

I jumped, spinning around and dropping the boxes in the process as I stepped back, only to tumble backwards and into one of the boxes. I yelped in pain, staring at my legs that were sticking up in the air.

Quiet footsteps approached, and a shadow fell over me. My heart thundered as I looked into a familiar pair of smouldering amber eyes.

"Theon…"

I gripped the side of the box, trying to get my footing so I could get out of it, but failed miserably.

"Need a hand?"

"No thanks," I shot back icily, remembering how he had walked off an hour or so earlier. He simply crossed his arms, watching me.

"Go right ahead. Get out."

I gave him a dirty look and pushed the box over, landing on my side and pushing the box away.

"Nice underwear," Theon remarked, making my cheeks burn as I quickly pushed my dress down and glared up at him.

I stood up, smoothing my hair. Theon stepped closer. Reaching over, he slid my strap that had slipped down my shoulder back up. His fingers that brushed my skin left a trail of sparks in their wake. My heart pounded, and I looked up at him, a flash of hurt clenching in my chest.

"Why did you turn away?" I asked quietly.

He remained silent, looking around the room instead. So I began to pile the boxes to one side. If he wasn't going to answer me, then I wasn't going to pay attention to him.

"Why did you leave the banquet?" He raised an eyebrow, taking the key out of the door, shutting and locking it from the inside, his eyes on me. My heart raced as I held his gaze, trying not to let him see how he was messing with me.

"You know why," I replied, turning away. I walked towards the window to close the curtains. I turned back, gasping to see Theon was right behind me. "Goddess! Don't sneak up on people like that!"

"Why did you leave? You knew Alpha Andres was going to make me Beta." He was serious, and I could tell from the glimmer in his eyes he was not messing around.

"Yeah, but to announce it like that… it doesn't matter, but he honoured Dad by mentioning him… but he didn't seem to care to remember that before anything else, Dad put his family first. He was the best father one could ask for," I whispered. My eyes glittered with unshed tears, and I looked around the room, trying to remain strong.

A memory of Mom cooking through the archway to our kitchen came to mind. I remembered Dad and I were having a pillow fight, and Mom was shouting from the other room, only to come and join in. That night, the meal was rather overcooked… but we had a good laugh about it.

"I have already told the Alpha I'm happy with my current living space. You won't need to move out of here."

"I don't need anyone's sympathy. I'm moving," I stated, about to push past him when he suddenly blocked my path and caged me between his arms, his hands firmly on the wall behind me.

"Why are you so impulsive, little storm? You know you're attached to this place."

"I'm not… I mean… I'm attached to the memories here… but I won't stay where I don't belong. They can take away the Beta position, they can take away this home… but they can't take away the memories I hold. I'm going to move. I have the money, I just need to find a place."

"Sounds like you have it all planned out."

"I do," I replied defiantly.

"Good." His gaze flickered to my lips, and I found myself licking them.

"So… why did you come? You walked off earlier, remember?"

"If I didn't, I would have ripped that bastard's head right off for touching you. Who do you want, little storm? Because I assure you, I don't fucking share."

His eyes shimmered gold, and my stomach flip-flopped, but confidence sparked inside of me. I stepped away from the wall and into his personal space. I tilted my head up and bravely cupped his neck.

"I think you already know the answer to that," I whispered, pressing myself boldly against him. His hands left the wall, taking hold of my wrists and pulling my hands away from his neck.

"A little too confident, aren't you?"

"What do you want from me, Theon?" I asked softly.

"One night. This will be nothing more than that," he said, making my cheeks burn at his reply. I already knew that, although it stung a little. I was ready for that…

"I assumed as much." He inched forward until I was forced against the curtain behind me.

"Good."

His eyes dipped to my cleavage, suddenly pinning my wrists above my head. Stepping back, he took a look at me, slowly letting his gaze trail over my bare legs, his eyes flickering as they lingered on my thighs... I pressed my legs together, trying to satiate the desire that was building within me.

"I have two rules; don't get attached, and don't expect me to treat you like a princess, because I plan to treat you like my little whore."

There was definitely something wrong with me. I was sure any other girl would have been shocked or insulted at his words... but they only made my core throb harder. I could feel the wetness pooling between my thighs.

"I won't. I know that's all I am to you. It's my body you want," I replied, rolling my eyes. A flicker of something crossed his eyes, but he simply cocked a brow.

"Glad to hear we are on the same page for once," he murmured huskily.

"Yeah, because you're an annoying ass most of the time," I shot back, trying not to melt completely.

"One you're soaking wet for," he countered seductively.

He ran his knuckles down the centre of my neck. My eyes flickered shut as he leaned in, his nose brushing the crook of my neck, making me shiver. He inhaled deeply, making my heart thunder. He kept my hands firmly behind my back. The knuckles of his other hand ran down the centre of my collarbones. *Cherish the moment…*

A sigh escaped me as his fingers brushed between my breasts before continuing their descent down my stomach.

"Tell me… how many have you been with?" His question caught me off guard, despite the burning fire of pleasure that was consuming me.

"Does it matter?" I whispered back breathlessly.

"Not really." His lips brushed my neck ever so lightly, yet it made me whimper.

I relaxed a little, wondering why he had asked, but the moment his hand caressed my thigh, slipping under my dress and brushing my ass, I moaned loudly, my mind going blank. His heart was racing too. His hand travelled over my hip and down between my legs until his fingers grazed my pussy.

"So, fucking wet..."

Touch me.

But he took his sweet time, his fingers lightly playing with the fabric of my panties.

"Theon..." My hands were still pinned behind my back, and even when I struggled, wanting to feel his body beneath my fingertips, he refused to let go of me. I loved it, feeling completely at his mercy...

"What do you want... use your words," he whispered seductively, sucking the corner of my neck.

I gasped as the pleasant sensation made my entire body react. His hand slipped under my panties, and then he slid one finger between my smooth pussy lips. I moaned loudly, parting my legs slightly.

"Fuck me, Theon," I whimpered. "Don't tease."

He moved back, his finger slowly and agonisingly circling my clit. Yes, I had pleasured myself in the past, but this... this was something else.

"Getting a little ahead of yourself, are you not?" Before I could even respond, he pulled away, letting go of me and stepped back, looking me over once more. "Strip."

I blinked, not expecting him to say that. Wasn't that supposed to happen as we made out? But his command was absolute...

To my surprise, he went and took a seat on the sofa, placing his arms across the top. My heart was pounding as I stood a few feet away, facing him. I swallowed hard, my cheeks burning, and he smirked.

"Want to back out?"

"Not at all."

Sticking my chin out in defiance, I reached for the zipper on my dress and slowly pulled it down. I slowly tugged at my straps, letting the dress slip down. I kept my eyes fixed on him as I slowly peeled it off my breasts, satisfied when his eyes blazed gold.

My heart was pounding as I tried to cover my chest with one arm, shimmying the dress down to my hips, but one hand wasn't enough to push it down completely, and I turned my back to him as I hooked my fingers into the dress and pushed it past my hips and allowed it to fall to the ground.

He muttered something I didn't catch, and I bit my lip, trying to resist a smile. Knowing that he was enjoying this gave me confidence. Crossing my arms over my chest, I turned back to him.

"Happy?" I asked softly.

"Don't hide from me," he simply replied, his face emotionless, yet I could see his hard shaft straining in his pants, making my stomach coil. Goddess, it looked big.

I removed my arms. Instead, I wrapped my right arm around my waist, not knowing what to do with myself. My heart was racing as I stood there completely exposed in my heels and lace thong as Theon devoured me with his eyes that held an unmasked hunger that only made my core clench harder.

"Turn."

I obeyed, slowly making a turn, but when I turned back, he was no longer seated but standing there. My heart thumped, and I looked up at him when he closed the gap between us. I mustered the courage to ask the question that was on the tip of my lips.

"Like what you see?"

"Far better than I imagined, actually," his cocky, cold reply came as he took hold of my chin.

"So, you've imagined me naked?" I whispered back.

"I've done a lot more than imagine you naked," he replied, making my eyes widen. "And I'm about to show you exactly what I have imagined doing to you."

With those words, his arm snaked around my waist, and the other hand let go of my chin and tangled in my hair, yanking it back roughly. Then his lips were on mine, setting off a stream of euphoric pleasure that lit every ounce of my body alight with a burning desire that only he could satiate...

Win-Win

THEON

Yileyna de'Lacor. A girl who had grown into a woman that was every straight man's dream.

I hated it. I hated her and the effect she had on me, but at the same time, I couldn't get rid of the thoughts of exactly how I wanted to fuck her and ruin her. The very thoughts that fuelled the urge to fuck her with everything I had and destroy her at the same time consumed my mind constantly.

I hated distractions. I hated anything that took me away from my goal. Yileyna was just that, a temptation worse than anything else on this planet. From those seductive grey eyes to those plump, pouty lips that were made to be wrapped around a cock. She was made of every man's dirtiest thoughts, the ideal doll to fulfil even the filthiest of sins.

She wasn't built like most women, from her creamy, blemish-free skin that never seemed to change no matter what the weather was—a canvas for me to paint with pleasure. Her slender shoulders and that dainty neck that made you want to choke her every fucking time she was around were gorgeous. Then there were her boobs, which were round and firm, and her narrow waist, which emphasised her jutting hips, completing her perfect hourglass figure. Her legs were as hot as the rest of her, with sexy lush thighs.

Everything about her fucking irritated me and appealed to me.

She stood there before me, covering her boobs with her slender arms. They didn't cover much, but I wanted to see those nipples of hers. What was the exact shade?

"Happy?" She asked in her seductive voice.

"Don't hide from me," I commanded emotionlessly, although all I wanted was to fuck her until she dropped.

Her eyes dipped to my crotch, and I knew she could see I was hard for her, to the point that it was painful. I needed something, or in better terms, I needed to be buried in that pussy of hers.

Ever since I laid eyes on her tonight in that skimpy lace dress as she danced with Bolton, something inside of me snapped. Her boobs were spilling out of it, and it just about covered her ass as she smiled at him. It had made a wave of anger burn within me, and it took every inch of self-control to keep myself under control.

I watched her slowly lower her arms, her cheeks dusted with a pink hue. I swallowed, admiring those light pink nipples of hers. I shouldn't have expected anything less. There wasn't an inch of her that wasn't appealing.

Oh, little storm, when I'm done with you, I'll have made you feel even more embarrassed than you feel right now. But would one night be enough to satiate the hunger she unleashed within me?

"Turn."

My cock twitched as I took in that ass, one I had gotten a glimpse of a few times but never like this... round, perky, and the perfect size to spank until it was fucking raw. I stood up, and, when she turned back to me, she looked startled for a second.

"Like what you see?"

"Far better than I imagined, actually." I took hold of her chin, her gorgeous blonde curls framing her face.

"So, you've imagined me naked?"

Keep talking like that, and I'm fucking you right now.

"I've done a lot more than imagine you naked, and I'm about to show you exactly what I've imagined doing to you."

I wrapped my arm around her waist. Letting go of her chin, I threaded my fingers into her lush curls, yanking her head back roughly, and then I kissed her, unable to control myself any longer. A sensation I had never felt before coursed through me. No kiss had felt so sinful, sweet, and tempting, and still made me fucking harder than I already was. I assaulted her mouth, sucking hard on her tongue. Her hands gripped my arms as I squeezed her ass, deepening the kiss. I twisted my hand in her hair tighter, making her whimper.

I tugged her over to the dining table and pushed her back onto it, watching her boobs bounce as she gasped.

"Ouch, rough… I like it," she whispered. Reaching for my shirt, she began yanking the buttons open. She was on the last button when I pulled her arms away, pushing her flat onto her back and pinning her wrist, biting into her shoulder and sucking hard.

She cried out in pleasure; the sound alone was better than any other woman I had ever fucked. I kept her wrists pinned above her head, my other hand running up and down her waist before I grabbed one of her breasts, the perfect size in my hand. She whimpered, and I claimed her lips once more, twisting her nipple and making her back arch off the table. I broke away, kissing and sucking every inch of her that I could reach. I knew I was squeezing her breasts painfully, but her cries only turned me on even more.

I had told her I was a beast, she had the choice to walk away, but she had only fuelled the flames of desire. I sucked hard on the side of her breast, yanking at her thong with one hand. The scent of her arousal hung in the air like a fucking drug that I was getting addicted to.

"Theon…" she moaned, wriggling as I bent over her.

I looked down at her pussy, the fabric pulled between those smooth lips of hers. So damn perfect… I ripped them off her just as she sat up, pulling open my shirt fully and reaching for my belt.

I didn't like women touching me... but I watched her. My eyes narrowed as she undid my belt and unzipped my pants. That was enough. I grabbed her wrist, pulling her hand away.

"Hands to yourself," I growled.

Tonight, I'd fuck her, and then tomorrow, I'd put this behind me. I had a goal, and I didn't need any distractions. A flash of anger ripped through me, a reminder that she was a dangerous distraction that I didn't need… I hated how she made me feel.

Disobeying me, she slipped her hand into my pants, making me cut off a groan of pleasure. I grabbed her throat, pulling her close.

"Since you're so fucking desperate, let's skip the foreplay."

"Perfect," she whispered, my grip on her throat cutting off most of her oxygen.

I pushed her back onto the table, my hand still around her throat, and with the other, I freed my cock from my pants. I took in the way the woman before me looked spread on the table. Her legs were parted. Red marks covered her thighs, breasts, and waist where I had gripped her tightly. Hickeys and bite marks covered her body.

The image of fucking perfection.

I looked up into her grey orbs. There was a vulnerability in them. Her heart was racing. Her scent reminded me of the fresh sea breeze and spring mixed in with the intoxicating scent of her arousal, creating a haze around me.

Time to get this pretty little body all dirty. I ran my fingers between her soaking slit, rubbing my thumb on her clit. She whimpered as I shoved my thumb into her, letting her juices coat my finger before I slipped it out and slipped my thumb into her mouth. Instantly, she wrapped those pretty little lips around it, swirling her tongue around it. *Fuck...*

I wanted her on her knees with my cock down that throat... but it was pushing the boundaries that I had set for myself. I didn't want to get attached to the nymph before me. *Fuck her like you would a whore, and then leave.* I pulled my thumb from her mouth, pushing open her thigh.

"Spread those legs for me like the bad girl you are," I commanded huskily.

She obeyed, despite her heart continuing to beat super-fast. I rubbed my cock at her tiny entrance, making her moan hornily. *That's it.* I tightened my hand around her throat just as I rammed into her. Her eyes flew open, her entire body tensing as her eyes stung with unshed tears. I didn't go easy on anyone.

I groaned in pleasure, relishing the way she felt so tight, wrapped around me. Her hot juices coated my dick as I began thrusting into her hard and fast. Her eyes rolled as she gripped my wrist around her throat, one hand gripping the edge of the table as I railed her. Each thrust hit her g-spot, but apart from her choked gasps and moans, there was nothing but the sound of skin slapping erotically against one another.

I closed my eyes for a moment, forgetting it all. Everything but how fucking good it felt. She stopped struggling, and I let go of her throat, allowing her soft moans and whimpers to fill the room. Her heart was thumping, one hand loosely cupping her left breast, one hand to her head. Her eyes were closed, and her breathing laboured as I pounded her.

I inhaled deeply, wanting to burn this memory into my mind when I tensed. The coppery smell of blood reached my nose, and I looked down sharply, noticing the blood that was smeared on her pussy and my cock. My heart thundered with a foreign emotion I couldn't place washing over me. She was a virgin.

Fuck.

"Keep going… I'm close," she whimpered, her eyelids fluttering open.

I clenched my jaw, irritation flaring through me. I had asked her, and she hadn't told me. She got what she deserved.

I pulled her up, my lips crashing against hers in a bruising kiss as I carried on fucking her, my own release near. I could feel her walls clamping around me as she wrapped her arms around my neck. Her moans and cries got louder, her fingers running through my hair. I groaned into her mouth as I rammed into her, brutally triggering her release. Her orgasm shook her entire body. Her scream filled the air, and I was sure anyone in the area would hear it.

She bit down on my neck, and I groaned, pulling out roughly and pumping my dick as I coated her stomach with my white cum. I kept my arm around her, supporting her body as she caught her breath, resting her head against my chest as she weakly clutched my open shirt. I ran my hand up and down her back. A thin sheen of sweat coated her body.

She wasn't the first virgin I had been with… but she had been the first I had treated so harshly. I felt sexually satisfied, but there was just something bitter about it. Her lie. I grabbed her by her hair and tugged her face up.

"I hope your first time was exactly what you wanted," I found myself saying coldly, letting go of her and turning away, but not before I saw the flash of hurt in those eyes of hers.

"It was with who I wanted," came her softly reply.

"Win-win, then."

I zipped my pants up and walked to the door, not wanting to be there any longer. I unlocked the door and stepped out, letting it shut behind me with a snap.

For the second time in my life, I couldn't simply remove the image of the girl I had just fucked and left behind from my mind…

A Raid

YILEYNA

I WATCHED HIM WALK AWAY, leaving me on the table, my heart thundering as I realised that was it. I knew it wasn't going to be anything more than sex, but to leave me the moment we were done…

I clamped my hands over my mouth, muffling the sob that left my lips. I didn't know what I was expecting… but I wasn't anticipating him leaving like that. Why had he felt disgusted at the end? Why could I feel his anger?

I pulled my legs to my chest, rocking myself as I tried to control the pain that was suffocating me. I felt even more alone than I had before I gave myself to him. I cried softly into my knees, the sharp throbbing between my legs a stark reminder of what had happened. A moment of pleasure with the man I had liked for so long... *Was it worth it? Had it been worth it?* I didn't know the answer to that...

At the time, I couldn't think of anything but the pleasure. It felt like a dream come true, and I couldn't deny that I felt like I was in heaven. But now I just felt lonely and scared.

Stop wallowing in self-pity, Yileyna. I took a deep, shuddering breath and brushed away my tears. *You do not need anyone.*

I slid off the table, my legs giving way, and I fell to my knees. I grabbed the table's edge, getting to my feet. My entire lower body felt heavy as lead and pain throbbed in my lower regions. *Was it meant to hurt this much?*

I looked at the table that contained a few streaks of blood and remnants of our sex juices. I'd clean it after I showered.

I made my way to the bathroom and stared at my reflection in the mirror. I looked… a mess. My eye make-up was smudged, leaving black circles around my eyes from all the crying. My lips were bruised, and my smudged lipstick only made them look worse. I realised it was bleeding a little, too… as for my body, I was a canvas of marks and bruises.

I turned away from the mirror, stepped under the shower, and turned it on. I touched my stomach where he had come all over and looked at my fingers, tears spilling down my cheeks and mingling in with the warm water.

It felt bittersweet. I just wished he hadn't left like that.

I don't know how long I remained under the water, but it was a long time. I soaped my body and washed my hair before I finally stepped out, feeling exhausted as I wrapped a towel around myself. I returned to the living room and began to clean up the mess. My tears had all dried up, but I was in a lot of pain. Was it meant to hurt like this?

I picked up my discarded clothes and placed them aside. Once I was done with the cleaning, I staggered to my bedroom, just wanting to sleep.

First thing tomorrow, I would start packing and get out of this place.

I jolted upright, feeling confused as I looked around. It was morning. The sun was shining through the window, accompanied by the sound of the birds and cockerels. I was naked in bed, the towel having come off. The pain between my legs made last night rush back to me, and I looked down to see dried blood coating my inner thighs. Theon had been huge; no wonder I was suffering now.

My heart skipped a beat, and I sighed. No matter how sad I felt that he had left me, I couldn't stop the fluttering in my stomach at the memory of last night. He may have been cold and uncaring, but he knew how to fuck.

I heard some sounds from the living room, and I frowned, looking around as I got out of bed. I quickly grabbed a gown and wrapped it around my bare body before exiting my room. To my surprise, there were several of the Epsilon-ranked guards ripping the place apart.

"What are you doing?" I exclaimed. "I would have moved soon!"

"Please step outside, Miss," one of the men ordered.

"This doesn't look good..." Nikolai's disgusting voice came from Mom and Dad's room.

My heart thumped. *No! Don't touch that place!*

I rushed to the door of my parents' bedroom and froze at the state it was in. They had torn it apart. The bedding was strewn on the ground, the bed was upturned, and the drawers were all opened and emptied. Even I hadn't changed anything in their room, from the way Mom had left her clothing on the rocking chair, I hadn't touched them...

"Stop it! Get out!" I cried.

"Step aside, Yileyna. We are doing our job," Nikolai smirked, blocking my path. His eyes raked over me, but I didn't care.

"Don't touch that!" I hissed, pushing past him and yanking a picture frame from one of the men's hands.

"Calm down, or you will be punished," he growled.

My eyes widened as I realised that I was staring at none other than Delta Zeridaan Blackmore, the head of the kingdom's security... the commander of the supreme army of Astalion.

What was he doing there? His black braided hair framed his face. The scars that littered his face only added to the hard look in his dark eyes. He was tall, and the sheer aura surrounding him made me back away.

"May I know what is going on, Delta Blackmore?" I asked quietly.

"We received information that your parents were traitors and were working for the Obsidian Shadow Pack. Get out of the way and allow us to do our job," his deep voice thundered. My heart skipped a beat, and I looked up at him sharply. Never.

"That's not possible. My parents loved this pack, they died protecting it! How can you -"

"They died protecting you, not the pack!" He cut in coldly.

"Regardless... they were not traitors, you can ask the king! He wouldn't allow this; he had known my father since he was a child! Hey, stop that!" I shouted, turning as Nikolai pushed aside the cabinet containing Mom's ornaments.

"Get her out of here, and if she keeps this up, lock her in the cells for the night," Zeridaan growled.

"I said to stop mistreating everything! When you find there's nothing here, you will regret this! At least handle their things with care!" I hissed, yanking Nikolai back and slapping him across the face. How dare he come here and touch my parent's things with his filthy hands.

A murderous growl from across the room didn't make me turn. I don't care who I pissed off. You do not disrespect my deceased parents.

"Take her to the cells!" Zeridaan roared.

"It'll be my pleasure," Nikolai smirked, grabbing me roughly by my arms and yanking me towards the door.

"Let go of me!" I hissed. I didn't trust him, and I was not going to allow him to take me there. Not alone. "I will go with someone else, Delta Blackmore!" He didn't reply, crouching down behind the shelf as he observed the wall.

"Come on, let's go…" Nikolai whispered, his hand caressing my waist as he pulled me out into the living room.

Last time I was exhausted… not this time. I elbowed him in the ribs, turning and kneeing him in the crotch with everything I had, not caring about the strain I felt in my lower region. He hissed, grabbing my hair.

"You will pay for that. It's treason to hit a guard!"

"Well, since I'm in trouble already." I grabbed his hair, yanking him down just as I brought my knee up, ready to smash his fucking nose, but he jerked back, and I missed, only managing to scuff his jaw before he threw me back, backhanding me across the face I fell back onto the ground. I clutched my gown that had come loose as I glared up at him, the taste of blood now in my mouth.

"I think a good lashing will fix that attitude; the daughter of a traitor deserves far worse," he hissed. His gaze trailed over me, and I knew he meant a punishment far sinister. Reaching down, he yanked me by my gown and dragged me to my feet. I could feel everyone watching as they searched the place. "Let me show you what punishment is befitting for a disobedient bitch like yourself."

"I don't think that is your decision to make now, is it, Levin?" A cold voice that sent my heart racing asked.

I turned to see Theon standing there, as emotionless as ever, as if yesterday had never happened. His eyes were fixed on Nikolai, shimmering gold as he came over and pulled me from his hold. I stumbled, hitting his chest. I closed my eyes, inhaling his intoxicating scent.

He may have left me last night… but he was always there for me. I wouldn't ask for more, I'd take what he gives me…

"Soon-to-be Beta, you need not concern yourself here. I was handling it."

"I could see exactly what you were doing. This doesn't involve her. Do your job," Theon replied, his voice dangerous and holding a hint of finality.

"Delta Zeridaan asked for me to take her to the cells."

"Do I need to school you on rank?" Theon asked coldly, still holding me by the arm. His warmth and scent made me lightheaded.

"I... I'm sorry. I was only following orders," he replied with gritted teeth.

"My parents are not traitors; they would never do anything to harm the Silver Moon Pack!" I snapped.

"We shall see about -" Nikolai was cut off by one of the men in the lounge.

"We found something, Delta!"

My heart thumped as I frowned. That's ridiculous. I turned to see they had pried off one of the floorboards. My eyes widened in shock. I had never known that was there.... The warrior began removing books, files, and some small sacks.

"What is it?" Zeridaan asked, stepping out of the bedroom.

"Our source was correct. There are blueprints of the city, patrol schedules, and letters from someone from outside of Westerfell."

An ominous silence fell in the room, and my stomach twisted. It was clear many of the warriors there weren't expecting it. Even Zeridaan seemed stunned.

"So, William was betraying us," he muttered.

"No. No, this is a lie. I know my parents! They would never do this!" I shouted, fear gripping me in its hold. *This was a lie, it was a lie!*

"Yileyna," Theon's quiet voice came.

"No. No! My parents are being framed or something! This is a lie!" I pleaded, staring up at him. He didn't reply, simply reaching down and wrapping my gown tighter before knotting my belt firmly. "Theon, listen to me!"

But he didn't speak. I turned desperately, only to see no one was listening. They were gathering around, and from the looks on their faces, I knew no one was going to believe me. I knew my parents weren't like this. They loved this place. They loved their Alpha and pack. *It's not true. It could not be true...*

It felt as if my head was going to burst. Everything was going wrong...

"You're bleeding," Theon murmured.

Why wasn't he listening? The pain in my body was far more than the slight bump from Nikolai. I was about to reply when I felt something trickle down my leg. I looked down to see a bit of blood on my thighs.

"I don't care, my parents were not traitors," I whispered, grabbing his shirt. *Please listen to me.*

"Shall I take her to the cells, Beta?" Someone asked him.

My vision was darkening, a sharp pain rushing through me. *Listen to me...*

"She needs a healer..." I heard Theon say before my body gave out and darkness welcomed me. A strong pair of arms caught me, and I knew who they belonged to...

Theon.

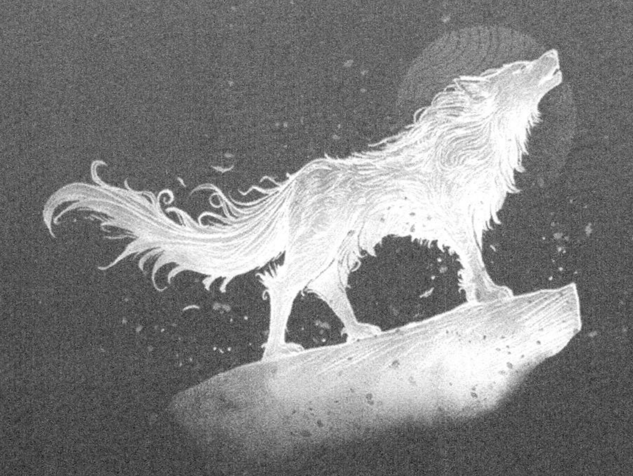

A Planned Journey

THEON

I caught her before she collapsed, looking into her beautiful face, as flawless as ever, even when in pain. The urge to brush back her blonde locks was strong, but I simply lifted her into my arms as Nikolai stepped forward.

"As Beta, you should handle the evidence. I'll take her," he said with that face of his; you wanted to punch him every time you saw it.

"As an Epsilon-ranked guard, you should learn when to keep your mouth shut before I have to do it for you." I looked him square in the eye. **After what you attempted… you should be worried about your position because when I become Beta, you are a goner.** His eyes flashed as I spoke the latter through the link.

My family is far too powerful for me to be stripped of my rank for something you have no proof of. Besides, she is the daughter of traitors. Her only value is to be treated like the whore she is.

My eyes flashed. That blistering anger that always swam beneath the surface was threatening to rise and kill the man before me.

She isn't a whore. Call her that once more, and I assure you I will cut your dick off, inch by fucking inch. So don't try me, I hissed.

Or does the Beta want her for himself?

I paused but didn't turn back to him, knowing that I would only end up killing him. I left the apartment, that foreign feeling consuming me once more.

The timing for them to find evidence wasn't what I was expecting, but I didn't really care. I had far more on my mind right now…

I looked at her inner thighs, her tiny gown barely covering anything, seeing the blood smeared between them. She shouldn't still be bleeding… I knew I had been rough… but she should heal. She was a werewolf, even if she hadn't shifted.

I hated how I was still drawn to her. One night hadn't been enough. I didn't even sleep last night because all I could think about was her... the way she felt wrapped around me, the feel of her boobs against my chest, the sinful pleasure that actually felt fulfilling but still left me craving for more, and maybe… just maybe, her presence… as long as she kept her mouth shut.

I entered the hospital wing of the castle and spotted Ulric looking through some files.

"I need a female doctor to look her over," I commanded emotionlessly.

"Right away, Master Theon. Take her through to room three," he replied before hurrying off to find a female healer. There were werewolves working there, and some were basically the communication link between the healers and pack members. I walked past him until I reached the room.

I pulled back the bedsheet and placed her down, about to move back, when I realised her hair was caught in the chain hooks of one of my necklaces. I stared down at her as I slowly untangled it from my necklace, letting the strands of hair fall by her side.

Her plump, kissable lips were slightly parted and slightly moist... her chest was rising and falling steadily, her cleavage on show. After seeing them last night, all I wanted was to see them again. I forced my gaze back to those tempting lips, and I bent down about to kiss her, when I heard footsteps and moved back swiftly.

"Beta Theon." The woman bowed her head before walking around to the other side of the bed.

Beta… a title that was far below me… I couldn't wait for the day I didn't have to keep this pathetic façade up.

"She's bleeding," I said, motioning with my eyes towards her legs. Her eyes widened with understanding before she gave me a brisk nod.

"Ah! Did something happen? Was she in a fight? How did she become unconscious?" She asked, about to move the sheet, when she hesitated. "Umm, will you turn away, sir?"

Like I haven't seen her naked. I resisted the urge to roll my eyes and, crossing my arms, turned my back on them.

"Not entirely. She had sex for the first time last night… yet this morning, she seemed to be bleeding again. That's not normal, is it? Plus, she may be a little stressed." I didn't need to be looking at the woman to know she was blushing profusely.

"Ah! I see it… it can happen, and she hasn't shifted, her healing is slower. Um, maybe there was some internal bruising… especially if the, umm, intercourse was rough…"

Obviously, it was rough. I didn't know the girl who enjoyed peeping on people having sex was a virgin.

"I will heal her, but I will need to ask her some questions when she wakes up. Why is she unconscious?" I turned back, only to see her with her hands on Yileyna's stomach, a pale green glow around her hands.

"You can ask her. Inform me when she awakes and leaves," I replied coldly and walked out.

Why were women so stupid? *Now to go tolerate and try to teach another stupid one.*

I made my way through the halls and stopped outside the princess's room. Last night, I saw her try to argue with her father when I was announced as Beta. Her love for her friend was pretty strong. It was a shame they didn't really have as much time together as they thought…

She stepped out of her room, her usual smile missing.

"Good morning, Theon," she said quietly.

The so-called treasure. There was nothing special about her. From the day she shifted until now, I didn't sense any strong aura from her. She was as ordinary as any she-wolf.

I led the way to the training ground, debating whether I should talk to Andres.

Alpha Andres, as you know, certain incriminating evidence may have been found at the previous Beta's house… what do you intend to do with Yileyna**?** I asked through the link.

She is innocent, regardless of what her parents have done. I don't know yet. I will have a think… I trusted Will… I need to see if there's

anything that can put him under suspicion first. I will not believe this until I have the proof before me. Zeridaan is on his way.

Of course, he was your closest confidant. However, I would advise that you make it clear that no one is to bother her, I replied, keeping my voice indifferent. He was silent for a moment.

Come to my office after Charlene's training.

I knew what he wanted to talk about, why I was so concerned about Yileyna. I wish I knew the answer to that too. She was just a pawn in this game. I guess it was only fair that I showed her some compassion...

I stopped when we reached the training court, and I turned to Charlene.

"As future Alpha of this pack, you really are lacking. Warm up, and then get in position."

She nodded, and I turned my back on her, frowning. I glanced at the clear sky. The sun was beginning to rise, and I knew many would still be asleep after last night's festival. Another peaceful day in the City of Westerfell...

The tides were changing, and the people didn't even realise...

Everything will unfold as it should... as planned.

I stood opposite Andres in his office as he sat back in his seat, staring at me with a thoughtful expression on his face.

"You wanted to see me, Alpha."

"I did. Theon, you have potential for a lot more. I must have done something right for the goddess to have you come to my pack. With no one coming to find you for the last two years. It means you were meant to be here."

If only you knew.

"If it's alright, may I ask what the relationship between you and Yileyna is?"

Not that it's your business.

"Why does the Alpha ask?" He grinned, running his hand through his straggly hair.

"Like I said, you have potential... last night, I had hoped that you and Charlene would be mated. It was a low probability, but I did wish you two were true mates. However, obviously, that isn't the case. You could, however, perhaps consider a future by taking Charlene as a chosen mate. This kingdom needs her to have a strong man by her side. You have potential, I can see it. Don't waste it." *I won't be wasting anything.*

"I appreciate the king considering me so highly, but I'm not really thinking of settling down yet. There's a lot I need and want to do, and with the threat rising from the sea as well as the Obsidian Shadow Pack, I need to stay focused without any distractions." He nodded in understanding.

"I see. I understand, you are correct, actually." He sighed and sat back. "So, I presume there is nothing between you and Yileyna..."

I raised an eyebrow. I wasn't going to answer that.

"Anything else, Alpha?"

"Ah... is Charlene showing any signs of awakening her powers?" He asked. *As much as a dead doornail.*

"I'm afraid not."

He sighed, and I had to admit it was weird that someone as powerful as him had a daughter who was, simply put, useless.

"There is a mage who will be able to see if she is the child of prophecy, the treasure of Kaeladia. He resides in the Purien Isles. I think it may be ideal if you take her to him. If she is the treasure, he will confirm it. If not, then perhaps it was just not meant to be..." I frowned. That wasn't possible. The prophecy was absolute. The one who holds the heart holds unfathomable power, an Alpha female.

"That's not possible. You said there was a prophecy, which was absolute."

"This is not widely known, but the queen has had two miscarriages... perhaps the child of prophecy is gone," he said quietly, looking at his hands.

The news derailed me too. This was...

"Will the mage be able to check even if her power is sealed?" I asked.

"Yes, he will. He is blind, but he has the gift to see what we cannot. He will confirm it. I sent a letter to him, and he is willing to see her despite being in ill health. He may not have long left, so I would rather you set out soon. Ideally, immediately after your passage of the Beta ceremony."

"I think making me Beta and then having me leave the palace would be more questionable. Hold off on the ceremony for a while." I pushed the thought that had come to my mind away, *It was not because of her.*

"That's true... I can't trust many people. It will be a small team. You will travel by ship, and we all know what the waters hold. Keep training Charlene on the journey."

"The Purien Isles are at least a ten-day journey away, and that is if there are no stops."

"I know, but we have no other choice," Andres sighed and stood up. "We need these answers. Give me three days. I will have a ship and a trusted team to make this journey." I gave a curt nod.

A trusted team… alone at sea for that long… the king's trust in me was admirable. Now to see how good a judge he is in the rest of his choices.

"Is that all?"

"Yes, thank you for your time." Andres nodded.

I turned and left the office. I might just go and see what was happening with Yileyna. The healer had sent a message via someone to inform me that she was healthy and had left the hospital wing earlier whilst I had been training Charlene.

She still owed me an answer.

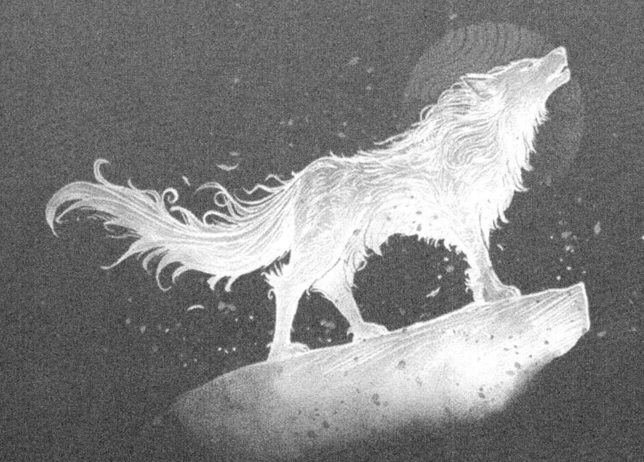

Broken Memories

YILEYNA

THEON HAD TAKEN ME to the hospital and had unashamedly told the healer I had had sex the night before. So, there I was with a mug of hot milk as Healer Shayna looked at me. She sat on the edge of the bed, her hands clasped together, concern clear in her warm brown eyes.

"Was it consensual? From my examination, it seemed it was rather… brutal."

"Yes, it was," I replied quickly, blushing at her question. She nodded, her curly blonde hair bouncing.

"Good. And are you on contraception?"

"No…"

"Would you like a contraceptive charm?" She asked.

It was humiliating… but I remember Mom telling me that when the time came to make sure I got one…

"Um, yes, please," I said, staring down at the steaming mug.

"I will have one prepared for you. Just come back monthly to have it renewed. Do you have any items you would like the charm to be put on?" I looked down, realising I was still wearing Mom's rings I had picked out last night.

"I have this," I said, my stomach sinking at the thought of everything most likely being ruined back home…

She nodded.

"That will be perfect as long as you plan to keep it on all the time," she said. "Otherwise, you can bring a necklace or bracelet from home. I work until nine in the evening."

"The only thing that looks good wrapped around your neck is my hand."

Theon's words echoed in my mind, and I felt my cheeks heat up.

"No necklaces. This ring is fine," I said, taking off the thin band with small gemstones along the entire length. She took it and stood up.

"Drink that up, and I'll have this ready for you." I nodded, and she left the room, leaving me with my thoughts.

Why had Theon come back this morning? Did he come to strip the place like the rest? Maybe...

Did Charlene know? I doubted it...

I sipped the milk, thinking of everything I needed to do. *No more wasting time. No more pitying myself. I will do what I need to.* Thanks to the healer, I felt much better. I was ready to get my life moving.

I planned to speak to the Alpha about the allegations too, but with my new status, I'd probably have to make an appointment. The Alpha wouldn't just see me anymore; it was clear he had cast me aside.

"All done!" Healer Shayna said, re-entering the room and holding out my ring.

"Thank you..."

I don't think I'll be needing it again anytime soon, but it's better to be safe.

"Now, tell the handsome Beta to take it easy." She chuckled, making my eyes fly open, mortified.

"W-who said it's him?" I stuttered. She raised an eyebrow.

"Really? Well, for someone who has nothing to do with you, he asked me to let him know how you are."

My heart skipped a beat, and I wasn't able to stop the small smile that crossed my lips, not saying anything. We were nothing. It had just been one sizzling hot night that felt far too short. Well, time to go home...

It had been worse than what I had expected. When I got back, the door was open. A group of humans and omegas who worked in the castle were glancing in through the broken door, discussing what had happened. When they saw me, they fell silent, but I knew that soon enough, the entire city would know of this event. I had entered our quarters, but I wasn't able to shut out their voices.

"She'll have to leave the castle."

"She's a disgrace."

"I heard no one will give her a bed or house. No one wants to be linked to traitors…"

"Oh, yes... they say the evidence was so shocking, the king is devastated…"

It seemed that after that 'evidence' was found, they had ripped apart everything else. There was not one piece of furniture that had not been upturned. Some of the dishes were broken, and the cooling box was wide open, the vegetables and milk spilt across the floor, and everything else had been dumped on the floor. No inch of the house had been spared.

It was devastating to see it like this. I wasn't even able to close the door as they had ripped it off the hinges, although I was sure I didn't lock it last night. I made do with it and propped it against the door frame. After getting dressed in some lingerie and an oversized shirt of Dad's, I got to work.

I started with Mom and Dad's room. I couldn't take everything, but I would take the most precious things. I got Mom's music box out and put on some music. I tried to remain strong as I got to cleaning up the mess that my own pack had made.

I was already an outsider…

I kept a few items of Mom's clothes that held meaning and some of Dad's before placing the rest aside in some sacks. I'd donate them to the orphanage.

I collected Mom's jewellery from the floor, placing them all in her broken wooden box. *I'll get this fixed. Dad got this carved for her…* I sat there, running my fingers along the leaves. I had a smaller one like it… I snapped it shut, pushing the emotional thoughts away, when I heard the creak of wood from the living room.

I tensed, my heart thudding as I got up.

"Whose there?" I called.

I was about to step out of the room when Theon appeared in the doorway. My stomach fluttered as I froze. I didn't know what to say.

Last night flashed to the forefront of my mind, remembering how he looked with his shirt open. I had wanted to touch him… but he hadn't allowed me… I had a taste of him, but I had wanted more… so much more…

My gaze flickered to his lips, remembering the intoxicating taste of his mouth, the way he had kissed me…

"Are you just going to stand there staring at me? This place is a mess. You should get back to packing," he said arrogantly, making me blink.

"I wasn't staring," I huffed, turning away and praying he didn't realise what I was thinking. I began to gather the pictures and placed them gently into the box.

Why was he here? I should ask him, I mean, this is my house…

"Why are you here?" I asked boldly, folding a blanket into the box of items to keep and placing some undamaged ornaments in there. I had to try to keep the bare minimum… they had destroyed so much, though. Was this their respect for their Beta?

I fought back the pain that threatened to consume me once more. His eyes met mine, but he didn't reply for a moment, a small frown furrowing his brow.

"I had a question, actually. I didn't think this place would be in such a state," he remarked, turning his back to me and my eyes fell on his ass…

One I didn't get to see last night, even his dick… we were so caught up in passion and desire that I didn't get to admire it. All I remember was that it was huge, and I had been slightly terrified at the fact that it would be my first.

"What question?" I asked as I began folding up the blankets from the ground.

He didn't reply for a moment before he glanced back at me and then turned to walk over to me. Without my shoes, I felt even smaller and stepped back, almost stumbling on a small chest of drawers that had been tipped over. I stepped onto it and crossed my arms, smirking as I realised I was a few inches taller than him.

He raised an eyebrow and crossed his arms.

"I'm glad to see that adding some height makes you feel better. I could push you, and you could snap that fragile neck of yours on the bedpost right behind you," he mocked, stepping closer, forcing me to move back on the chest of drawers that was on its side, not giving me the best balance.

"I should have been more afraid that you didn't end up crushing my neck last night. I don't think a fall will kill me." I rolled my eyes. My heart was a mess of nerves, my chest was heaving, and I knew my nipples had hardened… I just prayed he didn't notice that. "Why do you always think of me breaking my poor head and neck? Do you want me dead?" I asked, frowning.

He tilted his head, his gaze dipping to my breasts. He didn't reply, simply looking back into my eyes. We were only a few inches apart, and my mind was getting light.

"Breaking you has its allure," he whispered huskily, looking into my eyes. "It's a shame you don't heal as fast as I would prefer…" My core clenched at his words, and I pressed my thighs together, trying not to let it get to me. His gaze dipped to my neck, and I knew the marks from his hold still remained, although they had faded.

"You haven't broken me. No one can break me," I retorted, firmly pushing him back, only for my own feet to slide on the upturned drawer I was standing on. I almost grabbed onto him for balance, only for him to grab a bunch of my shirt and yank me back towards him.

Focus. Focus, Yileyna.

His smouldering eyes met mine, and, like always, his thoughts were a mystery to me.

"Don't tempt me to take that challenge because I assure you I will win," he murmured, taking hold of my chin. His gaze lingered on my lips before he let go and turned away.

"Are my parents really being accused of treason?" I asked quietly.

Just like that, the suffocating tension between us lifted, and I felt like I could breathe again.

"Yes, but you are not. The king knows that… but I would agree that moving out might be for the best."

"It's nice to see you care," I remarked lightly. He turned sharply, looking at me as I got down from the box.

"Don't mistake this for kindness… I assure you, the only one who will feel disappointed in the end will be you," he replied coldly. "In a few days, I'll be leaving on a trip. If you don't find a place to stay, you can use my place outside of the castle."

My heart thundered as I realised he was offering me a place to stay. I knew it was going to be difficult to find accommodation. The people at the door earlier were right, no one would want to house me…

"Thank you… I'll take your offer. I'll pay rent."

Our eyes met, and although I didn't know what we were, one thing was clear: if anyone had my back, it was Theon, even if he didn't want to admit it.

"My question…" he began, glancing away for a moment before looking down at me. "Why didn't you tell me?"

"Tell you what?" I asked, brushing my hair back and trying not to notice how handsome he looked standing there. It was hard to believe that last night we were kissing, our bodies crushed together… fucking…

"That you were a virgin," he replied with a withering glare.

"Did it matter? I don't think it mattered…" I turned away, only for him to grab my arm and yank me back around.

"That would have been my decision to make," he growled, his eyes flashing gold. I raised an eyebrow.

"I gave my first time to you because I wanted to. That was *my* decision. Don't try to act like you had a say in that." I rolled my eyes. I didn't regret it. It just hurt that he walked off after… but he came back. I was about to turn away when I paused and smiled deviously. "What's wrong, Theon? Did you feel guilty for being so rough?" I didn't know what to expect, but really, I had not been intimate with anyone to know what I should or should not have been expecting.

"Don't give yourself so much importance. I don't feel guilty. Ever."

"Oh? Are you sure about that, Theon?" I smirked, crossing my arms.

"Very sure. You really are irritating, I prefer you when you're not talking," he growled.

"Oh well, that's a shame because I talk a lot and pretty often. I also don't like -" I was cut off when his hand tangled in my hair, tugging my head upwards.

"Don't push me, little storm," he warned me, his eyes darkening dangerously.

"I'm shaking with fear," I taunted, my heart thumping as our chests grazed one another. The electric spark sizzling between us was almost visible as his eyes blazed gold. I felt goosebumps rise on my skin. His heart was thudding, and it only made my stomach knot.

"We both know there are a lot more ways I can leave you shaking," he said, his eyes flickering down to my body. I blushed, feeling my pussy clench, and I glared up at him despite my burning cheeks. "And once again, you're aroused," he whispered seductively into my ear. His lips brushed the tip, and my breath hitched, a soft whimper leaving my lips.

"Yileyna!"

My eyes flew open as Theon let go of me smoothly and stepped back, leaving me a mess of nerves as Charlene rushed into the room. Her face and arms were littered with fading bruises, telling me her training was indeed rough. She closed the gap between us, hugging me tightly.

"Thank the goddess, you're okay, Leyna! I'm so sorry... I just found out now."

I hugged her back, reality hitting me like a bag of bricks. What am I doing? Why did Theon consume me so? And above all... what did he want from me?

Our eyes met over Charlene's shoulder before he looked away, his cold exterior once again back in place...

Looking Forward

YILEYNA

A few hours had passed since Charlene had come, and Theon had once again become the quiet, cold, stoic, arrogant jerk he always was when we weren't alone. Charlene had helped organise the stuff whilst Theon had stood outside the apartment, leaving the two of us alone, but with the door broken, I knew he could hear everything.

She had been so upset with what had happened and refused to believe my parents would do such a thing. Goddess, I loved her. She wasn't just saying it to appease me, she genuinely believed it. I just wished her father also realised his friend would never do that to him.

"Are these all for donating?" Charlene asked, pointing at the sacks I had stacked to the side.

"Yes," I replied, feeling a wave of sadness wash over me as I looked at one of Mom's dresses peeking out.

"You are doing exactly what they would have wanted you to do," she whispered softly. I nodded, getting back to brushing up the broken crockery. "Are you okay, Yileyna? I mean, obviously not… but…"

"I'm fine. Things happen."

"I heard you were taken to the hospital today…" I tensed, my heart thumping. Did that healer tell everyone about Theon or her assumptions? I hoped not.

"Yeah, I'm okay, though." I glanced at the door. Charlene seemed to click on, and she nodded. I would tell her about Theon, just not when he could hear our entire conversation.

"Theon!" Charlene called. My heart skipped a beat, wondering what she wanted. He stepped inside, giving her a cold glare.

"What?"

"Could you fix the door, please?" Charlene asked with a small smile, although it didn't reach her eyes. I guess there were things we both needed to talk about. It wasn't like her not to be so warm towards him.

"I'm not a builder nor your servant. Don't call me for unnecessary things." He was about to turn when he paused, glancing back at me. "The Alpha wants to see you in an hour."

I nodded, my stomach sinking. I was going to request a meeting today, but for him to call for me… I wondered what he wanted to say…

"It's going to be okay. Dad does not blame you," Charlene said confidently.

"Hmm. I hope so. I didn't think he'd blame Dad either." Our eyes met, and she walked over to me, giving me a tight hug.

"One day, the truth will be revealed, and Dad will feel guilty." I nodded. *I truly hope so.* I'd hold onto that because I would prove my parent's innocence. They died protecting me and this city. I would not let their name be tarnished.

Everything was done by the time I had to go see the Alpha. Charlene looked at the boxes.

"I will have these donated. Where will you go?" She asked as we stood near the front door. She had mind linked some Omegas to come help. If it had been me, no one would have come, but no one would disobey the future Alpha.

"I'm going to go to one of the -"

"She has a place down by the woods. If you're done, Princess, shall we head back?" Theon cut in, his eyes on me. Did he not want her to know he was allowing me to stay at his place? I wasn't going to mention it…

"Then we'll get someone to take the stuff. Are you sure it's a good place?" Charlene asked me, concerned.

"Yeah, it's okay. I mean, it's nice. The owner was very sweet and considerate to allow me to stay there," I smirked. Theon's jaw ticked, his burning amber eyes meeting mine. I raised an eyebrow, crossing my arms. *Deny it, handsome.*

He turned his back on us. I smiled slightly.

"I'll make sure someone takes her stuff. Now let's head back. Besides, she needs to see the Alpha," he said icily.

"Thank you, Theon," I replied sweetly, brushing past him as I headed out the door. My breasts grazed his arm, and I felt him tense. Our eyes met before his flashed gold, my stomach did a somersault, and then the moment was gone.

The reality of the upcoming conversation with the Alpha King weighed on my mind as I stepped away from him.

Well, let's get this over with.

I stood opposite the king's desk as he ran a hand through his brown hair, his sharp grey eyes on me and his brows furrowed in concentration.

"Do you want to take a look at the evidence?"

"Have you seen it?" I asked quietly. He nodded and sighed heavily.

"It's in Will's writing. The maps... the notes... and it is my fear that he had been dealing with none other than the Obsidian Shadow Pack."

"Dad would never do that."

"I want to believe it, I truly do, but I assure you I have seen far more in life than you, Yileyna. Giving in to greed and betraying your loved ones isn't that hard. I didn't want to believe it, but the truth is before us." My heart clenched, anger beginning to rise.

"Things are not always as they seem, Alpha. Do you think my parents would keep such incriminating things in our house? This all seems far too coincidental." Anyone who knew my parents would know something wasn't adding up. The king nodded and gave me a small half-smile that held no happiness.

"I want to say the same thing, but the truth is, why would anyone try to frame them after their death? What's the purpose of it? There isn't any reason which points to your father knowing I'd always trust him. He probably knew that was one place I would never search. The one place no one would ever accidentally stumble onto. Only he didn't realise he'd die trying to save you."

With each word, my faith in our Alpha was crumbling. I understood he had a kingdom to run, a pack to answer to, and peace and control to uphold, but did he not have any compassion?

"Then there is nothing for me to see." He nodded dismissively, as if he didn't really care.

"You will not be punished for your father's crimes. Although many wanted me to make you an Omega… I will not punish you for his crimes. You are Charlene's greatest confidant, and she wouldn't be able to forgive me if I did that to you. Plus, there are others who seem to have your best interests at heart. I don't know how you do it, Yileyna, but you know how to win people over."

"Is it a bad thing? Or is it that maybe if I wasn't Charlene's friend, you would happily cast me aside? Strip me of everything and make me an Omega?" I asked quietly, unable to stop the words from leaving my lips. His eyes changed, turning the pale yellow of his wolf, but I held his gaze.

"I'm still your Alpha, Yileyna, and I will not tolerate disrespect." His voice was deeper, darker, and more dangerous, but it didn't bother me as it once would have. Everything that had happened… it only made me feel worse.

I thought I wasn't being treated right, but, okay, I guess I didn't have my wolf. I didn't deserve the Beta title… but then labelling my parents as traitors? There was a fine line between wronging me and completely abusing me, and expecting me to stay silent.

"Of course you are. I just wished as Alpha, you realised I'm just an orphan who has lost her parents, then her birthright, and was cast aside mercilessly. But thank you for not beheading me for my parents' crimes. I am truly grateful," I said quietly, trying to keep the bitterness from my tone.

"I do realise that, Yileyna, that is why I wanted to ask you if you want to see the proof, perhaps when you see Will's writing -"

"But you automatically included Mom in that? Was there her writing in the evidence?"

"You know the law, mates are one. If one commits a crime, then the other, by default, is guilty."

I clenched my jaw. A law that needed to be abolished. A law that disgusted me. It would be better to lock criminals up rather than kill them and punish their innocent counterparts. Finding your fated mate was both a blessing and a curse…

"As I was saying, if you saw that it's Will's writing, perhaps then you would be able to accept it."

"No, thank you," I said, clasping my hands behind my back, trying to remain passive as I stared at the Alpha. After a moment, he nodded and stood up.

"The choice is yours. Well, anyway, the second reason I called you was because Theon and Charlene are going on a trip… I have already told them both, and well, Charlene wants you to accompany her. I think perhaps having some female companionship will be good for her."

"A trip?" I asked. Maybe some time away from the city would do me well. I loved travelling with Dad whenever I'd had the chance.

"A trip to the Purien Isles. In fact, I think this might be something that would suit you. Your father always said you were impressive with mapping and had good knowledge of terrain, seas, and rivers. I think you will be well suited for this trip."

The Purien Isles… that was a dangerous path. If, as I'm guessing, he wasn't planning on spending months taking a detour, something told me he wanted to make a direct journey there.

"Alpha, then you would trust me when I say that the journey is rather dangerous?"

"I know, but it's a necessity. You see, there is a mage there, and time is short…"

He sat down again as he began to explain…

The meeting with the Alpha lasted under an hour, and although we did not discuss my parents after that, it wasn't something I would just forget. I walked through the halls and stopped outside my old home. The setting sun shone through the curtainless windows, illuminating the dust particles in the air. As promised, everything was gone.

I stepped through the broken door. The scent of Mom's candles lingered in the air, the last hint of her there… I ran my hand along the walls as I looked around one final time. I brushed away a stray tear that I didn't even know had escaped me with my free hand.

I paused at the door to my bedroom. The small knife dents that Dad made to measure my height every summer remained. I smiled, fighting back the storm of tears that threatened to stream down my cheeks. I slowly dropped to my knees, brushing my finger down the door frame until I saw the first mark. *I was one year old when Dad made this one...*

Even as an adult, he continued the little tradition. I remember complaining last year that I was too old for it. *Oh, how I'd let him do it forever if he was here...*

I stood up, walking over to the sack of broken cutlery I had gathered up earlier. Taking out a broken piece of glass, I returned to the door frame and stood against it, keeping my chin up. Reaching up, I nicked the wood before stepping away and looking at the difference from last year, just about an inch.

"I grew, Dad, just like you said I would... even if it's just an inch..." I murmured, my voice echoing slightly in the empty room. Silence. I smiled sadly as I glanced into all the rooms one final time.

When I step out of this room, I will be stronger. I will make my parents proud. I will prove to the world that they were innocent, prove that Yileyna De'Lacor is her parents' daughter, true to her people, her pack, and her kingdom, even when wronged...

I promise you, Mom and Dad, I will do better.

I walked to the front door, pausing and looking over my shoulder. My gaze lingered on the dining table, a place that held one memory that overrode the rest. Theon...

The walls... the kitchen... the memories. I wouldn't forget the time I spent there with my family. Ever.

I turned away and, with a deep breath, I stepped out of the quarters that were once my home...

"Goodbye..." I whispered before I walked away, not turning back. No matter how many times I wanted to cast a final glance back at the Beta quarters, I wouldn't. I couldn't. From here on out, I would only look forward.

In Three Days

YILEYNA

I stared at the small cabin that belonged to Theon, seeing the glow around the edge of the window, meaning someone was there… My heart skipped a beat. Theon would stay at the castle, right?

Did he know I'd be going on the trip too?

I looked around. There was a scattering of cabins, each with its own garden area, trees, and low fences surrounding each square of land. It was a nice area… I hadn't paid attention last time.

Taking a deep breath, I knocked on the door. I didn't hear anyone coming to the door, so I knocked again, frowning. Surely he was in there. I knocked again, louder, before the door was yanked open, and Theon stood there, giving me a withering glare.

"If no one answers, it means it's unlocked," he stated icily, turning and walking off.

"How was I meant to know that?" I retorted, stepping inside and shutting the door behind me.

The smell of something delicious filled my nose, and my eyes scanned the kitchen counters. I was starving, only just realising I had only had milk in the morning. As if on cue, my stomach rumbled loudly, making my cheeks flame up. His eyebrow shot up, and I pouted.

"I haven't eaten all day…" I explained sheepishly.

"Shame, I only bought food for myself. I said I'd give you a roof over your head, not hot meals," he said, sounding as irritating as he did sexy. He grabbed the brown paper bag from the counter and dropped onto one of the two chairs at the table.

"I never said I wanted your food," I replied icily. "So, where are my things?"

He tilted his head, and that tension that always seemed to settle between us filled the entire cabin, making my heart race. I stood there, a flash of that night returning to me as I remembered how he had looked me over as he sat back…

"Bedroom," he replied after a moment.

I managed a nod before I hurried through to the bedroom, shutting the door behind me. Instantly, I was hit with Theon's masculine scent, and it made my core knot. Theon's bedroom… *Did that mean he was letting me sleep here? In his bedroom...*

Focus, Yileyna! I shook my head, thinking I would go get myself some food and maybe some groceries. He was right; he had given me a place to stay, but I needed to pull my weight. The urge to take a long bath tempted me. I wanted to just relax, but then I was also starving… I looked at the boxes of my belongings and rummaged around until I found my purse.

I left the bedroom to see Theon pouring himself some wine, his long legs sprawled out in front of him. I wanted to climb on top of those muscular thighs and kiss him.

"There's leftovers," he remarked, motioning to the paper bag, bringing me from my thoughts. I raised an eyebrow, feeling my cheeks heat up. I'm glad I didn't go too red, even when I blushed, my cheeks only went a little pink. Thank the goddess!

"No thanks, I can get my own food." I wasn't going to accept his food after he had been a jerk. I was about to walk to the door, thinking night had fallen, meaning it'd be colder too...

Oh, the pie smelled good…

"Go ahead," his mocking reply came. I turned and frowned. Wouldn't he stop me? When it was clear he wouldn't, I glared at him.

"Then again, we shouldn't waste food," I replied in a clipped tone.

He raised his eyebrow, picking up his wine glass and swirling the liquid in it, but he didn't say anything as he drank some. My gaze dipped to his throat as he swallowed. I forced my gaze away and instead went to the kitchen area.

I took out a plate and fork before I returned to the table and sat down opposite him. I tensed when my knee touched his leg. I quickly pulled away, my heart thudding as I put some pie into my plate and quickly took a bite, not looking at him. I moaned in satisfaction. Goddess, it was delicious!

I felt his intense gaze on me as I scooped another fork full, and my eyes snapped towards him, my fork near my mouth. His glass was to his lips, but he wasn't drinking, and his eyes were pure gold, but what made my core clench was the raw carnal hunger in them. My heart thumped as I quickly shoved the pie into my mouth and looked down at my plate. He stood up suddenly, making me jump, but he didn't even look at me as he walked over to the sofa in a few long strides, grabbing his jacket.

"He wants me to go with you and Charlene on this trip," I said suddenly. I wouldn't say the Purien Isles out loud, knowing it was strictly confidential and, you never know, sometimes the walls had ears. He paused, turning back to me sharply.

"The Alpha?"

"No, the guardsman. Yes, the Alpha, but it was Charlene who wanted me to go..." I said, my hunger suddenly dissipating.

"Perfect." My heart skipped a beat as I looked at his back. "Two idiots to mind. Can it get any better?" He added, coldly glancing at me. I cocked a brow. His tone was scornful.

"One idiot you seemed to have a lot of dirty thoughts about," I teased with a small smirk. *Two can play this game.* His eyes flashed. I knew I was playing with fire, but I didn't really care. "Tell me, Theon, am I wrong?"

He tossed his jacket back onto the sofa and advanced towards me. I couldn't deny that sparks of excitement and pleasure tingled through me. I stood up and stepped away, crossing my arms.

"You tell me... do you like pissing me off?" He grabbed my neck, stepping closer as he pushed me against the wall. "Because to me, it seems you like me getting physical. And I assure you, next time, I'll be punishing you." Pleasure rippled through me, making my core clench. I pressed my thighs together, trying not to focus on the ache that had settled there.

"It doesn't sound like a bad idea," I whispered, uncrossing my arms and running a hand down his abs. His eyes flashed, and just when I managed to stroke his package, he crushed his body against mine painfully hard, his eyes a dazzled gold and I was forced to pull my hand free.

"I told you, I will break you. We agreed on one night." His minty breath, laced with the scent of wine, fanned my face. Oh, how I wanted those lips on me.

"You said that. I didn't," I whispered, unable to ignore the throbbing of his manhood against my stomach. He wanted me too…

His free hand gripped my waist, pressing me fully against him.

"You're not heeding my warning…" he whispered huskily. "Don't tempt me."

My eyes fluttered shut as pleasure rushed through me. Our beating hearts were like thunder in this silence. Can you break something that already feels broken?

"You can't break me," I whispered seductively. I needed him. The distraction he provided made me feel happier… alive.

I ran my hand up his waist, loving the feel of his taut skin beneath my fingertips. I wanted to feel him, to be able to kiss every inch of him.

"Don't be so sure about that. I'll never be able to give you more…" His gaze flickered to my lips before looking back into my eyes.

"I'm not asking for more."

He scoffed, his hand tightening around my throat, and with the other, he brushed back my hair from my face, sending tingles through me.

"Then do you promise to never fall in love, little storm?"

"Really? Fall in love with you? Theon... I admit you are incredibly handsome, but you're not really lovable material, are you?" I asked, raising an eyebrow. *I'll try not to, but I don't want you to turn away from me if I say that.*

"Good, because if you do… it will only hurt you."

"It won't happen," I whispered, my chest heaving as it pressed against him. Our bodies fit so well, as if made to be one. But dreams didn't come true.

"Have a think about it… because once you become my plaything, you will be opening the doors to something you never expected, and I assure you, there will be no escape."

"I don't mind," I replied softly. His eyes met mine, and after a moment, he let go of my throat.

"I'll give you three days to think about it. Then you can let me know your decision." He turned away, making reality settle in.

"Three days?" I blinked.

"Like I said, it's not a small decision." He picked up his jacket and went to the door, leaving me feeling weak and giddy.

"Okay…"

"Oh, and one more thing. Make sure you don't tell anyone about this." He looked over his shoulder at me, his burning amber eyes holding a silent warning. I knew even if I wanted to, I couldn't tell Charlene because if he found out… he would be beyond pissed.

"Understood."

"Three days. Let's see exactly how reckless you are." With a final cold glance, he left, shutting the door behind him.

I looked around the house, my home from now on… or until I found somewhere else… but if Theon and I did go through with this arrangement, did that mean I could stay here? Well, either way, it was always good to have a backup in mind, just in case.

Three days… I had already made up my mind, but if he wanted to give me time, then fine. I'd give him three days. I was not going to change my mind. Deep down, I knew it may not be the wisest choice, but I had nothing to lose, and I knew what I wanted.

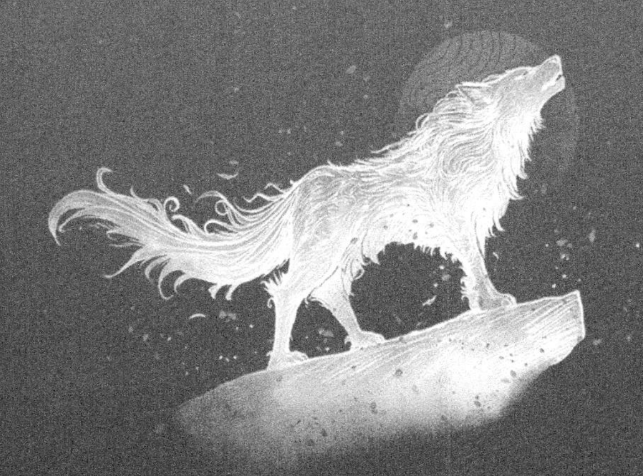

The Siren Killer

YILEYNA

THREE DAYS HAD PASSED, and I had been immensely busy. Not only was Theon's Beta ceremony delayed, much to the court's surprise, but we had been notified that we would set sail at sunrise on the fourth day.

The king had found a crew to take us. In total, there would be twenty-two of us on board The Siren Killer, a name that intrigued me. I was not expecting the king to have chosen something like that for our trip, but I guess a ship that was going to brave the journey had to be as dangerous as The Siren Killer looked. The body itself was dark and sleek; it looked like a formidable beast. I could see it was equipped with heavy weaponry and its three masts had deep red sails.

The crew consisted of nine men and three women, which included the captain of the ship. I didn't recognise any of the ones I could see from Westerfell. They all looked as threatening and hostile as the ship itself. From their tanned skin, tattoos, and sharp eyes, I doubted any of these werewolves were from our pack. I would ask Theon about their origin when I had the chance.

Aside from them, there was Raiden and the son of the other Gamma, Ryan. Then there was one of the king's mages, Madelia, and four of the king's most trusted royal guards, which meant our trip included the two future Gammas, the future Beta, and the rest who were hand-chosen by the king, well aside from me. It was obvious that this was no small mission or trip.

The future of Westerfell was on the ship; although Charlene had come onto the ship in disguise before dawn and was currently waiting under the deck in her room. No one was to know that she was making this journey. She was the future of the Silver Storm Pack and the Kingdom of Astalion. No one else apart from Theon, Madelia, and I knew the true purpose of our journey.

I stood to the side on deck. The cold morning wind blew through my hair that was braided into a loose fish plait, my hands folded behind me, dressed in a long-sleeved jacket with matching deep blue coloured pants and knee-high boots. Under my jacket, I wore a black corset top that left plenty of my cleavage on show. I planned to give Theon an answer today, and I wanted his attention on me.

The smell of the sea filled my nose. Like always, it elated me. I loved the sea, and it was the perfect time to enjoy the time we had there. We would be at sea for almost a month, an adventure my heart yearned for, something to keep my mind distracted from everything else.

The fifteen of us on deck watched each other wearily. Raiden was standing next to me with Ryan on his other side, both of whom seemed to be assessing the nine crew members that were on the opposite side.

"You're a pretty one. What's your name, lass?" One of the women asked me. She had cropped brown hair, brown eyes, arched brows, and plump lips, wearing fitted pants and a tunic. From the piercings on her face and the way she was playing with the little knife in her hand, I could tell she wasn't the type you would want to cross.

"Yileyna, and yours?" I asked.

"Cleo." She crossed her arms and jerked her head to her teammates. "Bobbie, Jack, Aeon, Leto, Barbara, Sam, Zen, and Anton." Each one gave a little nod save Barbara, whose blue eyes seemed to be fixed on the far end of the ship where Theon and the Captain were talking.

"Raiden, Ryan, Madelia, Bruce, and Nate," I introduced our own people.

"Handsome bunch," Cleo smirked. "Who's he?"

I glanced to where her attention was fixed on Theon, and I felt a flare of jealousy shoot through me. It was weird, I should be used to it. Theon's cold behaviour only made him a fan favourite of the she-wolves in Westerfell.

"Our leader and the one in charge of this trip, Theon," Bruce said with a nod.

In his black pants, white shirt, and jacket, he looked incredibly handsome, as always. He had his arms crossed, and just then, as if he knew we were watching, his smouldering amber eyes met mine. My heart thumped. I knew everyone here could probably hear it. Well, all the werewolves present anyway. I hadn't been around him alone since that day in his cabin when he had given me three days. My stomach knotted as I watched his eyes skim over me.

The spell only broke when he looked away, making me let out a breath I never knew I was holding. I looked away, quickly feeling several other pairs of eyes on me and one pair that belonged to Raiden… I wonder what he thought. He had seen Theon walk off that night at the festival. He had seen the state I had been in about the Beta title. If anyone, he knew there was something between us.

"Alright, who is ready to set sail?" The captain shouted, and for the first time, I got a proper look at him. He looked to be in his late thirties. He was large and muscular with tan, weathered skin. Scars littered his face, but the most prominent was the long, thick, puffy scar along his neck. He smirked, flashing his gold tooth at me, and his piercing green eyes bore into me. "That's a story for another night, lass. Now tell me, what is your pretty name?" His voice was deep and guttural, and he had a rough accent. Theon's dangerous glare turned on him.

"She's off-limits," he said coldly, walking past the captain and towards us. "Call the rest of your crew on board. I will have a word with them," he added, crossing his arms as he looked at the captain.

"It's Yileyna, Captain," I replied, ignoring Theon. The Captain grinned.

"Pretty name for a pretty lady. I'm Flynn."

"Nice to meet you, Captain Flynn." I smiled sweetly, trying to suppress my giggle at Theon's growing irritation.

"Barbara, call the rest," Flynn said, his eyes not leaving mine. "Nice to meet you too, Yileyna." He rolled my name on his tongue, and although it sounded nowhere near as amazing as it did from Theon's lips, it was satisfying to see Theon's jaw tick.

We smiled at each other before I made the mistake of glancing at Theon. My heart skipped a beat at the anger in those eyes. Something told me I'd be paying for that later. Well, we weren't together or anything, so I could talk to whomever I wanted.

I turned when Barbara returned with a young boy who looked about my age, and to my surprise, the woman next to him was one I recognised.

"Ailema?" I asked, stunned. She chuckled.

"Ah, my sweet, it's a pleasure to see you again."

"You two know one another?" Flynn asked sharply.

"Yes, we do, I was selling some goods, and she was my one and only customer." Flynn shook his head.

"You never get business. I don't get why you even shop when we travel."

"You need not tell me what I should or shouldn't do." She waved her hand. "Oh, you are as pretty as ever, but something has changed... what is it..." Her eyes ran over me thoughtfully, and I felt guilty, as if everyone would find out about what happened that night.

"Enough," Theon's cold voice cut in. "Everybody has been informed of our journey to the Purien Isles by order of the king of Astalion. I expect everyone to obey the rules that I set out."

"Aiy... I'm captain... but Commander Theon here is in charge." Flynn forced a smile. I knew he was probably not happy with that, but I was sure the king was paying him a pretty penny for this.

Theon's face remained impassive as his eyes pierced into each person present. Only Charlene and two guards weren't there, but I had a feeling they were getting the message through the mind link.

"There will be no playing around. I expect everyone to do what is expected from them. The Silver Moon Pack members will respect the crew of the Siren Killer, and I expect the same treatment back. The women of the Silver Moon Pack are off-limits. If I find anyone even trying to get close..." Raiden chuckled slightly before coughing to cover it up.

"That rule surely doesn't go for us, though, right?" He smiled.

"We are on a mission, Bolton. This is not a joke," Theon replied. His eyes flashed, and Raiden simply nodded. I could tell Theon's anger was at a breaking point already, so I dared not add anything to trigger him. "This is a vital and dangerous journey. Be prepared for the worst. As for the rest, just obey the rules you were given prior to boarding," he finished, turning away. "Yileyna."

"Yes?" I replied, realising he was done.

"Follow me."

I raised an eyebrow as he began walking towards the lower deck. I glanced at Raiden and gave Flynn a nod before I followed a few steps behind him, making my way down the narrow stair ladder carefully. I was almost to the bottom when Theon grabbed my arm, roughly yanking me off the steps and into his arms. A hand clamped over my mouth before the scream of panic could even leave my lips...

COUNTING AND PLEASURE

YILEYNA

MY HEART POUNDED AS I stared up at Theon. I could hear the captain shouting orders as we made to set sail. His scent filled my senses, and the feel of his hand against my lips felt good.

I tried to pull away from his vicelike grip, yet he didn't let go. He held me off the ground as I struggled fruitlessly, poking my eyes out at him. He didn't say anything, walking down the narrow hall and stopping outside one of the rooms.

"Do not make a sound," he warned, his deep sexy voice making my stomach flutter like always, his eyes blazing gold in silent warning.

I nodded, and he slowly removed his hand from my mouth. My heart was racing as he slipped a key from his pocket and unlocked the door, still not letting go of me until we were inside, and he pushed the door shut, locking it.

"And to what do I owe the pleasure of being dragged into a room so unceremoniously?" I asked, narrowing my eyes. I tried to yank free from his hold, but instead, he slammed me up against the door.

"I don't intend to make it pleasurable. What were you doing out there?" I smirked. So there we had it. Did Theon really not realise how possessive he was behaving?

"He was handsome. You know, I was thinking over what you said, and maybe you were right… one night was what you wanted. I think there's plenty o- ouch!" I gasped when he threaded his fingers in my hair, yanking my head back.

"So you were doing it to get a reaction from me... guess what? You're getting it." His hand closed around my neck, his arm pressing against my breasts, and my core knotted.

"Good," I whispered seductively. "I've made up my mind; I'm not backing out. I want this, even if it's just physical..."

His eyes flickered gold, his heart thudding. His gaze dipped to my lips and then back to my eyes.

"Oh?" His arm loosened around my waist, running down my back until it rested on my ass. "Then I hope you're ready for your punishment," he growled huskily.

"I wouldn't-"

"Theon?" Ryan's voice came from outside, making me tense. Theon squeezed my ass, his eyes meeting mine before he let go of me.

"What is it?" He asked coldly.

"The captain wanted to assess our first stop and discuss it with you."

"We just talked. He can wait for a while," Theon replied coldly. "I have something I need to tend to right now."

"Okay, I'll tell him," Ryan's voice came before I heard his footsteps retreat.

"Tend to what?" I asked, feeling the slight sway of the ship beneath my feet.

"Your punishment, little storm. Strip," he commanded, making my heart thud.

"What? Now?" I asked, my cheeks heating up.

Theon smirked, backing away until he reached the bed and sat down, resting his hands behind him, his gaze on me as I stood there, my heart hammering. I slowly took my jacket off, watching him. His eyes were on my breasts as I slowly dropped my jacket to the ground and reached for the button on my pants.

"Come here." My heart pounded as I walked towards him, stopping in front of him. "Turn and pants down."

I turned slowly, knowing my ass was right in front of his face as I slowly lowered my pants. I had just gotten them to my thighs when he stood up and grabbed my hair, pushing me down against the chest of drawers that was bolted to the wall next to the bed. I gasped as he buried his nose in my neck.

"Bad girls get punished. Spread those legs for me."

My stomach knotted as I braced my forearms against the drawer, my hands spread palm down on the smooth wood as I parted my legs, well, as much as my pants that were between my knees allowed me to. I didn't know what was going to come, but the excitement inside of me was already heightening.

"Then punish me," I whispered, looking at him over my shoulder. He yanked me back by my hair, and I tilted my head up, wanting him to kiss me, but he simply smirked slightly.

"This is a punishment, little storm." He pushed me forward on the chest of drawers. I could feel the heat of his body behind me, smell my arousal in the air... "You really are remarkably made..." My eyes fluttered shut as his fingers ran over my ass cheeks. I had worn tiny panties that were swallowed up by my ass, and I knew they were already on the verge of getting damp. "Flawless..." he murmured, just as his hand met my ass in a sharp slap. My eyes flew open as the sting of pain shot through me.

"Count," he commanded coldly.

"One..." I mumbled, my cheeks burning as he palmed my ass where he had just spanked me. Another sharp tap made me jolt, pain shooting through me and making my core throb. "Two," I whispered. The sensation was different... his hand met my ass again, and I whimpered as I counted.

"Will you continue to misbehave, little storm?" He whispered, his lips grazing my ear.

"I...fuck!" I gasped when his hand met my ass again. My core throbbed, and I didn't understand, *How is this turning me on?*

"Keep counting."

Another sharp tap, and then he massaged my ass, making me moan, giving temporary relief to my sore behind. His fingers brushed between my ass, and all I wanted was for him to touch my pussy.

"Seems like you're enjoying this. It's a punishment, remember?" Another slap, and I was unable to stop the wanton moan that escaped me.

"Fuck, Theon..."

"Wrong. You're counting, remember?"

"Seven," I whispered as his hand met my ass again. His fingers rubbed my soaking panties, and I closed my eyes, wriggling my ass. He continued, each slap that met my ass stung, yet it was accompanied by a deep, delicious round of pleasure that was making my pussy drip.

"Fifteen…" I moaned. My legs were weak, and I felt like I was going to come at any moment. "Don't stop…"

"What's wrong… turned on?" He whispered, massaging my stinging behind. "You're soaking. I'm sure if you don't wash up, everyone on this ship will know what a fucking dirty little whore you are."

"You're turned on, too," I whispered, reaching behind me and managing to brush my fingers along his hard shaft, smirking with satisfaction when he grabbed my arm and twisted it behind my back. "And I'm not that turned on," I added, biting my lip when he ran his finger between my thighs, sending sizzling rivers of pleasure to my core.

"Your body says otherwise…" he whispered at the same time he shoved two fingers into my dripping core, making me cry out.

His other hand clamped over my mouth as he began fucking me with his fingers. Pleasure rocked my body, and my core knotted, feeling my orgasm rising. It hurt a little, but it was nothing like when he fucked me. This was so enjoyable…

"Fuck," I whimpered, groaning loudly when his lips met my neck, sucking hard. He let go of my arm, reaching around and grabbing my breast roughly. "I'm coming," I whimpered, doing my best to keep my voice down.

"Who said you could come?" His seductive, sinful voice came in my ear, and before I could even comprehend what was happening, he slid his fingers out, leaving me empty and aching for a release.

I turned sharply, my eyes meeting his as he raised the two fingers that had been inside of me moments earlier to his lips and slowly ran his tongue along them, his eyes not leaving mine as he tasted me on them, making my pussy clench. Fuck, that was hot…

"Delicious, don't you agree?" He gripped my throat and slipped the same two fingers into my mouth, making me moan softly. "Taste yourself…"

I wrapped my lips around his fingers, swirling my tongue along his fingers and tasting myself on him. My cheeks burned, and my core knotted as his eyes darkened. I knew the same thought was going through his head that was going through mine. *How would it feel to have his cock in my mouth?*

He slipped his fingers from my mouth, and despite the fact that I wanted to kiss him, he simply turned away and walked to the small door that led off from his room. He paused at the door and looked back at me, once again that coldness returning.

"Make sure you do not touch yourself. From this day on, you come when

I say you can." With that, he shut the door, and I rolled my eyes, slumping back against the chest of drawers. My entire body felt extra sensitive, and he had left me unsatisfied.

I slowly pulled my pants up, knowing I would need to go to my cabin and clean up. I pulled my jacket on, fixing my clothes. I unlocked the door and peered out before I hurried down the hall. I had the room on the other side of Charlene, who was right next to Theon's.

Goddess, what if she heard something? I had to be careful.

Darkness shrouded the starless skies, and the weather had become extremely cold. Night had fallen not long ago, and several of us were on deck. The crew were sitting and laughing as they played a game of cards. Two of Charlene's guards, Bruce and Valentin, had joined in whilst Nate and Patrick were stood not far from where Charlene and I were standing, holding large mugs of coffee with a blanket draped over our shoulders. Even for werewolves, it was extremely cold.

Theon was at the bow of the ship alongside Flynn, Raiden, and Ryan, all four of them discussing something that I couldn't hear as the wind was carrying their voices away from us. Plus, they were speaking very quietly.

Theon… I hadn't spoken a word to him since what had happened in his room, but I couldn't help feeling the excitement simmering inside of me. Theon opened the doors to something more, something where I didn't know what to expect next, and I liked it. I'd had to wear a scarf around my neck after I had cleaned up, not wanting anyone to see the marks he had left.

I rested my head on Charlene's shoulder, and her head rested on top of mine. I felt guilty not telling her… I wanted to tell her…

"What's wrong? You've been quiet," I asked her, staring at the group on the far side, who were drinking beer and playing their game.

"I'm scared," she whispered so quietly that even the guards standing a few feet away wouldn't be able to hear us, thanks to the rowdy group opposite. "You know Father expects me to awaken this power… I'm scared I'll fail. Yesterday, Theon pushed me off the cliff, but even then, nothing happened, and he had to catch me before I cracked open my skull. I'm scared I'm just normal." I looked up at her, my heart aching for her.

"Don't say that, my queen, you are not normal. Power or not, you are a queen, our queen, the future Alpha queen. Always remember that," I whispered, looking into her green eyes. She smiled and nodded.

"You always have faith in me."

"If not I, then who else?" I asked, smiling, when suddenly an odd sense of unease filled me, and I felt the hair at the back of my neck stand up.

"Well, that's true. You are my queen, too…"

I turned sharply to the water, Charlene's voice fading into the distance as I stared at the water that looked black. My heart pounded as I stared at the ripples, the urge to lean over and touch the black liquid overpowering me.

A whisper of the wind brushed through my hair, and I felt the blanket slide from my shoulders as I leaned over the edge, staring deep into the bottomless sea…

Into the Water

THEON

"I don't understand why you want to go straight through the Lifeless Abyss, it's a death wish," Flynn said seriously, a frown on his face as he looked at the map in his hands. I crossed my arms, raising an eyebrow.

"You were chosen because, apparently, you are the most capable captain out there. Don't tell me the Alpha made a mistake." His jaw ticked, his eyes flashing as he stared at the map.

"Yes, I'm capable, not stupid. We can take a side route and then detour heading west towards the Aethirian Ocean," Flynn advised.

"I'm with the Captain on this one," Raiden said quietly. "The waters of the Lifeless Abyss are dangerous, and we won't make it through it in one day. Being there at night is a death wish. No man has survived a journey through it."

"So, The Siren Killer is scared to brave Siren-infested waters?" Ryan asked mockingly.

"It's a reckless move, is what I'm saying," Flynn growled.

I wasn't stupid. I knew exactly what those waters held… I also knew the risk, and Flynn wasn't wrong, it was a death wish... but only if you let it be. I had travelled those waters in the past when I wanted to find someone, and maybe deep down, I wanted her to make her appearance once more… I looked out at the dark water as the three discussed it.

To find her... to get revenge for what she did... her face was one I wouldn't ever forget. A burning surge of anger flared inside of me, and my eyes flashed with hatred.

"We go through the Lifeless Abyss. End of discussion," I spoke with finality. Turning away, my eyes fell on Yileyna. She was gripping the edge of the ship, leaning over dangerously. Charlene stood next to her, seemingly saying something, but the two guards didn't seem to be paying attention to Yileyna. My heart skipped a beat, and a wave of worry rippled through me. It almost looked like she was intrigued by something...

"Yileyna!" I growled,

Her head jerked up with a start, and she moved away from the edge, her chest rising and falling heavily as I brushed past Ryan and Flynn. I pushed away the mix of emotions inside of me, focusing on my anger which replaced everything else. *I feel nothing.* The only thing within me was hatred, rage and anger. That was all I needed, the only thing that would fuel my goal.

"Yileyna, are you okay?" Charlene asked, cupping her friend's face. She had just been standing there without a care, and now she was going to act worried? Useless.

"What were you doing?" I asked Yileyna harshly, yanking her away from Charlene. She looked up at me. Her face looked pale, her eyes full of confusion, as if she herself had no idea what was going on. "You should be more responsible. When will you ever grow up?" I asked coldly.

"I don't know; I didn't mean to. I was just looking at the water," she mumbled.

I could feel all eyes on us. Everyone knew that Charlene was the daughter of the Alpha and Yileyna was her friend. Although both were as useless and stupid as one another. Well, almost. At least Yileyna was a good fuck for distraction, but even that in itself pissed me off.

"You both need to be more careful. If I see anything stupid again, I will make sure you are both kept in your cabins," I finished coldly.

"Honestly, stop acting like something happened. I'm fine. What is your problem?" Yileyna shot back, irritation clear in her voice.

I clenched my jaw. Even Raiden and Ryan didn't disrespect me, yet there she was. I guess being of Beta blood still made her think she was fucking equal to me. Well, Beta or not, she wasn't.

"My problem is I'm the one who has to answer to the king. But then again, I'm sure he won't fucking care if we are one member less. If you really want to die, carry on as you are. In fact, I wouldn't mind pushing you overboard myself." She tried to pull free, but I only pulled her close.

"Let go of me, Theon," she growled, and I saw her gaze flickering to everyone who was silently watching.

"Once you realise who is in charge, I will. You can start with showing some respect," I replied coldly. She raised an eyebrow.

"Or what?"

I clenched my jaw, hearing a snicker that was quickly stifled. My eyes blazed gold. It was clear no one realised I meant what I said.

"Since everyone is finding this a joke…" I looked down at the woman in my hold before twisting us, and, in one swift movement, I picked her up and threw her over the edge. A piercing scream left her lips, her eyes wide with horror as she stared up at me.

"No!" Charlene screamed. A few gasps followed, and the large splash as Yileyna hit the water reached us all.

"What the hell…?" Flynn muttered.

"This is not a joke," Raiden growled, and the next thing I saw was him jumping into the water.

Fucking losers.

That in itself made it clear he had far too much interest in her, only adding to my anger. I turned to the rest, glaring coldly at each and every one of them.

"I'm in charge here. If anyone crosses me, disobeys me, or even so much as shows me disrespect, I won't falter from getting rid of you. Remember that," I warned, my voice so cold and menacing that I felt the tension and a wave of fear in the air from a few of them. They may not have been expecting this side of me, but the mission was not a joke.

I can't find her, Theon! Raiden's panic-filled voice came into my head.

My heart thudded, and a sliver of worry filled me again. I hated this feeling. I hated how she awoke this emotion within me. I walked to the edge, scanning the abyss of darkness, trying to remain calm.

You can't see her? Her hair isn't hard to miss…

No, Theon… I swear, I can't fucking find her! This was not a fucking joke!

"I need to get her!" Charlene shouted. Bruce held her back as she struggled to jump into the water. Pathetic, she couldn't even take care of herself.

"I'm not braving that," Flynn said, frowning.

I didn't need him to, fucking idiots. Why couldn't Raiden find her?

I pulled my jacket off and stripped my shirt. It was obvious if I wanted shit done around here, I had to do it myself.

"Have a rope ready," I ordered coldly before I jumped into the water.

It was far colder than I expected. Far too cold, considering it wasn't the coldest of seasons yet. It bit into my bones, and I felt it numbing me instantly.

Where was she? She hadn't shifted yet. Did she sink? Worry for her began filling me once more. *No, I am not worried, it's only because we are at sea, nothing more.* It simply brought back memories of something from long ago… *Fuck, Yileyna, where are you?* I knew I shouldn't have thrown her over, but she irritated me.

Theon, I can't see her! I didn't reply to Raiden, mind linking Ryan instead.

Get Madelia to illuminate the sea. Any light will help, I commanded, diving deeper. *Where are you, Yileyna…?*

A glow illuminated the sea, but it didn't help as much. I kept swimming farther down. The sea itself was devoid of life. No sea life seemed to be around, and that's when I saw it, her hair. She was still, her eyes shut as she slowly sank lower. Even in this state, her beauty was breathtaking. Her skin seemed to glow in the darkness of the water, and her hair floated around her.

Fuck, Yileyna…

Found her, I mind-linked the others, keeping any emotion from my voice despite the relief that had flooded me.

I swam over to her and wrapped my arms around her waist, frowning at the look of contentment on her face. Was she just unconscious? I pressed my ear to her chest; her heartbeat was strong.

I almost exhaled in relief, but instead, I swam upwards, the cold squeezing at my head. I was running out of oxygen too. She whimpered, and her eyelids fluttered open. Our eyes met, and a small, weak smile crossed her lips. We were almost there… I could see the glow of the light above, and finally, we broke the surface.

"There they are!" Flynn shouted as we both gasped for air.

"Thank the gods!" Madelia exclaimed, getting rid of the light she had created. I looked at Yileyna, gripping the back of her head with my other hand.

"Yileyna?" I called her.

"Theon..."

Our eyes met, and the urge to kiss her almost consumed me. She locked her arm around my neck, and I grabbed the rope, allowing them to pull us up.

"Yileyna!" Charlene cried out the moment we reached the top. I flipped my legs over, refusing to let go of the woman in my arms. I placed her down on the floor, breathing hard.

"Give her air," the hybrid woman, Ailema, said, waving the men away. Charlene dropped by her side, clearly worried.

"I'm okay," Yileyna said softly to Charlene before turning her gaze to me.

"Thank the goddess," Raiden muttered. Ailema checked her pulse, and I stood up as I brushed back my soaking hair from my eyes.

"Take this as a warning... next time, I'll leave you to drown," I said coldly. Charlene's eyes flashed as she jumped up and stood before me.

"You can't do that ever again! You could have killed her!" She hissed. Interesting, it wasn't often that the woman got angry... maybe using Yileyna was the way to trigger her into awakening her powers.

"You may be the future Alpha, Princess, but until you prove you are capable of that title, watch that tone of yours," I replied coldly. She clenched her fists.

"You are never to touch her again," she hissed, dropping to her knees and wrapping a blanket around Yileyna's sexy body.

That would be my fucking choice, Princess, not your useless empty threats. The blanket covered her up, and Charlene hugged her. Shame I couldn't see her look all fucking sexy, dripping wet.

"I'm fine, Charl," Yileyna whispered as Ailema brushed her hair back.

"I don't care, that was dangerous."

"It was," Flynn agreed.

"He is so hot," I heard one of the women mutter.

I could feel their eyes on me. Ignoring them, I crouched in front of Yileyna. Reaching over, I took hold of her chin. Even soaking wet, she looked entirely fuckable. Her eyes widened in shock, her heart thudding, and I was aware of everyone having their eyes on us.

"I'm sorry," I whispered with a cold smirk. Confusion flitted through her gorgeous grey eyes, and I tightened my grip on her chin, not missing the way she flinched at the force in my grip. "Sorry you didn't actually die. It would have been one less burden," I finished harshly, standing up and ignoring the flash of hurt in her eyes. Sharp intakes of breath came from the women on board, but I didn't really care. Grabbing my shirt and jacket, I walked off towards the lower deck.

I didn't like the emotions she evoked within me. She was a dangerous distraction. Like I said, I'd break her… physically and mentally. She'll regret ever agreeing to our arrangement. I stopped at the top, not turning back.

"We keep south towards the Lifeless Abyss." With that final command, I walked down the steps, having had enough for one day…

A Breeze in Comparison

YILEYNA

I stared at the wooden ceiling of my cabin, the events from earlier replaying in my mind. I could hear the faint sound of the sea from outside, the sway of the ship. I wasn't sure what time it was, but I knew I had been lying awake for hours.

Charlene had been absolutely fuming earlier, and as much as I loved her, I needed to be alone. The way he threw me overboard… the way he said if I died, I'd be one less burden…

I felt the trickle of tears seep from my eyes, but I refused to blink or give in to them. His words had hurt more than him throwing me into the water…

Rolling onto my side, I placed my hand under my head and sighed heavily. I hated that he did that… Theon was… he was right. He wasn't the type of man I should ever fall in love with. This crush… or infatuation with him, blinded me. But that dip in the sea, well, it opened my eyes to the fact that Theon was borderline unhinged or something. Was looking for a distraction from one pain, worth risking myself getting hurt in another way?

No, it wasn't.

I knew the answer to that, and I hated it. But there was just something about Theon that consumed me.

I closed my eyes, trying to let sleep overcome me, but no matter what I tried, I couldn't. I remembered the water enveloping me, and then I remembered how the panic that had filled me when he had tossed me into the water seemed to vanish. The cold had probably made my mind go numb. It had been strange, but I had felt… at peace. When Theon had wrapped his arm around me in the water, he had been so cold, but I didn't even feel it. Yet when we were on deck, I had felt the cold… strange. There was something about the water…

I sat up, pushing off the blanket that covered me and slipped out of bed. Unlocking my door, I slipped out of my room. The two guards outside of Charlene's door glanced at me. I just gave them a small nod before I headed up to the deck.

It was cold, and I was only wearing a white cami and shorts. Wishing I had grabbed something to wear on top, I wrapped my arms around myself and silently made my way to the opposite side, where I could see Leto at the helm, not wanting to run into anyone. I looked over the side of the ship, staring at the black abyss below.

Why had I felt that odd pull earlier?

"You really shouldn't be so close to the edge, Yileyna," Raiden's voice came, startling me. I spun around.

He gave me a small smile and, removing his jacket, he placed it around my shoulder, instantly reminding me of the time Theon had given me his jacket. Why did everything remind me of him? I smiled back at him, his scent enveloping me. It was pleasant, but it didn't consume me.

"You're right, or Theon may just get his wish," I joked lightly, looking out at the river. I saw him frown as he leaned on the edge, looking over.

"That was beyond crazy of him." We fell silent, and I slowly stepped back to the edge, resting my arms on the side and looking out.

"Hmm." I nodded. I was angry at him too. Maybe I should spank his damn ass. I smirked at the thought, but it faded away. There was no humour in it. What he did was wrong… I sighed, feeling Raiden watching me.

"Yileyna, can I ask you something?"

"You already just did," I replied, glancing into his blue eyes. He smirked.

"Then let me rephrase. May I ask the beautiful maiden a few more?" I smiled.

"Yes, you may, kind sir," I joked. He chuckled, turning and leaning back against the side. He rested his elbows on the edge as he looked at me sharply, as if not wanting to miss my reaction.

"What's the relationship between you and Theon?" My heart thundered as I looked at him sharply. Although I did think he was going to ask something about Theon, I wasn't expecting something so straight up...

"The relationship between us?" I looked at the dark water thoughtfully. "There isn't one. He's just helped me a few times."

"Helped?" He didn't seem convinced.

And hurt me too. But I didn't say that. Theon came with a warning. He told me from the start that he'd only hurt me...

"More than once, but he saved me from two men who had tried to assault me. I know it's no excuse for what he did, but it's complicated," I said, my stomach twisting. I felt cold at the memory. His eyes flashed, and he stood up straight.

"Who were they?" He asked coldly.

"Relax, I'm fine...and it doesn't matter," I reassured him, sighing as I looked out at the water again. It's not like they'd be punished. "Theon has always made it clear who he is... I just..."

"Do you have feelings for him?" My heart thundered, and I looked up at him. Our eyes met, and his returned to their normal blue. I brushed my hair back, praying I looked unbothered.

"No, of course not." He gave me a half-smile that didn't reach his eyes. He didn't believe me.

"I don't want you to get hurt, Yileyna. You deserve so much more. Don't ever feel like you have no one. Charlene, myself, and my family. If you need us, we will be there for you."

"I know, and you don't need to worry. I'm not in love with Theon or anything. I just..." I sighed, smiling slightly.

"It's complicated, huh...? Just know I'm here."

He reached over, tucking a strand of my hair behind my ear. His fingers ran gently through my hair. His touch was the opposite of Theon's.

I wished I could be attracted to someone like Raiden; he was handsome, charming, and caring... but there was no pull or that thing that made me feel light-headed. No adventure of what might happen next, no excitement of the unknown. Raiden was like a gentle breeze on a summer night, whilst Theon was a storm at sea, ready to destroy all in his wake and consume me...

There was something wrong with me that drew me to someone like him, but I couldn't help it.

"Thanks, I'll keep that in mind," I said, smiling at him.

I wouldn't give false hopes. I wasn't looking for a safety net; I was looking for adventure, something that would devour me entirely. As much as I knew Theon was an utter dick, he was the only one who made me feel that way.

"I'm going to head inside," I added, looking at Raiden. "Thanks for tonight."

"Anytime. I mean it." He winked at me, and I turned away. Pausing, I slid the jacket off and held it out to him. He took it, and I could tell he wanted to say something, but instead, he simply smiled. "Goodnight, Yileyna."

"Night night, Raiden," I replied before I walked away.

I was almost at the steps to go below deck when I sensed I was being watched. My heart thundered. I knew who it was. I could feel his burning gaze upon me, even if I couldn't see or hear him.

Well, if he thought I was just going to brush what he did under the rug, he had another thing coming. I was attracted to him, but I was not stupid.

Tomorrow I am going to get revenge, consequences be damned.

Anger in the Darkness

YILEYNA

THE FOLLOWING MORNING DAWNED darker and colder than the previous day. I dressed warmly, wearing brown leather pants, a white corset, and a leather fur-lined jacket on top. My hair was pulled back into a ponytail, not wanting the wind to blow it into my face all through the day. I had just pulled on some socks when there was a knock on the door. I stood up and, unlocking it, pulled it open.

Charlene stood there, all bundled up in a long fur coat, her hair elegantly braided. I had to admit she was talented despite having Omegas to help her back home.

"Morning, my darling. Damn, look at those boobs," she said, winking suggestively at me, making me giggle.

"Good morning from these cushions to their favourite lady," I said as she hugged me, laughing lightly. I pulled away after a moment and plopped onto the bed to put my other sock on.

"How are you feeling?" She asked me seriously.

"I'm okay, why?"

"What do you mean, why? Do you remember what happened last night?" I glanced at my heeled boots and sighed, pulling them on.

"Yes, and I plan to get revenge. What he did was not okay." I looked up at her.

"Yeah, exactly. Just stay away from him, Yileyna, don't mess with him. I swear, if he wasn't my guard, I feel like he'd have killed me by now. You know, sometimes when he looks at me…" She sighed, staring at her boots. "I feel like he hates me." I raised an eyebrow.

"Theon? He hates everyone, Charl, remember? Have you seen him towards me?" I asked, pulling the laces that were along the front of my boots tight and tying them.

"I don't think the way he looks at you is the same as the way he looks at me."

My cheeks heated up, and I kept my gaze down, tying my other boot up. I looked up at her sharply after a moment of pondering her words. Why did she feel he hated her?

"What do you mean?" I asked seriously.

"I just feel like he gets angry at times when we are training... he keeps calling me useless and weak. Sometimes it's like he's fighting with his own emotions not to just rip me apart... maybe I'm crazy, but I don't think he likes being my guard. On this mission, he isn't my bodyguard, and he doesn't even care what happens to me." I tilted my head, standing up and cupping her face.

"I'll try paying a little more attention, and from tomorrow I'll attend your training, even if it's just to watch, okay? I won't leave you alone." If he was venting his anger on her, then I was not going to let her suffer alone.

"Thanks, but I don't want him to say anything to you."

"I don't care, I'll handle him. Now… do you have any ideas of how I can punish him? I think maybe I should get, like, a spatula or something from the kitchen and spank his ass." I snickered as we left my room. Charlene stopped in her tracks, staring at me as if I had grown an extra head.

"Yileyna! This is serious."

"I know, I know, don't worry. I don't forgive so easily… actually, I might have an idea…" Step one, ignore him. I won't be the one to talk to him, but when he tries to talk to me, I will flip, but to keep his attention on me and rile him up, I should add a sexy touch… "One second, I'll be right back!"

I rushed back to my room and rummaged through my things until I took three delicate necklaces out and put them on. *There, that's better.* I looked down at the little crystal on the longest chain, nestled nicely between my breasts.

I may have agreed to be your fuck partner, Theon, but I didn't give you permission to treat me like that.

I had ignored him; from the moment I saw him over breakfast, I decided I wasn't going to give him any importance. I flirted lightly with Raiden, who I saw was finding it amusing and enjoying it. With each passing hour, I was pissing Theon off. He was getting snappy; his anger was clear from the way he was talking to anyone who approached him.

I chatted with the crew members when he sent Raiden to do some jobs. I didn't even spare him a glance, getting to know the crew better and doing my best to ignore him entirely. Cleo was funny; she was straight up and crass. I enjoyed talking to her. She was thirty-two, and I learned her mate had been killed by a rogue. That was when she decided to travel the seas. They had never marked each other, promising one another that they'd carry on and live their lives if one of them was to die.

It had hit me hard and made me think about Mom and Dad. I never realised there were people who would even consider that. To refrain from completing the bond, so the other doesn't die if harm befalls one…

"Don't look so down, girl." She smiled, smoking her cigar. I smiled back and nodded, but I couldn't deny that her words had affected me.

I glanced out at the sea, about to turn away, when I saw Barbara standing and talking to Theon. He stood there, legs slightly apart, arms crossed, one hand resting under his chin, and to my surprise, his eyes were on her. A flare of jealousy washed through me, and I did a once over. She was wearing a cropped top and fitted pants. From her body language, I could tell she was totally flirting.

I turned away. I was not going to bother with them, but… I planned to get my revenge. What exactly that was going to be or how I was going to accomplish it, I wasn't sure. Now, where was Raiden?

"Have any of you guys seen Raiden?" I asked. I didn't bother turning back as Charlene raised an eyebrow curiously.

"Nope."

"He went to get something from the hold," Ryan added.

"Oh, perfect, I'll go check. Thanks, Ryan."

I smiled before I sauntered off, slipping my hands into my pant pockets, making sure to make use of my curvy hips and ass. What better way to get attention? I felt him watching me and almost smirked. He was so predictable. I knew Theon would follow…

I headed below deck, walking down the hall and towards the hold. Going down the ladder, I looked around the dark room. The entire place was full of boxes, sacks and crates. I pulled the little lantern on, letting it cast its bleak light.

"Raiden?" I asked, thinking it was so dark in there. "Where is he?"

I had planned to make Theon jealous... but how do I do that if he isn't around? I'll go look elsewhere. I was about to turn when a voice came from behind me.

"You forget that I can mind link, unlike you. He isn't here," a cold voice I recognised came, and then we were plunged into darkness. My heart thundered as I spun around, hearing him descend the steps.

"You told him to leave?" I asked icily. Crossing my arms, I turned my back on him. A flare of anger rushed through me.

"Yeah. Shame you can't call anyone. It's just you and me, little storm."

I spun around, looking at him, or what I could see. My wolf hadn't awoken, so I couldn't see as well in the dark as a shifted werewolf. This wasn't the plan. I wasn't meant to be stuck alone with him.

"What do you want?" I asked coldly. "After what you did last night, I'm impressed you can show your face in front of me." I stepped away, hitting my foot on one of the crates.

"What were you expecting? An apology?" His cold voice asked. My irritation was growing, and I glared at him, or where I thought his eyes were. I hated the fact I couldn't see.

"From you? No. You don't know what an apology even is," I hissed. "But if you think you can throw me into dangerous waters, and I'm going to just be okay with it, then you are in for an awakening."

"Dangerous waters? This place is fucking dead. There was nothing dangerous out there. If you had swum, you would have been fine out of there," his icy reply came.

"Are you actually justifying what you did?" I asked. *Goddess, wasn't there a light down here, or was the one at the top of the step ladder the only one?*

"I don't have anything to justify. You disrespected me in front of the entire crew, and I punished you." I felt him come closer, and I stepped back, hitting another box and almost falling.

"You can't punish me for speaking up. You are not Beta yet, Theon, remember that," I reminded him coldly. My eyes flew open when his hand wrapped around my throat, his minty breath fanning my face. I could feel that he was standing extremely close, his chest almost grazing mine.

"I am still in charge of this mission, Yileyna. I told you, regardless of our agreement, don't expect special treatment from me," he replied coldly. I scoffed.

"I wasn't expecting special treatment, but throwing me overboard? Really, Theon? I saved -" I stopped, realising what I had been about to say and tried to yank his hand from my throat. "Just let go of me."

"No."

"Theon! Let me go," I hissed, trying to pull away.

"No. Calm the fuck down."

"Don't tell me to calm down when you fucking put me in danger!" I snapped, trying to hit him blindly. He grabbed my hands, holding them tightly against his chest, his other hand still around my throat.

"Can you stop being so fucking dramatic? I pulled you out, too," he growled, making my stomach flutter. *Not now, Yileyna, focus.* No matter how he made me feel, I was still angry.

His eyes were glowing gold now, and I could see he was trying to control himself.

"That doesn't excuse you," I shot back venomously.

He had to realise I was fucking pissed. I could feel his anger radiating off him, when suddenly he let go of me. One arm snaked around my waist, the other grabbing me by the back of my neck.

"Fine. I was pissed, and I took it out on you. You went and flirted with Bolton all fucking morning. We're even?"

"We are not even!"

"Then what do you want me to do?" He replied huskily, making my eyes fly open in surprise. My heart thudded.

"How about you start with an apology because -"

I froze when his lips met mine. Tingles of pleasure coursed through me, my heart thumping. His lips moved against mine slowly, grazing against them painstakingly slowly, and my mind went blank. A strange, intense wave of sparks rushed through me. This kiss was different… it wasn't fast or heated… it…

My body involuntarily arched against him, his hand running down my waist under my jacket. My breath hitched, but just as my eyelids were about to flutter shut, they flew open, my anger returning with a vengeance.

No, I will not give in.

With my anger fuelling me, I brutally bit into his plush bottom lip. He growled, ripping away from me, his eyes blazing with anger.

"Do not fucking think that will get you off the damn hook!" I hissed, clenching my fist and punching him straight in the jaw. In the darkness, I saw his eyes widen in shock. I froze with surprise, too, not expecting him to not block that.

The taste of his blood lingered in my mouth. I could feel it dripping down my lip, but I refused to wipe it, waiting for him to react. We stared at each other for a moment, neither of us moving, when suddenly the door opened, and the light was turned on...

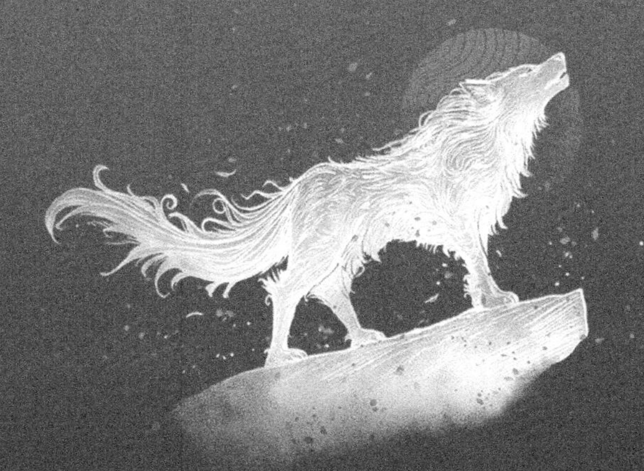

A Violent Storm

YILEYNA

My attention snapped to the door to see Ailema standing there, holding a basket in her hands.

"Oh, I do apologise for interfering. I just needed to grab some potatoes…" She smiled as she walked down the steps, her eyes flickering from me to the blood on Theon's lips.

I dared to look at him, just in time to see him brush his thumb along his lip, wiping away most of the blood. His cold amber eyes flickered to me. In the orange glow of the lantern, they seemed to burn like embers, making my stomach flutter with nerves. His tongue ran along his bloody lip.

This conversation wasn't over… I knew that.

"Ah, young commander, could you help me with this?" Ailema asked as she tried dragging a large sack of potatoes. Oh, she could drag it. I knew she was giving me the chance to leave, and I was going to take it.

He didn't reply. Walking over to her, his gaze flickered to me. I raised an eyebrow, wiping the blood from my lip and keeping my gaze locked with his as I licked my thumb slowly. His eyes flashed gold. I smirked smugly as I spun around and headed for the exit. I was halfway up the steps when I was yanked back. A scream left my lips as my back hit his hard chest. One hand cupped my neck, tilting my head back.

"This isn't over," he whispered in my ear. His other hand ran down my stomach, making my core knot as a ripple of pleasure thrummed through me, and I shivered. Just when I thought he'd let me go, he ripped the necklaces from my neck, making my heart thud, the stinging pain where they had cut into my skin making me gasp. "I told you, the only thing that should be around this neck is my hand."

He let go of me and turned away, leaving me frozen for a moment. Didn't he care that Ailema was right there? Or was he so confident she wouldn't say anything? After all, he was the one who didn't want anyone to know about us.

Not replying or daring to look at the woman, I rushed up the stairs, trying to clear my head and didn't even notice that someone was in front of me until I hit a rock-solid wall and tumbled backwards.

"Got you." Raiden's voice came as he grabbed my waist, stopping me from falling and steadying me on my feet.

"Thanks," I said with a smile, smoothing my hair and jacket.

"The princess said you went looking for me?" He asked, concerned. I smiled sneakily at him.

"You already know why I said that." He sighed and nodded.

"Yes, I do. Clearly, I don't understand the entire reasons, but be careful," he advised with a small smirk.

"I will."

Charlene. She had said something similar, but I knew what I was doing. I felt satisfied having punched him, but even then, the way he kissed me… it was different. It made me feel light-hearted at just the thought. It was almost as if it had been fuelled with emotions, but it was probably my wishful thinking that it was meant to be a kiss of apology.

Stupid Theon. He had a mouth and a tongue, surely he could have used them to say the damn word instead of using it so seductively... argh, he was an ass, one that knew how to kiss.

I returned to the deck only to find that the sky was dark and rain had begun to fall. How had the weather changed so dangerously fast? Wasn't it meant to be clear for at least several more hours?

"Stay inside!" Someone shouted to me as another struggled with the mast. I glanced out at the water, the waves were getting bigger, and the ship was moving a lot more violently.

"Where is Charlene?" I asked just as a blast of wind made me raise my arms, shielding my face.

"In her cabin, being watched over," Nate called back. *I should go to her...*

Raiden brushed past, winking at me before jerking his head downwards. "Go stay with the princess."

I nodded, about to turn, when I froze. A soothing whisper reached my ears, and I spun around, hurrying back up the few steps and stepping out into the open. I scanned the deck and the sea beyond it. My heart was thundering as I realised that I had felt something similar before that Siren had attacked Charlene and me. Were we already in the Lifeless Abyss? Surely there wasn't meant to be Sirens out this way?

I edged closer to the edge of the ship, looking at the roaring waves. The sounds of the crew shouting, and Sam, one of the crew mates, was standing at the edge, a silvery glow around him piquing my curiosity. Was he a hybrid? It seemed so. I wasn't sure what he was doing, but the glow took on the form of silvery wisps that ran across the ship, creating a weblike layer across the entire ship.

I heard footsteps behind me, and a hand closed around my arm, pulling me back.

"What are you doing out here? Go stay with the princess," Theon growled. His voice sounded animalistic. I had never heard him like this, and to my surprise, I could see the canines in his mouth.

"I was just..."

"It's dangerous," he barked, pulling me towards the steps.

"Theon, listen to me! I think there are Sirens out there."

"There are no Sirens here. We are still a ways from the Lifeless Abyss. If there was, we would have picked it up!" Flynn's voice came. *Damn werewolf hearing,* I thought I was the deafest one on the trip! "Take your pretty lady to safety, commander!" He added with a wink, and I knew if it was any other time, I would have blushed, but I had more important things on my mind. I knew I sounded crazy. I mean, surely the crew would know if there were Sirens approaching.

"Yileyna, can you, for once, just listen?" Theon growled roughly. I glared at him.

"Why should I? Leave me be! You wanted me dead, remember? One less burden?" He closed his eyes, clenching his jaw.

"I am not doing this with you now," he hissed, and just then, a strong pair of arms wrapped around my waist.

"Hey!" I shouted, glaring up at dumb Bruce. "Let go of me! Your job is to guard the princess, not me!"

"Orders are orders," he grunted.

"It's dangerous out there!" I don't know how I knew, but my instincts were screaming at me.

"Exactly, hence why it's no place for an unshifted wolf," he thundered.

Goddess, what am I doing? Nothing made me feel like this when there was an attack on the city... *So why now were these instincts of mine screaming at me?*

"Bruce, listen to me! They are in danger!"

"Calm down, Yileyna. What will you do by going up there? You will only get in the way." He asked, making me freeze. He was right... What was I going to do?

"I..."

"Listen to me, pup, you are only going to make matters worse. Let them handle this."

I didn't argue further. He was right. What would I be able to do? He placed me on my feet, a hand on the small of my back as he led me down towards Charlene's room. The same pull to turn around and go to the water seemed to wash over me, and I stopped moving. The faint whisper of an enchanting song reached my ears, making my heart pound.

A Siren.

"I'll go to my room..." I murmured, turning to look at Bruce. To my surprise, his eyes looked glazed, and he was dragging his feet. "Bruce?" No reply. I stepped away from him, but he didn't react.

Werewolf hearing. Could he hear the Siren's song!?

Turning, I ran back the way I came and up to the deck. The moment I was out in the open, I was hit with a shocking downpour of rain. The waves were higher than the ship, crashing onto the deck ruthlessly. Thunder roared in the sky, and lightning flashed dazzlingly. I could see Barbara fiddling with a thick rope. Cleo was shouting something at the captain, who seemed to be unmoving at the helm, the wheel spinning wildly out of control. Sam was leaning over the edge of the ship. To my horror, I realised apart from the two women, everyone seemed frozen.

Where were Theon and Raiden? I ran out onto the deck, rushing to Sam first and yanking him back from the edge.

"Take the wheel!" I heard Theon shout.

"Aiy!" Cleo yelled, running across the deck just for another huge wave to hit her, knocking her back.

I couldn't see him, but if he needed someone to control the ship, at least I could try to do that. How hard could it be? Quickly tying Sam's ankle to some rope so he didn't end up being flung into the sea, I rushed through the crashing waves and the violent jolts of the ship. A soothing whisper reached my ear, and I frowned.

Don't focus on it. Don't focus on it. Get to the helm!

I gasped as I was knocked backwards. My head hit the ground as another strong wave of water filled my lungs, and I choked. Coughing, I rolled over, tumbling to my feet clumsily and pulling off my jacket that was weighing me down.

Goddess! What was going on? Where was the Siren?

I was almost to the captain when the same eerie, beautiful song made me stop. It was powerful, ethereal, and I felt my eyelids becoming heavy. Sirens. I had been right… *They're here…*

No. I am Yileyna De'Lacor, and there was no way on Kaeladia that a Siren's song was going to get the better of me! I clenched my fists, letting my nails dig into my palms, the pain keeping my mind clear.

"Yileyna!" I heard Theon's shout.

I didn't look back, barely able to keep my balance as I finally managed to get to the captain, pushing him out of the way and grabbing the spinning wheel. Fuck, I didn't think this out, It was far too powerful. I braced my feet, trying to steady it. I wasn't enough. My arms screamed as I held on with all my might. I gritted my teeth, feeling the ship steady a little. Another huge wave crashed onto the deck.

"Yileyna, turn portside!" Cleo shouted, her voice sounding a little dreamy.

"Okay!" I shouted back, my heart thumping as I shifted, using all my weight to turn the wheel. Never had I imagined it to be so hard.

The Siren's song was getting louder. The captain tried to move towards the edge, and I stuck my leg out, tripping him up to slow him down a little before he jumped to his death.

"Dear mother, Selene…" Cleo gasped.

I made the mistake of turning to see what was going on, only to see a Siren there amongst the waves. My heart pounded as I stared at her. She was beautiful, from her flawless skin that seemed to glitter to her long blonde hair swirling around her. Her tail was a stark contrast to her light hair and skin, shimmering a deep red and black.

Her eyes snapped towards me, and I looked into her glowing red ones, our gaze locking. Her eyes, which had moments ago been cold, seemed to fill with an emotion I couldn't make out. Then in a flash, a huge wave hit the shore, and she was before me.

"Yileyna!" Theon...

I heard a murderous growl, but it felt far away. Had I been manipulated? All sound but the haunting tune of the Siren's song lingered in my mind, but I was still aware, still gripping the wheel with all my might. The Siren's long hand reached out to me, and she tilted her beautiful head to the side, cupping my jaw. Her touch was icy. A flicker of curiosity flitted through her eyes, as if searching my face for something.

"Let go of me!" I hissed, trying to bring myself back to reality and using all my willpower, I shoved her away. Her eyes widened, and a surge of anger seemed to roll off her. As much as I wanted to back away, I couldn't.

The ship was already caught up in the storm, and I needed to keep my hold on the wheel, just like Cleo had asked of me. My teeth were gritted as I held on with all my might.

"Tempest," she hissed. She raised her hand, and my eyes widened at seeing the waves grow higher behind her.

I flinched. The moment she was about to lunge at me, I saw the body of a magnificent deep copper wolf fly over my head, its huge paw ripping through the Siren's chest and stomach. She screamed, falling back into the water, blood splattering over me as the wolf landed a few feet ahead. He turned towards me, my heart beating wildly as I stared at Theon's wolf, a wolf that looked on par with the Alpha King himself. A true beast...

I gasped as the wheel broke free from my hold, the ship careening violently. The Siren may have fallen into the sea, but the storm was still raging. I grabbed onto it as the wolf pounced, landing next to me. Theon shifted back, and then he was behind me, placing his hands over mine and gripping the wheel tightly, his arms caging me in. My heart pounded, but this time it wasn't because of fear, but his closeness. His bare arms brushed mine, his scent overpowering the smell of the sea. Two scents that I loved...

"You're fucking crazy," he hissed breathlessly in my ear, my heart leaping as he turned the wheel with ease. The back of my head touched his bare chest, and I dared not focus on the fact that he was standing so close in utterly nothing.

"And you're fucking naked," I retorted defiantly, looking up at him.

"Not that you're complaining. Seems like even the god of death doesn't want you. How many fucking times will you face death and survive?"

"Well, what can I say? Even the mighty haughty Theon couldn't resist me," I replied haughtily.

"No fucking idea why..." he murmured, making my heart skip a beat.

I looked up at him in surprise. His hair was soaking, falling in front of his eyes, but what took my breath away was the tiny ghost of a smirk that crossed his lips...

A Tankard of Two of Ale

YILEYNA

Night had fallen, and it was still thundering, but things were back in order, although we had some bruised crew members. Ryan had come and given Theon pants quite quickly, but despite that, Barbara kept staring at his lower regions and licking her lips ever since. I wondered if Theon even noticed because it was really irking me, an annoying blue-eyed brat, but I realised Theon had been very distracted. He was usually quiet, but it was almost as if he was mulling something over in his mind.

Most of us were in the Mess as Ailema handed us all mugs of ale. It was silent, the weight of what had happened fresh in all our minds.

"How did it not affect you?" Flynn asked Theon sharply. It was obvious he was just a bit salty because he had fallen for the Siren's enchantment.

"It's a good question, that is," Ryan agreed, tilting his head as he looked at Theon. "We all know that it is harder for women to fall into their trap."

"But even women can fall victim to their song," Leto murmured, gulping down his ale. The light from the lantern hooked above cast shadows over his face. I wondered what crossed his mind…

"Yeah, they can," Theon added, a flash of something in his eyes catching my attention, but he looked away.

"Aiy, tis true," Nate nodded, sighing heavily.

"So, how do you stay focused, Theon? I think we can all use the tip," Charlene persisted. She was sitting next to me. She had given me a scolding for being reckless but then told me she was proud of me. Theon didn't reply for a moment, staring ahead at the far side of the wall as he gulped his Ale down. My gaze dipped to his Adam's apple.

"Pain. As long as you are in a lot of pain, your mind won't allow you to shut it out," he replied. He glanced at me for a second, and like always, his gaze melted me.

"Pain alone can't keep you focused. You need to have a very strong resolution," Valentin added, looking at Theon thoughtfully. He was one of the older guards and seemed to be sizing Theon up as he scratched his beard.

"I guess it depends on your inner strength, then," Theon responded.

"Maybe you could teach us some time. I wouldn't mind learning how to resist the deadly charm of Sirens," Barbara added flirtily. I snorted, rolling my eyes, quickly covering it with a cough.

"I'm with Barbara on this one," Charlene nodded.

"Shame I'm not here to teach anyone anything. Just keep a dagger close. If you hear a Siren's song, use it to stay focused." Theon sat back, his voice emotionless. "Tomorrow, we will reach the Lifeless Abyss; it is far more dangerous, and there will most likely be Sirens."

"I still don't think it's the ideal way to go," Flynn muttered. Madelia tilted her head.

"I will work with Sam and Ailema to put some protective spells up. Fae magic will help," she added, smoothing out the velvet skirt of her dress.

"I was trying to weave my magic into the ship, but it didn't work. I didn't manage to complete it," Sam sighed, staring at his calloused hands.

"You tried, that's the main thing," I comforted him gently. He had been there, trying his best regardless of whether he had been successful or not.

"Yeah… maybe so. Cleo here told me you tied me down before you went for the wheel. Thank you, kid." I smiled. Despite being called a kid, I was just glad he was okay. Looking around, it was obvious everyone was happy to be alive.

"I got to agree. If it wasn't for you taking the wheel, we could have suffered a lot more damage," Flynn remarked, giving me a smirk. "To our pretty little damsel with a heart of courage!" He raised his tankard, and Charlene smiled as everyone present raised their glasses, everyone but Theon, that is.

"To Yileyna!" Charlene cheered.

Everyone downed their drinks, making my cheeks burn due to all the attention. I didn't do anything that required such attention. I glanced at Theon. Our eyes met, and then, to my surprise, he raised his tankard ever so slightly, making my stomach flutter with a swarm of butterflies.

"This deserves another round! Here girl, drink." Cleo grinned, passing me a fresh tankard of ale.

"I think I have had enough..." I murmured but gave in.

Everyone was happy after that terrifying, unexpected occurrence. I didn't blame them. It hadn't been expected, and with the upcoming journey through the Lifeless Abyss, I think everyone wanted to cherish the happy moment of surviving one near-death experience. I smiled as I raised my tankard and downed it all as everyone cheered.

Leto began tapping his hand against the table and, to my surprise, began singing a sea shanty. I couldn't help but smile at how good he actually was.

"Oh, at sea, we sing to all the adventures we be seeing..."

Charlene began clapping as some of the other crew members joined in the singing. Barbara stood up and began dancing. I tapped my foot and moved my body to the music as Madelia whispered a little enchantment, and the room filled with music.

"That's how you do it!" Raiden grinned, accepting another round of ale from Cleo. The mood had instantly lifted, and even Flynn joined in with the singing.

"Come on, let's show them what we got," Charlene whispered, motioning with her eyes at Barbara, who was dancing directly in front of Theon. He was sitting back on the chair, his face as passive as ever, a sexy pout on his face, his left ankle resting on his right knee. He was the only one who hadn't joined in with everyone's enthusiasm.

I placed my empty tankard down, letting Charlene pull me up as she began dancing. Compared to her and Barbara, I was shorter, but I didn't let it bother me. I swayed my body to the music.

"When the nights were lonely and cold, did you miss me, or did you find another?" They sang.

I spun around, turning my back towards Theon and shook my hips sensually before spinning around and smiling at Charlene, who was singing along to the song. She took my hand, whirling me around, both of us flicking our hair as we blew kisses at the men.

"Were you missing me at sea? Or did you find another love?"

My eyes met Theon's, my heart skipping a beat. I gave him a wink before turning away.

"...In your arms to hold. Nay, all I could think of was you, my lassie..."

The song came to an end, and everyone clapped and cheered. I hugged Charlene, unable to stop the fit of laughter. I didn't think we had done anything as fun as that together in a while.

"Goddess, that was fun!" I giggled as Charlene nodded.

"I know!"

"I think it's nice to have more women on board. Don't you agree, boys?" Flynn chuckled. Barbara didn't look impressed, and I felt Theon's anger before he even spoke.

"The Silver Storm women are not for your entertainment," he remarked.

"Ah, of course not. Don't worry, I wouldn't dare take what you have claimed." Flynn grinned. I had a feeling he had had a bit too much to drink. Although, as a werewolf, he had a high tolerance, it seemed he had indeed reached his limit. Theon didn't respond, but Raiden smirked at Flynn's remark. Charlene looked at me, and for a moment, I wondered if she had an inkling that something was going on between the both of us.

"Well, it's been a long night. I think I'm going to head to bed," I decided, suppressing a yawn.

"Me too. Thank you, everyone, for all your constant support and for taking this trip with us," Charlene said before Valentin and Patrick stood up to accompany her.

We left the room together, and I hugged her farewell outside of her door as the two guards hung back, giving us a little space, although they'd be able to hear everything either way.

"Yileyna..."

"Hmm?" I asked, about to turn away. She tilted her head and gave me a small smile.

"I don't want to lose you... don't do anything so careless next time," she whispered pleadingly.

"You won't lose me."

"Leyna, please, I'm serious."

"Charl, if I didn't, this ship could have been damaged or worse, it could have turned over and sunk."

"I know... but you could have been killed by that Siren. You know, it's an omen… that's two times now. It scares me."

"I know, I'm facing death and surviving." I smiled, but it didn't reach my eyes. Maybe a Siren was an omen of death… but so was I… it was because of me that my parents died. I ran my fingers through my hair. "If we live our lives always questioning our every action, we are simply surviving, not living… I don't fear death, Charlene, but I fear losing anyone else I love." Her eyes softened, and she cupped my face.

"Yileyna, don't scare me. Promise me you won't be so reckless?"

"I can't make a promise I can't keep," I replied with a small smile, giving her a gentle hug. I saw the flash of hurt in her eyes, and I took her hands, gently kissing them. "I'm sorry." She shook her head.

"Don't apologise, I understand."

"Thank you," I responded before we both went to our own cabins.

Closing the door behind me, I removed my boots, sighing heavily as I took out one of Dad's shirts. I put it on the bed before removing the shirt and pants I had gotten changed into after I had gotten drenched earlier. I looked in the small mirror. The cuts that had been made by my necklaces were half-healed, with only thin red lines remaining. For someone who said they wanted me dead, he sure was concerned about my safety.

I frowned as I turned away from the mirror and unhooked my bra. I slipped the shirt on and sat down on the bed, thinking about what had happened.

"Tempest."

What had the Siren meant by that?

I sighed, about to get into bed, when there was a knock on the door. I stood up, pulling the door open, expecting Charlene, but to my surprise, it was Theon. My heart began racing, and before I could even say anything, he slipped inside, shutting and locking the door behind him.

"Theon!" The guards were outside!

"Keep it down," he replied, frowning.

"Well, what do you want?" I asked. I hadn't forgiven him entirely yet. I crossed my arms, doing my best to summon the most scathing look I could.

"Our conversation earlier wasn't over." He crossed his arms, but I instead turned my back to him. If I didn't look at him, I would be manipulated by his hot looks.

"If you can't apologise, then there's nothing more to say." I shrugged, stretching slowly before remembering I was only wearing Dad's shirt and quickly put my arms down. I could feel his intense gaze on me. He didn't speak, and after a moment, I turned sharply, staring up at him curiously. Why did I feel like there was something going on?

"Yeah, I won't, besides you bit me. We're even," he shot back icily. Strange...

"Umm, one little bite and being tossed into water that proved to be dangerous today are entirely different, handsome," I shot back, realising a moment too late that I had called him handsome, but he didn't seem to notice, or he didn't care.

"Fine then, enjoy the night. You aren't the only woman on this ship, Yileyna." He gave me a cold smirk, and my heart thudded, knowing Theon was the type of man to follow up on his threat. Barbara...

"And you aren't the only man, remember that," I shot back, trying to push away the clenching pain in my chest. *Yes, I'm that crazy too.* His hand froze on the door handle, his eyes flashing gold as he turned back towards me.

"Excuse me?"

"You heard me. Threaten me with other women, and don't forget that there are many men who want me, too," I replied icily.

We weren't a couple, I didn't even know what we were, but it was obvious he didn't like anyone flirting with me or getting close to me. He stepped closer, and I stood my ground. I was not scared of him.

"If any man even lays a finger on you, I swear I will kill them," he hissed, grabbing my neck.

"Shame. I would have already fucked them by then." I batted my eyelids innocently. His eyes blazed gold, his jaw clenched, and I could feel his anger raging around us.

I understood Theon a little more... and the one power I had over him was my body. One he craved... he desired... and one that only I had the power to grant him access.

"Don't push me, little storm." His grip on my neck tightened. I resisted the urge to sigh and instead raised my finger to trace those plush lips of his.

"Then, what is it going to be? An apology from these perfect lips, or shall I call Raiden? Actually, Raiden's a better option since I'm sure he'll stay to warm my bed for the night. We could cuddle! You should really go -"

"You want a fucking apology, then I'll give you one in my language." His voice was a murderous growl, his eyes full of anger as he grabbed my elbows, yanking me to the bed and pushing me onto it.

I gasped when my back hit the mattress. I was ready for him to climb on top of me, but instead, he cupped my thighs, yanking me to the edge of the bed before he knelt down, making my eyes fly open as I realised what he was about to do. My core throbbed, my heart pounding as my eyes locked with his.

"So, tell me, little storm, what's it going to be?"

My cheeks burned, my heart thundering as he knelt between my legs, his gaze fixed on mine. My core throbbing, I slowly parted my legs, my chest heaving in anticipation, my entire body tingling with nerves. A sexy, arrogant smirk crossed his lips, and in one swift movement, he ripped my panties off before shoving them into my mouth and pushing me back onto the bed. Then his lips were on my pussy, making my eyes fly wide open. A groan of pleasure escaped me as an intense wave of ecstasy rushed through every pore of my body…

In his Arms

YILEYNA

His lips brushed my pussy in a sensual, slow kiss, his tongue flicking out, making me whimper as pleasure rushed through me. My cheeks felt hot, and I didn't know how to feel knowing he was so close to me down there. His hand ran along my thigh as he slowly ran his tongue between my soaking slit. Goddess, the sensation was too powerful.

My chest was heaving. If he hadn't shoved my panties in my mouth, I knew I would already be a moaning mess. The moment his tongue found my clit, my eyes flew open, and I grabbed his hair as pleasure washed through me.

"I think you're not getting the idea here," he whispered, pulling away. "If you want me to continue, I want you to keep your hands to yourself." I couldn't respond even if I wanted to, because I knew for a fact that he wouldn't be pleased if I removed the panties from my mouth. So instead, I nodded and placed my hands on my stomach.

He reached up, ripped the shirt down the middle, and yanked it off me, leaving me entirely naked in front of him. His eyes flashed gold as he looked me over, pulling me up by the back of my head and removing the shirt completely.

"I prefer you naked," he murmured, running his knuckles down the centre of my neck and over my left breast, my hard nipple feeling extra sensitive where his fingers grazed it.

My eyes fluttered shut. He had once again succeeded in getting me where he wanted. I may have control over him, but he had the very same control over me. His hand was on my stomach, my core throbbing in need, when he suddenly let go of me. Picking up the torn shirt, he turned me and pushed me down on the bed. Then, to my surprise, he used the shirt to tie my hands together.

I gasped when he spanked my ass once before flipping me back onto my back, my hands now tied behind me. I wriggled a little, resting my wrists under the small of my back. He stood over me, and I wished he was naked.

"Much better," he replied, approval clear in his voice.

I wanted to tell him to take his shirt off, but I couldn't. Instead, I could only watch as he went down once more. This time he wasn't slow or gentle. He used one hand to part my lips, and then his tongue was ravishing me. I moaned as he flicked my clit hard and then sucked on it, pressing my legs wide open against the bed before plunging his tongue straight into my slick folds, pleasuring me so fucking well.

My muffled moans filled the room, and I grinded against his face, the pleasure growing with each passing moment, but he kept me pinned down. Fuck, he was so good at this... I closed my eyes, allowing the pleasure to consume me entirely.

I felt powerless, and I loved it. Giving in to Theon and his dominant ways felt good. I wouldn't mind being his toy forever... this feeling...

My orgasm was building, the knot in my core growing. When his thumb penetrated me, his tongue flicking my clit, my orgasm ripped through me, making my eyes fly open. My back arched, and my entire body convulsed with the pleasure that electrocuted my frame, making me let out a muffled groan.

He moved back his finger, replacing his tongue as he rubbed my clit, his thumb still inside of me.

"I knew you were a dirty little whore. Look at how fucking turned on you are...." I heard him murmur huskily as my juices squirted all over him, making me blush in embarrassment. For a moment, I felt mortified, my heart thundering, but when a satisfied smirk crossed his lips, and he slapped my pussy hard, I relaxed a little. "Perfect..."

His eyes darkened, and he grabbed my hips, yanking me off the bed until only my shoulders were on the mattress and ran his tongue along my soaking pussy, taking one long lick of my juices before he dropped me, grabbing me by the hair and pulling me upright. My entire body was still trembling from that incredible orgasm.

"So, tell me… apology accepted?" He asked, tilting his head as his eyes roamed my body. I nodded as his eyes flicked to mine. My cheeks were burning, but he simply replied with a single word that dripped with arrogance and seductiveness. "Good."

He pulled my panties from my mouth, and I gasped, breathing hard as I stared at the hard shaft in his pants.

"I want to taste you," I said, instantly wondering if he was expecting that anyway. I wanted to taste him, see him melt with pleasure above me. He turned away, pulling his shirt off, which I had squirted all over.

"I don't trust you right now."

"What do you mean?" I pouted. He came over and gripped my jaw, his gaze falling to my lips.

"I doubt you would know what to do. Tell me, little storm, how many cocks have you taken in this pretty little mouth? None, right?"

"Please, I've taken enough, more than you can count, actually," I lied with a roll of my eyes. He cocked a brow.

"If you're going to lie, at least make it believable," he smirked mockingly, slipping his thumb into my mouth. I wrapped my lips around it, sucking on it and enjoying the way his eyes darkened as he swallowed.

Oh, handsome, you want me to take your cock in my mouth. Just admit it. But I didn't say anything, sucking on his thumb seductively before he slipped his thumb out, his dangerously cold eyes fixed on me.

"We'll leave that for another day." He reached behind me and untied me. Our eyes met, and I just wanted to kiss him, but I couldn't…

I stretched my shoulders as I wiped my thighs with the torn shirt. Theon's habit of ripping stuff was not good. He stood up and walked to the small adjoining bathroom without another word. I sighed, wondering why he was so closed off; it was almost as if he wanted me, but at the same time, he didn't want to let his guard down…

I stood up and took out some fresh panties, satin, floral red pyjama bottoms and a matching cami with it. I pulled on another shirt just as Theon exited the bathroom. He had washed his face, but it was clear he still had a hard-on in his pants. I walked past him without a word, knowing that when I stepped out, he'd be gone.

I quickly washed my legs and dried myself before getting dressed and leaving the bathroom. Re-entering my bedroom, I froze to see Theon lying on the bed, his arms behind his head and his eyes shut, with his long legs hanging off the edge. Goddess, the man was huge...

"Why are you still here?" I asked, unable to hide the shock from my voice. His eyes fluttered open, those gorgeous lashes of his making my heart skip a beat.

"The guards are right outside. I sent them away when I came in. I don't think I can leave without them seeing me, so I'll sleep here. There's plenty of space for you," he said coldly, gesturing with his eyes to the place next to him.

My heart began pounding. I didn't know what was wrong with me. We had already been intimate, but sleeping with him? He raised an eyebrow.

"For someone who wanted to call Bolton over... what's wrong, scared?"

"Not at all. I was just thinking you're pretty overgrown. I like space when I sleep," I replied haughtily, despite my mess of emotions. I tossed my hair over my shoulder and got onto the small bed from the end, then squeezed into the gap next to him. His scent filled my nose, and I almost smiled.

"So tell me... did you stay because your jealous I said I'm calling Raiden?" I asked smugly, placing a hand under my head and propping myself up. His eyes opened once again, and he turned his head to look at me.

"I already told you the reason. Don't tell me you lost some brain cells after that orgasm?" I blushed and glared at him.

"No, I heard what you said. I don't believe it, though. Turn the light off, I'm tired," I shot back, turning my back to him, knowing that his attention would instantly go to my ass that was straining against the fabric.

He didn't respond, but the light was switched off, and I smirked at the fact that he obeyed. I placed my hands under my head, ready to close my eyes when the bed creaked as Theon turned onto his side. To my utter surprise, his arm snuck under my head, the other one slipping under my shirt until it rested on my stomach, and he pulled me flush against him. My heart was thundering as I lay there, completely frozen.

Goddess, I was sleeping in the arms of none other than my long-time crush: Theon. My heart was racing, my entire body tense. Was I dreaming?

I heard him scoff, his hand running down my stomach as he leaned over, his lips close to my ear.

"Really, Yileyna, for someone who talks so big, what's making you so tense?"

"Nothing," I replied, trying to control my crazy heartbeat.

"Good, because you need to get used to it."

His words made my eyes fly open, and it took my all to hide the smile that almost crossed my lips. My heart was leaping with a happiness I didn't know I'd feel. I didn't respond, relaxing into him. Although my core ached for more, I was content, lying there in the arms of the man I always wanted. Maybe, just maybe, there was some happiness waiting for me… just maybe.

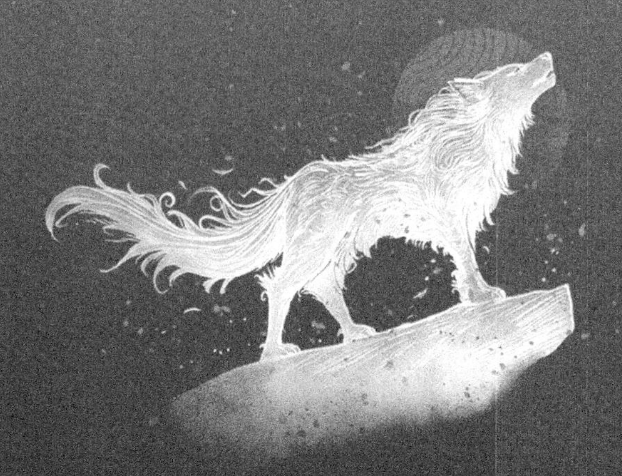

Memories of Pain

THEON

I couldn't sleep. Long after her heartbeat steadied, when her struggle not to press against my cock stopped and the exhaustion of the long day overcame her, I lay awake.

The distant sound of the waves seeped through the walls of the small cabin. Her soft rhythmic breathing was accompanied by a random whimper or tiny moan when she adjusted her position, wriggling her ass as she pressed herself into my cock. She was a minx, and I knew, if given the option, she'd love to play and have her way with me. I looked down at her, her creamy breasts pressed together in her silk top. One of her hands cupped the wrist of the arm that was under her head.

I had ruined her life in more ways than she knew. If all she wanted was a little comfort… I could give her that…

But deep down, I knew it wasn't why I had come to her room, and that same reason was keeping me awake. A night from long ago replayed in my mind. The events of today had brought back those painful memories…

Seeing Yileyna at the helm, her hands tied, helpless as she stared into the face of death… I didn't know what pull she had on me, but I didn't want to lose her, not yet. She was proving a good distraction from the turmoil in my mind. She wasn't scared to piss me off, and when I was around her, it distracted me from the storm within my head. It had almost been a decade since then, but the memory was still fresh in my mind…

Closing my eyes, I pressed my lips to the back of her shoulder, enjoying the feel of her cool skin against my lips. For a werewolf, she was always cool rather than hot, but I liked that, feeling her against the heat of my body, heat that she awakened within me. Her fresh scent of sea breeze and spring confused me, just like the sea. I loved it as much as I hated it.

Werewolves preferred land, but growing up, I enjoyed travelling by sea, enjoying the adventure, until that event anyway… love and hate. That's how it felt. Yileyna was the same. I hated her, yet I desired her. I don't know how it worked… wanting to rip someone apart for consuming me and then wanting to protect that person no matter the cost…

I sighed, staring up at the ceiling. My head was pounding, but no matter how many times I tried to push the memory that raged at the forefront of my mind away, it was futile. A memory of a tragedy that had happened not far from here… a memory from long ago…

ALMOST A DECADE AGO

The smell of blood filled the air. A few bodies with their hearts ripped out littered the deck – the bodies of our men.

"Theon! Hide!"

"I am not leaving you alone!" I hissed, staring into the beautiful blue eyes of the strongest woman I knew.

"That's an order," she whispered back, her voice gentle yet her command absolute.

The seductive, haunting song that was filling my ears was lulling me to sleep. I knew we were the only ones left. The pack had died protecting us…

"Mom, I have my wolf. I'm fine," I hissed. I had shifted far faster than most, and I was not going to sit aside and do nothing.

"Theon, your life is worth far more than mine. Protect your sisters." Her voice was anguished, and, although I didn't let it show, it fucking terrified me.

"I…" I nodded. It was my duty to protect my family… Mom was right. Besides, she had more of a chance against them than I did. Dad was meant to meet us… where was he?

Mom pulled out her sword, and I picked up my sisters, but my legs refused to budge. I needed to go below deck. Our ship, if you could call it that, was tiny.

The crew were all dead. The rain was pouring down, and both my sisters looked as terrified as I felt inside. Fuck, this wasn't good.

"Theon... I'm scared," Thea, my seven-year-old sister, whispered, her amber eyes filled with fear, her black hair falling in front of her face.

"I know. We are going to be o-"

My eyes flew open as the waves rose high in the air, and the enchanting song seemed to seep into every part of my body.

No, Theon, focus! *I reached for the small dagger that Thea carried and slammed it into my hip, making Thalia scream.* Focus!

The smell of blood filled my nose, but my mind felt clearer as the pain shot through my body.

Theon, take the girls through the portal. Use the crystal, now! *Mom screamed through the link*

"Let me go," Thalia whispered. Her blue eyes glazed as she looked ahead towards the Siren that had taken out our entire crew alone.

My heart skipped a beat at how beautiful the monster was. Was it possible that everything I heard was maybe just a lie? Long pale blonde hair fell to her waist, large breasts that were completely bare, and a narrow waist that led to a tail of scales, scales in shades of blue and silver. A beauty that lures you to your death.

THEON! USE THE CRYSTAL NOW! Mom's voice shook me from my numb state.

The crystal? Our last resort. Dad said to only use it if we had no other option. The chances of surviving the transportation spell were less. But for Mom to scream at me to use it... meant we could die here anyway.

I looked up at Mom. She had shifted, but I could tell she was losing the battle. The Siren's hand dripped with blood as she slammed Mom to the ground.

Anger rushed through me. I put Thalia and Thea down, shifting as I lunged at the monster before me. She laughed sardonically.

"Ah... the blood of an Alpha... it's what I crave..." she whispered seductively, raising her hand. A wave of water slammed me down, the wood beneath me splintering at the sheer force. I growled, getting back up.

"Theon, look at Thalia!" Thea screamed.

I turned, and it was almost as if I was watching it all in slow motion. Thalia was climbing over the edge as if she wanted to jump into the water. Fuck!

I saw Mom forced to shift back; her body was covered in bloody gashes as the Siren*'s beautiful laugh filled my ears as she looked down at Mom.*

I was torn. Mom or Thalia...

I ran towards the edge of the ship, just about to grab Thalia, when a blast of water pushed me away from her, and to my horror, I saw her jump.

No*!*

I rushed through the water that had thrown me back and to the edge of the ship, staring out into the havoc of the storm. I couldn't see her! Where is she?

Fear consumed me, paralysing me.

Thalia! Thalia...

Theon... the crystal... *Mom's hoarse voice came through the link. I turned towards her, my heart thumping.*

Mom! Thalia! She -

Is dead, *Mom's emotionless voice answered. I felt cold. I didn't want to believe it.*

No, she isn't! *I shouted.*

This can't be happening. It just can't...

The crystal.

I refused to believe that! She was only five! I shifted back, staring at the water. Do I jump?

I glanced back at Thea, who was clinging to a post, fear clear in her shaking body.

I looked out at the water, anguish and conflict filling me. I couldn't think straight. What do I do?

I had to save everyone! Just then, my heart leapt when I saw her white dress. Thalia! A huge wave lifted her up and tossed her tiny body onto the ship.

"Thalia!" I ran to her. My happiness faded instantly, fear and horror replacing it when I saw the reality before me.

Thalia's body lay before me, her eyes shut as if she was just asleep, her copper hair framing her tiny face, but the only thing I could stare at was the large, gaping hole in her chest where her heart had been ripped out. I backed away, the harsh truth that she was dead hitting me hard.

Mom...

I looked towards Mom, who was on her knees. The Siren had one hand on her cheek, the other plunged deep into her chest, and before my eyes, she ripped her heart out, tossing it into the ocean before turning her attention to me.

"Now, my true prize... I smelt that there was an Alpha on board..." she whispered in a seductive voice.

I backed away, unable to comprehend the vast hurricane of emotions that were killing me from the inside and making it hard to breathe.

An Alpha on board, she came for me... she came for me.

Mom... Thalia... as much as I wanted to kill the monster before me, I wasn't strong enough...

Thea... she only had me now. Turning, I ran to her, yanking the crystal from my neck.

"Ara shor mei kharaas!" I echoed the words Dad had drilled into me, grabbing Thea as a blast of light filled the stormy skies.

"No!" The Siren screamed.

I felt the barrier rise to the skies, and I wrapped my arms around Thea as I felt it wrap around us, sucking us into its abyss. Deep down, I knew if I had listened to Mom, Thalia would have been alive. I was responsible for her death. For Mom's...

My heart was thudding painfully, the excruciating pain in my chest threatening to suffocate me. I sat up, clutching my head as it squeezed painfully with the memories.

"Theon..."

I froze, remembering I wasn't alone. For the first time in years, I had allowed someone to remain beside me, but it hadn't been a smart idea. I could never share the truth with anyone...

She placed a hand on my back, the dreaded sparks of her touch clearing my mind.

"Are you okay?"

She was on her knees next to me, her hand on my shoulder, the concern in her eyes so fucking clear. I wasn't stupid; I knew she cared for me more than she let on, and I pretended not to see it so I could hold onto this for a while longer.

"Theon?"

My heart was racing, and there was no way I could say it was nothing. Looking into her grey eyes, I pulled her into my lap, tangling my hand into her hair as I yanked her close. My lips crashed against hers in a kiss fuelled with a thousand emotions. The desperation for a distraction from my own mind was consuming me...

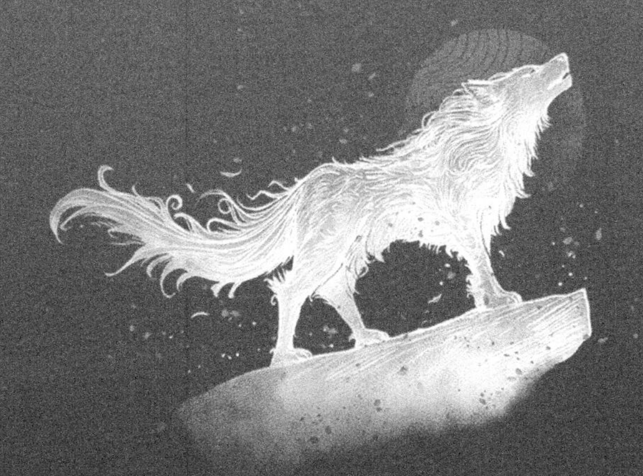

Together in Silence

YILEYNA

I GASPED FOR AIR, BREAKING away from him, my heart pounding and my head feeling dizzy. I had craved his kiss, and now it was as if he didn't want to let me go. Even as I sucked in some oxygen, his lips were on my neck, kissing and sucking on it as if wanting to claim every part of me. He had one hand under my top, stroking and kneading my skin.

I whimpered in pleasure, but I was also worried. Something had happened to Theon. His heart had been beating wildly.

"Theon? What's wrong?" I whispered, kissing his jaw, running my fingers through his hair as he sucked on the corner of my neck where one's mate's mark would go.

He tensed, freezing just as his lips touched my ear. His hand that was tangled in my hair yanked me back painfully, making me hiss in pain. My heart thudded when I saw his burning gold embers filled with rage.

His gaze flicked to my hair, and I don't know what it was, but he just seemed to get angrier as he twisted a few strands in his fingers.

"What a disgusting colour," he murmured before shoving me off his lap and onto the bed.

My heart squeezed painfully as he got up. His words rang in my head, and I felt my eyes prickle. I didn't know what had happened… but the anger and hatred in his eyes killed me. I didn't know what I had done, but he was looking at me with pure hatred.

He cast one last look over me, his eyes snapping to mine, and, for a moment, I thought I saw a glimmer of regret. Then he turned and left, the door slamming shut behind him. My eyes stung, but I refused to cry.

"You're stronger than this..." I told myself slowly, lying down on the bed.

The narrow bed now felt far too big and empty. The happiness I had felt having him there had just been pulled away. *No, I'm not going to sit here and feel sorry for myself.* Something had happened, and I needed to know.

Standing up, I left my room, not caring that Valentin and Patrick were watching me keenly as they stood outside of Charlene's cabin. They could probably see the marks that covered my neck, but I didn't have time for them right then.

I was about to try Theon's door handle when Valentin cleared his throat. I glanced at him sharply, only for him to motion down the hall with his eyes. Theon had gone that way...

"Thanks," I whispered before hurrying down the cold corridor.

Where did he go? I glanced towards the steps that led above deck, but I didn't think he went there. If he wanted to be alone, where would he go?

The Hold. That was the one place no one would go down to at this time of night. Quietly, I made my way towards it and, reaching the door, slowly opened it. My heart thumped as I stared into the darkness.

"Theon?" I whispered.

No reply. I switched the lantern on and scanned the area below. I was about to turn away when I hesitated. No... I should check first. Padding down the ladder, I walked around the boxes and crates. I stopped when I saw the pair of long legs sprawled across the ground.

"Theon..." I whispered as he came into view. His head was back against the wall, a bottle of alcohol in his hand and his eyes were his usual amber.

"Was me leaving not enough to show you I want to be alone?" He remarked coldly. I wanted to joke that I was blonde, and we are said to be a little more dense, but after his comment about my hair, I couldn't bring myself to say it.

"I'm not that easy to get rid of," I stated instead, and confidently, without waiting for an invitation, I sat down next to him.

He was still shirtless. I wondered if he was cold or not. I could feel the heat from his body as my arm grazed against his, and I leaned against him lightly. He tensed for a second but said nothing, so I didn't either.

I knew Theon didn't want to talk about it, and that was alright. Whatever was on his mind that was troubling him was something he didn't want to share. But I could still support him and show him that he wasn't alone by just being there. Just the way he had been for me.

I don't know how long we sat there, but he had relaxed, not even caring that his arm touched my breast as he drank his bottle of alcohol slowly. His anger had calmed down, and although at times I could sense it rising, he was more at ease.

"Won't you share that?" I asked when there was just a little left in the bottle.

He raised an eyebrow, tilting his head to look down at me. I batted my lashes innocently, squeezing my boobs together. His gaze dipped to them, but he simply looked me back in the eye before turning away.

"No, and your seduction skills need work," he said, making my mouth fall open.

"Meanie," I pouted, elbowing him sharply just as he had gulped the last bit down. He coughed, almost spitting out his mouthful, and I giggled. "Karma," I added smugly, only for him to yank me onto his lap.

"I think you deserve a punishment."

"I do not! I didn't even do anything wrong!" I huffed, feeling my cheeks heat at the thought of him spanking my ass again.

"Oh?"

"Yes, in fact, I thin- ah!" I gasped when he suddenly began tickling my stomach, my heart thudding as I giggled, struggling to free myself from his hold. "Theon! Stop!" He was relentless, tickling me nonstop. I couldn't breathe as I writhed in his arms, my breathless chuckles the only sound in the silent room.

"So, going to admit your mistake?" He asked, grabbing my ankle as I tried to kick him.

"No, I was nice to come down here, and you were being mean," I retorted, breathing heavily as I stared up from where I was flat on the floor.

"Shame, that was your choice to come," he replied coldly, his eyes flicking to my foot. "Tell me, little storm, are you tickly on your feet?"

"No, nope, not at all," I lied, my heart thudding as he bought my foot up. *Oh, Goddess, no.* I dared not yank out of his hold, knowing he would realise I was ticklish.

"Oh?" I nodded, trying to appear calm as I was panicking inside.

"Mhmm." I nodded as he glanced at my feet, a wicked smirk crossing his lips. "Theon…"

I closed my eyes, ready for him to tickle my poor foot, but instead, my eyes flew open when he ran his tongue along the base up towards the toes torturously slowly, making me gasp as I tried to pull free. A tingle of pleasure rushed up my leg, and I bit back the sigh that almost escaped my lips.

"Theon, what are you doing?"

He didn't reply, taking my toe in his mouth and biting down gently. Just then, he tickled my foot, making me shriek. I used my other foot to kick his stomach, and he finally let go, grabbing my legs and yanking me close until my thighs were draped over his.

"So, you are tickly," he stated, pulling me upright, and I found myself straddling him.

"Maybe a little. You are such a jerk," I replied, placing one hand on his shoulder for balance, daring to slowly run my fingers through his hair. "Theon… did my hair remind you of someone else's?" His eyes instantly became cold, and I got my answer. He didn't need to admit or deny it... but something about my hair had triggered him.

"No," he replied coldly.

"Okay," I replied softly, cupping his face as I claimed his lips in a soft, passionate kiss. The delicious sparks of pleasure rushed through me and went straight to my core.

He didn't need to tell me. Maybe one day he would… but I couldn't stop wondering who it was. I couldn't think of anyone back home with hair the same shade as mine.

His arms snaked around my waist, one hand wrapping around my neck as he began to kiss me back, taking control of the kiss. My eyes fluttered shut, enjoying the moment when suddenly there was a huge bang, and something hit the side of the ship, throwing us to the ground and making my heart leap in shock.

The entire ship shifted violently, making us both tumble across the floor. Theon's arms wrapped around me tightly, and my eyes widened in horror as I stared at all the crates and barrels over his shoulder that began tumbling straight towards us…

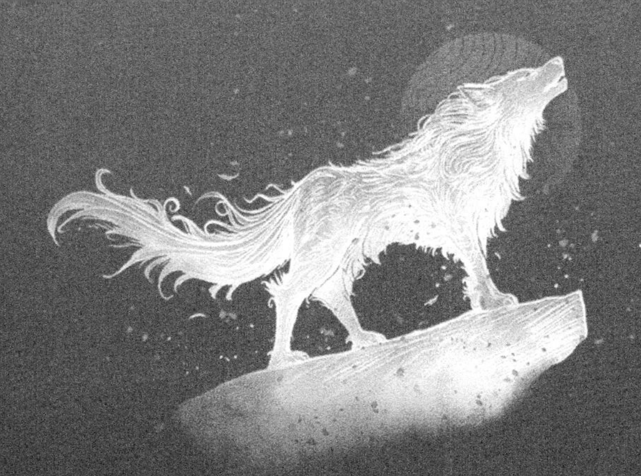

Resentment

THEON

"Theon, behind you!" Yileyna shouted, wrapping her arms around my head just as something slammed into us, the impact ramming us against the wall. The throbbing pain where the side of the crate had hit my head was intense. It was accompanied by the strong smell of blood.

Fuck.

I lifted my head from her breasts, and she slowly moved her arms. Letting go of her, I turned and shoved the crate that had hit us away and pulled her to her feet. Blood covered her arm where she had protected my head, and a flash of guilt filled me. She stood there unbothered about her injuries, gripping the wall as the ship lurched again.

"What's happening?" She asked as she was thrown to the side. I grabbed her around the waist, pulling her close as I tried to make my way to the ladder.

"We may have reached the Lifeless Abyss," I replied as another sharp lurch threw us to the ground.

Two crates crashed against one another. One of them splintered open, and a pile of apples and melons tumbled out in all directions.

"Well, it definitely does not seem to be lifeless," she muttered. I kicked away another barrel, pulling her towards the steps once more.

"You knew that," I remarked.

"Obviously, I just don't get why it's named the Lifeless Abyss."

"Because no one survives a journey through. Thick with Sirens and sea monsters, it's a nightmare for all sailors," I replied, lifting her up so she only had a few steps to climb.

"True…" she murmured, grabbing the ladder and climbing. I kept hold of her thighs, making sure she didn't fall; she was fast, and despite the violent movements of the ship, I took a moment to admire her derriere.

Once she was out, I climbed up and shut the door behind us, wondering how much food would be damaged down there.

"Go to your cabin," I commanded her, making her turn to me in surprise.

"No," she replied as if I was saying something unbelievable.

"Yileyna, this time, just listen," I said, clenching my jaw. I get that she helped, but I couldn't have her out there, not when we were probably already in the very sea where I lost two of the most important people to me.

"No." She turned stubbornly, about to go towards the deck, when my eyes flashed, my anger raging through me. I grabbed hold of her arm, spinning her around and against my chest. She was about to argue when I placed a finger to her lips.

"Not this time," I whispered, hitting the pressure point in her neck hard, instantly making her eyes roll before she fell unconscious in my arms. The ship lurched once more, and Ryan's voice came into my head,

Theon! There's something attacking the ship! Could use you up here right about now!'

Coming, I replied shortly, walking down towards our cabins. I stopped in front of Valentin and Patrick, both of whom looked tense.

"Take her to the princess," I commanded coldly, passing her to Valentin.

"Yes, Beta," he replied, bowing his head to me.

I didn't wait any longer, hearing them knock on the door before it was pulled open. I knew the marks on her neck and my scent still lingered on her. As much as I wanted to keep our agreement a secret, I didn't think that was going to be the case for much longer. I didn't want to be associated with her or anyone in that way, but it was a bit too late to change that now.

I ran up onto the deck, grabbing a sword as I went. I doubted wolf form was going to help. The moments from earlier replayed in my mind, and I frowned. What was I even doing tickling her? Sure, I liked the view of her breasts moving, but… who was I fucking kidding?

I pushed the thoughts away as my eyes fell on one of the large black tentacles that was wrapped around the mast. A Kraken.

"If my ship goes down, I'm taking you with me!" Flynn growled. I didn't bother responding to him.

I didn't come here to die. We were going to make our way through this, sea monsters, Sirens, or bad weather. *I am not the child I was ten years ago.* My eyes blazed as I broke into a run, spinning the huge sword, and, with full force, swung, slicing off the tentacle that was wrapped around the mast. A screeching roar of agony filled the tumultuous, stormy skies as the ship was hit wildly from the left.

"Madelia! On my signal, burn it!" I shouted.

"Fire on a ship! Are you crazy!" Flynn thundered.

"I know what I'm doing," I replied icily.

Some of the crew members were firing at it using the ship's cannons, but I knew what I had to do. With Yileyna safe, my mind felt at ease, and I was the calmest person there. Breaking into a run, I jumped, using the mast as leverage, and gave Madelia the signal…

Twenty minutes later, I dropped onto the deck. Not far from our now steady ship, the Kraken's burning body was sinking into the water. Its sliced-off tentacles floated on the surface, and its dark-coloured blood poisoned the waters of the Lifeless Abyss.

"You are more than you look," Flynn muttered, observing me.

I didn't respond, staring at the dead monster. The true potential of my powers had been sealed away before I had gone to Astalion. No one was to know who I really was. My Alpha aura was blocked away. The only thing that gave away any sign of my power was the size of my wolf, something that could not be hidden.

"You did well," I said emotionlessly, glancing at Madelia.

"Thank you," she replied with a small bow of her head. The respect they already had for me when I wasn't even officially the Beta… rank and a title weren't what made a leader a leader. It was capability.

"He is amazing."

"The Alpha King did well to choose him as the future Beta."

"He could be more…"

More. I knew exactly what they were insinuating, to take Charlene as my mate just as Andres had wanted me to, but she was the last woman on Kaeladia that I would ever take as my own. The daughter of the Alpha King…

My anger flared inside of me like a fire that had just been fuelled by oil. It irked me more than anything, having to pretend like this. But in life, I had always been robbed of everything. My family, status, power, and rights. If I wanted to attain something, then I had to make sacrifices, and I was ready to make every sacrifice needed. I was no longer a child, and despite my rage, I had to play this out carefully. Without distractions or emotions, I would fulfil my goal and have vengeance on all who had wronged the Hale family.

Turning towards the crew on board, I crossed my arms.

"We are already in the Lifeless Abyss. Stay vigilant and remember anything can attack at any time. From here on out, until we make it through these waters, we are in danger. Remember that."

Not giving them time to respond, I walked past them and headed toward the lower deck. I was covered in the Kraken's blood, and it was already dawn. I needed to shower and get some rest. *Who knows what else we might face over the next few days…*

I had just stepped out of the bathroom, a towel around my waist, and pulled open my trunk when there was a knock on the door.

"Who is it?" I asked, the irritation seeping into my voice.

"Charlene." I pulled my towel off and slipped on my sweatpants.

"It's open," I said coldly, turning as she opened the door.

I had a pretty good feeling about why she was there. I crossed my arms, watching her impatiently as her eyes flitted over me. Women.

"Hurry up, I want to sleep." She shook her head, now looking away.

"Theon, it's about Yileyna," she said, no longer able to meet my gaze. I cocked my brow, waiting.

"I don't have all day." My voice was icy as I glared at her. She nodded and took a breath, braving the chance to look me in the eye.

"Are you two… together?"

"What are you getting at? Besides, shouldn't you ask your friend, why are you asking me?" I asked mockingly.

"She's asleep, or unconscious. Patrick said you gave her to them and that he saw you leave her room in the night." A flash of hurt went through her eyes, and I smirked, advancing towards her.

"What's wrong? Jealous?" I had never been blind to both their antics. Like most young women, they had fawned over me since the start. Pathetic.

"No… I would never be jealous of Yileyna. She... I'm just scared. Why now? Why when her parents are gone?" She asked quietly.

"She's a woman now. I never thought much of her before, but I'm sure we can both agree that she is the most appealing woman in Westerfell," I replied arrogantly. I didn't know why I was even answering her, but the urge to cause her pain was appealing. I hated her. A small smile crossed her face, which only made me angrier.

"She is, and I hope you aren't using her. Theon, she lost her parents. She is going through so much. Please don't end up hurting her." She was speaking quietly, but her voice was sincere as she pleaded for her friend. Their bond irked me. I smirked coldly.

"She knows the risk, and she's taken it. Tell me, Princess, how much would it hurt you if I broke her?" I asked coldly. Her eyes flashed with hurt, and I smirked, getting my answer. A lot.

I could have chosen her. I could have destroyed her even if she wasn't as appealing, but the only reason I couldn't bring myself to was that I was disgusted by whose blood ran through her veins.

"Yileyna is just a plaything, and she knows that."

"So, is that all she is to you?" She asked, her green eyes full of pain. I turned away from her, trying to control the anger that was raging within me.

"Obviously. There's no way a wolfless female would be worth anything more to me than to be an object to use and discard when I'm done," I replied harshly. I heard her gasp, but before I could relish in the satisfaction of causing her pain, I realised someone else had heard what I had just said. I had been so caught up I hadn't even noticed her.

My heart raced as I turned quickly, just in time to see the flicker of blonde hair and the silent footsteps as she tried to slip away unheard.

Fuck.

A flare of guilt rushed through me as I stared at the crack in the door, no longer paying attention to what the princess was saying. The only thought in my mind was that she had heard what was not meant for her ears…

LIMITS

YILEYNA

“Obviously. There’s no way a wolf-less female would be worth anything more to me than to be an object to use and discard when I’m done.”

His words rang in my mind, and I sighed as I locked the door quietly behind me. I looked around my cabin, feeling exhausted, and dropped onto the bed. His scent still lingered. I closed my eyes, not wanting to think about anything, but I couldn’t stop the thoughts from swirling in my mind.

At times, it was as if he cared… and then at others… I curled into a ball, taking deep, steady breaths. I would not let it affect me.

A light knock on the door made me sigh.

“I’m trying to get some sleep. What is it?” I called out, really not wanting to talk to anyone, but I knew it was Charlene.

“Open up, darling,” her soft voice called.

Sighing, I got up, unlocking the door and getting back into bed. I heard the door open and Charlene sigh softly as she locked the door, then sat down on the bed.

“I’m angry at you, Leyna,” her soft voice came. I sighed, pulling the blanket down from my face, and looked over at her, feeling guilty.

“I know.”

“Theon, want to share?” I sighed again and sat up. It was a conversation

I knew was going to happen at some point.

"Not really," I mumbled, keeping my arms hidden under the blanket. I didn't need her worrying over my injuries.

"Since when?" She asked quietly.

"Since the festival," I muttered, staring down at the blanket. I heard her gasp, and I looked up to see the wave of sadness in her eyes.

"Since then, and you didn't tell me?"

"He didn't want anyone to know," I whispered, feeling ever so guilty.

"But... not even me?" She asked. I don't think I had ever felt worse.

"I'm sorry, I truly am, my queen," I whispered.

"When I told you he was interested in you, you vehemently denied it!" She exclaimed as if suddenly remembering that and frowned at me.

"I know! But I'm sorry... are you... umm, are you okay with it?" I asked, knowing that she had liked Theon for ages too. "I know it's stupid that I'm asking this now... after stuff happened..." I felt awful.

"I want to say I am. I mean, I'm jealous too! But I'm just a bit concerned... are you sure he's serious? I don't want you to get hurt," she replied, ending hesitantly. His words rang in my mind, and I lay back down.

"We have an agreement. It's just physical," I replied quietly. Her eyes softened, and she sighed.

"You know, I would say go get it, girl, and enjoy that piece of sexiness while you can, but why do I feel like you will get hurt?" She asked softly.

"I won't. I know he considers me nothing more than trash," I said, feeling my stomach twist at those words.

Then why was I allowing him to have me when he couldn't even respect me? I remembered our moment from down in the hold, the way he playfully tickled me and licked my foot. *Do you do that to someone you consider trash? Maybe?* I didn't know.

Charlene moved over and wrapped her arms around me tightly as she slipped under the blanket beside me.

"Goddess, this bed smells of him!" She yelped. I couldn't resist the smile that crossed my lips as I rested my head on her shoulder.

"Well, he did sleep here for a bit," I giggled.

"Wait, did you do the deed in here?"

"No, relax! We've only done it once." We didn't do much on this bed, and what we did do, she didn't need to know.

"Once? On the night of the festival?" I nodded.

"Yeah…"

"So, is he good? He seems rough if your neck is anything to go by," she teased. "I can't believe you have actually kissed Theon!"

"He is rough," I admitted, staring at the ceiling.

"Well, details! Since he is now claimed by my friend, the least you can do is share the details. Wait! Wait… is he big?" She whispered. I blushed and nodded.

"Yes, although I haven't really seen it much, it was all just so fast…"

I frowned, thinking we had actually only fucked once... for someone who wanted to simply use me, he sure hadn't taken advantage of that.

"Well, next time then," she replied with a gentle smile, brushing my hair off my face before we both snuggled down, letting sleep come to us. She fell asleep first, whilst I couldn't help but mull over everything that had happened…

Night had fallen, and I had stayed in bed, saying I wasn't feeling too great. Ailema had delivered some food, but aside from that, I had decided to stay in my room. I just needed a little space. If Patrick and Valentin knew about us, then I was sure the rest of those from the Silver Storm Pack knew as well.

I had kept my arms under the blanket, but I knew I needed to get up and make sure there were no splinters from the wooden crates stuck in my arms.

Charlene had spent most of the afternoon with me, but I had lied that I was feeling a little under the weather, and she had left me when night had come. Raiden had popped in earlier to ask how I was doing, but I hadn't entertained him for long, just wanting to clear my mind and be alone.

The lantern cast shadows on the wall from where it hung in a bracket. The slight sway of the ship was lulling me to sleep when I heard the door open and shut, followed by the key scraping in the lock. My eyes snapped to the door, all traces of sleep vanishing, and I sat up sharply. My eyebrows furrowed when I saw it was none other than Theon.

"I'm not feeling great, I don't have time to entertain you," I said, trying to keep my voice level.

"Then don't," came his short reply.

"I want to be alone," I added icily, sitting up. I frowned, looking at the two mugs of what smelled like coffee he was holding on a small tray.

Don't fall for it.

I kept chanting that in my head. He placed the two mugs down and crossed his arms as he crouched beside the bed.

"Everyone is saying you're not well. What's wrong with you? You look perfectly fine to me." I gave him a withering glare.

"That's because all you see is the fact I'm sat here with intact boobs and a vagina. That's all you care about," I hissed, raising my arms and showing my arms that were still not fully healed from when I had protected his head. "Now, if you can show yourself out, I'm not in the mood."

His amber eyes were on my arms, and to my irritation, he took hold of them, twisting my arms in front of him so he could get a look at the injuries. He brushed his thumb gently over the part that had almost healed, sending little tingles through me. *Not this time.*

I yanked free from his hold.

"Leave," I commanded coldly, glaring into his eyes. How could amber eyes, which were such a beautiful shade, look so cold?

"No." He took hold of my right arm, frowning as he looked down at it. That one was worse. "Why didn't you get these checked?"

"Theon, you can stop pretending to care," I whispered, pulling out of his hold.

His eyes met mine, but I looked away, trying to mask my emotions the best I could. He stood up, and I lay down, pulling the blanket over my head. The hollow emptiness in my chest was excruciating, but I wanted him gone.

I heard the door open and shut. I kicked the blanket off, rushing to lock the door, only to see he had taken the key. I clenched my jaw, irritation seeping through me. Should I go get it back, or is that what he wanted?

As I struggled to decide what to do, the door opened again, and to my utter dismay, he was back, holding a small box. He shut and locked the door, slipping the key into his pocket, only making me even angrier. He placed the box on the bed, then, without a word, grabbed me by my upper arm and tugged me towards the bed.

"Stop touching me," I hissed, feeling my anger rising.

Once again, he ignored me, opened the box and took out one of the bottles. Pouring some of the disinfectant or whatever it was onto the gauze, he dabbed it surprisingly gently over my partially healed injuries, making them sting. I hissed, and he paused, glancing up at me as if waiting for permission to continue.

"Don't worry, I'm used to pain. I'm sure you don't care if it hurts or not. Why be so gentle when you are rather brutal in general, aren't you?" I snatched the gauze from his hand and roughly scrubbed it down my arm. My eyes stung as I reopened the injuries that were partially healed. I was clenching my jaw to stop myself from crying out, but I just needed to get my anger out.

"Yileyna!" Theon grabbed my wrist, stopping me from doing further damage to my arm. A flicker of surprise was clear in his eyes.

"Then leave. You've done enough," I spat. I had never felt so angry at him as I did then.

"What I said earlier -"

"You like to hurt me on a daily basis, Theon, and we both know that I'm stupid enough to still put up with you, but to insult me like that to someone else? That, I won't tolerate. I may have agreed to give myself to you, but I have not agreed for you to ruin my reputation. Now get the fuck out. Seriously, I think I should never have ever agreed to this arrangement." His eyes flashed, and he smirked coldly.

"I told you, once you're in, there's no turning back." He tossed the gauze on the bed and stood up. "Think what you want. I don't give a fuck." He left the room, the door shutting behind him with a snap. I cradled my sore arm, trying my best to control my emotions.

He tried to help me... he was cleaning my injuries.... No, he was also being a dick. I knew, deep down, he had his hot and cold moments, but I couldn't deal with them. Not right then.

Angrily, I pushed the box he had brought in onto the floor, not caring as its contents spilt across the floor, and I glared at it in anger.

I hate you, Theon.

Turning, I threw myself down on the bed, refusing to cry. I turned on my side, my eyes falling on the coffee that stood on the dresser. For us...

Feeling guilty, I closed my eyes, trying to make sense of the havoc of emotions inside of me. *I don't know what I'm doing, I honestly don't know...*

My Advice

YILEYNA

THE FOLLOWING TWO DAYS, I avoided being alone with Theon like a wolf avoiding silver and wolfsbane. I stayed with Charlene when I could or locked myself away in my room after having to ask Ailema for a second key.

Theon would train Charlene in the mornings, but I asked Raiden or Ryan to accompany me to watch as well. Theon would make one of the men train with Charlene, but he, too, didn't talk to me. At times I saw him watching me, and at others, I could feel his intense gaze upon me, but I didn't entertain him. However, even then, the emotions coursed through me. Every time our eyes connected, I felt the intense rush of desire take my breath away.

Theon was a dangerous addiction and one I was consumed with. I knew if he tried, the chances that he would break my walls once more were high, so I didn't even try to rile him up. Even when Leto begged me to sing along to his sea shanty, I refused.

Mom said my voice was beautiful, and she always asked me to sing for her when she was doing the laundry or something. She used to joke that my voice was too precious to share with others. It wasn't that I didn't enjoy singing, but it reminded me of Mom, and I didn't want Theon to get all possessive.

Charlene was made to stay in her cabin most of the time due to being in dangerous waters. Apart from the occasional moments when she was allowed to come above deck or to train, she was kept inside, and I accompanied her, for the most part, anyway.

It was obvious Barbara enjoyed it. She spent a lot more time trying to talk to Theon. He would reply, but by the end of the first day, it was obvious he had grown tired of her and made his displeasure clear.

Today the sun was shining, and, despite the dark waters beneath us, it felt good not to have to layer so many pieces of clothing on, although it was still rather chilly.

It was early morning, and we had just had breakfast after Charlene had gone through more brutal training at the hands of Theon. I saw what she meant, that sometimes he seemed to look at her with hatred. But it was fleeting, and I often doubted if it was just my mind playing tricks, but why would Charlene and I see the same thing? I do believe he was just venting all his anger out on her.

The jerk seemed to have plenty of it bottled inside. I guessed the lack of sex might just be making him grumpier. Although I was sure if he wanted, Barbara was more than willing to cater to his needs. Even though that made my chest squeeze, I was not going to let it bother me. We would see what happened when we returned to Westerfell, but right then, I needed some space away from Theon.

I leaned on the edge of the ship. I was wearing a white top with a black corset around my waist and pants. I enjoyed the wind blowing through my hair, which Charlene had braided from the top.

From there, I could hear the discussion Theon, Flynn, Aeon, Sam, Ryan, and Raiden were having, and it captured my attention. I swear it may sound weird, but my hearing seemed to be getting better lately.

"I wouldn't advise it," Aeon murmured.

"We need to rest," Sam said, sighing heavily.

"The ship's port side has minor damage; we are almost out of supplies, and I don't think we will make it through without stopping," Flynn added.

"I get that, but if we stop now, wouldn't that just cause us further delay if we took a detour off route?" Theon's sexy, emotionless voice came, a voice that made my core knot. *Goddess, please help me get over him.*

"It might add a few days, but there is a small island that we can stop at for supplies. It's a pirate island if I am honest, but we do need to stop," Flynn reasoned. Pirate Island? I had a feeling they meant Bellmead...

"And delay us by three or so days?" Theon repeated, the irritation in his voice obvious.

"Well, there's no other option. We need to head northeast from here and then back en route to the Purien Isles so -"

"I am not going to stop just for everyone's leisure. We can survive with scarce food until we reach the Isles," Theon cut in icily.

I frowned. Bellmead... so if he's saying northeast... I looked up, staring at the mountains in the distance. An idea came to me, and I pushed myself away from the boat's edge, walking over to the group. Squeezing between Sam and Ryan, I looked down at the map they had open before them.

"There's a way that can lead us to Bellmead through the mountain pass; it's wide enough for our ship and safer, plus it won't take time from our journey or delay us. We will still be on course," I put forward, pointing a finger to a narrow mark on the map. I felt all eyes on me, but I refused to look at Theon, feeling his intense gaze upon me.

"Are you trying to lure us to our death? Going through a narrow pass... what if the ship gets stuck?" His icy voice came. "There could be a cave-in or a blockage on that route."

"No," I said, shaking my head as I looked up at him, probably the first time we were exchanging words since that night. "The pass is wider than it appears. I have studied the rivers and seas around Astalion very deeply, my father made sure I knew every route, and I loved to learn about our ocean. That pass is not well known because everyone avoids the Lifeless Abyss."

"I have heard of it now that you mention it." Ryan frowned as he looked down at me before massaging his jaw. "I think she's right."

"So, are we going to go into this on blind faith, just to save time?" Flynn added doubtfully.

"It's not just the time, it's safer. In a narrower setting, we will be more aware if something big is coming," I persisted, pointing to the exit through the mountains. "Look, Bellmead Island is here. These mountains do have a pass. See that? That's our exit."

Theon bent down slightly, placing his hand on the map not far from mine. His scent filled my nose, and my heart skipped a beat. *Focus.*

"Are you confident enough, knowing that if you're wrong, everyone dies?" He asked, looking directly into my eyes. My heart skipped a beat, knowing the weight of the responsibility of this decision was not a light matter. All life on board would be on me.

"We are risking death by travelling through the Lifeless Abyss directly, too," Raiden added in my defence.

"The difference is, I'm ready to take responsibility. Is she?" Theon countered coldly.

"Unlike you, I'm not standing here trying to rush this mission at the cost of casualties. I genuinely believe that this would be safest. They say the Siren Kingdoms lay in the thickest and deepest parts of the oceans; by going through the river pass, it's safer," I replied confidently. "I may not have a wolf yet, but I am still the daughter of our Beta who -"

"Was a traitor," Ryan muttered. Theon and Raiden's eyes flashed, but I didn't react.

"Who taught me a lot. Just this once, trust me," I said quietly, looking at Theon. He was the one that was in charge. I couldn't read him, but he seemed to be considering it.

"The pass may not be safe," he replied quietly, but I could see he was struggling with something.

"I think we should do it," Raiden said. "What do you think, Captain?"

"Well, her logic makes sense, *if* there's a pass," Flynn mused.

"There is," Theon said icily, his eyes on me as if sizing me up, but there was no anger. "We go through the pass. We should reach Bellmead by noon tomorrow."

He turned and walked away from the group. I felt confused. I had expected him to get angry, but he hadn't.

"Alright, we are heading to the mountain pass! Towards Bellmead, folks!" Flynn shouted before turning to me. "Well, lassie, I hope you know what you're talking about."

I nodded, hoping I was right. I glanced at Theon. It wasn't like him to be so… quiet. He was standing staring at the mountains in the distance, but it was the look in his eyes that made my stomach twist. It was almost as if he was thinking about something painful.

His gaze flicked to mine, and for the first time since I had met him, his eyes looked… troubled. I didn't even know if that was the right word, but he looked… upset or something. It was only there for a few seconds before he turned and vanished down the steps…

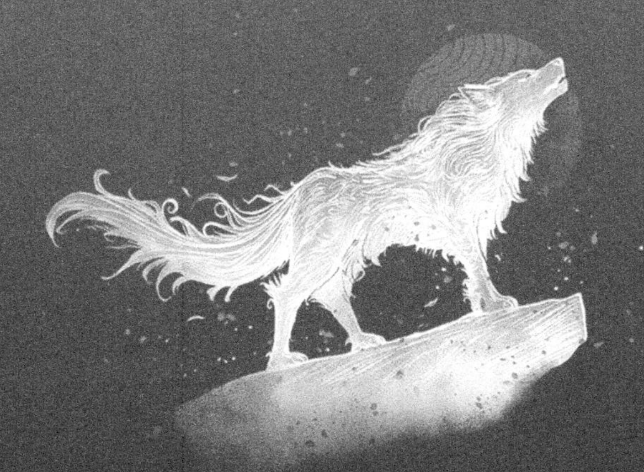

A Single Tear

YILEYNA

Raiden had told Charlene and me to head below deck soon after that. I didn't see Theon again. Hours had passed, and, when I felt the ship slow and the coldness grow, I knew we had probably reached the pass.

"I'm just going to go check on how things are," I told Charlene, standing up.

"You shouldn't go out there. It's dangerous."

"I told them to take the pass, I should be up there. There's a split several miles in, I just want to make sure they know where they are going."

"You told the captain that already," she protested, clearly not wanting me to go up.

"I know, but just in case. Don't worry, I'll be fine, my queen." I gave her my best innocent smile, wanting her approval, and after a moment, she sighed.

"Fine!" She crossed her arms, huffing in annoyance. I winked at her before opening the door, leaving her with the book that she had been reading.

"I need a book prince to come to life and keep me company," Charlene pouted as I was about to shut the door.

"Oh? Who's the charmer in that one?" I asked curiously.

"Declan of House Storm. He is perfect, cocky and mocking, yet charming," Charlene sighed dreamily.

"Ah, *His Caged Princess*." I smiled before shutting the door and walking down the hall, unable to stop the shiver that ran through me. *Goddess! It's freezing out here.*

I rubbed my arms, which were only covered in the thin white cotton of my top. I climbed up onto the deck and looked around. Everyone who was there was silent, so silent that I could hear the water rippling loudly. The few lanterns that were alight didn't help much against the darkness that enveloped us.

A few of the men were holding weapons as they looked out at the looming ice mountains that were beginning to close around us. Madelia and Sam were scanning the surroundings sharply as if ready to use their powers if needs be. I saw Theon standing next to Flynn at the helm, and I walked towards them. The sound of my heels against the floor and the creaking of wood made a few of them glance at me. The silence was deafening. I could hear my own heartbeat.

"You should be below deck," Theon's cold voice came without even turning towards me.

"I just wanted to make sure we take the correct turn ahead. There are two, the other one will be too narrow."

"We know that," Theon replied, his voice suddenly sounding much colder.

"Okay… great…" I turned, ready to walk away when I made the mistake of looking into his smouldering eyes.

A wave of pain rushed through me. I hated how I couldn't live without him. I hated how I wanted his arms around me… his lips on mine. But I also hated how he hurt me with his words, time and again…

"There's a morbid story about this area, one I heard took place years ago," Raiden remarked, coming over and giving me a warm smile.

"A story?" I asked, curious to hear it before I had to go. I watched him scan the area.

"Yeah. I was trying to remember where I heard of the mountain pass. A long time ago, one of the most haunting tragedies of the sea took place right here. Apparently, a Siren single-handedly took out all the passengers and crew on board, including an Alpha's Luna and his children."

"Single-handed?" Madelia asked sharply, glancing at Raiden.

"Aiy, I know the story." Flynn scratched his jaw. "But it's hearsay. It isn't confirmed it was here."

I glanced at Theon, who was silent. His back, which was towards us, was rigid as he stared out at the water.

"There are only a few Sirens who would have that much power," Cleo responded thoughtfully.

"Yes, she must have been from the imperial family then. They say they can control the very sea and even the weather to do their bidding," Bobbie added, his voice ominous in the darkness that surrounded us.

"The imperials. The one family that rules the seven seas..." Flynn sighed. "Let's not talk about omens. Come on, focus!"

"I'll be back," Theon said quietly to Flynn, his voice as emotionless as ever.

The captain nodded, scanning his crew as he scolded and shouted out a few orders, telling everyone to get back to work. My gaze followed Theon, who was heading towards the back of the ship. He was acting strange...

I couldn't stop myself. Even when my legs began carrying me down the path he had just taken with my head screaming at me to stop, I didn't.

He was there, leaning against the side, his head lowered, his back to me. My heart was racing, and I wondered what he was thinking. The urge to ask him if everything was okay was on the tip of my lips when he spoke,

"What do you want?"

I blinked, shaking my head to clear it. I walked over to him, keeping a good three feet between us, and leaned against the edge of the boat, tilting my head so I could see his face.

"Are you okay? You seem..." I couldn't say upset or stressed; he would deny it. "Tense or something."

"It's your crazy imagination that thinks that," he replied, his eyes meeting mine. My heart skipped a beat, and I nodded, looking away first.

"Okay...if you say so. Are you worried about the journey? I have a good feeling that we'll be okay. Look, we survived a Siren and a Kraken attack. This is an adventure that one day we can tell others about. You know, werewolves prefer land, so there are many who would never have experienced what we have. Adventures to always remember."

"Adventures? Are near-death experiences a game to you, Yileyna?" My heart thudded as I looked at him, not understanding why, suddenly, anger seemed to rage within him.

"They are conquests that we have come out victorious from," I replied, feeling tense as if I was taking an exam and one wrong word would result in him getting angry. I hated it, and it only told me that I was right. Avoiding Theon was the smartest thing to do. If I had to be careful around someone like this... then that was a big warning in itself.

"Conquests..." He scoffed, his eyes full of contempt as he looked me square in the eye. "And what about those who die? Are they a part of the conquests you speak of?" I frowned.

"No one died. That's why I said they were adventures… Theon, what's wrong?"

"Nothing," he replied coldly, looking away and running his hand through his hair. Something was wrong, even if he didn't want to talk about it.

"Okay, if you just want to talk ever… I'm here," I said hesitantly, pushing away from the edge. I turned away when he called me.

"Yileyna." I paused, my heart skipping a beat as I turned back towards him. He was still looking out at the water.

"Hmm?"

"What I said to Charlene, it wasn't right," he replied, glancing up at the towering mountains.

My eyes widened in surprise. I wasn't expecting that from him. I remained silent. If he wanted to apologise, then I wasn't going to say it was fine. *Show me what you've got.*

"I know it doesn't justify what I said, but my intention was never to hurt you."

"Then what was your intention, Theon?" He moved away from the edge, his dangerously sexy eyes on me as he advanced.

"To hurt her," he replied quietly as he stood before me. He towered over me, making my heart thud from a thousand things. I sighed, shaking my head.

"Hurting Charlene hurts me, just the way attacking me would upset her. So directly or indirectly, you still hurt me," I explained quietly, my voice sounding more breathless than it was meant to. He was standing too close. I needed him to move back, but I wasn't going to move and show him he was getting to me.

"I didn't mean to."

Our eyes were locked, and despite a thousand things I wanted to scream at him, I couldn't. His attempt at an apology had thrown me off. So, I simply nodded.

"Don't do that again."

"I can't promise that, but I can promise that I will try not to insult you." His face was emotionless, his eyes hard as he held my gaze.

"Well, I'll see how long that lasts, but… I don't think I want to continue with our agreement." My voice ended in a whisper, the pain in my chest suffocating me. Why did it feel like we were breaking up? We weren't even together; we didn't even really go through with our agreement... that night was all we had.

His eyes softened slightly, and he nodded.

"Yeah, I don't think we should. Like I said, I would destroy you," his husky reply came.

His gaze dipped to my breasts for a moment before he closed the small gap that was left between us. My breath hitched, but before I could put more distance between us, his hands cupped my face. Neither of us spoke, simply gazing into the other's eyes. His attention flickered to my lips for a split second.

I knew he could hear my heartbeat, and I could hear his… both beating as one. I didn't move, my stomach fluttering as we stood there so close… yet so far away.

"You're still the most beautiful woman I've seen," he whispered before he pressed his lips against mine.

A small gasp escaped me, making my eyes flutter shut as pleasure swirled through me like a storm, igniting a thousand emotions within me. His lips moved against mine slowly, as if trying to memorise the feel of my own. The way his lips felt… the way his touch consumed me…

Before I could kiss him back, he had stepped back, letting go of me.

"Go below deck," he commanded quietly as our eyes met. Once more, his were as cold and hard as ever.

He turned and began to walk away, not waiting for a reply, leaving me standing there with a million emotions coursing through me. *Why? Why did you show me there's more to you when you pushed me away?* I raised a hand to my chest, trying to control the pain I was feeling deep inside.

A single tear trickled from my eye.

I refuse to cry.

Reaching up, I wiped it away and stared down at my fingertip, my teardrop glittering like a single jewel. Why was something that was caused by pain so beautiful?

"Theon… what are we?" I whispered into the night sky.

"Heaven and Hell," his faint reply came, and I froze, not realising he had heard me.

I turned just in time to see him vanish around the corner, leaving me feeling so very alone all over again…

Down a Cobbled Street

YILEYNA

The journey through the pass had been uneventful, and everyone was beyond surprised at that. The tension had grown as the hours had passed, but I was just relieved that there had not been any attacks. We had reached Bellmead just before sunset the following day and would spend the night at a local inn.

The crew were dealing with mending the minor damage to the ship's exterior, and those from the Silver Storm Pack would spend the night in the inn, whilst half the crew would stay on the ship to make sure no one sneaks aboard.

Theon had made it clear to everyone that no one was to discuss our journey, where we were headed, or where we were from. To keep it vague and simply state that we were from Astalion if anyone asked.

The town itself was small, and on every corner, there were people leering at us. Curiosity and suspicion had been clear in their eyes from the moment we stepped off that ship. Theon had taken the lead, with Charlene and I right behind him, and the others had flanked us. I wish I wasn't squashed in the middle, curious to observe the little island.

We had ordered some dinner downstairs before we retreated to our rooms to rest and have a proper hot bath. It was night, and the sounds of violins and a woman singing seeped through the cracks in the window. There was a tavern just across the cobbled street where the music was coming from.

I had napped at first, allowing Madelia and Charlene, with whom I was sharing a room, to bathe first.

"Can we go to the Tavern?" I asked, tilting my head as I peered through the window, towel-drying my hair.

"The princess needs to stay here," Madelia replied, smiling slightly.

"You go," Charlene added with a knowing smile. I pouted hesitantly.

"I'm sure Commander Theon wouldn't approve," Madelia added after a moment's pause. I knew the four guards were on duty too. I was sure if I went for a bit, no one would notice.

"He will be fine as long as Charlene is here. I just want to explore the streets a bit, I'll make sure to stick to areas that are busy. Fear not, I just want to have a little look around."

She nodded and didn't argue. After all, I was no longer of any importance. I wasn't complaining because I could handle myself if something came up, and, like a child allowed to go to the candy shop, I quickly got dressed in a white buttoned shirt with balloon sleeves that I tucked into wide-legged grey pants. I wrapped my damp hair into a bun on top of my head before sliding two small daggers into my boots. I picked up my pouch, putting in some essential items and my purse of coins, deciding that I would buy something as a souvenir. *Who knows if I'll ever visit Bellmead again?*

I left the room, slipping the bag over my head and letting the strap sit comfortably between my breasts as I left our room.

"Where are you going?" Patrick asked wearily.

"Just for a walk. Take care of Charlene," I said quickly before I walked off, hoping they didn't push further.

Stepping out onto the cobbled streets, I was welcomed by a cold breeze. The ground glistened due to the rain from earlier. I could feel a very faint sprinkle still falling, but it was not enough to dampen anyone's spirits. The weather was typical for Bellmead. The smell of smoke, cigars, and something or other cooking, filled my nose, and I was unable to stop the smile that crossed my lips.

Excitement filled me as I began to stroll down the streets. Peering into the open shops, it was obvious Bellmead was a trading point, and many of those trades were of illegal items – Items that were probably stolen, rare, or forbidden to sell.

I stuck to the open traders, but even then, the 'charms' and items all seemed rather strange or suspicious, so in the end, I simply chose a notebook each for Charlene and me. The covers were made of special Fae material that seemed to sparkle whenever it caught the light.

I ignored the obvious stares and the vulgar comments that were thrown at me by the men, most of whom were drunk. It was not a werewolf town, and deep down, it was nice to see so much diversity in one place, even if most of the men were pigs. Back in Westerfell, even though it was the capital, it was still mainly a werewolf city.

"That's fourteen gold coins each," the man behind the counter told me.

"Fourteen each? That's crazy. I won't pay more than seven each!" I stared at the diaries in my hand. I knew he was ripping me off.

"Look, lady, these things aren't cheap. That is material made only in the fae kingdoms. Either you take it or -"

"That's fine. I won't buy them then. Here you go. Thank you for your time," I replied, placing the diaries down without even a moment of hesitation. No matter how much I wanted them, I was not paying twenty-eight coins for them! Besides, I knew how traders worked.

Three… two…

"Alright, alright! Come back, woman!" The man growled, and I smirked, schooling my face into innocence before I spun around and raised an eyebrow questioningly.

"Yes?"

"Ten gold each." I shook my head.

"I'm afraid I only have eighteen coins on me," I sighed. "It's fine, I don't need them." I smiled innocently, about to turn away again when he slammed his fist on his table of items, making them all rattle.

"Deal then, eighteen for both!" I paused, not wanting to make it look like I was eager.

"Sixteen. I need to buy something else too." I crossed my arms.

"How about eighteen, and I will throw in this locket?" He held up a pretty pendant, but it wasn't exactly what I was looking for. However, I had pushed enough; eighteen for both plus the locket was fair, I guess.

"Alright then, you've robbed me," I grumbled dramatically, making sure not to let my purse tinkle as I took out eighteen golds. "Now I only have a few silvers left," I sighed.

"I robbed you? You robbed me!"

"Well, you insisted I purchase from you." He frowned, wrapping the books in a square of brown paper.

"Aiy, I couldn't let a pretty customer just walk off," he muttered, clearly not pleased.

"Oh, how sweet. You really are a true gentleman, and those are very hard to come by." I batted my eyelids, and to my surprise, his cheeks flushed. I resisted a chuckle.

"Not really, aiy… but yes, I say the same to my woman back home." Men were so fickle.

"Thank you for these. I will remember your kindness," I said. Taking the parcel he had just wrapped and waving, I walked off. It was then I realised I had ventured rather far out.

I best turn and head to the tavern for a good tankard of mead or rum! That would let me sleep well in a much more comfortable bed.

A few minutes later, I was making my way back, going through the streets, when I stopped. It felt as if someone had called me. I looked around, but save the sounds of chatter, shouting and drunken songs, there was nothing more…

Strange…

Shaking my head, I continued walking when I stopped, turning my attention down a narrower cobbled path. My mind was telling me to head to the tavern, but my instincts were telling me to walk down that dark alley. I hesitated, trying to brush the feeling off again, but it came even stronger. No, I had to check it out.

I silently hurried down the path, not even stopping, just following my instinct. Goddess, did I wish I had the mind link.

Wait, I should do this carefully… I took out my two daggers, placing my package on the ground in a niche between two walls for safekeeping before I continued down the dark streets.

The sound of the men on the streets and music had faded to a distant hum. Soon it even stopped. I carried on, and by then, I had forgotten where I was going or my way back. I stopped, looking around, and wondered if I should turn back when suddenly a strangled sob reached my ears. My heart thumped as I spun back around. There was someone down there.

A mix of terrifying thoughts filled my head, and I silently hurried along, trying to keep my heartbeat as calm as possible, praying that it was just someone who had hurt themselves, but the moment I heard the sound of gruff laughter, my stomach sank. The worst thought was coming to me. Nikolai and Kyson's faces leered in my head, making me feel sick.

I slowed down when I saw the glow of light ahead. Keeping close to the walls, I peered out into the small opening.

"That's it, get that one right there," one of the men muttered. A muffled shriek of pain followed.

"Oh, shut her the fuck up!" Another rough voice came.

It took me a moment to realise what was happening and to comprehend the scene before me. My eyes widened in horror. Tied to a post, her arms twisted behind the post and a cloth in her mouth with tears streaming down her cheeks was none other than a Siren. Unlike the ones I had seen before, she was smaller, perhaps around twelve or thirteen. Her long brown hair fell in her face, but what made my stomach twist sickeningly was the blood that pooled heavily around her on the ground.

Poachers. Although killing Sirens was encouraged, taking their scales was a crime, but they were sold for high prices on the black market.

Her fin was nailed to the ground, making me flinch, and to top it off, two of the men were bent down next to her as they ripped out her shimmering green scales. I clamped a hand over my mouth. Yes, Sirens were monsters, but this was wrong. They should have killed her first. This was not right...

Suddenly, her green eyes snapped to mine, and despite her being gagged, I heard her voice as clearly as if she was standing next to me. Her soft, whispery voice resonated in my head,

"Help me."

The Darkness in the World

YILEYNA

What do I do? I mean, I needed to help her, but how? Doing a quick scan of the situation, I frowned. Seven men… two were mages, some werewolves, but most were fae. The fae are the one species who were immune to a Siren's song. One thing was clear; they were all dangerous. Each one of those men would kill me without a second thought, but I can't just let them do this.

"Make sure she feels the pain," an eighth man hissed, making me shudder. There was something odd about him, and I felt as if my entire body recoiled from his voice.

"Of course," another added.

How many of them were there? There was no way I'd win in a match against them all… I could count thirteen now.

This wasn't Astalion, where wolves stuck together. This was a place entirely different, with a mix of species working together, but I wouldn't let it fool me. It was only for their own goals. I almost gasped when I realised the raspy voice belonged to a Naga… my stomach churned.

If they discovered me, I'd be dead within minutes… *Think quick, Yileyna…*

Maybe if I somehow caused a distraction, I could -

Suddenly a hand clamped over my mouth, and a strong arm wrapped around my waist, lifting me off the ground as I was pulled away. I struggled. My heart was thundering in my ears, panic flaring inside of me. Did they see me?

"Calm down," my captive whispered. His warm breath on my ear made my stomach flip. I relaxed, relief flooding me. I slumped against his chest, my heart pounding hard. *Oh, thank the goddess.* "What the hell are you doing here?" He asked ever so quietly.

I turned my head, looking up at him, trying not to focus on how good his body felt against mine. *Focus, Yileyna!* Why did he make my body go crazy like this? I tried to pull free from his hold, but he didn't let go, only removing his hand from my mouth. His other hand still gripped my waist tightly.

"I heard a girl cry for help. You saw them, they're torturing her," I whispered quietly, knowing even though he had moved us away, we might still be overheard.

His amber eyes narrowed calculatingly, and he loosened his hold on me. Although I was unable to pull away, I was able to turn in his arms and look up at him, my chest crushed against his.

"You do know that she's a Siren?" He murmured; his voice was so quiet I could just about hear him.

"A young one. She doesn't deserve this," I countered.

"She will grow to become a killer."

"I know, but they are torturing her."

"Don't tell me you were about to go in there to protect one of the very monsters that have tried to kill our kind countless times?" He asked coldly.

"I… no, it's…" Yes, I was going to because I didn't think. All I saw was a young girl being tortured. "She's not even in water. Her body wouldn't become foam if they had just killed her first… so why are they doing this?"

"Because monsters deserve to be punished," he replied coldly. His eyes seemed to darken with hatred.

"Theon, she's a child," I whispered, glancing down the alley where I knew exactly what was happening.

"Who will become one soon enough."

"Innocent until proven guilty. She has done nothing."

"Yet."

"And until she has… we can't call her a monster. They are causing her so much pain."

"What do you plan to do, Yileyna? We are only passing through; we can't afford to put the rest of the pack or crew in danger," he whispered coldly.

We were so close. I didn't know when his hands went to my waist or when he had drawn my lower body entirely against his. Our faces were only inches apart, and the urge to kiss him made my core knot. The only thing keeping me sane was the concern for the young girl not far from us.

"I know, but they are torturing her." I felt torn. "Please, Theon, let's do something. She's just a defenceless child being killed by monsters." Something flickered in his eyes, and he looked away. For a moment, I actually thought he was considering it.

"Stay here," he commanded, his eyes simmering gold.

"Theon, where -" He placed a finger on my lips.

"Don't move. I'll be back." His gaze raked over my lips and breasts before he turned and walked back down the alley.

The urge to follow him was tempting, but I also didn't want to piss him off. Was Theon actually going to help her? Maybe we could toss her back into the ocean…

Shouting ensued, and then Theon was back. Alone.

"Run," he said quietly, taking my hand as he pulled me down the street. Taking a sharp left, he pulled me through an archway until we were in a narrow, neglected, small garden.

"Theon, where are we going?" He didn't respond to me, pulling me in through the open, broken door of a small, abandoned building. "Theon, where's the girl?" He looked down at me, his face emotionless as he uttered a single word that felt like a harsh slap across the face.

"Dead."

How do you respond to that? I felt as if the breath had been knocked out of me. A flashback of him telling me that my parents were dead hit me full force, and I backed away from him.

"What…"

"I killed her so that she wouldn't feel any more pain," he said, his voice cold and normal as if he had just told me the weather. I stared at him, unable to believe what he was saying.

He killed her…

No wonder there wasn't an uproar. He had just killed her. They were free to rob her of her scales…

"She was a child," I whispered, feeling my chest squeeze.

"Yileyna…" He closed the gap between us, and I backed away.

I wasn't able to understand how killing children made us any different to those Sirens. I had asked him to save her, not kill her…

"Stay away from me." I heard myself say. Like always, he didn't listen. He gripped the back of my neck with both hands, his thumbs brushing my cheeks as he cupped my face.

"What I did was the only option. At least she is no longer in pain. Sometimes death is better than a life of torture. She would have been kept as a prize, sold to the highest bidder, or even simply held prisoner until she grew more scales. The cycle would repeat until she died." His voice was low, yet his eyes bore intensely into mine.

The sounds of the men had faded, clearly not wanting to risk anyone else learning of their deeds. My irritation rose, and I felt so useless.

"Theon, are you trying to justify what you did?" I hissed, "Well, it's fucking normal for you, isn't it? You can never admit when you are wrong. All you do is believe that you are correct!"

My anger was at boiling point, and it was ready to burst. I slammed my hands against his chest, trying to push him away, but he didn't even budge. His eyes flashed gold as he let go of my face and wrapped his arms around me.

"If it was my fucking choice, I would have left her to suffer. I fucking killed her for you. I didn't give a fuck what happened to her, but for you, I put her out of her misery," he growled, one hand tangling into my hair, making my bun come undone. Anger flashed in his eyes, and it took me a moment to comprehend what he had just said.

"For me."

In his own twisted way, he thought he had done something good. I knew Theon, like most werewolves, hated Sirens. He was right… no one else would have cared… I stopped struggling, fighting back the pain that threatened to envelop me.

"She was so young," I whispered, looking down at his neck and staring at the tattoo that wrapped around it.

"Her life ended the moment she was captured. Forget about her."

I won't ever be able to forget her. The look in her eyes as she begged for help would remain in my mind.

He pulled my head close, pressing my forehead against his chest. I let him. My fists that had been hitting his chest became limp. Was I really the only one who thought like that? If that was the child of a Naga… a Fae… a rogue… I wouldn't be able to kill any of them. *Maybe everyone is right… I am not worth the Beta title…*

Was I the only one with this mentality? I closed my eyes, a memory from long ago flashing through my mind…

TEN YEARS AGO

"Dad, look! I collected daisies!" I exclaimed.

"Oh my, those are pretty! But not as pretty as my beautiful princess."

I giggled as I turned away, staring out at the field of grass that reached my knees. The sun shone brightly, making me squint to look around. The warm weather and pleasant breeze made me feel happy.

"I'll go collect buttercups now, and I will then make flower chains for the girls at the orphanage! We can give them to them when we go to donate the food Mommy is making!" I stated, about to run off when Dad caught me and pulled me into his lap, placing a big slobbery kiss on my cheek.

"That's my girl."

"Ewww, yucky!"

He chuckled, "Shall I tell you what makes me most proud of you, little one?"

"You're proud of me?" I asked, my heart leaping with happiness as I stared up at him. The corner of his eyes crinkled, and his laughter lines from smiling so much were prominent on his face.

"I am always proud of you, but what I'm most proud of is your pure heart," he said, tapping two fingers gently on the centre of my chest. "I am proud of how you always think of others. Don't let that ever change." I clambered out of his lap, tilting my head as I bent down, searching for little yellow buttercups.

"How will that change, Dad? You always teach me to be kind to others."

"Life changes us… growing up changes us…" He sighed heavily, and I felt confused before he smiled once more. "Always follow your heart, little one. No matter how dark the future looks, I know my little princess has the purest of hearts out there." Hmm, that all sounded so confusing.

"Don't worry, Daddy, I will always follow my heart."

"Good, promise me you will always be that light in the darkest of places." Daddy doesn't make any sense…

"I will always help and care for those who have no one, I promise, okay?"

"Okay!"

Life wasn't as happy as it seemed long ago… but I promised him to always follow my heart. To bring light to the dark. Dad had more faith in me than I deserved…

I closed my eyes, listening to the beating of Theon's heart. Light to darkness… Theon had a darkness in him, anger that seemed to consume him. Why was I drawn to him? Why did I wish to stay in his arms forever, even though I knew it wasn't the smartest choice? But the way he was gently massaging the back of my head, his other hand caressing my back… he had a heart, even if it was hidden away.

"Let's go back…" I whispered, pulling away.

He gave a small nod, and we broke apart. Instantly I wished I was back in his arms. We both looked away, and a tense silence fell between us. I led the way out into the night when a sudden thought came to me. Pausing, I looked at him sharply.

"Theon, what were you doing out there?" He didn't reply, brushing past me when I grabbed hold of his arm. "Hey, I asked you a question."

"And I don't plan to reply," he replied mockingly.

"Were you following me?" I taunted mockingly. Surely when I teased him, he'd spill the truth, but to my surprise, he froze. My eyes flew open in shock. He was following me. "Why?"

"Because you have a knack for getting into trouble, remember?" He replied icily. I couldn't resist the smirk that crossed my lips as I looked up at him.

"Aww, was the mighty, heartless Theon worried about me?" I teased, raising my eyebrows suggestively. He glared at me, but his silence was enough of an answer. My heart skipped a beat as he turned away.

"Let's go get a fucking drink. You are annoying," he growled, walking off.

I nodded, although he couldn't see me. I followed him, unable to stop the flutter of my heartbeat or the glimmer of hope that settled into the pit of my stomach. No matter how much he denied it, there was a part of him that cared.

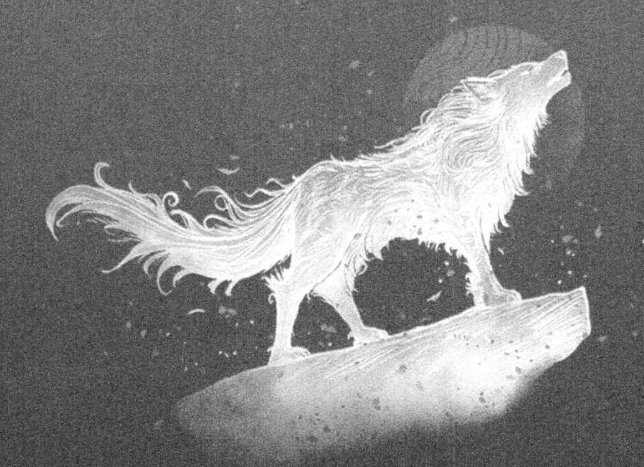

Losing his Control

YILEYNA

"And then I cut off his tail before slaying him on the spot!"

"Bravo!"

That story was overly exaggerated… I resisted rolling my eyes as I drank my tankard of ale. Theon and I were at the Tavern, and although I was enjoying listening to the stories, some were a little too overly colourful. We had faced a Kraken and Sirens, but it hadn't been colourful, although it was an adventure.

"He's lying right out of his ass," someone scoffed, making a rumble of laughter go through the room.

"What did you just say, you rotten piece of dog shit?" The werewolf who had been speaking growled.

"Alright, boys, play nice, or I'm kicking you all out," the buxom, middle-aged owner of the tavern warned, pouring a few drinks. She was a pretty woman with brown curls and hazel eyes. Her top left her cleavage on show. Like the rest of the ladies serving here, her outfit was provocative, and the men didn't hide their approval of seeing the women sashaying their hips around teasingly.

"Why can't they have any handsome, shirtless men serving?" I remarked without thinking, then sighed as another woman walked past. Theon, who was sitting opposite me, looked up at me, his face emotionless as ever.

"You really do like perving at people, don't you?" He asked me.

"Don't you?" I countered with a pout.

"Not really," he remarked, his eyes flickering to my breasts. I had my elbows on the table, and I was sure he was getting a pretty good view.

"Only at certain people, it seems."

"Yeah, unlike you, who seems to obviously love staring at anything with a dick, I don't feel the need to look at everyone with a pair of breasts," he replied mockingly.

"I don't look at everything with a dick…" I shuddered at the thought. "I only like to look at them if they are incredibly handsome, with the perfect body that was carved to precision, covered in ink that only makes them look like a sculpture of art… oh, and if they have the perfect jawline and eyes… eyes that burn into my soul."

Theon. I was describing him. Yes, I looked at a fine specimen if they walked past, yet none made my heart skip the way he did. None made my core clench in a desire that only he awakened, and none made me drown in emotions that were so intense I couldn't think straight. He was the one that still called to me, but I couldn't go down that path. Not until I knew what I meant to him, and above all, for him to realise what he truly wanted…

I looked down at the tankard clutched in my hands; we were so different… would we ever be more? Could we ever be more? And I didn't mean just the agreement.

Stop it, Yileyna, you ended it for a reason.

Shaking my head, I pushed the thoughts away and glanced over at the playing instruments, and a woman sat on a stool as she sang. She was beautiful, with ebony skin and dark, lush curls that fell to her shoulders. Her voice was stunning, but I couldn't make out what species she was. Perhaps a hybrid of some sort…

A new tune began, and it was much deeper and darker than the previous ones. Even the rowdy men became slightly silent as they listened to the music, a few of them singing along or tapping their feet to the music.

"Treat me like your last breath, treat me like your last poison… I want to be your addiction even if it kills me…"

I felt Theon's intense gaze on me, but I didn't look at him, knowing if I did, I would once again fall captive to those amber eyes of his. I ran my fingers through my hair that he had made come undone earlier.

"Mind if I buy your friend a drink?" I turned to see a handsome yet rugged man standing next to Theon, and although he was addressing Theon, his piercing dark eyes were fixed on me.

"Move along," Theon replied coldly, not even sparing him a glance. Wasn't it my choice to make that decision?

"I see no harm in it. It's not like you two are together," the man pushed, clearly not bothered by Theon's hostility. Theon's frown deepened. Although we weren't together, something about trying to make him jealous no longer appealed to me.

"I already have a drink, thank you," I replied, holding up my tankard. He gave me a smirk, but it was the way his gaze leered over me that made my skin crawl.

"Well, I'm sure you can hold a lot more than just one drink in that pretty little body -"

A menacing growl filled the room, cutting him off as Theon grabbed his throat, slamming him up against the wall. My heart thumped, not expecting that. The singer had stopped, and silence filled the room as everyone stared at Theon. So much for passing through.

"You will watch how you talk to her," Theon hissed, his grip tightening on the man's neck.

"Don't give me that. No decent woman comes into a place like this in the middle of the night if she's a good one," the man smirked, clearly not scared. Wrong answer, mister.

"She's with me, and even if she was alone, degrade her in any fucking way, and you will answer to me." Theon's voice was dark and cold, the rage in it sending a chill down my spine. I needed to step in.

"Theon, let's leave," I said, standing up and walking around the table. I knew Theon's anger, but these men didn't. Pissing him off after a warning didn't fare well.

"Why the rush, sweet tits? I'm -"

Blood.

Blood splattered across me, the smell strong in the air as I stood there frozen in shock. Theon had just ripped his throat out, letting blood splatter everywhere.

A ripple of shock rushed through the room, my heart thundering as the weight of the situation dropped on me. This was not the plan. He was telling me about laying low! He had just killed someone in a room full of witnesses!

Theon let the body fall to the ground mercilessly, placing his foot on the man's chest as he took his last breaths, his body spasming before it stilled. Theon bent down, wiping his hand on the man's shirt before he reached over, picking up his tankard with his bloodstained hand. Downing the rest of it, he placed it down with a resounding thud.

He scanned the room, his eyes still burning gold. They met mine, and suddenly it felt like my emotions had returned. My heart thundered as he reached over, wiping the blood splatters from my cheek, causing my body to react to his touch.

"Anyone else want to insult her?" He asked quietly, looking around the room once more. His voice dripped with a cold, deadly threat, and, despite the hostile looks he was getting, no one spoke. After a moment, he smirked coldly. "Good. Let's go."

Not waiting for me to respond, he tossed a few gold coins on the table, far more than our drinks were worth, but he did just leave them a body to dispose of. Taking hold of my wrist, he pulled me towards the exit.

"You don't just come here and kill who you want, son," a deep voice growled, and a huge man blocked our path. Although he was slightly shorter than Theon, I could sense the power from him.

"Try me," Theon replied coldly. I knew he meant it too.

"Step aside, Oden..." the owner said quietly.

I glanced over at her. Any playfulness that had been on her face for the last hour was gone. Oden stepped aside, and I was unable to say anything, staring at Theon's back as we stepped out into the darkness.

"What the hell was that?" I hissed the moment the tavern door shut, knowing that inside there was going to be an uproar.

"I'm sure you saw what that was. Or is your lack of brain cells now extending to lack of sight, too?" He replied, pulling me away from the tavern and inn.

"Theon! This is serious! You said to me we can't risk our mission or crew and pack members! You just killed someone in front of a group of people!" He didn't bother replying until we were down a quieter alley. I tried to pull free. He sighed, yanking me into his arms, one hand pinning my arms behind my back as he pulled me against him, chest to chest once more.

"Calm the fuck down. The difference is, I took a stand against someone insulting you; you were merely taking a stand for a monster," he replied arrogantly, his scent helping me lose focus on the coppery smell of blood that was a dark reminder of what had just taken place.

"She was being tortured, Theon. That man just insulted me! There's a huge difference!" I hissed, but despite that, I couldn't deny that my shock and panic were dissipating. Trying not to focus on the bulge in his pants that was pressing firmly against my stomach, I glared into his eyes, but his next words derailed me completely.

"You're worth is way fucking more. So yes, there is a difference."

"So… it's okay for you to insult me but not others?" I asked softly, swallowing hard despite the fact that I was losing control of my emotions.

"Pretty much," he replied arrogantly, licking his lips sexily as he looked at me challengingly. Leaning closer, his lips brushed my ear, making my breath hitch. "Because we both know you like it when I call you my little whore."

My heart was pounding. Any sense of logic had left me, and all I wanted was to rip his clothes off his body to feel him against me. I slowly looked up into those eyes that devoured me, only to see the unmasked lust in them. Neither of us cared that there was blood smeared on us or that we were in the middle of a dark alley on a dangerous island.

It was just him and I.

"Fuck me, Theon," I whispered breathlessly.

A dangerously sexy glint filled his eyes before his free hand tangled into my hair, pressing me up against the stone wall, and then he was kissing me hungrily, sending off a voltage of delicious pleasure coursing through my veins. He kissed me so deeply that it felt as if he had been deprived of something for far too long and was ready to quench that thirst…

This Pull

THEON

Her tempting scent intoxicated me. From the moment she asked me to fuck her, there was nothing else I wanted than to drown in the pleasure I had only ever felt with her. As much as I hated it, she had become a drug I craved every time I laid eyes on her.

I broke away from her plump lips, leaving her breathless as I kissed every inch of her neck, leaving my mark. We were both covered in splatters of blood, but I didn't care. I liked painting her pretty skin with colour anyway…

I ran my hand down her waist, reaching for one of the knives I carried. I let go of her arms that I had pinned behind her back, and with one flick, I cut the strings down the middle of her corset, making her gasp as it fell to the floor, leaving her in nothing more than her shirt, a shirt that did nothing to hide her stiff nipples through her skimpy bra.

The feelings that rushed through me as I pulled open her shirt and admired her almost naked body were unexplainable. Fuck, if only she knew just how strong of a fucking effect she had on me…

Her hands ran up my waist as she pressed her body fully against me. *Fuck.* I throbbed against her, twisting my hand into her hair again. I grabbed her left breast in my hand, moaning as we kissed once more.

How did we get in this position once again?

The question snuck into my mind for a moment, but when temptation was before you, offering itself to you, how do you fucking say no?

Yileyna was that temptation. From her creamy smooth skin to the way she responded to me. All women did, but there was just something so different about her whimpers of pleasure, the feel of her skin against mine, the need to mark every inch of her with my touch, and the way she looked as I pleasured her... and as much as I hated her for having this effect on me, every time we were close, there was this magnetic pull that neither of us was able to deny.

I yanked her bra down, revealing her tits, and sucked on her nipple as she leant against the wall, moaning. Her arousal scented the air, and the heat on her usually cool skin felt perfect against mine, just the way her nipple felt against my lips. I flattened my tongue against her breast, slowly letting it flick over her nipple, making her whimper in pleasure.

My eyes flashed as I ran my tongue up her neck before wrapping my hand tightly around her neck, claiming her lips in a rough, bruising kiss once more. She moaned into my mouth, her hand going to my pants. I let her, my own hand massaging her pussy, feeling the dampness already beginning to create a patch on her trousers.

"Fuck, Theon," she whimpered, gasping for breath as her gaze flickered to the large bulge in my pants. "I want to..."

My eyes flashed, tightening my hand around her neck, making her gasp. *What exactly do you want, little storm?* Her eyes darkened with obvious lust as she ran her hand over my hard cock.

"I want to have a taste," she whispered, making me smirk coldly.

"Just like the little whore you are..." I whispered, kissing her roughly and plunging my tongue into her mouth, making her moan helplessly against my touch. "Now, how about you get down and show me what this pretty little mouth can take?"

"Yes, please," she whimpered. Smirking, I shoved her to her knees, my hand still tangled in her silky hair. I pulled my dick out, making her lick her lips as her eyes roamed over it.

"I'm going to fuck you so hard that your throat's going to be fucking sore when I'm done."

Her heart pounded, but when she stuck her tongue out with need, my eyes flashed. Not waiting for an invitation, I thrust my dick into her mouth. Instantly, she wrapped her lips around me and never had she looked as fucking good as she did then. I growled, feeling white-hot pleasure sear through me, and I slammed my free hand against the wall behind her.

Her seductive grey eyes were staring back up at me, filled with such pure lust, which only made me fucking throb harder as she began sucking my dick, her head bopping with every thrust, the tip of my cock hitting her throat.

"Fuck," I muttered, thrusting harder and faster into her mouth.

She moaned, gasping as I throat fucked her. The pleasure was like intense currents rushing through me. Feeling it build up, everything else faded away. All I could focus on was us and the dam of pleasure that was building with every passing moment.

"Fuck, Yileyna, that's it."

Like the good little temptress she was, she began sucking harder, sensing I was near. Then my hips bucked, my release ripped through me like a crashing wave, and my thrusts became jerkier as I released my load into her mouth. She didn't pull away, even though my hold on her hair was looser. She simply kept sucking me off until I had to yank her back, trying not to growl at how fucking good that was.

My eyes blazed gold as I stared at her mouth, full of milky white cum. She licked her lips, swallowing it. I pulled her up and slammed her against the wall, making her gasp from the slight pain of the impact.

I slipped my thumb into her mouth, and she sucked on it despite her lips looking plumper and clearly raw. I ran it along her lips roughly before wrapping my hand around her throat once again. Sliding my other hand into her pants and massaging her dripping pussy, I thrust two fingers into her, my thumb rubbing her clit. She moaned; her eyes locked with mine.

She felt so damn good.

"Oh fuck… that's it, Theon," she whispered. Her voice sounded a little hoarse, but that was to be expected after that mouth fuck.

"Yeah?" I whispered back, my nose brushing hers, and I pressed my lips against hers. She kissed me back, moaning into my mouth as I hand fucked her harder and faster.

Her cries became louder, but I didn't give a fuck if anyone heard us. In fact, I wanted everyone to fucking know she belonged to me. She was mine, and although we kept clashing, the constant push and pull between us was never-ending. As her eyes rolled back, her face the image of pure pleasure, I realised that I needed this. Even if being a part of my life ended up killing her, I was far too selfish to let her go. She was mine to use and pleasure as I wished.

She screamed as her orgasm rocked her body. I smirked in satisfaction… I loved seeing her like this. I never bothered pleasuring anyone else. It was always taking what I wanted, but with her being so fucking sexy, watching her writhe entirely at my mercy was a pleasure in itself.

"Goddess…" She gasped as I pulled my soaking fingers out of her and tapped her ass before I wrapped my arm around her waist, supporting her shaking body.

Our shirts hung open, and our bodies had a thin layer of sweat coating them despite the coldness of the weather. Our hearts pounded as we stared at each other. Not knowing what came over me, I let go of her throat and instead caressed her cheek before cupping her face and pressing my lips against her beautiful ones.

Her eyes fluttered shut as she locked her arms around my neck, but just before I could deepen this fucking amazing kiss, I heard footsteps approaching. I pulled away, recognising the scent, and slipped my cock back into my pants before pulling Yileyna against my chest, not wanting anyone to see her in the state she was in.

What do you want? I asked through the link.

Theon, we need to leave. There's been a killing in the tavern, and… was it you? Raiden's voice asked.

Yes, it was, I replied coldly, just as I felt his presence behind us.

I looked over my shoulder, my cold eyes on him as I felt Yilena's heart beat wildly, but I refused to let her go, not missing how Raiden's gaze ran over us. I knew he could probably smell the air. If he had any fucking doubt left, he would know exactly what was happening here.

"Are you just going to stand there? Or finish whatever the fuck you were saying," I asked coldly.

"Yeah… sorry… I was actually looking for Yileyna... there's an entire group ready to kill. Everyone is already on or almost on the ship. You had your block up… I couldn't mind link…"

I was busy. Leave. We'll be on the ship within ten minutes, I replied coldly, feeling anger flare through me at the conflicted look in his eyes as he stared at the back of Yileyna's head. He nodded and turned, walking off.

I let go of her and she quickly pulled her bra up over her breasts.

"Are you in danger?" She asked, her cheeks now dusted with a faint, pretty hue of pink.

"You really are dumb. How would I be in danger? I guess we are leaving so I don't paint the entire island of Bellmead in rivers of blood," I replied coldly as I buttoned her shirt up swiftly before closing my own. Taking hold of her wrist, I led the way out of the alleyway, my mind still reeling over what we had just done.

"Wait!" She suddenly stopped.

"What is it?" I asked.

"I bought something! Can we grab it? It's not far from where you found me earlier…" I glared at her in frustration, but the hopeful look in her eyes made me agree.

"Fine."

Ten minutes later, she had grabbed the package, clutching it to her chest. She looked a mess. Her neck had my handprint around it, along with several hickeys. Her hair was ruffled, her lips looked raw and so fuckable that I was tempted to go for a second round.

"Thanks." She smiled at me, sending a flash of guilt through me, and I turned away, not replying. *I won't get too close.*

Sex was sex, and although she was the lethal poison I could never get enough of, she was also the glass vial that I didn't want to break. My stomach twisted at the thought that had just slipped through my mind, and I frowned.

I was right. I would keep her at an arms-length, well, unless I was fucking her... because if she knew my truth, I was pretty sure not only would it shatter her, it would completely destroy her.

"Come on. We better hurry," I said icily, hearing the distant shouting of the search party.

Theon! How long?

I'm there, I replied to Raiden before grabbing hold of Yileyna's wrist once more and pulling her in the direction of the sea…

Mine

YILEYNA

Back at sea, without even one night of enjoying the comfort of a warm bed, everyone on board was irritable and crabby, especially since they had to grab supplies in a rush and hadn't completed the fixing of the ship's side, let alone even getting a moment to simply sit back and enjoy a tankard of ale or mead. Luckily, they had gotten the ship mostly fixed up. The damage was minor, so it wasn't too bad.

As we moved away from the island of Bellmead, I glanced back at the lights and the dark cobbled streets, remembering the little Siren and how her scales were being harvested. That was something I wouldn't ever forget. Then, Theon killing that man, and our hot moment…

We had only been on the island for a few hours, yet so much had happened. I doubted I'd see this place again, but I wouldn't forget it.

"Someone get the luggage and supplies below deck!" Flynn growled, clearly pissed off about his day to relax being cut short.

"Aiy, Captain," Sam replied as he and three other men began taking the supplies.

"I hope your men got everything I need," Ailema murmured as she looked at the crates, peering into a few boxes.

"Not as much as you wanted, but it will do until we get to the Purien

Isles," Cleo sighed. I glanced over at her, and our eyes met before she looked me over. I suddenly felt naked being observed like this.

I had left my shirt hanging out, not wanting anyone to see the damp patch on my trousers, but without my corset and with my hair a mess, it wasn't hard to know what I had gotten up to. It was beyond embarrassing.

And Raiden, his eyes kept coming back to us, that knowing smirk on his lips never left. As for Charlene, she had been by my side, raising her eyebrows at the marks along my neck that I did my best to cover with my shirt and hair.

"So, we continue on course towards the Purien Isles. I am presuming there are no more stops before then, are there?" Flynn asked Theon.

"Yes." Flynn sighed, his irritation obvious.

"Aiy, Commander… and how long are we to stay there? We will need to fix the ship and gather supplies properly. Please don't go around killing -" Theon's cold glare turned upon him and he instantly shut up, averting his eyes.

"I don't give warnings, but this time I'll give you one. Remember who you're talking to," he said, his voice so cold I felt a shiver run down my spine, feeling his raging anger cut through the air, and I saw Flynn baulk. I almost smiled at seeing the tough captain seem to shrivel under Theon's anger. Theon was Alpha material!

I tilted my head, looking at the sexy huge man before me; tall, strong, powerful… imagine if he was the son of an Alpha and had no idea! But wait, that can't be true. We would have known if an Alpha's son was missing or something. The Alphas all come to meetings at court. They had seen Theon many times.

My sudden train of thought dissipated, and I realised it was too far-fetched. I sighed, running my hands through my hair, looking around. Everyone had gotten to work quickly after Theon's threat.

"Come on, shall we go?" Charlene asked as she nudged me.

It was obvious she just wanted the details of what had happened. I nodded, picking up my parcel as well as my bag, which had been brought on board. We began making our way towards the steps to go below deck when Ryan, who was standing with a map in hand, glanced up at us. His gaze flitted over me before he whistled quietly.

"Nikolai was saying you get around. I didn't believe him at first," he said quietly.

My heart skipped a beat thinking about Nikolai and Kyson, and it took me a second to comprehend what he had just said. I felt a rush of coldness wash through me, realising what he was just insinuating. I had only given myself to one person… that did not mean I got around. Charlene growled.

"Ryan, you are speaking -"

"To Yileyna. The rumours may be true that there's Omega blood in -"

Both Charlene and I gasped when Ryan was slammed against the nearest pole, Theon's hand wrapped against his neck tightly. Blood dripped down his neck where Theon's claws were digging into him. Anger was radiating off Theon, and the sheer weight of it was making me shudder.

"One more word. One more word, Sanchez, and King Andres will be looking for a new potential Gamma," he hissed, making my heart thump. Ryan raised his hands in surrender, his face turning a dark shade of purple as Theon cut off all his air supply.

"Theon. Stop," I said, realising that his anger was growing. He ignored me, his hand tightening around Ryan's neck.

"She's mine. Insult her one more time, and I fucking swear I will rip you apart." My eyes widened in pure shock as Theon's words resonated in my head. *She's mine.* Goddess, he said I was his…

I could see Charlene's wide green eyes staring at me from the corner of my sight, but I didn't look at her as Theon let go of Ryan. His blazing gold eyes met mine, and I was unable to stop the pounding of my heart.

I stared at him; my mouth slightly parted in shock, unable to form two words. The anger seemed to lessen, his eyes returning to their dangerous amber, and the faintest ghost of a smirk crossed his plump lips. He reached over and placed two fingers on my chin, pushing it up and forcing my mouth closed. My stomach did a somersault knowing that everyone there was watching and had heard his words.

He said I was his…

Goddess, what does he mean? His plaything… or?

I was unable to control the storm of emotions within me as he closed the gap between us and leaned down slightly.

"Keep that mouth open, and I'll put it to better use, little storm," he whispered so quietly that I just about heard him. A strong rush of heat washed through my body, making my heart skip several beats. If I died tonight, I'd die happy.

Our eyes met, and for a moment, it felt like it was just the two of us on board… he and I and nothing more than the pleasant crashing of the waves. His gaze dipped to my lips for a moment before he turned and walked away, leaving me standing there with a shell-shocked Charlene and a humiliated Ryan.

An hour later, Charlene had finally allowed me to return to my own room after she had questioned me thoroughly. It felt so surreal… even Charlene had been ecstatic at his words, saying she felt so much better knowing he was staking his claim. I had just readied for bed, wearing a thick gown as I combed my hair, trying not to smile at the fact Theon had said I was his.

I bit my lip, placing my brush down, then leaned against the wall and placed a hand on my pounding chest. Theon…

She's mine.

I smiled. Never had I felt so light and giddy as I did then. I looked at the wrapped package and was about to unwrap it when the key slipped out of the lock, and I heard the door being unlocked. I turned sharply just as Theon stood there, making my eyes widen. He still had the key…

"Have you not heard of knocking?" I asked despite the beating of my heart.

"I don't see the point of knocking when I have a key," he remarked, entering the cabin and shutting the door behind him with his foot. I did not miss how he pocketed the key as he advanced towards me. I crossed my arms, rolling my eyes.

"A stolen key. You should try being a little subtle with it," I said haughtily.

"I'm not one for subtlety, am I, little storm?" He asked, placing his hands on the wall, caging me between the walls and his muscular arms.

"No, you're not…" I said softly. The urge to ask him what he meant outside was on the tip of my tongue… but… I didn't want him to say something that may break me.

"What's wrong, little storm? At a loss for words?" He taunted, bending down.

"Not at all, just curious as to what you meant out there," I answered quietly but watched him sharply. His eyes glinted as he removed his hands from the wall and instead wrapped one around my neck, sending jolts of pleasure through me.

"Were my words not clear enough, little storm, or would you prefer I carve them into you?" My eyes widened as he held up one of his small knives with his free hand. A seductive yet predatorial smirk played on his lips.

"Theon…"

"You're mine, little storm. You will always be mine or no one's," he whispered huskily into my ear. My heart pounded as he pressed the flat side of the blade to my plump lips, my breath hitching when I felt the sharp side slice into my skin.

"Yours," I heard myself murmur, feeling the droplet of blood trickle down my lip. He leaned in, his tongue flicking along my bottom lip as he licked up the blood, making me moan.

"Good girl," came his husky reply before he tossed the dagger aside, tangling his hand into my hair and yanking my head back so he could look directly into my eyes. The dangerous glint that lingered in his eyes made my heart skip a beat. "Welcome to this world of mine that I call hell."

No matter how dark his words were, they ignited something inside of me, making my heart leap with happiness. Theon…

You said that we were heaven and hell…but I promise I'll bring light to your darkness. I'll be that ray of hope and happiness for you, even if you become my destruction… I promise.

GIRINOR

YILEYNA

"FUCK! THEON!" I WHIMPERED, trying to gasp for air as he fucked me against the wall.

He held me with ease, one hand tight around my neck, the other hooked under my knee as he rammed into me. Every thrust hit my g-spot, knocking all the air from my body. Pleasure was sizzling through me like a thousand jolts of lightning. I remember him vaguely asking if I was on any form of contraception, and I remember nodding and showing my ring. He had muttered a, "Perfect" before kissing me hard.

I tried to control my screams of pleasure, knowing that the walls weren't so thick. His lips met mine in a bruising kiss as he cut off my air entirely, squeezing my throat. Pleasure erupted within me as I reached my climax, my orgasm rushing through me. Fuck… I felt so good…

The spasms of pleasure that washed through me were euphoric, and I felt as if I was flying on cloud nine. He released his load into me, kissing my neck as he did so. My vision blackened, a sky of white dots dancing behind my closed lids.

"Fuck," he growled, placing rough kisses up my neck.

I wasn't able to respond, the aftershock of our lovemaking still igniting fireworks of pleasure through me. I felt him let my leg down, releasing his hold around my neck, his strong arms wrapping around me as he carried me to the bed. I wanted to open my eyes, but I was so… so tired…

"Yileyna…"

"Nh…" I managed to moan in reply.

"Fuck," he muttered, placing me on the bed.

No, keep holding me…

I felt the coldness touch my skin the moment he let go, and I forced my eyes open a little. He was holding one of our discarded shirts as he wiped himself down, his eyes on my pussy. My cheeks heated as I watched him pull his pants up. Goddess, he looked so… hot... I don't think that covered it. He was utterly drool-worthy.

"Give me," I murmured, holding my hand out for the shirt.

"As much as I was tempted to wipe you down, I actually enjoy watching my cum dripping out of you."

I felt my cheeks burn. The urge to press my thighs together and hide away from him was tempting, but instead, I simply parted my legs slightly, giving him an even better view. The pain that throbbed through me was a pleasant reminder of our session of hot sex. My heart was pounding as he stood over me, his eyes filled with obvious approval and hunger.

"Keep it up, little storm. I'm ready to tear you up," he growled, climbing on top of me. I bit my lip, locking my arms around his neck and smiling softly.

"As tempting as teasing you sounds, I will pay attention to that threat," I replied, running my hand down his back. "So let me get my shirt so I can cover up."

"You're sleeping naked," he said, dropping onto the bed next to me, making my eyes widen in surprise.

"But…"

Our eyes met, and I knew he meant it. His gaze dipped to my breasts before he reached over and squeezed one of them. I rolled onto my side, my back to him as I bit back a moan. Goddess, I did not need to get all horny all over again. He kissed my neck before wrapping his arms around me.

"Sleep, little storm."

I smiled, nodded, and closed my eyes as I snuggled into him, in the arms of my love.

Please don't let this be just a dream.

We reached the Purien Isles a few days later.

Theon and I didn't talk much when on deck, despite his eyes always being on me. Even if I didn't catch him looking, I could sense it. When alone, there were moments when we'd make lighter conversation, but it was rare, and we usually ended up ripping each other's clothes off. Goddess, just thinking about Theon made my pussy clench.

Barbara had not been happy. Ever since Theon had made it obvious I was his, her irritation and jealousy rolled off her. She made her disdain so obviously known, but it only made Charlene want to giggle.

I yawned as we walked through the beautiful streets of the city of Girinor. The weather was warm, with a pleasant, cool breeze. The mango trees that surrounded us were full of ripe mangoes, and the urge to steal one was rather tempting. The floor was made of earth, but most of the roads were lined with flowers and rocks. The buildings were all spacious, made of a beautiful grey selenite stone that seemed to glitter when the sun hit them. I stifled a second yawn, feeling my pussy ache from last night's sex.

Goddess, Theon was a beast.

"Late night?" Charlene teased.

I smiled slightly, nudging her and poking my eyes out at her, knowing Theon could hear us as he led the way just a few feet ahead of us. She giggled and nudged me back.

We would be having a meal before we all split ways to 'explore'. Although Theon, Charlene, Madelia, and I would be going to see the mage. I could see Charlene's nervousness, the fear that she tried to mask. I knew she was scared. If this mage saw her and said she had no gift… it would break her. I was nervous, too, for her, knowing that there was so much riding on this meeting.

"This looks like a good place," Ailema remarked, staring at an open restaurant that had several long tables right outside. A low wall and a garlanded archway surrounded it welcomingly. Soft country music was playing from somewhere inside, and it really did look appealing. I just wanted to sit down and have some delicious grilled meat.

"Yes, it's perfect! Let's eat here," I suggested.

"Ah! The decision has been made," Flynn added happily.

"Commander Theon hasn't approved…" Barbara added, earning a frown from her captain.

"His lady approved; he won't say no to her, will he now?" My heart skipped a beat as everyone looked at Theon. He simply gave Flynn a cold glare.

"You're too fucking loud," he replied icily before leading the way through the small archway that was at the entrance to the restaurant area. He had to bend down to get through, and I tried not to smile as we all followed him in. He didn't argue with my choice…

We were all taking our seats along one of the long tables, and I was sitting next to Charlene. To my surprise, Theon took the seat on my other side, making my heart skip a beat. I looked up at him, grey eyes meeting amber ones, and I felt my stomach flutter. He raised his eyebrows questioningly at me, and I shook my head, fixing the strap to my sky-blue corset bustier. The weather was warm, and I had opted not to wear multiple layers. I was wearing cropped white pants with it, and my hair was in a high ponytail. Charlene and I had spent quite a while trying to cover up all the marks that Theon loved to leave on me; I knew by nightfall, they would fade away only for him to create many more.

I saw his gaze flicker to my cleavage before he looked away after a moment. His arm brushed mine, and I felt the tingle of pleasure make goosebumps rise on my skin. But there was something that could dampen my spirits; to my utter dismay, Barbara took the seat on his other side. I resisted the urge to sigh in frustration.

"Hello and welcome to Girinor, and we pronounce that Jee-ree-nor! Now, what can I get everyone on this fine afternoon? I am Oliver, and I see the journey was long, and many of you look rather tired!" A cheerful young man said as he stood by our table with some menu cards in hand and a small notebook and pen.

"Thank you for the nice welcome, son. We are all ravenous, and I am hoping you keep the food coming because most of us eat like a pack of wolves!" Ailema grinned, clearly happy with her joke. All the men save Theon chuckled.

"Ah, of course, and we will. Please check the menu, and when you have chosen, we will make sure the food supply is endless!" He left rather quickly, and I had a good idea he was about to tell everyone who worked here that a huge order was on its way.

"The weather is really nice. It's actually lovely to be able to simply enjoy the warmth," Barbara commented, brushing her hair over her opposite shoulder and giving us all a view of her smooth skin. It was obvious she was trying to get Theon's attention. What an annoying woman…

"The weather sure is, although it will get colder as the days pass," Leto agreed, looking up at the sky that had scarcely any clouds.

"Then we should enjoy it whilst it lasts. I swear I prefer the sea to land any day," Cleo remarked as the waiter returned with a tray holding jugs of iced juice. Oh, that looked divine!

"I love the sea too, but a small break harms no one now, does it?" Flynn added.

"True, I love the sea, but I love the land as well. I think I'm a mix of loving both," I added.

"I prefer land," Charlene said with a small smile. "I mean, I don't mind a swim, but the sea is not for me." I nodded. Not everyone was a water person, and that was their preference, even if I didn't understand it.

"Now these fish platters..." Sam mused.

"And the meat grills," Valentin added.

"Okay, we need a mix of everything on the menu, I'd say," Bobbie, who didn't talk much, added.

We all talked and discussed the menu, deciding what to eat, aside from Theon, who sat there emotionlessly, not bothering to join in on the conversation or to give his input.

When the first batches of grilled seafood and meat platters arrived, we all started helping ourselves. Theon didn't join in, waiting for those around him to help themselves. Seeing this, I decided to put some on his plate, but just when I was about to add some fish, Barbara also had the same idea, picking up some crab and placing it on his plate at the same time as me. We both stared at each other, still holding the fish and crab with the tongs as our eyes met. I felt a pang of irritation as she let go of the crab, placing it on his plate and casting me a small annoying smirk.

"Would you like some salad, Theon?" She asked, giving him a flirty smile. The urge to grab the salad bowl and dunk it on her head was truly very appealing.

"I'm sure he can help himself, Barb," Cleo added as Theon ignored her and picked up his fork.

Please don't eat the dumb crab...

I tried to remain passive as I placed some fish and grilled meat cubes on my own plate. To my utter dismay, Theon stabbed his fork into the crab, making my stomach plummet with disappointment. To make matters worse, the victorious smile on Barbara's face felt like a slap across the face.

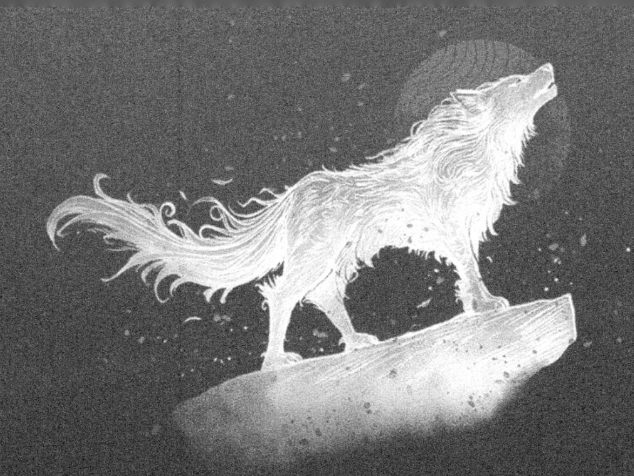

The Mage

YILEYNA

Trying to remain indifferent, I grabbed the jug and poured myself some juice just as Theon lifted the crab. Rather than eating it, he used his knife to push it off his fork, letting it fall rather unceremoniously back onto the platter, tossing his knife back down onto the table. His irritation was clear in his actions.

"Don't push my fucking boundaries," Theon's icy voice warned, and the anger that radiated off of him made the entire table fall silent, but despite the tension that settled around the group, I couldn't help but feel happy. I was about to put the jug down when Theon reached over and took the glass I had just filled up.

"That was mine," I said, poking my eyes out.

"Now it's mine," he replied with an 'I don't give a fuck' look, gulping down half of the juice in the glass and placing it down again.

"Everything is yours," I muttered, but despite my mock annoyance, my heart was soaring.

"Yeah, it is."

Our eyes met, and my heart pounded. Like always, his gaze consumed me. I turned back to my food just as he took the fish I had placed on his plate and bit into it. I couldn't stop the smile from crossing my face and turned towards Charlene, who was watching with eyes wide open in excitement, and I knew she wanted to squeal with happiness. I did my best not to look at Barbara, although I did want to see her expression. Oh well, we can't have everything we want.

Feeling far more content, I decided to enjoy the delicious meal before me...

A while later, after we had all eaten a lot, Oliver wasn't as jolly as he was by the end of our meal and the poor man looked as if he had run a hundred miles. Well, that is what happens when you have twenty or so customers, and the majority are all werewolves. We could eat for Astalion itself!

The mood that had settled over us during lunch was gone, the severity of the reason behind this journey weighing down upon us. Theon was quiet, and Madelia was frowning deeply.

"This mage, will he do a spell of some sort?" Charlene asked the two who were walking slightly ahead.

"No, he is in no health to perform any magic. He is a seer. He may not have the sight to see anything of this world, but he sees what we cannot. Now, Princess... please do not ask such questions out in the open."

"Yeah, I -"

"As future Alpha, shouldn't you know that without having to be told?" Theon asked, his voice cold and that familiar hatred seeping into it once more. How had I never noticed that hatred towards Charlene before?

"Okay, calm down," I said, frowning at his back and glancing at Charlene. I hooked my arm around hers and rested my head on her shoulder. "She gets it."

He cast one look over his shoulder, and Goddess, if looks could kill, we would both be dead. The rest of the walk there was quiet, with the steep hills becoming tiring, and soon I was beginning to feel it in my calves.

We had been going on for ages. Theon and Madelia seemed to have been given some sort of direction because they were not asking anyone for any help, help I do think they needed because, at times, they seemed to stop and ponder over the small letter in hand.

"How much longer?" I asked when my foot skidded on some pebbles, and I glared at the narrow rocky path.

"Not long, but if you didn't get relaxed with your training, this would have been a pretty easy trip," Theon's cocky voice came.

"Oh, please, this has got nothing to do with my training. It's been forever. Do you two even know where we're headed?" I asked, my voice equally icy. I was met with no answer. Theon obviously didn't think I needed an answer, but even Madelia decided to ignore me. I stayed silent after that, deciding to ignore Theon.

After another hour, we finally reached the home of the mage. It reminded me more of a shrine. The nervousness and seriousness of the situation settled back in me, and I took Charlene's hand as we made our way to the entrance.

"Welcome to Master Wenyu's home," a young man greeted, bowing deeply.

"Thank you, may we see him? How is his health?" Madelia asked politely as he led us inside. I wondered if the Alpha sent her to at least have some courtesy because Theon clearly lacked that.

"The master will be happy to have you here," the man replied. "His health is deteriorating very fast..." The gravity of his words was obvious, and I knew the man we were to see would not live for much longer.

We followed him down the wooden-panelled halls. The floors were covered with rugs with modest patterns, and the smell of orchids and mangoes filled the air. Beside me, I could feel Charlene's body shaking with nerves. I gave her clammy palm a slight squeeze. I looked at her and gave her a smile of encouragement.

"I'm here with you," I whispered as quietly as possible, not wanting anyone else to hear, although I was sure Theon probably could. She nodded, forcing a small smile that didn't take away the worry in her eyes.

"Always."

I nodded, then looked ahead to see Madelia and Theon had stopped outside a door. The man who was accompanying us had gone into the room, closing the door behind him and telling us to wait a moment.

"You knew him?" Theon asked Madelia. She nodded, looking around the hallway.

"Yes. Before he retired up here, he was my mentor." She explained, "I was raised and taught by him from the day I was found at an orphanage." Theon simply gave a small nod in reply before the door opened, and the man stood aside.

"Come on in."

Theon led the way in. Even when he was simply calm, he oozed dominance and power. The moment I entered the room, my heart sank at the state of the man on the bed. He was far frailer than I had imagined. His breathing was heavy, and his milky white eyes were staring at the ceiling.

"Welcome to my home," he rasped, holding his hand out.

Theon walked around to the left side of the bed. He seemed tenser. It was obvious the weight of what we were there for was getting to everyone. He stepped back, his arms crossed, and allowed Madelia to step forward.

"Master Wenyu," Madelia murmured, taking the mage's outstretched hand and kissing it. It was obvious the woman was near tears as she did her best to remain composed.

"Madelia… I may see many things, but I did not think I would have the happiness of meeting you once more. A royal mage to House Aphelion… it is no small feat. I am proud, I am proud…"

"Thank you, master, it is all your teachings. Today we are here, as you know -"

"Archeron, leave us," Wenyu cut in.

The man who had led us here bowed his head before he left the room, the door shutting behind him with a quiet click.

"I know why you are here. I received Alpha King Andres's message," Wenyu added as Theon jerked his head at Charlene to step forward. She didn't let go of my hand, holding it painfully tight. Goddess, shifted wolves were so powerful! *No wonder they say I'm lacking!*

We both stepped around the other side of the bed to Madelia and Theon, whilst Wenyu turned his gaze towards us.

"Does she have the gift, Master?" Madelia asked quietly.

Charlene stared at the blind man in bed. His unseeing eyes seemed to bore into us. Even I felt myself becoming unsettled as his gaze didn't shift.

"She has the gift. It dazzles brighter than the sun," Wenyu proclaimed, making both Charlene and I let out a breath of relief as I hugged her tightly. Her heart was pounding, but the look of relief on her face made me smile.

"That's perfect!" Madelia exclaimed, turning to Theon, who was frowning. His jaw was taught, and his eyes were sharp and cold as he stared at Charlene. Well, I bet it must hurt knowing the one you insulted is the heart of our world. I smirked smugly before winking at Charlene.

"However, it is not all good news…"

"What is it?" I asked, my heart pounding.

"The power is suppressed. There is a seal stronger than anything I have seen upon her… I have not seen magic of this kind..."

"You're saying her powers are blocked?" Theon asked, frowning sharply.

"Yes… and I am afraid I have no idea of what will undo it. You must find the one who cast it…" His eyes fluttered shut, and his breathing became shallow before he began coughing violently.

"Master!" Madelia shouted in panic.

I grabbed the silver jug from near the bed, biting into my lip as the silver stung my skin, and poured him a glass of water whilst Madelia helped him sit up. Charlene rushed to the door to get help. Only Theon stood there unmoving. Wenyu gulped some down, his coughing easing as Archeron returned with Charlene. He rushed to his master's side, and only when Wenyu settled back against his pillows did he step away from the bed.

"We will take our leave," Madelia said, although it was obvious that she didn't want to leave.

"Yes… I will rest." Wenyu said.

"We'll give you a moment," I told Madelia, knowing she at least needed a few moments to bid her master and mentor a final goodbye…

Theon left the room first, with Charlene and I following behind him. We had just reached the door when Wenyu spoke once more, making me pause in the doorway.

"Remember, the heart of Kaeladia belongs to all…"

Colours

YILEYNA

We were heading back down the rocky path when Theon grabbed my wrist, making me gasp as he turned my hand, palm upwards.

"What is it?" I asked, trying to ignore the tingles I felt at his touch and how close he was standing. He frowned as he uncurled my fingers before looking up at me after a moment.

"I thought the silver jug would have burned you."

"I don't think it was fully silver, it only stung a little," I replied, my heart skipping a beat, and I couldn't resist smirking as I looked up into those smouldering amber eyes. "Were you worried about me?" I added teasingly as I leaned into him, placing my free hand on his chest. My heart pounded as our gaze locked.

His eyes narrowed, and he wrapped a hand around my neck, making me gasp. I could see Madelia and Charlene watching us, and when Theon bent down, his lips brushing my ear, I tried not to sigh in pleasure.

"No, I just don't want a burned hand wrapped around my cock later," he replied arrogantly before letting go of me. Oh, whatever, that was a total lie. We both knew it would have healed by nightfall…

"So, what now, Beta?" Madelia asked as we all continued trudging down the path.

Beta… that title used for another still stung a little. I wanted to prove my worth… but with Theon as the new beta-to-be… I felt… confused.

"Did he say anything more after we left the room?" Theon asked, ignoring her question.

"Nothing regarding the prophecy or Charlene. We just said goodbye," Madelia replied, trying to remain emotionless and professional despite the sadness in her eyes.

"He saw the gift in her but said it's sealed. The question is, who would have done that?"

"I'm afraid the mages closest to the king will be questioned now. I fear what this will do to the court," Madelia replied, her worry clear.

"Either way, it's not something small that we can just brush over. It needs to be thoroughly looked into. Besides, he said it was magic he doesn't fucking recognise; I don't see how it can be a mage then," Theon replied coldly. "It might actually explain why the princess is pretty much useless." I was about to speak when Charlene grabbed my arm and shook her head.

"He has a point," she said quietly.

"It doesn't mean he needs to be harsh," I grumbled.

"The princess has an excuse. What's yours?" He asked icily, looking at me over his shoulder. I glared back at him, but he had already turned away and carried on down the rocky path.

Jerk.

Charlene smiled at me.

"I'm just glad I'm not an entire disappointment," she whispered, linking arms with me.

"Power or not, you are never a disappointment," I said firmly. We smiled at each other, and Charlene raised her eyebrows at me playfully.

"So… what did he whisper in your ear that made you blush?"

"Nothing at all," I replied with a pout, trying not to think of what he had said. My cheeks turned light pink. Was it bad that I was looking forward to tonight? She laughed at my expression. I shook my head as we carried on down the path.

I was relieved, knowing what this meant to Charlene, and the fact her powers were sealed meant they couldn't keep pushing her so ruthlessly in training. The king and Theon had to just find a way to break the seal.

Evening had fallen, and we would be here in Girinor until the day after tomorrow. The ship would be fixed, and supplies would be fully stocked. Currently, Charlene, Ryan, Raiden, Theon, and I were sitting together, with the rest being given a little time off to enjoy themselves. Both Charlene and I were wearing matching dresses we had purchased earlier.

Charlene's was a pretty mint net with little metallic hearts all over it. The skirt was full, and it reached above her knees with a matching net sash. The bottom layer was strapless with a slight sweetheart neckline and ruched balloon sleeves in the net. Mine was made of the same fabric but in sky blue. It was a halter neck with a cut-out section between my breasts, the waist was fitted with a thin leather belt, and the skirt was full like Charlene's with an extra little ruched trim at the bottom. We both wore very similar heels and had our hair styled with a double braid crown and the rest curled.

When we had stepped out of the hotel room hand in hand, it was obvious that all three men weren't able to keep their eyes off us. Theon's eyes had flashed gold as they had raked over me. I felt good, knowing that his eyes were for me and me alone. I just hoped he'd open up a little too…

"I think we have eaten far too much," Raiden said as he ate the cube of grilled meat.

"And yet you are still eating," Ryan remarked, drinking some of his juice.

"Well, we deserve it."

"I think we all do," Charlene agreed as she sipped her water. I was sitting between Theon and her, with the two future Gammas opposite, and although Theon had barely said a few words, his scent and closeness made me happy.

"So, did you guys get what you needed done?" Raiden asked lightly.

Theon nodded as he leaned over, taking a lamb chop from the platter just as I reached over for my glass. Our arms knocked together, and he looked down at me, a cold glare on his face, but instead of my face, his gaze fell on my breasts. He clenched his jaw, looking away as if nothing had happened. *Yes, remember you love these.* I smiled slightly, taking my glass.

"Let's play a little game," Charlene suggested.

"A game? Like?" Ryan asked, raising an eyebrow curiously.

"Ten questions." Charlene smiled. "We spin this empty bottle. Whoever it lands on can ask the other person a question, and if you don't want to answer, we take a strong shot of this Girinor special alcohol."

"Sure, I wouldn't mind knowing a little more about the pretty ladies," Raiden winked. I smiled back, despite knowing Theon would get riled up pretty fast if Raiden continued to flirt, even if it was subtle and just playful.

"Sure, why not?" Ryan shrugged.

"And of course, I'm in," I said, smiling as Charlene cleared a spot on the table, spinning the small bottle. We all watched it as it stopped on Raiden, and Charlene smiled.

"Okay, Raiden! As it's the first question, I'll go easy on you; favourite colour?"

"I always thought it was blue, but then one day I realised there is a shade of grey that is the most beautiful that I've ever seen." He smiled, his eyes fixed on mine, and I don't think anyone needed him to explain what he meant. I felt Theon's irritation as the other two stared at me.

"Nice... um, okay, your turn, spin the bottle!" Charlene said quickly, glancing at Theon. Raiden smirked as he spun it. It landed on Theon, and his smile only grew.

"Theon, what's your favourite colour?" He asked, and I knew he was trying to get a reaction from him. Honestly, did these men have to get all cocky? Theon gave him a scathing glare as he cocked a brow.

"I don't remember saying I was fucking participating," he replied icily.

"Oh, come on, it isn't that bad. Loosen up," Ryan added. Although they weren't intoxicated, they were still a little looser tongued than normal. I hoped it didn't get them into trouble.

"Red. Want to know why?" Theon asked coldly.

"I have some ideas, but do enlighten me," Raiden asked, amusement dancing in his eyes. Theon's eyes blazed, dark, cold anger radiating off him, and before he even spoke, I had a feeling none of us would like the answer...

"It's the colour of blood, and I would love nothing more than to paint this entire restaurant in yours."

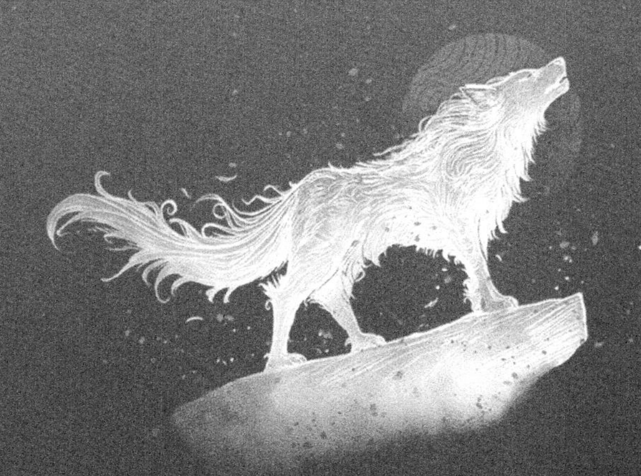

This Feeling

YILEYNA

Raiden still managed a small smile despite the threat that was spoken in a tone so poisonous that we all felt it. He picked up his cup, taking a rather big swig, and cleared his throat.

"I think I like the interior colour they already have here," he said lightly, looking around the restaurant. Theon didn't reply, simply sitting back as he was and looking as cold and uncaring as always.

"So… your turn?" I said, looking at Theon. His cold glare turned on me, his eyes flashing gold, making my heart skip a beat.

"You do it. Like I said, I'm not playing," he said, and to my surprise, he reached over and ran his knuckles down my cheek, making my heart pound as he left tingles in his wake. "You looked pretty beautiful with blood smeared all over you too." His eyes dipped to my lap, making my cheeks burn as I realised what he was hinting at. My virginity.

He was getting back at Raiden, that was obvious. I looked away, brushing a curl over my shoulder and turned towards Charlene only for Theon's hand to wrap around my neck, tilting my head backwards until it hit his chest, and then his lips met mine, sending dangerously delicious sparks of pleasure through me. Even though I was far too shocked, my lips automatically moved against his, and when his other hand wrapped around my waist possessively, making my core clench, I wasn't able to pull away. His touch and caress, like always, were irresistible…

"Damn," Ryan remarked lightly. "I think I need to find myself a lady for the night."

Theon finally let go, leaving me a giddy mess as he indifferently picked up some more meat from the platter.

"Well, that was a clear point made," Raiden smirked as he raised his glass. "To Yileyna and Theon, our Beta couple." He winked at me, and I smiled slightly.

Beta couple… it sounded… odd. We were something, but what that was, I had no name for it. I reached for the bottle and spun it, waiting for it to stop. It finally slowed and landed on Ryan.

"Ryan… what is your worst fear?" I asked after a moment.

"I have none," he scoffed. I raised an eyebrow.

"Really, I don't think that's true," I said suspiciously.

"Yeah, we all have fears," Raiden agreed, whilst Charlene nodded her agreement.

"You can tell us. We are only the future heads of the Silver Moon Pack. Your secret is safe with us," she encouraged him gently. Ryan simply took his small cup, filled it with the strong alcohol mix, and downed it in one go.

"Right, I took my shot." He glared at us as Raiden and I jeered.

"That was silly of you! It was just your fear," Raiden scolded.

"Yes, you are no fun!" I agreed as Ryan simply gave Raiden the finger and spun the bottle…

Much later, we had all left the restaurant together, and I was still mustering my courage to ask Theon if we could go for a walk because I knew the moment we were in our room, there would be nothing but us submitting to our desires.

Theon had actually booked us a room together this time, and I had to admit it made me happy to know I wasn't just a secret of his to hide. Despite some of the men lightly teasing or joking with Theon, none pushed it, knowing that although Theon didn't give a reaction, he could flip in seconds.

We were about to walk up the stairs to our floor when I grabbed hold of his arm, making his gaze snap to me. I glanced at the other three, who had stopped, but I didn't speak, waiting for them to get to their rooms.

"Make sure the princess's room is watched," Theon commanded emotionlessly. Raiden nodded as all three continued up, and Charlene gave me a small wave. Once they had disappeared from sight, I turned back to Theon.

"Umm, could we… go for a walk?" I asked quietly, although we were alone. Suddenly, it felt like a test. If he refused, I was nothing more than his sex doll, and if he agreed… just the thought made my heart skip a beat, a ray of hope flitting through me.

He didn't reply, turning around and walking back towards the entrance. I smiled, happiness rushing through me as I hurried to keep up with him. He had stopped outside the front doors, and I came to an abrupt stop so I didn't go slamming into his back. He gave me a cold smirk as I glared at him knowing he found it amusing.

"What's the rush?" He mocked, carrying on down the path.

"Well, if you were a gentleman, you could have walked a little slower," I retorted. He raised an eyebrow.

"I never said I was a gentleman, and we both know it's not a gentleman you crave," he replied arrogantly, making my stomach flip.

"Hmm… true. You win this round."

Because you agreed to the walk.

I smiled, wanting to lean into him, but I didn't move, walking beside him with no destination in mind. The wind whispered past us in a pleasant breeze, and the occasional person walking past cast a curious gaze our way. It was obvious that we were foreigners in this city.

"Theon…"

"Hmm?"

"Do you ever wonder where you are from? Or if you had a family?" I asked bravely. A frown flitted across his face, but he kept moving.

"What's the point in delving into something that I don't have?" He asked, his voice emotionless and hard.

"You must have had one somewhere… maybe they thought you had died," I persisted gently. He clenched his jaw.

"Or they're dead already." His eyes were cold and hard as he stared ahead.

"What if -"

"If I had a family, Yileyna, wouldn't they have come to look for me?" He had stopped now, glaring coldly into my eyes.

"Maybe they actually thought -"

"I am not having this conversation. Drop it."

"I'm only saying, what if you have a family out there? Maybe we can try -"

"I have no one." His cold words clenched my heart painfully, and I could almost feel the agony in his voice.

"That's not true. You have me," I whispered, placing my hand on his chest. I was ready for his anger, for him to push me away or to scoff that I was nothing to him, but instead, he just looked... uncertain. His eyes held several emotions before he looked away. "Theon..."

I had lost my family too. The pain of losing almost everyone you love and feeling alone was something I understood.

"Don't tie yourself to me, little storm. You will only regret it," he said quietly.

"It's far too late for that, Theon... I..." My heart pounded, my nerves making me feel sick as I grasped onto the front of his shirt as he tried to turn away from me. "I love you."

There, I said it. My heart was thumping with nerves. I admitted my feelings, feelings I never knew were so strong until that very moment. A flicker of surprise crossed his face before he frowned deeply and shook his head.

"You don't know what love is. Trust me, this infatuation with me is not love. One day, both of us will wake up and realise that that was all it was... a fleeting moment of infatuation." He ran his fingers through my hair, slight tugging on my braids and threading his fingers into the locks at the nape of my neck. "Don't add meaningless names to this, Yileyna, because in the end, it's only going to hurt you."

Don't add meaningless names... but it wasn't meaningless... I knew, in his own way, that he cared and that I had truly fallen for him.

"Theon, my feelings won't change. I know what I'm feeling, and it's my choice," I whispered, but something about the look on his face told me I was losing this conversation.

"Nothing is forever, little storm. Nothing."

"Theon -"

He cut me off, cupping my chin with his free hand before claiming my lips in a sizzling passionate kiss...

Think what you want, Theon, believe what you want, but this was my decision. I could love whomever I wanted, and my heart chose to love you... I'll stay silent. If those are words you don't want to hear, then that's fine. I'll show you through my actions. I'll express my feelings for you in ways that don't include me speaking those words...

I promise you.

The King's Decision

YILEYNA

I OPENED MY EYES AND smiled, seeing Theon lying there, his eyes closed, his one arm under his head, the other one loosely draped over his chiselled stomach. Sexy, hot, and absolutely divine from every angle. I had a god in my bed, and I was not complaining, or more like he had me in his bed, considering this was his cabin.

I looked around the room and smiled. We were finally home.

We had arrived late the night before and had all retreated to bed. The journey back had taken eleven days. In that time, there had been three attacks on the ship, but to everyone's shock, we had made it back without anyone dying or being seriously injured. Everyone joked that having the Alpha King's daughter on board must have brought us luck. It was obvious that life at sea was extremely dangerous, and in the last decade, the number of ships lost at sea only grew, but it was clear that luck had been on our side for this journey.

I lifted my head, rolling onto my side so I could look at his handsome face, and propped myself up on my elbow. *Goddess, you sure didn't hold back when creating him...* The urge to run my fingers down his jaw overtook me, and, reaching up, I brushed my fingertips down his perfectly carved jaw, only for his hand to grab my wrist a moment later, and his eyes opened. They met mine, and I smiled, slightly tilting my head to the side.

"Morning," I said softly as he removed his arm from under his head and pulled me on top of him.

"What are you doing?" He asked, his gaze raking over my body. I was wearing a cotton shirt of his that I had pulled on after last night's shower. It had been rather cold, but to my relief, he hadn't made a remark about me sleeping naked. I guess he must have been tired after that long journey. The shirt strained against my breasts, emphasising the pinks of my areolas, making my stomach flutter as his eyes darkened.

"I was only admiring you," I replied, my eyes darkening as I tugged my hand free from his hold and bent down, letting my hair curtain our faces. "I'm rather jealous that you were given so much attention when you were created."

I kissed his neck, closing my eyes and cherishing the moment, knowing that it was one of those rare moments he seldom allowed me. I smiled as he yanked me back by my hair, and I looked into his gorgeous eyes. *See, so predictably Theon.*

"Then perhaps you need to look in the mirror and realise what true beauty is."

My heart skipped a beat. Theon never reciprocated my feelings for him that night. He never vocally said much unless we were in the throes of passion, and he'd compliment me. However, when it came to my beauty, he didn't hold back. It was obvious he found me very appealing, and that made me happy, but deep down, I wanted him to love my personality too. Love the person I was inside.

My eighteenth birthday had happened on the ship, yet only Charlene remembered it, and I had asked her not to tell anyone else. It hurt remembering what Mom and I had planned for it. I was meant to have a party, a grand one, but… it wasn't meant to be.

I don't know if Theon knew or not, but he didn't mention it. That night, I had simply told him I'd be sleeping with Charlene, and he had not even bothered replying. Yet the following day, when I had been about to say something, he had growled that tonight, I was his.

My possessive man.

I could call him mine, right? Barbara had shamelessly tried to flirt several times, but Theon hadn't given her even a moment of attention, so it was clear he only had eyes for me, right?

"Oh, I know I'm beautiful, and I don't need to look in the mirror for that. You remind me of it often enough," I replied smugly. He narrowed his eyes, pulling me close and slapping my ass hard, sending a stinging pain through me. "Ouch."

"Don't get too cocky, or I'll have to teach you a lesson," he growled, kissing my neck.

Yes, please.

I blushed at the fact that I enjoyed it. I was about to say something when he kissed my lips roughly, flipping us over so he was straddling me. I gasped against his lips as his hands slipped under my top, squeezing my breasts hard. I moaned loudly, feeling my core throb when suddenly he pulled away, irritation clear on his face.

"What is it?" I asked, my heart thumping and my entire body tingling from his touch.

"The Alpha wants us to report in," he replied coldly, tapping my thighs. He moved back before he went down between them, making me gasp when he bit my inner left thigh, sucking hard and sending pleasure coursing through me.

"Fuck!" I moaned, wanting him to devour me, but instead he moved back, a tiny arrogant smirk on his face before he turned his back on me.

"As appealing as that sounds, we only have fifteen minutes before we are to meet the Alpha." Fifteen minutes?!

"Shit!" I gasped, jumping up from the bed. I rushed to my trunk and began rummaging inside for something to wear…

Twelve minutes later, I had washed up, brushed my teeth, and pulled on a black high-neck, long-sleeved tunic dress which had a slit down from my waist, with a red corset around my waist and knee-high boots. I wrapped my hair up into a bun as we walked down the palace hall, half walking, half running to keep up with Theon's pace.

Shit… I wonder if the Alpha would realise that we had been together. I'm sure we smelt of one another… Oh well, it was too late to think of that, and I wasn't a child…

"Can those legs of yours move any faster, or are they simply only good for wrapping around my waist?" Theon remarked, looking back at me. I shot him a glare.

"Well, it's not my fault your long poles for legs move so fast." I frowned. I didn't mind, though; the view of his broad back and that ass was very appealing… I just wished he would let me enjoy his body, but Theon was the type to always want control.

"Faster, little storm. If you carry on at that pace, I'll be tempted to train you myself, and I assure you, I won't take it easy."

"I know you won't, but I don't think I'd mind," I whispered as he slowed at the door to the king's office.

I reached over, about to touch his abs, when he grabbed my wrist, twisting me around and pulling me against him. My back pressed against his chest. My eyes widened, spotting the two guards that were trying to remain emotionless and professional as they guarded the king's office, but I could feel their eyes on us.

"Theon!" I hissed.

"Not everything will be pleasure, little storm," he whispered seductively.

Even pain is welcome, big boy.

I hesitated, knowing the two men could hear, and for Theon to not even care about the guards surprised me. Did he forget what people in Astalion thought of me? The daughter of traitors… didn't he care for his own reputation?

"Point taken," I whispered after a moment and tugged free from his hold. He gave me an arrogant look, knocking once on the door before simply opening it and entering the King's office. Charlene and Madelia were already there. The happiness on the king's face was obvious as he slapped a hand on Charlene's shoulder.

"I knew it. I knew it!" He said, grinning as he turned to the both of us. I shut the door as Madelia looked at Theon.

"There's more, your majesty," Madelia tried to speak, but the king just nodded.

"As long as she is the heart, then there is no fear. We just need to wake her abilities -"

"Her powers are sealed by magic that even the mage said he had never come across before," Theon cut in, his voice cold and sharp. The king's smile vanished, and he turned sharply to Madelia.

"And you didn't think to tell me that?" He growled viciously.

"I was trying to, Your Majesty. Forgive me for not stating it fast enough." She bowed her head, and I raised an eyebrow. It wasn't her fault…

"Yes, so making Charlene go through such intense and cruel training was wrong of you. She isn't the one at fault for her powers not awakening," I stated, making all eyes turn on me. Walking over to Charlene, I placed my hands on her shoulders and looked at the king, who frowned deeply. "Am I wrong, Alpha?" I challenged.

"Yes, you are. Intense emotions are often a way to break seals and barriers.

So we will continue with it. In fact, maybe we need some more extreme measures…" the king replied to my shock. Charlene tensed, her heart thundering as I stared at the king.

"What?" I asked quietly, but the king turned to Theon, clearly not bothered about my reactions or opinions.

"I am correct, am I not, Theon? What do you think we should do?"

"That is true. Intense pain or emotions can break magical seals, but there's also a risk of death," Theon said, his tone as normal as if he was stating the weather. Madelia frowned, looking at Charlene and me with concern.

"She is the heart, she won't die," the king replied briskly, crossing his arms. I shook my head, irritation rising within me. I looked at Theon. Was he really not bothered?

"Are you in agreement with this?" I asked him quietly. Our eyes met, but he just looked away indifferently, making a stab of pain go through me. I hated how he treated Charlene so coldly.

"We could perhaps look for a way to break this seal," Madelia suggested. The king shook his head dismissively.

"How? Time is short. The threat from the sea and the Obsidian Shadow Pack is growing by the day. Do you really think that we can just look for answers to something that we didn't even know was on her? Never has any mage picked up on it, and if Mage Wenyu himself has never seen such magic, the chances of finding a solution are low and an utter time waste."

"Why would someone place a seal on me to start with?" Charlene asked quietly.

"Sometimes as revenge for something our parents may have done," I said icily, clenching my jaw. I heard Madelia gasp at my ill-hidden disrespect, but the king didn't react. I dared a sneaky look at him and saw him frowning deeply.

"Has the king perhaps made an enemy that we don't know about?" Theon's emotionless voice came, and I realised his voice had become slightly softer around me. But when we were somewhere publicly, that coldness returned with full force.

To my utter surprise, the king didn't reply, running a hand through his hair, his heart beating a little faster than before, but the most shocking thing was the guilt that filled his eyes, guilt he tried to mask, but it was far too late, and with it, the blaring question left my lips before I could stop myself.

"Is there anything that comes to mind, perhaps, Alpha?"

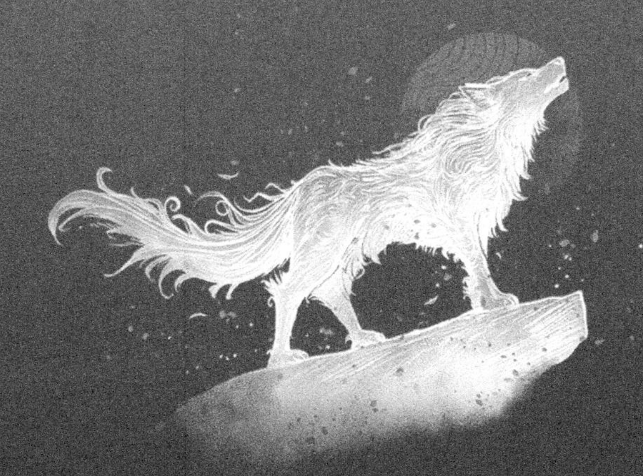

A Monster

THEON

Charlene gasped, and a tense silence fell over the room. Yileyna's question hung in the air. It was impressive how she had asked that so bravely, a question that had been on my own mind. Maybe she was losing that innocence.

I liked it.

"Nothing. I have done nothing," he said quietly, but despite his words, he frowned deeply as he swiftly walked to the window, staring out into the distance. That was not the reaction of someone who had done nothing. Andres was the type to have Yileyna thrown into the cells as a punishment for accusing him, unless of course, it hit home.

Out of the corner of my eye, I saw Charlene look up at Yileyna, poking her eyes out at her – a silent warning not to instigate the king. But the blonde bombshell simply shrugged and glanced over at me. Our eyes met, and her heart began racing.

She looked incredibly sexy in that little dress, and the way that corset wrapped her tiny waist…

I frowned, looking away. I hated how she distracted me.

The king's words before I left, regarding Charlene and myself, crossed my mind, and the fact that I had returned to Astalion in some sort of relationship with Yileyna... I was sure he wouldn't take it well, but his daughter was someone I'd never choose, even if she was the last woman left on Kaeladia.

Yileyna played with a strand of her blonde locks, catching my attention once more. Recently... there was something about her that made my mind go blank, and it irritated me. I looked away and towards Andres, watching him calculatingly.

"Maybe it was something you didn't think you did wrong... or perhaps something you don't want to talk about? But if there is something or anything that you can think of, isn't it better that we know so we can prepare rightfully for it?" I asked, emotionlessly. The king sighed, turning back towards us.

"I have many enemies, Theon, many... do you know that any pack that conquers the middle land becomes the ultimate king? I have far too many enemies..."

How many crimes did you commit for power? I resisted a scoff and nodded.

"Understood, however, by sharing it, we can work on a solution to this problem or at least be able to narrow down who may have cast a seal on the princess." He nodded, his brow furrowed.

"You women may leave," he ordered.

I almost smirked. He was trusting me... he was so concerned about a threat from the outside that he didn't even think the greatest threat had already infiltrated these walls. All I needed was to light the match and watch as the entire city burned. With every passing day... that time was coming closer.

"Father..." Charlene murmured. "As future Alpha, shouldn't I be here?"

Some Alpha she would be. There was nothing about her that was fit for that position. Sealed power or not.

"I am alive, Charlene. Leave," Andres commanded. Madelia bowed her head and listened to Andres instantly, however the other two hesitated.

"But with the threats growing, if you want Charlene to learn to be a capable leader, you should allow her to observe such matters," Yileyna added. I frowned slightly. Was it just me, or was she speaking up far more than she used to as well? I tilted my head, observing her keenly.

The day she turned eighteen, I had felt her aura. It was faint, but compared to before, it was there. I wondered if she was getting ready to shift and, with it, her wolf's presence was perhaps giving her more confidence...

either way, she was a lot mouthier than before, and I wasn't sure if it was a good thing or not...

Not that I'd mind punishing her more often if she ran that mouth...

Andres walked over to the girls and looked down at Yileyna, a cold glare on his face.

"There's something different about you," he growled, his aura rolling off him. "But I will not tolerate disrespect."

"I know, Alpha, I wasn't trying to be rude," Yileyna said quietly.

"Dad! She's right. How can I learn to be the perfect successor when I don't have any real-life experience?" Charlene asked, quickly standing up and placing herself in the line of her father's wrath, whilst my much shorter doll moved to the side so she could see the Alpha, not standing for her friend to protect her.

"You need not worry. I will find you a mate who will be capable of running this kingdom," Andres thundered, making Charlene flinch. Yileyna frowned, but when Charlene was about to leave, clearly giving up, Yileyna grabbed her arm and made her stay in her spot. Andres growled in frustration and turned to Yileyna. "You! Get out!" He shouted, his aura raging around him. A flash of anger rushed through me.

"She's staying," I said coldly before I could stop myself.

Fuck. All three turned to me, and I made sure not to even look at Yileyna. *Why the hell did I speak?*

"Why would she stay? She is nothing more than an outcast," Andres said coldly, his eyes blazing as they burnt into me.

"She's our future beta female!" Charlene blurted out, making both Yileyna and I look at her sharply.

No, she was not.

"Theon will be Beta, Charlene, and I will make sure those rules stick even when you become Alpha," he threatened. She nodded in agreement.

"Of course, Father, I mean, Yileyna is now Theon's woman, so she'll still be Beta female..."

"Charl!" Yileyna hissed, her eyes widening as she looked at me. Our eyes met, and the look of uncertainty and worry in her eyes surprised me. She acted so confident, yet...

I tilted my head, unable to resist the tiny smirk that crossed my face at the look of shock on Andres's face. I wouldn't address it, but I wouldn't deny it either.

"Can we get to business?" I asked. "We have been at sea for nearly a month, I would ideally like to go for a run and get back to my training regime."

Andres looked at his daughter, a flash of anger clear on his face before his gaze turned upon me.

I see you as a son, Theon, don't make this mistake for a woman's looks, he said icily through the link.

If I'm to take a woman, at least she should be one I find appealing. There is no use for women other than for pleasure and entertainment.

I appreciate the concern, but I would prefer it if the king did not intrude into my personal life, I replied emotionlessly. He frowned, sighing with clear irritation before he walked to his desk and took a seat behind it.

Very well, but I have been there.

I didn't bother replying to him. I saw Yileyna glance at me, but I ignored her as well, wondering what the king was about to tell us. Would he mention what he had done long ago, or did the Alpha King have a lot more skeletons in his wardrobe?

"What is said in this room stays here," he said quietly after several moments, running his hand through his straggly hair. None of us spoke as we waited for him to continue. "Many, many years ago, long before I met Soleil, I crossed paths with a woman, one who had a charm that was undeniable. It was just a short meeting, yet when I told her that was all it was, she took offence and promised that she would get her revenge for betraying her." I frowned. Sounded like a woman scorned. What had that got to do with anything? Where was this headed?

"Would she even be capable of such magic, or asking someone to get revenge in this manner? That alone doesn't seem to make sense." I stated, crossing my arms.

"Oh, she would… in her anger, she took her true form. She was no woman but a monster of the sea. A siren." The girls gasped, and my eyes widened in surprise. The king nodded, sighing heavily.

"When you said a magic that the mage did not recognise, I fear that it was from her. If that is the case, then I truly don't know any other way but to push Charlene to her limits and ultimately break the seal upon her powers."

The room fell silent, but the story just seemed… empty. Unless of course, there were parts he wasn't telling us. I glanced at the girls and then back at the king.

"Well, if we are done... if you ladies could leave, I need to discuss something with the Alpha," I said. Both girls exchanged looks before Yileyna nodded, and the king snorted, his irritation obvious as he lit himself a cigar.

"They listened to you, yet not me," he growled when the door snapped shut behind them.

"Hmm," I said, watching him sharply. "Would you like to tell me the real version of that story?" Andres froze, before looking at me hesitantly. He sat back in his seat, making it creak slightly.

"This is why I am telling you to choose your future wisely. Theon, you have great potential. I can see you as the future Alpha King." So could I, but I didn't need a woman to get that title. "Yes… I lied. That woman… monster, whatever you wish to call her, came to me when I had gone for a walk. It was night. Soleil told me she was pregnant for the third time. After two miscarriages, I was giving up hope, and I needed an outlet…"

So he didn't want to mention that fact in front of Charlene. His infidelity to his true mate was something I wasn't expecting, but then again, it wasn't so uncommon. I remained silent, letting him continue.

"She was very alluring, beautiful, and she seemed to understand what I was going through, despite obviously being rather drunk." He sounded disgusted. "One thing led to another, and even though I knew Soleil would know what was happening, I didn't care. I was angry that she was unable to even bear one child. The following day, I awoke to the water coming up to my knees, and to my horror, where her legs should have been was nothing other than a tail." I felt sick at the very thought. I was surprised he was even alive after fucking one of those monsters.

"Realising what I had done, I tried to choke her to death, but she awoke and the reality of what happened settled in. I thought I saw fear and panic in her, but she was probably acting the part as she begged for me to let her go. We struggled, but soon she managed to free herself and her true colours were revealed. She told me that I needed to take responsibility for my actions. I tried to kill her, but I failed, and she survived by jumping into the ocean and vanished. I never saw her again, but the last words she spoke were that she would get her revenge." He shook his head, and I frowned, trying to digest everything the king had just said.

Did that siren return to land to get her revenge? Wouldn't killing the king's daughter have been more suitable? If that was true… it meant she had to be from the imperial family. They were the only ones who were able to walk on land. Was that siren part of that family? I'm sure she must have been. Did they know about the prophecy? Was she able to see the gift in Charlene and sealed her powers away until they could make sure of it? There were too many questions and my knowledge wasn't enough.

"It must be her… she has a grudge…" the king's muttering brought me from my thoughts.

"So, let's say it was her. Why would she seal the princess's power rather than simply kill her? I feel there's more to this." Andres nodded gravely.

"Yes, I feel the same, unless of course there's a reason behind it… Charlene has always been heavily protected since she was a child. I do not see how anyone could have gotten past the walls to the city."

"More questions but no proper answers…" I mused thoughtfully.

"Yes… and I think Charlene's extreme training must begin as soon as possible. We need the ability of the heart. The Obsidian Shadow Pack is moving very fast..."

I zoned him out, pondering over the information he had given. I needed the princess's ability to reveal itself. Whoever held the heart of Kaeladia, held the power to conquer the world. I needed advice…

I think it is high time that I contacted him.

A Home Where You Are

YILEYNA

"I don't think dad told us everything," Charlene sighed as we walked down the hall. I nodded in agreement, our voices echoing in the halls. The windows were frosted, a sign that winter was truly here.

"I agree," I replied, sighing. "That comment about finding you a man to handle the Alpha title…"

"Yeah, it annoyed me too. Hey, wait, surely he'll tell Theon the full story right?"

"I'm guessing so. He loves him far more than me," I replied, rolling my eyes. The Alpha seemed to dislike me more and more as of late.

"But Theon loves you! So, you can seduce the answers out of him and then share with me?" She nudged me, blinking hopefully. I stopped and planted my hands on my hips.

"Seriously, my queen? Do you think Theon would spill?"

"I'm sure he spills enough. What are a few small secrets?" She winked suggestively at me, and it took me a second to realise what she meant. My eyes widened as I blushed.

"Charl!" She burst into laughter, and I shoved her lightly.

"Ouch, you are getting stronger," she said, laughing.

"I wish."

"No, I'm serious," she persisted, her laughter fading, and she looked at me curiously.

"Hmm, am I?" I asked, smirking and flexing my muscles.

"No, I'm serious… look." She pulled up her sleeve, showing me the small mark on her arm where I had shoved her. "Maybe… maybe you're getting closer to shifting." She smiled warmly at me, and I felt a flicker of hope inside, the same hope in her beautiful green eyes.

"Hmm, I don't feel different, maybe… who knows?" I hope so. *Please let it be so.* "Well, I need to go get my contraception charm renewed! See you!"

"Ooo, I am jealous you get to have some of that fine, sexy ass every day!" Charlene pouted. "You are yet to tell me the full details!"

"I told you enough! What do you want me to tell you? Every little thing?" I replied, laughing.

"Well, it would at least be nice to know exactly…" She turned and waved her hand in farewell, motioning with her eyes to the side, and I turned to see Theon walking down the hallway. "Bye!" Charlene ran off, and I pouted.

"Can I help you?" I asked, looking him over. My eyes fell to the front of his sweatpants. *Goddess, those should be illegal...* Why did he look so dangerously sexy all the time?

"No, but if you and the princess spent a little less time talking about sex and more actually training, perhaps the Silver Moon Pack may have a better reputation for its future," he replied, arrogantly brushing past me. My mouth fell open at the insult, and at the fact that he had heard us.

"We don't always talk about sex…" I protested, sticking my tongue out behind his back.

"Childish and horny. Perfect traits, little storm," he added sarcastically before he walked off.

Ass.

Well, I better go get this renewed, and then I would go to the market before I headed home. I paused mid-step, a soft smile crossing my lips. Home is where the heart is. I glanced down the hall, the way Theon had gone, and felt a pleasant warmth fill me. Our home.

Turning, I ran towards the hospital wing…

Looking around the kitchen, I smiled sheepishly. I had gotten a little carried away… okay, very carried away, and lugging everything home had been exhausting!

There were baskets and bags full of fresh vegetables, fruits, eggs, flour, spices, and many other items to make some baked goodies for dessert, as well as some bottled juices and an entire bag of meat and poultry. The house was literally empty, and it had nothing to do with us being at sea. It was obvious Theon didn't cook.

"Okay, where to start…" Put the shopping away and organise it? Yes, Mom always did that first.

I began going through the bags, deciding what to cook and placing what I would use onto the worktop. Once I had made up my mind, I wrapped the extra meat and poultry up and placed them into the cooler box. I would make sure to use that up over the next two days so nothing went to waste.

I got to work dicing the onions once the shopping was all put away and took out one of the new pans I had bought. I began humming as I worked, remembering the sea shanties Leto and the others would sing. I wondered if I'll meet any of them ever again. I didn't miss Barbara, but I'd like to see Cleo, Leto, Bobbie, even Flynn again.

I opened the window above the sink, despite the sharp wind, and glanced at the time. Good, I still had a few hours until Theon would return. Training and his other duties would take him a while. After coating the chicken with spices, I set it aside and added mince to the pan, whilst throwing some vegetables into a second. I smiled. I just hoped Theon would like it…

Two hours later, I had just taken a shower and slipped into a simple yet figure-hugging strapless black dress. I left my hair open and, after some hesitation, settled on winged liner, a touch of blush, and red lipstick. I picked up the small studs I had selected from Mom's jewellery box and a few bracelets, putting them on and finishing with a spritz of fragrance. Did I look like I was trying too hard?

I sat there, suddenly feeling vulnerable. Staring back at me was a woman I didn't recognise. I looked so in control and confident, yet deep inside I was scared to lose him. I didn't want to push so hard that he backed away, but at the same time, I wanted to do things for him…

I shook my head, I needed to stop being doubtful. I should check the roast chicken in the oven! I stood up and left the bedroom. I had closed the window not long ago as it had begun to rain. The hearth was blazing, and the entire cabin was glowing. The table was set with the juice bottles, which I had placed in the cooling box, and two place settings. I hoped Theon would be here soon because the food was ready.

I plated the servings of chilli and rice and carried it to the table. Setting the bowl of salad, sauces, and roasted chicken in the middle, I finished by placing the roasted vegetables in the centre.

The sound of rain beginning to patter down was welcoming in the background, and I hummed a song as I adjusted the dishes on the table. The door opened, and I turned to see Theon standing there. He was halfway through the door, ducking slightly as if not wanting to get soaked, but he had stopped in his tracks. His eyes scanned the cabin, lingering on the kitchen where the chocolate cake I had made stood ready for us, and then to the table, full of food, before his eyes finally settled on me.

My heart hammered as I held his gaze, suddenly feeling as if maybe I shouldn't have done this. I couldn't read what was going on in his mind as he stood there, his eyes fixed on mine. Rain began pouring down faster but he didn't move. I wasn't sure how long we stood there before his eyes trailed over me, and I wondered if the dress really was too much.

My stomach twisted when I saw him glance over his shoulder, almost as if contemplating to leave.

"It's raining. Close the door," I said, my voice coming out softer than it was meant to. He frowned slightly before he scanned the cabin once more.

"What is this?" He asked. His voice was cold and harsh, sending a sharp stab of pain through my chest.

"I just, I missed a home-cooked meal and I -"

"I told you to be responsible for your own food, not mine," he cut in coldly. My heart pounded, and I felt the familiar prickle in my eyes. *Do not cry.*

"I didn't know that arrangement still held," I whispered, looking down at the food I had cooked. I could feel his eyes burning into me, but I refused to meet his gaze. "It's okay… I'll drop off the extra tomorrow at the orphanage. I'll wrap it up!"

I hurried to the kitchen area, my heart pounding as I crouched down, opened the cabinet with shaking hands, and took out the few scarce containers he had. I stood up, gasping and dropping the tubs when I realised Theon was right in front of me. I stepped back, staring into those unreadable eyes that glinted with emotions I couldn't read.

"You usually argue. What happened today?" He asked quietly. There was no hostility in his tone, and my heart clenched. "Don't cry."

"I'm not crying!" I turned away from him, brushing under my eyes, not wanting him to see them. "But I don't think you deserve my hard work," I added lightly, trying to hide my heartbreak. I was about to bend down to pick up the fallen containers when his arms wrapped around me from behind, pulling me roughly into his chest and knocking the breath from me.

"Maybe not, but since you've set the table..." His lips touched my bare shoulders. My heart pounded, but I didn't know what to make of it.

"Are you angry with me?" I asked, pulling out of his arms and looking up at him. I couldn't pretend this didn't happen, I needed to know...

He frowned before looking away.

"No. I just... I'm not used to this," he said quietly, a deep frown furrowing his handsome face as he scanned the cabin.

My heart ached at his words, and I realised he had just been taken by surprise. Theon's reflex was to put his walls up. I smiled gently and stepped closer. Although I wanted to cup his face, I knew Theon wouldn't allow me to do that, so I simply tossed my hair over my shoulder and looked up at him.

"Well, if you treat me well, I could help you get used to it?" I suggested casually, with a small shrug. "I'll be here for as long as you let me."

He didn't reply, but I was beginning to understand that the conflicted look in his eyes was him fighting his emotions. *You need to take the next step, Theon...*

I placed my hands on his chest, our eyes meeting. After a moment, he ran his fingers through my hair before twisting his fingers into my locks and yanking me closer. *Now my turn.*

Amber met grey, and this time I was the one to lean up, pressing my lips against his, sending off fireworks through my entire body. His free arm wrapped around my waist tightly and he deepened the kiss, taking control. Our bodies pressed together so perfectly, and for a moment I truly felt that we were made for one another.

Were we?

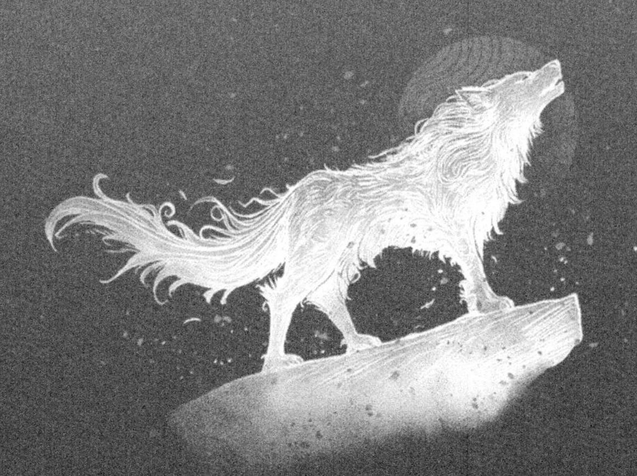

A Disappointment

YILEYNA

We broke apart, my arousal scenting the air and the large poky thing that was pressing against my stomach told me I wasn't the only one who was turned on.

"As much as skipping dinner sounds very appealing, I am starved," I whispered, running my hand over his package. His eyes blazed and he kissed my neck hungrily, making me whimper.

"I plan to have you for dessert anyway," he replied. His hand was still holding the side of my neck and face as he moved back slightly, his face inches from mine, our eyes locked. I looked away from his intense amber eyes and led the way to the table. I took a seat, and Theon sat down opposite me, scanning the table. "I never knew you could cook. Unless of course, it just looks good… I'm mentally prepared to be food poisoned." I gave him a pointed look.

"You won't get food poisoning! Besides, you're a werewolf. You can eat raw meat and live. But you don't need to worry because my cooking is very good. I'm good at many things, actually. Apart from shifting, I have excelled in every field, but I guess it doesn't matter when the most important thing is where I'm lacking," I sighed, picking up my fork.

"Do you feel any different lately?" He asked as he began eating. Why did everything he do look so hot? The way his lips wrapped around that spoonful of his chilli…

He cocked an eyebrow, and I quickly cleared my head.

"Different? Not really, but Charlene said I'm stronger now," I replied, taking the cork out of the juice bottle and pouring it into two glasses.

"She has a point." I looked at him, almost dropping my fork.

"Did you actually just agree with Charlene?" He didn't reply and picked up his glass.

"I've noticed it during sex," he stated bluntly, making my heart skip a beat.

"Meaning?" I pouted.

"Meaning your wolf is probably awakening."

I nodded, my hope soaring inside. I looked at him thoughtfully, wondering if I should ask him if the king had said anything else in the room after I had left. Deciding to go for it, I took a roasted potato and bit into it slowly.

"So, what did the king say once Charlene and I left the office?" I asked. He raised an eyebrow.

"And why would I share that?"

"Oh, come on, I won't tell anyone."

"Really? At least say something that is partially believable." I pouted.

"Well… the king doesn't treat Charlene or me seriously. This involves the entire kingdom, he can't just not share it with us," I said, watching as Theon broke some of the roast chicken off and placed it on his plate.

"Hmm, because what he did was something he wasn't proud of."

"Well, obviously, he told us that, wait! Are you about to tell me what the king said?" I asked, unable to hide my curiosity.

"Sure, because after you hear it, you won't have the guts to tell the princess," he said, smirking coldly. I frowned, my excitement vanishing. What did he mean…

"The king lied. That siren he cheated with wasn't before he met his mate. The Alpha, rather than celebrate and pamper his queen when she'd just found out she was pregnant with the princess, decided to go and sleep with someone else." Theon didn't hide the disgust in his voice, and I didn't blame him.

I felt… I placed my fork down, no longer having any appetite. Any respect I had for the king was diminishing as I tried to look for logic or reason that would save his reputation.

"Sirens are seductive creatures. Maybe he was seduced…"

"Maybe, but not once did he say he was lured into her charms. He, in fact, didn't seem to try and even hide that part," he replied, eating his food unbothered.

"That's appalling… Luna Soleil is his true mate, which meant she would have felt him cheating," I mumbled, feeling so bad for the Luna. Theon simply gave a small nod. He was right, there was no way that I was going to tell Charlene that.

Dinner was over, and I was still lost in thought. What I had hoped to be a light and pleasant evening had turned rather gloomy. I cleared the table as Theon put some milk to heat in the pan without even asking me, and I smiled. I loved having the coffee that he made.

I placed the dirty dishes in the sink and packed away the leftovers.

"Can you pass me the knife?" I asked, pointing to the knives in the pot near the cooker.

He looked down at me, giving me a once-over before he stepped back slightly, allowing me to squeeze past. I rolled my eyes at the tiny space he was allowing me. I slid past him, trying not to focus on his body heat behind me and grabbed the knife, very aware of his body brushing against my ass, sending a ripple of electricity through me. It made me crazy.

"Careful not to get burnt," he murmured huskily, his hand on my stomach as he pressed me into him, making my heart pound. His lips met my neck for a moment, and my heart fluttered before I slipped away from his hold and looked up at him.

I love you.

I wanted to say it out loud… every night and every morning… but I couldn't because I didn't want him to push me away.

"So, was the food edible at least?" I asked, trying to get rid of the sexual tension that had fallen over us.

"Did my four helpings not answer that question?"

"A simple 'yes I liked it' would have sufficed," I smirked as I began slicing the gooey chocolatey cake. "Do you not know how to answer a question directly?"

"I do. I just don't do compliments unless it involves you being a good girl in bed." My eyes widened, and despite the blush that coated my cheeks, his words shut me up completely. I was smiling.

He turned the cooker off, pouring the milk into the two mugs and mixing them into a pleasant froth. I picked up a slice of cake with the knife and my finger for support and placed it onto a plate before placing a second slice on another. I was about to reach for a paper towel when Theon grabbed my wrist and raised my hand to his lips. My heart pounded as he ran his tongue up my finger, licking off the slightly sticky chocolate ganache from my finger.

"It's good," he said quietly, his eyes trailing over me as he let go of my hand and took the knife from me. He brushed his finger up the blade, scooping up the bits of cake before slipping his finger into my mouth. "Don't you agree?"

My core knotted, and I only managed to nod as I tasted the chocolate cake that I knew Mom would be proud of. He placed the knife down without even looking away and slowly slipped his finger out, tracing my lips with it

"Oh, and one more thing... you look beautiful tonight."

The following day, I awoke to an empty bed. I was naked, remembering how amazing last night was, although I was feeling it now, along with the fading marks that covered my body.

Theon was gone, and I assumed it was for training. I decided to head out to do some training too. After all, I had become rather relaxed, and a theory had cropped up in my mind. Just the way they wanted to push Charlene to break her seal, would exerting myself result in my wolf awakening? It sounded like something that might work. Why not try? Should I ask Theon to train me? Maybe his gruelling training would help me... *Maybe I'll try it.*

I had just gotten dressed and was rummaging through Mom's jewellery box when I picked up the small brown square – the pendant from the trader in Bellmead. The image of the siren girl came to mind, and my stomach filled with guilt.

I sighed as I unwrapped the brown paper and removed the locket. It was a dark metal. The chain was delicate yet strong, and the oval charm at the end had an intricate pattern of swirls and leaves all wrapped around a slightly dull brown gem. *I think a little clean-up of it would make it look a lot prettier than it is currently.* Hmm... was it a stolen item?

It was heavy, and the chain was rather long. I think it would fall to just below my breasts. It looked like under all the grime, the quality may be good… *I'll soak it in some vinegar.* That would get it a little cleaned up.

I quickly left the bedroom and walked over to the kitchen area. I took out the vinegar bottle I had bought yesterday and poured some of it into a bowl. If it was made of cheap metal, it would get ruined, but there was no point in me keeping it if it was of no use. I rinsed the top layer of dirt off before drying it and dropping it in the vinegar, placing the bowl on the windowsill before I left the cabin, locking up behind me.

Feeling watched, I turned to see two young women watching me from over the small fence.

"Can I help you?" I asked as a vicious wind blew past me, making my hair blow around me. They exchanged looks before the older of the two cleared her throat.

"We just hope you know what you are doing. You are ruining Beta Theon's reputation by living with him," she said haughtily.

Yeah, that was one thing that I did not miss at sea. In fact, it was foolish of me to think that things would be normal again when I returned. Nothing had changed. People hadn't forgotten what had happened. It was a shame. People forgot the good fast, but when it was something bad… no one forgot, which was a reminder that I still needed to prove Mom and Dad's innocence. Somehow.

"I'm sure your precious Beta isn't a child and knows what he wants or doesn't. Perhaps it's better if you advise him instead," I said. I walked past them, not waiting for a reply. I was not going to let anyone get me down.

I looked around. The occasional person walked past, minding their own business, all bundled up in thick fur coats. I was surprised people were already wrapping up so warmly, I didn't find it too cold yet.

I looked at the dark grey skies and frowned slightly, thinking of what the king had said. That threats were growing ever stronger… I needed to shift so I could at least be part of our ranks and fight for my city and for my kingdom…

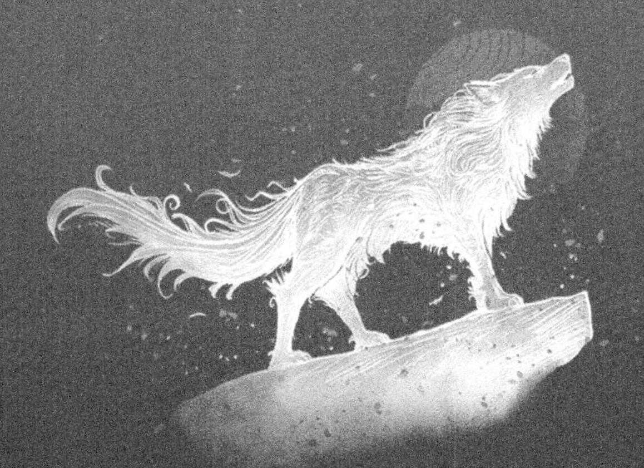

Love and Thoughts

THEON

Last night still replayed in my mind, and although another day had come and gone, I couldn't bring myself to return to the cabin. It had felt too… intimate. Against my better instincts, I had been unable to hurt her by walking out. That in itself should be warning enough for me. She was having an effect on me, far more than she should. I should have walked out last night but seeing the hurt in her eyes… fuck, I wished I could say it was how ravishing she looked that made me stay, but it wasn't.

I didn't want to see tears in her eyes. Unless, of course, they were caused by when we were getting physical…. Just the thought of her naked body made my dick twitch.

Was I falling for her? Was I even capable of that?

I had spent years trying to squash all my feelings, so why was she able to break the impenetrable shield I had placed around myself?

"Here you go, handsome," the blonde who had just placed a fresh tankard in front of me said in a flirty tone. I cast her a cold glare, not bothering to even spare her a word.

That was another issue. I was someone who had no shame in admitting that I didn't mind admiring a sexy body when I saw one, but that was until Yileyna came into the picture…

I wasn't the only one who thought so. She was the most talked-about woman, especially among the epsilon-ranked warriors when they were drunk or unmated. I had heard enough about her. There was no such thing as getting enough when it came to Yileyna. I closed my eyes, trying to control my anger that was beginning to rise.

I had loved once...but it had been different than what I have with Yileyna. I always put it down to simply desiring her, but last night, my actions proved that wasn't the case.

I picked up the tankard, gulping it down in one go and slamming the empty tankard onto the table.

Yileyna... *What will happen when she learns the truth? Was there a part of her that would side with me? Will she forgive me for what I have done? Do I care?*

"I love you."

Her words rang in my mind, and I almost believed them, even if I knew she was just delusional...

Love.

Iyara...

The music in the tavern faded away as my mind went back to the young girl I had once opened my heart to...

FIVE YEARS AGO

"I've shifted now. Are you excited for the full moon tonight? Do you think maybe we are mates?"

"Does it matter?" I asked, looking up into her chocolate-coloured eyes as she straddled me.

The sun was shining brightly as I lay on the grass, arms behind my head. Her dark hair bounced around her in pretty curls. She was tall and slender, with a toned body and beautiful ebony skin, the daughter of one of our strongest warriors. I wasn't sure how we ended up talking, but it became something more.

We hadn't taken the final step... but I thought it was only a matter of time before she gave herself to me.

"Not really... I think it's better... if we're not mates?" She mused, looking up at the sky. She was gorgeous. Right then, the way the sun was shining on her... fuck, she needed to get off of me. I sat up, pushing her off lightly.

"Yeah?" I said, not looking at her as her eyes filled with concern.

"Yes, and the only reason I'm saying that is because if something were to happen to me, I don't want you to die," she whispered, twisting her fingers in her lap. I smirked, looking over at her.

"Yeah, and do you think if I took you as my mate that I'd let anything happen to you?"

The smile that lit up her face took my breath away, and I was unable to stop myself from giving her a small smile of my own...

I frowned remembering how we didn't end up being mates, but she confessed her love once more. That night, when she gave herself to me... I realised I couldn't do it. She was far too innocent for what I was planning to do... I took her first time, but then I walked away, telling her that it had been a mistake. I broke her that night... but I had stayed away after that, cutting off all contact with her.

Why couldn't I do that with Yileyna? Was it because she wasn't as innocent and gentle as Iyara? Was it because no matter how rough or twisted I became, there was no fear in her sinful eyes? She craved more... she welcomed my anger and rage... almost as if she was the perfect match...

The door slammed open, and the sound of loud talking made me glance towards it, only to see Nikolai, Kyson, and a few of their cronies enter. A blistering flare of anger rushed through me, remembering what they had done to Yileyna. I wasn't one to forget my enemies... Nikolai and Kyson would be the first I'd kill when the time came.

"Sana! The usual, beautiful!" Nikolai called out, blowing a kiss at one of the women. I lifted my empty tankard, and instantly one of the women was at my side, filling it up for me.

"Can I get you anything else, Sir Theon?" She asked.

"No," I replied coldly as Nikolai and his group took a seat at the only table they could find in this crowded place, a table that was right in front of me. I think it was time I got out of here. I picked up my newly filled tankard when Nikolai spoke.

"Rumours are going around, Beta-to-be Theon, that you have taken the traitors' daughter as your whore."

Our eyes met. His smirk faltered when he sensed the murderous intent in my gaze. I wanted to vent my frustration and it looks like I just found my distraction.

"I've given the warning time and fucking time again, yet it's obvious that it's not getting through to you," I replied coldly. And as much as I wanted to rip him limb from limb right then, I had to wait. I couldn't ruin my mission because of my anger.

I stood up, dropped a few coins on the table, and walked over to Nikolai. I grabbed him by the scruff of his collar, his smirk vanishing as the other men around him tensed.

"Yileyna De'Lacor is not my whore but my woman and possibly your future Beta female. So, make sure you learn to respect her. Do you know the punishment for disrespecting your superiors, Levin?" I hissed, twisting my hand and tightening the fabric around his neck viciously, cutting off his oxygen supply. I knew it would only give birth to more rumours, but I'd had enough. He grabbed my wrist as he struggled to get free from my hold.

"Let him go!" Kyson growled, so I turned my murderous glare on him. He looked away, and I slammed Nikolai back violently, knocking his chair onto the ground, his head hit the floor with a satisfying crunch. The smell of blood filled the air. He groaned in pain.

"I hate repeating myself, but I'll do it this one more fucking time. Disrespecting Yileyna means disrespecting me, and I don't tolerate any kind of disrespect. Do I make myself clear?" Silence and the beating of several hearts followed. I fucking thought so.

Turning, I left the Three Horseman's Tavern, glancing up at the night sky. I hoped he got my message soon. I needed to meet him before we took our next step…

Hot and Hard

YILEYNA

THEON HAD ARRIVED SOMETIME late at night. He seemed rather quiet, and that was saying something for Theon. He had told me Charlene's training was beginning today, and it would be under Madelia and himself. I had just asked if I could attend too.

"You won't be able to handle seeing her go through it."

"What do you mean?" I asked, concerned, as I removed the pendant from the vinegar and began scrubbing it. Wow, it was looking so much better, and the stone was beginning to look a little less dull brown. I carried on scrubbing it firmly.

"Let's just say the techniques are usually used for torture," he said, drinking his coffee from where he was sitting at the table, looking as godly as ever. I frowned deeply, a flare of anger going through me.

"Does the king know?" I asked sharply.

"Yeah, he's the one who recommended several of the methods. We had a meeting with the princess yesterday afternoon too. She knows it's going to be brutal, but we need her powers to awaken."

"But then… at least let me come so I can give her moral support," I insisted, feeling my irritation towards the king rising as I brushed my hair out of my face.

"No, you will just get in the way." His voice held finality, but I wasn't going to back down that fast.

"What if I participate in the training?" That caught his attention. He looked at me sharply.

"You don't even have a wolf."

"That is my point. What if this same intense training helps me awaken my wolf and shift?"

"You mean to force the shift?" He asked quietly, watching me with a very calculating expression as he placed his mug on the table. I nodded.

"Yeah. Like you said, you can feel my aura a little, and I'm already eighteen. I need to shift soon. Yesterday, I went for training, and you and Charlene were right, I am stronger now."

His frown deepened as I continued scrubbing at the pendant and rinsed it. *I think another day or two in the vinegar might help break up the layers of dirt that had built up.* Emptying the old vinegar out, I poured in some fresh and dropped the pendant back in, placing it on the windowsill.

"What is that?"

"I bought it in Bellmead. Well, the man actually conned me of several coins and gave me this necklace, but it's really filthy. I'm trying to clean it."

"You could bin it. I'm sure it's not worth the time."

"That's my choice. Since I paid for it, I should at least see if it's worth anything. Besides, it's rather heavy, surely it must be worth something." It cost me gold!

"I never knew you were so stingy," he remarked mockingly. I rinsed my hands and looked at him. Going over, I took the mug from the table and placed it on the worktop.

"Although Mom and Dad left a good amount in the vault at the bank, I no longer earn anything as I am not the future Beta or even a warrior. So, I need to spend my money wisely."

"Yet you splurged on all these groceries and food products," he reminded me pointedly.

"Those were for us," I replied, "but I haven't received even one gold coin from the king since Mom and Dad died, even when I was still the prospective future Beta...." Seeing his eyes turn cold and a frown crossing his face, I changed the subject. "Anyway, can I take part in the training then?"

Right then, I didn't want him to say anything hurtful. It was painful as it was, the fact that I hadn't seen the warning signs from the king. Not to mention that talking about Mom and Dad hurt enough without any additional issues being brought up. I looked over at him when he didn't reply, a frown on his face.

"Are you listening?" I asked.

"You never thought to question the Alpha or go to the Pack accounts manager?" I was surprised he was fixated on that part.

"Money was the last thing on my mind." I shrugged. "Besides, it's not like I'm doing anything for the Alpha."

"You went on a trip. Everyone on that trip was paid for risking their lives." His voice was cold, and I could feel his irritation rising. I dried my hands and walked over to him, smiling softly.

"Tell me, Theon, are you angry for me?" I teased, perching on the edge of the table in front of him. He raised an eyebrow.

"No, just a little concerned at your level of stupidity. You won't get far in the world if you carry on with that mindset," he said coldly.

Lie.

"Okay, I'll try to keep that in mind," I said, looking down at his lips. Goddess... his lips were so kissable…

"I can see exactly how long that stayed in your mind. A little distracted, aren't we, little storm?" He reached over, wrapping his hand around my throat as he pulled me closer.

"You distract me," I replied, slipping off the table and straddling him. My heart was pounding as his eyes blazed, his lips crashing against mine in a hungry kiss. His free hand squeezed my ass, making me moan as my core throbbed. "Theon…" I whimpered, grinding against his crotch.

"Fuck, I had somewhere to be," he growled, attacking my neck with rough kisses.

"And you haven't agreed to let me… attend," I moaned, trying to focus when pleasure was erupting through me. He let go of my neck, grabbing my breast as his lips travelled down my collarbones.

"I don't see why I should agree," he replied huskily,

I could barely focus, feeling the hard shaft in his pants that made my pussy clench with an insatiable hunger.

"I can make it up to you…" I whispered, raking my nails down his chest and leaning in. I kissed his neck sensually, feeling him throb. "Agree, and tonight I'll treat you like the king you are, fuck!"

Something in my words had made his eyes flash, and he stood up, turning me and pushing me down on the table. With one swift movement, he yanked my pants down, unzipping his own and slamming into me so harshly that it made me cry out in pain. His hands ran up my thighs before he grabbed a fistful of my hair in one hand.

"Don't try to tempt me, little storm, because I assure you if I lose control, I will fuck you so hard you won't be able to take it," he whispered huskily, making my pussy clench.

"Try me," I shot back, trying not to cry out.

"As you wish," came his dangerously animalistic growl that only made pleasure swim through me as he thrust into me impossibly harder.

Fuck, I couldn't breathe...

I could hear the screams that left my lips and the sound of our skin meeting. His one hand fisted in my hair, the other gripping my hip painfully. The table creaked violently beneath me, and I was sure it wouldn't hold for long as he continued to fuck me mercilessly.

Tears stung my eyes at the intensity of his thrusts, the pain giving way to pleasure, and my cries became more and more erotic. The pressure inside of me was building into an incredibly powerful high. I could feel my juices trickling down my legs, and I knew we were both going to need a shower after this.

"Seems like you enjoy being fucked hard," he growled.

Oh, Goddess, yes.

I couldn't reply, but my body was screaming with satisfaction. I couldn't explain how good this felt... *Fuck*!

"I'm so fucking close!" I moaned hornily. "Fuck, baby... nh..."

"And so fucking wet."

He was nearing, too, his voice breathless, and when a quiet moan left his lips, I bit my lip, savouring that sound. I never wanted another man's touch, just his, only his. Explosive fireworks erupted inside of me.

"Theon!"

I screamed. My release ripped through me with such intensity that my vision blackened. Moments later, I felt his seed coat my insides, and a low groan escaped him.

"Fuck," he hissed, pulling out and letting go of my hair. He placed his hands on the table, palms downward on each side of my head. His lips touched my shoulder, making me shudder as it sent another river of pleasure through me. "You're fucking lethal."

I don't know what I did that triggered that reaction from him, but I was not complaining. That had been one brutal, hot, fast round of sex.

The table creaked loudly, and Theon pulled me up just as it collapsed, making me stare at it, mortified.

"You broke the table…"

"We broke it," he corrected, and I could hear the amusement in his voice, his lips touching my neck once more. "I have never been late, but thanks to you, I am now late for training."

"I don't regret it," I replied, placing my hand over his that was pressed against my stomach as he supported my shaking body.

"Me either."

"So… can I join her training?" I asked, putting on the most doe-eyed expression I could muster and batting my eyelids coquettishly. He clenched his jaw, knowing exactly what I was doing, and frowned deeply until I reached up, running my fingers down his neck. "Please?"

"Fine. If that is what you want, don't come crying to me later." I smiled victoriously. It seemed whether he was doing it intentionally or not, he was beginning to give in a lot more often… "Let's get cleaned up."

With those words, he lifted me up bridal style and carried me to the bathroom…

Within the Castle Walls

YILEYNA

I REGRETTED AGREEING TO TRAIN. I could barely walk straight, holding the fur coat tightly around me so it didn't blow all over the place. It was beginning to snow, and I was sure a blizzard was headed our way. I had to drag my legs to move against the vicious winds.

Theon was wearing a knee-length grey fur coat. It made me look him over whilst trying not to lick my lips in approval. He looked very regal and sexy, the coat only adding to the princely look he was displaying. His coppery hair blew in front of his forehead, yet he seemed unbothered by the cold. His breath was coming out in visible puffs.

I think my wolf was really awakening because I didn't feel as cold as I once would have. Another roaring bout of wind whipped against me, and I almost flew back from the sheer force. Theon's arm wrapped around my shoulders, and he looked down at me with those eyes that seemed to burn into my soul. Even in the cold, he made me feel all warm inside.

Once again, the words were on the tip of my lips, but I wasn't brave enough to say them. *I love you.*

I leaned into him, not caring that I was smiling helplessly, feeling utterly content. Even the wild weather couldn't dampen my spirits.

We approached the castle, and I wondered when Theon would let go of me. I felt the eyes of the epsilon-ranked guards upon me as we walked through the courtyard. The smile on my face was gone. I hated seeing the mixed looks on the faces of those we passed, some of hatred, disapproval, irritation, anger, and then some of jealousy.

Was I ruining Theon's reputation by being with him? Did he not care? He removed his arm from around my shoulders as we approached a group of guards who had just finished their training. *I guess that answers my question.*

But to my surprise, he took my hand, lacing his fingers with mine and raising it to his lips before pressing them to my hands for a single moment. He made my stomach flutter before dropping them by our sides, yet he didn't let go.

"Theon." One of them bowed his head to him just as Raiden walked over to them. Despite the weather, he was shirtless, clearly having finished an extreme round of training.

"Ah, my favourite couple," he said with a smirk as he wiped his forehead.

"Raiden." I smiled.

"Yileyna." He gave me a wink, his eyes flitting to our combined hands before he grinned. "Theon."

Theon didn't bother replying, leading me past the gates. I gave Raiden a quick wave, ignoring the rest of the men, before Theon pulled me into the inner courtyards, but instead of going straight through, he took a sharp right, leading me away from the castle.

"You don't need to be so mean towards Raiden. He's a nice guy."

"Hmm, since when have you liked nice men?" Came his cold reply. I smiled in amusement.

"Jealousy looks good on you, Theon," I whispered teasingly. He gave me a cold glare but said nothing more. "Where are we going?" I asked after a moment.

He didn't respond as he kept going farther and farther through the narrower side paths of the castle before he pulled out a key and unlocked a gate.

"Theon?"

"Do you really need to question everything, little storm?"

"Yes, what if you're taking me somewhere isolated and far away? Then when we get there -"

"I fuck you senseless?"

"No, I was going to say kill me off," I replied, thinking that his sounded like a much better option. He looked down at me and smirked coldly.

Turning towards me, he pushed me up against the stone wall behind me.

"There are people I intend to kill, but I assure you, you aren't on that list... unless, of course, we are talking about fucking you to death?" My eyes widened as I looked up at him. The snow that was beginning to fall was getting thicker, and it tickled my face as I stared up at him.

"That wouldn't be a bad way to die." I shrugged carelessly, about to cross my arms when he grabbed them and pinned them against the wall, making my coat open, and he looked down at my body. That familiar carnal hunger filled his eyes.

"I don't plan on getting rid of my favourite toy yet. There is still far too much that I plan to do to you," he whispered huskily in my ear as he cupped my pussy, making my breath hitch. Rivets of pleasure rushed up through me, and I wondered how, despite having had a taste of him not long ago, the feeling never ceased. I always craved more of him.

"I can't wait," I whimpered as he massaged me down there. I wished I wasn't wearing such thick pants. He simply smirked before giving me a sharp tap on my pussy and moving back.

"You're making me late again." He frowned in disapproval. "I should punish you for that."

With those words, he turned, his cold exterior returning as he made his way through the gate he had unlocked. Soon, we reached a rather derelict old garden. Dead vines hung around the walls and latched onto the cracks in the stone. An old stone bench and empty flowerpots were scattered around. Two broken statues of gargoyles stood on either side of an iron door that was standing slightly ajar.

"In here."

My curiosity was piqued. I had explored this castle so many times; the fact that such a place was here and I hadn't known of it was strange.

"It's so weird, I've never seen this place," I murmured as we entered through the iron door, taking a moment to adjust to the darkness. I could hear water dripping somewhere. How strange.

"You can only find it if you know about it."

"Magic."

He gave a curt nod, leading the way further and further in until we came to another door. He pushed it open, and I saw Charlene and Madelia waiting there.

"Hi!" I said, smiling at them both, but Charlene only seemed to pale, concern clear on her face.

"Why are you here?"

"That's not like you. Don't want to see me?" I pouted. Going over, I hugged her, and she hugged me back. Her heart was thundering, and I became concerned. Why was she so worried?

"I'm serious, Yileyna, you shouldn't be here."

"I've come to take part in the training too, or whatever forced methods we are going to try out here to see if I can awaken my wolf," I replied quietly, cupping her face. Her eyes were filled with worry, but she sighed.

"I see... Goddess, Yileyna... why do you take risks?"

"I'll be fine, but like you, I need to do this too." *Besides, I'll be here for you, even if it's just for moral support.* Our eyes met, and she cupped my face, shaking her head.

"I could lose everything in this world but you," she said, about to hug me when I was yanked away from her and straight into Theon's arms. His eyes shimmered gold as he held me possessively. What the heck? Was he seriously jealous of Charlene? Well, he could carry on! She was my soul sister! I glared up at him, trying to pull free.

"Let's get to the first attempt," he growled.

Madelia nodded, squaring her shoulders as she stepped back and took out a scroll. Opening it, she placed it on the floor before looking at us.

"As you know, these... spells, or trials, are made to push you into the depths of despair and force you to react. These may be triggering, but we won't stop until we feel we need to. The first one isn't too bad. Theon... are you alright with this?" He frowned coldly, and I gave up struggling.

"Why wouldn't I be?" He shot back, but his arm tightened around me.

"You know why." Madelia glanced at me pointedly.

"She'll be fine. Besides, she wanted to come," he remarked icily, making me smile. I looked up at him, my heart skipping a beat.

"Won't you worry for me?" I whispered quietly as Madelia began explaining something to Charlene, who was smiling as she cast sideways looks at us.

His hands slipped under my fur coat, squeezing my ass as he pulled me tight against him. Goddess.... My stomach fluttered, and the urge to stay snuggled against him was very strong.

"No," he replied arrogantly.

"Meanie." I pouted. His gaze dipped to my lips, and I couldn't resist licking them slowly. "Well, I'm not worried because you will be right here." Something flashed in his eyes, his heart thudding, and he let go of me suddenly.

"Don't hold so much faith in me," he said very quietly as he looked away. He crossed his arms and backed away, leaving me confused.

"Let's begin," Madelia said as I watched him curiously for a moment. Why did he always seem to think he'd hurt me or wasn't worthy of being trusted or something?

"Get ready, Yileyna, this training is brutal. Unlike Charlene, who has her wolf, you do not."

"I'll be fine," I said confidently, taking off my coat and placing it down.

I was wearing a brown blouse with black pants, and although it was cold, I knew once we started working out, we would warm up. Madelia chanted a spell, and suddenly fog filled the stone room as the temperature dramatically plunged.

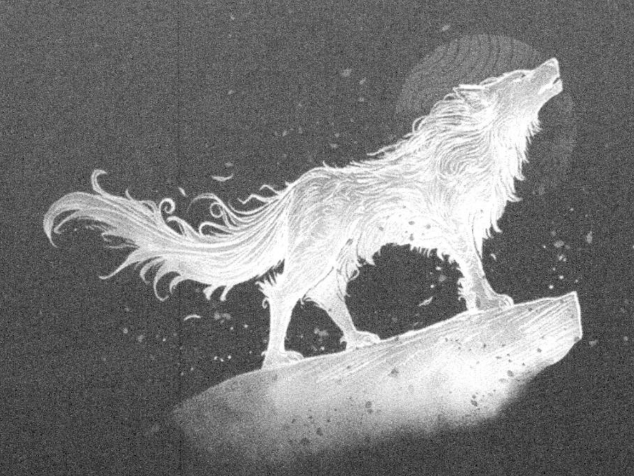

Our Limits

YILEYNA

The temperature dropped several notches. I felt it biting into my bones.

"Ah..." I heard Charlene groan from somewhere nearby, but I couldn't locate her.

"The temperature will continue to drop until your body will not be able to continue to function... good luck."

"When will you stop?" Charlene asked tensely.

"Stop? There is no stopping unless you find Madelia and are able to stop her yourself," Theon's cold voice answered. I nodded in concentration.

Of course, they wouldn't stop until we were near dead or passed out because they were trying to get Charlene to break the seal on her abilities.

Things became colder and colder until I felt it become painful. They were lowering the temperature faster than I could focus. *What do I do?*

A cry from Charlene made my heart thump. I couldn't see her, but I needed to find her! She sounded like she was in agony. I closed my eyes, trying to sense where she was, listening to her heartbeat despite the cold. It was becoming far more bearable than I had expected. Maybe it was easing up?

"Princess, you need to get up. There is no one to help you," Madelia's voice came from all directions.

I frowned. Wait, I hadn't moved from my spot… did Charlene? If she hadn't, then surely I could find her. Following my instincts, I moved forward in the direction I last saw Charlene standing before the fog had settled in.

"How is she moving?" Theon's murmur came. I frowned. Unlike Madelia's voice, his came from the far side, so they both must be standing over there.

Where was Charlene?

"Charlene?" I called out.

A groan was my only response, but it was enough for me to pinpoint her location. I rushed over, almost tripping over her, and realised that she was on her knees on the floor. I wrapped my arms around her body, which was ice cold. She felt like a block of ice…

"You can't help her, Yileyna," Madelia's voice came, and the temperatures dropped further.

"Come on, Charlene," I whispered, my heart pounding.

"I… it's so cold…" she whispered, her teeth chattering.

"Fight it," I urged her.

I was a little disappointed that Madelia wasn't doing the same to me. Did she think that I couldn't handle it because I didn't have a wolf? I frowned and turned in the direction I had heard Theon's voice, knowing they were probably standing together, ready to snap at them, but I couldn't do anything. Charlene needed to do this.

"You are going to be okay. Come on, shift if you need to. Let it go. Take control. Don't hold back," I urged her, rubbing her back. Even her thick coat was cold to the touch.

"Yeah, you're right," she muttered, groaning as I felt her pull away and try to stand up. I still couldn't see her, but I was glad she was trying to fight it.

I backed away and glanced in the duo's direction, or where I thought they stood.

"Can you guys turn it up for me too? I can handle this," I sighed.

"How cold are you, Yileyna?" Theon asked.

"Not that cold, so please."

A low growl made me tense when I realised Charlene must have shifted, or was trying to shift. I smiled, glad she was trying her best, but then I heard a thud and Madelia's sigh, followed by running footsteps.

"She's out cold." I heard her say.

"Don't end it yet… focus it on Yileyna. Keep going."

"But… I don't even know how she's still standing," Madelia muttered.

"Exactly why I want you to keep going..." Theon replied emotionlessly. I frowned. Why were they both talking as if I wasn't here?

"Yileyna, are you okay?" Madelia's voice came, and I heard something being dragged along the floor.

"Yeah, I am," I replied.

"Okay... I'm going to keep making it colder," her hesitant reply came.

I heard her whisper an enchantment as the temperature plunged lower. I just stood there, wondering what I was supposed to do. My clothes began to feel stiff as a layer of ice seemed to coat them over. However, it wasn't affecting me...

"I can't lower it anymore," I heard Madelia's strained voice come.

"Yileyna, follow my voice and come here," Theon's cold, sexy voice ordered. Frowning slightly, I followed his voice.

"My word..." I heard Madelia whisper.

"Pass me the dagger," Theon commanded. I paused hesitantly. What was he about to do?

I heard a rustle, and then I felt the whistling of the dagger coming straight towards me. It was at that moment that I felt something inside of me, like a faint ripple of something in the pit of my stomach, and then it was almost in slow motion. I moved my head sideways, allowing the dagger to whiz right past before it hit the far wall behind me.

Madelia chanted something, and the room cleared, then once again, I could see them. Both were watching me calculatingly. I frowned at them.

"I wanted the same amount of pressure as Charlene. I don't have a wolf, but I can handle it," I replied with irritation. "I think I felt something."

"You were able to handle far colder temperatures than the princess," Madelia murmured. "I'm not a water or wind elemental mage, yet those spells were extremely powerful. I used one first, and then I used two for you alone. That was incredible, Yileyna." I frowned at her words, feeling confused. I looked at Charlene, who was lying on the ground unconscious.

"Maybe the seal on her has sealed away some of her wolf's abilities," I said, concerned.

"Maybe. I do think it's a possibility, considering she has no alpha aura," Madelia said with a nod. Theon was watching me thoughtfully, a hand on his chin. Our eyes met, and he stepped closer, touching my neck, only for him to jerk his hand away.

"You're fucking cold." I didn't feel that cold...

"Madelia, the princess's training is over for the day, but if it's alright with you, Yileyna and I will continue for a bit," Theon murmured, and although it sounded like a question, it wasn't one. His eyes were fixed on me with an interest that was not the usual sexual kind. In fact, it unnerved me a little.

"Of course, just take it easy. I'll report to the king that today didn't go as well as planned."

"Yeah, however, keep it at that. There's no need to add anything more to it. We don't want him to feel angrier towards the princess if he compares her to a wolfless woman."

I frowned at him, feeling suspicious. His words of concern for Charlene couldn't be true, he was always hateful towards her...

Madelia nodded.

"Yes, good point. I will keep it short. We will meet here tomorrow at the same time again. The planned time," she said, glancing between us. I felt my cheeks heat up a little, wondering if she had an inkling of why we had gotten there late. Theon cast her a cold glare, not even giving her a nod of agreement before she bent down, lifting Charlene and carrying her out.

I turned to Theon, whose eyes were running over me as if assessing me for the first time.

"I wonder if the rumours that you may not be your parents' daughter hold any truth..." he said quietly, making my eyes widen in shock.

If my blood wasn't cold before, it felt ice cold as I stared at him, trying to squash the flare of pain that filled me inside, but my moment of shock and hurt didn't last long, giving way to my anger.

"I am my parents' daughter!" I snapped coldly, my chest heaving as I tried to control my anger. His gaze snapped up and he raised an eyebrow challengingly.

"You look like neither," he said, his voice icy and emotionless.

"So? Many of us don't look like our parents!" I shouted back. How dare he!

Nikolai's remarks returned to me with a vengeance, what the king had said about not seeing Mom pregnant... these thoughts made the pain inside double as I glared at Theon with frustration and anger. How could he, of all people, say that?

"How dare you!"

He closed the gap between us, his hand wrapping around my neck. The next thing I knew, he had knocked my legs out from underneath me and pushed me to the ground. His hand was still around my neck as he straddled me, one hand pinning my wrists above my head as I tried to push him off, ignoring the pleasure that coursed through me.

"Calm down. Why are you getting so worked up? Unless, of course, deep down, you feel there may be some truth in my words," he said icily.

"There is no truth in it. It's just lies that I can't believe you are actually entertaining!" I replied, hurt. He tilted his head, looking down at me.

"I'm just saying, there's no way the princess, a shifted wolf, couldn't handle the cold, but you could. What if your father maybe had an affair, and it resulted in you?"

That was it.

I felt my anger rise once more, and, using all my might, I shoved him off, taking him by surprise, or he had simply not been holding me as tight as I had thought. He was thrown off, making his eyes flash as he watched me.

That same feeling swirled in my stomach as I glared at him.

"I knew my parents more than anyone else did! They were not traitors, nor would my father or mother ever have an affair and cheat on the other! They were not like that! Not everyone is like the king!" I hissed angrily.

Theon stood up, his eyes still blazing gold as he looked down at me emotionlessly. Taking hold of my chin, he forced it up roughly.

"Then explain to me why a werewolf seems to hold elemental powers?" He whispered threateningly.

I frowned in confusion, and he motioned to the floor with his eyes. I turned my head, staring at the ice-covered floor, but the most unnerving part was that it was spreading from beneath my very own feet...

My Purpose

THEON

THE MOMENT FROM EARLIER still played in my mind. She had gasped, backing away from the ice that was thickest beneath her feet, and then it was gone. I had tried to get her to call upon it again, but she didn't manage it. She was unnerved and confused, but as for me? I was simply intrigued.

Was she part mage or fae? The odd thing was, usually, you could tell, but with Yileyna, you could only sense her werewolf side. There was something missing… and I needed to know what it was.

She had been angry and hostile towards me for the comment I had made about her parents. I needed to do some digging into her parents' past. She may have gotten offended when I stated the truth, but it was obvious she looked nothing like her parents. That surely meant something. Her hair, eyes, facial features, and even build were entirely different. We all inherited something of our parents, even if it was subtle.

She had been distracted since then, asking me not to mention it to the king. I didn't plan to. If she was part mage or fae, I wondered if the king would want her on his team. I just knew he'd use her as collateral damage, and Yileyna would happily agree, simply to feel that she was needed and able to do something, but I didn't plan on letting her be killed so soon. My only issue was Madelia had also seen how she had coped with the cold…

Was allowing her to live safe?

For now, I'll let her live as I need her, but the moment she becomes a threat to Yileyna, I'll get rid of her.

Another blast of wind slammed against me, and I wrapped the grey fur coat I was wearing around me tighter. I had received the signal that he was here, ready to meet me. I had told Yileyna I would be back late as I had work to attend to and not to wait up for me.

Although she was still upset about my comments, I did not plan to apologise for stating what was a fair statement. On the other hand, I was glad that she didn't ask me where I was going... but the fact that she was simply falling so perfectly into my life... that was beginning to worry me. From wanting her as my whore, to somehow being concerned when she was upset... to claiming her openly... to the thoughts that crept into my mind that I should claim her by marking her... something I wouldn't do.

I couldn't deny that I enjoyed her presence. I slept better for the most part, despite the constant desire of wanting to fuck her repeatedly.

I trudged along in the snow, the blizzard pushing against me and the howling wind louder than everything else. My footprints wouldn't remain with this strong wind and snow, and I was glad for it. It would save me time from having to cover my tracks.

I had left the city through a hidden passage, making my way further and further away from the city and into the forest. I hadn't seen him in eighteen months... but I knew I would have to tell him about Yileyna. She...

"Theon." I froze, not even having sensed his approach. A cold blade pressed against my neck, and I heard his sigh of distaste. "Don't tell me you have become as weak as the pack you are now part of." Shit, I was too distracted by my thoughts.

"Not at all. I didn't sense an enemy," I said emotionlessly, turning and looking into a pair of amber eyes that were so similar to my own yet so different.

The man was almost my height, bulky, muscular, and wore a dark coat with his hood up, partially hiding his face. A speckled beard could be seen and an angled jaw.

"Smart answer," he replied, his deep baritone holding power despite keeping his aura suppressed. "What was so important that you risked calling this meeting?"

"There've been a few problems. That's why I had to," I clarified quietly. "I told you not long ago that the princess is the heart, but the problem is, her powers are sealed. There are chances it was a Siren's doing."

I quickly and quietly began explaining to him everything Andres had told me. He growled with irritation.

"One step closer and two steps back. Maybe it's better to simply kill her," he said, the fury in his voice barely hidden.

"I don't think that's going to help us take over the middle kingdom. You want that position, and I plan to get it for you," I replied quietly. A smile curled his lips, and he slapped my shoulder, sending a fair amount of snow flying.

"To get it for us. Not me, us," he corrected me before stepping closer and hugging me.

"Yes. To retake what should have been ours."

"That's my son."

I hugged him back. The familiar feeling I once used to associate with home was no longer there. Yes, he was my father, but things had changed. I guess eighteen months apart did that. He moved back, and we both became serious once more.

"How is Thea?"

"Well. She knows not of this meeting." I frowned and nodded. That made sense. "How is your relationship with Andres?"

"Good, he trusts me more than most," I replied, smirking coldly. Approval was clear in Dad's nod.

"You need to get rid of the rest of his confidants. We can set up another attack or do something just like we did last time. The aim is for him to feel that you are his only friend, the only one he needs. Just the way we removed the Beta couple from his side." I frowned; a sliver of guilt washed through me.

"Yeah."

"It was smart of you to know exactly where their daughter would be. You timed the attack and gave the signal so precisely. You were sure they would end up dying for her, and you were correct." Dad's approval was obvious in his voice, but I didn't feel the satisfaction I once had… "Andres bought the set-up, didn't he?"

"Yes, they think they were traitors," I replied quietly.

"Good, good. So, in your last message, you said you were to become Beta. What happened to their daughter?"

"She hasn't shifted, but I don't think she's their real daughter. She's a hybrid of some kind."

"Oh?" The intrigue in his voice made a flash of possessiveness fill me inside, as if I had to make it clear that she was mine.

"Yes, however, I've taken her as my woman for now." He looked at me sharply, his eyes flashing, and I knew he was doing his all to not let his aura out.

"Why would you do that? Are her powers strong? Can she be manipulated or be of any use to us?"

"I am a man, and I rather not have the reputation of a player if I am to keep the king's respect and trust. She is useful," I lied coldly. He cocked his head, and, like always, I felt as if he was peering deep within me.

"I've heard she's a scorned reject, stripped of rank and power. An outcast. That would ruin your reputation with Andres, Theon." His voice was dangerous, low, menacing even.

"She's good in bed," I shot back, my eyes flashing. "I'm keeping her."

"Keep as many women as you want. If Andres likes you so much, I'm surprised he hasn't offered you his daughter." I looked at him, hatred filling my eyes.

"I would never take her as a mate," I hissed coldly.

"But becoming potential Alpha before the takeover will help greatly. Having the heart as your chosen mate would be perfect." I tried to remain emotionless, my heart betraying me before I managed to quickly regain control of my emotions, but something told me I was too late.

"I can't even stand being in the same room as her, and you wish for me to take her as my own? That would require a lot of self-control."

"You have control, Theon. You know it's a fair point, unless, of course, this other woman is the problem." His voice was calm and nonchalant, yet I knew the underlying threat that lingered.

"She isn't. I can kill her if need be," I said coldly.

The moment the words left my lips, I knew it was a blatant lie. It left a bitter taste in my mouth, but I also knew that he had the power to have her killed if he wanted. Even from out here, he didn't need to be in the capital to have it done.

Then I also knew if she knew my truth... she'd want me dead.

"Good. You will get Andres to agree, and I know it won't be so hard. A little bird has already told me he is extremely fond of you and already hopes you take her as your mate." How did he know that? I remained passive, frowning as I pondered on my answer. I needed to be careful…

"I am unable to even stay in the same room as her, knowing how her father tried to destroy us," I tried again.

I was trying to tell myself it wasn't Yileyna. That she wasn't the reason… but why was it her face that was at the forefront of my mind? Was it that it was the thought of her that squeezed at my heart?

"Because we need her for the revenge that I have waited for, for years. He owes us so much, but if the heart is a person, then we need that person under our control. Make it happen, Theon."

He had a point… to use the heart, we needed her alive…

My mind was a turmoil. I knew I had gotten far too involved with Yileyna than I ever should have.

"Your hesitating, son."

"Not at all. I know what I need to do."

"When I had your powers sealed for this mission, we decided to seal the mate bond alongside it. It was for your benefit, remember? Mates are a weakness. Theon, women are a weakness. I had that spell performed on you so -"

"So, I never fall victim to the mate bond. I won't feel it. Even if she stands before me and proclaims that I am her mate, I won't feel anything. I know."

"Good. So don't let another woman ruin that. You are Theon Alexander Hale, son of Theoden Hale. Make me proud." His voice was powerful and strong, I turned and gave him a nod.

He was right. I was no coward who would let a woman come in the way of my goal… I'd do the right thing.

"I will make you proud. We will defeat everyone who has wronged us, from Andres to the Siren who killed Mom and Thalia. The Obsidian Shadow Pack is the strongest pack on Kaeladia, and we bow to no one."

Copper eyes met copper, and it felt good to see the burning flames of approval and pride in his eyes. This was my purpose, the only goal that I had in life.

Vengeance.

And I would destroy anything and anyone who came in the way of it. No matter what.

INSECURITY

YILEYNA

I AWOKE WITH A START, jolting upright in bed. I scanned the room frantically.

Alone. I was alone.

My heart was pounding, and once again, the nightmare of the night my parents were killed was replaying in my mind. I ran my trembling hand through my hair, closing my eyes as the emotions that I tried to control hit me full force.

Focus, Yileyna, it's okay. It's going to be ok…

No, it wasn't okay… they died saving me and were marked as traitors. They were not traitors! I had to prove their innocence! I had to… Goddess…

I wrapped my arms around my legs, burying my head in my knees.

Focus.

Breathe…

What time was it? Where was Theon? Was he still not back?

"They're dead."

Theon's words from that night rang in my head, I felt the crushing agony in my chest break its restraint and hit me brutally.

It was my fault. They died because of me.

I won't cry.

I can't.

But I was unable to stop the tears from streaming down my cheeks as

I pressed a fist against my chest, trying to control the pain that threatened to drown me. It was my fault. They died because I was out there... Dad came to protect me. A strangled sob left my lips, and I curled up, dropping onto my side.

The memories of that night, the wolves... the bodies... the fire... they played before my eyes like a horror show on repeat.

Stop. Stop, Yileyna... think of something else...

Why did I have these odd abilities? How was it possible? The daughter of two werewolves having elemental magic?

I didn't look like them. The fear of the unknown terrified me, and I wanted it all to just go away.

The bedroom door opened, and I quickly tried to cover my face, hoping Theon thought I was asleep.

"Yileyna."

I tried to turn away, not wanting him to see my tears, but he was stronger than me, taking hold of my arms and forcing me to turn towards him. A frown creased his brow. His shirt was hanging open, his hair was a mess as if he had run his fingers through it repeatedly, and the distinct smell of alcohol was coming from him.

I looked away, not wanting him to see the tears that were streaming down my cheeks.

"What happened?" His voice was husky and low, but it was missing the coldness it usually held, almost sounding concerned. I hated being weak. I hated him seeing me like this.

"Nothing. Nothing happened," I whispered, trying to pull free from his hold, but he refused to let me go, pulling me upright and straight into his arms. My breath hitched. I fought to control my emotions as he held me tightly.

"What's wrong, little storm?" He whispered, stroking my back.

I was unable to control the sob that left my lips. I couldn't reply, knowing, if I did, I would lose all control of my emotions. I locked my arms around his neck, and he instantly pulled me closer, sitting back on the ground with me straddling him. My breasts were crushed against his chest, and his arms felt like a shield, protecting me from the world as he gently rocked me in his lap.

It didn't seem like it was something Theon would do. Sure, he was comforting, but the emotions and concern that seemed to be in his eyes and touch… maybe it was the alcohol in his system, but I didn't care. I needed something to keep me tethered from drowning in my pain, and he was there for me.

He rubbed my back, sending sparks of pleasure through me, burying his head in my neck. We remained like that for a while, his scent and touch giving me the strength I needed to regain control of my emotions.

"Talk to me, Yileyna."

I know we argued earlier, but I was ready to open up to him. I was tired of keeping it inside, but I couldn't talk about them when they were branded traitors.

"I miss them," I whispered, pulling back so I could look into those amber eyes that I loved so much. His eyes shadowed, and he looked away.

"I know…"

"I don't care… I don't care if one of them or both are not my blood, they are still my parents. They were my world," I said quietly. I knew the revelation from earlier had only triggered these emotions within me, but I couldn't stop them.

He nodded but didn't say anything. Instead, he reached up and cupped my neck, his thumbs brushing away my tears, only for more to fall in their place.

"I lost them… then I felt like everything was being snatched from my grasp. I know you deserve to be Beta... but when it was taken away from me, I felt like the last part of Mom and Dad I had was taken from me too."

I couldn't look into his eyes anymore. I hated feeling so vulnerable, but I wasn't able to control these emotions. I was breaking, and I needed to tell someone. I gripped his wrists, the pain of my memories twisting within me.

"I'm scared of losing everything I love…" I said quietly, looking up into his shimmering eyes. *I'm scared of losing you. I love you.* I didn't need to say it because I knew he understood.

Would I push him away by acting so vulnerable and needy? I wasn't sure, but I couldn't keep it inside of me any longer. It hurt so much…

"Your parents…" I wasn't sure what he was going to say, but he took a deep breath, looking at me sharply, and I knew he had changed his mind. "They were traitors. Let the pain go." I shook my head.

"No, they were framed. My parents are not traitors. Something or someone did this. I knew my parents. They would never do this," I said desperately. How could he say that? He knew my father! "And I'm going to find out the truth." He frowned, his eyes sharp as he tilted my head up slightly.

"You might regret what you find out," he said quietly.

"No, I won't because I know they were innocent." Our eyes met, and he didn't reply, before clenching his jaw and nodding slightly.

"You're strong, Yileyna… even when the world turns its back on you, I know you'll be okay," he said quietly, almost as if he was speaking to himself over me. It confused me, but I still nodded.

"I will." *As long as I have you, I will be.*

"Promise me that no matter what happens… you will always stay strong," he whispered huskily, his gaze dipping to my lips.

"I promise." *Because I have you.*

His warm breath fanned my face, his scent intoxicated me, and my heart pounded.

"You're my beautiful distraction, little storm," he murmured, his lips grazing mine, letting an intense, electrifying spark course through me.

And you have become my world.

"I love you," I whispered.

His heart was thudding, his grip on my neck and face firm as he pulled me close, sealing our lips in a deep, intense kiss that was fuelled with emotions that were far too many to ever put into words. His hand tangled into my hair, our lips moving against the others. My tears still trickled down my cheeks, yet I was drowning in his touch. His tongue ran along my lips, seeking entrance, and I slowly parted them, moaning when it slipped into my mouth. My pussy throbbed as he drowned me in pleasure that only he could inflict upon me.

His free hand raked down my body, squeezing my ass and kissing me harder. Pulling me down on top of him, his lips never left mine, as if kissing me was his very lifeline. His hand slipped under the nightdress I was wearing, tugging at my lacy panties. He broke away suddenly, a growl ripping from his lips before he flipped us over. My back hit the cold floor, and I stared into his shimmering gold eyes for a second. His heart was racing, and a deep frown was on his face. With one pull, he ripped my silk nightdress off, and I reached up, tugging open his shirt, letting my gaze run over his chest, admiring every ridge and curve of his godly body.

I ran my hand down his chest, loving the feel of his firm body beneath my fingers, but the moment my fingertips grazed against his nipples, making me whimper, he had my hands pinned to the ground. His body was on top of mine, his free hand cupping my thigh as he caressed it. Biting into my shoulder, he kissed me sensually.

I cried out as pain and pleasure rippled through me. His tongue flicked the blood from the bite before he placed another hungry kiss there, letting go of my wrists, only for me to seize the moment and flip us over so I was on top.

"My turn," I whispered. He yanked my head down, kissing my lips once more before I pulled away, kissing him along his jaw. Goddess, he was perfect...

I ran my hands down his chest, not caring that I was digging my nails into him. The way his eyes flashed and he throbbed in his pants told me he liked it. Bending down, I kissed his neck, sucking hard in the most sensitive spot. His hand tangled in my hair, yanking me back.

"Fuck," he growled, flipping us over. He looked down at me with those eyes that were full of pure desire and hunger.

I struggled, but he had my hips between his knees, reaching for the belt in his pants. I licked my lips. My core clenched as he slid his belt out, a dangerous glint in his eyes as he pulled the belt taut in his hands.

Fuck me, baby.

"My turn," he said in a deep sexy growl, making my eyes widen. He gave me a small smirk and bent down, placing tantalising teasing kisses along my neck and massaging me over my soaking panties. "Tell me, little storm, do you trust me?"

I didn't need to think about it.

"Yes. Yes, I do," I whimpered, my eyes flying open as I stared into his glowing orbs. Those emotions... but he closed his eyes, and it was gone, replaced by a dangerous predatorial smirk as he sat back, yanking me up and rolling me onto my stomach.

My entire body was tingling with anticipation and pleasure. My heart was pounding as he kissed the back of my neck.

"Perfect," he whispered, and then he pulled both of my arms behind my back, tying them up with his belt. "Then let's play."

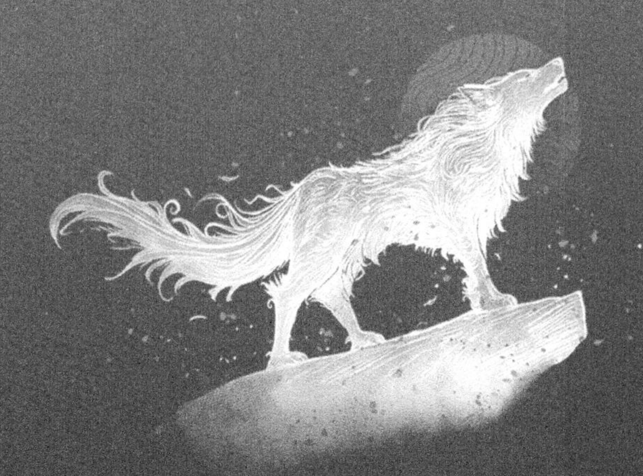

Like a Season

THEON

I NEEDED THIS. I NEEDED an outlet for the tornado that was destroying my mind from within. Grabbing her nightdress from the floor, I ripped a strip from it and, reaching over, covered her eyes. If she couldn't see me, then I didn't need to try and hide the emotions from my eyes. She was always trying to search them, and I knew she was looking for any signs that I had any feelings for her.

I pulled her up, pushing her onto her knees facing the bed. Her breasts were pressed against the mattress, and I yanked her head backwards. She moaned softly, and I smirked, kissing her neck sensually from behind. She looked perfect, her legs slightly apart… arms tied behind her back. Her ass was in nothing but panties that she was going to lose soon enough.

"Keep those legs apart. I'll be right back," I whispered seductively, running my free hand down her ass, making her moan.

"Yes, my king." My eyes blazed, and I growled lowly. Fuck, I liked it when she called me that.

"That's my girl." I spanked her ass, making her gasp before I stood up and walked over to my bottom drawer. A little something that I had picked up the other night… *I wasn't planning on using these yet, but…* I pushed the thought away and took out the box. I took it to the bed, placed it down, and flipped it open.

I stepped back over to her and removed my shirt, my eyes never leaving her perfect ass. The red mark I had left on her ass was the first of many. Tonight, there was not going to be an inch of her that would be left unmarked. Tonight, I was going to make her mine…

I ran my hand down her ass and slowly slid her panties down. They were soaked, and the scent of her arousal was driving me crazy.

"You're such a dirty little whore. Look how fucking wet you are," I murmured, massaging her smooth pussy with my fingers. She moaned loudly, her back arching as she parted her legs more. I stopped, delivering a sharp tap to her ass.

"Did I tell you to part your legs further?"

"Sorr- ah!"

She gasped when I shoved two fingers into her, making her moan loudly. With my other hand, I reached into the box, taking out a pair of leather ankle cuffs, swiftly cuffing her and restricting her movements. Her heart was pounding, which only excited me. My dick was hard in my pants as I fucked her slowly with my fingers, enjoying the way her soaking insides coated my fingers.

"Oh, fuck, Theon… faster," she whimpered. Reaching up, I yanked her head back, making her cry out.

"I prefer it when you call me -"

"King. Fuck me harder, my king," she begged, cutting me off. I smirked. She learned fast.

"Good girl, but I'm not sure you deserve to be fucked just yet," I whispered huskily, slipping my fingers out and, instead, parting her ass cheeks, I admired her. "Now, how about I have a taste to see how good my little slut tastes." I kneeled behind her and plunged my tongue into her soaking core, making her whimper loudly.

"Oh, fuck…"

Oh, fuck was an understatement. She tasted so fucking good. Her moans and whimpers of pleasure only drove me to fuck her harder with my tongue, using my thumb to rub her clit. Her legs shook from the pleasure as more of her juices began to leak from her, and just when I felt her nearing, I pulled back, licking my lips.

"You taste perfect," I growled. Reaching into the box, I took out the black leather flogger. "I think it's time to whip this ass so hard that you aren't able to sit for a few fucking days. How does that sound, little storm?"

"I- ah!" She whimpered when I flogged her ass lightly,

I rubbed her ass, making her whimper loudly before whipping her ass again, this time harder. Each strike, each contact only made me throb harder, watching her body react, the whimpers and moans of pleasure mixing with the pain. Watching how her juices trickled down her legs and the way she wriggled against her restraints.

She was the perfect plaything. Pleasuring her gave me satisfaction beyond anything else. Ten flogs later, I massaged her sore ass, kissing her shoulder. The bite upon her shoulder from earlier was half healed. I bit into her shoulder right next to the previous bite, wanting to mark every inch of her perfect skin. My gaze flickered to the corner of where her neck met her shoulder. The place where one's mate mark would sit…

Would she move on?

I clenched my jaw, my eyes blazing, and I pulled her around, wrapping my hand around her slender neck. I pushed her head back onto the bed behind her before I kissed her roughly.

"You're mine," I growled possessively. I pushed away the thoughts that threatened to consume me. *I don't care… I don't care about what's to come… tonight, she is mine.*

I deepened the kiss, not caring as she gasped for breath, sucking hard on her tongue before ravishing every inch of her sweet mouth. *Mine.*

"Theon…" she whimpered when I broke away, her lips parted as she gasped for air.

"Tell me, who do you belong to?" I asked quietly, running my hand down over her perfect, firm, round breasts, her hard nipples standing to attention, and cupping her pussy. I bent down and sucked on one of her nipples.

"You."

"Remember that," I growled, sucking on her other nipple before squeezing her breasts in my hand as I slipped two fingers back into her pussy. She moaned in response, and I smirked as I began fucking her with two fingers.

"Don't stop, please," she begged.

"What do you want?" I asked, enjoying the faint blush that coated her cheeks.

"I want you to make me come," she whispered, and despite the blush, her words were as enticing as the rest of her.

I could feel my dick wanting its release. The pleasure inside of me only grew, and I began fucking her harder. Wrapping my free hand around her neck, I fucked her fast, slamming my fingers into her rough and hard. Her screams were loud, and I was sure that everyone in the area would be able to hear her, and although I didn't care, I clamped my hand over her pretty plush mouth.

These beautiful sounds were only for me to hear.

Her juices squirted over my hand as her orgasm ripped through her. I pulled out, slapping her pussy hard as I claimed her lips in another bruising kiss. She could barely keep up, her body still recovering from her orgasm. Standing up, I unzipped my pants and pulled my cock out.

"Tongue out beautiful," I commanded.

Her heart skipped a beat as I leaned on one knee near her head, tangling my hand into her blond locks and pulling her head up. She obeyed like the good girl she was, and I smirked, shoving my dick into her mouth.

"Now, suck like the good little slut you are."

She moaned, wrapping her mouth around my cock. I pushed her head back on the bed, resting both my knees on either side of her head and began face fucking her roughly. I groaned as pleasure fucking knocked me out of my senses. My eyes blazed as she worked the magic of her tongue.

"That's it," I growled in approval, looking down at her as she took me all in. Her plush lips stretched around my girth as she sucked on my dick. Even when I shoved myself fully into her, she simply took it, gagging for a moment before she adjusted. This was my kind of girl.

I held onto her hair tightly as my release slammed through me, making me swear in pure fucking ecstasy. For a moment, I saw fucking stars as pleasure rocked my entire body. I pulled out, pumping my dick, squirting the rest of my cum onto her face and breasts. She gasped, sticking her tongue that was already coated in my cum out needily. She moaned, licking her lips hungrily before I tapped her face lightly. A soft smile spread on her face that was glowing from her orgasm, and I caressed her cheek with my thumb.

Perfection…

Bending down, I kissed her slowly, not caring that I could taste myself on her. Her sweet taste lingered, and I nibbled on her lower lip. It was so fucking soft, I had drawn blood several times from it. I bit into it, making her breath hitch as I sucked, licking her lip slowly and sensually.

The pain in my chest returned with a vengeance, my heart thudding as I closed my eyes. *Mine.*

I did it before... why was it so much harder this time? Why couldn't I just walk away? Why was this pain consuming me?

"Theon," she whispered against my lips. I looked at her blindfolded eyes, and as much as I wanted to look into those gorgeous grey eyes as I fucked her, I knew she would see too much in my own…

"Time to fuck this pussy until you pass out," I whispered, stepping away from her. I removed my pants and pulled her up onto the bed. I unhooked her legs, tossed the cuffs aside, and flipped her onto her stomach. "On your knees."

She obeyed, her shoulders and head pressed against the bed. I positioned myself behind her, grabbing hold of her bound wrists, my eyes on her ass that contained many angry welts. Several hickeys littered her back, and I smirked with approval. I had left my mark.

Yanking her up by the arms, I slammed into her with one hard, brutal thrust, making her cry out. Then I began fucking her roughly, so fucking hard that I'd make sure no other man would do it for her.

"Fuck!" She screamed breathlessly.

I would give her so much pleasure that even when another man tried to touch her, she'd remember me. I'd ruin her for everyone else. She was mine and mine alone…

An hour had passed since she'd passed out. I had carried her to the bathroom when the first rays of dawn appeared through the curtains, and I had washed her off before placing her into bed. I had then spent an hour in the shower myself, unable to collect my emotions...

In the last round, before she had passed out, I had untied her blindfold and looked into those beautiful eyes of hers. Grey... maybe it was becoming one of my favourite colours…

I dried myself with a towel and exited the bathroom.

I warned her that I'd break her…

I warned her that I'd ruin her…

Yet she kept pushing…

How do I tell her that this was it?

I entered the bedroom. Her hair was still wet since I hadn't dried it, and with the slight ray of light that seeped through the curtain, her skin seemed to glisten breathtakingly. She really was beautiful…

I crouched down by the bed, running my fingers through her light blonde locks and caressing her cheek. The sound of her gently beating heart made the howling wind from outside fade away.

Her moans were my favourite sound, her voice was my favourite song, her breathing was my favourite lullaby, and her beating heart was my favourite rhythm. Now and forever. I leaned forward, pressing my lips to her forehead softly.

I was nothing more than someone passing through her life, just like another season... and before the end of this winter, I hoped she would forget me just like one would forget a season long passed…

A Cold Morning

YILEYNA

I awoke to find the bed empty, feeling a pang of pain inside of me. I know he had a lot to do, but I did wish I could at least wake up to him next to me, even if it was just occasionally.

My entire body felt sore and achy, yet the lightness that I felt in my chest was immeasurable. A smile played on my lips and my cheeks burned as I thought of last night. It had been different, and even if I was blindfolded, it only heightened my other senses. I felt as if we had somehow become closer. It was almost as if we had opened ourselves to one another in an entirely new way.

I was sure Theon felt something much more for me than he admitted. He couldn't put it into words, but I was positive he was falling for me. I smiled happily, hugging the blanket to my chest. He had cleaned me too. No one did that unless they truly cared. I closed my eyes for a moment, feeling utterly happy and content.

My Theon… just like I was his…

My heart leapt when I heard the sound of movement in the other room, and I jolted upright, wincing at how sore my behind and core felt. He was home!

I kicked the blanket off and quickly got out of bed, almost falling over my legs that felt like jelly. I opened the drawer to grab a shirt or something to put on, when I realised it was half empty. I frowned. Most of Theon's clothes were missing…

Feeling confused, I pulled on a t-shirt before I closed the wardrobe and pulled the curtains open. The window was entirely frosted, and from what I could see outside, the snow was still falling strongly, and it was extremely windy.

I stripped the bedding, the stains from last night a reminder of everything that we had done there… I don't think I'll be able to come into this room without remembering it. My heart skipped a beat as I held the bundled bedding in my arms and made my way to the bedroom door.

I opened it to see Theon standing over a trunk, wearing black pants and a black shirt, which hung open, and his hair brushed back. He turned his gorgeous amber eyes towards where I stood, his eyes trailing over me, and I could feel my cheeks burning up under his gaze. It was almost as if he was undressing me entirely, and the shirt I was wearing suddenly felt too small...

My heart skipped a thousand beats when our eyes locked.

"Morning," I said, my stomach all fluttery.

"Morning," he replied, his deep sexy voice making me feel giddy. Goddess, what was going on? I was feeling even more nervous than usual…

He turned back to the trunk and tossed in some clothes. I frowned, remembering the wardrobe that was partially empty.

"Are you going somewhere?" I asked, walking over to him. There was over a foot difference in height between us, and although I wanted to pull him down and kiss him, he had turned back to the trunk.

"I'm going to be moving to the castle for a while. I have to take the Beta title soon. The ceremony should be coming up, and then my workload will increase. It makes sense for me to take up my old room at the castle," he replied, his voice emotionless and cold. My stomach sank at those words, and deep down, I wondered if he'd invite me too.

"So, do you mean permanently?" I asked, taking the clothes he was shoving in and beginning to fold them. My eyes fell to the red welts on my arms where he had tied me up. They were fading, yet the reminder of what happened remained. Making an illicit desire throb in my lower regions.

"Pretty much. You can keep staying here. No one will remove you." I froze, my heart thundering at what he had just said. *Why did that sound like…* It didn't sound right.

"You're speaking as if you might not even come back here," I replied lightly, raising an eyebrow. He looked down at me. Reaching up with his hand, he cupped the left side of my face, brushing his thumb over my cheek.

"Who knows." He smirked arrogantly. I frowned.

"That's mean," I huffed, pushing his hand off. His smirk had eased me. "I'm sure you'll come to see me at least."

"Hmm, well you are a beautiful distraction." My heart skipped a beat.

"I'm glad I am," I replied softly. His smirk vanished and he frowned.

"Although I will be busy over at the castle, I do want to see if we can push to awaken whatever you are and maybe your shift... without anyone else knowing." My unease vanished and I nodded, internally scolding myself for feeling paranoid.

"Thanks, I'd appreciate that."

Our eyes met and, stepping closer, I reached up, locking my arms around his neck and pressing my entire body into his. My heart pounded as I felt him tense, but it wasn't even a split second later when his hands wrapped around my waist and he stood up straight, lifting me off the ground completely and crushing me against him. I smiled, kissing his jaw softly. He nudged my face away, kissing my neck sensually instead. I resisted a moan and his hold on me tightened before he inhaled deeply, burying his nose in the crook of my neck.

For a few moments, he didn't move. I wrapped my legs around his waist, enjoying his embrace and the steady beat of his heart. He exhaled slowly and placed me down.

"Are you going now?" I asked as he continued to put his things into the trunk.

"Yeah, I'll be leaving. Don't wait for me, alright? I won't be coming back." I suddenly felt cold inside, but I nodded. He slammed the trunk shut and closed the buttons of his shirt before he put on one of his big coats. "Every evening at ten o'clock, down by the White Dove, starting tomorrow, meet me there."

I nodded, feeling a flash of confusion. Why was he acting like that was the only time he'd see me...?

He picked up the sack and trunk and walked towards the door. Stopping, he placed something on the shelf by the front door before opening the door. Instantly the howling wind became louder, and I flinched as the blast of bitter cold rushed through the cabin. Theon stepped out and pulled his trunk out behind him. He paused for a moment as I walked over to the door.

"See you..." I said softly.

He didn't reply, and after a moment, he walked off in the deep snow. I watched him until I could no longer see him, and closed the door to the cabin, locking it.

This was... strange... was he really gone? Not all the higher-ups lived in the castle. Sure it was easier, but the sudden plan to move there...

I turned to the shelf, wondering what he had put there. Pushing aside the small box that stood on the shelf, my heart sank when my gaze fell on the key. The key to the cabin... I looked at the door, my heart thundering as I realised both keys were here. Why did he leave his key?

Fear enveloped me, and I unlocked the door, running out into the snow in nothing but the shirt I was wearing.

"Theon!" I shouted, but my voice was drowned out by the howling wind. "Theon!"

Surely, he'll hear me! He couldn't have gotten far with his luggage. I looked down at the snow-covered ground that was eleven inches deep and saw his tracks. Not caring about the cold that was biting into my feet, I ran through the blizzard, my heart leaping when I saw his back in his dark fur coat.

"Theon!"

He stopped in his tracks, and I ran over to him, brushing away my hair as the wind blew around us violently. He turned to look at me and I gave him a small smile, despite the cold that was sinking into my skin.

"You left both keys," I explained, holding it out to him. "One was in the door." He glanced down at my hand. I stood there, hand outstretched. He didn't take it, and I realised his hands were full. "Shall I put it into your pocket?" I offered, stepping closer.

"No. I don't need it. I left it on purpose," he replied emotionlessly. My heart skipped a beat and fear began to settle into me.

Don't think negatively, Yileyna; he probably doesn't trust it at the castle... or something...

"Oh! Okay, um, what if you come when I'm not around or -"

"I'll knock on the door if I do come, but it's not necessary. I no longer need the key. The place is yours. Consider it a gift." I frowned, confusion filling me.

"Theon, you're scaring me. It's almost as if you're not coming back," I said with a small, forced chuckle. He didn't reply. He simply looked at me. "Theon?" *You're really scaring me. Say something.*

Silence ensued, only the sound of the screaming wind and my pounding heart filled my ears.

"Like I said, as future Beta of this kingdom, I need to focus on that. I realised when we were late for training that I can't afford to have distractions. I need space from anything that holds me back from reaching my full potential, and if that includes you, then so be it."

I felt as if someone had just wrapped their hands around my heart and were crushing it. He was leaving me.

Goddess, he was leaving me.

"I… I'm sorry if I made you late, I promise I won't do it again -"

"You're wasting my time right now; I have a meeting with the king in half an hour." It felt as if he had just slapped me across the face. I looked up into his eyes, my own stinging with hot tears that I refused to let fall.

"I'm sorry," I repeated softly, stepping away. He didn't reply as he continued walking away, the pain in my chest worsening.

I felt alone. So, so alone. The fear of abandonment raged within me, mirroring the storm around me. The wind blew harshly, and I backed away, staring at his receding figure. *Do I really mean nothing to you, Theon?*

I was praying for him to turn around, just one look… one reassuring nod. To look at me and tell me he'll be back. But he didn't.

I backed away slowly, the pain in my chest stronger than ever, and when the first tear spilt down my cheek, I turned and ran back to the cabin. The one I had thought was our home.

Once again, those that I loved had left me alone in what was just a house… I stepped into the warmth, slamming the door shut and locking it before I clamped my hands over my mouth, muffling the painful sob that wracked my body.

I looked around the small cabin. The fire was blazing, casting warmth around the room. Memories of our time here consumed me. The table was gone… a reminder of that moment... the two chairs and a small makeshift table stood to the side, and there, on the kitchen counter, stood a single steaming mug of coffee. I walked over to it, wiping my tears away. Did Theon forget to have it?

His coffee… I would miss it. I wrapped my freezing hands around it when my gaze fell to the sink. A matching mug sat there, and I looked down at the one in my hand. He had made it for me…

A single tear splashed into the mug, and I wondered what was wrong with me that not even one person wanted to stay by my side. What had I done that I deserved to be deserted?

I let go of the coffee mug, dropping to my knees and resting my head against the kitchen cabinet. I felt empty and alone.

He said we would meet for training, right? It means something, right? The fact that he made coffee, surely I meant something to him… *Right, Theon?*

Stop it, Yileyna. I was only trying to make myself feel better, but the truth was that I just wasn't enough.

A Sacrifice

THEON

I entered the king's office, trying to do my best to remain emotionless. The burning rage of resentment and hatred bubbling beneath the surface of my skin was growing ever stronger.

I couldn't remove the image of her from my mind in that thin white shirt as she stood in the cold with concern and fear clear in her grey eyes… I hated it, hated that I had left her when I could see her breaking before my very eyes. She had only wanted one small gesture of reassurance that I wasn't leaving her, but I was, and I couldn't string her along any longer than I already had. It was one of the hardest things I have ever done in life, but I had to.

She was a distraction from my goal.

"Theon, are you alright?" Andres asked, frowning as he looked up at me from behind his desk. I gave a curt nod.

"You wanted to see me?" I said. Never had I detested him as much as I did at that moment. He was the reason for all of this.

"I did, but if now isn't the right time, we can postpone our meeting…"

"Just carry on. I'm fine," I said through gritted teeth. He observed me for a moment before he nodded.

"It was regarding your Beta position; I was thinking about the upcoming ceremony. I wanted to ask you a final time… are you sure?"

I looked into his grey eyes coldly and frowned. It was the first fucking time I realised his eyes weren't much of a different shade than Yileyna's. The only difference was that I hated this pair with the same vengeance as I did the man they belonged to.

"Sure about what?" I had a feeling he was asking if this was the position I was happy with. Dad's words rang in my head, but I felt sick at the very thought of having this man's daughter as my mate.

Remember the goal.

"About my offer. Charlene may not be the same as Yileyna, I know she is very popular when it comes to her beauty and personality, but Charlene would make a good mate. Besides, I know you are very chivalrous, Theon, and this is for the betterment of the kingdom. We need someone worthy of being Alpha."

Alpha… it was the position I needed. I could take her as my mate, and then, with me as Alpha… no one would be able to disobey. The plan was for the attack to happen before this winter passed… that wasn't too long a time. If I just…

The image of Yileyna flashed through my mind; her blonde hair, her soft, plump lips, her gorgeous grey eyes… and with it, the clarity that I had indeed strayed hit me like a fucking avalanche.

She was ruining everything.

"You are right. This kingdom needs a strong Alpha, and despite Charlene being your daughter, she doesn't have the will of an Alpha," I said coldly. "I guess I will accept this deal." The guilt that washed through me as those words left my lips was suffocating.

Andres didn't do anything to hide his happiness, his eyes lighting up as he let out a raucous laugh, standing up and slamming his hand down on the table.

"Are you agreeing? Ah, you are! That's my son!" He walked around the table, wrapping his arms around me in a tight hug, only making my hatred flare through me viciously.

I was no fucking son of his. The day I killed him and his fucking daughter would be the day I'd be happier than ever.

I clenched my jaw, my eyes flashing as I did my all not to shove him away from me. He patted my back, his happiness as clear as the blizzard outside.

"I'm doing this for the kingdom," I said coldly, looking into his eyes.

"Of course! Theon, you know you can keep Yileyna on the side if you so wish -"

"Keep her as a whore and humiliate her in the process? I don't think so." I clenched my jaw, unable to hide the venom in my voice. Andres's smile vanished as he looked at me with a concern that almost looked real.

"Do you love her?" He asked after a moment.

I stared at the wooden table in front of me. I knew enough to know that if an Alpha didn't want something or someone in their way, they got rid of it. He could do anything to Yileyna... just as Dad could...

"No," I replied without hesitation, instantly seeing how he relaxed. "She's nothing to me, but I prefer not to humiliate her."

"That's understandable. Fear not. I'll keep her busy with work. I realised I haven't really assigned her anything, and after talking to you about it last time, I have decided I will make her a Zeta-rank, a warrior. I'll make sure she gets her pay and everything on time. She'll be happy, and she'll have the chance to keep busy. I have already talked to Raiden to have this all in order by the end of the week. "

Zeta-rank... just below the royal guards... so she won't be around the palace. I guess that was better. Being Zeta-ranked would mean she had some level of protection from bastards like Levin. I nodded.

"That sounds ideal. We will continue with the princess's training as planned, and hopefully, soon, her abilities will break free. What exactly are we looking for? What kind of ability is the heart meant to possess?" I asked. The prophecy never said more than the one that held the heart possessed the ability to control the middle kingdom.

"We aren't sure. It has never been said anywhere, but whatever it is, it will bring great power and prosperity."

It was too vague... far too vague for me to know if I needed Charlene alive and by my side or if I could just throw her in a cell and use her as a weapon. Although I still had no idea what kind of weapon she would be, she was plain useless.

A sudden thought came to me, and I tilted my head, looking at the king calculatingly.

"Charlene knows of the relationship I had with Yileyna. Do you think she will agree?" I asked.

She didn't have a spine; she was meek and pretty much useless, but I had seen her anger when it came to Yileyna. I was sure the one person she wouldn't want to hurt was Yileyna...

"Charlene will agree. Before a friend, her duty is to her pack and kingdom," Andres replied dismissively.

"She and Yileyna are close." Charlene was the only person Yileyna had left, but I guess we all know that even the closest friends can betray one another. I was letting Yileyna come in the way of my revenge…

"I will talk to her. Fear not, she will agree. We need to do this for this kingdom. She will understand. We will make the announcement at the planned ball at the next full moon." I gave a curt nod.

"Fine."

It wouldn't be for long... soon, this kingdom would bend its knee to me. This pack would become mine, and the Obsidian Shadow Pack would take its rightful place as the ruling pack, and then, everyone who had wronged us would pay.

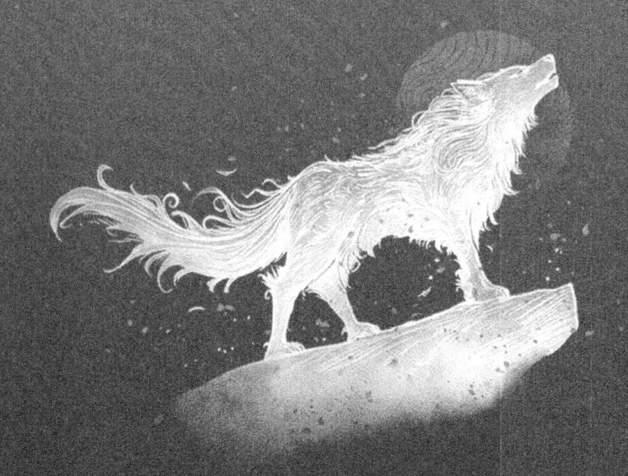

A Failure

CHARLENE

"Really, Charlene, can you pay a little attention? You need to choose a dress." Mom scolded, flipping through the samples of fabrics that sat on the sofa next to her.

I frowned as I stared out at the blizzard outside. We were currently in the sitting room of our quarters, and Mom was trying to have our dresses finalised for the upcoming ball.

Was Yileyna okay? I heard Theon was moving back to the castle. This time of year was brutal in terms of how cold it got. I didn't get why Yileyna hadn't moved to the castle with him as well. It had shocked me when the staff said it was just Theon alone. What was going on? It wasn't like either of them to be separated.

Theon was so possessive of her. Everyone could tell from the way he looked at her, he was even going around making it known, so it was strange she wasn't at the castle. It was worrying me. Did they argue again? I wished she had the ability to mind-link so I could at least talk to her.

"Charlene!" Mom snapped, making me jump.

"Mom, relax. Choose whatever you like," I said quietly. I felt restless, and I knew it was because of the news of Theon coming here alone. Goddess! I needed to do something.

"Charlene, as the future ruler of this kingdom, you need to be a lot more proactive about what is going on around you," Mom reprimanded me icily. I frowned.

"Choosing a dress when we are threatened by war and attacks isn't really being proactive," I murmured, but of course, she heard.

Her heels clicked on the floor as she strode over to me, pulling me by my arm and turning me viciously. She raised her hand. My eyes flew open as I stared at her, and she brought it down, stopping inches from my face. Our hearts were thumping. She had never hit me...

She looked shocked by her own actions too. She lowered her hand, clenching her fist, and twirled away, her anger so obvious that it worried me.

"You need to act like you are at least an alpha female!" She hissed.

"I don't understand why you're saying that, Mom. I'm doing my best." I didn't understand what more she wanted from me.

"You aren't. Your father is so worried about the future of this kingdom. Why? Because you aren't up to the standard needed," she said, worry and anger on her face. "Growing up, we both know you were always second to a certain someone. At least now, try to live up to the expectations we need from you."

I felt a pang of pain inside. Yes, I knew I was always compared to Yileyna by Mom. Yileyna was always better at everything, and Mom would always make remarks about it. That only stopped when I shifted, and Yileyna didn't. But lately, with the growing threats, it was only becoming more and more stressful for us all.

I worked hard. I was trying to awaken my abilities. I was trying to be involved and learn about the kingdom from Dad. I mean, as future Alpha, he should involve me, but he didn't. There was only so much I could do on my own.

Mom simply stared at me, clucking her tongue sharply in frustration.

"You need to be the daughter he needs, Charlene. You need to care for the kingdom. This ball is an important event, with your father choosing Theon of Westerfell as our Beta." Theon of Westerfell... I had heard that title going around, binding him to the city since he had no memory of his past... I sighed heavily and nodded.

"Yes, Mother, you are right," I said, not wanting to argue.

At least when Theon became Beta, Yileyna would, by default, become Beta female, and then we could spend much more time together. I missed her. Since her parents had died, we didn't have as much time as before, and now that Theon's in her life…

Yes, I was a bit jealous that my soul sister was taken from me, but as long as she was happy, I was happy. She deserved happiness.

I forced myself to look at the fabric swatches that were scattered on the sofa. I flipped through a bundle, unable to focus on what I was seeing, and stopped at a silver fabric.

"I will wear silver," I said emotionlessly, not wanting to argue further with her. She paused before she nodded, smiling with approval.

"That's perfect," Mom said, and I breathed a sigh of relief.

"We can go for some accents of green," I offered, not wanting to upset her any further.

"See, that wasn't so hard, was it?"

"No. Of course not." She smiled in approval just as the door opened and Dad entered the sitting room.

"Andres," Mom said, standing up as she walked over to her mate and, cupping his face, kissed him softly. Dad kissed her back, but I could tell he'd had a long day; he looked tired but somewhat still happy. I guess things were going well.

I smiled politely. I was so glad that I did hold the power of the heart of Kaeladia within me, it made me feel far less useless. I just wished I could break the seal on my powers soon. It would at least help me make my parents happy and help the people of the city.

Dad grinned when he broke away from Mom, cupping her face for a second.

"I have good news," he said, kissing her neck. I looked at him curiously, wondering what this good news was that had gotten him so excited.

"Oh?" Mom asked as Dad sat down, pulling her into his lap.

"Yes. Theon has agreed to take Charlene as his chosen mate."

My stomach dropped, my heart thumping as his words rang in my head. I stared at him in utter disbelief and anger.

"What?" I asked, my voice coming out hoarse.

"Theon will be your mate," Dad repeated, his smile vanishing, the command in his voice making me shudder.

"He's with Yileyna."

"Not anymore. He agreed to take you as his," Dad smirked.

I clenched my fists, my heart pounding as I stared at Dad, summoning every inch of my courage.

"No."

"What?" He asked, his eyes hard.

"I said no. I will never take Theon as my mate. Ever," I said bravely, despite the fear I felt as Dad's aura raged around him like a beast ready to wreak havoc. Goddess, give me the strength to stand up to him.

"Say that again," Dad threatened, slowly pushing Mom onto the sofa as he stood up. I squared my shoulders, jutting my chin out defiantly.

"I said no. I will *never* take a man that belongs to another as my mate. I don't care if Theon agreed, I don't agree," I said clearly.

"You will. You are not worthy of the position yourself!" Dad warned. "This kingdom needs an Alpha."

"Then let him be Alpha. Make Theon your heir! Why are you tying me to him? He can still be Alpha, I don't want the position!"

"Charlene!" Mom hissed, standing up, her eyes flashing. I frowned as Dad let out a laugh, as if I had just made a joke.

"Make him my heir? Oh, if it was only that easy! Do you really think it is? I need an Aphelion on that throne! I need my blood to continue on! I fought for that throne! How childish and ridiculous are you that you think the Alpha title is a joke that you can just pass on to someone else!"

"Then let me choose another mate. There are so many potential Alphas, Father! Please, don't tie me to Theon. I don't like him!" I pleaded.

Why had he agreed? I didn't get it. Was he really casting Yileyna aside? I couldn't believe it…

I had a crush on Theon from the moment I had first seen him… but when I began to see the attention that he had only for Yileyna, I accepted that he belonged to her. I would never be jealous of what was not mine, what belonged to my sister, and I would *never* take what is hers. Ever.

"Another Alpha? When we have Theon, who is far better than any young man I have come across?"

"It just shows how much she is lacking!" Mom added.

"Then… at the ball, you are having Alphas from all around. What if my mate is there? At least let me have the chance to find my true mate?" I begged.

"You will be bound to Theon, by mark and by marriage," Dad added with finality. His raging eyes glared at me, and I was forced to lower my head in submission to him. He let out a scoff. "An Alpha, my daughter, yet she cannot even defy my command ..." He stepped closer to me, taking hold of my chin. A dangerous glint in his eyes made my heart pound in fear. "I'm warning you, Charlene, if Yileyna is the reason behind this, I will make sure she's out of the picture," he whispered menacingly. A threat he truly meant. My eyes stung, but I didn't blink.

I will not show him I'm scared. Nothing can happen to Yileyna. If Theon isn't in her corner, then she has me. Even if I am useless or not good enough, a failed daughter and a failed Alpha... but I swear by Selene, I will not be a failure of a friend.

I nodded in silent agreement that I had understood him.

"At the ball, we will announce their union," Dad added, turning to Mom, who smiled and gushed about how Theon was perfect for me. I frowned.

The ball... that meant I had a little time. I needed to talk to Theon and Yileyna. Immediately.

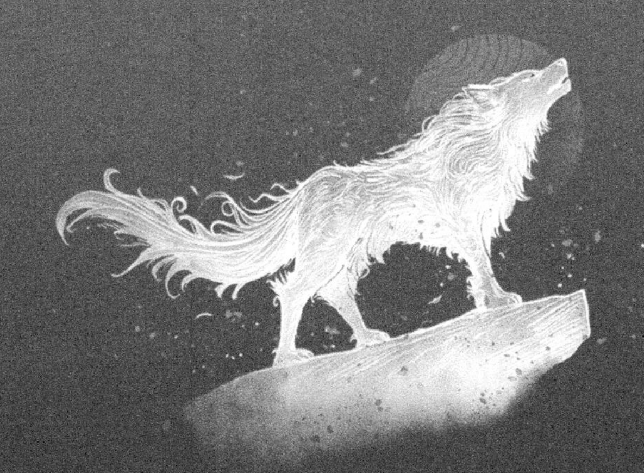

Stopping for a Hot Drink

YILEYNA

I FELT NUMB. OVER TWENTY-FOUR hours had passed, but as he said… he didn't come back. I spent the night before pacing the cabin, wanting to see him, to go to him, until I realised I didn't hold that right…

I was a distraction and one he didn't need…

I didn't sleep that night, unable to enter the bedroom after what had happened there just the night before. His emotions… he… there was more to last night. I knew it… but where I thought he was falling for me… he was actually saying goodbye…

I ran my hands through my hair once more, staring out at the blizzard. The fire in the hearth had died down yesterday afternoon, and the cabin was cold, but I didn't care… I don't think anything felt as cold as it was inside my heart.

Ten o'clock tonight. He said he'd meet me… and although I was counting the minutes, what was I to do? Pretend to be normal? When Theon himself told me it was over… it made clear all I was to him: a simple pass time.

I couldn't just sit there doing nothing, but then why did I feel like I didn't want to do anything but wallow?

"Well, even if you want to, you can't," I told myself, sitting up and taking a deep breath. "I am Yileyna De'Lacor, and I am not going to let a man make me lose sight of my goals."

I had been played and used. Regardless of whether there were emotions involved or not… I had to stop. I really needed to stop letting him hurt me. Maybe tonight I'll see how he is, but unless he says that he made a mistake, I will not give him the time of day. I will stop thinking about it. I will try to be strong and act like I am not affected. I missed him, and deep down, I did want to see him again, but his actions would confirm many things tonight…

For now, I would go and ask the Alpha for the proof of my parents' crimes. Nodding with determination and a sense of purpose, I quickly ate some food and got dressed in white leather pants, a pale grey shirt, and a white corset belt.

I picked up my empty dishes and carried them over to the sink. I was about to place them in the sink when my eyes fell on the glass of vinegar.

"Oh, shit!"

I had forgotten it. I quickly split it in the sink, wondering if the vinegar had destroyed the metal. Turning the tap on, I rinsed it off before applying some washing-up soap to it and giving it a good scrub with the sponge. Once I had scrubbed it thoroughly and rinsed it off with warm water, I looked at the chain in hand. My breath hitched; I wasn't holding just a rusty, dull trinket. I didn't need to take it to a jeweller for confirmation that I was holding a precious stone in my hand, something worth far more than a few gold coins.

The jewel in the centre that had looked a dull brown under the layers of grime and dirt dazzled a gorgeous burning amber. I ran my fingers along the chain; where it had once looked grey and dirty, it shone a pale gold. I had hit a gold mine. Was it a stolen item? Or perhaps he had found it somewhere? Obviously, he didn't realise how pretty it was! I'm sure he would have tried to charge far more.

I was about to put it down when I hesitated. If it was worth a lot… then I should wear it and keep it safe. I dried it with a dishcloth and slipped the long chain over my head, tucking it into my shirt and letting it nestle itself between my breasts.

Theon's face flashed to mind, the memory of his touch making my body betray me. My stomach reacted, and that ache settled inside me once more. I took a deep breath, grabbed my coat, and squashed the thought. *Focus, Yileyna.*

I pulled open the door to the cabin and stepped outside into the blizzard. It took me a moment to keep my footing as the wind pushed against me violently. Goddess, the weather was getting worse. It seems worse than usual, despite the cold not seeming as bad.

Locking up behind me, I slipped the key into my pouch and placed it into the large inner pocket of my coat, then began trudging through the snow. The snow was deeper than yesterday too…

It took much longer to make my way toward the castle, but it gave me time to ponder over how I would approach the topic with the king. I sighed heavily as I approached the busier streets of the city. The snow was far less here, with lots of foot traffic making it melt away. However, this made parts of the ground rather iced. I could feel the cold now. My legs felt rather numb too.

"Yileyna!"

I stopped, surprised to see Charlene standing there in a white fur coat and hat. The tip of her nose was red, but the relief, worry, and happiness in her eyes made me concerned and delighted to see her all at once.

"Charlene!" I smiled, giving her a big bear hug. She hugged me back, and I smiled, feeling a little better in her embrace, but she was the future Alpha. I couldn't really rely on her. The king indirectly made it clear he only tolerated me because of Charlene. I knew for a fact that if I shared my problems with her, she would only put herself in more trouble and take more stress due to it.

"I was actually coming to see you, but I had training with Madelia first," she explained, taking my hands in her gloved ones. "Goddess, Yileyna! Why aren't you wearing your gloves!"

"It's not that cold, I'm okay," I said.

"You will get frostbite!"

"I really won't. So, tell me, how was training? And why was I so lucky to have you come visit me?" I asked. She looked around, as if checking if anyone was listening.

"How about we get a hot drink?" She suggested with a smile, but there was something worrying her. I could see it.

"Why not? We can go to Madam Marigold's," I suggested. It was always very packed, and you could have a conversation there.

She nodded, and we both made our way down a side street before we approached the small café. Steam was blowing out from the chimney, and the promise of warmth and a hot cup of coffee was calling. *Coffee… maybe not.*

We exchanged looks, a smile crossing both our faces before we hurried to the door. Charlene skidded on the icy entrance. I grabbed hold of her as she yelped in alarm before we burst out laughing.

"Oops, careful," I giggled as I pushed open the door, and we stepped inside.

Instantly I was hit with the smell of coffee, roasted walnuts, and so many more delicious scents. Music played in the background, blending in with the hum of chatter.

"Did you ladies not see the warning outside to be careful on the ice?" Madam Marigold questioned, raising a brow sceptically.

"No," Charlene and I said in unison. We hadn't.

"Oh, that sign is long since covered by snow, Marigold!" Someone called out, making the woman roll her eyes.

"Right, but I don't need the king to be out for my neck if his daughter gets hurt on my premises," she scolded lightly before jerking her head towards the back.

"Really?" Charlene asked. It was rare to get a back room in here.

"Yes, go. It's too rowdy in here for pretty girls to be around. I don't need the extra drama!"

Ah, perfect. We needed a place where we could simply talk. It was almost as if she had read our minds! Behaving ourselves, we made our way to the back. Only one of the booths was empty, and, taking off our coats, we took our seats.

Zarian, the young fae man who worked there, walked over to us. He was probably a good few decades older than us, but he looked as if he was not a day over twenty. Muscled, lean, beautiful violet eyes, and silky black hair that held a purple hue to it, fell to his shoulders.

"And hello, ladies, it's been a few months. How are you both? Looking as ravishing as ever."

"Hello Zarian, we are well, thank you," Charlene said, as I smiled slightly. "Can we get two mugs of hot chocolate?"

"Is that all? Are you sure the beautiful ladies want nothing more?" He asked with a small flirty smile. I raised an eyebrow.

"That is all," I said, trying to suppress my giggle as Charlene blushed, embarrassed. He let out a small chuckle before he gave a nod.

"Well then, I'll go get those two mugs of hot chocolate, but if you do want something else… I'm not far off." He gave a final wink, and I shook my head.

"I swear he wasn't this flirty the last time we came..."

"Well, he did joke that if we were a wee bit older, he would consider us," Charlene giggled, shaking her head.

"Well, he is... beautiful," I said, trying to ignore the sadness inside of me.

"Hm." Charlene's smile seemed to vanish at the same time as mine before a frown creased her forehead. "Yileyna, what's going on between you and Theon?"

My smile vanished, the pain in my chest hitting me like a tonne of bricks. I couldn't lie because she had seen the look on my face. I shook my head, trying to compose myself. I would have told her, maybe... but this wasn't the way I was expecting it to be brought up.

"Darling..."

"He said it's over..." I said quietly with a small shrug. She frowned, her eyes flashing.

"How dare he... did he give a reason?"

"He said I was a distraction." It hurt, so much, but what could I do? She looked at me, clearly conflicted, as if she wanted to say something but wasn't sure. "It's fine, Charlene, I'm over him. I mean, I'm not, but I will be. I gave him enough chances," I whispered, knowing that he had such a hold on me that my sanity went out the window when he was around. She frowned deeply, staring at the table,

"Yileyna..."

"It's okay, Charlene, it was my fault. I shouldn't have allowed myself to get trapped in this. I'm fine. Really." She hesitated before nodding.

"I am going to have a word with him," she said quietly, her eyes cold and serious.

"You don't need to," I said quickly, waving my hands, knowing that Theon was even nastier to her. Just then, Zarian returned with our drinks, and we stopped talking. Charlene looked extremely upset, and after that, she was far more lost in thought, barely touching her hot drink.

"I'm truly sorry, Yileyna," she said quietly, looking up into my eyes with sorrow and guilt.

"Don't be. You aren't responsible for him being a dick," I said, gulping down my hot chocolate in one go. "I'm afraid I have a lot more to do than wallow in self-pity. It's time I did some digging."

"Digging?" I looked around before leaning forward and lowering my voice.

"The truth about my parents; I know they weren't traitors, and I intend to find out exactly what happened," I whispered quietly. She frowned, a flash of determination in her eyes as she nodded.

"Sounds like a plan. I'm with you. We are going to do this together," she whispered. I smiled as our eyes met, and I knew we would always have one another. Men could break your heart, but sisters… sisters didn't.

"Thank you, my queen." She smiled at me, taking my hand and giving it a gentle squeeze of encouragement.

"Always, my angel."

I was truly grateful to the goddess for at least giving me Charlene.

Her Pathetic Attempt

THEON

I had just showered after having trained with the men. I hadn't even been able to face the princess so had told Madelia to handle training her today. My anger at just the thought of being tied to her made me physically sick. I hated her with such a vengeance that I wished I could just kill her. I was sure I could take over without the fucking heart of Kaeladia.

I wrapped a towel around my waist just as there was a knock on the door. My heart raced for a second, and deep down, I prayed somehow that it was Yileyna, just to look into those beautiful grey eyes of hers. I wanted to see her again… but at the same time, I knew I couldn't. I had to push her away. I opened the door, and my mood instantly darkened when I saw the woman before me.

"Theon, may I have a word?" Charlene asked, her eyes fixed on my face. The look of determination in her eyes was something that you didn't see often from her.

No, you fucking can't.

"Make it quick," I said, turning away from her. She stepped inside, partially closing the door. My eyes flashed as I turned, glaring coldly at her.

"Why did you agree to Dad?" Her voice was serious, her eyes full of anger. I raised an eyebrow, smirking coldly. *So this was what she was here for.*

"Why are you so angry? If memory serves, you were always pretty infatuated with me," I remarked coldly. Her eyes flashed, and she glared at me.

"The moment you and Yileyna started a relationship, those feelings were gone. Why did you agree? Why are you hurting her? She is such a good person, Theon. You are lucky to have her," she whispered, keeping her voice low. I crossed my arms, not bothering to reply, but her words weren't that wrong...

I was lucky, because she did provide me with a mental break from the storm within my mind. A beautiful distraction.

"Please, Theon, don't hurt her. What did Dad promise you? Because I promise you, when I'm Alpha, I will give -"

"When you're Alpha? Really? You're so useless, Princess, that even your own father has no faith in you. I'm doing this for this kingdom, so when the time comes and that throne needs an Alpha King, it will have one who is worthy of it. If you weren't so incompetent, this would never have happened. So, congratulations, Princess, thanks to your uselessness, I decided to drop her." Her heart was beating fast, her eyes filled with guilt, but she still shook her head.

"No. No, I'm not marrying you. I don't care, I will never let you mark me. Yileyna doesn't know yet, but I'm going to tell her."

"Won't that just hurt her?" I asked coldly. "Her knowing won't stop it from happening, now, will it?"

"I'd rather she knows from me before she's hurt, just like you and Dad hurt her at the festival when Dad announced you as Beta," she spat.

So she had some fire in her. Unfortunately, it only seemed to show when it came to her beautiful friend. I smirked coldly. It was satisfying seeing her in pain.

"And tell me, what will Yileyna think when she finds out it's her own friend who will have her man?" I taunted mockingly. Her face paled, but she frowned.

"That's the thing, Yileyna and I trust one another before anyone else. She will believe me, and I won't do this. I won't. I may not be strong, but I won't... I won't..." She was shaking her head, her voice cold and determined. "I came to you because I thought we could come up with a plan. I thought... I thought Dad was threatening you, so you agreed, and I... we could have planned something. You deserve to be with who you want. Yileyna deserves some happiness... you made her happy." She was whispering now, looking at my indifferent mask. Her hands began shaking as she realised how wrong she was.

The only thing was, she didn't realise she was pretty close to the truth. Yileyna... both my father and hers wanted Yileyna out of the picture if she came in the way of their plans. She didn't deserve to become collateral damage. My heart squeezed at the thought, and I looked at the angry princess.

"Well, it's a shame that your visit was futile. I'm not backing down. This engagement will happen as planned," I said coldly. My stomach churned at the thought, and I turned away from her.

"Theon, please, if you have even an ounce of feelings for Yileyna, and I know you do, then -"

"Get out," I interrupted coldly.

"Theon, she only has you!" She stepped in front of me, blocking my path. Her eyes were full of fear and worry as she looked up at me, begging.

I was right, she was just useless. For an Alpha she couldn't even protect her friend. I wanted to say more, but I heard footsteps in the corridor.

"She doesn't. I don't need her…" I trailed off, my heart thundering as I realised who those light footsteps belonged to. What was she doing here? This was the higher-ups' section of the castle; I had only been given a room here yesterday…

"She needs you, please," Charlene whispered. I had to take the chance… I swallowed hard.

"I'm done with Yileyna," I said clearly, and loud enough that I knew she'd hear. "I think it's high time we told the entire kingdom about us, that we are to be mated. Don't you agree, Charlene?" I continued arrogantly, the words feeling like poison on my tongue, but if I was going down in Yileyna's eyes, then so was Charlene. She didn't deserve Yileyna as a friend… and I didn't deserve her in my life either.

Charlene looked confused as I took hold of her jaw, painfully tight. From the corner of my eyes, I saw the shadow of someone stopping at the door. Charlene was too riled up in her own emotions to notice. Perfect.

"Theon, we need to -"

I cut her off, pressing my lips against hers. Anger flashed through me, and even when she tried to shove me back, I didn't let her move, holding her face in place.

I heard the small gasp and the sound of footsteps silently retreating, before she turned and ran. Only then did I move back, shoving Charlene away from me and wiping my mouth.

"Get the fuck out," I hissed venomously. Her eyes pooled with tears as she wiped her mouth with shaking hands.

"I hate you," she whispered before she ran from the room, slamming the door behind her.

"I fucking hate you more," I replied to the empty room.

The pain in my chest was crushing me. I had fucking broken her, or more like whatever there was left to destroy. *Congratulations, Theon.*

I clenched my fists, before quickly grabbing some clothes and pulling them on. I needed to at least see if she was okay… in this weather, I didn't want her to end up on the roof of the Goddess' temple. I pulled my shoes on, almost at the door when I realised I couldn't.

If she realised… if she noticed me…

If she was in front of me, it fucked me up. I needed to stay here… away from her. I removed my hand from the door handle and moved back. I needed to cut all contact with her, and I mean all… which meant I would break the promise to meet her tonight…

I sighed, leaning against the door and dropping to the ground, resting my head back against it. Why was it that everything I was doing was at her expense? I had told her I'd destroy her, and I had practically succeeded, but then, even with the warning given, why did I feel fucking guilty? I closed my eyes, inhaling deeply.

Even back then, it didn't hurt this much when I ended things with Iyara… was it because we hadn't gotten so deep? Or because she had her parents? Or that I ended it the right way?

All I was doing to Yileyna was hurting her time and time again. She deserved someone who would cherish her, someone who could make her fucking happy, and there was one person who did come to mind, but I had been too selfish to stay away from her. Someone who didn't judge her for her parents' actions and deaths; even those were things she didn't deserve to be blamed for. It was all my doing.

I hated thinking that she deserved someone else... but at the same time, I knew I was killing her.

I hung my head, staring at the shadows on the floor. My heart was too dark for her. I was not right for her, and I was far too twisted to ever give her anything but pain upon fucking pain. My goal in life was revenge. That was the only goal I had and the only goal I needed to focus on.

I leaned my head against the wood of the door and stared out at the darkening skies, the snow still falling. In a few weeks, Yileyna would learn of my truth, and she, herself, would turn her back on me. Then, whether I ever meant anything to her or not, it wouldn't matter because she would only have hatred left for me.

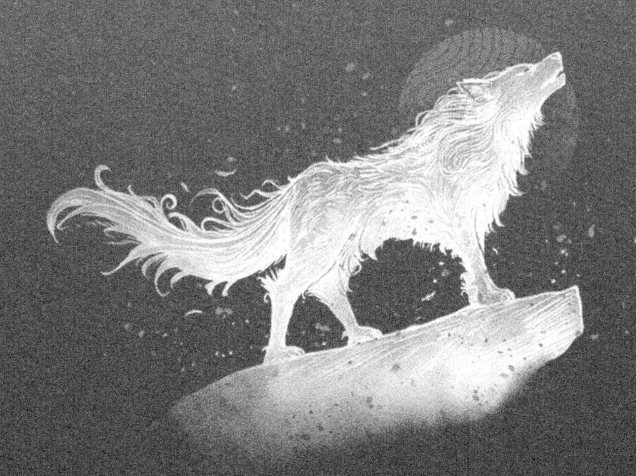

Refusing to Believe

YILEYNA

After meeting Charlene, we had gone our separate ways. I had first walked around the city for a while, trying to relax my mind, before I requested a meeting with the king. I now waited patiently for the guard to tell the king that I had requested an audience.

"The Alpha said he is busy, but what is it regarding?" The man asked me coldly.

"I wanted to see the evidence against my parents," I said quietly, knowing the king obviously didn't want to see me anymore. I just wasn't worthy of his time. The man quirked an eyebrow before looking at me scornfully.

"Are you actually wasting the Alpha's time with your pathetic requests? You should be grateful he hasn't demoted you to an Omega," he muttered scornfully. I frowned, about to reply, when I heard footsteps.

"That is not your place to decide, Gerald. I'll let the Alpha know, and I will take Miss De'Lacor where she needs to go. You are speaking to a Zeta-rank guard, even if you are an Epsilon… treat her with respect," Raiden's smooth, calm voice came, yet it held a clear warning. I turned, feeling relieved to see him. Although I don't think he realised I'm nothing, not a Zeta-rank or anything, so I had no idea why he said that.

He gave me a small smile before motioning for me to follow him. I gave Gerald a small nod before following Raiden. He was quiet, and I had a feeling he was mind-linking the king.

"Come on, he said I can show you the proof," he said, giving me one of his killer smiles. I forced a smile back, not missing the concern in his eyes.

"Thanks. Did the king agree?"

"He said you can take a look. Besides, I was actually going to come find you later. The king has decided to make you a Zeta-rank warrior. Congratulations. I think your wit onboard the Siren Killer must have reached him," he said, giving me another smirk.

I nodded, wondering why the king had done that. It wasn't like him to care. Had Theon said something? Maybe I was being hopeful, but it just felt too coincidental...

I followed him through to the wing which had our old quarters, the Gammas' quarters, as well as the king's personal library, office, and other important rooms. The wing next to this one was the Alpha's personal living quarters.

"So, the evidence is kept in the restricted area, but I will have to stay with you whilst you check it," Raiden explained.

"Oh... I'm sorry, you probably have a lot to do, right?"

"It's not much, I'll get it done. Besides, I didn't have to come find you myself. That saved me time." He winked at me, and I nodded as he entered the library.

There were many people scattered around, some searching for books, others mulling over maps and records. Far more mages than werewolves. They all lowered their heads to Raiden. I remembered a time I had been shown that same respect. I looked down, thinking I was okay with the insult and rejection, but I wanted at least my parents' names to be cleared.

Raiden told me to wait before he went over to the desk. The man behind the table was a serious elder mage, and his hard eyes turned to me before he nodded to whatever Raiden had said. He took out a key from his huge ring of keys, as well as taking another bunch and removing one small one from it. Raiden thanked him before returning to my side.

"I got the keys. Come on," he said, leading the way.

Once inside, he shut the door after us. The room was a lot smaller, yet it was far fuller. Boxes and chests were also stacked to one side. The shelves and cabinets were all locked and labelled.

Yileyna." I turned to look at him, and he walked over to me, making my heart skip a beat at the seriousness on his face.

"Raiden," I said, narrowing my eyes. He chuckled before crossing his arms.

"Tell me what's wrong? You aren't your usual sparkling firework self tonight," he said softly. I shook my head.

"I am fine, really. They say you reap the consequences of your actions. I paved this path for myself, and now I'm walking it," I replied with a humourless smile.

"He hurt you again, didn't he?" He questioned sharply, his eyes flashing green.

"It doesn't matter. Can we get to the evidence?" I asked, turning away.

"Yileyna." I looked back at him, and he frowned slightly.

"What is it? I said I'm fine," I said, trying not to sound irritated.

"Hmm, you did, but I just wanted to say I'm here even if you just need a friend to listen. No judgement, no expectations, just someone to listen," he said quietly. My heart squeezed, and I looked down at the ground.

"I'll keep that in mind, but I'll be okay," I said, turning away. That was a lie I was telling myself again and again. Even when I felt like I was crumbling inside, I wouldn't admit it...

"Alright, let's get to this," he said, briskly walking past me and unlocking one of the small metal cabinets. The mood became darker as he took out a bunch of letters, maps, and reports. "It's all here; the letters he received and sent, as well as the blueprints and maps of the city and castle," he said quietly.

"He didn't do it," I replied firmly. "I know my parents."

I took the things from him, not wanting to hear anything more, and turned my back to him. Walking over, I sat down at one of the three tables in the room and placed everything down carefully. I could feel him watching, but I refused to look at him. *I came here for a reason...*

I looked at the letters Dad had apparently received; plans for an attack, plans to usurp the Alpha from the throne, to take over the middle kingdom...

Lies. Dad considered Alpha Andres his best friend, there was no way that he would have done this. I stared at the letters, taking a calming breath before I picked up the first letter. Although I knew it just couldn't be Dad, the fact that everyone said it was him made my stomach churn.

I looked at the letter I had just unfolded. It was a letter he was meant to send soon, it seemed. It was Dad's handwriting, or extremely close... but no,

Dad couldn't do this. I skimmed the letter, a letter that stated he was enclosing the maps and a clear route into the castle. Stating that he needed more time, and that the planned attack needed to be delayed. I read it quickly.

'We need to hold out... I fear that the king may know something... Yours, W...'

I frowned, staring at the last part.

It just didn't make sense. If Dad was planning to send this letter out to tell them to hold off the attack, then why was it even here? Shouldn't he have posted it as fast as possible? I know one could argue he didn't get the chance, but... but still, something wasn't right.

I stared at the writing, trying to find even one small sign to tell me it wasn't Dad's, but even after staring at it, I found nothing. It looked just like his...

I folded it away and picked up the letters that were sent to Dad, not that even one was addressed to him. They talked of plans to storm the capital from the sea, how the king's time had come and how the Obsidian Shadow Pack would take their rightful place. There wasn't much, as if they were speaking about casual topics, but there was no deeper evidence, none that referenced any solid plans and dates. Maybe they were destroyed, but if that was the case, why would Dad even keep these? He was a Beta-rank, he wasn't stupid enough to get caught...

"If Dad did this, he wouldn't keep such files in our home," I said, my voice coming out icy and angry. Raiden was silent for a moment before he sighed.

"They said it's the one place that would never have been raided or found."

"Yet they somehow received a tip-off? Do you know who it was or how?"

"That's classified information, I'm afraid, my ice queen." I glared at him before sighing. I felt guilty. I was taking my frustration out on him. "Probably one of the king's own spies," he replied after a moment, "but it's not something we should be discussing."

"I still don't believe my father did this," I said, standing up. I wanted to swipe a letter. Raiden might be charming, but he was sharp, and his eyes were currently on me.

"Me neither," he said quietly, a small frown on his face. I looked at him, my heart skipping a beat, and I gave a small smile.

"Thank you." He gave a curt nod before we put everything away and left the room.

"So… I'm assuming you don't have a date for the upcoming ball?" I frowned. Theon becoming Beta was becoming a grand affair, wasn't it?

"No, I don't," I said quietly. "I won't attend."

"But as a Zeta-rank, you should be there; besides, I don't have a date either. Want to go with me?"

"Really? Have you already been through all the single women in Westerfell?" I remarked with a smirk. He pouted.

"I've been behaving rather well, actually, especially since that voyage." I couldn't resist a smile.

"Oh, have you now? I'm proud of you, but has that changed since we returned?" I asked, slightly amused.

"Yeah, I even refused the she-wolf on board. However, on a serious note, I realised that there's a huge difference between love and lust." He winked at me, and my smile faded. Love and lust…

Had I been blinded when it came to Theon? Was there really nothing more than lust between us? My heart sank, and Raiden stopped.

"Come with me to the ball, if not as a date, then as a friend. You don't need to suffer alone. Charlene will be at the Alpha's table. You need someone by your side, and I'm sure my brother would love to see you again. So, what do you say?" I hesitated before sighing in defeat.

"As a friend. Don't expect more." He smiled and nodded.

"I won't." He winked before taking my hand and placing a soft kiss on it.

"Raiden," I warned.

"As friends, I promise." He became serious, letting go of my hand. "Besides, I won't take advantage of your emotions and try to pull a move."

"Thank you. I don't want to hurt you or use you." I smiled softly, his words making my heart skip a beat.

"What if I want to be used?"

"Raiden!"

"Sorry." He chuckled. "Anyway, I'll send a messenger with your duties from Monday. Make sure you go to the pack tailors and get your uniforms." I nodded before he paused, clearly being mind-linked.

"Everything okay?" I asked when he frowned.

"Yeah, I just need to go. Dad and the king want to see me regarding some security plans. Will you be okay going from here?" I nodded.

"I grew up in these halls, too, remember?"

"Yeah, I know. We played together, remember?" He replied in the same tone that I had used.

"Yes." I smiled slightly.

He gave me a final smile and wink before he walked off, and I decided to take the shortest route out. I didn't want to go anywhere near Theon's room. I made my way down the hall, passing some guards, and took a left from the gamma quarters.

It was a lot quieter here; I was about to open a door that led to a staircase, which led to a side exit, when I paused, hearing familiar voices talking. My heart skipped a beat when I realised who that was…

Theon…

"… you please." Charlene?

"I'm done with Yileyna. I think it's high time we told the entire kingdom about us, that we are to be mated. Don't you agree, Charlene?" Since when did Theon call Charlene by her name?

Wait... mated?

I calmed my heart, realising what was happening. Charlene must have come to try to talk to him for me. Goddess, didn't she realise he'd just be mean to her? Worried for her, I made my way towards the room where the voices were coming from. I stopped at the door, shocked to see Theon was holding Charlene's chin. Confusion filled me, and I looked at the side profile of the man before me, having to confirm if it really was Theon.

"Theon, we need to -"

Charlene was cut off when Theon bent down and claimed her lips in a deep kiss. Shock slapped me in the face, accompanied by the sharp pain of rejection and betrayal.

I wasn't able to stop the sharp intake of breath, my heart pounding as I backed away. He kissed her…

What was going on? *I…. No… he…* Nothing made sense…

My head was about to burst. I turned and fled, unable to stay there any longer. The pain in my chest was overwhelming, crushing me painfully. Theon kissed Charlene…

I was halfway down the stairs when I froze, turning back towards the open door at the top, fear enveloping me. I knew my best friend enough to know she wouldn't do that… but what if Theon forced her? *He isn't like that… but still, I was scared. I need to make sure she is okay.*

I heard the sound of a door slam, my heart pounding in fear, then Charlene's sobs as she ran down the hall. I pressed myself against the wall, hoping she wouldn't sense me. Thank the goddess she was okay…

I looked down at the stone steps, trying to fight back my tears. Theon really was done with me...

The urge to comfort her was overwhelming, but I knew she'd also feel terrible if she knew that I saw what had happened. I couldn't go to her.

Theon, of all women; my friend? I won't cry.

After a moment, I quietly made my way down the steps and out into the cold. My heart was racing painfully fast, and I felt that sharp pull within me once more. It hurt. The image of Theon kissing her was screaming in my head, and my eyes prickled.

"I think it's high time we told the entire kingdom about us, that we are to be mated."

Confusion was bubbling within me, but the pain that was overpowering everything was unbearable. The howling wind and the vicious rain that began pouring down drowned out my soft sobs as I rushed toward home…

A home that wasn't mine…

Would I ever find where I truly belonged?

Truth & Decisions

YILEYNA

My head was screaming with agony when I woke up. I looked around, realising I was in the cabin on the floor in the kitchen area. A few bottles of wine lay scattered on the floor, and my entire body was aching.

What happened last night? I remembered crying, but then I had gone to the spot Theon had told me to wait for him. I just… I had needed to see what he'd say, if anything. I waited until twelve. For two hours, I waited in the cold, promising myself that if he didn't come today, I would truly never forgive him, and he didn't.

He hadn't come. I was a fool to think he would. But wasn't that exactly what I was? I was always foolish when it came to Theon.

I pressed a hand to my forehead, feeling broken. I was an idiot… I really was…

I got to my feet, running my fingers through my hair. What time was it anyway? The pain of last night was still there, but the throbbing in my head was overpowering it, and I welcomed it.

It was then that my heart began pounding when I realised the entire cabin was covered in a layer of frost. Right beneath where I lay, a thick white layer of ice was spreading outwards.

"What on Kaeladia..." I murmured.

My heart thundered with fear as I stared at the ground, remembering what had happened back when Madelia had done that spell... *Did I do this?*

I got up and rushed to the door to unlock it, but it was stuck. I had to give it a hard push before it opened, and I stared outside. It was far worse than what I was expecting. It was obvious yesterday's storm had been far worse. The snow which had covered the ground was now entirely frozen, and everything, as far as I could see, was covered in ice. The trees were coated with ice as long icicles hung off them. I stared at the snow right outside the steps of the cabin. My stomach lurched as I stared at the ice that paved as far as I could see. Solid ice.

I backed away from the door, fear enveloping me. Was it crazy that deep down, I felt like I did that? I shut and locked the cabin door, staring at the frost that covered the table, the worktops... the walls... the logs in the fire...

My heart was thundering. If I did this, surely there must be a way to undo it. What if someone saw this? The confusion within me threw me into turmoil. Fae and Mage magic didn't work like this... what were my abilities?

I took a deep breath, placing my hand on my chest. The necklace still hung around my neck, and I wrapped my hand around it for comfort, taking a deep breath.

Breathe, Yileyna...

I closed my eyes, trying to focus on something, but I didn't even know where to pull my abilities from. There was something in me, I was sure of that. After all, Theon saw that himself...

I tried again, but nothing. After several minutes, I gave up and decided I needed to just heat the place up. Getting some fresh logs, I placed them in the hearth and lit the fire before I began to clean the cabin. My head was still pounding from the alcohol, and my heart was still aching from all the thoughts. Theon...

I decided to make myself something for my hangover as the ice began to melt in the cabin. It was going to take time, and it was all going to be an awful soaking puddle when the frost melted. *Goddess, what have I done?*

I sighed heavily as I gulped the drink I had prepared before adding a few extra logs to the already blazing fire and going to shower. Once I was done, I cleaned the place up, not wanting it to smell of alcohol. Every corner of the cabin held memories of Theon, and as I cleaned, I realised what I needed to do.

Leave.

I wouldn't accept anything from him. Not this place, not his help or sympathy.

From this day forth, I needed to just step away from him in every way, and I really couldn't keep saying this. This time, I needed to stick to my decision no matter what.

I was being given a chance to show everyone that I was something, to be a Zeta-rank warrior. If I tried my best to work on this power, I could truly make my parents proud. *Maybe I should ask Madelia for help…* She was a mage, and if I was one, surely she could help me. Or maybe I should ask someone else…

Who though…?

Zarian! He was fae, and unlike Madelia, who was close to the king, it would be safer to ask him.

I could do this. I had to.

Two hours later, I had finished cleaning, gotten dressed, and was packing my things. I would find somewhere else to stay from today onwards. I was bundling up the last of my beauty products, such as my shampoo, soap, and stuff, when there was a knock on the door. I tensed, my heart thumping as I wondered who it would be. The first person who came to my mind was Theon, but he wouldn't come here.

Taking a deep breath, I looked in the mirror first. Staring back at me was a girl with slightly reddened eyes, a pale face, and her hair knotted in a messy bun atop her head. I looked okay, I guess. I walked over to the door and unlocked it.

My heart skipped a beat to see that it was none other than Charlene standing there. She looked… worse than I did. Her eyes were red and tired. Her hair hadn't been combed because, unlike me, who could get away without combing it, Charlene couldn't. The most noticeable thing was the guilt and regret in her eyes. I smiled softly at her, stepping out into the cold. I hugged her tightly. She didn't know I knew, but I knew why she was here. She had come to tell me what had happened.

"Yileyna," she whispered before hugging me tightly.

"Charlene, why did you come out here in this weather?" I asked softly, tugging her into the warmth of the cabin. I had mopped up the water, and it looked rather presentable, despite the pile of boxes that were gathered in the centre of the room.

"There was a dangerous storm last night, but it's gone today. Even the snow has stopped," she said, shutting the door slowly as she glanced around the cabin, looking at the boxes. "You're leaving."

I smiled and nodded, leading her to the kitchen chair as the sofa was still wet. *Goddess, what have I done?*

"Yes. This is Theon's place, I don't see any reason to stay when I'm not with him. You were right, Charlene; all he does is hurt me, and I really don't need him in my life." She didn't reply, staring at her hands in her lap.

"Yileyna, there's something I need to tell you." Her voice was low and full of pain. My heart skipped a beat, and I crouched down before her.

"Tell me, my queen," I whispered encouragingly.

"My father asked Theon to take me as his chosen mate, so he can take place as the next Alpha… because the kingdom needs someone capable…" I frowned, my stomach sinking. *That's what he meant… 'the world should know we are to be mated'…*

"When did this happen?" I asked quietly, wondering if he had that thought when we were together…

"I don't know, but I found out the day Theon returned to the castle."

My heart clenched. The day he didn't plan to return. He ended it with me and decided to take my friend as his chosen mate. It would be a lie if I said it didn't hurt.

"And… are you okay with that?" I asked her gently, giving her a warm smile. She looked confused before her eyes flashed.

"No. Even if there were some feelings there, and there aren't! I promise! I wouldn't because once he took you as his woman, that was it," she said, her eyes full of determination and stubbornness. Her words filled my heart with warmth. At least I had my friend. I smiled gently.

"He's… harsh… and call me hypocritical, but you deserve someone who loves you for you, not your title. As for him getting the Alpha title... are you okay with that?" She sighed heavily.

"I'm not good enough… but I am never going to allow Theon to be my mate. I will take someone else as my mate. If I mark someone else before the ball -"

"Whoa, no. You are not going to mess your life up like that. You deserve true love. We all do...." I whispered, feeling the pain in my heart squeeze.

"Yes. We do. Both of us, and we will get it. Theon... he was our infatuation for the last few years. I guess him being around us didn't help... but he's just that... an infatuation. You don't deserve to be hurt, Yileyna, and after, after his recent behaviour, he doesn't deserve you." I smiled softly, tilting my head.

"Why? What has he done that has pushed you to hate him even more?" I teased lightly, knowing until she told me it would eat her up inside.

"He hates me... he always has and made it clear... but... yesterday, after talking to you, I wanted to try to talk sense into him, I know that he cares for you, and he... he..." She swallowed, and I gave her hands a gentle squeeze as I stood up slowly.

"He kissed you to prove his point. I know, and it's okay. It was him, and... we aren't together anymore anyway," I said quietly. Realisation dawned on her, and she jumped up from her seat.

"I'm so sorry."

"Don't apologise for something that wasn't your fault," I said, and I had to admit, talking to her did make me feel better, even if I did know it wasn't her fault.

"No, still... because of me and this title, he probably ended it with you... I feel Dad has more of a say in this," she muttered, clenching her fists. I frowned thoughtfully.

"What do you want to do? I mean, about the title and all?"

"If Dad told me to pick anyone but Theon... I would have agreed and done this for the kingdom... but..."

"So, if it wasn't because of me, you'd be okay with Theon, right?"

She frowned and shook her head fervently, but I knew she would be for the kingdom. However, Charlene stuck with Theon would be... terrifying. Unless he treated her better, but after everything, I had lost faith in him, and his hatred for Charlene was so strong.

Sure, it hurt, so much... but the truth was he had the most potential as a Beta, but he was a born Alpha, in my opinion. From his dominating personality to his ability to lead... Theon was the kind of person who could rule.

"He first took your Beta title, and now, trying to take mine? No way. I hope that I find my mate at this ball. If I find my true mate, Father can't force this union," Charlene said, bringing me from my thoughts. "If not, then I'll take someone else, anything to -"

"This is going to be hypocritical coming from me, but don't be reckless, Charlene. Promise me, whatever we do, we do it together. We come up with something together...."

"But what can we do? We hold no power," she whispered. "My training isn't working. Dad is getting angry. He doesn't even eat with us anymore, saying he's disappointed in a daughter like me." I scoffed.

"Disappointed to have a daughter like you? Well, he should be grateful for a daughter like you. I'm sorry, but my respect for your dad is just constantly dropping," I said icily. She smiled weakly.

"Yeah... me too..."

"Don't worry, we will come up with a plan. We have time yet, not much, but we do. We'll figure something out...." I murmured.

But she was right. What could we do? We were just two girls with no plan...

We needed help, but who? Who could help us?

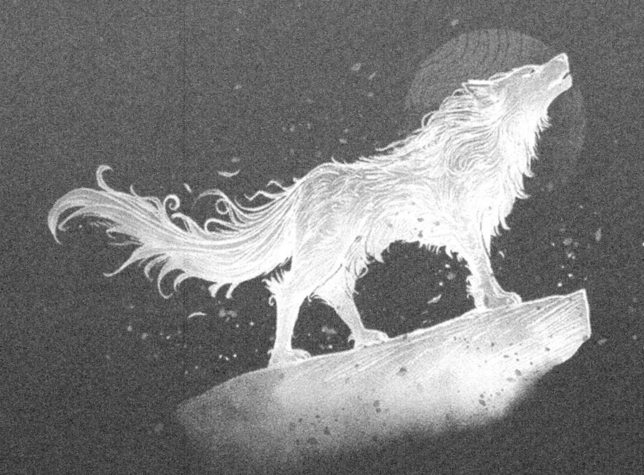

Finding Solutions

YILEYNA

"And that's why the sofa and everything is wet," I finished.

I had spent the last hour telling Charlene about my powers, how Theon assumed I might be part mage or fae, and about the frost all over the cabin.

"Dear Selene… that's… amazing," Charlene whispered in awe.

"I don't know if it is, but I was thinking of asking Madelia or maybe Zarian to see if they could help me channel it or something?" I mused as I stood up from where we had both been sitting cross-legged on the floor.

"Hmm, I think Zarian is the better choice. Madelia is far too close to Dad. She obeys his orders without question, and if you don't want Dad to know, then I would say avoid her," Charlene said. "You have become stronger since your birthday, even I can sense it… Yileyna, do you think you made the odd storm happen last night?" I almost laughed.

"A storm? I highly doubt that."

"I'm serious… like you said, the entire place was frosted. The storm came on suddenly and was crazy all through the night, and it only calmed considerably after three in the morning…" Charlene said thoughtfully, "which would rule out you being a mage. Without casting a spell, there's no way you can draw upon your magic…"

"So, you think I'm part fae then?" I asked, tilting my head.

"Yes! Oh, my goddess! You must be, you are so beautiful it makes sense!" She exclaimed in excitement, cupping my face.

I raised an eyebrow before my amusement faded away as the reality set in that one or both of my parents may not be blood-related to me. As if realising what was on my mind, Charlene hugged me.

"Our blood does not make us who we are, just as I consider you as my sister." She gave me a squeeze, and I smiled. She was right; no matter who or what I was, my parents were always going to be my parents. I was the daughter of William and Hana De'Lacor, and no one else.

"Right, so let's do this. We first find a new apartment, and then we talk to Zarian," Charlene decided.

"Aren't you going to be missed at the castle?"

"Not yet, I have a few hours free before I need to return, and we need to think of a plan too…" She tapped her chin. "This ball… I wish you would come."

"Oh, I am coming," I said as I laced up my boots. She turned sharply towards me in surprise and excitement.

"Really?"

"Yes, Raiden asked me to accompany him," I said as Charlene smiled.

"Ooo, from one handsome man to another handsome but also charming young man! He's liked you for so long!"

"Let's not forget that Raiden is the biggest playboy in the city. He's slept with most women here. He only teased me and flirted," I reminded her.

"Oh, I know, but -"

"Charl, I'm not ready to think of anyone romantically," I whispered, trying to hide the pain in my eyes.

"I'm sorry," she replied apologetically.

"It's fine, let's go," I said, picking up my coat and putting it on.

We left the cabin together; our first plan of action was to find somewhere for me to stay. We made a quick stop at the bank, where I filled up a bag of coins from our family vault, and I saw that the king had indeed given me a good lump sum for the trip we had made.

"Okay, let's ask Madam Marigold if she knows a place! I'm sure she may have some rooms above the café, too."

"That's true, we can ask her. I'm sure she may know someone or other who is offering a place. If they even accept me with my reputation as the daughter of a traitor. I can't wait to remove this mark from my parent's reputation," I responded thoughtfully.

"She is one person who doesn't care about anyone's opinion or background. I'm sure she'll happily help."

It was true she had a mix of people working for her, yet still, her cafe wasn't any less busy. It was a place where everyone could just enjoy the sweet treats and hot drinks without discrimination. We made our way there, with Charlene saying she couldn't wait to have a hot drink with this blistering cold.

"Finally!" She breathed a sigh of relief when the café came into sight.

"You really are cold," I said, sympathetically looking at her red-tipped nose. She looked over at me, looking me up and down calculatingly.

"Do you think your element is the reason you don't feel cold? I mean the ice," she whispered, leaning closer.

"Goddess knows." I shrugged, thinking over her words. "That is an interesting point. Recently, I haven't felt as cold as I used to. I assumed it was because my wolf was awakening...."

"Exactly. I really think it plays a huge factor," Charlene said thoughtfully. A sudden thought came to me, and my stomach twisted.

"Charlene, do you think, if that's the case, that I won't have a wolf?" I whispered quietly. Sure, the king had people of all species working for him, but they weren't in the pack. Would that mean if I didn't have a wolf I'd be thrown out?

"You are most likely a hybrid; I can sense you are a werewolf. Trust me, I have done extensive research on this matter. If anything, you may not be able to take werewolf form, but most werewolf hybrids can mind link," she explained confidently.

I frowned and nodded. She was right... the few hybrids we had in the pack were extremely rare; I think there were only three at most. However, only two of those three could shift, but the third also had the mind link. I wanted my wolf, I really did....

We reached the café soon after and requested if Madam Marigold could give us a few moments when she had time. She looked at us suspiciously before giving a curt nod.

"Alright, now go to the back booth. Zarian will bring you something to eat. You are both a sight," she ordered as if she knew we hadn't eaten anything, but then I guess we didn't look like our normal selves.

"Thank you," I said as Charlene smiled gratefully at her.

Once settled and after placing our orders with Zarian, we waited for him to return. We planned to ask him when he brought our food.

"I love those pastries," Charlene said, licking her lips as she referred to the pastries we had just ordered. Madam Marigold had some delicious pastries that she only served in the morning hours, and they were delicious crispy pastries filled with a special cream and jam in the centre.

"Me too," I said, playing with the fur of my coat that now sat on the booth beside me.

Zarian soon returned. His silky black hair held two small plaits that came from the back and fell by his side, and a few strands were left out, framing his face. He was indeed a very beautiful man. He flashed me a smile as I observed him.

"Distracted, beautiful?" He teased as he placed our tray down.

"A little," I said before smiling sweetly. "I actually had a favour to ask..."

"Oh? What favour can I do for the beauty before me?" He looked curious, glancing between us before he crossed his arms, watching me with sharp interest. As expected, he wasn't just a beautiful man. I think I was right coming here. Something told me he'd be able to help us.

"Yes, can we talk in private once you are free?" I asked quietly, glancing around the café. He tapped his chin before he nodded.

"You are in luck; I am finishing early today anyway," he replied with a wink.

"Perfect," Charlene said just as Madam Marigold came over, and Zarian walked off smoothly.

"I do hope you pretties are not distracting my waiter. Now, what can I help you ladies with?" She asked, sitting down beside me and folding the tea towel she was holding with a huff of relief.

"Busy morning, I see," Charlene said, picking up one of the pastries.

"Extremely. I await the day I retire, yet I love this place so much I don't see it happening any day soon."

"Well, we are glad to hear that. This is the best café in Westerfell," I said, exchanging a look with Charlene before continuing, "We won't take too much of your time. The thing is, I was looking for a place to stay. A permanent place. It doesn't need to be big..." Her eyebrow shot up, and she looked me over.

"Weren't you living with the soon-to-be Beta?" News indeed travelled fast.

"She isn't anymore. We were hoping you knew of a place that would offer a room. You are always so knowledgeable." Charlene smiled warmly, trying to divert the conversation away from Theon and me. Just the mention of him made my heart squeeze with pain. Madam Marigold sighed as she sat back as if thinking before she turned to me.

"You know, with the upcoming ball, many places are fully booked out. Even I don't have any rooms that I can give you full-time. However, I have a friend who has made an inn down by the coast, and yes, I know it's a bit of a risky place, but it's cheap, very easy on the eyes, and it's doing well. Besides, as long as you don't go down to the coast at night, it's fine," she said briskly.

Charlene and I exchanged looks; I knew which place she meant. It had been getting constructed for a while now.

"It's more catered for travellers, and since it's on the outskirts, it's a bit more away from the hustle and bustle of the city. He is offering some permanent residency too, and if I write you a letter, I'm sure he will happily allow you to stay."

"Could you do that? I would be grateful," I said, feeling a little hopeful.

"Should we not take a look first?" Charlene asked worriedly.

"No, it's fine. I'm sure it'll be perfect," I replied. I just needed a place.

"Well then, you girls carry on enjoying your food and I will have it written up for you. I need to get back to work too!" She stood up, and we both thanked her for her time and effort before I looked at Charlene.

"I guess we could hire a cart to get my stuff down to the coast."

"I don't know, Leyna, it's not the safest place."

"It's going to be fine. Trust me, I have faced sirens more than once and lived." Charlene relaxed visibly.

"You know what? You are right. I think that, in itself, is one of the greatest achievements. If Dad knew, I'm sure he'd want you guarding the coast!" She shook her head. "But seriously, Yileyna, you do need to be careful if you live down there..."

"I'll be fine, my queen. Trust me," I said. As I picked up my mug of coffee, my smile faded, the reminder of Theon once more hitting me hard.

I am done with you, and I pray the moon goddess gave me the strength to face you, to hold myself with strength and grace...

A while later, Zarian was finally free to leave. He had taken us to the staff quarters in the back of the café, where we wouldn't be overheard. Madam Marigold had given us a letter to show the inn owner, which at least sorted the first of our problems.

Charlene and I wondered where to start, and I took a deep breath after making him promise not to share this conversation with anyone else.

"I take an oath on Etaar themselves," Zarian said, placing a hand on his chest. He was referring to the fae deity, a being that was neither male nor female but held such beauty that it was said that no mortal could look them in the eye.

I nodded and, taking a deep breath, I told him how I had recently felt a shift in myself after my eighteenth, but rather than getting my wolf or anything, I told him about the two occurrences of power, leaving out the fact that it was actually Charlene's whose abilities we had been trying to awaken the first time, simply making it out as if it was performed to help awaken my wolf. I also told him how we assumed I was a hybrid and asked if he could help me train or at least fully awaken my abilities or help to channel them.

"So... I was wondering if you could help," I finished.

"I don't think she's part mage... we think she may be part fae. She's beautiful too," Charlene finished as Zarian watched us with a small smile lingering on his lips.

"As beautiful as she is, she is not fae." My stomach sank as he said those words.

"Are you sure? She can't be a mage because even before learning to use their abilities, they need to refer to the books of their elders. Her power is more elemental, she didn't -" Zarian raised a hand, cutting Charlene off.

"There are many races in this world of ours, Princess Charlene. I assure you, Yileyna is not of fae blood."

"Then what could I be? If it is the fact that I need to show you proof of my powers, I can try," I said, feeling as if I had once again hit a wall.

"You need not prove anything to me, beautiful. I believe you, but I can only tell you that you are not fae." He reached over and caressed my cheek. I pulled away, frowning at him as I watched him sharply. He chuckled, running his fingers through his hair. "I have... some theories, but they don't really make sense. Time will tell. As for training you, I don't see why not. If, as you say, it's elemental, I can perhaps help somewhat...." He was watching me keenly, and I felt a little self-conscious under his gaze. "What do you enjoy?"

"Enjoy?" I asked warily.

"Your preferences of day or night, land and sea, song or dance," he explained as if it was obvious, and I should know what he was talking about. I frowned slightly, thinking about his question. It was clear he wanted an answer. Fae were sly creatures, and I knew I needed to answer properly.

"I prefer night… I love both land and sea, yet I do love the freedom of the sea, the smell of the fresh sea breeze, and as for song or dance… I love to dance, yet I can sing well," I answered, feeling as if there was some sort of a trick question in there. Even Charlene was scrutinising Zarian sharply. He smiled and nodded, tilting his head and letting his silky dark hair fall over his shoulder.

"Now tell me, my beautiful blond hybrid, what are the species of this world?"

"Werewolf, human, mage, fae, naga, and siren," I replied, "they are the intelligent species." His smile grew.

"Indeed, and what species is the weakness or fear of the other?" I glanced at Charlene confused.

"The Naga fear mages and sirens… the werewolves' greatest enemy are themselves or the sirens…" I mumbled feeling lost, I had never ever considered this.

"The mages fear the werewolves, correct?" Charlene added. Zarian gave a nod.

"Correct, and the fae dislike the naga, for they hold strong elemental power. Now, tell me, what race do the sirens fear the most?" Charlene and I exchanged looks. Neither of us knew the answer. "Fae," Zarian said. I frowned.

"That makes no sense. You said the naga fear sirens, and fae fear the naga…" I mumbled.

"It may not be common knowledge here in Astalion since it is not a fae kingdom. However, the sirens' song has no effect on a fae. We are the only species that are superior to them." A wicked smile crossed his face, and, for a moment, he wasn't just the beautiful man we knew but a fae who knew exactly what his worth was. I nodded slowly.

"That's incredible, considering how much damage they can do," I said, frowning. I wondered where we were going with this.

"Perhaps… but every species has a weakness." He gave me a dangerous smile as he took hold of my chin in his long slender fingers. "And that is why I will agree to train you."

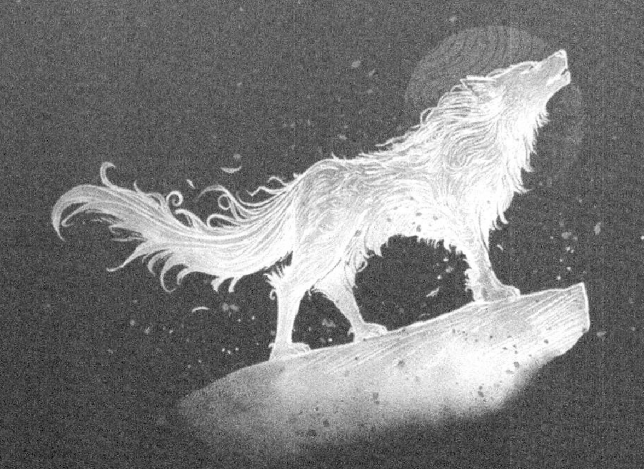

Zarian's Training

YILEYNA

I HAD MANAGED TO SECURE myself a small room and bathroom at the new inn, which was called The White Mist. The inn owner had simply given me a once over before telling me he expected me to pay the rent on every full moon. He warned me that if I was even a day late, he would boot me, and so I had paid for six months in advance, which appeased him greatly. The room was nice and clean, with simple furnishing and an adjoining bathroom. It was warm too. I had gotten all my things brought over for me.

I had placed the keys to the cabin with a small note into an envelope and had left it on the table at the cabin. That moment had felt like a resolution. When I had left my childhood home, I had promised to be strong, yet I had fallen so deeply into things with Theon that I once again let my heart be broken, losing sight of what I wanted. It still hurt. Every night he lingered on my mind; his gaze, his touch, the comfort and emotions he awakened within me, but I refused to let them overpower me.

The following day, after securing my room, I had gone for my uniform fitting. The Zeta-rank wore a dark grey uniform with black accents to it. None of the standard sizes fitted me, and so the tailor had told me to come back to collect it in three days' time.

It had been four days since the day Zarian had agreed to train me, and he did so every day, sticking to his words and the only promise he had asked of me was to stay committed.

"Again," his smooth voice ordered as I breathed heavily. I was bent over on all fours, fighting the fatigue that consumed me.

Zarian may not be a warrior, but he knew how to push me to my limits until my body screamed for reprieve. He was good with weapons and with his element, using them both together in a way that intrigued me greatly. I wondered what he was back in his own kingdom or what he once was long ago. He was a mystery that I knew nothing of.

There were two training sessions; the morning one was lighter, and I was able to function after, but the evening training was far more extreme, leaving me exhausted. It required trust, and when Zarian had asked me that first session if I trusted him, I had said yes. I had to because when he was done, I often held no power to even move.

Right now was the evening session, and we were far away from the safety of the walls of Westerfell as Zarian stood over me, arms crossed as he stared down at me. His wind element whipped around him powerfully, and I could feel it swirling around me.

There were eight elements; wind, water, fire, earth, ice, lightning, shadow, and light, each one powerful in its own right.

"What's wrong? Feeling useless?" His hard, cold voice asked as I struggled to pick myself up.

Emotion. It wasn't even our second lesson when he realised that only when I was emotional could I call forth my powers, and I had managed to do so in last night's session, but it was only a small display of power, similar to the ice I had created in the hidden area of the castle.

"I'm not useless," I said coldly.

"Really? Then why are you not Beta? Why were you unable to keep your rank? You really are a disappointment." I knew what he was doing, he was trying to trigger me off, but even then, it hurt. I could handle insults.

"I'm not," I said. Despite trying to push my emotions, the pressure of his powers pushed me to bow my head before him. He crouched before me, taking hold of my chin and forcing it up to look into his violet eyes.

"Really? Then why did Theon of Westerfell cast you aside? Even he did not want you. Tell me, my beautiful student, aside from your beauty, is there anything more to you?" Anger flared through me, and the crushing reminder of Theon's betrayal rushed through me.

"You were nothing more than something to use and cast aside. If he really cared, he wouldn't have left you... but that is all you are worth. Nothing more. You are a shame to the De'Lacor name."

"I am not a shame to my parents' name!" I snapped. The pressure of his power was crushing me, and I pushed against it with all my will. It was all I had.

"You are. Right now, despite being a Beta-rank wolf, you are bowing before a fae. I wonder what your parents would think. Would they be disappointed in the daughter they had high hopes for?" My anger flared, and I glared at him.

A sudden, painful pull ripped through my stomach, and I gasped as lightning flashed in the sky above.

"Useless, pathetic, and wolfless," Zarian said, his eyes glinting with scorn. "You can't even withstand the small amount of my powers that any wolf would be able to."

I'm not weak. I am not pathetic!

"I don't blame Theon for leaving you. No one wants such a weak woman by their side."

I wasn't weak or useless!

"Trash."

"You're wrong! I was foolish to fall for Theon, but I am not worthless! I am worth more, far more. A man's opinion counts for nothing!" I snapped, pushing against his power. My patience snapped.

Using all my will, I managed to stand up, pushing his powers back. A flash of lightning illuminated the sky, striking the ground inches from where Zarian had stood moments earlier. A swirl of wind whipped around him in a protective shield.

A blast of wind knocked him off his feet, and I felt the temperature drop. Looking at the ground, I saw the ice spreading from beneath my feet and out across the ground. From the corner of my eyes, I saw Zarian regain his balance, crouched on the ground, holding his stance as I felt my anger swirling around me.

I was going to hurt him.

I gasped, and the flashing lightning in the sky vanished. The whipping wind around me stilled, and I staggered back from the ice that was beneath my feet, but in every direction, as far as I could see, there was a layer of ice covering the ground. I suddenly felt as if I had been hit by a huge boulder, feeling exhausted. The agony in my stomach eased up, and I fell to my knees, shaking.

Zarian waved his hand, getting rid of the barrier created by his element, and stepped closer to me.

"Impressive. How do you feel?"

"Annoyed." I glared at him, my voice coming out as a hoarse murmur.

"My apologies. You really are hard to rile up." He smiled sexily, and I simply made a face, feeling drained. "Where are you drawing your powers from?" He asked, crouching in front of me as rain began pouring down, drenching us both.

"It feels like my stomach..." I whispered, clutching my stomach. He nodded.

"And do you feel it spread through you when you summon it?

"Summon? No... I just feel a pull and intense pain, like something is being ripped inside of me." He frowned.

"That doesn't sound right... may I take a look at your stomach?" I nodded, reaching for my shirt with shaking hands, when I realised I was wearing a corset.

"Allow me," Zarian offered and reaching over, he began to undo my corset. I knew if I wasn't feeling so exhausted, I would feel very self-conscious, but I didn't. Once he had removed it, he pulled my shirt up to my breasts, looking at my stomach. "Hold it," he commanded.

I nodded as I tucked my legs under me and sat up straight, holding my shirt up from my stomach. Even that felt like a task. He placed his hand on my stomach, closing his eyes, and I felt pressure in my stomach. He glanced up at me as if trying to look for a reaction.

"Does that hurt?" I shook my head.

"It just feels like a pressure."

"Strange... I might need to do some research. Something isn't right."

"Great, now I'm a malfunctioning hybrid, too," I sighed, unable to keep the bitterness from my voice. He smirked as he looked up at me.

"You are anything but malfunctioning. It's almost as if something is blocking you from using your abilities," he said thoughtfully. I frowned.

"Like a seal?" Wasn't that the same issue that Charlene was having?

"Yes, which makes me think someone wanted to keep your... other side a secret. How many people know of your abilities?"

"Just you, Charlene, and Theon. Oh, and maybe Madelia, one of the royal mages. She saw I could withstand a very low temperature."

"Make sure you don't tell anyone further, at least until I find some answers," he said, brushing his fingers down my stomach, making a tingle of pleasure rush to my core. I blushed as I realised he was still touching me and swatted his hand away before I quickly pulled my shirt down, making him laugh. "I was enjoying that."

"You're a pervert." I frowned, but I didn't feel angry. "What element do you think I have? Ice?" I think it was, anyway. I looked at the ground, staring at the ice that was melting away due to the rain.

"Ice, water, so much more… I don't really know, but it's definitely not just one, which is very unique…" I looked at him curiously as he brushed back his soaking hair, looking at the rain that was pouring down. "Sit back, calm yourself, and clear your mind," he said, standing up.

As much as my body was groaning for rest, I wanted to learn and do the most I possibly could. If Zarian was taking the time to train me, then I would be the best student, and so, I didn't question him. Sitting down on the cold, wet ground, I crossed my legs and took calming breaths, clearing my mind. I focused on nothing but my own heartbeat, emptying all thoughts from my mind…

"That's enough. Well done."

I opened my eyes. I don't know how long I had been meditating, but the rain had stopped. He gave me a small smile and offered me a hand.

"I admire your resilience," he said quietly.

"Thank you," I replied. He bent down, picked up my corset, and, without asking, slipped it around my waist, swiftly tying it up.

"Who knew you were such a good help at getting dressed too?" I teased, adjusting my soaking shirt.

"I admire this waistline," he joked before a faint smile crossed his face. "My mother was a tailor, and I was often given the job of adorning the mannequins," he added, surprising me.

"Oh? That's an interesting little piece to learn about you," I said, staring into his gorgeous violet eyes.

"If you want, I don't mind sharing far more with you." He winked, giving me a seductive smile. My heart skipped a beat, and no matter how much my heart yearned for the attention of an amber-eyed heartbreaker, I couldn't deny that the man before me was very handsome and charming.

"That doesn't sound like a bad idea," I whispered softly, knowing I was playing a game I would lose.

A hint of a dangerously sexy smile crossed his lips, and he slowly reached up, brushing my wet locks from my face. He cupped the side of my face, stepping closer until my chest brushed against him. Both of us were soaked by the rain, and the heat from his body was inviting. Our eyes remained locked, our hearts beating in rhythm. I leaned up, closing the gap between us, when I suddenly felt a dangerous aura swirl and surge around me. I felt Zarien tense ever so slightly, his hand going to my upper arm protectively as we both turned to look at the intruder.

My heart was thundering as I stared into the shimmering gold eyes of none other than Theon himself – eyes that were full of burning hatred as he looked at me with such rage that I felt a sliver of fear rush through me.

"If you're done being a whore, I need to have a word with you."

A Clash in the Rain

YILEYNA

I slowly pulled away from Zarian, my heart thundering a thousand miles as I looked at Theon. His words stung, but his anger was oddly satisfying.

"Sorry about this," I said to Zarian, feeling very aware of what I had almost done. My gaze dipped to his lips, and he leaned in, placing a soft kiss on my cheek.

"We'll continue after our guest leaves," he said with a wink.

I couldn't resist the smile that crossed my lips or the fluttering in my stomach. I couldn't deny that Zarian was extremely charming, even if he didn't drown me the way Theon did…

My smile faded as I looked at the man that took my heart, then crushed it and tossed it aside, time and time again.

"What do you want?" I asked, crossing my arms.

I frowned, realising that despite the cold, he, too, wasn't wearing a coat. Zarian and I hadn't worn any due to our training, but why was Theon out here like this? His shirt was soaked, sticking to him like a second skin. The fabric was now sheer, thanks to the rain, displaying his god-like body beneath. My core knotted as I glanced down at his pants, the visible bulge making my heart pound. Why did he have this effect on me?

I looked into his eyes, and he brushed his soaking hair back as fresh rain began to fall.

"As I said, a word," he replied icily the moment our eyes locked, his blazing with rage and fury. The murderous aura around him made me nervous, but I wasn't going to show him that.

"I can hear you. Talk," I replied defiantly. His eyes flashed, and he looked at Zarian.

"Leave," he said, his voice cold and full of venom.

"I'm afraid I'm not a werewolf, and as long as I abide by the laws of Astalion, I don't need to listen to you," Zarian replied with a smirk. Theon's eyes darkened, and something inside of me twisted. That look in his eyes was almost a silent threat...

"I'll be fine... could you wait here for me?" I asked, not wanting Zarian to be the target of Theon's anger. I had seen it before, and something told me Theon held grudges.

"I don't fear him, beautiful," Zarian replied lightly, and I didn't miss the way Theon's eyes flashed at his words.

"I know, but I won't be far," I said softly, smiling up at him. I appreciated his help in training me, but I was not going to let Theon make life hard for him because of me. I walked over to Theon, stopping a foot away.

"What?" I asked icily. He seemed to hesitate for a moment, as if wanting to say something before deciding against it.

"What the hell is the meaning of this?" He asked, holding up a soaking paper, one that he had been crushing in his hand.

'I don't need your gift or charity. Keep your cabin – Yileyna'

"That's pretty self-explanatory, is it not? Or have you forgotten how to read?" I asked airily. Despite the heavy rainfall, his scent was invading my senses. He consumed me, and deep down, that terrified me... why did I lose myself when he was near?

"Where are you staying?" He asked, swallowing hard.

"That's personal. Who are you to me that I should share my business with you, future Beta- oh, I'm sorry, future Co-Alpha?" I spat coldly. "You know what's funny? You are literally going from one woman and title to the next. What's wrong, Theon? Can you not do better than steal others' titles?"

"This isn't a fucking joke. Answer my question, where are you staying?" He hissed. I was surprised he didn't lose it after my last comment.

"No, it isn't, but I moved out days ago. It's funny you just found that note now," I said quietly.

"There was a break-in at the cabin. It's why I... I thought I'd check if you were okay," he said coldly, looking away from me. I smiled sadly. Why check if I'm okay when you're the one who hurt me the most? Keeping my voice level, I replied,

"Oh, I see. I had left the door open, I guess that's my fault. I hope nothing was taken or damaged." He looked into my eyes, and I did my best to hide my emotions. "If we are done, I'll be leaving. I have better things to do than talk to a manipulative, heartless man," I added harshly. Not even a flash of emotion crossed his face before he stepped closer. The urge to step back was strong, but I remained rooted in my place, glaring at him in warning.

He tilted his head before looking down at my breasts. I knew my blue bra was showing through, but I wasn't going to act like I cared.

"Good luck finding a man who makes you feel half of what I did," he said, placing a finger under my chin and tilting it up. I scoffed at the arrogance he held. He left me!

"I found someone better already," I lied, satisfied when I saw the flash of anger in his eyes. "We are done, Theon. I don't have any more time to waste on you, and I'm sure you have places to be, titles to steal, people to use, and all the other crap you get up to." It hurt to say those words. It was causing me pain too, but nothing compared to what he made me feel.

The image of him kissing Charlene flashed in my mind, and I looked up at him emotionlessly as I pulled away from his touch. He smirked coldly, his eyes glittering gold.

"You know nothing about me."

"No, I don't, and I really don't care. Besides, you were the one who ended things. You broke my heart, so you have no right to come back into my life and try to hurt me again. We are done."

"Don't play the victim. For someone who was apparently heartbroken, you seemed to move on pretty fast," he said icily. I was no longer sure if Theon even cared or if I was just a possession to him, one to be used and hurt by him and him alone.

"Oh, I did, especially when I realised there are men who actually treat me better." I brushed my wet hair away from my face. "Now, if we are done, I want to go get down and dirty, just like the whore I am," I added sarcastically.

Our eyes met, and for a moment I thought I saw a flash of guilt in his, but it was definitely just my imagination. I turned away, looking at Zarian, who had heard every single word. If he had felt any type of attraction to me, it was surely gone now. I was about to walk towards him when Theon grabbed hold of my arm and spun me around.

"Where are you staying?" He asked, my heart pounding at our proximity. What did he want? *Goddess, leave me alone, Theon.*

"Far from you," I said coldly.

"Then a word of warning, little storm, do not trust every man you come across," he said, glancing at Zarian with eyes full of pure hatred.

"I learned my lesson when I trusted the worst of them all," I shot back, feeling pain squeeze inside my chest as I looked into those amber eyes that still pulled at my heartstrings. He didn't respond. I ripped free from his hold and walked toward Zarian. I could feel it, his eyes burning into me, the sound of his heartbeat that brought me contentment and pain. Walk away just as he walked away from you…

"Yileyna."

"I will see you at the ball, Theon. Until then..." I looked at Zarian, who was watching me with an unreadable look in his eyes. "Let's go."

He always made sure I was safe and in my room before he left, and I was truly grateful for it. I suddenly felt exhausted, not only physically but mentally. Zarian placed his hand on the small of my back as we walked away. The feeling of being watched didn't leave until we had rounded the bend.

"I don't want to go home right now, especially with him watching. I'll go to the local tavern or something," I said, crossing my arms. He raised his eyebrows, looking down at me.

"You're tired, emotional, and soaking wet. As much as I wouldn't mind joining you for that drink and getting drunk, I don't think you will appreciate your actions in the morning," he said quietly.

A voice of reason. One I didn't want right now.

I stopped in my tracks and looked up at him. He was slightly shorter than Theon, but his leaner frame made him look equally as tall.

"I don't care," I said, knowing I sounded stubborn and childish, but I really didn't care right then.

I turned and began walking in the opposite direction towards the city. I heard him sigh as he grabbed hold of my wrist and spun me around into his arms. *Goddess, what is with these men yanking me like a damn doll!* His arms tightened around me, and he looked down at me seriously.

"You don't want to return home, correct? Then you may stay at my place for the night," he suggested, looking down at me. My heart was thundering as I realised our bodies were moulded together firmly.

"I don't think that's a good idea..." I said, my chest heaving rapidly. He tilted his head.

"We both know it's the smarter of the two choices that are before us," he said quietly.

I knew I wasn't ready to move on. Seeing Theon's appearance reminded me of how I felt for him... but if by any chance, he was still watching me... then I wanted him to see me go home with Zarian. I wanted to hurt him just like he had hurt me.

"Fine, why not," I whispered, slowly pulling away as we continued through the rain...

"Here is a towel and some clothes. I'm afraid I have nothing that will fit well," Zarian said, holding a bundle out to me.

We had just gotten to his place. It was actually a nice house in the more luxurious part of the city, with high walls and good privacy. It wasn't too big, but it was far from small also. He jerked his head to the bathroom of the room he had given me before he left.

"I'll have hot drinks ready," he said.

"Okay, thank you!"

I entered the bathroom, pausing for a moment as I looked around the house. For someone who worked as a waiter, his house was... very nice. I shook the thought off. After all, he was goddess knows how old, he must have saved over many years, or perhaps family wealth...

The moment I stepped into the shower, I let everything wash away. The thoughts, the emotions... everything... but his face didn't leave. The look in his eyes, the way his touch still left an imprint like a ghost. I leaned my head against the wall behind me and sighed. I needed to stop letting him get to me, but how do you do that? How do you stop the emotions that have no bounds?

I spent a good while in the shower before stepping out and wrapping a towel around myself. I looked at the clothing that Zarian had given me. A shirt which was clearly his and one that I knew would not close on my chest, and a gown which at least covered me entirely. I brushed my hair with my fingers before I left the bedroom and went to find him.

The smell of coffee led me, I found him already showered and seated in the living room, wearing a fresh pair of pants and a shirt which he had left open. His hair was pulled into a ponytail as he looked through some scrolls.

"Ah, there you are. You suit purple," he remarked. I looked down at the black satin gown, realising it had a purple border.

"Thanks, I guess," I said, taking a seat. The gown slipped open, and I didn't miss his gaze flicker to my thighs before he looked away smoothly. My stomach did a flip as I reached for one of the mugs. "I apologise for you having to see all that earlier."

"Not at all, I think we can all agree that the man is deeply infatuated with you."

"I don't think so. I was just a passing moment for him." I shrugged, feeling very aware of his gaze upon me.

"Ah, well, I guess I just assumed wrong then. So, you're going to the ball then."

"I am, yes, with a friend," I said with a nod.

"I'm sure Theon of Westerfell will feel incredibly jealous."

"Well, too bad for him then." I shrugged when a sudden thought came to me. The idea made my heart skip a beat as I jolted upright, not caring that my unrestricted breasts had just bounced.

What if I managed to push Theon to his limits, and he caused a scene which could result in Charlene openly having a reason to refuse this relationship? I knew it was reckless, and it would only make me a target for the king's wrath, but I didn't care. I would talk to Charlene about it, and maybe it was time to fill Raiden in as well… maybe he'd help.

"Dare I ask what's going through that mind of yours?" Zarian asked. I smiled slightly.

"Let's just say I think I have an idea to save my friend…"

"I see," he smirked, picking up his mug and not asking what I was saving her from. We fell silent as we sat there sipping our coffees, whilst my mind reeled with a thousand ideas. There was no way Theon was going to get away with trying to ruin mine or Charlene's life. Not on my watch.

"I just need to purchase a dress that would bring every unmated wolf to their knees," I mused. Zarian let out a light chuckle.

"I assure you, you don't need a dress to do that. However, I think I might know someone who can send us the perfect dress."

"Really? Thank you. The price won't be an issue." I smiled gratefully at him as I finished off my coffee.

Bring on the ball. I was ready to show Theon that I may not be as strong as he was, but I held power.

An Unexpected Reaction

YILEYNA

THE DAY OF THE ball had finally arrived, and my nerves were running wild. The plan wasn't the best… but it was all we really had, and we were going to risk it.

Raiden had needed some persuasion. He didn't think my putting myself at risk was worth anything; however, in the end, I had managed to convince him.

Then there was Charlene, who had been an entirely different story, saying she didn't want to pretend to blame me and how her father wouldn't be happy with me either. She didn't want me hurt, but I had managed to get her on board. The chances of Theon actually playing up weren't even solid anyway, plus I was sure the king would be angry at him, although Charlene didn't agree with that. We were just going to try and see what happens.

I was a little worried for Raiden, though, not wanting him to get in trouble. Although Zarian had offered to accompany me, Raiden had said he was the safer option as he was the son of one of the Gammas.

I had ended up telling Raiden about my abilities, although Zarian had not been happy with that, but I trusted Raiden, and so he had begrudgingly agreed. The two often seemed to clash, as if there was an unspoken competition between them. Men. I will never understand them.

Aside from that, I was doing my patrol duty as well as training with Zarian. It was becoming increasingly obvious that somehow, I was able to manipulate the weather, something which was beginning to cause a deep fear within me… giving birth to a chilling terror, for the only species on Kaeladia that could bend the weather was not one I ever wanted to be associated with.

I pushed the thought away, not letting the fear get the better of me. Not tonight.

I pulled at the top of my dress, staring into the mirror. I swear if I bent over, I feared I'd spill out of it, or my nipple would peek out to greet the world.

"You look beautiful," Zarian said as he entered the room.

I was at his place as I had gotten ready there. He was the one who had ordered the dress for me from none other than his mother from his own kingdom. It was exquisite, different from the Astalion designs, and, dare I admit, very sexy.

The underlayer was a fitted nude strapless bodysuit, which pushed my breasts up even more. The dress itself was a delicate fabric with silver beads and clear crystals. I was worried that I'd tear it. On top of that, Zarian refused to take any payment for it.

"Allow me," he said, coming over and fastening the two hooks I couldn't reach at the back. "You look incredibly ravishing…" He looked in the mirror over my shoulder as I smoothed the fabric over my hips.

I touched my neck; I still wore the necklace. The inn wasn't the safest place. Although I had not been bothered by anyone, there were questionable visitors, and when I had taken the necklace to a jeweller to sell it, I could tell from the greedy look in his eyes it had been valuable, something he was trying to trick me out of, so I had changed my mind, refusing to sell it at all. I'd keep it safe for now. Maybe in the future, when and if I needed money, it would be a good investment. I could feel the pendant between my breasts and adjusted the chain a little.

"You won't remove your necklace?" Zarian asked, his gaze dipping to my breasts. For some reason, I hadn't shown anyone it, but he had seen the chain often enough.

"No, it's precious," I said, turning to face him. "Distracted somewhere?" He smirked, stepping closer. My heart skipped a beat. Since that day, we hadn't had any more moments, and in a way, I was relieved.

"You are a welcome distraction." He winked, but my stomach twisted.

Distraction… that was the reason Theon left me.

"Well, today, I hope I am a distraction enough."

I turned back to the mirror, gazing at my reflection. My hair had been styled by a friend of Zarian's who had her own beauty parlour here in Westerfell. She was a mage, and after seeing her work, I knew if it wasn't for her race, she would be the most popular beautician in the city.

Spending time with Zarian made me realise that there was such a high level of discrimination toward other species that I had never known of. It was appalling. When Charlene was Alpha, I would address the issue, or even when things calmed down a little, I could talk to Raiden and Charlene. It wasn't fair.

My hair had been put up in a low bun, with a braid which was entwined with a hair vine and sparkly gems scattered around it. Although I had wanted my hair open, Zarian had immediately said it was a bad idea. My hair wasn't that bad, but he refused to change his mind, saying to trust him. Zarian had been the one to make every decision tonight. I had wanted to keep my make-up simple, but even that was something Zarian had refused, saying we needed to go all out. Although I had had my make-up fully done for the moon goddess festival, something about me had changed from all those months ago…

I looked different, even more like a woman than I did back then. My breasts looked slightly larger, although that may just be the dress, my hips were curvier, and my face looked more mature. A silver sparkle covered my body, and a touch of shimmer was brushed over my cheeks.

My heart thudded as I stared at myself once again, that sliver of fear settled into me. I looked like… dare I say it? *No.*

The only other jewellery I wore were dangly drop earrings that glittered brightly. It would be a lie to say I was not nervous. I just hoped Raiden didn't get the brunt of this.

The doorbell rang, and I knew it must be Raiden to collect me.

"It's time," Zarian said, holding out my grey fur coat to me. I took a deep breath as I took it, ready to face them all…

The queen had gone above and beyond to create the perfect venue for the extravagant ball. The Astalion and Silver Storm banners hung from every wall, a proud reminder of who was in power. Garlands of white flowers, vines, and lights adorned the grand chandeliers, pillars, and railings. Dangly strings of crystals hung in rows across the ceiling, and when the light hit them, they dazzled brightly.

The guests were all dressed up. The nobles of Westerfell wore the colours of their house, whilst Alphas and other guests wore their pack colours.

I had my hand hooked around Raiden's arm, trying to soothe my heart as we stepped into the grand hall of the castle. I hadn't been here in days... and although I hadn't seen Charlene, Raiden had been the link between us, passing her messages, and it was nice to hear from her, even if it wasn't in person. She had been very busy lately, and although it was because she was busy, I had a feeling her mother was stopping her from leaving the castle. One of her greatest wishes was that she would find her mate tonight, but the chances of that were low.

Raiden really was a gentleman. Although he had openly checked me out when Zarian had opened the door, he was now doing his best to keep his gaze on my face and, even then, kept looking away. It was a little amusing. I was sure I didn't look that different with all the makeup. He, himself, looked handsome in a black and gold patterned jacket.

"You look... really different tonight," he said as we made our way through the crowds. Eyes followed us, and I was sure my rather revealing dress was going to be a source of discussion now, but I just hoped it had an effect on a certain someone. I raised an eyebrow, looking up at Raiden.

"You have said that three times already. I'm beginning to worry I don't look good," I replied, amused.

"No... there's just... you just do..." he trailed off, sighing. "Let's go pay our respect to our Alpha," Raiden said with a wink at me.

"Let's go," I said. My heart was thudding as I looked towards the royals.

The king and queen looked regal, and for once, the king had his long hair braided back, and a crown sat upon it. He was dressed in smart pants and a patterned black and silver jacket in the colours of the pack. The queen, too, looked regal in silver and purple, with a crown upon her head, but Charlene, my queen, looked the most beautiful. She was in a stunning silvery grey dress with a tulle-layered skirt and a white floral detail scattered down from her waist. The bodice was nude with flowers along the top. A tiara sat upon her head, and her face was glowing as she smiled politely at the couple her parents were talking to.

I saw several Alphas glance my way, unmated. I resisted the urge to roll my eyes. They were like a pack of hungry wolves...

Theon was standing with Ryan a few feet away, looking handsome in black pants, a shirt, and a jacket similar to Raiden's, but in black and red. I saw him pause, stiffening slightly as we approached, and I knew he had sensed us. I stepped closer to Raiden, pressing my breast against his arm.

"You look handsome tonight," I said softly, knowing that even with the music and chatter, he'd hear us.

"Why thank you, but you already told me," Raiden replied in a seductive whisper.

"Raiden! Yileyna!" Ryan called, coming over to us. "Yileyna, may I say you look incredibly beautiful tonight? I'm sure you will be the talk of the ball or more like the desire of every unmated werewolf." He took my hand, kissing it just as Theon turned.

His heart rate quickened slightly as he looked me over, his eyes flashing gold as they raked me from my feet to my waist, then to my breasts. Raiden's arm snaked around my waist possessively, and I placed my hand on his chest, smiling up at him, trying not to focus on Theon.

"Thank you, Ryan, you look handsome, yourself," I said, looking over at him.

This is it, look at him and act like you don't care...

I turned towards Theon, my heart betraying me as it began pounding. Our eyes met, and I tried not to pay attention to the way his breathing was heavier. His eyes, which were entirely gold, bore into mine, a frown on his handsome face. His anger was palpable, but it was the fire within his eyes that made my core knot, the way a strand of his hair flicked in front of his forehead sexily. Those eyes that devoured me were drinking me up, and the way he licked his lips, swallowing hard, made me feel lightheaded. Through my own storm of emotions, I felt satisfied.

Perfect. I had his attention...

"Theon, hi," I said lightly, smiling as innocently as I could.

His nostrils flared, and when his gaze flicked from my lips to my eyes, I knew he knew exactly what I was trying to do. Before each one of us could say anything more, Raiden squeezed my waist, making me look at him questioningly. Before he could even reply, I sensed the powerful aura of the Alpha and heard the royal family approaching.

"Raiden, Yileyna, it's lovely to see you two together," Alpha Andres's deep voice came.

"Thank you, Alpha. You look beautiful, Luna Soleil, Princess Charlene," Raiden said as I pulled away from his hold, turning towards the Alpha family.

"Alpha, Luna," I said, smiling politely, but his reaction was not one I was expecting. The moment his eyes fell on me, his smile vanished. *Great, now what have I done?*

I smiled at the queen and Charlene, wanting to crush her in a hug! I had missed her, but the king's reaction disturbed me. His heart was beating violently in his chest, and his face was pale as he stared at me.

"Alpha, are you alright?" I asked, concerned, stepping closer to him. He stepped back as if my touch would burn, looking me over head to toe before he turned and walked off. I stared after him as I felt all eyes on me, and the queen tutted.

"I'm sure your aim was to seduce many men tonight, Yileyna, yet your attire is indeed an insult to the king. Obviously, with such a dress, all men would lust after you," she spat before she turned and stormed off.

I frowned as I stood there, confused. I knew a look of lust, and the king was not looking at me like that. The queen's thoughts were disgusting. The king may not like me, but he had never looked at me in that way. But I couldn't blame her; Theon had told me he had cheated on his true mate… perhaps she was just insecure…

What concerned me more was why the king had reacted like that.

I suddenly felt lost and confused, not even realising when Charlene closed the gap between us and hugged me tightly…

Losing Control

YILEYNA

I WAS SO CONFUSED… I don't know what happened, but I was unable to shake the king's reaction from my mind. Why had he looked at me like that?

"I'm fine…" I whispered to Charlene, giving her a tight squeeze. Where would I be without her? She moved back slowly, concern and sadness in her eyes as she brushed a strand of my hair from my face.

"You look beyond beautiful tonight, so beautiful that even the moon does not compare," Charlene complimented me, trying to cheer me up with a small smile on her face, and I tried to smile back.

This wasn't what I was expecting. This wasn't how it was meant to go. Sure my dress was revealing, but so were many other dresses tonight. The only difference was mine was in the fabric and designs from the Aerean Kingdom, the Fae kingdom Zarian hails from.

"Thanks," I said, trying to regain control of myself. I could still feel Theon's burning gaze upon me. The intensity of it made me a little confused. We parted, and I gave Charlene's hand a gentle squeeze as Ryan let out a low whistle.

"I wonder if the king is okay. That was… strange," he said, massaging his jaw.

"Don't let Mom's words get to you, I'm sure Dad just…" Charlene tried, but even she had no answer.

"I don't think the Luna was wrong. What was your aim, De'Lacor, by dressing like that?" Theon spat coldly, his voice full of rage, resentment, and venom.

My heart skipped a beat, a flash of pain filling me as I looked into his amber eyes. Amber eyes that were so similar to the shade of the pendant I wore that I wondered if that was why I subconsciously kept it close. Because of the colour, a colour that reminded me of him...

I glanced down at the floor, trying not to let his words get to me. *You should know me better than that, Theon...*

Focus, Yileyna, remember the plan.

"My only aim was to look good for my date. Besides, I don't need to dress in a certain way for men to fall at my feet, right, Theon?" I mocked, knowing I sounded horrible, but the urge to make a jab at his infatuation with me was far too strong for him to deny, and as much as I hated behaving like this... he deserved a taste of how it felt to be mocked. His eyes burned gold, his anger rising, and Raiden pulled me close.

"Good is by far an understatement, Yileyna. You look so stunning even the moon would be jealous of you," he said, trying to defuse the rising tension between Theon and me.

Theon scoffed, and from the corner of my eye, I saw him turn his gaze away. It showed that my plan was working, Theon's anger was radiating off of him, and I wondered what exactly it would take to break his self-control...

"How about we go take our seats? Dinner will be served soon..." Ryan trailed off as Theon turned and stormed away. He looked at Raiden, his smirk vanishing. "Raiden, you know you are slated to be Beta, why are you doing -"

"I already said I don't want that position, so I'll behave as I deem fit," Raiden cut in. My heart skipped a beat as I looked at him in shock. Why didn't he tell me?

"What?" I asked.

"With Theon's engagement, the Beta position -"

"Enough, Ryan," Raiden said. His voice was calm, yet the finality in it made Ryan shake his head.

"No offence, Yileyna, but it would be beneficial for us all to see Raiden in that position. If -"

"Ryan, I said enough. This has nothing to do with her," Raiden growled. It was the first time I had seen him so angry, his eyes flashing as he glared at Ryan.

"Okay, stop, the both of you," I said, pulling Raiden away. "Excuse us for a moment." Charlene nodded as Ryan crossed his arms with irritation clear on his face. I led Raiden away towards one of the doors leading to the courtyards.

"I'm fine," he said, giving me a small smile that didn't reach his eyes as we stepped out into the cold. "Let's go back inside, Leyna, you know you aren't even wearing a coat.

"I don't feel cold," I said, refusing to listen to him. I tilted my head and raised my eyebrows, crossing my arms. "But I'm upset with you, Raiden." He looked down before shaking his head.

"I'm sorry, but know that I would never accept that position. I would never -"

"Raiden," I cut him off, placing a hand on his arm. I looked up at the man I considered a friend and smiled gently. "I'm upset because you are letting an opportunity you deserve slip from your fingertips." He looked at me sharply as fresh snow landed in his hair.

"That's your birthright, Yileyna, and no matter what, it feels wrong to accept it. I won't do that to you," he said quietly. A serious Raiden made me nervous. I often forget that he was indeed a man, one who could be many things...

"It was, but I am not fit for the position. We need a Beta who is just, loyal, and hardworking. In fact, you remind me a little of Dad. He was always caring, wanting his best for our people and to work hard... I'm sure he would have been proud to know you would be his successor," I said quietly.

The ache in my chest was because of my parents. As for the beta title... a few months ago, I would have been hurt, but it all felt so childish now. A title was a title, one that should be held by who was worthy, and although I once felt it was my only attachment to my parents, I realised that regardless of the Beta title, I was still their daughter. I was still Yileyna De'Lacor and I would still make them proud.

"Yileyna, it just doesn't feel -" I placed a finger on his lips and shook my head.

"No. It's the right thing to do. If I had known, I wouldn't have come with you tonight... I can't let you ruin your life and opportunity because of me. I thought we were friends, Raiden. You should have told me," I said quietly as a sharp wind blew through my hair, but I ignored it.

"I'm sorry, but it was not necessary when I wasn't going to accept it," he said, flashing me a charming smile. "But if you want to make it up to me, you could honour me with one dance."

"Raiden…" He was trying to change the subject.

"One dance with the most beautiful woman around. Although I'm uncertain if your appearance is a luxury or a punishment tonight…" he murmured huskily. His eyes dipped to my dress, and I felt my heart skip a beat as I blushed under his obvious meaning.

It was nothing like Theon. Raiden was far different… warmth, comfort, and security, and that was why I would never hurt him. But I could tease him, right?

I smiled brightly and stepped closer, wrapping my arms around his neck and almost laughing when he tensed.

"So tell me, shall we dance here? All alone, away from hundreds of prying eyes or… want to go inside?" I whispered, pressing my chest against him. He looked at me suspiciously before a smirk crossed his face, clicking on to exactly what I was doing.

"Ever the tease, Ms De'Lacor. I think you forget that Raiden Bolton is rather experienced in this field," he replied, wrapping his arms around me and pulling me against him firmly. I gasped, tightening my own hold on him as our bodies pressed against one another entirely. His scent invaded my senses and I laughed softly.

"Who can forget that Raiden Bolton was the biggest playboy in Westerfell?" I raised an eyebrow, looking into those deep blue eyes of his.

"I would at least have hoped that you would," he said with a wink as he began swaying to the music that was playing inside the hall. I raised an eyebrow.

"I actually remember you grabbing your pants as a certain she-wolf's father chased you away onto the streets. Charlene and I laughed over your naked butt for a good few weeks," I smirked as he groaned.

"Damn, fathers hate me."

"Well, is that why I'm your latest pursuit? Because you don't need to worry about a father?" I asked, amused, despite the small pang inside at the reminder that I was an orphan. His smile vanished and he shook his head.

"Actually, you were never just a pursuit…" He reached up, brushing his knuckles down my cheek. "You aren't just a pursuit. You are different, Yileyna. I know that you only see me as a friend, so I shall respect that, but you will always be my favourite girl." My heart thumped as I looked into his eyes. He meant it, I knew that. I just wished I wasn't. I wished I wasn't the one he wanted…

"You have a mate out there," I whispered. "She may be waiting for you."

"We both know a mate does not equate to love. I'm not asking for more, Yileyna. I just hope you know you are worth so much more. Never settle for anything less." Our faces were inches apart as we gazed into each other's eyes.

"Thank you, Raiden," I whispered. "Any girl would be lucky to have you as their mate."

"Yeah?" He said, but his eyes said more. Just that the one girl he wanted wasn't interested… I felt guilty as I stared up at him.

"I'm -" He cut me off, placing his finger on my lips.

"It's fine, don't say anything," he whispered, his hair tickling my forehead.

My heart thundered, and suddenly I was very aware of how close we were; our bodies moulded as one, his left arm wrapped around me as he pressed me against him, his right hand lingering on my neck as he cupped my face.

"Okay," I whispered back, as our noses brushed. Just enjoy the moment…

Deep down, I wished I didn't fall for the one man who had only caused me pain, but we didn't get to choose who we fell in love with. My obsession with Theon was born the day I first saw him. He was within inches of losing his life as I braved fighting that Naga to save the young man in his hold. And then, the moment he began to give me attention, I fell hard…

I closed my eyes, pushing the thoughts away. *I will no longer let him make the choices in my life…*

The heart, mind, and body wanted different things…. My mind wanted to be loved and protected. My heart wanted Theon. It desired him, his touch his caress, his embrace… and my body… my body craved pleasure…

I could hear Raiden's heart racing, and I made the mistake of opening my eyes. The depth of the emotions in his blue orbs knocked the breath from me, and without realising it, I tilted my face up. A look of confusion flashed in his eyes, but it only lasted for a mere fraction of a second before his soft lips pressed against mine.

A soft whimper left my lips as tingles of pleasure rushed through me, before his grip on my neck tightened, pulling me closer. His hand slid to the small of my back as he pressed me against him firmly, his lips moving against mine in a soft kiss as if I might break. I tightened my hand around his neck as I deepened the kiss, kissing him harder.

For a moment… even if it's just a moment, I wanted to forget…

I felt him throb against me, and my core ached with need. My stomach was fluttering like crazy when his hand dipped an inch before he froze, tightening his grip. I knew he was fighting to control himself. I reached behind me with one hand, grabbing his wrist and guiding his hand to my ass, satisfied when I heard him groan. Neither of us cared that we might be seen. Right then, all that mattered was the pleasure and sensation that rippled through us.

He ran his tongue along my lips slowly seeking entrance, and I parted them. Kissing Raiden was different... the fresh, sweet taste of his mouth was pleasant.

I gasped when his tongue slipped into my mouth, but before I could melt into it, I was violently ripped away from him and thrown to the ground roughly. I gasped as pain shot through my arm, the biting cold sinking into me as I lifted my head from the ground.

"Theon," Raiden growled, his eyes blazing with anger.

His gaze snapped to me as the smell of blood reached my nose, and I looked down to see blood staining the snow. I sat up slowly, looking at my elbow to see that I had hurt it, but I didn't get to ponder on it as I felt the dangerous aura that now surrounded the man who had pulled me away. Theon.

"No one touches what's mine," he hissed, his voice more animal than human. His words dripped with venom and rage.

His back was to me, but to my utter horror, I saw that his claws were out, his entire body shaking with uncontrollable fury. Fear enveloped me as my gaze snapped to the doors to the hall, where I could see a few people were already looking our way.

I knew Theon. I knew what he was capable of. I had seen him kill without a second thought… but I had never seen him this angry… ever…

"Theon. She isn't yours," Raiden growled, but it was futile.

Stop, Raiden… He was in danger, and it was all my fault.

"Wrong. She's mine or no one's," Theon growled, and then it all happened so fast.

My ears rang and my heart thumped as I stared at the scene unfolding before my very eyes. In a flash, Theon was in front of Raiden as several screams filled the air. The sound of a sickening crunch followed, and the smell of blood filled the air…

A Downward Spiral

THEON

From the moment I had laid eyes on her, I was unable to focus on anything but the temptation and beauty of the goddess-like woman before me. Her dress clung to her every curve, made to fit her to perfection. Nothing was left to the imagination, from the perfect ass that I wanted to grab and pull against me, to her breasts that were spilling out of her dress. Everything was on display in the sexiest, most enticing way.

I hadn't been the only one with my eyes on her. Every unmated man, and many who were mated, were watching her with a look of pure lust in their eyes. The urge to rip them all apart was appealing, and seeing none other than Bolton holding her…

It had taken every ounce of willpower to control myself. Even holding back the hatred I felt for Andres didn't compare to the amount of control I was fighting against to not murder anyone who set their gaze upon her.

She was mine and mine alone.

When she had turned towards me, it felt as if time had stopped. She had looked ever more breath-taking… the type of beauty you could simply sit back and admire. Not one flaw… not one imperfection… I had swallowed hard, unhearing as she said something from those soft lips of hers.

All I fucking wanted was to rip her from Bolton's arms and mark her there and then. To show the fucking world who she belonged to.

It was all a fucking haze since then, trying to fight my emotions. For once, I was glad that Andres came over, but his reaction was… intriguing. It snapped me from the rage and jealousy within me.

Did it matter I was to be engaged to the fucking princess right now, when the woman I desired was on another man's arm? I was trying to talk myself into calming down, the urge to kill them all right now…

Do it.

I frowned, struggling to keep myself from shifting. *Fucking hell, focus, Theon.*

I leaned against the wall of the courtyard, struggling to regain control of myself. It was then that I heard her voice reach my ears as she talked to Raiden. Jealousy reared its ugly head, and it was as if I had been bitten by a poisonous snake. My eyes flashed gold, my claws came out, and the urge for blood overcame me.

I told her, I fucking told her she was mine and mine alone. I didn't fucking care if I left her. She was still mine.

Unable to hold myself back, I followed the sound of her voice when I froze in my tracks. There, right in front of me, she was in the arms of none other than Bolton, and what made it a thousand fucking times worse was that she was kissing him.

A red-hot rage engulfed every inch of my body. Anger burned through me, and all I fucking saw was death. *Tonight, I'm fucking painting the snow with blood that belonged to none other than that bastard.*

In a flash, I was behind her, ripping her from his hold and throwing her to the ground as I turned my attention to the scum before me.

"No one touches what's mine," I growled; my voice was barely recognisable. To hell with it all. There was no way I was going to allow her to be with anyone else.

"Theon. She isn't yours," Bolton had the fucking cheek to growl back. I smirked murderously. He just fucking sealed his death.

"Wrong. She's mine or no one's."

I lunged at him, grabbing him by his neck and slamming him to the ground with enough force to split his head open, but the bastard wasn't as weak as I had predicted. His eyes blazed green as he placed his hands behind his head, saving it from being split open. Several screams ripped through the air as blood spread from the back of his skull, staining the snow ever so beautifully. Satisfaction filled me as I smirked coldly.

"Theon," her hoarse whisper came.

My heart was thumping, and my rage unquenched. All I wanted was to keep smashing his head into the ground until it split open. I wasn't done. I raised my hand, ready to end this fucker's life. A small part at the back of my head told me that I should let him live for her… but I was far too possessive to let her go and far too fucking angry to let him go.

I wasn't a fucking hero. I didn't care if she hated me for becoming the villain in her eyes. Maybe she'd learn to stay away from all men, or they'd suffer the consequences.

I let out a menacing growl, plunging my hand towards his chest as our eyes met, and suddenly the wind began howling and the snow whipped around us as it began falling heavier.

"Don't touch him!" Yileyna's voice came trembling with anger. Then I saw her in front of me as she shoved me away with more force than I had ever felt from her. Through the blizzard, I thought I saw something different in her eyes, but I wasn't sure.

"Move aside," I warned her dangerously, unable to recognise the look of hatred in her eyes. That was an expression that she had never directed at me before or anyone else...

"No. What I do has nothing to do with you!" She hissed, standing before the bleeding man like a shield, only angering me more.

I closed the gap between us, about to grab her throat when she raised her hand, and I felt ice beginning to wrap up my ankles, restricting my movements. My heart thundered as I realised she had far more control over her powers than back then. That Fae had indeed done a good job, but she was risking herself by displaying her abilities. If anyone saw beyond the blinding blizzard as to what she was doing, she'd be judged far more.

"Stop it," I growled.

"I will not let another person die because of me," she whispered back, and for a moment, that burning fire of anger was replaced by sorrow and guilt. *If only you knew all those people you thought died because of you were dead because of me…* "Get him to a doctor!" I heard her shouting. "Now!"

Those who had been watching the scene unfold seemed to suddenly unfreeze, and I saw Ryan and Charlene rush forward, along with the bastard's father. I knew the repercussions of my actions were going to create an obstacle in my path, but I didn't really care right then. All I could see was the way they were kissing, replaying again and again in my mind…

When she first came into the hall, I had thought she was trying to piss me off, but to kiss him out here when she was alone… it wasn't just a game to her. She had wanted it. She was crouched down near Bolton, her heart pounding as she cupped his face, only creating more resentment in me.

"He'll be fine. I'll take him," his father, Henry, said curtly. His voice was hostile and cold as he glanced at me before lifting his son with the help of one of the guards.

I broke away from the ice shackles and closed the gap between us. I grabbed hold of her arm, making her head whip towards me.

"Do not touch me!" She hissed.

"Don't push me. You brought this on yourself," I said venomously, yanking her close. She scoffed bitterly.

"I hate you, Theon, get out of my life," she spat.

"Calm the fuck down," I whispered. Her ability was getting out of control, and something told me this raging storm that was brewing was her doing. How though? She wasn't speaking any enchantments, nor was it in a fae's capabilities to do so…

There was only one species on this planet that could manipulate the weather like this.

My heart thrummed as I stared into the beautiful, fearless face of the woman before me. My stomach twisted, and I didn't realise my grip had loosened until she had wrenched free. My mind was too consumed by the thoughts in my head.

Why had I never realised it…

The way the droplets of water seemed to glitter like gems when they clung to her… hair, a colour so rare for our kind… a body that enticed all men…

No.

This was some sick twisted reality. I wouldn't believe it. I couldn't. There was no way that I would fall for a…

The signs had been before me. Had I really been that clueless, or had I just been too blinded?

She faced a siren and lived… her love for the sea…

I ran a hand through my hair, unable to focus on the shouts of the onlookers. I looked up at her slowly, watching the princess say something to her. She was shaking her head, my own head squeezing with the shock of the revelation.

She smelt like a werewolf, though… was she a siren hybrid?

Something orangey peeked out from between her breasts, capturing my attention, but before I could focus on the item that was a stark contrast to the rest of her ensemble, I sensed Andres' aura.

"What is going on?" He thundered, his eyes assessing the area, taking in the blood that stained the snow before he scanned the sky. His face, which had looked pale, seemed to turn even ashier. Something in his eyes changed, and I felt a flash of fear as his gaze moved to Yileyna. Was he making the link?

The urge to divert his attention made me step forward. My own mind was a reeling mess, but I couldn't allow anyone to figure it out.

"Forgive me, Alpha. I lost control and ended up hurting future Gamma Raiden," I said coldly, my voice clear and hard. I didn't want forgiveness, nor was he my fucking Alpha. I didn't care for repercussions; he had deserved it, and I wanted to do far more to him than I already had.

"I…" The king cleared his throat. He seemed disturbed, the same as he had been when he had walked away the moment he had seen Yileyna. "What was the cause for this behaviour, Theon? I wasn't expecting this from you."

"I have no excuse for my behaviour. I'll accept any punishment -"

"Punishment? You deserve far more than that! You almost killed him!" Yileyna snapped, stepping forward. To my surprise, Andres said nothing. I frowned, refusing to answer her.

"Father, I refuse for this union to take place. There is no way that I will ever take this man as my mate," Charlene added, and I resisted a smirk. Like I wanted her. She was nothing more than trash.

"It was over her…" someone murmured in the crowd.

"She was with the Bolton boy…"

"Ah, so there we have it! He is not to blame. It's obviously her fault," Soleil spat, making my eyes flash.

"It is not her fault!" Charlene snapped back at her mother.

"Can we please take this elsewhere?" Ryan added quietly. For once, he fucking said something wise.

"Tonight is a big night, my king. We need to carry on. We can deal with this incident later. Let's have the ceremony over with," Soleil said, placing her hand on Andres' arm.

The ceremony… I needed it to happen. I scanned the crowd behind Andres, wondering if one of my father's spies was here…

Would he learn of what happened over a woman? Over her?

I looked at her; she still looked as beautiful as ever, even with the blood staining the skirt of her dress and her chest heaving in anger.

"You have to give Charlene until the full moon is at its peak to at least see if her mate is present or not," she said to the queen. "How can you simply want to pair her off with a man who almost killed one of our own?"

"Hold your tongue, child," the king said quietly before turning to the guests. "Leave us!" Was he that fucking shocked at my actions that he couldn't even speak?

"Hold my tongue, Alpha? I have said nothing wrong. How can you tie your daughter to a man who can't even control his anger? He isn't one of us. This proves it," Yileyna shouted, her words stinging, but I remained silent.

"Silence, you insolent filth!" Soleil snapped, and to my surprise, she stepped forward and slapped Yileyna across the face hard. A menacing growl left my lips, and I was by her side in a flash, grabbing the queen's hand, the urge to crush it in my hold overcoming me. My wolf's rage was beyond anything I had felt from him before.

"Mom!" Charlene gasped, but Yileyna remained indifferent, as if it'd had no effect on her. She looked up at me, and our eyes met, but all I saw was anger.

"I can hold my own," she said coldly before stepping away from both Soleil and me.

I let go of Soleil's wrist, and she clutched it to her chest, massaging it as the bruise began forming. Her face was pale, as if she had not expected that from me.

"Let's return to the ceremony," Andres said quietly.

"What about what happened to Raiden?" Yileyna asked coldly. "By taking his attacker and applauding him, you are showing that it's fine. Where are your duties to your people? What will the Boltons think, that their years of loyalty are not even valued?"

"Yileyna, not now." Andres's voice was strained as he stared at her.

Soleil scoffed, "Andres, what is wrong with you? She is insulting us!"

"I am not insulting anyone! I am stating the truth! Raiden almost died, and it was my fault -"

"Ha! Exactly! It was your fault! You caused this! Like your parents, you are simply a conniving…" Soleil trailed off, frowning as her gaze fell on something.

"I'm not conniving… I didn't mean for him to get hurt… that wasn't -" She was cut off when Soleil jumped forward, grabbing the chain that hung around Yileyna's neck.

"By Selene…"

My eyes flashed. I was about to intervene when my gaze went to the pendant that Soleil was holding up. Even through the falling snow, the amber jewel dazzled clearly. A pendant that I would be able to recognise anywhere...

How did she have it?

My stomach twisted, my heart pounding as my gaze snapped from the necklace to Yileyna's face, a look of confusion clear on it, and with a sinking realisation, I saw she had no idea what she possessed. But her innocence wasn't going to be enough.

I don't know where and I don't know how she got that necklace, but she had just sealed her own fate.

My head was squeezing as I stepped back involuntarily, trying to reign in the storm of emotions that were tearing me apart inside.

"That is…" the king murmured.

"The very insignia of the Obsidian Shadow Pack! She is a traitor! She is the daughter of a traitor! For those who had any doubts about the De'Lacors, here is your proof they were traitors! Throw her into the dungeons!" Soleil screamed to those who had remained, Ryan, Gamma Grayson and his wife. Several guards, including Madelia and another Mage.

"What? No! I got this -"

"I always had a bad feeling about you!" Soleil screamed, slapping Yileyna across the face again. The urge to snap her hands off and break every fucking finger by fucking one was growing ever stronger.

"Mom, stop it! It can't be true! Let her explain!" Charlene cried.

"Take my brat to her room! She is far too blinded to see logic! Throw this traitor in the dungeon, now!"

All sounds faded from around me, and for a moment, I felt as if history was repeating itself. Yileyna's horrifying truth screamed in my mind, but even then… where I should have been repulsed and angry, I wasn't. All I could think of was the accusation that was thrown at her.

Two guards grabbed her arms as the queen tried to rip the necklace from her neck, slicing into her skin, but still, the necklace didn't come off. It wouldn't. It was made from the strongest metal on this planet…

I stormed over to her as her blood seeped from the two long cuts made by Soleil's violent pull. Taking it from the queen's clutch, I pulled it off over her head. Our eyes met, and she shook her head slowly as she looked away, refusing to hold my gaze.

"I'm not a traitor," she whispered softly, making something in my chest tighten.

I said nothing as the men pulled her away, leaving me standing there holding the necklace that, once again, was tainted with the blood of someone that I truly cared about…

I watched as they dragged her away, yet not once did her eyes hold fear. Determination, anger, and confusion were in them.

Look at me. Come on...

I needed to see if she was alright, but not once did she even glance my way.

Once again, I just stood watching as someone who meant something to me was in need of help, but all I could do was stand there like a coward. And what fucking irked me the most was, I triggered this off. Do the right thing for the greater good…

I was doing the right thing – the logical thing, right?

The storm faded away and I stared down at the pendant in my hand. I couldn't pay attention to the murmur around us, the questions, the cries of outrage, or the sobs of someone who truly cared for Yileyna. My own mind was wreaking havoc within me.

Where the fuck did you get this necklace from, Yileyna?

A question that no one had fucking given her a chance to answer.

The buzz of talk only grew louder as Ryan forced Charlene to go with him. Everyone else was talking about what had just happened, but my attention went to the king, who was gripping the stone pillar next to him, his face greyer than I had ever seen it. It wasn't his appearance that caught my attention, but the words that he whispered ever so quietly that perhaps no one would have heard them.

"What have I done?"

These Emotions

THEON

"Like her parents, she's a traitor!"

"Who would have thought someone so beautiful and sweet was working for the Obsidian Shadow pack?

"Is it true the amulet belonged to the Hale family?"

"To the Alpha family of the Obsidian Shadow Pack? Who would have thought."

"They should have her beheaded!"

"Publicly!"

"I knew she should never have been allowed to become an epsilon-rank warrior!"

"It's because of her that Gamma Raiden Bolton is in critical condition!"

"He tried to protect her from Theon of Westerfell, and this is what happened…"

"Yes, yes, Theon of Westerfell must have realised she was a traitor!"

The distorted versions of the truth were already sifting through the crowd as a path split through the throngs, allowing us to pass. How foolish were they blaming her for something I did? I needed to stick by Andres' side; he was the only one who had power over Soleil's command, the only one who held the power to not have Yileyna beheaded.

Make sure Yileyna De'Lacor is unharmed and untouched. Place her in the cells, and Patrick, I want you to watch her until the Alpha has further orders, I said through the link, knowing Andres hadn't given any further order. He was one of the men I trusted enough to know he would not disobey me.

Yes, Beta!

I frowned. Beta… a title I didn't claim. If the princess and I had gotten engaged… I could have killed the king soon after and taken the throne. It had been so simple. I had been telling myself repeatedly to go through with it and then kill the Aphelion family. They deserved to die. Because of them, I had lost so much…

"Andres, Alpha Andres!" Soleil's voice hissed as she grabbed onto Andres' arm. His head jerked towards her as if suddenly brought out of a reverie. There was something off about him…

"What is it?" He asked curtly, but he lacked his usual power and arrogance.

"The engagement," she said coldly.

"Now isn't the time," I replied impassively. Soleil turned, glaring at me for speaking, but before she could reply, Andres turned as we reached the entrance doors to the hall and looked around the room.

"Take rest, there will be no engagement tonight! But fear not, this engagement will happen!" He called loudly and clearly. Not waiting for a reaction or reply, he turned and left the grand hall swiftly.

"Theon, as your future mother-in-law, tell me, what is with you and De'Lacor? You are to marry Charlene, yet you seemed to be besotted by the traitor," Soleil hissed, now turning her attention to me, her voice shaking with rage. The day I slit her throat would be a day I was going to enjoy thoroughly…

"Soleil, go to our quarters, I have much to do. This engagement will happen, don't worry about that. Just give me time to sort this mess out," Andres said dangerously.

"You are acting strange, Andres."

"Soleil, go." His command was absolute. He removed the crown from his head and shoved it into Soleil's hands. "Grayson!"

"Yes, Alpha?" Grayson stepped forward, his eyes serious yet his face was as emotionless and professional as ever.

Andres paused as if trying to think of what he needed to say or do, only making me watch him sharply. His words 'what have I done?' stuck with me… his reaction to everything that had happened was intriguing. Had he figured out her truth? But if that was so, then why was he not ordering for Yileyna to be killed? It was something else… but what?

"Make sure the Boltons are alright… check up on Raiden, and I will talk to Henry when he is ready," Andres sighed heavily. "Theon, I will have a word with you now. In my office."

My brows furrowed. I was missing something, but what was it? I gave a small nod, walking past him and up the stairs, heading towards his office.

Enjoy your time giving commands, Andres, for soon this crown, this title, and this kingdom will be mine.

The door shut behind Andres with a snap and he walked to his chair, dropping onto it as if carrying his own body had been exhausting. He ran his hand down his face, exhaling sharply.

"Theon… Theon… why?" He questioned silently. Our eyes met, and I crossed my arms. He didn't need to announce what he meant. Even if he had handled it calmly or didn't react, it wasn't a small matter.

"I have no excuse; I lost my temper, and I attacked him." He looked troubled before he placed his head in his hands.

"Theon… you are to be the future Alpha alongside Charlene. You cannot hurt your future Gamma. Raiden is a good man."

I don't really give a fuck.

Yileyna… what was to happen to her? I looked down at the pendant in my hand, my heart clenching. How did she have it? This should have been lost at sea…

My heart was thundering as I pushed away the grief that threatened to seep through… I never thought I'd see this pendant again. Was it a sign that Yileyna had it? Memories from long ago rang in my mind, and I swallowed hard as the voice filled my head.

"This? It's very precious, son…"

"It's beautiful…"

"It is, isn't it? One day I will give it to you to give to the woman you love…"

"Woman? Yuck, I'm never going to fall in love…"

"Oh, is that so?"

Mom's pendant… gifted to her by my grandmother and to be worn by the Luna of our pack… a necklace she had always worn, a necklace which she was wearing when she had been killed by that siren, a necklace which should have been lost at sea...

My stomach twisted as suddenly the siren's face leered in my mind, a face so beautiful yet so evil… a face which looked so like Yileyna it made me sick. Fuck, was my mind playing tricks on me? Blonde hair…

No, they didn't look alike.

I ran my hand through my hair, the sheer reality of Yileyna's truth hitting me once again. Fuck.

Did she know? Her having the necklace… my heart began hammering as a thousand possibilities came through my mind. I needed to ask her. I needed to know where she got it from. Was this why she felt so compassionate towards the young siren back on Bellmead Island? No. She couldn't fucking know… right?

I turned, needing to see her now.

"We are not done, Theon," Andres said, his voice sharp. My eyes flashed. It took me a moment to calm my anger before I placed an emotionless expression on my face and looked back over my shoulder at him. "I'm waiting for an answer."

"I have no answer, I lost my temper…"

"It's the girl, isn't it?" His voice was quiet, and I clenched my jaw, turning around fully.

"Yileyna… what do you plan to do with her? I don't believe she is working alongside the Obsidian Shadow Pack," I said quietly.

"You are not answering my question," he replied quietly, but there it was, those emotions and that… was it fear?

"Is something troubling you?" I asked, raising an eyebrow.

"Worrying me? I… no… it's…" His face looked haunted, and he closed his eyes. "It's nothing… answer your Alpha, Theon. You said this girl was a mere distraction… are you sure it's not more?" I clenched my jaw. Her life was already at risk… but to deny the obvious…

"I don't know," I said quietly. *She'll hate me soon enough anyway.* He sighed heavily, standing up.

"Theon, throwing away your potential for a woman -"

"I already agreed to this union. Leave Yileyna out of it," I growled, my eyes flashing dangerously. The king's expression darkened.

"Do not disrespect me, son. Remember, I am still your Alpha," he growled. Like hell he was my fucking Alpha. I clenched my jaw but didn't reply.

"I said I'd accept the punishment for hurting Bolton. What will happen to Yileyna?" The king looked away.

"I do not know yet… she… I will talk to her first. I want to see what she says," he said, taking me by surprise. Something was off. I nodded.

"Give her a chance to explain." It was a statement.

"Theon… you know I trust you with everything. Did anything about Yileyna seem… odd to you?" My heart fucking betrayed me, and the king looked at me sharply. "Ah… so it did." He chuckled humourlessly. "Yet you will not speak of it. You are far too deeply infatuated with her it seems."

"I'm not," I refuted dangerously.

"Deny it all you want, but whether you admit it or not... or if it's just the magic of her temptations…" His voice became bitter as he trailed off, and I saw the flash of anger in his eyes. I knew what he was insinuating, and although neither of us said it aloud, we were on the same page.

He knew she was part siren. It must have been her display of power. I had hoped no one would notice but they had. Who else had seen her?

"I will take Charlene as my chosen mate, as promised. Let's leave Yileyna out of this," I said quietly. He knew she meant something to me, no matter how much I denied it. Right then, she was in his grasp…

"Theon, being king means we make hard decisions. If I find that this… girl... is coming in the way of my plans, you know the consequences. I will handle it swiftly before the problem becomes far too -"

"She will not come in the way of any of your plans. As long as Yileyna is unharmed… I will do as you say," I cut in, trying to control the flaring rage within me at his obvious threat.

He knew she meant something to me, and he was willing to use her against me. *So these are your true colours.* I hated him with a vengeance, and until I destroyed him, I would not rest. A small smirk crossed his lips.

"Good. Very good… you are dismissed."

Without even a second look at him, I left the room, controlling the rage within me. I wanted to shift and rip them all to pieces, but we didn't need a rebellion…

I made my way through the castle, heading towards the dungeons. My heart was thudding, and my hands were shaking with anger.

"Leave us," I commanded to the guards as I walked down to the cells, her scent guiding me. My fists balled with anger. Sea breeze…

I slowed down as I took a deep breath, spotting Patrick standing there near her cell with two other guards. Behind them, I saw Yileyna on the floor behind the bars, still in her dress. Her hair was half down as if someone had yanked on it, making another wave of anger rage through me. I was like a storm waiting to be unleashed, and I wasn't sure I'd be able to hold back for much longer.

"Queen's orders, no one can see the prisoner!" One of them said, blocking my path. My eyes flashed, and I grabbed his throat.

"You are speaking to the future Alpha. I'm here to question the prisoner," I growled. "Leave!" His eyes widened in fear. His heart beating irritatingly loud. What would it feel like to rip his heart out? But before I could ponder on that thought, Patrick stepped forward.

"Yes, sir, we will leave you," he said curtly as both he and the third guard pulled the guard free from my hold.

I let go, satisfied with the blood that dripped down his neck. The three men were about to walk past when I held my hand out.

"Key," I said coldly.

The two hesitated before the man who had dared bark at me passed me the key. I didn't move until they had all left. The dungeon door slammed shut, and we were left in silence. Just the two of us…

I swallowed hard as I slowly made my way over to the silver-barred cell. She sat there with her knees tucked under her, her face turned away from me. For a moment, I pictured her with a siren's tail, and my stomach churned at the image.

She's a hybrid, not a full siren… she isn't a monster…

I unlocked the door to the cell, letting it swing open. The hinges creaked, and the sound echoed in the cold, damp dungeons. She tensed but still refused to look at me.

"Yileyna."

"What do you want?" She asked quietly.

"Look at me."

She refused, making my eyes flash as I closed the gap between us and crouched down before her. I took hold of her face, forcing her to look at me. My heart skipped a beat as I saw the tears she refused to shed. She lowered her gaze, and I eased my grip. I reached behind her, taking out the few pins that held up her half-loose hair, allowing it to fall free around her shoulders.

Neither of us spoke. All I wanted was to pull her close… tell her it was going to be okay... but was it? I had hurt her time and time again…

"Where did you find the necklace?" I asked. I still had it in my pocket.

She looked at me sharply, and although she tried to pull free, I didn't let go. Fuck, she was beautiful…

"I don't want to talk to you. When I am tried, I will speak then," she replied coldly, pulling free from my hold. She stood up and put as much distance as she could between us. But the cell wasn't that big…

I advanced towards her, her heart racing as she watched me sharply. For a second, I couldn't even recognise her. Where was that girl who looked at me with adoration and love?

"Answer me, Yileyna; you know not everyone around here gets a trial. You were wearing the crest of the Hale family… that's no small matter. Now, will you talk? Or do I need to force it from you?" I asked quietly, placing my hands on the walls and caging her between my arms. She looked away, pursing her lips. When I thought she wouldn't reply, she frowned.

"It's the necklace you saw me cleaning. The one I bought from a merchant in Bellmead," she said after a moment. I scowled, looking down at her, only for my gaze to fall to her breasts. I averted my gaze.

"So you had no idea what it was…"

"Obviously not, or do you think I would wear it openly? I am not a traitor." She glared at me, trying to push me back. Her hands felt good on my chest, and to piss her off, I stepped closer. Chest to chest, our hearts beat as one as we stared into the other's eyes.

"So it was a mistake…" Obviously, I knew she wasn't a traitor…

"So you believe me?" She asked with disbelief. I cocked a brow, looking down at her.

"When have I ever doubted you, little storm?" Little storm… was it ironic that the name suited her so well now?

They said only the imperial sirens could control the weather. My heart thumped at the sudden thought, but before I could delve further into my thoughts, she smiled, scoffing as she shook her head.

"Now that you got your answer, leave me alone. What you did to Raiden is something I won't forgive you for. Ever," she whispered, her voice full of rage.

"I told you time and time again, the moment you agreed to become mine, that no other man could touch you," I growled dangerously. She raised an arched eyebrow.

"That deal was off the moment you walked out of my life. I will do whatever I want, with whomever I want, and I would like to see you try to stop me," she spat as she shoved me away from her, and this time she managed it. I was forced to move back, the sheer strength in her push taking me by surprise. Had the fae managed to awaken her powers?

"No, I can't stop you, but I will fucking kill anyone who dares to touch you," I growled possessively.

"Don't you dare try to claim me when I am nothing to you!" She said, pushing past me. The tingles of pleasure that danced along my skin as she brushed against me were something I had missed. I growled, grabbing her arm and slamming her up against the wall, making her breasts bounce. She gasped as I pinned her wrists to the wall.

"Do not push me, Yileyna, or I swear I will paint this fucking city in the blood of every man who dares to approach you," I warned darkly, "or better yet, I wouldn't mind painting you with it. You look good covered in blood," I whispered, leaning into her, my lips brushing her neck. She shivered in response. I didn't care if it was from fear or pleasure. She was mine…

The urge to kiss her… claim her, and fuck her was overpowering me, but I forced myself back. I smirked arrogantly, and her eyes flashed. I saw the iridescent multi-coloured shades that painted her irises. Beautiful…

Her plump lips curled into a smirk as she looked me over.

"The thing is, Theon, I realised that my feelings for you weren't enough. Not enough to keep you happy, and so I let you go. You no longer hold any claim over me. Touch anyone ever again, and I swear…" She left her threat hanging, her chest heaving with anger. "Move aside, or you will regret it." Her voice was soft, yet the coldness reminded me of the harshest winters. That aura around her was there again, the temperature plunging, and then ice began spreading from beneath her feet.

"Enough."

We both froze. We had been so caught up that neither of us had noticed when the king had arrived. His voice was powerful and dangerous, his aura swirling around him so strong I wondered how I had fucking missed it.

I looked into Yileyna's eyes, which had returned to her usual beautiful grey, before I looked down at our position.

Fuck.

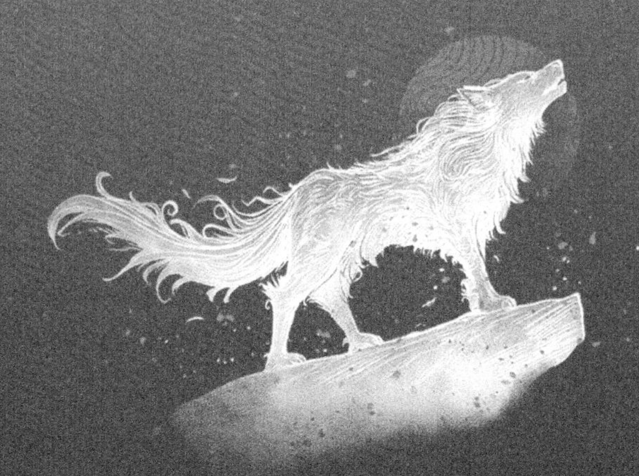

His Strange Reaction

YILEYNA

Theon moved away smoothly, yet I didn't miss how swiftly he had backed away from me. I almost smiled bitterly.

That was all I was to him, something to play with when night falls and darkness blankets the city… something to hide and use when he pleased. A plaything to enjoy and toss aside when he was done, so the world never knew. That is why I was done with him.

All he did was come and go as he pleased, but I couldn't deal with it anymore. How many chances did one person deserve?

My gaze snapped to the ice on the ground. It glittered under the moonlight that seeped through one of the tiny gaps in the walls. It was obvious it was spreading from beneath my feet… *Goddess… how am I going to explain this?*

I turned my attention to the king, who stepped into the cells, his hands clasped behind his back. Without his crown, he had lost his regal look, but he now looked even more menacing and dangerous. His glowing eyes were on me as if he was trying to look into my soul. I held his gaze as he approached, but what unnerved me most was the look in them. An emotion that seemed familiar…

I could smell something mixed in with his usual scent when he stopped a foot away, and then it suddenly dawned upon me what it was. *Fear.*

Why though? The king didn't care for me, nor did he care about Charlene's attachment to me, so what did he fear? And it was obvious it wasn't my abilities, as he had approached without care.

"If I say I'm not a traitor, you won't believe me, will you?" I asked quietly. He didn't reply for a moment before he tilted his head slightly.

"Leave us," the king commanded Theon without turning towards him. Theon narrowed his eyes, and I saw the distrust in them as he looked at the king.

Why are you confusing me, Theon? It was almost as if he cared...

He was one of the king's most loyal followers. His reaction made no sense to me. But then again, he only feared another man touching me. Did he think the king would? I doubted that.

I knew the looks of lust, hatred, love, and so many more. The only person I was never able to read properly was Theon. His signals were so mixed that I had become entangled with him. I knew better now.

"I will not hurt her," the king snapped, now glaring at Theon. *Like you care, Theon.*

Theon looked at him sharply, staring at him for a moment before his gaze flicked to me, calculating before he looked back at the king. His frown vanished, and a look of understanding dawned upon his handsome face as he stared at me. His chest was heaving, and the look of pure disbelief on his face unnerved me. He shook his head slowly as if denying something to himself.

My stomach lurched sickeningly. The fear that I had doubted came back to me with a vengeance. What if they had come to the same conclusion and realised what I may be? *Please, no...*

"Please," the king said quietly, taking me by surprise.

Theon looked at the ground. His heart was racing as he glanced at me once again as if seeing me for the first time, but what shocked me the most was the look of hatred that flashed in his eyes as he did a once-over of me. What was it? Why was he looking at me like that?

Not saying anything, he turned and strode out of the cell. I watched him walk away. He paused at the end of the hall, and my heart skipped a beat when he looked at me over his shoulder, but my blood ran cold when I saw the hatred in his eyes. Theon...

The king sighed heavily. I turned my attention to him. I knew he hated me...

"Yileyna, where did you get that amulet?"

"From a merchant in Bellmead. It was filthy, and I'm sure he didn't know its worth. He sold it for a mere few gold coins. Once I had cleaned it, I even took it to a jeweller to ask about its value! You can ask him if you want proof," I said, suddenly realising I had someone to vouch for me. "And Theon! He saw me when I was cleaning it."

"I'm not asking for an alibi," he replied curtly, staring at me so intensely that it was beginning to unnerve me. His eyes were boring into my face as if he, too, were seeing me for the first time. He was making the link...

I tried to hide my fear as he slowly looked at the ice that covered the floor.

"How long has it been since you discovered this... ability?" His voice was grave and dark. His eyes were cold when he looked back at me.

"Not long... since my eighteenth birthday. The cold became easier to bear as well, but you don't need to worry; my powers are blocked anyway," I assured him quickly.

"Blocked?" He asked sharply, something flickering in his eyes.

"Yes, so you have nothing to worry about," I replied.

"Who said they're blocked?" I didn't want to mention Zarian.

"Just someone who was helping me with my powers. I realised I could be a hybrid of some sort, and so I sought out help." I didn't trust the king enough to tell him everything.

"Tell me, Yileyna, what kind of hybrid do you think you are?" My heart thumped, and a sliver of fear rippled through me at the look in his eye.

"I don't know, Alpha," I lied quietly. His eyes darkened dangerously. He reached out, taking a strand of my hair, making my heart thump in fear.

"Hair lighter than most in Westerfell, beauty that is indeed the talk of the town, and the ability to manipulate ice and the weather..." His words were quiet, yet with each one that left his lips, my stomach began to sink. He knew... Goddess, he knew...

He let go of the strand of my hair and placed his hand on top of my head just as he used to when I was a child.

"How did I not see it...?" I frowned in confusion, but he simply turned away, sighing heavily.

"Speak not of your abilities or your heritage. I will handle this myself."

"My heritage?" I asked quietly. Why did he sound so grave and almost defeated?

"We both know what you are, or dare I say it, the three of us, including Theon, know. Tell me, Yileyna, does anyone else know of your abilities?"

"Raiden, Charlene, and… Zarian, the fae whom I sought help from," I answered quietly.

"I will have a word with them myself. I will give the order that no one is to come to see you."

Without another word, he left the cell. Shutting the door with a loud resounding clang, he locked it before he paused and glanced at me.

"Make sure you speak to no one until I summon you," he warned once more.

I nodded as his footsteps retreated. I slumped against the wall, letting myself slide to the ground. I locked my arms around my knees and closed my eyes. This was not how I was expecting the night to go…

Raiden, was he okay? It was my fault that he was hurt. It had never been the plan to kiss him for a reaction. That had happened on impulse, and I didn't hate it. I sighed as I opened my eyes, leaning my head back against the wall. *I'm sorry, Raiden.*

Theon's words still rang in my mind… if any man touched me, he would kill them. A ripple of anger washed through me, and I shook my head. There was no way I would allow him to dictate what I should do with my life, but before that, I needed to be free from here.

I truly was bad luck…

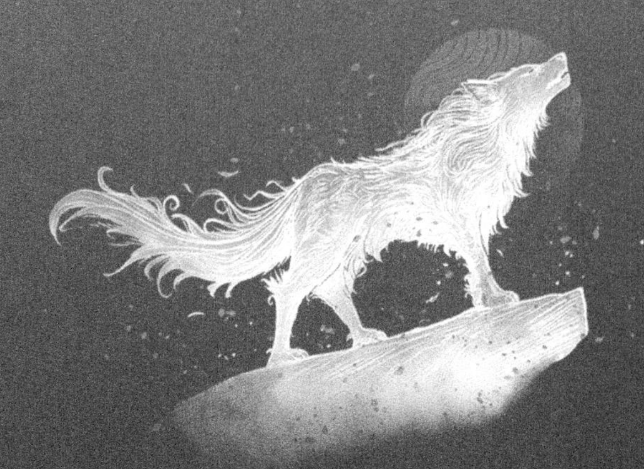

Buried Truths

ANDRES

She was mine… my daughter, and I hadn't even realised it. Why had I not seen it? Did William know that she was mine? Is that why he never told me she was adopted?

I had not realised nor suspected it, not until tonight. The moment she had turned, I thought I was seeing my past…

A secret that I had not told anyone. Not even when I told Theon had I revealed the full truth. Deliana had not been a one-night stand…

The memories of long ago haunted me, and no matter how much I wanted to push them away, I couldn't. We had met by accident; I had been injured by some rogues, and I was by the coast at night. I had heard her singing, and it had drawn me, yet instead of ripping my heart out, she had helped me when she realised I was injured, stemming my bleeding and wrapping my wounds.

She had been the most beautiful woman I had ever seen. Goddess, there was no woman who held even a candle in comparison to her beauty…

Despite being a siren, she seemed to be innocent and pure-hearted, curious to learn about our world. That night, she kept me company. Since I couldn't move from my injuries, I had put up with her, knowing she could kill me within seconds. The wolfsbane in my system stopped me from mind-linking for help, too…

NINETEEN YEARS AGO

"Are you waiting for me to heal so you can rip my heart out?" I asked, wincing in pain.

The weather was warm, and the only reprieve was the slight warm wind that sometimes blew past on this hot humid night.

She giggled, batting her big, gorgeous, deep blue eyes rimmed with thick dark lashes. Her tail was a pretty silver and blue, and although I knew she could kill me with ease, I was helpless.

"Why would I kill such a handsome man?" She ran her hand down my chest, and I flinched, feeling sharp pleasurable sparks rush through me. She removed her hand instantly, cupping my face. "Are you alright?"

"Yeah, don't touch me," I growled.

Why did I feel those intense sparks? I only felt them with Soleil…

I stared at her, trying to ignore the intense emotions that rushed through me. She tilted her head, a huge smile spreading on her lips. Her teeth were pearly white yet almost normal, but I knew those could transform into extremely sharp ones if she wanted.

"Is my appearance scaring you?" She questioned.

"No, sirens don't scare me," I shot back, watching before my very eyes as she transformed into a woman. It was more dangerous than before as she stood there in all her beauty, but this time accompanied by a very appealing, sexy lower half of a woman's body. That awakened something deep within me, blood rushing south as she did a slow twirl.

"Tell me, Alpha Andres, do I look pretty now?" I swallowed hard, trying not to look at her pussy.

"You may look like a woman, but you aren't acting like one… cover up," I muttered, sounding rather grumpy.

She giggled, "You are so adorable."

But she didn't bother covering up as she sat down by my side, cross-legged. At least her hair covered her perfect breasts, but her smooth lower region was still distracting me. So, I instead stared at the ceiling of the cave she had brought me to. The sound of the waves lapping against the rocks filled my ears. Something she said came to my mind and I paused, looking at her sharply.

"How did you know my name?" She blushed lightly and looked down.

"I just do…" Her eyes softened, and if it were not for her beauty, I would have almost forgotten that she was a siren…

"What do you want in return for helping me tonight?" I asked instead. "Or are you just waiting to rip my heart out the moment I'm healed?"

"No, I already told you I won't do that, but I request you spend one night with me every week for four weeks. To tell me about your world, your kind, how things are on land." I narrowed my eyes as I sat up, holding my chest, trying not to grunt in pain.

"Why are you so curious about it? Are your people not trying to kill us?" She looked at me and shook her head.

"No, we just want what is ours, what the people of land stole. I want to learn so that, in the future, we are friends." She smiled brightly, and I wondered how many sirens were truly like the one before me...

One night a week became two... then three...

She and I had a connection that confused me. It was almost parallel to the mate bond but far more intense, but I guess it was the seduction of a siren that made me feel like that.

I continued to walk through the silent halls of the castle, the very castle she had always wanted to see. Yileyna... she was my, our daughter...

The signs had always been there, but I never thought it was possible. Growing up, I kept her at arm's length because she reminded me somewhat of Deliana. I had never actually thought she was ours; it was just her hair colour that had irked me.

Soleil had also never questioned my nights away. Although she knew I was cheating on her, a true mate would always feel it... but she never said anything, not until she was pregnant with Charlene, telling me that I needed to cut it off with whoever I was seeing, saying she had given me the heir I wanted...

I also knew I needed to. I was the Alpha, and our enemies were the sirens, the Dark Fae Kingdom, the Rogues, and above all, the Obsidian Shadow Pack...

I knew that no one could find out about what I had done. She was a monster...

Keeping that in mind, I had drunk plenty before I had gone to see her, to end it once and for all. She had been waiting for me, dressed in a small blue dress that revealed half her breasts and most of her thighs. She had been happy, unknowing as to what I was there for, wrapping her arms around my neck as she tiptoed and claimed my lips in a sensual kiss that had consumed me. She had asked me how I was.

She had worried over me, concerned about my silence, and questioned if I was okay, but I had reassured her that all was fine. I wasn't able to end it straight away. Being with her had a powerful pull on me and so we had gotten intimate once again.

Making love to her was very different from making love to Soleil, and so I had given in, relishing in it for the last time. Yet when I had told her this was the end of our relationship, she had lost it…

"What? How can you end this? We are meant for one another, don't you feel it?" She whispered, her panic making her aura swirl around her.

"No, we are not. I have a fated mate. In fact, we are about to become parents, too," I told her. Her heart was thundering as she shook her head vigorously.

"No! You can't do this to me! You are mine!"

I could see her sharp teeth now become prominent, and her eyes, glimmering with hues of silver, blues, and purples, burned with rage as she began to show her true colours.

"Now you reveal yourself for who you are," I said coldly.

"No, Andres! You can't do this to me, I can give you an heir!" She clung to my arm desperately. "My father has already become suspicious, I may have to leave the sea. I thought you would let me come home with you!" I cocked an eyebrow.

"Allow you to come with me? You look like a siren, Deliana, everyone would realise what you are," I said, frowning. I could not have her linked to me in any way. What if the other packs found out? I had just about won the crown…

No, I couldn't let her ruin my life.

"Please, Andres, my father will kill me if he realises I have had an affair with a werewolf." She looked horrified and full of fear as she clung to my arm.

"I'm sorry, Deliana. Just don't tell him, but it's better to end this completely from here on. My kingdom and my crown mean everything to me," I said coldly. Her face paled, hurt was clear in her eyes, and I could feel her anger rising.

"Betray me, Andres, and I will let the world know what you did!" She spat.

I frowned, wanting to leave her right away, but I had to be careful… I needed to make sure no one learned of this. A plan crept into my mind, and I looked into the beautiful face that was full of rage and sighed heavily, stroking her hair.

"Calm down, you are right. I can't leave you like this," I said quietly. She hesitated, searching my eyes, but it wasn't hard to show my love for her when it did exist. She broke into tears, throwing herself into my arms.

"I love you, Andrés. Don't leave me." She looked up at me with eyes that begged for reassurance.

"I won't," I lied.

I stepped into the snow and sat down on the stone steps of the courtyard. A wave of guilt washed through me. I had formed a plan. I had no intention of staying by her side. I had waited for her to fall asleep, and then I had tried to take her life…

She had lost it, switching back to her siren form, unable to retain her legs. The weather became violent… but I didn't stop. It was my only chance to kill her before she got away. But she was powerful; she had gotten away, but not before she promised that she would release her wrath upon the werewolf kind, that she would get her revenge.

That was why I made sure my men began searching for any sirens, to kill them all. I hoped she was killed in the process and our secret would remain buried forever… but clearly not before she left this child on shore…

I sighed as I looked at my hands. I had almost taken the life of my daughter that day…

But what do I do now? I couldn't kill her, that much I knew the moment I saw her in those cells. She was my daughter, and unlike Deliana, I didn't see myself being able to kill her. But people had seen what had happened. I had to form a plan. I needed to protect her. I needed to make sure no one found out the truth because if they did -

"So, she's your daughter."

My thoughts came to a crashing stop as I turned slowly to look at the man that stood against the stone pillar. A man I had begun to see as my closest confidant, but at that moment, he held a power over me, the power of a dark truth, something I did not like one bit.

A confident glimmer shone in those amber eyes of his as he watched me, almost as if he knew the hold that he now had upon me. For the first time since I had met him, I felt as if maybe I couldn't trust him…

"Theon."

A Sickening Reality

THEON

When I left the cells, my mind was spinning…

I had slept with the daughter of my enemy. She was the daughter of a siren… I was still able to deal with that somewhat, but his daughter? I felt sick and angry at myself for even allowing it to happen. I had never made the link between them…

Even those eyes that I loved were the same shade as his. Fuck this.

I punched the stone wall of the pillar in front of me. Pain jarred up my arm, and a crack appeared in the stone. I clenched my fist in anger. Andres' daughter…

A sudden thought came to me, and I frowned, deep in thought. Her powers seemed to be blocked… the heart was sealed…

Yileyna was obviously much more powerful than Charlene and held power. Was there a possibility that she could be the heart? The mage was blind. My heart thudded as I turned, realising he had looked in the direction of….

Both girls. They had been together.

"Remember, the heart of Kaeladia belongs to all."

An Alpha female… Yileyna was definitely more of an Alpha than her sister. Fuck, Yileyna was the heart… I was sure of it. The one thing my father was after… what we needed.

I exhaled, running my fingers through my hair, remaining silent when I heard the sound of footsteps. His scent reached me, and I knew it was the king. He didn't even seem to notice me as he walked out, looking like a man defeated. He deserved it…

He sat there on the steps, deep in thought and almost forlorn. I liked seeing him like this, and this was only the beginning.

"So, she's your daughter." He turned to look at me, and I was satisfied to see the glimmer of fear in his eyes.

"Theon." I schooled my face into one of slight concern.

"I'm sure it must be hard to get your head around, but fear not, we will find a solution," I said quietly. He visibly relaxed at my words and sighed.

A sudden thought cropped into my head, and I stepped over to him. As long as he didn't think Yileyna was the heart… this might work. I sat down on the stone steps a foot away from him and placed my hand on his shoulder. *One day I will take his life with this very hand…*

"Alpha, don't worry too much. We will come up with a solution. Perhaps we should move her to another city for now? Somewhere away from the accusation's upon her." He shook his head.

"No, we can't. Theon she… she might be the heart. Did you not feel her aura?" He looked at me seriously. Fuck. He had figured it out. I frowned smoothly, pretending to think before feigning subtle surprise.

"You might be right. Then what is your plan?" I wouldn't get to take her away without a fight or reason.

"There is only one option… I announce the truth: that she is my daughter, but we keep her… other side a secret," he said, frowning coldly. I raised an eyebrow.

"You will let everyone know?"

"Yes, if she proves to be the heart, then I will," he said quietly.

"And if she isn't?" Maybe if we could make sure it wasn't revealed -

"She must be. She said a fae by the name of Zarian said her powers were blocked."

"But if she is not, then?" I asked quietly.

"Then… I'll make sure she's taken care of, of course, meaning I'll send her far away," he replied, changing his sentence midway as he watched me warily. I frowned slightly. Would he really try to kill his own daughter? His eyes met mine, but apart from anger, I felt nothing. She was his daughter. Why should I care about her fate? I tried not to think of her, not wanting those foreign emotions to consume me.

"Zarian… the fae, he may know more. Find him and bring him to me immediately." I nodded curtly.

"I know who he is. I'll bring him to you immediately."

I stood up. The fact that Andres had realised she may be the fucking heart still irked me. However, I needed to listen to him… I needed to keep this façade up. If Yileyna's powers were awakening, it meant victory was ever closer.

My stomach twisted as I realised what I was implying. Dad wanted to manipulate the heart… but unlike Charlene, I couldn't see Yileyna bending to anyone. Maybe, just maybe, she'd listen to me, but I wasn't so sure. The dark truth was that she was already part of all of this long before any of us realised it.

I left the castle and shifted. I went to find the fae bastard, my mind still reeling with the weight of the revelation.

What kind of sick game was this? Not only did I get involved with a siren-hybrid, but also with someone who was the daughter of the man I hated the most. The mere thought repulsed me.

I first went to the café, but Zarian wasn't there, and so I got his address and headed to his home. I knocked on the door, scanning the garden. He was richer than one would think. Why was he working as a waiter then? Something was off.

I shifted back, pulling on my pants that I had carried along before I banged on the door with the golden door knocker once again. Something was very off… who exactly was he?

The door opened to reveal Zarian himself, wearing a black satin shirt and black leather pants. A flash of anger ripped through me, remembering how he and Yileyna almost kissed that night.

"Ah, Theon of Westerfell himself. To what do I owe the pleasure?" The snow was falling fast, and it was extremely cold.

"The Alpha King wishes to see you," I said emotionlessly. He smirked as if he was expecting that.

"Oh?" He asked, crossing his arms. I glanced at him sharply as another thought came to mind. Should I ask him not to reveal anything to the king? But what if he was one of Dad's men? No, I couldn't say anything. I couldn't trust anyone.

"Yeah, so let's leave now," I said coldly.

"My, at this time of night... what is it regarding?" He asked, moving away from the door and grabbing a coat.

"He has some questions," I answered shortly.

"Would you like a coat?"

"No," I replied coldly. He chuckled, pulling on the black coat as he stepped out and locked the door behind him.

"So, how was the ball? Do I get to congratulate you on your engagement?" My eyes blazed gold as I looked at the other man, trying to contain my rage.

"You're a little behind, are you not? There was no engagement," I almost spat with resentment. His smirk only grew.

"Ah, she did look ravishing…" My eyes flashed, and I grabbed hold of his coat.

"Do not try to fucking antagonise me before I end up killing you," I threatened.

"You will do well to respect the people of your soon-to-be kingdom, no? As future Alpha, is it not your duty to your people to protect us?" He asked, still as calm as ever. "I am the one who dressed Yileyna tonight, and she looked even better than I had envisioned. If me complimenting my work is an offence, then please do enlighten me as to how so."

"You dressed her?" He smirked in response, and I let go of him roughly.

His words hit me hard, and I clenched my jaw, trying not to let my emotions show. *Trust no one…*

I didn't bother saying anything more to him. I wondered if he knew what she was… fae were the one species that were immune to the siren's song.

We soon reached the palace, and I led the way to Andres's office, knocking on the door.

"Enter," Andres's voice called.

The two guards at the door looked at Zarian with interest that they tried to hide. Opening the door, I stepped inside, and he followed. One of the guards shut the door behind us, and I turned my attention to the king.

"Alpha Andres, it's an honour to meet you in person," Zarian greeted him with a gracious bow.

"Please, take a seat." Andres motioned to the seats opposite his desk, picking up his tankard of ale. Was he drinking due to the revelation?

"Yileyna De'Lacor. Do you know her?" Zarian raised an eyebrow.

"I'm sure the Alpha King knows the answer to that," he replied with a smirk. Andres frowned.

"Then I will skip to the matter at hand. Tonight, at the ball, Yileyna De'Lacor displayed some rather... interesting powers. You wouldn't know anything about that, would you?"

"Well, I'm sure the Alpha King knows the answer to that, too. Isn't that why I was summoned?" He asked, raising an arched brow.

"Yes, you were helping her unseal her powers. Yileyna told me that you said there was a block on her abilities." For the first time, Zarian frowned slightly.

"Where is she?" He asked.

"In the cells for treason, and unless you can give us some answers, she will remain there," Andres threatened coldly. Zarian's brows creased deeper as he glanced up at the king sharply.

"I do not need to answer anything without knowing why. Why was she imprisoned for treason?" He asked sharply.

"For wearing a possession from the Obsidian Shadow Pack," Andres replied coldly.

"No, her ensemble is from Aerean, I assure you. I ordered them myself," Zarian said, and I narrowed my eyes. So he didn't know about the amulet...

"She had a necklace which she said she brought on a journey at sea. Tell me about her abilities and this block that you assume is upon her." Zarian seemed to hesitate.

"She is a good person, Alpha..."

"I know. She is the daughter of someone who was a good friend to me despite turning out to be a traitor. I have always had a soft spot for his daughter," Andres' reply almost made me scoff.

Like hell you did. Aside from threatening, belittling, and isolating her, you did nothing more. Not that I was any better, but I had always been open with her and warned her that I would destroy her... but now that just felt even more real. Avenge my family by wiping out the Aphelions. That included her too. I pushed the thoughts aside, crossing my arms.

"However, her having this amulet after what her parents did is no small matter. If you can help me with what you know, it can, in turn, help me to help her," Andres continued. Zarian cocked a brow.

"How would you knowing about her personal matters benefit her?" He asked, almost mockingly. If he wasn't such a dick and didn't try kissing Yileyna, I actually wouldn't have minded him.

"I am her Alpha, and your reluctance makes me wonder what exactly you are hiding?" Andres's eyes flashed as he looked at Zarian, slamming his tankard on his desk, the liquid sploshing everywhere.

"I'm hiding nothing," Zarian replied. His voice was dangerously calm, but I could tell he was tense. He knew her truth… I was sure of it. Otherwise, why would he fear telling the king if he presumed she was part fae or mage?

"Then do you wish to rot in the cells?" Andres growled.

"What is my crime?" Zarian asked, his gaze flickering to me.

"For defying your king's command. I asked you what you knew of her abilities!"

"We know what she is," I cut in, having had enough of this. Zarian's face dropped. I saw the worry in his eyes as he looked at the king and then at me.

"She is innocent. She, herself, doesn't know what she is."

I hated how he was defending her. A flash of jealousy rushed through me at his defensiveness toward her, but I no longer cared. She was Andres's daughter, and that was not someone I'd ever care for. Right?

Denying it felt like a lie… *Don't go there, Theon, remember who she is.*

"Then, tell us of her abilities that are blocked," Andres growled. Zarian sighed, seeming to realise there was no way out.

"There seems to be a type of powerful sealing spell upon her. She's able to draw some power by force, but I think this seal is suppressing everything about her. Only when she displays intense emotion is she able to draw upon her power," he replied grudgingly. Andres frowned.

"The ability to bend the weather... do you know the rarity of that?"

"Of course. Only the imperial family of the sea are able to do so," Zarian replied quietly as Andres nodded.

I frowned as I turned away, remembering that night from long ago, my stomach sinking as I remembered the sudden change in the weather. It had been so unpredictable that fateful night. It was meant to be a clear night; the sea was calm too. The imperial family…

If Yileyna was from it, then that meant she was also related to the monster who had killed Mom and Thalia that night. My eyes flashed as disgust consumed me.

Pale blonde hair...

The similarities, despite the Siren's face being contorted with rage and her sharp teeth, were there... I felt sick as the truth hit me.

I had become entangled with something that was related to what I detested the most. Andres and that monster, both of whom were responsible for destroying my family…

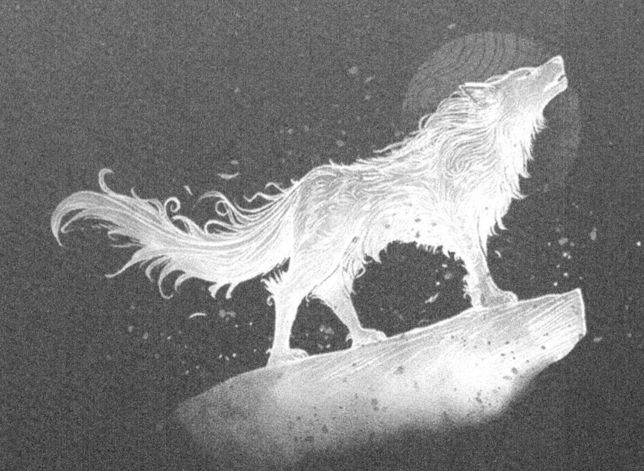

Disbelief

YILEYNA

The sound of keys and metal screeching made my eyes snap open; it took me a second to realise I was on the floor in the cell. I turned, my heart thumping when my eyes met Theon's.

"The Alpha wishes to see you," he said emotionlessly, looking away from me.

I nodded as I got to my feet, pulling my dress up from my breasts. I probably looked a mess, but there was little I could do about it. He didn't even look my way again. Something about the coldness oozing from Theon unnerved me. He led the way from the cell and up the stairs at a swift pace as I followed.

I wanted to know how Raiden was. I didn't think asking Theon would be the smart thing to do. I'd ask the king… I wondered what his verdict was going to be. Why did the king want to see me anyway? I felt a mess, and those who passed us in the halls were looking at me. I wondered what state my face was in.

"I need to pee," I said suddenly.

"Hold it."

"What?" I stopped in my tracks. I heard him exhale before he turned and glared at me.

"You're a fucking woman, hold it."

"I held it all night," I snapped back. Was I actually having this conversation with him?

He clenched his jaw before he carried on walking, and I followed. He stopped when we rounded the corner, and I was relieved to see the door to the restroom on the opposite wall.

"You got two minutes." He glared as he looked me over. Yeah, right, it was going to take me two minutes just to undress to even use the toilet.

Not replying, I quickly rushed to the door, relieved that it was not occupied and shut the door behind me. I locked the door and began stripping.

Once I had used the toilet, I washed my hands and stared at my reflection. My makeup wasn't as bad as I had thought it would be. Grabbing the soap, I cleaned the makeup off my face and ran my fingers through my hair before getting my dress back on. I left the bathroom, spotting Theon leaning against the opposite wall, his arms crossed. He raised an eyebrow seeing me but said nothing.

By the time we reached the king's office, I had thought of a hundred scenarios of why he had summoned me, each one worse than the last. Theon opened the door and stepped aside, allowing me to enter. I paused, looking up at him. Even if he was angry at me, I still felt safer with him here than not...

Like last night, the king said he wouldn't hurt me and only then did Theon leave. I couldn't forget the look of hatred in his eyes before he left, though. I pushed my thoughts away, taking a deep breath as I turned my attention to the king, who was standing facing the window.

"Take a seat," he commanded.

I obeyed as Theon shut the door. I could feel his eyes on me, but I didn't turn, waiting for the king to speak.

"This may be a lot to take in, however..." The king frowned as he turned and took his seat behind his desk. "It is obvious that you are part siren, and we all know that. The worst kind of beings on this planet." My stomach lurched as my heart began racing. Fear wrapped around me like a blanket, suffocating me. Was me being part siren going to be my doom? "Calm down, and listen well," the king commanded. I nodded, trying to control my emotions as I tried to give him my full attention...

He seemed to find it hard to speak, looking at Theon almost as if for assistance. I heard him step forward before he moved the chair that was next to mine a little away, sitting down and stretching his long legs out.

"As you know, long ago, the king had a one-night relationship with a siren. That story wasn't entirely correct," Theon began. My heart skipped a beat as I looked into Theon's amber eyes.

I knew the truth, Theon himself had told me. It had been when the queen had found out she was pregnant with Charlene… which meant…

My stomach sank as I realised where this was going.

"It was shortly after the queen became pregnant with Charlene. You and the princess are sisters, and the Alpha is your father." His voice was cold, yet the look of disgust on his face was so similar to the way he looked at Charlene…

I glanced at the king, who was staring at his hands, trying to contemplate what Theon had just said. The king was my father?

I felt as if someone had just dumped a bucket of cold water over me, my mind spinning a thousand thoughts. Charlene was my sister? I was the result of the king cheating on his mate? The Luna would be devastated... what would Charlene think? How could I be his daughter? There was not enough proof!

"We have to keep this a secret," I said quietly. The king frowned, looking at me sharply.

"Yileyna, as my daughter -"

"No, this changes nothing. I am still who I am. The Luna and Charlene don't deserve this," I said. I was not going to be the reason behind someone's family getting ruined.

"That is not your choice. Besides, there is a strong chance that you are the heart." The heart? It took me a moment to let those words sink in.

Goddess… no. I shook my head, refusing to believe it. I stood up, backing away from the desk.

"There is no chance! The mage himself…." He had turned his head in our direction… but he was blind…

These powers… no, it just can't be.

This was Charlene's right; she had been so happy to know she held the power to gain the king's approval.

"Yes, he turned in the direction of both of you. Do you not understand that you are that heart? You hold immense powers, and something tells me that once the seal is broken that you will be even more powerful. You have always been better at everything than Charlene. You only lack a wolf and a shift, a shift that may or may not happen once the seal is broken, but you are still the heart. Your mother must have had your powers sealed to hide your siren side and blocked off everything," the king said in his rough voice. "I'm just shocked she didn't kill you." The last sentence was barely audible. I looked up at him, feeling my irritation growing.

"And so, what? Do you expect me to just accept that? This is Charlene's birthright. I am not going to take anything from her!"

"Her birthright? She isn't what I thought she was! You have no choice, you are the heart of Kaeladia! The one thing that will get rid of all the threats that we face! The one thing that can protect this kingdom!" The king growled, clearly not happy with my refusal.

"By threats, you mean sirens, too, correct? Do you forget that I am apparently part siren?"

"Keep your voice down!" The king hissed, glancing at the door. My heart skipped a beat as I realised that I had spoken loudly.

"That is something that you should really not go around and announce to everyone," Theon remarked, so calm compared to the king and me. Our eyes met, and my stomach fluttered. I forced my gaze away, refusing to let him get to me.

"Understood. However, I don't consider myself your daughter, nor do I consider -"

"Do not try me, girl!" The king growled, standing up and slamming his hand on the table. I flinched when a large crack appeared in it.

"All I'm saying is you have always disliked me. That won't change. I am not the heart. I really can't be. An Alpha female would be born with abilities, correct? There is no way for a second child to be an Alpha over the first. I may have abilities, but those must only be because of my siren side. Charlene could be the heart. Give her a chance," I reasoned quietly.

I didn't want to anger him any further, but I refused to believe this. I know my reasoning was weak, but there was logic. No second child is born an Alpha, surely that rule applied in this case, too?

The king exchanged looks with Theon and, to my surprise, seemed to actually be considering my words. I resisted a small smile. Thank the goddess...

"I've seen daughters of Alphas who have powerful auras, something I've never sensed from the princess, whose wolf is nothing impressive either. Is there any chance that Charlene is not your daughter?" Theon asked, tilting his head. For a second, I thought his voice held some mockery, but it was fleeting. The king and I both looked at him, my anger only rising.

"Of course she is!" I snapped, but the king was frowning as he slowly sat down. "You are not going to consider that are you?" I stared at the king in disbelief, but he simply ignored me.

"You may be onto something, Theon. When Soleil miscarried twice, I was told that it was... no, that doesn't add up." He shook his head, trailing off as he became lost in thought for a moment before looking up. "However, perhaps it's time I talked to Soleil... I have never felt her cheat on me, but there are ways for that to be overcome."

I shook my head, unable to understand how he could accuse his own mate of cheating on him. Not everyone was as lowly as him. Listening to the appalling conversation before me, my opinion of the king was only dropping. I looked at him coldly.

"Regardless of anything, Charlene is still your one and only daughter," I said quietly.

"You cannot change your fate, Yileyna. You will be the next Alpha," the king warned me menacingly, his eyes blazing as he tried to control his anger. I shook my head.

"No, I will not take away Charlene's right. Even if I am the heart, I can use that ability from the side-line. She has worked so hard to please you, Alpha. She trains to do her best; she deserves to be the next Alpha."

"She actually doesn't. She's not showing any sign of good leadership or strength," Theon added, only adding to my anger.

"Oh, and what does a good Alpha need? Because, as far as I know, it's compassion, strength, and the ability to rule fairly," I snapped, glaring at him. Something both these men lacked.

"Hmm, and she lacks strength," Theon added. The king sighed before looking at me seriously.

"Well, you have no say. The kingdom will know you are my child from an affair, but we will keep your mother's truth a secret. Yileyna, you know, by accepting this position, you will be the one to marry Theon." I scoffed in disbelief. Did the king actually think I'd betray Charlene for a dumb dick?

"Him? Who said I want him? If I'm ever to be a ruler, I wouldn't pick someone like him to be by my side," I spat scornfully, not missing Theon's face darken and his eyes blazing gold.

"Do not disrespect me, little storm," he growled, standing up. I stepped back from him, glaring at them both.

"I am not disrespecting you; I am stating facts, and if you two can't see that, then you can carry on. If this is as far as loyalty goes and all it means to the two of you, then I pity this kingdom. I will have no part of it," I said coldly. Not waiting for an answer, I rushed to the door.

"Yileyna! Stop!" The king thundered. His alpha command rolled off him, grinding into my bones, but it didn't have the intended effect on me. My anger outweighed it as I ran down the hall.

I needed to talk to Charlene before the king did or said something that would hurt her. I knew him well enough to know he didn't care to break the news gently to anyone. I just needed to -

I gasped when someone grabbed my arm and slammed me up against the wall, making me groan as pain rushed up my back and head. His familiar seductive scent and the tingles that I felt when he touched me told me who it was. Theon.

I opened my eyes, glaring at him for manhandling me so roughly, trying not to focus on how close he was standing.

"What do you want?" I spat.

"Don't fucking show me attitude, or I will bend you over and punish you," he hissed, anger clear in his eyes. Like always, my body betrayed me, that sinful ache in my core returning at his words. Mustering all my willpower, I pushed him away.

"News flash, Theon, you no longer have any right to punish me!" I said coldly, making to walk off when he grabbed my arm, twisting it behind my back as he spun me into his arms.

My back hit his chest as he wrapped his free hand around my throat. My heart pounded at the familiar move that always drove me crazy with desire, and when his lips brushed the lobe of my ear, making my breath hitch, I tensed, hating the effect he had on me.

"News flash, the Alpha just ordered me to be your personal fucking bodyguard, and that means I get to do whatever the fuck I want."

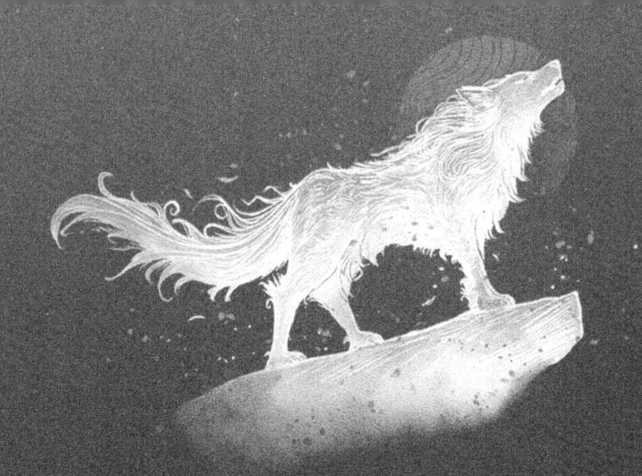

My Anger

YILEYNA

His words reignited that illicit desire within me. I used all my willpower to pull free, and, turning, I faced him.

"He commanded you as my bodyguard, which means your job is to follow me around wherever I go. Right now, I am going to go see Charlene, and then I'm going to visit Raiden. Mess up and interfere in what I do, and I swear I'll tell the king that I don't want you as my guard," I replied, warning him. Theon frowned, glaring coldly at me.

"Yeah, the only thing is the king said you are not to see Charlene until he has had a word with the Luna." My heart skipped a beat.

No. I needed to tell Charlene first, before the king.

"Well then, guess what?" I whispered, stepping closer to him, planning to throw him off guard, but he didn't fall for it. Frowning, he grabbed hold of my arm and held me at arm's length. I resisted the urge to roll my eyes. Shame it didn't work.

"What are you trying to pull?" I shrugged, pulling free and turning away.

"Nothing at all. Just no one can stop me from seeing Charlene." With those words leaving my lips, I broke into a run.

"Yileyna! This is not a fucking game," Theon growled.

"Well then, don't try to stop me!" I shouted back.

I ignored the looks of contempt, disapproval, and irritation as I rushed through the halls, weaving through other people. Being smaller than Theon gave me the advantage, and I was able to get by a lot easier.

"Yileyna!"

He was pissed. I could hear it in his voice. I couldn't stop now; I just wished there was a way I could mind link Charlene… I needed to find someone who would do it for me.

I rushed out onto one of the open balconies and grabbing the rail. I flipped over the edge and dropped onto the balcony floor below, quickly pushing the doors to the adjoining room open. I looked around, my heart thumping. I was in one of the side library rooms. I felt relieved, spotting one of the elder guards looking through some scrolls. He looked slightly curious to see me before it changed into one of suspicion.

"Sir…" I couldn't remember his name. "Sorry for intruding in like this, I was looking for the princess."

"Hmm?"

"Could you mind-link her and tell her Gamma Raiden is allowed to have visitors and to bring the daises?"

Bring the daises – a code we used as a child. I just hoped she remembered it and came immediately. He looked at me for a moment, and I gave him the most innocent smile I could muster, batting my eyelashes. He cleared his throat, turning a little red before he turned away.

"Okay, okay." He went silent. I knew he was mind-linking her, but I also knew Theon would find me at any minute. "She said right away."

Perfect.

"Thank you." I almost exhaled in relief.

I went back out onto the balcony, gasping as Theon landed in front of me, his eyes blazing gold. My heart thumped, and, not wanting to alert the guard, I smiled at Theon.

"Theon! You found me," I said cheerily. "Come on, let's go see Raiden at the hospital."

He frowned suspiciously at me. I knew he wasn't dumb. He glanced at the guard who was leaving the room. For a moment, I thought he'd stop him and ask him if I had said anything or that he might make the link… but he didn't. *Thank the Goddess.*

He didn't respond, grabbing hold of my arm as he yanked me to the door.

"Do you expect me to actually believe you have suddenly given up on seeing her?" He asked, his voice so dangerously calm that it made my stomach twist.

"Oh, I'm going to see her, but I think we can stop at the hospital wing first, considering you need to apologise to Raiden." His hand firmly wrapped around my arm as he scoffed.

"I won't apologise for something I'd do a hundred fucking times over."

"And that is exactly why you will never get far in life," I muttered.

His grip tightened painfully, but I didn't react, not wanting to give him the satisfaction. The tension between us suddenly became suffocating. It felt like it all returned at once...

How had things become so complicated? From those days of Charlene and I sneaking away for a swim... to my parents' being framed despite everything they had done for this pack and city and finding out that they weren't my birth parents? It didn't change anything, but it still hurt to know my life had been somewhat of a lie. Did my parents know the truth? They still loved me for me... but I knew even if they knew that wouldn't change, because they were the truest, most loving people I knew.

Everything the king and Theon had said suddenly felt like a huge burden upon my shoulders. How do I take this all in alone? I felt the familiar sting in my eyes, wishing they were here by my side. There are different types of parents on this planet, but mine were the type that could never be replaced.

Theon came to a stop, and I frowned, not even realising when he had loosened his grip. Once again, he was completely cold and stoic.

"You can get changed before we go to the hospital," he stated, his eyes skimming over me. If I wasn't feeling so upset inside, I would have lost my temper, but instead, I shook my head.

"No, I want to see him first."

A flash of irritation filled those eyes as he glared into mine. That sexual air between us was still there, even if it felt so confusing now. He turned, took hold of my wrist, and pulled me along to the hospital wing.

I shook my head, glancing at the mark he had left on my arm. There was a time I welcomed the marks he left upon me... but now? Now, I didn't want him to touch me...

I looked ahead, staring at his back. What did I feel for him? I still loved him.

My heart squeezed at the thought, and deep down, I knew those feelings wouldn't go for a while, but they were no longer the same. No longer pure and innocent, no longer clouded by dreams of how I thought I would win the heart of my first love, but they were now tainted by his betrayal...

I would keep my heart encased in a dome of the strongest armour. I really was done. Yileyna De'Lacor needed no man.

We reached the hospital and were instantly directed to Raiden's bed, a curtain surrounding the cubicle. I tensed, realising his parents were here... so was his brother.

Goddess, I didn't think this through...

Neither Gamma Henry nor Andrea looked pleased to see us. A wave of guilt washed through me; this was my fault...

"May we come in?" I asked quietly. Gamma Henry frowned but nodded as Rhys flashed me a smile.

"Hey, Yileyna!"

"Hey," I replied, smiling at him as Andrea tried to keep her emotions in check.

Taking a deep breath, I looked at Raiden. His head wasn't bandaged, to my relief, and he looked to be just sleeping. Thank the gods for healer mages. I walked over to the bed, my heart pounding as I looked down at him. He was still a little pale...

"Did the healer say anything?" I asked quietly.

"No, just that he almost died," Andrea replied. I saw her gaze flit to Theon, who simply stood there, arms crossed, that mask of indifference plastered on his arrogant face. "He hasn't awakened yet."

I looked down at Raiden, gently stroking his hair for a moment. I could still see slight traces of blood that they had not washed off. I looked down at his bare chest before slipping my hand into his that lay on the bed by his side and giving it a gentle squeeze. *Forgive me, Raiden, because of me, you suffered.*

I could feel Theon's irritation, but I refused to give him any attention. Instead, I looked at Raiden's parents.

"I'm so sorry. I know it's not enough, but this was my fault... I should never -"

My eyes widened when I felt Raiden's hand tighten around mine. My attention snapped to his face, my heart pounding as his eyelids fluttered open.

"Don't apologise for something that I wouldn't mind doing ten times over," came his raspy reply. I almost laughed at the irony of his words. *Men.*

"Raiden!" My heart leapt with relief, and although I wanted to hug him, I settled for raising his hand to my chest and holding it close as I kissed his knuckles softly. "Thank the gods and goddesses!"

"Rai!" Rhys exclaimed.

"My son…" Andrea whispered, jumping up from her seat. I instantly lowered his hand, stepping away to give his family space as they crowded around him, hugging him. I didn't have that right over him. I smiled, watching them all together. A wave of nostalgia washed over me, but I was just glad he was okay.

"I'm completely fine, don't worry," Raiden reassured Andrea. I could feel Theon's anger growing, and I looked over at him.

"Apologise," I mouthed to him, but he simply cocked a brow, turning away.

"If you're done, shall we go?" He asked icily. Raiden sat up, seeming only to realise now that he was there.

"What is he doing here?" He asked, his blue eyes darkening as he looked at Theon, his gaze hostile.

"Watching me," I said quietly, not wanting something to happen again. Raiden looked confused, and Gamma Henry sighed.

"Yileyna was found wearing the amulet of House Hale, the Alpha family crest of the Obsidian Shadow Pack and is awaiting trial… yet the Alpha is trusting your attacker," he said quietly, clearly displeased.

"I agree," I said. Although I know no one here really trusted me, Theon did deserve a punishment too. The king favoured him too much.

Raiden took hold of my wrist, my heart skipping a beat at the intimate way he caressed my wrist with his thumb.

"What's going on?" He asked quietly, his eyes flitting from the mark Theon left on my upper arm to my face. I shook my head.

"I bought it in Bellmead… I didn't know what it was," I explained quietly. He nodded.

"I believe you." I smiled softly, and our eyes met for a moment before I slowly pulled out of his hold.

"Thank you. I'm glad you're awake. I'm sorry on Theon's behalf and my own for all of this," I said. I should give him and his family some time alone. But where was Charlene?

"Don't keep apologising," Raiden replied with a wink, which made me smile. I turned away, frowning as Theon smirked coldly.

"Shall we go so the Boltons can have some time to enjoy their precious reunion?" He asked, his voice dripping with mockery. I clenched my jaw and nodded as I gave the Boltons a polite bow of the head and stepped out.

"What's wrong? Wondering why Charlene isn't here?" He taunted. My smile vanished as I stared at his cold smirk. He had somehow found out…

"What did you do?" I hissed.

"I just made sure she didn't leave her quarters… you're welcome." His arrogant face was irritating me.

I needed to be the one to tell her. Did he get how this could devastate her? How dare he wear that smug look on his face.

"Calm down," he warned, his smile vanishing, and I realised the temperature was dropping.

"Fuck you, Theon," I hissed, feeling the painful tug in my stomach before a blast of wind slammed him across the hospital.

He flipped in the air, regaining his balance as he knelt on the ground, his claws out, digging into the stone as he held his ground, the wind whipping violently in the room. Everything was being thrown around, but I was far too angry to care. His gold eyes were blazing as he watched me without even an ounce of fear.

He wants to play? Then let's fucking play.

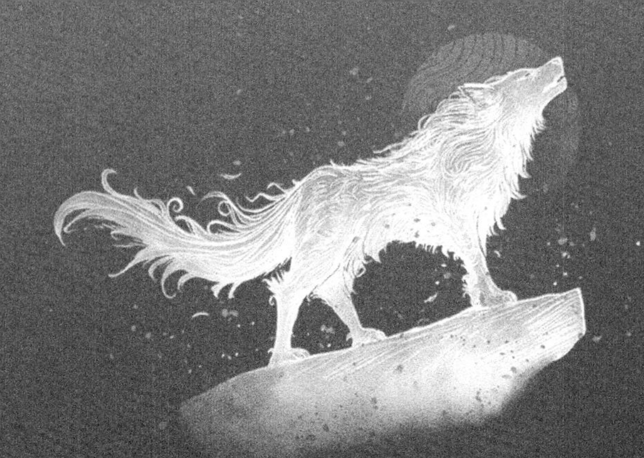

Unfaithfulness

ANDRES

I had barely slept all night, remaining in my office, yet I now returned to my quarters to speak to Soleil. A lot weighed upon her answer. Unlocking the door to our quarters, I stepped inside.

You might want to make sure Charlene stays home. Yileyna just tried to get her to sneak out, Theon's voice came through the link. I closed my eyes, exhaling deeply.

What would I do without him? Theon was a great help, although the colour of his eyes often unnerved me.

I will handle it. She is far too disobedient, I replied through the link before mind-linking Charlene. **Stay in your room until I summon you. This is very important.**

D-dad… is Yileyna okay?

Perfectly. Fear not, I will not have her punished. It was a mistake — the pendant, I mean. It was strange to think Charlene was not mine.

"Andres! You didn't come home; I was worried you had your block up! What is going on!" Soleil said, coming over.

Like always, she was dressed perfectly, upholding the image of the perfect queen and Luna. She had known I had been unfaithful but never asked who or where… yet knowing that she may have been unfaithful to me… it opened an entirely new perspective. If it is deemed to be true, what should I do? Rejecting her would destroy us both… and punishment would only affect me since she was my true mate…

"A lot is going on," I said as she kissed me. The familiar sparks rushed through us both.

"What is it?" She asked, her green eyes filled with concern at my expression. "Is it Theon? Can he not get over Yileyna? Maybe you need to have her taken care of! She is a traitor who we do not need anywhere around us!" She turned away in frustration, and I rubbed my jaw.

"Yileyna isn't going anywhere."

"Meaning?" She asked, looking over her shoulder at me. "Are you planning on leaving her in prison? With Theon here, I wouldn't advise -" I simply nodded, waving my hand.

"I'm going to ask you something, Soleil, and I want the truth," I cut in quietly. As my mate, she may be able to defy my command, but I prayed that in good faith, she told me the truth that I was becoming more and more certain of.

"Of course, anything, Andres. You are worrying me."

"Is Charlene really mine?" I asked clearly. My Alpha command rolled through my words that shook with power. I had put my all into it, now I could only hope for her to yield to the command and tell me the truth.

Her face paled, her heart thundering, and at that moment, I realised I did not need to use my alpha command upon her. Her reaction alone had already given me the only answer I needed.

I felt… cold and empty. I don't even know if there was anything for me to even feel angry about. We had both cheated on one another and had children with another. I have no idea what the moon goddess was thinking when she paired us… it was obvious we were not a good match. She never gave me happiness, and I, her.

"Andres… she -"

"I have gotten my answer. Were you planning on hiding it forever?" I thundered, my anger suddenly returning with a vengeance.

"You raised her as your own, Andres, forgive me! I…. we were so desperately trying for a pup, b-but it wasn't happening! You should be grateful to me! It wasn't me that was the issue! I am able to carry pups, there was something wrong with you -"

"So I'm to blame? Cheating was not the answer!" I roared. She flinched, backing away. I looked around, ripping the huge artwork from the wall. It hit the floor, the wooden frame splintering.

"Andres, she, she'll hear!" She whispered.

"Who is the father?" I asked coldly, tearing the tapestries from the wall. My anger was raging within me, and all rationing was gone. My eyes blazed as I broke the cabinet that stood to the left. "Answer me, Soleil!" She was trying to defy it, her face paling as she clamped her hand over her mouth, refusing to speak. I strode over to her, pulling her hand from her mouth roughly. "Who is her father, Soleil?" She broke into sobs.

"It's it.... it... ah.." She was fighting it.

"Who is he?" I roared, and before my eyes, she finally succumbed to the Alpha command, falling to her knees.

"G-Grayson is Charlene's father!" She screamed, anguished.

My mind stilled.

Grayson.

My chest heaved, my heart thumping faster than it should. My own Gamma...

Was it karma that all those I considered my comrades were betraying me one by one? Was this the price I was paying for my sins?

I ran my hand through my beard, glaring at the woman before me.

"How long was it going on for?" I asked.

"You were always busy... always out...it was not long," she sobbed. Ah... back when his mate and son were gone to visit her homelands... the timing made sense.

"Does he know Charlene is his?" I asked murderously. She shook her head, sobbing.

"No! I told no one!"

"And how and when did you notice she was not mine?" I spat resentfully.

"I swear -"

"The truth, Soleil!" I roared.

"I was desperate! I needed to bear you a child, so you didn't entertain other women! I did it for you! To keep you!" She screamed in desperation.

"And so, you decided to become a whore and sleep with another man!" I growled, upturning the sofa that she was clinging to. She yelped, backing away with fear in her eyes as it smashed against the far wall. My canines were out now, my anger barely controllable. "I will only ask once more! When did you realise she was not mine?"

"She, she lacked an Alpha aura… when I became pregnant the first two times, I felt the power within my womb of an Alpha pup… but… I feared… but she may be yours! We can't be sure that she isn't!" She begged, crawling over to me. I shook my head. We both knew she wasn't.

"No. Charlene isn't my daughter. I was told a certain fact, which I hid in fear that one of our pups that died before they saw this world was the heart, but the prophecy said it would be my first-born female child. Charlene is not mine because my daughter is younger than her, and she already holds far more power than your daughter!" I hissed.

"Y-your daughter?" Soleil was confused and fearful.

"Yes, my real daughter. I have found her, Soleil."

I heard a soft whimper from behind me, and I froze. She was not meant to hear that…

I turned to see the child I had considered my own standing there, her eyes full of pain and shock as she stared at Soleil and me in complete horror. This was not the way I planned to break the news to her…

"Charlene," I said, withdrawing my canines and claws.

"Charlene!" Soleil scrambled to her feet, but the girl simply shook her head as she backed away, her heart beating violently before she ran into her bedroom, shutting the door with a resounding bang.

I clenched my jaw, about to unleash hell upon the woman before me, but first, there was one other who deserved to be punished.

Henry, I know you are busy with your son, but I need you to have Gamma Grayson Sanchez apprehended immediately for treason.

Alpha… that… we have a serious situation at the hospital to handle first.

What is it? I growled. What was more important that he wasn't even stunned that I was asking for my Gamma to be thrown into prison?

It's Yileyna De'Lacor.

My eyes snapped to the window, realising it was a lot darker. Selene…

The sky was dark, and all I could see was the menacing storm that was brewing. Over my own anger and shouting, I hadn't even noticed it. Something had triggered Yileyna to lose control.

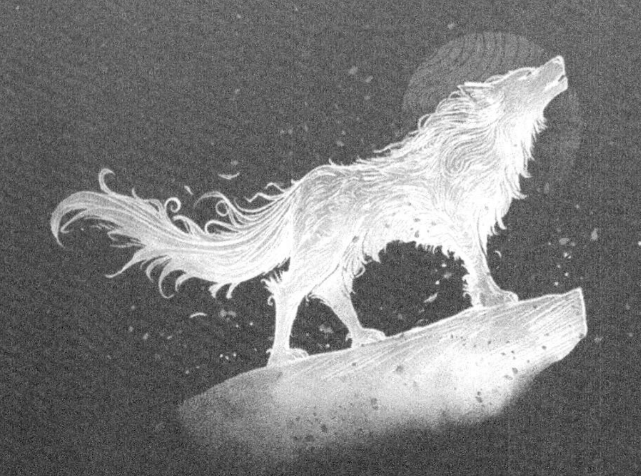

Out of Control

YILEYNA

"CALM THE FUCK DOWN, Yileyna," Theon growled as he pushed against the whirling wind.

My head was going to explode! He knew the king's attitude, and I knew that he would have gone to talk to Soleil. Charlene would be there, and he wouldn't take care to break it to her gently. We both knew the king was selfish, yet Theon stopped her from coming here. I could have done it in a better way! I could have told her in a gentler manner! She may or may not be my biological sister, but she was always going to be my soul sister regardless of blood.

I was scared, terrified that she would be hurt because of me… and Theon. He had to go mess everything up!

"Don't tell me to calm down," I hissed, clenching my fists as I stormed over to him, the wind whipping around us like a hurricane. "If I messed up something of yours, you would lose your shit! So don't tell me to calm down! This was so important, Theon!"

"The Alpha can handle her himself. Stop causing a fucking scene," he growled, glancing around the room before he grabbed my arm. I could see the Bolton's watching, looking at the wind that was beating around me.

"Calm yourself…"

Zarian's guidance ran through my mind, and I tried to take a steady breath. I had to be careful. I was indoors; there were patients here. I allowed Theon to pull me into the hallway, but the moment we were out, I punched him. He dodged, but I managed to snag a hit at his neck. His eyes flashed as he licked his bottom lip, looking pissed.

"I hope she does get hurt. Wouldn't that be fun?" He whispered tauntingly. My eyes flashed in anger.

"Why do you hate her? She's never done anything to you!" The nearest window slammed open, the skies darkening outside. "I hate how you belittle her! She is a far better person than you ever will be!" I snapped resentfully. My chest was heaving with emotions that seemed to no longer be in my control.

"Control yourself," he warned coldly, any amusement from his face going as he glanced at the weather outside. He looked back at me, and whatever he saw on my face made him frown. "Last warning, little storm. Control it, or I will fucking knock you out," he growled.

The pain in my stomach was growing, and although I was trying to focus, I couldn't. The havoc of emotions from everything was taking over. Unleash it all… I just wanted to scream and let it all out…

"Yileyna!" His voice was fading, but when he tried to grab me, I pushed him off, punching him.

He blocked, knocking my hand aside and flipping me. He skidded on the glassy ice on the floor and landed flat on his back with me on top. He didn't seem to be bothered by rolling us over, so I was beneath him. That must have hurt.

"Get off of me!" I hissed. This dress may have been made from a delicate fabric, but it was stronger than I thought it would be.

We slid on the ice. He was unable to hold his balance, something I was having no issue with. His rising irritation would have been amusing if I was not so angry. He growled as I twisted, slamming him onto his back, and this time I landed a solid punch on his handsome jaw. A satisfying crack made me smile.

"You know what I love more than hearing you groan in pleasure?" I whispered in his ear just as he managed to wrap his hand around my throat, yanking me closer. "It's the sound of me breaking your bones," I added darkly before slamming my free hand into his nose. I gasped as he flipped us, slamming me into the ice. My vision darkened as he straddled me, his eyes glowing, his coppery hair falling in front of his forehead.

"Shame you won't be breaking any more bones then," he whispered, pinning my wrists to the ground.

Wrong move.

The moment I was unable to fight against his strength, I felt another tug in my stomach, a gut-wrenching one that made me unable to breathe for several seconds.

He was thrown back by a powerful blast, the shimmering haze creating a barrier around me. The pain in my stomach was growing, and I heard the sound of thunder through the open window. Blinding lightning followed. I heard screams of panic and distant shouting, but I wasn't quite able to place where we were anymore. I flinched with pain that seemed to be tearing my stomach apart.

"Yileyna?" Theon called, but I was in too much pain to respond. I saw his shadow approach despite the vicious wind that now encased me. He pushed against it, trying to reach me. The wind cut into his skin, but he didn't seem bothered. He managed to take hold of me by my arm.

Fire.

The scene around me was changing. I was in the open castle courtyards... a hooded man in a black cape stood there... there was so much fire. Bodies were discarded all around...

What was going on?

The cloaked man turned. His glowing amber eyes met mine... I couldn't see who it was, but I felt like I knew him. He said something, but I couldn't hear... and then he threw a lit match towards me...

I screamed in agony as I felt my entire body burn, the taste of blood in my mouth, and then everything went cold... so cold. But I could see nothing, my powers making me fall to my knees. A scream filled the air, and I knew it was mine.

"Yileyna!"

"Everyone stay back!"

"Dear Goddess..."

"Yileyna, fuck, listen to me." Theon... His voice was soft, calm, and soothing, but I was no longer able to do anything, the agonising pain in my stomach crushing me. "Leyna..."

I gasped the moment I felt his touch on my arms. The scene with the blazing fire returned, and I knocked Theon away.

"Don't touch me!" I screamed blindly.

"Yileyna, calm down. Listen, it's me, Raiden." A calmer touch brushed my back, but I flung him away without meaning to. I couldn't see anything but the fierce wind and fog.

"Fuck, she's bleeding… I'll handle her, Bolton!" Theon's possessive growl came.

"What on Kaeladia…" Was that the king?

I could taste the blood in my mouth. My eardrums felt like they were going to burst.

"Stop! This might be it… the seal may break."

"She's bleeding!" Theon's dangerous reply came. "I'm knocking her out."

"Theon! She can do this! Let her," the king thundered, only adding to my irritation.

"No. Not like this." Theon's voice held finality as the king growled before his strong arms wrapped around me, and something hit the back of my neck. I gasped as everything began to go dark…

"I got you," his whispered promise came before I succumbed to the darkness…

My eyes flew open. I was in a bed… I couldn't recognise which room, but the bed was large, with heavy bedding. It was dark, the curtains were drawn, and I could hear faint talking. I pushed the cover off, realising I was only in the under-layer bodysuit, my dress gone. What happened?

It took me a few minutes for everything to come back to me. I closed my eyes, placing my head in my hands. I had messed up. I shouldn't have gotten angry or lost control like this… Zarian had told me I needed to control my emotions.

Did I hurt anyone?

I remembered Theon and Raiden were both there. Goddess! Raiden didn't get hurt again, did he?

"Yileyna, you're awake." My heart pounded. I gasped before I realised that Charlene had been sitting by the bed and had awoken with a start herself.

"Goddess, you scared me," I scolded, placing a hand on my heart. A smile crossed her lips, despite the sadness in her eyes as she flicked the lamp on. She had been crying.

My stomach sank, and I wondered if she knew. I wrapped my arms around her, and she hugged me tightly. Her heart was pounding, and she held me so fiercely it was as if she was scared she was going to lose me.

"Tell me, my queen, what's wrong?" I whispered. I could hear talking, and I didn't want to be disturbed.

"I'm fine. I'm just glad you are okay," she replied, moving back and brushing my hair back.

"Where am I?" I asked, glancing around the room.

"You're in the guest bedroom in our quarters," Charlene said quietly.

"Oh…"

I had never been here before. I usually spent time in the living areas or Charlene's bedroom whenever I stayed over.

"Yes, Dad didn't allow Theon to take you… and he refused to leave," she added quietly.

Theon had no right to act possessive. Dummy.

We fell silent, and I wondered if she knew anything about what had happened…

"Theon… he's the reason I got angry." I frowned.

"You called our code," she said softly. She had lost her usual positivity, almost sounding empty…

"I did. There was something I wanted to tell you before you heard it from someone else," I said quietly. She nodded.

"Oh, what was it?" How do I start? "If it helps… I think I already know," she murmured, giving me a weak smile.

"Y-you do?" She nodded.

"If it's the fact that I'm not… I'm not Dad's daughter." She looked down at me, and my stomach sank.

How had the king broken it to her? Was it gently? Did he comfort her and reassure her that no matter what, he'd always be her father? She seemed to notice my expression and tried to smile cheerily.

"It's okay… he…"

"Did he… what else did he say?"

"He hasn't talked to me… the castle's been crazy. He only commanded me to stay with you in this room. They got back a short while ago, but… I haven't talked to him."

"Oh… so aside from that, what else do you know?" I asked hesitantly. She sighed.

"Gamma Grayson is my dad," she whispered, making me gasp. I was not expecting that! My mind was reeling; the Luna and Gamma Grayson never seemed close…

"Ryan's your brother!" I hissed. She shrugged.

"Seems it… all I know is that they have taken Gamma Grayson to the cells. You know he's always been nice… he's a good gamma…" she mumbled, her eyes looking tearful. "Mom is not allowed to leave her room."

This was a mess, but the king locked the Gamma up for cheating… shouldn't he be locked up for cheating, too, then? Such a hypocrite.

"There's more... He said he has a daughter, a biological daughter that he has foun-" The door opened, and none other than the king's frame filled the doorway.

"Ah, my girls." A grin crossed his face, and I felt my stomach sink when I heard Charlene's heart skip a beat…

He never referred to me as his girl... *Way to go, Alpha.*

"How are you feeling, my dear?" He asked, coming over to the bed, with concern on his face.

My heart was thumping as I looked at Charlene. Our eyes met, and neither of us needed to say it out loud to know that the other knew the full truth… I could see the sadness in her eyes, the confusion. Behind that gentle smile of hers that tugged on my heartstrings. How do I fix this?

The king was speaking, but I didn't care. I couldn't focus on anything else. My only concern was for my soul sister, my best friend, my queen.

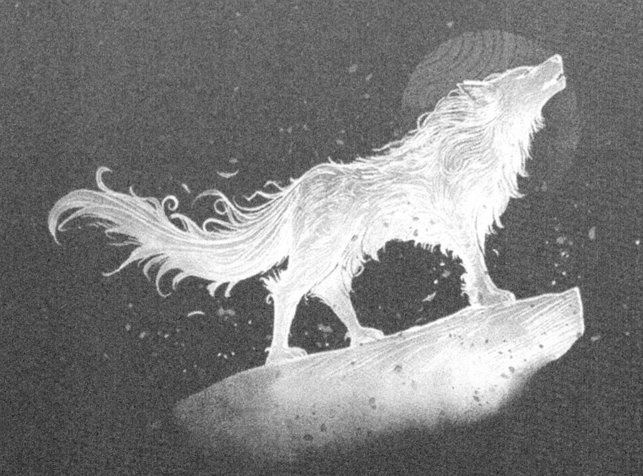

Sisters

CHARLENE

"Can you hear me, Yileyna?" The king asked, taking a seat on the bed, placing his hands on his knees as he turned towards us both. "I asked you, how are you feeling?"

"I'm fine," Yileyna replied, sounding hostile.

Although she was trying to control her emotions, it was obvious that she was angry with Dad. I looked between them, realising their eye colour was so similar. How was this possible? Who was Yileyna's mother?

"I heard you had Gamma Grayson locked away. What are his crimes?" Yileyna asked.

Gamma Grayson… he was my father. I swallowed hard, thinking, *What would happen from here on out? What would happen to me?*

"Betraying his king and having an illicit relationship with his Luna. It is an insult to me, the Alpha!" Dad growled, his eyes blazing. Yileyna nodded.

"Will you, too, serve prison time for your own illicit affair, which is an insult to your Luna?" She asked, blinking innocently. Dad's face almost turned purple at that blatant insult.

I almost smiled. There was a time I had to hold Yileyna back, knowing Dad would get angry, but now I could tell he was trying to keep his temper in check. He had to tolerate her now. *Go, Yileyna.*

"I am Alpha! I don't need to prove anything to anyone!" He thundered.

Yileyna shook her head.

"No, as Alpha, you are the one who should set an example... Gamma Grayson is a good person, and with the current times, you need all the support you can get. Gamma Grayson and Zoe were not fated mates... but you and the Luna were. Yet you both betrayed one another. If Gamma Grayson is in prison for cheating, then all three of you need to be there together," she said, crossing her arms.

An Alpha female. How had I not seen it before? Confident, proud, and just.

Dad glared at her yet said nothing for a moment before exhaling deeply. He then shook his head before grinning and slapping her on the back so hard she almost fell off the bed. I winced. Dad often forgot his own strength.

"Answered like a true Alpha!" He chortled.

I had never seen this side of him. I knew at that moment why Dad was acting the way he was. He was going to make Yileyna his successor. Her powers... She was the heart.

I was happy for her, I truly was. I think I am a little disappointed that we aren't blood-related, but it's okay. We are still sisters. We always have been, and we always will be.

I don't know what Dad wanted to do with me. Would he cast me aside? Would he order me to leave as he did Yileyna when her parents were branded traitors? Dad had always treated me well, although I never did as good as he wanted. It had always been Mom who looked down at me. To think she's the one who was my biological parent...

No, Dad didn't seem to have much faith in me, but I wondered what would happen from here.

It was frustrating to know Mom had treated me harshly when I was doing fine. For a werewolf, I'm sure I was doing well. How could she be like that?

I blinked when I realised Yileyna had taken my hand and pulled me up from my seat. She scooted aside, pulling me to sit between her and Dad. I felt out of place... until she wrapped her arms around me, giving me a warm embrace. I often thought her embrace felt like how Mom's would feel if she had been caring and loving...

I wrapped my arms around her waist, resting my head on her shoulder. This was where I felt happy. I pursed my lips, fighting the tears that were threatening to fall.

"Charl..." she whispered, her voice full of concern. Dad sighed heavily.

"Right, I think we need to have this conversation now," he said. I slowly sat up before scooting back so I could see Dad properly. Yileyna smiled gently as she pulled the duvet over us as we sat there, side by side.

I smiled back, things were confusing right now, but no matter what, we'd always have one another...

"First of all, save a select few who know the truth about your parentage, no one else will be told. As far as the pack and kingdom know, you are my daughter," Dad said, and although I felt happy that he was at least still calling me his daughter, I wondered if that rule applied to Gamma Grayson, too...

"What of Gamma Grayson?" I asked quietly. Dad's eyes flashed, his face darkening with anger.

"He will never know," he spat.

"That should be Charlene's choice," Yileyna said quietly, making Dad glare at her in irritation.

"Don't think you know everything." Dad frowned.

"I don't, but I know that should be her choice." Yileyna remained stubborn.

"Yet you want me to free the man." Dad glared at her. I looked at Yileyna, worried for her, but she was just looking at Dad calmly.

"Yes, of course."

"It's one or the other. I behead him for his crimes, but before that, he gets to learn the truth, or I consider pardoning him, and we bury this secret," Dad growled. "Which will it be?" My heart thumped, but Dad was right. It would just destroy one more family. Just the way mine had been torn apart today. I felt lost... empty, and confused...

"Dad's right. We shouldn't tell anyone. It's fine. Gamma Grayson deserves to be out of prison more than him learning about this... plus, I may not be Dad's real daughter, but -"

"You are his one and only daughter. My parents are dead. William and Hana were my parents, and that won't ever change," Yileyna cut in. "Your dad will always be yours." Dad wasn't happy with her words, but he said nothing.

"Sisters," I said, quietly giving her hand a gentle squeeze. She nodded before turning to Dad.

"I do think that if Charlene wants, Gamma Grayson should also be told.

I'm sure he won't tell everyone anyway."

"You are disobedient, girl," he growled in response. Yileyna didn't reply, and I watched her lock eyes with Dad, a silent move of defiance…

But I agreed with her. Even if I don't think I ever wanted anyone to know right now, maybe in the future, that would change…

"You may not consider yourself my daughter, but it doesn't change the fact. Tomorrow evening, I will make the announcement that you are my daughter and the future Alpha! I will have the Fae train you to learn control, you cannot keep losing control!" Dad stood up, frowning at Yileyna. "Don't push my patience because, I assure you, I have a low fuse." Yileyna frowned, but I squeezed her hand in warning.

She didn't respond, and Dad left, shutting the door behind him. We both sighed at the same time before exchanging looks and smiling. The tension Dad had left behind lifted, and I giggled weakly.

"Well, that didn't go well," I stated, dropping back onto the pillows and staring at the ceiling as Yileyna dropped back onto her pillows. She didn't respond for a moment, becoming serious.

"Hmm… Charlene, I'm sorry… I didn't want to be Alpha. I don't want to take what's yours," she said, turning her beautiful face towards me. The sadness, regret, and guilt were clear on her face.

"What's mine is yours, that's always how it is, and what's yours is mine. I think I'm luckier in that aspect, Leyna… I still get to be the Alpha King's daughter without the burden of having to unlock my powers and the pressure to run a kingdom when the Obsidian Shadow Pack and Sirens are out for us. We are in dire danger, and it scared me to think I was to handle it all… but… now you can, right? You're stronger than I am. I'll be here rooting for you, always… but you are better suited to lead," I said, smiling at her. She may be younger, but at times I felt like I was the younger one being protected by her. She smiled slightly, but I knew my words weren't enough to reassure her. She would still feel guilty, but with time that would change because she was born to do this.

"There's something else, too…" she said, turning onto her side and encasing my hand between two of hers. I copied, turning onto my side to face her.

"What is it?"

"My mother… although the king wants to keep it a secret, you know there's nothing I can keep from you. I'm part Siren, Charl," she whispered.

It took me a good few moments to process her words. Part Siren? What does that mean…. My eyes widened as it hit me like a hammer on the head.

"Part siren!" I gasped, staring at the duvet as if she had a tail hidden under there. My heart was beating as I jolted upright. "Goddess, Yileyna! No wonder you have always loved the sea!" I exclaimed.

It took me a few moments to comprehend what she had said, and all the pieces clicked into place. Dad's alleged affair with a Siren... Yileyna's beauty that didn't quite fit the standards of our pack.

"How do you feel?" I asked her after a moment. She shrugged.

"I had a feeling for a while now, but I didn't want to acknowledge it," she sighed. I looked at her sympathetically.

"You are still you," I said, holding my arms out to her. She smiled before she pounced on me, hugging me.

We laughed, and I realised that nothing had changed; we were still best friends, still sisters. We talked for a while longer, and I had just said I'd go get her food; she hadn't eaten all day.

"And some clothes too?" She suggested looking down at her tiny bodysuit from where she was standing.

"Yes, I think you need some. If I squint, it's almost like you're naked," I said, scrunching my eyes.

"I know..." She nodded in agreement.

"On it." I smiled, pulling the door open to reveal none other than Theon, who had been about to knock. My heart skipped a beat in fear, but his eyes were not on me, but on Yileyna. I stepped aside without realising, and he walked over to her.

"So, you're awake?" He asked coldly.

"No, I'm just standing here asleep," she retorted, despite the way her heart was pounding. "What are you doing here?"

"I'm your bodyguard, remember?" He asked mockingly, stepping a foot away from her. Yileyna rolled her eyes.

"No, you're not. I'm talking to the king about that."

"Fine, but I'm here for another reason."

"And what exactly might that be?"

"Revenge," Theon growled dangerously before he grabbed her by the neck, making me scream.

"Theon -"

Yileyna was cut off when he wrapped his arm around her tiny waist, crushing her against his body before he claimed her lips in a very hot, passionate kiss...

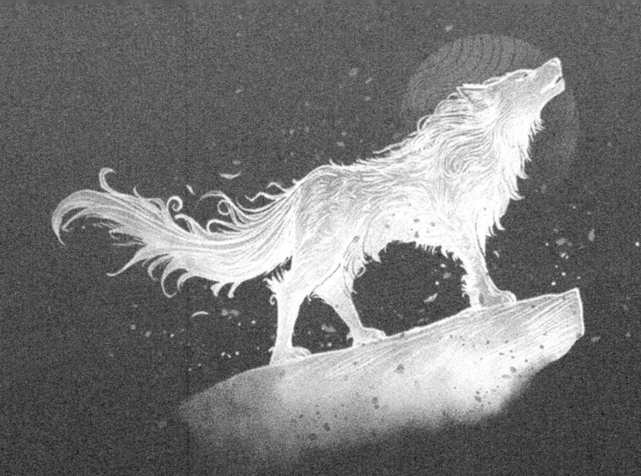

Confusion

YILEYNA

Sparks erupted through every ounce of my body, so intense that I wasn't sure where they started and where they ended. His hand that encased my waist, the way his hard chiselled body was crushed against mine, ignited that intense pleasure and desire that only he could. My core throbbed in response to his perfect plush lips moving dominatingly against mine. A soft whimper was on the tip of my tongue when reality hit.

Stop.

Using all my anger to give me strength, I pushed him away roughly, and no matter how much I had enjoyed that kiss of his, I placed a disgusted look on my face and made the obvious display of wiping my lips.

"How is that revenge?" I growled, sounding far too breathless for my liking.

I saw the tip of Charlene's hair as she fled the room, shutting the door behind her. This girl…

"Oh, why not? Did you happen to enjoy it?" Theon asked coldly, raising an eyebrow.

"No!" I denied a little too quickly. He scoffed lightly, his cold intense gaze on me.

"Earlier, you attacked me with your fists, and I'm not one to hit a woman… unless, of course, she takes pleasure in it. So I simply used my lips instead." There it was, that coldness and hatred in his eyes again.

"I hated it," I said, glaring at him. He had thrown me off, once again.

"And I hate you, so we're even," his reply came.

That stung. He had never said he loved me, but to express his hate so easily? That was harsh. Our eyes met before his gaze dipped down and I remembered what I was wearing.

"What do you want, Theon?" I asked, trying not to care.

"Aside from that, what you did today was fucking reckless. You say you care? You almost ripped that hospital apart."

"So, you came here to lecture me? You, who doesn't really give a fuck about anyone?" I asked, crossing my arms under my breasts. He clenched his jaw.

"No, I don't. However, the king expects me to train you alongside the Fae. He thinks you have the potential to actually become a true alpha, something that the fake princess does not have the potential for."

"She is not a fake princess." I glared at him. "Blood doesn't make us something, Theon. She is still the one and only princess in my eyes. The king is not my father, he did not raise me. He will never be my father." Something about my words made his cold frown soften slightly, almost as if paying attention to those words. He looked at the ground, before glancing at me.

"We cannot run from our fate though. You may not consider him your father, but he is still your blood." I shook my head.

"You don't get it, Theon. You never will. You and the king are actually more alike; your thinking, your mindset, and your values. Goddess, with the way he wants a powerful heir, he should just adopt you," I replied with contempt. He stepped closer to me, but I refused to back down.

"We are different," he said, looking down at me. My heart was pounding as I tried to not let his closeness affect me.

"You're not, really. You both get on like a house on fire. In fact, even your preferences are so similar, right? Right down to the fact that you both seem incredibly infatuated with women of siren blood." I knew it was a low blow, but I wanted to hurt him. "Funny coming from two men who apparently hate sirens." It had the reaction I wanted from him, hearing the way his heart thudded at my words.

"You have no idea how much I fucking hate sirens. Don't ever think that will change," he hissed. His eyes flashed gold as he glared at me.

"Hurts when I insult you, right?" I asked softly, stepping closer. "That's exactly how I feel when you insult Charlene." For a moment, our eyes met, hatred clear in his, and it felt like I was being crushed inside…

How did we get here?

"Think whatever the fuck you want."

I thought he was going to say more, but he simply shook his head, turning and storming out. The door shut with a resounding thud, and I exhaled, dropping onto the edge of the bed. Today had been too much to take in…

THEON

Her words still remained imprinted in my mind, even as I poured myself another glass of wine. The boisterous sounds of the Tavern were drowned by my own thoughts.

"The king is not my father, he did not raise me."

She wasn't wrong… but she was still of his blood.

I closed my eyes, trying to drill that into my head. Then why was I only seeing her for her? Why had that kiss felt so fucking good, despite knowing what and who she was?

I ran my hand through my hair, refusing to let it get to me, but it already was…

EARLIER THAT DAY

"I told you to let her do it. She would have been able to break the seal," Andres said seriously as I held the unconscious Yileyna in my arms protectively. She wasn't a monster… she wasn't a fucking traitor like Andres.

I wiped the blood from her nose and lip, my own anger threatening to unleash upon the bastard before me.

"You don't care that she was fucking bleeding?" I almost growled. His response was a grin.

"And you say you don't love her… well, it all worked out, did it not? You get to be with the one you wanted all along!"

Wrong… I didn't want to be with her. Not like this… not ever… right? Fuck, I was only kidding myself… I had fallen for her, whether I ever admitted that out loud or not, but there was no fucking future for us. The time was coming ever closer, and then she would become something to be used. A weapon for the most power-hungry...

Dad could do this without her. Why couldn't we just play this out without involving her…? But I knew neither Alpha would give up the heart.

I needed to protect her. I needed to talk to her.

I stood up suddenly, and I realised I couldn't do it. I sat down again, running my hand through my hair. What would I say to her? To leave? That she wasn't safe here?

"Did you hear Grayson Sanchez is in the cells?" A drunken voice asked.

"Ah, yes… what a shame. First the Beta, now the Gamma… they are all traitors!" I frowned, listening to the conversation behind me.

"Do you ever feel that we see nothing but ill luck here?" Another quieter voice asked his companion.

"Karma indeed." I frowned ever so slightly. Karma? What were they insinuating? A shiver of unease ran down my spine. Who were they?

Trust no one…

I licked my lips, remembering the way her lips felt against mine once more. The way her body reacted, the way she had involuntarily pressed herself against me. My dick throbbed at the thought. All I had wanted was to throw her onto that bed and fuck her…

But I was told to stay away from her, by both dad and Andres, and now she is the very same woman that they expected me to be with. It doesn't work like that… and knowing their reasons only makes me even more uneasy.

Yileyna was in grave danger, from my father more so. If he ever learned she was part Siren, he would make sure she died. I closed my eyes, but even then, her image flashed before them.

I should hate her.

She had become a thorn in my revenge. She had destroyed sex for me because no other woman appealed in the same way… she ruined my sleep with dreams of desires.

I downed another glass and refilled it.

The king still expected us to mark and mate… but it didn't feel right. Not without her knowing the truth that I owed her, a truth that I knew I would never tell her.

I stood up, tossing a few coins onto the table.

I needed to see her. Now.

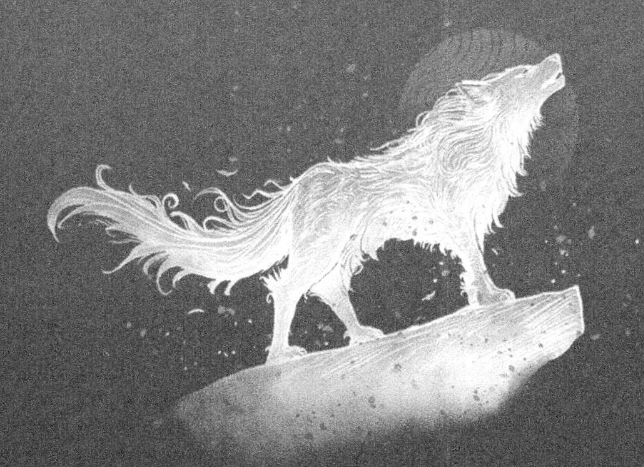

These Moments

YILEYNA

I AWOKE TO THE SOUND of something knocking against the window. I sat up and looked around. Charlene was still asleep on the other side of the vast bed. I stared at the window, seeing the shadow reflected on it. I frowned, getting out of bed and going over to it slowly. My senses were on alert as the figure stopped moving, and I could tell from the outline that it was a muscular man. My heart skipped a beat upon realising who it was.

Theon.

What was he doing here?

I quickly glanced back at Charlene and the closed door to the bedroom, my heart skipping a beat as I slowly unlocked the window. He instantly pulled it open, letting in the cold. Charlene stirred, and I frowned, looking at him. He smelled of alcohol. Was he drunk?

"I need to talk to you," he said huskily. Despite his voice being as cold and emotionless as ever, I could tell from his eyes that he may be slightly intoxicated.

"Theon, I don't want to do this right now," I whispered.

"We are running out of time, Yileyna. We need to do this now," he replied quietly. I frowned, glancing at the rainy sky outside. He was already drenched, his shirt sticking to him and water trickling down his face and neck.

I bit my lip, trying not to focus on how sexy he looked right then, and instead gazed down at myself. I was wearing a black satin nightdress that Charlene had given me with thin straps. I didn't have any other clothes to wear... not that the cold bothered me...

"Theon, I already have the king trying to control my every action. Can I at least sleep in peace?" I frowned. I almost expected him to argue, but seeing the struggle in his eyes I knew I needed to hear him out.

"Please."

Theon didn't say please. That one word made up my mind. My heart thundered with worry before I looked out at the narrow ledge where he was balanced with ease.

"Theon, you're drunk, and you're taking such a risk?" I hissed.

"Then come with me before I end up falling," he whispered softly, teetering slightly on the ledge. My heart leapt into my mouth, and I grabbed onto his shirt.

"Goddess, Theon!"

"Better hurry up, little storm," he whispered.

I glanced back into the room, hesitating. The rain was already beginning to soak me. Taking a deep breath, I slowly climbed out onto the ledge. The sky was dark and cloudy, and it seemed as if the castle grounds were empty. What time was it?

"Careful," he said, placing a hand on my thigh, making my heart skip a beat.

"So, how do we get down?" I asked. He smirked as he slid the window down, his arm slipping around my waist.

"Just don't scream," he said, pulling me against him. I raised my eyebrow questioningly as I wrapped my arm around his neck before he jumped.

The wind rushed through my hair, and he flipped me, carrying me bridal style just before he landed agilely on the courtyard ground.

"That worked," he said, standing up and placing me down.

I took a moment to get my breath back. Wow.

He smirked slightly before he took hold of my hand and pulled me along. I was barefoot, unlike him, and the rain was still pouring down, soaking me thoroughly. Now that the sleep had lifted from my eyes, I wondered if agreeing was a good idea...

"Getting cold feet?" He asked when he pulled me into the shadows.

"In a literal sense, yes, but I am wondering why I should listen to you at all," I replied, looking up at him.

He clenched his jaw but said nothing, leading the way from the palace. He took one of the paths that only had one guard at the gate. The man didn't bother sparing us a second look. Well, he wouldn't care until tomorrow when I was announced as the future Alpha. That still felt weird.

"Where are we going?" I asked, my heart thundering as I wondered if he was taking me to the cabin. There were far too many memories there...

"The Moon Goddess's Temple," he replied after a long moment when I thought he wouldn't.

His place...

We continued in silence until we got there. We climbed onto the roof of the temple, and I stared up at the rainy sky. It looked beautiful. I could feel his intense gaze upon me, and I wondered if this was just a dream...

I turned slowly, looking into those gorgeous amber eyes.

"What is it?"

"The Obsidian Shadow Pack are gaining more and more control of this city with every passing day. Their Alpha has vowed to destroy every one of the Silver Storm Pack. As future Alpha... you will become a target." I wasn't expecting that, of all things. His words sent a chill through me, my chest heaving at the confidence in his voice, as if he was absolutely sure that would happen.

"They won't be able to infiltrate this city. We will never let them win," I replied with confidence. He tilted his head and gave a small nod, as he stepped closer and cupped my face.

"But *if* they do... you will become the target. Until you have unlocked your powers, let me take you away from here." I pulled away, looking at him with utter confusion and surprise.

"Ok, I think I am dreaming," I said, brushing my wet locks back.

"I'm serious, Yileyna. You cannot be here." I shook my head.

"I don't get it, why shouldn't I be here? As the heart, it is my duty to unlock my powers and to protect this pack, this kingdom. Theon, I can't leave." He ran his hand through his hair.

"If I said..." He swallowed hard before looking away and exhaling, and then tilted his head back sharply. "If I said that I cared... that you mean something to me, no matter how many times I tell myself that you don't. Would you believe me then?"

My heart squeezed and the weakness that washed through me scared me. How did just a few words weaken my resolve?

"Why now?" I whispered, unable to get rid of the fear within my chest. He had broken me so many times that I was terrified.

"Answer me. Would you or would you not?"

"I don't know," I whispered honestly, my eyes stinging with tears. He was silent before he turned fully back towards me.

"This city may fall. If there's a part of you that believed in… us, then you will let me take you far away. Just for a short while, until you learn to use your powers." I shook my head determinedly.

"No. I won't leave this city, Theon. You're scaring me, almost as if the Obsidian Shadow Pack is going to attack soon," I whispered.

"It looks that way… I don't want you around when it happens."

"Who would have thought Theon of Westerfell cared so much? But I wonder… is it me you want, or my title?" I asked. My words hurt me too, but I had to say them. The corner of his mouth turned up in a small smirk.

"I'm not asking you to marry me, Yileyna. We both know I could get you into my bed if I wanted." I frowned, shoving him. Any weakness that I was beginning to feel was wiped away by his cocky words.

"Oh, whatever, that's not true," I snapped, crossing my arms in irritation.

"Oh, yeah?" His voice sounded like a challenge before he grabbed my elbow, yanking me into his arms.

I gasped the moment our bodies collided, my hands automatically going to his shoulders. For a moment, our eyes met, and I could hear our racing hearts. The way we reacted to one another's touch… we were each other's addiction, even when we weren't ever meant to be…

"Theon… fine. You don't want my title, then why?" He became serious once more, but he didn't let go of me.

"Like I said, they will attack, and this time it will be worse. We know they will infiltrate this city with only one aim, to destroy the Silver Storm Pack."

"I wish I knew why the Obsidian Shadow Pack wants to attack. Surely there must be another reason than simply for the power? If there was a way to resolve this without a war. Do they want to be given their land, to be recognised as one of the packs? I don't get it. Surely there's another way." His eyes flickered with an emotion that I thought was confusion or surprise... maybe both…

"Only you would think that would resolve things. No one believes in false promises or that things can be resolved. No one can promise that."

"I would. When I become Alpha, I'm going to be far better than the king. I will make this kingdom better; I will make it fair. One step at a time." His hand caressed my cheek.

"I can picture it, a crazy blonde going on a rampage, trying to fix everything singlehandedly." I couldn't resist a smile at his light joke.

"I won't be alone. I'll have my friends; Charlene, Raiden, Ryan, and, I hope… you," I ended hesitantly. I didn't know what we were but…

"Friends… you know this entire thing between these packs started in the name of friendship," he muttered, his finger grazing my jaw and leaving a sinful trail of tingles in its wake. My heart was pounding as I resisted melting into his touch.

"What do you mean, friendship?"

"This is just a story I've heard outside of Westerfell, the other version of what truly happened between King Andres and the Alpha of the Obsidian Shadow Pack…" he said hesitantly.

"Tell me." He looked uncertain.

"You know it's treason to talk of it."

"I don't care, I don't mind breaking rules. Remember?" He seemed to be searching for something in my eyes before he let go of me and inhaled deeply as he turned his back on me.

"Fine, I'll tell you, but be warned; it may change your views on this pack and your king forever."

I didn't care, I needed to hear it. There were always two sides to a story... or as my dad used to say; three. The versions of both parties and then the ultimate truth.

"I'm ready. Tell me."

Two Packs

YILEYNA

My stomach was a mess of nerves as I stood there in the pouring rain, looking at Theon's back. I wanted to hear the story he had heard outside of Astalion. Theon had travelled a few times and had seen far more of the world than Charlene and I ever had. I remember we would always wait for him to return, counting the days. There was just something fun about having a broody sexy man around…

Why did those times suddenly feel so carefree and childish?

"Do you know when the Silver Storm Pack took control of the middle kingdom?"

"It's said Alpha Andres took this land that was in control of the Dark Ones, saving the people from them over twenty years ago." The Dark Ones were mages who had become necromancers, so lost in their ways that the land had become poisoned by their evil deeds. "The king saved the people from them, and the land began to flourish once more as well, bringing peace and safety to the kingdom as a whole." Theon nodded.

"Yes, in under two weeks, it will be exactly twenty-one years since that day… the day this land was freed, but beyond these walls of this city, with Astalion itself, the hushed whispers of another version of the truth are that Alpha Andres didn't do it alone. He conquered the land alongside his closest comrade, his best friend, Theoden Hale. Two Alphas, two packs, one goal…." My heart thudded as I stared at his back.

The Alpha of the Obsidian Shadow Pack…

"A goal that they worked on together. They were said to be such good friends that they were willing to die for one another. Theoden Hale even took a hit for his friend in battle, resulting in him getting severely injured." Theon looked at the sky, and I waited patiently for him to continue. "It is said that it was Theoden Hale who took out the final and the most powerful of the Dark Ones and, in doing so, freed the land. Yet, against what was promised, where both would rule the middle kingdom, Andres Aphelion went back on his word. With Theoden being injured from the battle, he was weak, and at that moment, Andres tried to kill him."

I was unable to stop the gasp that left me. Theon turned around, brushing his fingers through his wet locks. The move alone made my stomach flutter, despite the severity of the conversation.

"And then what?" I asked quietly, looking into his amber eyes. He stepped closer, his gaze dipping to my body before he ran his knuckles down my arm.

"He didn't only try to kill him, also his wife and young son… but Nathalia Hale was not weak. She was rumoured to be the strongest female wolf around, a true warrior… someone who never backed down from a fight. They say she caused a distraction, shifting and carrying her pup in her mouth with her mate on her back. She fled, but it wasn't enough for Andres… not wanting the past to come back, he never rested, seeking out where the Obsidian Shadow Pack lived to the point where they were forced into hiding. The king's word is law, and they say he made sure everyone knew the Obsidian Shadow Pack were enemies."

Something inside of me twisted as I stared into those amber eyes that held far more emotions than they should have. Yes, the story was heartbreaking, but… it was almost as if Theon could feel that pain… like he was experiencing it himself. Was it not all hearsay?

"So, is that why the Obsidian Shadow Pack wishes to take over? They feel they deserve to be in control of this city?" I asked quietly.

"Hmm, revenge. Revenge for all that was taken from them. To show Andres that no matter what, he will pay for the crimes he has committed." His voice was low, sinister even…

My heart raced as I looked up into the amber eyes of the man before me. Amber… like the crest of the Hale family…

Fear enveloped me as I held his gaze. I was suddenly seeing him in a new light. A man who was worthy of being Alpha... a man who had a wolf like an Alpha's... a man who talked of vengeance and revenge often enough… a man who only came to this city two years ago…

"And does the Hale family want to take revenge on the family and pack of the Alpha King too?" I asked softly, trying to rein in my emotions.

The hatred towards Charlene… the look of hatred when the king had asked him to leave… was I overthinking it? What if Theon had never lost his memory? What if he came to Westerfell to get close to the king?

"What's wrong, Yileyna? Shocked that your king may not be the man you thought?" His gaze flicked from my lips to my eyes, and I simply nodded.

No, I'm scared that I'm right. What if Theon was somehow more than he was portraying?

"My father said there are always three sides to a story, in this case, Alpha Andres's, Alpha Theoden's, and the truth. What Alpha Theoden is doing is wrong…" I trailed off, my breath hitching as I placed a hand on my chest. "He was the reason behind my parents dying. In his revenge, he is also killing the innocent…" If I was right… then… then…

Theon must have known of the attack…

I looked into those amber eyes that were watching me intently, and for the first time in my life, they truly terrified me…

"Maybe so, but war always has casualties."

"It sounds like you know a lot, to a point it feels like you believe the version told by the Obsidian Shadow Pack," I said, trying to act normal. His eyes seemed to darken as he ran his knuckles down my cheek, making me shiver.

"Of course not. I was just telling you the other version. A version that no one really believes anyway," he said, turning away.

Everything seemed to ease up. I let out a breath of relief and a giddy laugh at my ridiculous thoughts. Goddess. Where was my mind going?

"Why do you look so scared, little storm?" Theon asked with a small smirk.

"Nothing. I'm crazy." I couldn't resist smiling up at him and the ridiculous thoughts that had crossed my mind.

"I already knew that," he whispered huskily, making me gasp when he squeezed my waist, tugging me slightly closer. "So… will you let me take you away from here?"

"Is my safety of that much importance to you?" He looked into my eyes, his face only inches from mine.

"Do you want it to be?" He asked, making my eyelids flutter shut for a moment as I tried to control my emotions.

"Don't play mind games," I rebutted with a roll of my eyes. The rain was trickling down his hair, dripping from his nose and lips. The urge to kiss him was powerful.

Move away, Yileyna.

I made the mistake of shifting slightly in his hold, my stomach brushing against his package, which I realised was semi-hard, making my own core clench. My stomach fluttered as I heard him suck in a breath. I blushed as our eyes met, the sexual tension between us feeling too much.

"So what's it going to be, little storm? Will you let me take you away from here?"

"I can't," I said softly. He frowned, exhaling in frustration. "It's nice to see you so worried, though, but you don't need to be. I mean, I'm more surprised that you haven't told your idea to the king. You and he usually love ganging up on me, and anyone else," I said, knowing I needed to pull away. My core was already aching at the proximity, and I feared that he'd soon smell my arousal.

"He wouldn't listen," he said quietly before letting go of me, his eyes raking over my soaking body. "Let's get you back." I nodded. "Oh, and one more thing, make sure what we talked about stays between us."

I nodded again. I understood that. After all, if it was treason to talk of it, then I wouldn't risk getting him in trouble… however, why would it be treason unless the king had something to hide…? I did need to talk to him…

I needed to know his full version. I would come up with a plan to get the truth out of him. Maybe, just maybe, I would break my promise to Theon. Dad always said to listen to all sides of the story before jumping to conclusions… I had never heard of the Obsidian Shadow Pack having a hand in securing this land.

We made our way back in silence, his hand wrapped around my wrist. He took me back to my room via the window, his hand on my lower back as I slipped into the bedroom.

"I'll see you tomorrow," he said emotionlessly once again.

"Hmm, don't think I'll agree to this engagement just because you were charming for an hour or so," I stated haughtily, reaching for the window when his hand clamped over mine, refusing to allow me to pull it shut.

"We both know charming doesn't do it for you anyway. Correct me if I'm wrong, little storm, but we both know it's anything but charming that gets you soaking wet." I gasped when his hand wrapped around my throat, tugging me towards him.

"Well, it's definitely not you anymore," I shot back breathlessly as he leaned in, his hand tightening around my throat.

"I can smell you, little storm. Keep playing hard to get, and I will take the challenge. I'll bend you over and fuck you like the dirty little whore you are." My pussy clenched at his words, and if he had been lying about smelling my arousal before, he definitely would now.

"Shame I don't want you to," I managed to reply, shoving him lightly, enough to make him let go but not enough to push him off the ledge. His eyes flashed, and I simply smirked, blowing him a mock kiss before I shut and locked the window quickly, letting out a sigh of relief.

I felt giddy. Theon was already weaving his way back in, and I refused to let him. I can't fall for it. Not again.

I looked around the guest room. I needed clothes. I better go sneak to Charlene's room and find something to wear. I made my way to the bedroom door silently, seeing that Charlene was still fast asleep. I opened the door, exiting silently, and closed it behind me as I made my way down the hall to Charlene's room, leaving a trail of water in my wake.

I slowly opened it and peered inside before turning the light on and stepping in. I went over to her wardrobe, opening it and taking out something that might fit when I heard footsteps from behind me.

"Oh, so you finally decided to return after whoring around."

I paused, turning to face my accuser...

The King's Rage

ANDRES

I looked at Grayson as he stood there, arms clasped behind his back. He turned and bowed his head to me as I approached.

"Do you know why you are here?" I asked seriously, my footsteps echoing in the silence. This was a grave matter. Not only had I trusted this man, I had dined with him, a man who had cheated with my woman behind my back…

"No, Alpha," he replied solemnly.

"I know of your affair with Soleil." I was unable to keep the rage from my shaking voice. "Give me a reason not to tear you to shreds right now." A frown flitted across his face, and he sighed heavily. It was not the reaction I was expecting.

"Good. It is a burden I was tired of carrying," he said quietly. I frowned.

"That's all you have to say? After everything you have done?" I growled.

"I was blackmailed. I had no choice."

"Blackmailed?" I asked sharply. "I want the truth." My alpha command rolled off me in waves, and he submitted, lowering his head in response. "Tell me the truth! The entire truth!" He took a deep breath.

"The Luna had always been infatuated with me, but she told me that if I did not yield to her demands, then she would make sure that I was ruined…

I still refused, yet somehow, she managed to get me in bed. When I awoke the following day, I was ready to tell you everything, but she told me that no one would believe me, and she would accuse me of raping her. We all know the king's Luna's word in the matter would hold more power over a simple Gamma's..."

I couldn't begin to comprehend the torrent of emotions that hit me. Was Soleil really this... conniving? She always appeared prim, proper, and supportive. Always there for me…

"From there, she told me that I better agree or she would tell Zoe and ruin my life and that of my young pup. She used to give you a sleeping potion so you wouldn't even notice her missing." And that was how I never felt her cheating. She had me unconscious…

My anger was growing, and all I wanted to do was end the woman who was meant to be my true mate. I could not; I had marked her. Her death meant my death. How had she had the audacity to use and blackmail one of my own men?

"And how long did it last?" I asked, feeling angry that this man was Charlene's father.

She was my daughter; I had raised her and watched her grow. What irritated me was that Charlene had always preferred Grayson and William over me growing up. Grayson was a quiet man, but he always took the time to greet her. Was it the unknowing bond of father and daughter?

"A few months. She suddenly decided I was of no use anymore," he said, frowning. When she became pregnant…

This was all Soleil's doing.

"Forgive me, My King. I am ready for any punishment you deem worthy. I only ask that you do not tell my mate." He lowered his head, and I frowned deeply.

"You will be let out at dawn. I will say I had a tip-off, and I had to question you for the safety of the kingdom," I said, turning away.

"Alpha…" I paused, waiting for him to continue. "May I ask how it was revealed now?" He asked hesitantly.

I tensed. How do I answer that? When I make the announcement tomorrow that Yileyna is my daughter… would he piece the puzzle together?

"I myself had an affair, and in her rage, she told me that she, too, had committed the same sin," I replied simply before I left the cells.

I had been here far too often in the last few days, and I did not wish to come here again for a while. It was late. Although I didn't want to return to my quarters, I needed to face Soleil. There was much I needed to ask her. How dare she…

YILEYNA

I looked at Luna Soleil, who stood at the door to Charlene's room. She looked distraught. Her face was makeup free, and her hair was a mess. Her eyes were red from obvious crying.

"What I do with my life has nothing to do with you, Luna. Especially calling me a whore when I think that would be more befitting for you, don't you think?" The words had left my lips before I had been able to stop myself.

Shit.

Her eyes flashed as she strode over to me, her fists clenched as she glared at me.

"Don't you dare! It was your mother who was a whore! Seducing my king and then giving birth to you… I always knew there was something about you that I just never liked." She grabbed hold of my jaw, squeezing it painfully.

"I don't know much about her, but I also know having an affair when you are mated is worse than me whoring around when I'm unmated," I said icily, pushing her hand off of me.

"If you had any shame, you would pack your bags and leave silently," she said with contempt.

"Shame? What have I done that I should be ashamed of, Luna?" I asked quietly. I had too much on my head to waste time with her.

"Don't think I don't know what went on with you and Theon! This position, this title, all of this belongs to Charlene, and you think you can stroll into here and steal her clothes too?" She spat, yanking the tunic I had taken from the drawer. "I always knew that Hana was a whoring bitch!"

"Don't you dare insult my mother!" I hissed, feeling my anger rise. She obviously didn't know that my mother wasn't my birth mother, but how dare she insult her?

"Well, like mother like daughter, don't you agree?" Soleil scoffed scornfully.

"My parents were the most in love couple I have seen, and it's something you could only ever hope to have. She would never cheat on Father. How dare you dirty her name," I shot back, my eyes flashing, and the windows rattled in the wind.

Breathe, Yileyna...

"In love? Yet she was able to spread her legs for her Alpha. What a good little slut -"

"Enough!" The king thundered, making both of our gazes snap towards the door. My heart was thundering as I focused on my emotions until the rattling stopped. The king seemed to do a quick sweep of my soaking clothes.

"Give her the dress, Soleil," he growled commandingly. The queen pressed her lips together before tossing it at me, her eyes flashing.

"Yileyna, go shower and change before you catch a cold. Did I not tell you you cannot leave these quarters?" He asked coldly.

"I went with Theon," I replied, knowing the king couldn't fault that. He trusted Theon and had made him my bodyguard. As predicted, he visibly relaxed.

"So I hope that tomorrow you agree to the union?" I frowned.

"I am capable of being Alpha without a man, if the Alpha King gives me a chance to prove myself." He shook his head dismissively.

"You know nothing of the truth of war. You need Theon. Go bathe, Yileyna, now."

I nodded, walking over to the bathroom in Charlene's room, feeling the king and queen watching me. The moment I was inside, I closed the door and stripped out of my nightdress. I turned the shower on, and that's when I heard the sound of angry talking from the room outside.

I paused, tempted to listen. Letting the shower water run, I slowly padded back to the door and pressed my ear to the keyhole.

"... everything, Soleil, or by Selene, I will have you thrown into the cells!" The king hissed.

"You wouldn't dare..."

"Don't test me. Answer me truthfully. Did you blackmail and seduce Grayson to bed you?" The king's Alpha command was absolute. It bit into my bones, and I heard Soleil whimper at the full force of it. I peered through the keyhole and saw Soleil on her knees. Unable to resist the command, she bowed her head.

How strange... I was told that true mates were almost equal... that even an Alpha's command would not work on his true mate.

"I… yes, yes I did," she hissed.

"Why?" The king growled murderously. She was struggling against it until she clamped her hands to her head.

"Because… he is my true mate!" Soleil screeched, making me gasp as I jumped away from the door. My heart pounded at the shocking revelation that I had just overheard. The king was silent, and I was sure neither heard my gasp, being so consumed by their own argument.

"What?" The king asked quietly, his voice devoid of all emotions. "You're my true mate…"

"No… I called up an enchanter to make it seem like you were. I… I wanted to be Luna, n-not the mate of a mere Gamma! This is the life I deserve, and I proved to be the perfect Luna, did I not?"

"That's why you never knew I was cheating…" the king murmured. "Why give me a sleeping potion if you knew I wouldn't feel you cheating?"

"So he spoke…" she muttered bitterly. "I used to give you a potion every night to make sure you were unconscious when I went to Grayson!"

"Did he know you were his true mate?" The king growled.

"Of course not. I made sure the spell was on him too. I am the Luna. I am meant to be Luna!"

"No, you're not. We aren't true mates, Soleil, which means even if I have you killed, it would have no effect on me," the king's cold, dangerous voice came, making my heart thud. I had never heard it sound so… sinister…

My head spun with everything I had learned, fear enveloping me. I needed to move away from this. I shouldn't have listened… but I was unable to move from my position. Would the king really kill the Luna for cheating on him? She was not a good person, but death?

"What is my crime?" She hissed as I watched through the keyhole, my chest heaving in fear.

"Betraying your Alpha."

The king turned his head sharply towards the bathroom door, and I quickly moved away from the keyhole, clamping a hand over my mouth, praying he didn't realise I had been eavesdropping…

Another Side

YILEYNA

I had barely slept all night. The morning came, and two Omegas were waiting to take my measurements for a gown.

"Colour, miss?" Odessa asked.

"Neckline, miss?" Leonora added.

"Let me see what there is, and then give me the options on which can be most easily adjusted on such short notice," I said, looking over at Charlene, who was looking through the gowns. I hadn't gotten to talk to her about what Theon had told me.

"Yileyna, I think you should wear silver," Charlene added suddenly.

I nodded, and the two women rushed to bring every silver gown they had brought with them.

"As commanded, we went to every designer in the city and asked for their best," Odessa stated. When I had been asked this morning, all I had said was to not exclude Fae designers.

"These all can be adjusted to your size, madam," Leonora added.

I looked at the gowns, although all my mind could focus on was how I would approach the topic with the king. I was lucky enough that he, himself, wanted a word before the ball in the evening.

"These two… one for me, one for Charlene. Charlene, choose first," I stated.

"They are meant for you, you're the one to who this night belongs. I will go for this satin gown," Charlene said, shaking her head as she held up a pink gown.

"Since when have we ever thought so hard? I was all dolled up on your night, Charlene," I reminded her.

"A night I didn't want," she whispered.

"And this is a night I want? These two," I said firmly, making Charlene sigh and smile in defeat, giving me a nod.

"I haven't worn anything from Fae designers… are you sure it's okay?" She asked hesitantly.

"Yes, the princess is correct… perhaps designs from our own people for a special ball." They didn't know what it was regarding yet. Otherwise, I knew they wouldn't speak up to me.

"The Fae are part of our kingdom. Why can't we wear their designs? They are our people too. Come, this will be the start of our statement as a kingdom that respects all its people." Charlene smiled and nodded, picking up one of the two dresses.

"I'll wear this one. You can wear silver. Frankly, I'm bored of being expected to wear grey and silver all the time."

We both laughed. She was right; growing up, she often had to wear the pack colour, something she got fed up with, being a girl who loved her summery colours. My laughter faded, that same wave of guilt washing through me. This should have been hers…

I hid my thoughts as Odessa discussed jewels and hair. Leonora had taken our measurements before taking the dresses and leaving. I was relieved to be free from it all. I glanced at the time. It was almost time to go see the king…

"Is there something important you want to discuss with Dad?" Charlene asked quietly.

"Kind of…" I said, glancing at Odessa. Charlene gave a small knowing nod. "Have you spoken to your mother?" She frowned, shaking her head.

"No… I'm not ready to talk yet," she said forlornly. I gave her a comforting hug.

"Take your time. I'm going to leave. Wish me luck!"

"Good luck to you both!" Charlene giggled as I left the room.

I glanced towards the queen's room, seeing the two guards that stood outside her door. The king hadn't decided what to do with her. When I had left the bathroom at night after showering, the queen was in her room, and two royal guards had been standing outside her door, but the king had vanished.

The fact that Gamma Grayson was her fated mate, and she had used an enchantment to hide that... she had planned it from the start. It was appalling, to say the least. Was that why she had miscarried two pups? Because she was not built to carry an Alpha heir? Those Alphas who didn't find their true mates often mated with Alpha-blooded females, so they could bear their heirs.

Lost in my thoughts, I found myself outside the king's office. Taking a deep breath, I knocked on the door. The two guards watched me until the king called for me to enter, and I stepped inside. His office was messier than usual, as if he had been searching for something.

"Ah, Yileyna."

"You wanted to talk to me?" I asked, glancing around at the books and scrolls that were now scattered everywhere. He nodded, brushing his long hair back.

"Yes, close the door and take a seat," he commanded. I shut the door and walked over to his desk, taking a seat as I watched him clear the shelf. He sighed in frustration and turned toward me. "As you know, tonight I am announcing you as my heir. There are Alphas invited and many more. With Charlene being born and raised as an Alpha's daughter, she knew what to expect. She has training you do not. Stay close and avoid conversation with anyone."

"Why?" I asked. I know Charlene was usually with her parents during these events, but she preferred it that way.

"They will grill you on your knowledge of the kingdom. Expect to see what makes you good enough as Alpha. You don't even have a wolf," he reminded me with a once over, as if he was second-guessing his decision. I frowned. My father always told me to be confident... I would do as I deemed fit. I've always talked to visitors at these events. Why would I change that now? "Good," he said, taking my silence as obedience.

"Now, I know you and Theon are in a relationship anyway, so I will also announce your engagement tonight. As future Alpha, you have a reputation. You shouldn't be seen with young men when they are not your mates." I almost smirked. Yet it was okay to have secret affairs...

"I don't wish to get engaged to Theon. He was happy to leave me the moment the Alpha position was offered to him. I will not marry him. If you want a man by my side, I'm sure you have others who could be potential suitors. Anyone but him," I said coldly. His treatment still stung...

The king let out a frustrated growl.

"You are a disobedient one. William always said you were a spark." I smiled softly at the mention of Dad.

"I always have been. Dad said never to change," I responded softly, trying to hide the emotions from my voice.

"Theon is not to blame. I know you hold a grudge against him. However, I may or may not have indirectly warned Theon to stay away from you, or I would make sure you were gone..." he said curtly, turning back to his shelf. I frowned as I stared at his back, my heart thundering.

"Excuse me?"

"I wanted him for Charlene, and you were a thorn in my side, one I did not need. He was more concerned about you than he admitted, even making sure I paid you for your trip abroad. I told him I would make you a Zeta-rank guard. That would give you the respect and security you needed, and so he agreed. It is obvious that you are rather popular among the young men..." He gave me a side-eyed frown. "But Theon is ideal for this position."

Theon... the man I loved for so long... the chance to have him as my mate was once something I would have only ever dreamt of... but after everything, I was scared, scared to let him in only for him to break my heart once again.

The king had threatened him...

My mind was split between that small part of me saying to give him a chance to the larger part of me not wanting him or any man, not as my mate anyway.

"You need not mark yet if it helps. Take your time. However, if the kingdom knows you have a man by your side, you will be secure. " I highly doubted that...

I looked at the king sharply. This was my chance... he was occupied with rummaging through a small metal chest on the shelf.

"Fine. I will agree to get engaged to Theon on one condition," I said, knowing that I was already boxed into a corner.

"What is it?" The king's irritation was clear on his face.

"I want to know the truth, the real truth of what happened between two friends. Andres Aphelion and Theoden Hale. How did conquering a kingdom side by side as two united packs change to becoming enemies?" I had mulled over my words carefully, and I was now watching the king sharply. He almost dropped the box, his heart racing as he turned to me with his eyes blazing.

"Where did you hear that?" He hissed, and to my surprise, his canines were out.

"In Bellmead. It was the talk in the tavern when I said I was from Astalion," I lied smoothly. My words didn't quell the king's anger, and he slammed his hand into the shelf.

"He is spreading lies…" he spat venomously. "What exactly did you hear?" I frowned slightly, repeating most of what Theon had told me. There were moments I saw the guilt in his eyes and others when there was outrage.

"I only turned on him because I knew him well enough! He was always power-hungry; it was obvious he would have ousted me," he spat. I frowned as I looked at him.

"If that was the case, then why did he protect you during battle?" I asked.

"I protected Nathalia! His woman! Did he forget to tell the world that?" He spat angrily before looking at me suspiciously. I knew that there wasn't much more I could say without it sounding like a blatant accusation, and I frowned. Who exactly was right?

"May I ask who told you that he was going to overturn you?" I asked the king, whose anger was rising.

"Do not pry in what you know nothing of! I am the king, I claimed these lands! Where is he if he helped? I will destroy these lands before I ever let him set foot here!" I flinched as he slammed his fist into the table beside me. He growled dangerously as the table shattered. I did my all not to cower under his aura. "I am king. Remember that," he hissed, grabbing my arm. "You may be the heart of Kaeladia, but you are just a pawn. A woman can be nothing more than one to stand by the side of her man. Theon will be king!"

So, the issue was never Charlene but the fact he wanted a man to rule… I didn't bat an eyelid. No matter how much his aura was willing me to yield, I fought against it. A flash of lightning filled the sky, striking the window. I didn't flinch even when glass shot everywhere, making the king jump back.

"Control your anger," he growled.

"Likewise, My King," I said, standing up as I glanced at the broken table pointedly.

Our eyes met, grey against grey, and I realised that perhaps there really was a better solution to this fight than to send our people to their deaths... I needed to find that solution. It's what Dad would have wanted me to do... he always believed in peace...

"If we are done, I will be going," I said coldly.

I will work night and day until I become stronger for my people. I didn't wait for a reply, turning and storming to the door. Let the kingdom know I am the heir. That alone would bring power. I would spend the night talking to our allies, and I would derive a plan for the betterment of everyone...

I still couldn't shake off the random thought I'd had of Theon either... but that was just ridiculous. I pushed the thought away, focusing on what was important; to figure out a way to reach out to the Obsidian Shadow Pack Alpha...

Inner Conflict

THEON

THE PREPARATIONS FOR THE evening event were in full swing. I had left the castle late in the afternoon, having things to do around the city. I blended in, sticking to the shadows as I made my way to a certain location where I was to meet Dad again. I had stopped at the jeweller's on the way there. Even if it was not real… I planned on giving her a ring that I paid for rather than one the king had chosen…

"You will be engaged to Yileyna." Andres' words from earlier echoed in my mind.

Yileyna…

There would be nothing disappointing in being tied to Yileyna… waking and falling asleep to her face every night. In an ideal world, that would be perfection, a dream come true… but there was so much more to this than that. A dream of a content and complete life did not exist.

She was a pawn to use in both Andres' and Dad's games… all for the ultimate goal; one of victory and power. A power that should have been ours from the start. But was it worth risking Yileyna's life over? No.

Fuck.

I had made the one mistake I shouldn't have: fallen victim to a woman's seduction. This was why my mate bond was sealed alongside my power.

yet I still fell for her. Hard. Last night, I almost messed up. I had almost blown my cover in my partially drunken state, but deep down, there had been a part of me that had wanted her to know…

Who was I trying to fool? I'd never had an issue with holding my liquor, ever.

I had wanted her to know that although I'm no fucking angel, we weren't the ones entirely in the wrong. The biggest thing was her parents… not only were they collateral in this entire situation, but I had wanted them out of the picture, having them killed to make sure the king relied on me with William gone. If she knew…

I sighed in frustration.

"What troubles you, son?" A deep voice said from behind me.

My eyes widened slightly. We were only a few metres away from the walls of the city, still in Westerfell. I wasn't expecting him to be here. We had agreed to meet down by the coast. For Dad to be so close at such a time when security was tight, he was indeed very confident in himself.

"Nothing," I said, turning quietly.

I walked deeper into the shadows until I stopped face-to-face with him. I saw the enchantment in his hand as he whispered something, activating the spell, and a dark smoke wrapped around us – a spell of concealment. No one would see or hear us now.

"Don't lie to me, son." His voice was calm, yet there was a clear warning in it.

"There is nothing troubling me. There's just been a lot of change within the castle, and I just want to make sure nothing comes in the way," I lied smoothly. He raised an eyebrow.

"Changes?" I wondered how much he knew…

"Andres's daughter, Charlene, isn't his. She was born from an affair Soleil had," I started.

Dad smirked, "I always knew that one was a snake. His loss. But then… does that mean… what of the heart?" His voice became serious, cold even, and I didn't miss the urgency in it.

"We can take this kingdom with or without the heart. We don't need it," I replied quietly. Dad shook his head, his brows furrowed together.

"We need it at all costs… there must be something. Didn't you say Wenyu confirmed it?"

"Yes, there was another girl present. That's something I wanted to tell you. She is proved to be Andres' daughter, born from an affair," I replied. I didn't want to tell him, but I should have known nothing would get by him.

"Oh? Interesting… who is she?" He asked sharply.

"The Beta's daughter," I forced myself to reply. "Andres is announcing her today as his heir, and he wants me to get engaged to her."

"The woman you were attracted to…" Yeah, he remembered that too. "Tell me, Theon. Your heart is not weakening you, is it? Are you worried that this fake relationship of yours should not start on lies?" His voice was harsh and rough, the dangerous underlying warning becoming clear.

"Not at all. This engagement is all a lie, all a goal to get what we want. Why would I feel guilty?" I replied icily.

"Good. Get engaged to her, mark her, and she is in your grasp, yours to use and control however you wish. Remember that is all she is."

"She isn't that easy… she's anything but meek, Dad, she's a fighter. Strong, confident, and just. She reminds me of Mom," I said quietly, trying not to let my irritation out. "She won't bend to anyone." He scoffed and slapped my shoulder.

"Your mother was one of a kind. No daughter of Andres can match to her," he growled lowly. "Your mother submitted to me; no matter how strong she was, she still knew I was her Alpha. Be a man and control her." I looked at him emotionlessly. They were words I, myself, would use, but now… they fucking irked me.

"Andres didn't raise her, nor is she fond of him," I remarked instead, hiding my anger. I don't know what I was trying to prove, but he was wrong about her. His hand clamped down on my shoulder, and he chuckled, a chuckle that held no humour or amusement.

"I actually want to meet this one. After all, despite my constant warning, you seem a little too attached. It intrigues me. You have always disliked people disobeying you, even Iyara was a gentle one. So I want to know what kind of magic this one has done on you." His voice became darker as he moved back.

"None," I said coldly. "She is nothing to me."

Our eyes locked, and I held his gaze, refusing to look away. After a moment, he nodded and turned away.

"Well, make sure this engagement goes through. If you get the chance to mark her, take it, but make sure she does not mark you." I nodded. I wasn't going to mark her. I needed her gone... "The heart is within our grasp. The power of this kingdom will be soon, too. Nothing will stop us from taking our place as the true ruling family." I glanced at him, seeing the rage and hunger for power in his eyes. Revenge...

"Anything more on the siren that killed Mom?" I asked. He looked at me as if pulled from his thoughts.

"Hmm? No, nothing yet." I nodded.

"I came here knowing that you would handle that. Finding Mom and Thalia's killer was far more important than taking over this pack -" A low menacing growl ripped from his throat, and he grabbed me by my arm. I twisted it, breaking free, my eyes flashing. "I may be your son, but I will not let you fucking disrespect me," I growled warningly, fuelling my irritation into this conversation.

"We need to be in power! Do you think the Obsidian Shadow Pack can roam the seas openly with the current issues?"

"I was, wasn't I? I was out there. I know taking over the middle kingdom is important... but finding the siren who killed Mom is far more. That is where vengeance truly lies," I said quietly. The blackness was lifting as the spell began to dissipate. Our time was over.

"Once I am Alpha, you are free to roam the seas," he replied, trying to control his anger.

"Hmm. So, in the end, it will still be me who needs to do it? Perfect. At least I'll get the job done," I replied, unable to keep the bitterness from filtering into my voice. Two years... wasted.

"Nathalia will be avenged. She was my true mate. I felt her death," he said gravely. I didn't respond.

True mate... yet, he had claimed her but refused to allow her to mark him just to save himself from an unforeseen death. It was something many chose to do... but now, when it came to Yileyna, although she wasn't my true mate, imagining marking her to claim her alone sounded... sick. How had Mom even allowed that? Questions that I would never have considered before were now flitting into my mind.

"I should go before I'm missed," I said curtly.

"I'll be watching, son; don't worry. We are so close. We will bring this city to its knees."

"Yeah."

I gave him a bow of my head before I walked away. The bright lights of the city were warm and welcoming, but they did nothing to pull me from the chilling thoughts that consumed my mind.

I had just returned to the castle, heading to my room to get ready for the night, when I stopped in my tracks, spotting Charlene standing outside my door with a small, uncomfortable smile on her face.

"Hey, Theon." I raised an eyebrow, unlocking my door.

"What do you want?"

It was strange. Someone I had simply hated for who their father was, was now of no importance. In some ways, I wished it was her who had the heart. I wouldn't care what happened to her… but Yileyna…

"I wanted to tell you something," she said, now holding out a bag she was carrying. "Sent by the royal tailors…" I took it from her, entering my room and looking at her coldly.

"What is it? Tell me and get out."

She nodded, staying in the doorway as if scared to be in the same room alone as me. Smart. The memory of what happened the last time she was here came to my mind.

"It's about back when you first came to Westerfell… back when I saved you from that Naga…" I frowned. Where was this going?

"Yeah, what of it?" I asked coldly. She took a deep breath, as if readying herself for something big.

"It was Yileyna who saved you. She was the one who risked her life that day… I was… I was scared, and I thought you were dead, but she, she refused to leave you, saying what if there was a chance you were alive." My heart thudded as her words echoed in my mind.

"Yileyna? But you both said it was you, remember?" I said sharply. A look of guilt washed over her face before she looked down.

"No… I just… you were handsome, and I wanted to be the hero, so I asked her if I could say it was me," she mumbled.

Yileyna had saved me that day… I was meant to end up on shore, injured but alive, but then a Naga had attacked me. In my state, I was unable to fight it and I had almost died…

Fuck, she had saved me…

"Why tell me now?" I asked quietly, unable to digest the new information. Why was fate pulling me to Yileyna every single fucking time?

"Because… you two are going to be engaged, and she really is someone with a huge heart. She's selfless and she deserves the best. I know you don't like me, and you only tolerated me because I was the king's daughter, and maybe because you thought I saved you. But I'm neither of those things. Please, treat her well. Don't hurt her again."

Their bond was so strong, but seeing it hurt. It reminded me somewhat of the bond between Thea and Thalia… a bond which left Thea broken after Thalia's death. I hated how it brought back memories of them, and the thought of how Yileyna would feel once Charlene was taken from her...

"Leave," I commanded. She nodded before obeying and shutting the door behind her.

My resolve and the road to revenge were becoming distorted. Yileyna may have been my saviour, but she was also becoming the reason behind my failure.

I entered the bathroom, stripping and stepping into the shower. My mind was still in turmoil as I got dressed in the suit that was given to me. Silver… the colour of this pack. I pulled on the shirt, which had a ruffle along the buttons. Where I usually would have cast it aside, I was far too caught up in my thoughts to care.

I looked at the small box containing the ring I had purchased earlier. If she knew my truth, she would cast me aside no matter who forced her to do this. She was already angry with me; I had hurt her plenty of times, and I was about to do so again… soon…

I sighed, snapping the box shut when a sudden thought came to my head. I knew what I needed to do. My heart thundered knowing this could get me trouble… but… I didn't care. I had to take the risk. I was losing my sanity knowing what was to come. I needed to try one last time to see if she'd see reason and if not… then I'd have to do this the hard way…

More Lies

THEON

THE GRAND HALL WAS lit brightly. I waited for her arrival, but to my irritation, Bolton came over. Clearly I hadn't hurt him enough, since he was up and walking again.

"Hey, so I heard the news," he said with a smile that didn't reach his eyes.

"Told you she was mine, one way or another," I replied arrogantly.

"Yeah, you did… as long as she wants you. Treat her well, Theon. She's a jewel that many would love to attain," he said, his eyes hard as he looked at me sharply. *Yeah, you have no fucking idea.*

"I second that statement, Yileyna is ravishing."

I turned my cold glare on Zarian. He smirked as he tapped his arm where he wore the band of a member of the royal court, Yileyna's trainer, and with it, untouchable – for now. I didn't bother replying before he shook hands with Raiden.

"It's an honour to meet you again, Sir Raiden Bolton."

"Likewise, Lord Zarian."

I ignored their petty exchange. So Andres had let the Gammas know that Yileyna was his? Well, it made sense since they had seen her display of power…

I saw Grayson standing beside Henry, but despite Andres being here, the queen wasn't... interesting.

The doors opened, and a silence fell as everyone turned their attention to the double doors that were kept only for the royals to enter from, and there she was... looking beyond breathtaking.

My heart skipped a beat as time seemed to stand still. The lights in the hall only made her glow even more. She wore a floor-length gown with a sheer bodice. It had long, sheer, fitted sleeves encrusted with diamonds, while the belted skirt was a shimmering silver.

I won't deny that my gaze lingered on her breasts for a few moments longer as she descended the stairs, the jewels on her bodice expertly concealing her nipples. *I wouldn't mind tearing that dress from her…* Blood rushed south, and I forced my gaze up to her gorgeous face. Her makeup was alluring, but it was lighter than the other night, working on highlighting her natural beauty. Her hair was styled up, and on top of her head sat a tiara, a blinding reminder of who she truly was...

She turned and smiled at Charlene before taking her hand when they reached the bottom. Both women walked towards where Andres was standing. He greeted them both with a kiss on the forehead, one that Charlene welcomed and Yileyna remained indifferent to. She was not his daughter by anything more than blood…

The music stopped and the chatter died down as he stepped forward.

"My people! Welcome once again. Tonight is a very important night, yet with it there are some concerning matters that I must address…" He placed an arm around both Yileyna and Charlene, both having different expressions on their faces at his move. Charlene smiled up at him whilst Yileyna pursed her lips, forcing a small smile.

I smirked. Goddess, she was so fucking beautiful and real. The allure of a crown and title didn't make her blind to Andres's antics. Just like the storm she is…

It seemed everyone noticed the king's gesture and her appearance.

"Isn't that Yileyna De'Lacor?"

"Why is she wearing a royal crown?"

"Why is the king with her…"

"As you can see, I have these two young women with me tonight. It is with great disappointment that I must share something that has recently come to light. My Queen, your Luna, has committed a great crime!" I raised an eyebrow. I wasn't expecting that…

Bolton exchanged looks with Zarian and me as we all listened to what the king had to say. Was he actually going to announce the queen's infidelity?

"A heinous crime that I could never imagine..."

Henry, Grayson, and their mates looked confused, too, as the king let go of Charlene and placed his hands on Yileyna's slender shoulders. "This woman before you, a woman who was accused of possessing an artefact of the Hale family, is innocent. You may have heard that I had Gamma Grayson Sanchez thrown into prison. Well, the truth is, I did." I frowned. Something wasn't right here...

A ripple of confusion flowed through the crowd as Andres nodded gravely.

"However, behind it all was the hand of none other than your Luna! Not only did she try to frame this young woman by giving her this amulet, but when Gamma Grayson, who suspected it, questioned her, she lied and said he was a traitor!"

A murmur of gasps rippled through the room, and I frowned. Painting Grayson as a hero...

Realisation of what he was trying to do dawned upon me. He was going to manipulate the entire situation to suit him. I crossed my arms, waiting to see what exactly he was going to do...

"As you all know, years ago, Soleil was not able to conceive, and so we decided to try other means to secure an heir. This was kept a secret and was always meant to be a secret. Soleil played along... playing the role of being pregnant," he said gravely. I narrowed my eyes. He was going to save his own reputation...

Yileyna looked confused as well, glancing over at Charlene. The crowd was buying it... I could see from the concern on their faces.

"We sought out a strong she-wolf to be the mother of my child, and she delivered!" He motioned to Charlene, who was pale, before he shook his head. "Or so we thought, for out of her jealousy, Soleil decided to betray me! She sent the she-wolf away and brought home the child of another."

And I didn't think you could fall any lower Andres. He was throwing Charlene under the cart. The expressions on both Yileyna's and Charlene's faces were opposite of one another. Yileyna's chest was heaving, her face livid, whilst Charlene looked devastated.

"Charlene... my dear Charlene... she is not my child, but I raised her as my own." He patted her back despite the fact she was fighting back her tears. He may think he was being loving, but he had just stripped her of everything in a matter of seconds.

"The queen was kept away from the public eye for her pregnancy..."

"No wonder... it wasn't only for her safety..."

"Who would have thought."

The king raised a hand as Yileyna took deep breaths, trying to calm herself.

"As for my real daughter. Once she was born, Soleil had her cast in the sea to die, and that was when William De'Lacor found and raised her as his own. Perhaps the only good thing he has done! I may not have known it, but my daughter has always been close. It has been confirmed that she is mine, and with it, she is my true heir!"

The sound of thunder in the sky outside was deafening, but despite it, Yileyna remained silent. Her anger was making her tremble, but she didn't speak... I wondered what Andres had said to her for her to listen to him when I could tell she was seething. I could feel her aura and see Zarian motioning for her to focus. Her eyes were locked with his, and her breathing became erratic as she fought to control herself.

"How shocking..."

"The Luna is despicable!"

"I hope she is punished... my, if not for her, we wouldn't have had to see this day..."

"And so tonight, I will take the oath, making Yileyna my true heir! And to have her engaged to Theon of Westerfell!" Everyone but Bolton and I clapped.

Charlene gave a trembling smile before she muttered an 'excuse me' and tried to walk away as gracefully as possible, but her expression was crumbling with each passing second. Yileyna pulled away from Andres, rushing after her friend. I could see the pain and guilt on her face, and it irritated me. Indirectly, Andres, the bastard, had hurt her as well.

"That was..." Bolton murmured.

"Low," I said before I walked towards the exit where Yileyna had disappeared.

An Exchange of Rings

YILEYNA

"Charlene!"

She had broken into a run the moment she was out of sight, but I caught up fast, grabbing hold of her arm as I battled my emotions, trying to calm the storm that was raging outside and within me. *Breathe…*

"My queen…" I said softly as she refused to look at me. I tugged her around gently and she turned. It killed to see the fat tears spilling down her cheeks. I pulled her into my arms, hugging her tightly.

"Just like that, he cast me aside," she whispered.

"Well, he just lost the only daughter he had. It's his loss," I said angrily as she pulled away.

"I'll ruin your dress," she said, wiping away her tears as she wrapped her arms around herself. "It hurts… not only have I lost Mom… but Dad, too…"

I frowned. Maybe Gamma Grayson needed to know… maybe he would be the father she needed. The king and queen were both disgusting in my eyes.

"He doesn't deserve to call you daughter. Don't let his words get to you," I comforted her, stroking her arm and brushing her tears away gently. She looked down and nodded, forcing a smile.

"Yeah… I'm just… the daughter of no one now… just an orphan who took the place of the true princess."

"I'm sorry, Charl."

"Don't. Why apologise for something you have no hand in? I'm just… upset with Dad…" she whispered. "Sure, he addressed me as his daughter, but at the same time, he insulted me." There was nothing to say to that.

How do I tell her he didn't deserve her or could justify any of this? His lies had been shocking. I gave her another hug as we heard footsteps. Charlene turned away, taking a deep breath as she patted her tears away.

Theon's scent reached me before he came into view, my heart skipping a beat as I looked him over. Black pants, a satin shirt, and boots, with a silver and black jacket on top. A chain was on the side of his pants, and I couldn't deny that he looked incredibly handsome, dangerously sexy… the expression on his face emphasised his chiselled jaw and cheekbones.

"You're staring," he said, making me blush before he added quietly, "Unless we both get to stare." My eyes widened, and I wondered if he had actually said that or if it had just been my imagination.

He was looking towards the window now, frowning at the storm outside, before he turned to me.

"I came to make sure you didn't lose control," he remarked, looking me over. My stomach fluttered when his eyes darkened with clear approval.

"Or he came to admire how beautiful you look," Charlene said, smiling as she gave my hand a squeeze. Apart from her eyes being slightly red, she looked normal. It didn't mean the king's words were forgotten, Charlene was just good at hiding her emotions.

"Or that," Theon said huskily, making me raise my eyebrow.

"Did you practise how to be charming all morning? Must have been hard work," I mocked.

"I already told you, charming doesn't work for you now, does it?"

"Excuse me…" Charlene remarked, suppressing a smirk. I glanced at her, poking my eyes out, but she simply winked. "I will leave the soon-to-be-engaged couple to it…"

"I'd appreciate that," Theon said, surprising me further. Charlene's footsteps faded away as I looked into the gorgeous amber eyes of the man before me.

"I'm left speechless with the change in persona," I mocked as he tilted his head.

"I assure you I haven't changed…" He stepped closer, making my heart skip a beat as I tried not to move back. "Relax, I'm not going to bite."

He reached out, cupping my neck as he ran his thumb down the centre. I swallowed, my heart pounding against my ribcage. Our eyes locked and the only thing I could think of was the marks that he used to leave on me, from a time that felt like so long ago…

"What's on your mind?" He asked quietly, his low, husky tone making my core clench.

"Not you," I managed to respond breathlessly. He leaned in, his lips grazing my ear, making my breath hitch.

"Just me fucking you?" I closed my eyes. My entire body was reacting to him.

Don't go there…

"Don't get so cocky…" I murmured, placing my hand on his firm chest and pushing him back slightly. He moved back, and something the king said came to mind. "Is it true the king threatened you with me if you didn't agree to Charlene?" A flicker of surprise crossed his face, but he masked it fast. I was getting better at seeing through that mask of his…

"Who said that?" He asked, frowning.

"The king."

"Because you refused to get engaged to me?"

"Maybe."

"Don't talk in a roundabout way, little storm," he warned, his hand tightening around my throat… "I see you didn't wear a necklace…"

"I forgot to," I lied; the truth was I had refused it on purpose.

"I'm sure," he replied arrogantly.

"Don't avoid what I'm asking you, Theon. Did the king threaten you?" His free hand ran down my arm painstakingly slowly, leaving a trail of pleasure in its wake before it snaked around my waist, making my breath hitch.

"It doesn't matter, Yileyna… but there's something I want to talk to you about," he said seriously as he let go of my neck and instead took hold of my chin.

"What is it?" I asked, hearing the thudding of his racing heart.

"Let's go somewhere -"

"Excuse me, but the king wants you two in the hall," Ryan said, interrupting Theon.

His eyes went to our position. We were crushed together and standing far too close. I quickly pulled away, my cheeks flushing lightly. Theon frowned, but I could see his irritation that he was masking rather well. I wondered what it was that he wanted to talk about.

"We should go. We'll talk after..." I suggested softly. He frowned and gave a small nod as he led the way back.

My irritation at the king returned with full force when I saw him standing there as if nothing had happened, as if his words had no impact on anyone. Did he only care for himself?

Charlene was standing by Andrea, who was asking her something and looked sympathetic as Charlene smiled gracefully back.

"Before we drink and feast, let us begin with the oath and then move on to the exchanging of rings!" The king said loudly.

I looked at Theon. It didn't feel real. Was I really getting engaged to him? Everyone gathered around, all eyes on us as we moved to the dais, and the king faced me.

"I bear witness under Selene's moon and before this audience that I take you, Yileyna Aphelion -"

"Yileyna De'Lacor. It won't work unless you take the name that I hold true to my heart," I said quietly, knowing that everyone could hear.

"She still holds the traitors' names... and wants to," someone whispered, but I ignored them as Andres frowned. No matter how much he didn't like it, it was the truth.

"I bear witness under Selene's moon and before this audience that I take you, Yileyna De'Lacor, as my heir. I acknowledge you as the future Alpha of the Silver Storm Pack and the ruler of Astalion, the middle kingdom. Do you, Yileyna De'Lacor, vow to uphold the rules, decorum, and values of this pack and those of this kingdom?"

Far better than you ever will.

"I, Yileyna De'Lacor, accept and acknowledge this position. I vow under the moon of Selene and before this gathering that I will always uphold the rules, decorum, and values of this pack and of this kingdom," I repeated before continuing, "and to always be true, just, and fair to all, regardless of rank, species, or status..."

I saw the small frown on the king's face, but it was fleeting as a murmur rippled through the crowd once more.

"Then I bind you to it by an oath of blood."

He took the knife from Gamma Henry, slicing his hand before I held mine out. He took it, making a deep cut along my palm. I made sure the blood didn't drip onto my dress as I ignored the sting of pain. We then shook hands, sealing the oath by blood. Everyone clapped, and Charlene passed me a cloth to wipe away the blood.

"Congratulations, my angel," she said, hugging me.

"Thank you, my queen," I replied, hugging her back tightly.

I held her close for a moment before I was pulled away from her, and everyone began congratulating me. Andrea, Zoe, Gamma Henry and Grayson, who looked a little pale despite everything, all gave their congratulations.

"Now we move on to the engagement of my daughter, Yileyna, and Theon of Westerfell," the king said clearly. "The rings." Andrea held out a glass tray that held two rings on it. "Theon..." The king said with a grin on his face, like a man whose birthday had come early. Theon frowned slightly before reaching into his pocket.

"I bought my own," he stated emotionlessly, taking not only me but several others by surprise. The king chuckled.

"Ah, of course!"

"Nice move," Ryan remarked. I stared at Theon as he flipped open the box. Theon got a ring... for me...

My resolve was crumbling, my heart pounding as he took the ring from the box.

Stay strong... this is only a political agreement...

I pressed a hand to my stomach, trying to control the wild fluttering that was taking place inside of it. Any resolve I had left melted the moment those smouldering eyes turned on me, locking with my own.

"So, shall we do this?" He asked, holding his hand out to me.

And just like that, the walls I had fought so hard to build around me shattered, the tidal wave of emotions hitting me hard as I looked at the hand that he now held out to me...

ALPHAS HUNTER

YILEYNA

I SMILED SOFTLY. I COULDN'T believe just that morning, I was beginning to feel doubtful about him to the point that I wondered if he could be a traitor. I shook my head and placed my hand in his.

"I guess we should," I replied airily, trying to ignore the sparks that softly tingled through me. A few guests chuckled whilst I heard someone say they should drink in mourning that I was no longer available.

I watched as Theon slid the stunning ring onto my finger. It was made from platinum white gold with a pale blue emerald cut diamond at its centre, surrounded by small clear diamonds that covered the double band of the ring itself. It was a perfect fit.

My heart was such a storm of emotions that I was no longer able to think straight. I took the ring for Theon from the cushion, my hand shaking as I held my hand out to him, his eyes burning into me.

"Any moment now," he whispered mockingly, making me try an attempt at a glare before I managed to slip the dark engraved ring onto his finger. The moment it was on, everyone broke into cheers and applause.

Everyone began to come over to greet us. It was all so fast that I was unable to remember who was who. Theon's arm slid around my waist protectively, pulling me to his side. Someone passed us drinks, but it was all a haze after that. People were introducing themselves, and others were asking questions about when the marriage would take place, asking the king when I would take over from him, when there would be an heir…

I replied when I could, trying to remain calm in the face of their obvious insinuation that I, as a female, was not enough and needed to produce an heir soon.

Congratulations!" Raiden said, now coming over, a smile on his face despite the glimmer of sadness in his eyes. "I'm happy for you."

"Thank you," I said softly. Pulling away from Theon, I hugged him. "Thank you for everything." *And I'm sorry… sorry I'm not the woman for you.*

"Nothing to thank me for," he said, giving me a tight squeeze.

"Well, well, well… congratulations."

My mood darkened as I recognised the voice of none other than Nikolai. I would never forget what he tried to do… ever. My heart thundered as Theon's eyes flashed.

"Thank you," I said icily.

"You look beautiful… Princess, now, right?"

"Keep talking, and you and your title will be dead soon enough," Theon said coldly, his eyes shimmering gold.

"I apologise for any insult caused. I'm only here to offer my congratulations…"

"Leave, Nikolai," Raiden said, frowning. Although he wasn't sure what was going on, it was obvious he could sense the tension. I ignored Nikolai's gaze that I could feel crawling along my skin, taking hold of Theon's arm.

"Come on, everyone's about to eat. Let's go talk," I whispered, placing my empty glass down.

"Yileyna, Theon, come on, it's time to eat," Charlene said. I glanced at Theon, who was frowning.

"Fuck, again," he muttered.

"We can talk later?" I suggested as he licked his lips and glanced at me.

"Doesn't seem like we have any other choice now, does it?" He asked, his hand caressing my waist. My heart skipped a beat as he yanked me close.

"Theon…" I knew we had a thousand eyes upon us.

"Yileyna…"

I smiled despite myself. I felt like I was on cloud nine, but a part of me was still scared. Was this really a dream come true?

The moment his fingers curled under my chin, tilting my head up and claiming my lips in a toe-curling, orgasm-inducing kiss, I lost all sense of reality. My entire body ignited with pleasure. I heard a small moan escape me, but it was so far away as I clung to him, gripping onto his shirt tightly. His lips moved against mine sinfully, my core clenching as he slipped his tongue into my mouth. Goddess…

I felt him throb against me, and he pulled away suddenly as if reality had just hit him, his eyes blazing gold, and I saw him scan the hall as if looking for someone.

"Everything okay?" I asked, confused. He nodded, looking into my eyes for a fleeting moment before he looked away.

"Yeah, let's go."

I was glad he kept a hold on my waist because I was sure if he had not been holding me, I would have fallen. My lips still tingled from his kiss, my heart still raced, and every nerve in my body seemed to buzz, feeling extra sensitive.

We walked to the Alpha King's table, and I was brought back to reality. I had not sat at this table for so long, but it still left a sour taste in my mouth. There were two empty seats on either side of the king. He motioned for Theon and me to take them. Theon took the seat where the queen usually sat, and I saw Charlene about to sit down in the seat next to her usual place. I walked over swiftly, flashing her a smile as I sat down on the other seat, pushing her towards her usual seat beside the king. She frowned slightly but sat down as the king gave me a disapproving frown. I ignored him, glancing over at Theon, who sat on his other side, looking as sexy and arrogant as ever.

I had somehow ended up back in his hold… but I couldn't deny I felt excited.

"How are you feeling?" I whispered to Charlene as the king made his small speech of thanks to the gods for the food before us. She gave me a nod and a smile.

"I'm okay," she replied, and I gave her hand a gentle squeeze, glad she was coping ok.

"So tell me, Princess Yileyna, how much do you know about the kingdom? After all, you were not raised to be an Alpha," one of the King's closest allies, Alpha Romeo, asked. He was a man a few years younger than the king and someone who had a powerful pack.

"I know enough to know that there are many things that need changing," I replied before the king interrupted.

"Now Theon here knows far more…" he said, making Alpha Romeo turn his attention to Theon.

"Goddess, the king should just marry Theon himself," I muttered, earning a giggle from Charlene and a glare from Theon. I simply smirked at him.

Both Alphas looked at me confused, as though they weren't sure if they had misheard. Neither asked. After all, it would be an insult to their mighty hearing if they couldn't hear properly. I blinked innocently, then returned to their conversation, and I, too, paid attention to it.

Dinner passed in a blur, but I was glad to realise that I knew rather a lot, and when I did give my input, even the King was surprised at times. I didn't shy away from speaking my mind or asking about something that I did not understand, and by the end of the meal, Alpha Romeo told the king that he felt I would make a good Alpha.

"You impress me," the king said to me with a nod of approval as an elder Alpha couple walked away.

"I am not trying to impress anyone," I replied, just as I heard heavy footsteps. I turned, instantly sensing the tension from both the king and Theon.

I looked at the man who was approaching, flanked by two men. Power oozed off him. He was handsome, rugged, muscular, and not much shorter than Theon. His brown hair, which was long on top, was sleeked back and tied. His taupe-coloured eyes were sharp, and he had a short beard with a scar across the bridge of his nose. He didn't look much older than Theon, dressed a lot simpler than most here, yet he dripped with authority and dominance.

"Alpha Andres, it's been a while." He smiled ever so slightly, but somehow it looked more challenging.

"Alpha Hunter Slade Carson… it's an honour. Yileyna, meet Alpha Hunter of the Iron Claw Pack. Alpha Hunter, my daughter, Yileyna, and her fiancé Theon."

Iron Claw… I now realised why they were so tense. The Iron Claw Pack was a neutral pack that didn't get involved with the political aspect of the kingdom, yet they were powerful and guarded the entire far border that separated us from Naraan – a Naga Empire.

"It's an honour, Alpha Yileyna, Alpha Theon…" He took my hand in his large calloused one, placing a rough kiss on the back of it before turning his attention to Theon. A small smirk crossed his lips before he stepped forward. "Congratulations," he said, giving Theon a manly hug, one which he returned emotionlessly.

"Thank you," Theon replied curtly.

Hunter smirked slightly before his dangerous gaze turned to Charlene, who stood behind me. I didn't miss the way he gave her a once-over, with that familiar look of lust and hunger that he hid well. Men…

"And this is your other daughter, correct?" He asked the king.

"Yes. My daughter, Charlene," the king said, pushing Charlene forward.

"It's a pleasure to meet you, Alpha Hunter," Charlene said gracefully.

"The pleasure's all mine," he responded in a deep voice that seemed to resonate from within his chest.

He held his hand out to her, and Charlene took it. He gave it a kiss, one that lasted longer than mine, his eyes locked with hers. I almost smiled, promising myself I would tease her later. She blushed as he let go of her hand and gave the king a nod.

"How is the eastern border?" The king asked, looking between Charlene and Hunter. I could almost see the cogs turning in his head as he looked at Charlene for a moment before turning his attention back to Hunter.

"The usual. Naga's being bastards, so we pick them off like the snakes they are," he said with a cold smirk. That was harsh…

"When they attack, of course?" Charlene asked as Hunter tilted his head, raising an eyebrow at her.

"Whenever they are too close to the border," he corrected her as the king nodded in approval.

"As it should be," he said, frowning at her.

Charlene and I exchanged looks but said nothing. Something about Hunter Slade gave me an unnerving feeling, but I wasn't about to argue with him. It was obvious things weren't as calm as they appeared here.

"Excuse us," Theon said coldly, placing a hand on my lower back.

The two men nodded as Charlene also bowed her head, giving me a wink and mouthing 'good luck' before she, too, excused herself and went over to where Ryan and Raiden were standing. I didn't miss Hunter's gaze following her.

I glanced at her as both Ryan and Raiden complimented her. I wondered how she felt knowing that Ryan was her brother…

Moments of Pleasure

YILEYNA

We walked out into the second-floor hallway. This part of the building had a little roof. We stuck to walking under the protection of the roof above our heads, watching the rain fall to the courtyard below. Despite it being quieter here, there were still many people talking and strolling around, so we took the next stairs up. Theon led the way, scanning the area as he went. It was clear he was looking for somewhere quiet to talk. He finally stopped when we were in a secluded area.

"Ah, this is perfect," I said, looking up at the open sky as I walked to the edge of the balcony that circled around the centre of the middle courtyard. We were on the third floor, and there was no one up here save from us.

"Just the two of us…" He said huskily, making my heart skip a beat.

"Yes." I turned my back towards him as I gripped the balcony rail, leaning beside me. He closed the gap between us, and I bit my lips as his scent hit me. He smirked, placing his hands on the balcony on each side of my waist.

"Who would have thought we'd ever end up engaged?" He remarked, glancing down at my breasts before looking back into my eyes. My heart squeezed before I sighed, the sprinkle of rain was hitting my back and arms, but I didn't care.

"Not me… you broke me when you left. I gave you everything," I said quietly, unable to hide the pain in my voice. He frowned, nodding slightly.

"I told you I'd destroy you… I'm not the type of man one wants for their mate." I shook my head.

"You need to give yourself some credit, Theon. You care, in your own crazy way, you have shown that... but what now? Will you leave me?" I looked into his eyes, hoping for some sort of reassurance. "Just promise me you won't do it again… that you won't leave me again," I whispered, placing a hand on his face. Because I don't think I had the strength to rebuild myself if it happened.

"You are my kryptonite, one I can't seem to live without. I don't seem to have the willpower to leave you… even when I should…" He frowned, looking down. That was all I needed to hear. "But don't get attached Yiley-"

"Not again, stop. I don't want to hear it. We're engaged, let's start afresh… I don't think I can handle another heartbreak," I whispered, leaning into him. I pulled him closer, about to kiss him when he nudged my nose with his. His heart was racing, and to my surprise, he didn't initiate the kiss. I leaned in, our breath mingling.

"Fuck, Leyna…" he muttered, one arm wrapping around my waist, the other tangling in my hair as he fought against himself.

"Kiss me, Theon," I whispered seductively.

I tilted my head up, pressing my lips to his. One arm snaked around his waist, the other on his chest as he kissed me like there was no tomorrow. I gasped when his squeezed my ass, pressing me hard against him as a low groan rumbled against my mouth. He kissed me harder and rougher. His tongue slipped into my mouth, exploring and ravishing every inch of it.

I moaned softly, my core clenching. As if in response, he throbbed against my stomach, his hand now squeezing my ass. The scent of my arousal filled the air, but I didn't care. I wanted him to know how much I needed him…

He pulled me from the balcony, pressing me against the pillar next to it and pulling up my dress. I moaned, my nails digging into his neck. He broke away from our lips, both of us breathing hard. Hunger and lust coated his eyes.

"We need to talk," he growled, his hand slipping under my dress, caressing my inner thighs. No, I wanted him now. I ran my hand over his rock-hard bulge, making him hiss. "Fuck."

"We can talk later," I whimpered, parting my legs slightly as his hand rubbed against my molten core. His eyes flashed as he ripped my panties off, his finger rubbing my pussy roughly.

I cried out, but he cut it off by claiming my lips in a bruising kiss once more. He yanked my hair, and I moaned, pleasure rushing through me as his fingers assaulted my clit. *Goddess, this pleasure…*

"Theon… fuck…"

He kissed my jaw and my neck, tearing my dress from my breasts as he took one of them in his hand. I whimpered at the pain and pleasure that mixed so perfectly under his touch as he squeezed my breast tightly.

"Fuck…" I breathed as he broke away and began to unbuckle his pants. I ran my hand over his hard shaft, my pussy clenching in need, only for Theon to grab hold of my wrist.

"Play with yourself," he growled, his eyes blazing as he glanced down at my exposed lower region.

My stomach fluttered as I pushed my dress up, parting my pussy lips with two fingers. I slipped my index finger into his mouth, letting him run his tongue along it before I placed it on my clit. There was no sense of logic anymore… I wanted him and he wanted me. This addiction, this passion, this obsession… it was everything and more.

The cool air fanned my exposed skin and I let my eyes flutter half shut as I rubbed circles on my clit. He watched me with hunger as he ran his hand along his delicious, thick long cock. I moaned.

"Fuck, Theon, fuck me…" I whimpered pleadingly as the pressure began building within me, my eyes on his cock as he stroked it slowly. Fuck, even in his hand, it looked so big…

"Eyes on me, little storm. Touch yourself and beg me to fuck you," he growled.

I forced my gaze away from his cock, and stared into his face, only for him to watch my pussy. The very thought that I was entirely exposed to him made me wetter, and I let my moans out, not caring to hold back.

He growled, wrapping his free hand around my throat as he stepped forward, crouching slightly as he positioned himself at my entrance before he thrust his cock into me, squeezing my throat so tight I couldn't even scream as his girth stretched me out. For a moment I couldn't breathe, but Theon didn't give me a moment to adjust as he began ramming into me brutally...

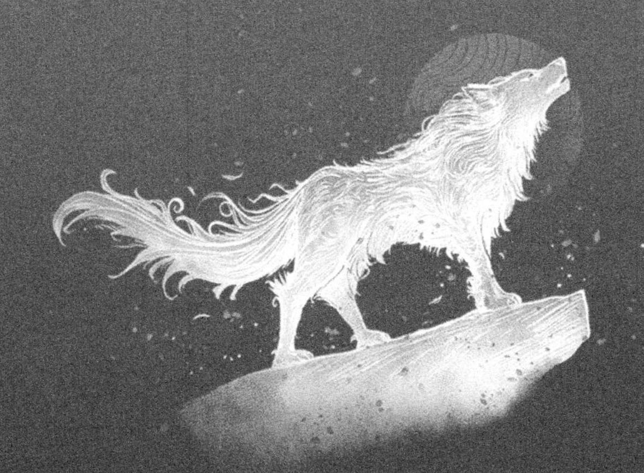

Unveiled Reality

YILEYNA

My eyes rolled as pain and overwhelming pleasure coursed through me, every thrust hitting my g-spot. His lips crushed against mine in a rough kiss as he pulled out before slamming in completely.

"Ouch… fuck, Theon," I whimpered, my legs trembling.

"Too late. You wanted me to fuck this pussy hard, right?"

"Yes... fuck, Theon…" I gasped, my vision darkening. He pulled out fully, leaving me gasping and feeling empty, before he delivered a sharp slap to my pussy. "Ah!"

"Turn around," he commanded.

I obeyed, clinging onto the pillar as he thrust into my pussy from behind. I gasped as he lifted one of my thighs, driving fully into me, his other hand around my throat as he kissed my neck and shoulders hungrily. Only the sound of his breathless grunts and my wanton moans filled my ears. I knew that we might be heard, even the rain and wind wouldn't drown us out, but I didn't care. Right then, all I wanted was this moment, this insane and intense pleasure that only he could drown me in.

The intense pleasure was nearing its breaking point and I knew he was close too, his hand digging into the flesh of my thigh as he pounded me hard and fast.

"Ah, fuck, baby," he groaned, "You are so fucking tight…"

I whimpered, unable to respond as I was thrown over the edge, pleasure erupting through me like a thousand bolts of lightning. A moan of pure satisfaction left my lips as he delivered a few harsh thrusts before he pulled out, and I felt his seed coat my inner thigh. He instantly caught my body that almost collapsed, kissing my neck hungrily as he breathed hard.

"Goddess…" I whimpered, feeling like a puddle of jelly.

"More like you are a fucking Goddess," he murmured huskily, making me shiver in delight when his tongue flicked my neck. His hands squeezed my breasts before he pulled the torn fabric up over my chest, covering me as he leaned in, claiming my lips in a soft yet passionate kiss. It was different, fuelled by intense emotions as he pulled me into his arms, holding me so protectively I didn't ever want him to let go. We broke apart after a few moments and he smoothly zipped his pants back up.

"I'm so tired now…" I whispered softly, leaning into his hard, firm chest, wanting to close my eyes.

"I need to talk to you, Yileyna, it's important," he said quietly. His heart rate had spiked. I frowned, turning to look at him. It must be something serious. He kept going back to it…

"What is it, Theon?" I asked as he guided me to the balcony, allowing me to perch on it as he supported my weight.

"Hear me out," he said, his expression darkening as he looked me in the eye seriously. "Give me a chance to explain…" I nodded, concerned as I looked into those amber eyes. "Before that… you once said you loved me… I wonder what power it actually holds… I'm not who you think I am, Yileyna. When I said to you that I'll destroy you, I meant it." Words that he kept saying, constantly… but… why did it feel like it meant more than what I was taking them for?

"What do you mean?" I asked softly, caressing his face as I placed a soft kiss on his jaw. "Who exactly are you then?" What did he mean he wasn't what I thought? He didn't respond, simply taking hold of my chin and giving a small knowing smirk.

"I think deep down, you know… last night… I'm certain that you clicked, but you're denying it," he said softly, his voice so calm… so dangerous…

My heart thudded as the thought that had occurred last night returned to me, and I stared into his amber eyes. Amber eyes that now looked so dangerous…

Tell me it's not true... please tell me...

His words from last night... his conviction that there would be an attack. I swallowed hard, letting go of his face, holding my hand against my chest. His eyes never left me, not even once.

"Who... who are you, Theon?" I asked quietly, trying to squash the thoughts that filled my mind once again. His expression didn't change as he simply watched me, his knuckles running up and down my arm.

"You already know the answer to that, don't you?" He whispered, brushing his thumb over my lips with his other hand.

"I don't," I denied.

"Try again," he said, his voice sounding ominous as his eyes flashed. I let out a small shaky laugh.

"Theon, is this a joke?"

"I don't joke... I told you not to get attached. I will destroy your world and I already have." His voice was so quiet I could barely hear it over the wind and rain from the open balcony behind us. Theon was... could he somehow be from the Obsidian Shadow Pack? I refused to believe it. Why would he tell me if he was?

"Fine, you're part of the Obsidian Shadow Pack, sent to infiltrate the Silver Storm Pack," I said, rolling my eyes. His eyes flashed and a small humourless smirk crossed his lips before he leaned in, his minty breath fanning my face as he whispered in my ear.

"Good girl." My heart thumped as I jerked away from him.

"I was joking." He didn't respond, simply watching me unblinking.

Fear began to spread through me. I needed to alert the king! I needed to-

"Now you know... so let me take you away from here. You don't need to be around when things go down. Pick your side now, you should know which one is the one to choose. I will protect you. I will make sure no harm comes to you. Just trust me, please."

I couldn't focus, even if his tone was soft, I just couldn't. My heart crumpled as I stared at him. Lies... all of it...

This couldn't be true.

"Tell me this is a sick joke," I almost begged.

Silence.

"Tell me this is a prank, Theon."

I took a shuddering breath; he was caging me between his arms. I was at his mercy, but he still didn't reply. My mind raged with havoc as I tried

to comprehend it all.

"So, for the last two years, you lied? Was that attack with the Naga staged?" I cried, feeling the devastating pain in my chest crippling me. Had I risked my life for a traitor who didn't need saving?

I pressed a hand to my chest, trying to focus on my breathing. The rain was beating down faster, and I knew it was my doing. He was just watching me with an unreadable expression on his face.

"No, that was real. You saved me yet you lied about it. Why?"

"It doesn't matter, me or her, it fucking doesn't matter! You lied and played us! Theon, tell me. Did you know about the attack that night?" I stared up at him, fear squeezing my chest. "Theon… the night my parents died! Did you know of the incoming attack?" I whispered, horrified. I grabbed hold of his shirt, shaking him as I stared up at him. My entire world was crashing down around me, but nothing beat the terror within me. "Theon, tell me… my parents, they weren't traitors… were they? They were framed, weren't they?"

"Yileyna, calm down. Look at the weather," he said quietly, glancing at the sky behind me, but my head was pounding, and I didn't care. I couldn't focus on anything but the sheer reality of this revelation.

"Answer me, Theon." He looked into my eyes, his arms still around me.

"Yes, they were framed, and yes, I knew of the attack." I couldn't breathe. My hold on his shirt went limp.

"Then… did you… did you frame them?" I asked, horrified. He was the one on the inside… the one able to do it…

Silence and that flash of guilt in his eyes…

I gasped as I pushed him away, clamping my hands over my mouth. I had gotten my answer. Not only was Theon a traitor in our midst, but he was also the one who tarnished my parent's name…

"Yileyna, listen to me. It doesn't have to be this way. I did that before -"

I raised my hand, my heart pounding as rage consumed me.

"Don't… just don't. Two wrongs never make a right… what you did… I'll never forgive you! You will not get away with this!"

I turned, ready to get as far away from him, when he suddenly grabbed my arm, spun me around, and bent me backwards over the balcony. A scream left my lips, but his hand clamped over my mouth, cutting it off. The only thing keeping me from falling off the balcony was his hold on me. If he pushed me, I'd fall.

"Calm down and heed my word of warning, little storm; tell anyone, and everyone in this city who has ever been in contact with you will die… from Zarian to Marigold and let's not forget the younger Bolton… by now, you should know the power that I hold."

My blood ran cold as I looked into his cold eyes, the rain pouring down just behind us.

"You wouldn't…"

"Wouldn't I? I'm sure by now you know I'm capable of anything," his dangerous reply came. "One last chance, Yileyna. Choose me, and we can live a life together."

No.

My world seemed to crumble. Once again, I had been so stupid... so, so stupid...

"If I am to die, then I will die with honour. Not by the side of a traitor."

"And yet you said you loved me," he said, his voice devoid of emotions.

"I do, I love the part of you that I knew… I could die for you, but I cannot stand by your side and see you do wrong. This is wrong, Theon." I tried a final time; my heart was shattered but I refused to allow myself to fall into the depths of despair.

"Then you have chosen," he whispered, caressing my cheek softly before his eyes blazed, and he stabbed something into my neck. I gasped at the rush of pain. My eyes flew open before I suddenly felt my body grow heavy.

"What… did…you…"

"I told you, little storm… I would destroy you…"

With those words, he suddenly pushed me, shoving me off the balcony. My scream pierced the air, the wind rushing through my hair as I went spiralling downwards…

Awakening

YILEYNA

I awoke with a gasp. My entire body felt heavy. My eyes flew open, my heart thundering with confusion as I looked around the room. Where was I? What happened? I felt delirious and confused, jolting upright in bed.

Where am I?

I looked around, trying to focus, and it took me a moment to realise I was in the guest room at the Alpha's quarters… *How did I get here?*

It looked to be mid-afternoon outside, but from the howling wind, I could tell the weather was rough. The cold was obvious in the room too. The huge log fire was lit ablaze. I placed a hand to my head just as everything came rushing back.

Theon… the Obsidian Shadow Pack… the truth…

My heart pounded, and I pushed the blanket off, stumbling out of bed. I needed to tell someone! Suddenly, the door opened, and my heart leapt seeing Charlene standing there with a few towels and a bucket in her arms.

"Yileyna! Goddess! Yileyna's awake!" She shouted in relief as she ran to me, dropping the bucket of water and catching me before I fell to the ground as the warm water splashed over our legs. I couldn't even feel my legs…

I heard footsteps before Theon appeared at the door. My heart thumped in fear as I stared at him. He pushed me…

His look of surprise changed to a deep frown as he came over quickly, taking me from Charlene. I opened my mouth to talk but no sound came out, it felt like I had swallowed handfuls of sand. Only a weak croak left my mouth.

"Bring her water!" Theon growled, carrying me to the bed as my chest heaved, staring up at him.

"Yes!" Charlene nodded, her eyes full of tears of happiness as she rushed from the room.

"So, you're awake…" Theon said quietly, running his fingers through my hair. Looking into his eyes for a moment, I almost thought I saw concern and worry, but it was just my imagination. *I… I needed to tell someone… Do I pretend I forgot that night?*

"What happened to me?" I asked, feinting a look of confusion. He smirked slightly, tilting his head.

"You don't remember?"

"No… I don't remember anything," I said, rubbing my head.

Calm down, Yileyna… His eyes glinted as he leaned closer, tilting my chin up before he pressed his lips to mine. A ripple of pleasure rushed through me despite the fear that was consuming me.

"Lies…" he whispered, making me gasp as I jerked away. "You remember it all…"

"Dad! Yileyna has awoken!" I heard Charlene say. I needed to tell the king…

"Let's keep that night between us. We wouldn't want anyone to lose their pretty head of ginger hair now, would we?" Theon asked softly, brushing his thumb over my lips. *Charlene…*

"You wouldn't," I croaked out hoarsely. He ran his fingers through my hair, raising an eyebrow, his face as emotionless as ever.

"We both know I would."

I stared at him. The man before me was unrecognisable, but I knew what he was capable of… he was the reason my parents were dead… he had pushed me from the top floor… he would kill Charlene if I opened my mouth.

"Yileyna!"

For the first time in my life, I was relieved to see the king, feeling safer with his presence around than with Theon. When he embraced me, I held on tight, I needed to give him a message… how?

The hug didn't last long enough for me to come up with an idea, and Theon was right there sitting on the bed.

"Here, my angel," Charlene said, passing me the glass of water as she sat beside me on the bed. I leaned into her, my heart pounding as she placed the glass to my lips, helping me drink.

"Thank the goddess, you are awake. After that attack, I was worried."

"Attack?" I asked, looking at Theon. He nodded.

"That night, when I left you to go to the bathroom, I heard the sound of a scuffle, and all I saw was the figure push you off the balcony. I caught you just before you hit the ground, however, he seemed to have used some sort of poison or spell on you so that you were unable to be awoken at all," Theon said emotionlessly. So that's the story he fed everyone?

"Oh. Well, I hope he's caught and castrated," I spat, my chest heaving with irritation.

"Careful, little storm. We don't want anyone getting hurt. You should rest."

"Theon's right. You have been out for a few weeks."

"A few weeks?" I asked sharply, looking at Charlene.

"It's the full moon tonight, Leyna," she replied with a gentle smile. I had been unconscious for that long?

"But it's fine, you are awake now. Somehow the culprit got away, but we are still looking," the king said seriously. "I have matters to attend to, so I will be going. Theon, enjoy the evening with your fiancé." Charlene looked at me, about to get up but something made her change her mind and she smiled, holding me tighter.

"I will stay, too," she said. "There's much I need to tell Yileyna."

"Of course," I said, holding her hand tightly. If I was able to give her a signal... I would. But Theon was right here...

He was sitting opposite us, his hand on my thigh as he leaned back on his elbow as emotionless and calm as ever.

"What have I missed?" I asked her, dragging my eyes from Theon.

"Well... Mom's in the cells... for treason, and no one is allowed to see her," she said quietly. "The Obsidian Shadow Pack have been sighted moving closer... we fear there will be an attack before the end of winter."

"I see..." I said, looking at Theon. If he had wanted to... he could have killed me... He wanted me to choose him. Maybe I could talk some sense into him.

Charlene continued, telling how two sirens were seen right up the coast last week.

"It was strange, like they were looking for something or someone." She shivered.

"Were they killed?" I asked.

"I killed one, one got away," Theon added quietly. I nodded before Charlene smiled.

"I'll have someone bring you food, you two could use a moment alone." She winked at me before pulling free. My heart thudded as I watched her leave, shutting the door behind herself.

"What are you planning to do?" I asked him.

"Nothing at all. You weren't supposed to wake up for at least another week… I was told that the enchantment was strong enough to keep an Alpha out for a month," he replied, frowning coldly. "Last chance, Yileyna. Think this over… we both know Andres is not the best king -"

"I don't care! Deceit, lies, and framing my parents? You are worse than him," I shot back resentfully. His eyes darkened as he looked at his wrist.

"As you wish," he said, glancing out at the sky. "Do you know what tonight is, Yileyna?"

"The full moon, Charlene just told me," I spat. I didn't want to talk to him. It hurt far too much.

"The last Full Moon of winter. Tonight will be a cold night. I guess we will have to keep the fires burning…" He didn't explain what he meant as I watched him stare at the tattoo on his wrist, massaging it slowly with his thumb. I didn't reply, not knowing what to say to someone who had betrayed and played me.

Theon had told me the Obsidian Shadow Pack would attack soon… I needed to warn the king about Theon somehow.

Night had fallen, and Theon left, telling me Charlene would die if I so much as tried anything. I didn't see her after that, and I felt worried. I had showered and eaten, but I still felt exhausted. Where was Charlene? I needed her safe…

It took me a while to realise that not even a servant was left to attend to me. I was entirely alone. How strange. I left my bedroom, finding it odd that no one was around. The entire Alpha quarters were empty… perhaps everyone was busy with something or other. I left the wing; the guards at the door were missing too. The castle felt too silent…

My heart skipped a beat as I looked down the dark halls. Something was wrong. I broke into a run. The castle always had someone walking around. Surely I'd bump into someone. I kept running, but I didn't run into anyone. The entire castle was as silent as death itself. Charlene, where was she?

The kitchens! There's always someone in the kitchens!

I ran down the steps, my bare feet padding on the cold stone as I took them two at a time. I neared the kitchens, slowing down, but I didn't hear the hustle and bustle that usually filled the lower halls. I inched closer. I felt like I was stuck in a nightmare.

I pushed open the kitchen door, the door creaking horrifyingly loudly, making me close my eyes before I peered into the darkness. Empty. What on Kaeladia…

"Attack! There's an attack!" The faint shouting made my stomach sink.

I ran to the doors that led outside just as the night sky was suddenly lit ablaze with fire. Then the ground shook violently, throwing me off my feet. I got up, my heart pounding as I made to rush out when suddenly someone grabbed me by my arm. I turned with a gasp to see Theon standing there. He was dressed all in black, right down to the cloak that was draped around him.

"You really need to learn to stay put," Theon growled, dragging me back inside.

"Theon! We are under attack! Let me go! It's them, isn't it?!"

He didn't respond, pulling me down towards the dungeons. My eyes widened as I stared at the cells as we passed them. Each one was full of guards and the castle staff.

"You… Charlene!" I gasped, spotting her red hair lying in the pile on the ground of one of the cells, but he pulled me away to the far end.

"Be grateful I didn't kill them," he said coldly, pulling open the door and pushing me inside. I spun around, lunging at the door, but he slammed it shut, locking it before I could reach it.

"No, Theon… don't do this," I pleaded, grabbing the silver bars and shaking them violently, barely noticing the slight sting of the silver. "We can stop this war. Together." The sound echoed off the walls, but Theon didn't seem to care that I was making noise.

"War is already here, and we can't stop it. This is far bigger than us," he said quietly, walking toward me, an emotion I couldn't comprehend in his eyes. "I never wanted you caught up in this, but… the time has come. Two years of waiting for this moment…"

He turned his head, glancing towards the small windows at the top of the cells. The full moon shone through the window as Theon closed his eyes, pressing his wrist and whispering a word. A brilliant amber glow surrounded him, and intense green runes weaved through the amber. I felt an immense surge of energy roll off him, and I realised he was breaking a seal, a seal that had been suppressing his Alpha aura, an aura so vast that it made my heart pound as I backed away from the bars.

His eyes blazed gold as he flexed his hands, as if relishing in the power that he had suppressed for so long.

"Goddess…" I whispered, fear and worry growing within me. He tilted his head as he looked at me, and our eyes met.

I realised in that moment that it was no longer Theon of Westerfell who was standing before me, not the man who used to get angry at our pranks, not the one who used to scold and mock us or protect us… but Theon Hale of the Obsidian Shadow Pack, a man who seemed to hold no emotion at all. A man that I truly did not know…

"One final time, Yileyna. Stand by my side, and I will protect you." I shook my head.

"I will never… never stand by the Obsidian Shadow Pack," I said, my heart heaving as I glared at him. "Please don't do this, Theon. We don't have to do this…"

"I'm afraid I do… the time for vengeance is here. This will be goodbye," he said quietly. Our eyes met, and confusion flitted through me. Goodbye?

But with a sudden cold awakening I realised what he meant. His gaze became colder, his eyes blazing with hatred and vengeance. I was losing the Theon I knew. Forever.

Doing What's Right

YILEYNA

IT HAD ONLY BEEN less than ten minutes since Theon had left, but it felt like years. I was trying to think of what to do. I had no way to contact anyone… whatever he had done to the palace guards and staff was beyond me. No matter how many times I shouted, trying to wake them up, it didn't work.

Think, Yileyna…

Shouting and the orange glow of fire seeped through the small, barred windows. Time was running out. I took a deep breath. I needed to get out of here now. Letting Zarian's words guide me, I began to focus.

Focus from within, Right now, my abilities were sealed, and so I needed to channel my emotions. That wouldn't be hard anyway. With a surge of determination, I strode to the bars, gripping them tightly and closing my eyes. I let every heartbreak and pain I had ever felt out; the pain, the sadness, the bittersweet moments. My eyes stung with tears as I used the pain that I had buried within me. The temperature dropped. I felt the ice spreading beneath me and through my fingertips.

My parents' death…

Theon's rejection…

His betrayal…

His lies…

A violent wind whipped around me, and, using every ounce of willpower I could muster, I pulled at the bars. The metal groaned, the pull in my shoulders and arms aching, then there was a violent tug in the pit of my stomach before they were ripped from the ground. My eyes flew open as I dropped the bars that were distorted entirely. The thick heavy metal clanged as it hit the ground, making it shake slightly. I rushed out, glancing at the other cells.

Raiden! Spotting him, I glanced around looking for the keys, but they were nowhere in sight. *What do I do…*

Taking a deep breath, it took me a moment to channel my abilities again to break the bars of the cells. I rushed inside, spotting Gamma Grayson and Ryan there too.

"Raiden!" I shook him but he was unconscious. Whatever Theon had done to them, there was no sign of them waking up. I went over to Charlene, fixing her position so she was lying on her back, and planted a kiss on her forehead. "I'm going to try to fix this, my queen," I whispered.

It was me alone.

I ran up the stairs, pushing the door. I grunted as I slammed into it, but it refused to open. Locked. I backed up and ran into it again, this time trying to focus on my rage. The door was slammed off its hinges by a violent wind.

"Hey!" A deep gravelly voice came, and I saw two other men getting to their feet. They were wearing black attire with the amber-coloured insignia on their left arm. Members of the Obsidian Shadow Pack…

"I'm afraid I don't have time to play," I growled, not wanting them to mind-link anyone.

I ran at the first one, spinning around and aiming a kick at his neck. A flash of ice spread across the ground, making the other one slip. I turned, snapping the man's neck as the other one grabbed my hair, yanking me back and throwing me against the far wall. I groaned as I hit the floor and got to my feet.

"Seems like we have a violent one here," he growled, yanking me by the back of my tunic.

"I'm afraid I need to resort to violence when we are under attack," I hissed, snapping his neck. He wasn't dead, but he would be out for a while.

The other man punched me, throwing me to the ground. I twisted, turning and knocking him back with my foot. He slipped on the ice, so I took the chance to pin him down and punched him across the face. His eyes flashed as he growled, his canines coming out before he shifted. I shoved him back. A thick layer of ice began encasing him, spreading from the tips of my hands and soon, he ceased struggling. I wasn't sure if he was dead but…

The screams were growing from outside. I took one of the discarded swords and ran up the rest of the stairs to the main floor. A child's cry made my stomach lurch, and as I rounded the corner, I saw two bleeding guards enter, I knew them by name but wasn't acquainted with them, holding none other than Rhys. His leg was bloody, and he was in obvious agony.

"Princess!" Kyle said, relief flooding his face. It took me a moment to realise he meant me.

"You need to hide," Valen whispered urgently, coming over as I looked at Rhys. Luckily, apart from an injury, he was okay. I gave him a small smile, which he returned with a brave one.

"That's my boy. Stay strong, okay? I can't hide, I need to go out there."

"No, you don't understand. It's Theon. He betrayed us," Kyle escaped quietly.

"I know…" I said quietly. "I need to stop him." I was about to run past, when Valen grabbed my arm, something that would be considered disrespect in normal circumstances.

"Princess, he's taken over. He is currently holding the Alpha and Luna in the centre courtyard! The entire city is under their control now. We need to get you out of here -"

"And abandon everyone down in the dungeons? No. Take Rhys to safety. Where are the Gammas?"

"Gamma Henry is wounded; Lady Andrea and Zoe are captive. As for Gamma Grayson, I have no idea."

"He, Raiden, Ryan, and Charlene are in the cells. Get those four, plus Rhys, out of the city, please."

"What are you planning, Princess?"

"I'm not sure. There's not much I can do about those outside, but if they are going to take over by killing the families in power, those will be their first move. Take the way through the lower gutters. I know Theon knows every way out, but it's the only chance we've got. If you can, mind-link any guard to come help -"

"The king gave the order to protect you and to get you out of Westerfell immediately. He said you need to live."

"They need me, they won't kill me," I said firmly, "but I can't guarantee anyone else's life. The king is currently is in their hold correct? Then I'm in charge, you will obey me." They hesitated, exchanging looks.

"Princess, please -"

"Don't waste time. Leave now," I commanded, and they lowered their heads before they ran towards the cells.

I ran in the opposite direction and out into the open, stopping in my tracks. The entire courtyard was covered in flames. Every tree... every flower bed was lit ablaze. The heat beat against my skin. My heart pounded as I realised the flames were beginning to spread across the stone, making their way up the doors and windows. Everyone in the cells could die...

I stared at the sky. The rain was falling, but it was doing nothing to stop the fire. This time, when ice began spreading from beneath my feet, I focused on letting it encase the entire castle. The flames hissed and fizzled as they touched the ice, yet I pushed further, pulling at every ounce of power I could from within. The desire and urgency to protect those whom I loved fuelled me, and the ice became thicker, blindingly bright as it withstood the flames that sought to destroy all in their wake.

I felt connected, feeling every part of the castle that was covered in ice, almost as if the ice was my sight. I enforced it in areas where the flames felt stronger. I looked at the castle behind me. No longer was it dull stone but a shimmering castle with the illusion it was carved from ice alone.

"What is going on?" Someone shouted, and I broke into a run as the rain began pouring faster.

Two guards came in my way, and I spun around, swinging the sword and slicing off their heads before they could even react. Another came and shifted, but I raised my hand, encasing him in a tomb of ice before I continued on my way. I had no idea how I was able to pull at my powers, but with the emotions that were a storm inside of me, I was able to focus on what I was trying to do, the will to protect our people stronger than anything.

I stopped the moment I reached the main courtyard, my heart thumping in my chest at the sight before me...

Bodies covered in blood were strewn across the ground, in the midst of the ever-lasting flames. I could smell the oil used to fuel the fire, and the terrifying flashback to the night my parents died returned to me, making my blood run cold. My heart rang in my ear as I tried to differentiate between my memories and the present.

Men and wolves of the Obsidian Shadow Pack seemed to have slain anyone who put up a fight, whilst others cowered to the side in fear. Where were the children? I raised my hands, sending a wave of water over the bodies of the injured, stopping the flames from burning them.

Suddenly, a terrifying roar filled the air, and one of the largest black wolves I had ever seen launched itself at me.

An Alpha.

I jumped aside, spinning on my heel and driving my sword into its left flank, but it did nothing to the wolf that took the blade in its teeth and threw it aside. One swipe at me sent me flying into the air before I twisted, ignoring the agony in my body as I landed on my feet, a strong wind whipping around me. His burning orange eyes were filled with rage as he launched at me once more. I jumped to the side as a bolt of lightning almost struck him. He jumped back, watching me with fury and rage in his eyes.

I wouldn't win this battle…

His Vengeance

YILEYNA

Just then, two men of the Silver Storm Pack attacked him. It was a suicide mission, but it gave me the time I needed.

"Run, Princess!"

I nodded, my heart squeezing as I knew their fate was death. I turned and ran through the flames, refusing to let their sacrifice be wasted, and stopped suddenly at the sight before me. There, in the middle of the clearing, were the king and queen, tied and mortally wounded. The queen was near dead, lying in a pool of blood, whilst the king was on his knees, breathing raggedly as he kept his head raised.

"So, you managed to escape…" Theon's cold, emotionless voice came.

My heart thudded as I stared at the hooded man that circled the king and queen, the sword in his hand dragging along the ground and grating against the stone. My stomach lurched as a strong sense of Deja Vu from the day at the hospital returned to me. Somehow, I had been forewarned of this moment… when Theon had touched me…

Fire…

Death…

Goddess…

"Don't do this, Theon," I whispered pleadingly. "Please, you have won. Don't taint your hands with the blood of so many." I wasn't close to either the king or queen, but this was wrong.

"I have waited for far too long for this moment to stop. Bow to your new king, Yileyna."

I was about to speak when the huge black wolf approached, blood dripping from his sharp fangs. His aura surged around him, and when Theon looked at him, I realised who it was. Theoden Hale.

Before my eyes, he transformed into a tall, muscular man. Scars littered his body, and his muscles rippled with every step he took. He was a man that oozed of power. Grabbing a discarded cloak and wrapping it around his waist, he approached the king.

"I told you, you would pay for your betrayal, Andres." His voice was harsh and cold, yet held vast power.

"Theoden..." the king spat coldly, his own aura swirling around him even if he was weakened. The two men who had started all of this... but what was the truth? *What do I do?*

Theon's eyes were on me, and I shook my head pleadingly.

Don't do this...

"You didn't even recognise my son," Theoden smirked coldly. "The power of a simple enchantment..."

"It's a shame... a shame that I let someone like him into our pack! You will suffer for this, Theon! And you, you will never be the king, Theoden," Andres growled. His breathing was heavy and laboured as he glared at the man that stood before him. Theoden smirked, yet it lacked any glimmer of emotion.

"I already am," he said, holding his hand out for the sword Theon held.

"Don't do this, Alpha Theoden!" I shouted suddenly, running forward. "You don't need to kill him, you have Westerfell in your grasp -"

"Do not talk to me, wench!" His eyes flashed, his aura radiating off him.

"Stay silent," the king growled, looking at me warningly. Despite his harsh tone, I saw the glimmer of fear in his eyes as he motioned toward the gates discreetly.

Run.

He was telling me to run. I couldn't...

"Yileyna!" Andres growled warningly.

I told you... I don't need a man... I will protect my people. I don't know how but I will try my best. I said nothing, simply shaking my head at the king. *I'm sorry, but I am no coward.*

Theoden raised the sword and, with one swift move, beheaded Soleil in the blink of an eye. The king flinched, and I ran forward. Another bolt of lightning struck the ground inches from where Theoden stood.

"Control her!" He roared at Theon, who was behind me in a flash, his arm tightening around my throat and waist. Theoden let out a terrifying roar of power as he beheaded the king right before my eyes. In the same moment, with his other hand, he tore his heart from his chest. My heart thumped as I stared at the horrifying scene before me.

I felt a huge wave of power within me, the transfer of the Alpha position. If there was any doubt that I was not the Alpha's daughter, it was gone.

I froze in Theon's hold as I stared at the king's head, that now lay detached from his body. Dead.

Suddenly, it felt like everything was lost. I felt lost, scared, and defeated. The king was the most powerful in our pack...

A raucous laugh left Theoden's lips. He slammed his foot down on the king's face as he bit into the king's heart, making me sick. This was a nightmare… this could not be true.

"You picked the wrong side," Theon whispered in my ear before throwing me to the ground roughly.

The sound of heavy footsteps approached, and to my horror, I saw the guards that I had ordered to take Charlene and the others being thrown to the ground by a group of Obsidian Shadow warriors. They were bloody and injured, but when Valen gave me the tiniest of nods, I felt a wave of relief flood me. They had managed to get the others out… or so I hoped…

"We saw these two bastards trying to escape!" One of the men shouted.

"I ordered them!" I hissed before Theon or his monster of a father could speak. "I'm the one who should be punished!"

"Then it's time you were taught a lesson. Theon," Theoden commanded dangerously. I glared up at both him and Theon.

"You're right," Theon said coldly, his eyes boring into mine and crushing my heart in the process. Theon…

There was no love nor emotions in the eyes of the man before me… only the flames of hatred burning brightly, consuming those amber orbs. Was I nothing to him?

"Tell me… what are we?" I asked softly. *Please…* The pain in my body was suffocating, and no matter how strong I tried to remain, I couldn't keep the pain from my voice.

"Nothing more than Heaven and Hell." His voice was equally cold, destroying the last of my resolve.

"Then kill me," I whispered hoarsely, trying to ignore the pain of betrayal that was tearing me up from within.

A ruthless smirk graced his handsome face. He crouched down, his fingers curling under my chin and making the sparks from his touch rush through me; pleasurable, yet equally painful. He was so close… yet so far away…

"That would be far too easy… but I assure you, when I'm done with you, you'll wish you were never born."

"You don't mean that…"

"Watch me." He turned away, pushing me back onto the ground roughly. My head hit the ground as he gave the command. "Burn her."

My heart sank, my head hanging as the pain of his rejection tore through me. Even when I was doused in gasoline, I didn't move, trying not to gag on the strong, pungent smell that cloaked me entirely, keeping my eyes clamped shut. Didn't he realise I was already burning in agony from the pain he had inflicted within me?

My eyes stung as I forced them open, watching him retreat, hoping… praying… that he'd turn back and change his mind. That perhaps deep inside of him, the man that I loved still existed. He once said that I was his kryptonite…

Was it all lies?

He paused. My heart leapt with a glimmer of hope, but then I saw it, the blazing match in his hand as his eyes met mine.

"Burn."

He tossed the match, and I watched as if in slow motion as the match came spinning through the air, straight towards me.

Memories of our time together…

Him rescuing me from Nikolai and Kyson…

Him making me coffee…

Kissing me…

Complimenting me…

Promising me he would destroy me…

And my innocent willingness, not knowing he had always meant so much more…

My vision blurred as the pain became unbearable.

He betrayed me…

Goddess, he betrayed me…

The emotions were too much…

I let out a scream of anguish as I felt the searing pain of something breaking within me. Suddenly a blinding, iridescent light blazed around me, obliterating the match before it even touched me and blasting everything away from me. A violent wind beat against everyone there, making them struggle to keep their balance as they shielded their faces from the storm that now swirled around me. I felt something snap, and several fearful voices filled my head.

What's happening… help us…. Goddess…

The mind link… Somehow, I had gained access despite not having shifted. This power… it ran through my veins like a charge of energy. My seal had broken.

My heart pounded as Theon looked at me sharply, his eyes cold and indifferent, yet my stomach sank as the most delicious, intoxicating scent filled my senses, and I felt the intense pull of the mate bond snap into place.

With it came the birth of a dark, twisted truth.

Theon was my fated mate.

END OF PART 1

PART 2

My Alpha's Retribution

Rising from the Ashes of his Vengeance

COMING DECEMBER 2022

GLOSSARY

SPECIES

WEREWOLVES

Werewolves are one of the fastest growing species on Kaeladia and, due to this, have become the ultimate species in power.

Appearance: Lean, well built, tend to be toned and muscular. Even the women will have more of an athletic build. They are usually more on the tall side. Omega-ranked she-wolves are more feminine in appearance and were originally only for mating purposes.

Abilities: They are extremely strong and fast in both human and wolf form, with heightened senses once they have shifted.

Shifting: The average age of shifting happens between 14-18, however, the earliest recorded shift was 13 years.

Lifespan: Werewolves live to about 200 years old.

Mates: They can find their mates on a full moon as long as both parties have had their shift.

Pregnancy: She-wolves can get pregnant, whether by their mates or another man, does not need to be marked to do so.

Deity: Selene – Said to reside on the moon itself, she cares greatly for her children. Known for her love and compassion.

Feared species: Sirens

NAGAS

A proud race who keeps to themselves. However, if you cross paths with them, it can be life-threatening.

Appearance: Well-built with a human upper half of the body with a scaled snake lower half, and range from anywhere between 5-8 feet when they are upright, however, depending on the actual length of their tails, from head to tip can be anywhere between 15-25 feet. They cannot gain legs on any account. There are different types of Nagas – Sea, Desert, and Forest, and this is reflected in their appearance and habitat.

Abilities: Keen senses, can also speak in snake tongue as well as the common tongue. They can see better in the dark than day. Their bite is poisonous, and they have incredible strength.

Lifespan: Live to about 500 years old.

Mates: Nagas do not have fated mates and tend to live alone, and the females are usually only used for mating purposes.

Deity: Nagina – A goddess known for her cunningness and deception. It is said whoever looks her in the eye would turn to stone.

Feared species: Mages & Sirens

SIRENS

They are not necessarily cruel, but they do have a tendency to look down upon other species, save the Fae. They are often playful with a strong sexual desire; however, if wronged, they will hold grudges.

Appearance: Extremely beautiful with full, large breasts and flawless skin. They tend to be 7-8 feet from head to fin with scales of different colours.

Abilities: The ability to enchant and control their victims through their music. They can see slightly better than humans but nowhere near as far as other species. They can, however, see perfectly underwater and in the dark, including the ability to see everything in colour. They can be of different elements. Most will be water, ice, or air; however, the imperial family often can control the weather itself.

Shifting: Members of the imperial family are the only ones who can take the form of man, however, they would be mistaken for Fae due to their extreme beauty.

Lifespan: They live around 300 years.

Mates: Sirens may often have true mates, and they can sense this by the intense bond towards their counterparts. It may not be as strong as a werewolf's bond, but it does exist.

Deity: Oshera – The sea goddess is said to be equally terrifying and beautiful, with her face of utter beauty yet her lower body a vast darkness of tentacles.

Feared species: Fae

FAE

A powerful species that is smart and powerful.

Appearance: Extremely beautiful, with a leaner and more graceful build. They tend to be tall with flawless features. Their features may often give away what element they hold.

Abilities: Elemental; they have the ability to bend their element and conjure it from thin air. However, taking from the surroundings can fuel their abilities.

Lifespan: Can live to over 1000 years.

Mates: It is rare for them to be mated, yet it has happened a rare few times in history.

Deity: Etaar - A being that was neither male nor female but held such beauty that no mortal could look them in the eye.

Feared species: Naga

MAGES

They are human in every aspect aside from having the ability to cast magic.

Appearance: Human as we are.

Abilities: Can cast spells and enchantments, may be stronger in certain elements than others. There are two types of mages, light and dark, and both follow separate gods. Dark mages are rarer.

Lifespan: Mages live slightly longer than their human counterparts and have an average life span of 150 years.

Deities: Hecate – The goddess of witchcraft (Light)

Dezeenath – The god of trickery (Dark)

Feared species: Werewolves

The eight elements

- Wind
- Water
- Fire
- Earth
- Lightning
- Shadow
- Light
- Ice

OTHER WORKS

THE ALPHA SERIES

Book 1 – Her Forbidden Alpha

Book 2 – Her Cold-Hearted Alpha

Book 3 – Her Destined Alpha

Book 4 – Caged between the Beta & Alpha

Book 5 – King Alejandro: The Return of Her Cold-Hearted Alpha

THE ROSSI LEGACIES

Book 1 – Alpha Leo and the Heart of Fire (2 Volumes)

Book 2 – The Lycan Princess and the Temptation of Sin (Coming 2023)

STANDALONES

His Caged Princess

Mr. CEO, Please Marry My Mommy

His Dark Obsession

THE RUTHLESS KING'S TRILOGY

Book 1 – The Alpha King's Possession

Book 2 – The Dragon King's Seduction (Coming 2023)

SOCIAL MEDIA PLATFORMS

Instagram: Author.Muse
Facebook: Author Muse

AUTHORS SUPPORTING AUTHORS

Check out these work from some amazing authors!
Chosen By The Dragon Kings – Jessica Hall (Amazon)
Beneath Her Darkness: The Alpha's Little Demon (GoodNovel app)
My Song To My Alpha's Heart – Willow Joy (GoodNovel app)

Printed in Great Britain
by Amazon